Eight Dime Novels

Edited by E.F. BLEILER

OLD KING BRADY

FRANK JAMES

NICK CARTER

DEADWOOD DICK

BUFFALO BILL

THE STEAM MAN

FRANK MERRIWELL

HORATIO ALGER

Dover Publications, Inc.
New York

Copyright © 1974 by Dover Publications, Inc.
All rights reserved under Pan American and International Copyright Conventions.

Published in Canada by General Publishing Company, Ltd., 30 Lesmill Road, Don Mills, Toronto, Ontario.

Published in the United Kingdom by Constable and Company, Ltd., 10 Orange Street, London W.C. 2.

This Dover edition, first published in 1974, contains the unabridged and unaltered text of the following works:

The Bradys and the Girl Smuggler, or Working for the Custom House, by "a New York detective" [Francis W. Doughty], published (as No. 79 of the series *Secret Service, Old and Young King Brady Detectives*) by Frank Tousey, New York, July 27, 1900.

Frank James on the Trail, published (as Vol. I, No. 46 of *Morrison's Sensational Series*) by John W. Morrison, New York, 1882.

Scylla, the Sea Robber, or Nick Carter and the Queen of Sirens, "edited by Chickering Carter" [Frederick van Rensselaer Dey], published (as No. 465 of the *New Nick Carter Weekly*) by Street and Smith, New York, November 25, 1905.

Deadwood Dick, the Prince of the Road, or The Black Rider of the Black Hills, by Edward J. Wheeler, published (as Vol. I, No. 1 of *Beadle's Half-Dime Library*) by Beadle and Adams, New York, 1877.

Adventures of Buffalo Bill from Boyhood to Manhood, by Colonel Prentiss Ingraham, published (as Vol. I, No. 1, of *Beadle's Boy's Library of Sport, Story and Adventure*) by Beadle and Adams, New York, December 14, 1881.

The Huge Hunter, or The Steam Man of the Prairies, by Edward S. Ellis, published (as Vol. XI, No. 271 of *Beadle's Half-Dime Library*) by Beadle and Adams, New York, 1882.

Frank Merriwell's Nobility, or The Tragedy of the Ocean Tramp, by "Burt L. Standish" [William Gilbert Patten], published (as No. 158 of *Tip Top Weekly*) by Street and Smith, New York, April 22, 1899.

Adrift in New York, or Dodger and Florence Braving the World, by Horatio Alger, Jr., published (as No. 45 of *Brave and Bold*) by Street and Smith, New York, October 31, 1903.

E. F. Bleiler made the selection and wrote the Introduction specially for the present edition.

International Standard Book Number: 0-486-22975-0
Library of Congress Catalog Card Number: 73-79744

Manufactured in the United States of America
Dover Publications, Inc.
180 Varick Street
New York, N.Y. 10014

Contents

Acknowledgments
vi

Introduction, by E. F. Bleiler
vii

THE BRADYS AND THE GIRL SMUGGLER,
or Working for the Custom House
FRANCIS W. DOUGHTY [1900]
1

FRANK JAMES ON THE TRAIL
[1882]
33

SCYLLA, THE SEA ROBBER,
or Nick Carter and the Queen of Sirens
FREDERICK VAN RENSSELAER DEY [1905]
47

DEADWOOD DICK, THE PRINCE
OF THE ROAD,
or The Black Rider of the Black Hills
EDWARD J. WHEELER [1877]
77

ADVENTURES OF BUFFALO BILL
from Boyhood to Manhood
COLONEL PRENTISS INGRAHAM [1881]
91

THE HUGE HUNTER,
or The Steam Man of the Prairies
EDWARD S. ELLIS [1882]
107

FRANK MERRIWELL'S NOBILITY,
or The Tragedy of the Ocean Tramp
WILLIAM GILBERT PATTEN [1899]
123

ADRIFT IN NEW YORK,
or Dodger and Florence Braving the World
HORATIO ALGER, JR. [1903]
157

ACKNOWLEDGMENTS

This introduction could not have been written without *The House of Beadle and Adams* by Albert Johannsen, an inexhaustible reference source, perhaps the strongest examination of any aspect of American publishing. Also indispensable were *The Fiction Factory* by Quentin Reynolds; *Frank Merriwell's "Father," An Autobiography*, edited by Harriet Hinsdale and Tony Landon; the bibliographies of Horatio Alger by Frank Gruber and Ralph Gardner, and the many contributions made by the collectors who have written in the *Dime Novel Round-up*, the trade magazine for the dime novel world. One may not share their enthusiasm for a particular story, but they have done so much invaluable spade work that between them and Johannsen, an editor is hard put to offer more than a point of view and a coordination.

Introduction

> BOOKS FOR THE MILLION!
> A DOLLAR BOOK FOR A DIME!!
> 128 pages complete, only Ten Cents!
> BEADLE'S DIME NOVELS NO. 1.
> MALAESKA;
> THE
> INDIAN WIFE OF THE WHITE HUNTER.
> By Mrs. Ann S. Stephens.
> 128 pages 12mo.   Ready SATURDAY MORNING, June 9.
> IRWIN P. BEADLE & Co., Publishers
> No. 141 William-st., New-York.
> ROSS & TOUSEY, General Agents.

This advertisement, printed in the *New York Tribune* for June 7, 1860, announced the birth of a major American phenomenon: the dime novel. It is the first statement of a plan that governed much of American publishing for about two generations and dominated the culturation of young America for this time.

Yet *Malaeska, the Indian Wife of the White Hunter* was not a new work; it had appeared in the *Woman's Companion* magazine in 1839, and it was not especially sensational. It was not the first inexpensive book, either. There had been earlier series, such as Ballou's, that had essentially been dime novels. What was so new about it, that it became the opening for hundreds of followers? Mostly marketing. And it came at exactly the right time, when tens of thousands of young men were settling in army camps and needed inexpensive entertainment.

The second, and possibly more important event in the early life of the dime novel came in October 1860 when the residents of the New York area suddenly noticed a disturbance in the environment:

> All of a sudden, all over the country, there broke out a rash of posters, dodgers and painted inscriptions demanding to know "Who is Seth Jones?" Everywhere you went this query met you. It glared at you in staring letters on the sidewalks. It came fluttering in to you on little dodgers thrust by the handful into the Broadway stages.... In the country the trees and rocks and the sides and roofs of barns all clamored with stentorian demands to know who Seth Jones was ... and just when it had begun to be a weariness and one of the burdens of life ... a new rush of decorations broke out all over the country. This was in the form of big and little posters bearing a lithographic portrait of a stalwart, heroic looking hunter.... And above or below this imposing figure in large type were the words, "I am Seth Jones."

This is from the reminiscences of Edward S. Ellis, who wrote *Seth Jones, or The Captives of the Frontier* at the age of twenty, while he was teaching school in Red Bank, New Jersey. It marked the beginning of one of the most productive careers in American popular fiction, and it also marked the beginning of true dime novel publishing: mass market sensational adventure. It is said that Beadle sold about 400,000 copies of *Seth Jones*—and from here on the dime novel was off to a racing start.

The biography of the dime novel in its heyday, from 1860 to about 1910, can be told in a number of ways. It is a facet of Americana, peculiarly American in some respects, and it is closely tied up with the cultural history of the middle nineteenth century.

First and foremost, the dime novel was big business. Never before or since has book publishing held a larger share of the gross national product. The first mass-produced entertainment industry of importance, it stood in the same relation to the average young American as television does today. It was also a phenomenon of prodigious productivity. Beadle and Adams alone, during the thirty-five years or so of its existence, published more than 7,500 novels, and its competitors were not far behind. There are, of course, no figures for the total number of dime novels printed, but it is not an unreasonable guess to say several billion. Horatio Alger alone accounts for about 250,000,000 copies!

In operation dime novel publishing was much like a gigantic poker game. The players were a few giants—Beadle and Adams, Frank Tousey, George Munro, Norman Munro, Street and Smith—and a host of smaller onlookers and drop-snatchers. Each publishing house frantically followed the successes and failures of the others. When it became obvious, for example, that Norman Munro's Old Cap Collier detective stories, the first important detective series, were skyrocketing, the other lines immediately established competitive detective lines. Tousey set up Old Sleuth as a rival; this was the first use of the word "sleuth," which properly means a bloodhound, to designate a human detective. When another publisher attempted to infringe on the word "sleuth," Tousey obtained a court order forbidding all other publishers from using the word "sleuth" in this sense. Whenever Beadle established a new format or a new library, the other publishers followed suit. When Street and Smith adopted the first garish full-color covers for dime novels, the other lines immediately dipped into the paint pots. It was an industry that published weekly newspapers with installment parts, quarto-sized booklets, small books, with tens of thousands of novels issued, reissued and subissued to the tireless public.

The dime novel was also a changing world in itself that had to follow larger and smaller reading patterns. For the first two decades of its existence —the 1860's and 70's—reading America was apparently obsessed with the frontier and Western life: Indian skirmishes, adventures among the wild animals of the plains, rough characters of the Old West, the cattle industry (somewhat transmogrified) and gold mining. Even *Malaeska, the Indian Wife of the White Hunter* qualifies as a frontier novel, despite the fact that the frontier here fell within the Catskills. Other dime novel areas were explored (Beadle strongly favoring pirated reprints), but the semihistorical Buffalo Bills, Deadwood Dicks and Calamity Janes and mythical Silver Sams, California Claudes and similar heroes and scalawags triumphed. The stands were soon filled with such titles as *Redpath, the Avenger, or The Fair Huntress of the South-West; The Ranger's Rifle, or The Wolf of the War-Path; Pepe, the Scout, or The Rangers of Sonora; Alapha, the Squaw, or The Renegades of the Border; Prairie Chick, or The Quaker Abroad; The Phantom Chief, or The Indian's Revenge;* and *The Trappers of the Gila; or Life and Adventures in the Far Southwest.*

For the next two decades of the dime novel —the 1880's and 90's—however, crime and its detection formed the bread and butter of the publishers. Crime was pretty much synonymous with the James gang, and the criminals of the big cities cut little ice. On the detectional side, Old Cap Collier was the first important thief-taker, soon to be followed by three or four major detectives—Old Sleuth, Young Sleuth, Nick Carter—and a horde of minor detectives. Some of these went to absurd lengths, as the titles of their adventures show: *Old Opium, the Mongolian Detective; Velvet Foot, the Indian Detective, or The Taos Tiger; The Pitcher-Detective's Foil, or Double-Curve Dan's Double Play; Harlem Jack, the Office-Boy Detective; Zeb Taylor, the Puritan Detective; New York Nat, the Knife Detective; Deadwood Dick's Dog Detective; Telegraph Tom's Winning Game, or The Messenger Boy Detective among the Bowery Sharps; Old Sledge, Blacksmith-Detective; Bert Adams, the Fireman Detective; The Hudson River Tunnel Detective;* and *Old Humpey, the Dwarf Detective.* Such detectives exist by the hundred.

Some of these detectives were conceived fairly realistically; others, the more popular sleuths, could disguise themselves with a hundred faces, outmatch Tarzan in strength, and penetrate the subtlest crime in a flash. The parentage of all would seem to be international: a full share of old English semifactual crime stories by "Waters" and MacLevy, more than a suspicion of Gaboriau and the French detective novel of the 1860's and 70's, and the background of America.

Toward the end of the century most of the Indians had been pacified, most of the criminals contained, and the dime novel world began to interest itself in self-improvement. Horatio Alger became more popular than ever, and a priggish prep school boy, Frank Merriwell, formed a nucleus for a new vitality. There had been previous school stories in America, particularly the British Jack Harkaway stories by Bracebridge Hemyng, who had been lured to America from England to establish an American line, but Harkaway was not too successful, and the real schoolboy explosion had to wait almost until the twentieth century. Somehow or other, posh prep schools, and the perpetual defeat of Harvard on the football field, year after year, came to be more attractive than the slaughter of Indians or the overcoming of criminals. The note of larger-than-life-size, however, remained.

Mentioning these peaks is, of course, an abstraction, since Westerns continued to be printed and reprinted (Buffalo Bill having a whole chain of late adventures), and the detectives never went out of business. But their creative force was no longer present.

Despite its strong peak interests, the dime novel, especially on the levels of lower quantity, was also incredibly varied in situation, virtually a microcosm of nineteenth-century life. Thus we read of *Neck and Neck, or Around the World with Nellie Bly!; La Mafia, the New Orleans Italian Fiends' Oath; Whiskey Bill, or The Road to Ruin, A Story of the Rum Fiend's Frightful Work; Jack Winters in the Zulu War; Young Sleuth at the World's Fair, or Piping a Mystery of Chicago; Yale Murphy, the Great Short Stop, or The Little Midget of the Giant New York Team; Al Schock, the Champion Bicyclist, or The Adventures of the*

Greatest Long Distance Wheelman of the World; The Liberty Boys' Good Work, or Helping General Washington; Mad Abe, the Scout, or Bivouac and Battle in the South; and *Young Klondike, or Off for the Land of Gold.*

When Thomas A. Edison received a new sheaf of publicity for one of his multitudinous inventions, a dime novel series starring Tom Edison, Jr. was born. When the lure of the big top was strong, a whole cycle of circus dime novels hit the stands. Each aeronautical disaster produced a horde of boys who solved the problem of flying. Boy fire fighters wax strong after Chicago burns; railroaders parallel the streaming rails; steamship stories, motor stories and so many other special categories keep emerging that it would be an almost endless task to list them.

The first dime novel, *Malaeska, the Indian Wife of the White Hunter*, was an adult story, reasonably well told, a competent example of early Victorian commercial writing. It would be pleasant to say that the dime novel held to this level, but it would not be true. The history of the dime novel, on the whole, is devolution. What began as a marketing venture for adult books ended as an almost entirely juvenile form. The language peculiar to dime novels appeared: the omnipresent declarative sentence, the bald statement of results rather than description of processes, and the capsulation of adventure in briefest form.

The classical dime novel had to die, although the exact moment of its death is probably multiple. In the last of the nineteenth century and the early twentieth century, it was reeling, and it did not have the vitality to fight off competition or attacks by the U.S. Postal Service. The book publishers, periodical publishers and moralists apparently lobbied, and suddenly the dime novel, which used to be mailed at the extremely low, subsidized second-class periodical rate, was declared not applicable. Mailing permits were revoked, and consignments of novels lay around at depots. The economic situation became painful.

Just as radio killed the pulp magazines, and television killed radio, in the early twentieth century the pulp magazines caused the final downfall of the dime novel. The pulp magazines usually contained several stories and possibly a serial part; they offered a great variety of subject matter, contemporaneity and greater sophistication. The pulps were simply better. They offered fiction that could be read by adults as well as adolescents, written by writers superior to the old dime novelists. The essential point of the dime novel, that it was a member of a series, was no longer an advantage. And finally, there was the generation gap. All the dime novel publishers depended heavily on backlist as a source of free material already set in type or easily adaptable. A boy of 1880 might be enthusiastic about Buffalo Bill; the same person, thirty years later, would probably not be. The boys of 1910, 1920 and 1930 had different tastes.

During the years of its heyday, however, the dime novel permeated young America, molding folkways in the same manner that television does today. It influenced the popular stage, and in turn was counterinfluenced. Its plots affected the early movies, and the detective series prepared the way for more sophisticated detective and mystery stories. They also offered a picture, perhaps distorted, of what was going on in otherwise inaccessible parts of the country: the Westerns exaggerated bloodshed, but did at least convey the psychological image of the Far West; the city stories reflected aspects of urban life. Farmboys read of the wonders of Manhattan and city millhands read of desperate criminals and superhuman crime fighters. Cowboys riding post read of the wild and woolly West.

The dime novels also reflected and served to reinforce the general cultural "myths" of the period: the ambivalence felt toward the successful criminal; admiration for the violent egotist; worship of physical strength; the Puritan ethic about wealth; the upward dynamism of progress; the righteousness of expansion; and a simplistic morality.

The novels, as is notorious, were regarded with great uneasiness by the more intelligent, the more conservative and the more religious adult elements, although for different reaons. It was vaguely felt that they were immoral, although the objectors were hard pressed to verbalize their objections. Sexuality was taboo in the dime novel, and the Ten Commandments were not conspicuously violated, except for the Sixth, which omission bothered few. Many of the publishers took the issue of morality very seriously and publicized the wholesomeness of their product. An interview with Orville Victor, one of the Beadle editors, in the *New York Evening Sun* around 1892 illustrates the concern the publishers claim to have felt for the Deadwood Dick series:

> I kept urging the author to make the stories less terrifically forcible in the language of his rougher characters, and gradually the sulphurous nature of their dialogues became moderate enough to need but little editing, and at the same time the torrents of liquor that flowed like rivers through his earlier manuscripts dwindled to rivulets under the influence of my appeals for less rum.
>
> The author urged the absolute truth of both the language and the amount of whisky-drinking that he attributed to his characters, but I begged in the interests of morality that the flow of both one and the other be curbed, and of course the stories were none the worse for his doing so.
>
> Deadwood Dick himself was also gradually re-

INTRODUCTION

formed and changed from the outlawed terror of the law-abiding to the deadly foe of the law breaker, and when once that transformation was achieved, his subsequent course in the path of virtue was an assured success. (Quoted in Beadle's *Half-Dime Library*, #816, *Deadwood Dick Jr.'s Rival, or Old Gideon's Wipe-out.*)

In the earlier days of the dime novel Beadle would occasionally bind novels in cloth and persuade ministers to read them. The novels often passed as individuals, but the category remained in damnation. At a later date Street and Smith cancelled its Jesse James series, when it seemed that public opinion was against the outlaws and their deeds. (It should be mentioned, though, that the Jesse James stories contained much cold-blooded killing.) It was also not uncommon for publishers to use several dummy imprints and addresses to avoid the condemnation of all story lines because of a single miscreant.

Today the dime novel is a matter of nostalgia and sociology of literature. It is a vast field of publication, so enormous that no one man could ever hope to encompass it. A speedreading researcher, working over a normal work week, at a thousand words a minute, would spend almost three months on Frank Merriwell alone—without having time to take notes. And so the dime novel, even if collections were available for reading, will long remain only a semi-explored wilderness.

For the enthusiast and the collector, however, it remains a solidification of rare nostalgia, capturing as nothing else can, the flavor of a dead era. It assembles thrills with minimal fuss, uses forceful language not overladen with subtlety, and depicts actions heightened beyond the size of life.

II

The eight dime novels that follow have been selected to show major tastes and trends, important authors and major series within the almost limitless sea of publication. Other novels, however, might just as well have been chosen, since uniformity within diversity was a characteristic of the dime novel.

Two detectives, Old King Brady and Nick Carter, show various styles of crime fighting; two Western figures, the necessary Buffalo Bill and Deadwood Dick, represent two major frontier adventurers. Among outlaws the James Brothers are easily preeminent, and among inventions, a steam man. In the ethics and morals branch, or rags to riches, "Burt Standish" and Horatio Alger obviously must be included. Other areas that might have been included are the early prank books and crude ethnic humor, pirate stories, general adventure, military and naval exploits, and special topics like circus life, railroading and goldmining in the Klondike. But one must stop somewhere.

The first novel in this collction, *The Bradys and the Girl Smuggler, or Working for the Custom House* [1900] was a member of a very popular series designed by the editors of Frank Tousey to take the market which two earlier detectives, Old Cap Collier and Old Sleuth, had already established. Old King Brady's author was Francis W. Doughty (1850–1917), whose accomplishments show that the authors of dime novels were not necessarily morons.

Born in Brooklyn, Doughty started to write at a very early age for the various dime papers, and from 1872 until close to his death he wrote intermittently for Tousey. All in all he wrote about 85 novels about Old King Brady. Doughty did not write all of Brady's adventures, since Tousey used the house name, "A New York Detective," to cover the work of other authors. But Doughty's work was the best in the series, and whenever Doughty relinquished Old King Brady, sales dropped, and he had to be called back again. Doughty was an intelligent man, who had serious numismatics as his hobby; he wrote at least one very creditable paper on archeology. In his later life he did some work for the movies.

Old King Brady, who appeared for the first time in a periodical in November 1885, was in some ways a reaction to the more superhuman sleuths of his day. As he is described in *99 99th Street, or The House without a Door*, his first adventure,

> He was a tall, spare man of about forty, evidently an Irishman. His clothes were plain and ill-fitting and his features large and unattractive, yet for all that there was something about the keen, penetrating eyes, the small mouth and firmly set lips which served to inspire the boy with the conviction that he was dealing with no ordinary individual.

Over the years Brady's image was bettered, but he still remains something of a soft-sell detective. He made mistakes; he was not a master of disguise nor a fantastic linguist; he was not a Hercules. But he was intelligent in a reasonable manner and had a wide knowledge of crime and human nature. In his later adventures he was accompanied by Young King Brady, who was no relation. Adventure and thrills were stressed in the series, rather than deduction; realism is usually characteristic of the crimes investigated, but there is an occasional story (such as *The Haunted Churchyard*) with unrationalized supernaturalism.

Doughty, who was an indefatigable traveler, took great pains to maintain correct local color and factual accuracy. If Brady walks down certain streets, the modern reader can be reasonably certain that what Brady saw really existed at the time. In part this was probably Doughty's personal penchant for accuracy; in part it may have been a device to raise local sales. The immigrant market, too, obviously concerned Doughty and Tousey.

There was no factual prototype for Old King Brady, but the James Brothers were still alive when their dime novel adventures started to appear. No other outlaws have ever captured the enthusiasm of young America as much as did Jesse and Frank James. Other highwaymen, train robbers, assassins, murderers, agrarian reformers or safecrackers like the Younger Brothers, Billy the Kid or Joaquin Murrieta may have attained temporary notoriety, but the Jameses far surpass all others as heroes and antiheroes in the world of the dime novel.

The first story about the Jameses was *The Trainrobbers, or A Story of the James Boys*, written by R. W. Stevens (John R. Musick) in the *Wide Awake Library* published by Tousey. The Jameses became so popular that the other publishers soon had to come to terms with them fictionally. Indeed, Street and Smith almost turned the Jameses into an industry with *Jesse James Stories* and *The James Boys Weekly*. Many of these stories were completely fictional, and had no relationship whatever to the historical doings of Jesse and Frank. A typical example is *Jesse James's Diamond Deal, or Robbing the Red Hands* by W. B. Lawson [1902], where Jesse destroys a criminal secret society and highjacks their loot. Of all the major publishers only Beadle refused to chronicle the nefarious doings of the Jameses.

So important were the Jameses in the world of the dime novel that even the other dime novel heroes had to pursue them. Young Sleuth sought them. Old King Brady tracked them in *The James Boys in Boston, or Old King Brady and the Car of Gold*. The most unusual experience of all, however, was probably Jack Wright's. Jack Wright, a boy inventor with many adventures of his own, was panhandled by Jesse James, who managed to extract a five dollar check from him. Jesse thereupon kited the check to five thousand dollars and tried to make a getaway. Young Jack chased Jesse and his band in an electric landrover, protected himself in inflated armor, exchanged shots with Jesse (using a pneumatic gun of a sort), and captured Jesse. Jesse, however, escaped later for more adventures.

As may be guessed, opinions about Jesse and Frank James varied greatly, and this ambivalence, which balanced the cruelty of the outlaws against their daring resourcefulness, permeates most of the novels about them. This is obvious in *Frank James on the Trail* [1882], which was issued in one of the lesser dime novel series, *Morrison's Sensational Series*. Its sadism is not untypical, but the venture into reportage at the close of the booklet is. The authorship of this piece is unknown, although there is a possibility that it is adapted from an earlier story by John Musick.

Nick Carter, today, is one of those characters whose name almost everyone recognizes, yet whose adventures few now know. The Little Giant, as he was nicknamed, was a small man, but so incredibly muscled that he could stand comparison with the great Sandow. His brain, however, was not muscle-bound, for he was master of many languages and skills, and his mental nimbleness enabled him to overcome with ease the elite of the world of crime. The titles of some of his adventures indicate his range: *The Thirteen's Oath of Vengeance, or A Criminal Compact; The Little Giant's Task, or Nick Carter's Wonderful Nerve; The Great Detective Defied, or Zelma the Female Fiend.*

Nick Carter's adventures fall into two major groups, stories of routine criminality and stories of fantastic criminality. The more romantic stories are the more interesting. Nick, in the course of his duties, visited lost civilizations in the Amazon drainage (where he fought in a gladiatorial arena and won a wife) and in a hidden valley in Nepal. He met strange inventions and criminals with weird abilities, such as Zanabayah, who used the "vitic force" to shock like an electric eel those who touched him. Nick had chains of adventures against particularly colorful villains of great mettle. These included the Dalney family of upstate New York, who were as much stronger than Nick as Nick was stronger than a child. They delighted in vivisection. There were adventures against Daazar, who perpetually confounded Nick by being a serial syndicate of villains (including a Tibetan lama and a Russian princess), and best known of all, Dr. Quartz. Dr. Quartz's first appearance was marked by the dispatch of a piano case containing four embalmed men playing cards. One of Quartz's obsessions is easily stated: "She was beautiful. I like beautiful girls. I like to cut them up. It is my passion." (*The Fate of Dr. Quartz, or Nick Carter and the Dissecting Room Murder*, 1895). As a result of these little touches, Nick Carter had the longest run of any American dime novel detective; only Sexton Blake, the English detective, appeared over a longer period of time.

Nick Carter first appeared in the old *New York Weekly*, the stamping ground of so many important dime novels that were later published in book form. He starred in *The Old Detective's Pupil, or The Mysterious Crime of Madison Square* [1886]. The series was created by John R. Coryell (1848–1924), who wrote the first three Nick Carter adventures, but Coryell was too busy to continue the series, since he was writing the multitudinous books of "Bertha M. Clay" for Street and

Smith, and the series was continued otherwise. In 1889 Frederick van Rensselaer Dey (pronounced "dye") took over Nick Carter, and over the years wrote more than 1,000 adventures, some 20,000,000 words.

Nick Carter became enormously popular, and his adventures were chronicled in several formats. Nick was probably the only important dime novel hero to survive the collapse of the form in the early twentieth century (since Frank Merriwell and others count really as resurrections), and original adventures of Nick Carter continued to appear (with some interruptions) up through *Nick Carter Magazine* in the early 1930's. Nick was then written by Richard Wormser. When *Nick Carter Magazine* died, occasional stories about Nick still appeared in other pulps. At the moment there is a paperback series called Nick Carter, but it has little to do with the original concepts. Over the years many men have written Nick Carter, but the Nick Carter amanuensis nonpareil remains F. v. R. Dey.

Frederick van Rensselaer Dey (1861-1922) was a pathetically interesting personality, whose life crystallized in a way the life of an "ideal" dime novelist. Born into a socially prominent family, he graduated from Columbia Law School, practiced law for a time with a future mayor of New York, took to drink, had a breakdown, and was forced to enter the treadmill of the dime novelist. Like a Southern colonel in appearance, portly, strong-featured, mustachioed, he drank and gambled away most of what he earned. In his later years he suffered from delusions of grandeur and would pose as a millionaire, ordering yachts and purchasing manors and railroads, until the time came for passing papers. His last exploit before his suicide in 1922 was a role:

> Before he killed himself he wrote to a friend telling him of what he intended to do. The friend got the letter and hastened to the little hotel where the "Colonel" was staying. As he had not registered under his own name, the visitor could not locate him and described him to the clerk.
>
> "The description fits a gentleman on the seventh floor," said the clerk, "but surely he had no thought of suicide. The man is a wealthy fruit grower in California. Why, last night before he went up to his room, he offered me a position in the fruit business in California."
>
> "That's the man I am looking for," said his friend.

It was. It was too late. Dey also wrote many other books and series, but they all vanished when the dime novel world collapsed. To indicate his working speed: his first Nick Carter novel he wrote in eight days; his second in five; his third in four, and his fourth in three days, which remained his usual speed for a 30,000-word short novel. Even at this speed his quality was superior to that of many of the other popular writers in the arena.

Dey acted out a role in life, but Edward L. Wheeler, who created Deadwood Dick, was posthumously forced into a role by his unscrupulous publishers. Wheeler, who had his stationery printed as *Edward L. Wheeler, Sensational Novelist*, was born in Avoca, New York around 1855. He spent most of his adult life in Titusville and Philadelphia, and his death must have occurred some time around 1885. Albert Johannsen, who rooted out the facts about Wheeler, discovered that Wheeler's name was used on novels long after his death, to maintain sales, even though the work of the deutero-Wheeler was much inferior to that of the original scribe of Deadwood Dick.

Deadwood Dick, who was based in part on a historical Western character named Richard W. Clarke (although there are other claimants for the role), entered literary life in October 1877 as the first issue of *Beadle's Half-Dime Library*, one of the most important dime novel series. Among the points which may have caused the success of *Deadwood Dick, The Prince of the Road or The Black Rider of the Black Hills* are its heavily dramatic structure, with a strong revenge and disinheritance plot, multiple identities and eventual justice for all. Even more interesting to the modern reader is the remarkable use of slang, a veritable gold mine of metaphor.

Well over thirty Deadwood Dick adventures were written, which were followed by a long series of Deadwood Dick, Jr. novels by other hands than Wheeler's. The success of Beadle and Adams's Deadwood Dick may be gauged by the speedy appearance of Street and Smith's Diamond Dick, which also became one of the leading chains of Western adventures. Other heroes on the same order were Gentleman Joe, Dead Shot Dave, Dakota Dan and Denver Dan.

Other historical figures of the Old West also entered the world of the dime novel: Grizzly Adams, Kit Carson, Pawnee Bill, Wild Bill Hickok and Texas Jack. Much the most important of all, of course, was Buffalo Bill, whose novels incorporate with enlargement and certain coloring the exploits of William Cody, the hunter, scout and showman. It was Ned Buntline, one of the more outrageous of the early dime novelists, who started the exploitation of Cody with *Buffalo Bill, the King of Bordermen*, which appeared in 1869. Many other adventures followed, some apparently written by Cody himself, but Buffalo Bill's chief chronicler soon became Colonel Prentiss Ingraham.

Ingraham (1843–1904), whose life rivalled his novels, was the son of the Rev. Joseph H. Ingraham, author of *A Prince of the House of David*, which in some circles had a standing only slightly lower than Holy Writ. (J. H. Ingraham was also a dime novelist of some celebrity.) After a good education Prentiss Ingraham served on the Confederate side in the Civil War, then turned soldier of fortune. He fought with Juarez against Maximilian, and also served in the Austrian and Egyptian armies. During the Cuban insurrection of the 1860's, he ran guns through the Spanish blockade, and was eventually captured. This swashbuckling life continued for a time, until Ingraham became acquainted with Buffalo Bill. Eventually Ingraham settled in New York (later Chicago), and apart from a brief period as publicity agent for Buffalo Bill's Wild West Show, he spent the remainder of his life writing dime novels. According to some sources he produced more than 1,000 novels, Buffalo Bill being his most important product. In them Buffalo Bill did not limit himself to adventures among Indians, but often escaped peril from Russian revolutionaries, anarchists, spies and rogues in general.

One of the bitterest complaints about Buffalo Bill and his fictional parallels was that their thrills and delights lured Eastern boys away from home to the wild and woolly West—and the parents had to pay rail fares home. I have never heard, however, that parents approved of the dime novels that interested their children in technology, invention and applied science. This was the Frank Reade series and its parallels.

The formula for these primitive science-fiction stories was generally simple: a boy genius invents something that is not too far removed from the science and technology of the day, and then has adventures which usually could have happened just as well without the invention. Aeronautics was especially popular, with assorted flying machines that worked by electricity, by steam, by new superbuoyant gases, or by an anticipation of the helicopter. Submarines, too, were popular, and through their mechanism much buried treasure was found and many sunken cities. In one such story Tom Edison, Jr. invents a Sea Spider, with which he destroys a Chinese pirate base, and then engages in a submarine duel with the Sea Serpent, an underwater vessel designed by the Chinese criminal mastermind, Kiang Ho. The Sea Spider is a globular vessel with retractable legs like a spider's; the Sea Serpent progresses by rotating its outer shell through the water like a screw.

The first of these early invention stories was written by Edward S. Ellis (1840–1916), the author of *Seth Jones*, the book that established the Beadle fortunes. Ellis long remained one of the most important authors of dime novels. He wrote both under his own name and under so many pseudonyms that today it is not certain what he did write, and aficionados still argue vigorously about his possible bibliography.

Ellis maintained a double career more than did most of the other important dime novelists, who tended to be complete specialists. He was a teacher and administrator in various New Jersey school systems for many years, and he wrote numerous textbooks. These range from elementary physiology and arithmetic to grammar, but the bulk of his work consisted of popular histories and biographies for school use. Most of his books, like his large anecdotal *Youth's History of the United States*, were intended for the juvenile market, but others, like his *Story of the Greatest Nations* (in collaboration with Professor Horne, who presumably provided the data which Ellis wrote up), are adult and ambitious. An outgrowth of this historical bent was a commission to prepare the scenario for a film history of the United States by Thomas A. Edison.

A sampling of these books shows Ellis to have been a fluent popularizer, without too much to say, or any great depth, but a good master of easy exposition. He obviously took his work seriously, as can be seen by a very odd lawsuit in which he was concerned. He had written a particularly low-level thriller under a pseudonym; when a publisher, who held rights to the work, insisted on republishing the work under the name Ellis, Ellis attempted to restrain him. Ellis lost the suit, thereby establishing the legal precedent that an author does not have the right to his own name.

Most of Ellis's fiction was frontier adventure of the hair-raising sort. One of these frontier stories, however, provided the germ for a new development in the dime novel. This was *The Steam Man of the Prairies* (No. 45 of *Irwin's American Novels*, 1865). It must have been a reasonably popular work, since it was reprinted at least six times under variant titles, as *The Huge Hunter, or The Steam Man of the Prairies* and *Baldy's Boy Partner, or Young Brainerd's Steam Man.* Yet Ellis and Beadle never followed up in this area, and it was left for the more aggressive Tousey to make real the potentialities of a new subdivision in the dime novel.

It was *Frank Reade and His Steam Man*, which first appeared in Tousey's *Boys of New York* periodical that established the invention story as a form. The first three Frank Reade stories were written by Harry Enton, a very young New Yorker, who used his earnings to pay his way through medical school. Enton then withdrew, since Tousey insisted on carrying the stories under a house name, "Noname," and Luis Senarens, also a very young man at the time, continued the series through many inventions, against some competition. (The reader who wishes more detail, particularly the relation of these stories to Jules Verne, may consult Sam Moskowitz's *Explorers of the Infinite*.) The ultimate outcome of this small stream of fiction, of course, was E. Stratemeyer's Tom Swift series.

While these invention stories have some interest as prototypes of later science-fiction, they are more important in reflecting the invention mentality of pre-modern America. Judging from that fine account of primitive automobiling, *Horseless Carriage Days* by Hiram P. Maxim, every other barn in America before 1900 housed the dream of a horseless carriage or a flying machine.

An even stronger symbolic figure than the inventor, however, was Frank Merriwell, one of the very few dime novel heroes who tried to make an adaptation to our modern world of radio, motion pictures and television. *Frank Merriwell, or First Days at Fardale* appeared in April 1896, as the first issue of Street and Smith's *Tip Top Library*. Documents survive showing that Frank was created with great deliberateness by the editorial staff of Street and Smith and "Burt Standish" as a countermove to the British school stories, which were enjoying one of their occasional successes in America. The publishers established Merriwell's life pattern: exploits at a fashionable prep school, an inheritance, travel, matriculation at college, preferably Yale, and further adventures. Merriwell was to be democratic in outlook, above the racial and ethnic prejudices that sometimes beset the British school story, and the novels were to deal more with characters than with hair-raising events. *Frank Merriwell, or First Days at Fardale* was a smashing success. It was followed by more than one thousand sequels.

These Frank Merriwell stories fall into two groups, the school stories set at Fardale or Yale, and adventure stories, in which Frank, with or without school chums, meets perils around the world. *Frank Merriwell's Nobility, or The Tragedy of the Ocean Tramp* [1899] has been selected to show the moral fervor that often animates Merry, typical personalities, and characteristic adventures. It should be pointed out, though, that Frank is not anti-French, for shortly after this adventure there occurs a sequence of stories in which Frank becomes involved in the Dreyfus affair in Paris. The anti-Dreyfusites cause a bomb to be hurled at Frank; he bites off the lighted fuse.

More than 900 of the 1,000 or so Merriwell stories were written by the original "Burt Standish," William Gilbert Patten.

Patten (1866–1945) was the last of the great dime novelists. A State of Mainer with limited education, originally destined for the ministry, he was driven by native ability into a long, profitable career as a writer. After trial ventures as a cooper, a newspaper owner and job printer, a reporter, he gravitated to New York, where he first wrote on commission for Norman Munro, then later on salary for Street and Smith. Patten's outlook on life was moral, even though he wrote ordinary adventure dime novels, and he considered Frank Merriwell a force for good and cherished him. After the dime novel world collapsed, attempts were made to bring Frank Merriwell back to life in other forms: in addition to an early film, *Frank Merriwell in Arizona* (1914), there was a Universal film, *The Adventures of Frank Merriwell* (1936), a comic strip in the early 1930's, and a radio trial. Television adaptations were long promised, but if they ever took place, they did not succeed. Patten himself attempted an adult novel about Frank, *Mr. Frank Merriwell* (1945), but it was a failure from all points of view.

William Patten alone of the great dime novelists has left us a fairly full autobiography, so that we know something of the external and internal experiences of a multimillion worder. I wish the same could be said of an even more important, even more widely published author, Horatio Alger. Not only did Alger fail to keep an adequate record of his eventless life, but the first biography of Alger was a hoax which interpreted Alger's life as a combination Horatio Alger novel and true confessions account. It disseminated many delightful incidents which never happened and created about a dozen Alger books that were never written.

Horatio Alger was the world's best-selling author for a long time. No one knows how many of Alger's novels were sold, since there were often many editions of the same book on the market, on a plate-rental basis, and publication history is very confused. Estimates range, however, from 100,000,000 to 300,000,000 copies. These hundreds of millions of copies are based on a little more than 100 novels, without counting a few score short stories, poems and lesser works. As a corollary to this frantic printing sequence, it is certainly safe to say that Horatio Alger must also have been one of the most widely read authors in all history, for no one in the 1890's would have bought a dozen of Alger's novels except to read them.

Much wish fulfillment must have entered the novels of Horatio Alger, for their author was very unlike the heroes of his books. A very small, slight man (until he fattened late in life), a man with severe sexual problems, with mental depressions, he probably earned a fortune, but managed to spend most of it unwisely. He delighted in giving presents to the newsboys with whom he lived at the Newsboys Foundation, and he seems to have been a sure touch for any attractive gamin with a good story. He died in near poverty.

Alger was born in Massachusetts in 1834, the son of a Unitarian minister. He graduated from Harvard, tutored for a time, did freelance writing, graduated from Harvard Divinity School, entered the ministry for a time, and was forced to leave because of scandals. From 1866 on he made his living as a writer in New York. While he had had several books and a fair amount of ephemeral work published earlier, *Ragged Dick* (1867) was his first important novel, a story which catapulted him to fame. As a result of it he became associated with various New York social and philanthropic activities. He died in 1899.

The selection for this volume, *Adrift in New York, or Dodger and Florence Braving the World*, is an abridgment of a novel which first appeared in 1889 in the *Family Story Magazine*, published by Norman Munro. It was republished at least twice between 1889 and the present edition, but it did not achieve book publication until 1904. It is one of Alger's lesser known works.

As *Adrift in New York* demonstrates, Horatio Alger was not a great writer. Even his collectors and admirers will occasionally admit this. His work differs, however, from that of most of the other dime novelists. Alger took it very seriously, and in turn he was probably taken very seriously by his readers. It would be impossible to measure the impact which he had on late nineteenth- and early twentieth-century America, or even estimate the degree to which his work mirrored contemporary mores. Today, beyond the story line, it has the virtue of offering a good, detailed picture of daily life in Victorian Gotham—horse cars, street venders, street crime, the Bowery, immigrants, mud, brutality, and over everything, the drive upwards.

These were the men who made the dime novels, hundreds and thousands of books, millions of dollars, and the reading time of young America for forty or fifty years. As can be seen, for the most part they were men of intelligence and education who assumed the incredible burden of creating an endless flow of fiction. There were, of course, other individuals who wrote for the large chains and the minor leagues—housewives in the Middle West, salesmen in New England, farmers in upstate New York, schoolboys, cowboys and others. But much the largest, most representative share was created by men like Dey, Ellis, Ingraham and Patten, men who worked hard yet did not find it too difficult to cope with a task that most writers could not have fulfilled.

They must be admired as mental athletes of a very peculiar sort, men who could emit novels as freely as a queen bee lays eggs, perpetrators of a colossal achievement. To entertain a million people for one thousand times, no matter on what level, is an achievement very few men can match.

E. F. BLEILER

March, 1973

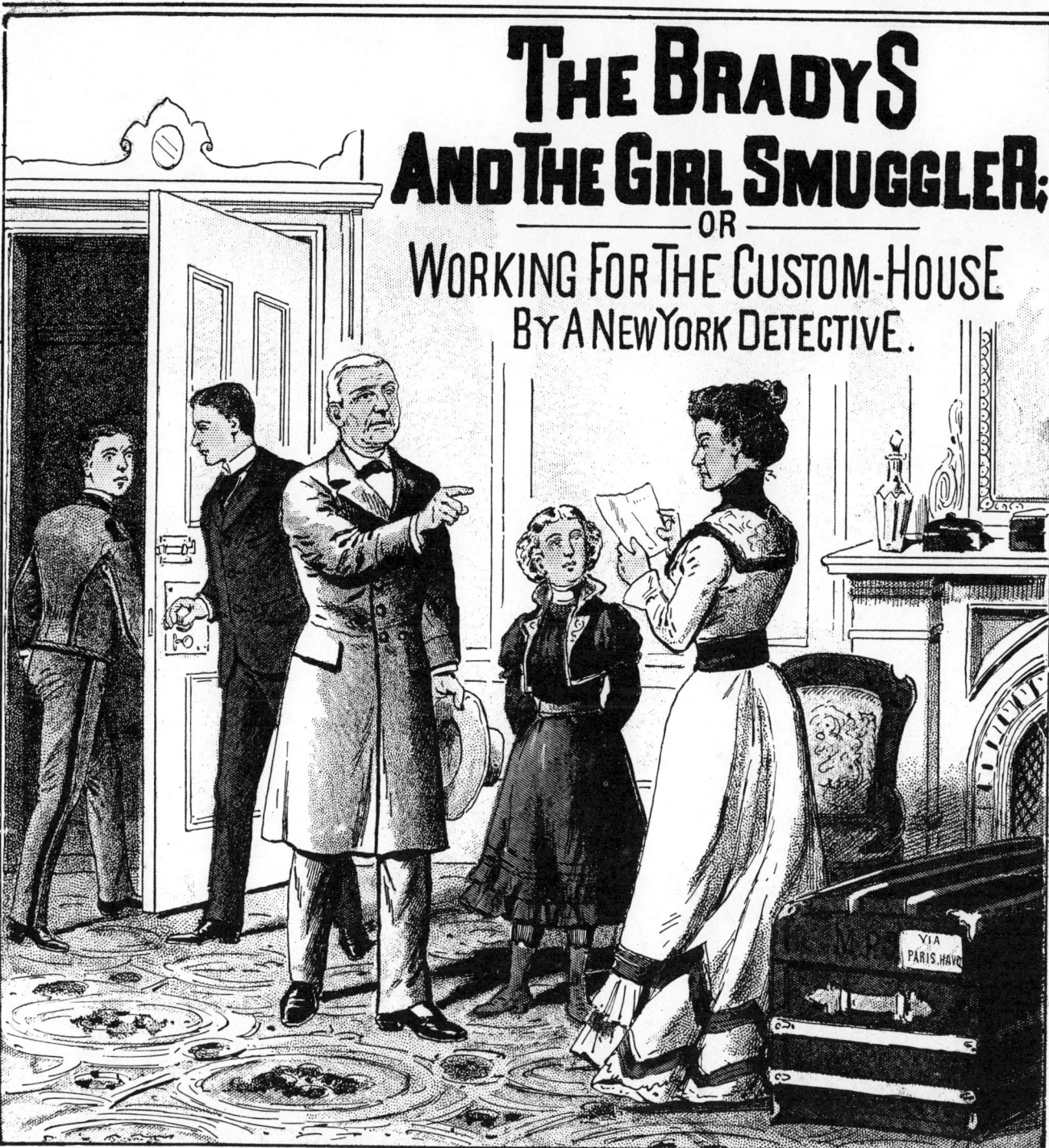

SECRET SERVICE.

OLD AND YOUNG KING BRADY DETECTIVES.

Issued Weekly—By Subscription $2.50 per year. Entered as Second Class Matter at the New York, N. Y., Post Office, March 1, 1899. Entered according to Act of Congress, in the year 1900, in the office of the Librarian of Congress, Washington, D. C., by Frank Tousey, 24 Union Square, New York.

No. 79.   NEW YORK, July 27, 1900.   Price 5 Cents.

The Bradys and the Girl Smuggler

OR,

Working for the Custom House.

BY A NEW YORK DETECTIVE.

CHAPTER I.

THE BRADYS AS CUSTOM HOUSE DETECTIVES.

The Collector of the Port of New York sat in his office in the Custom House with a look of annoyance upon his face.

Several of his chief inspectors were standing about the room with the most uneasy expressions, for they were being censured unmercifully.

"I tell you, gentlemen," the Collector was saying, angrily, "I am very much disgusted with the poor service your department is giving. I am determined to stop this wholesale smuggling. If none of you are capable of doing the work for which you are liberally paid, I'll have to get somebody to do the work for you. Do you understand?"

"But, sir," began one of the inspectors, humbly, "we've done our best——"

"And accomplished nothing!" snapped the Collector.

"How could we, sir? The smuggler you want us to catch does not resort to the usual tricks such people adopt to avoid paying duty on the diamonds and other precious stones, which you say are smuggled into this country. It's because he's such a sly and clever rogue, that we can't locate him. We've resorted to every known method to discover the villain, but can't make any headway."

"Then you admit you are beaten?"

"Yes," was the hesitating reply.

"Hum!" grunted the Collector, in tones of contempt. "A nice lot of government detectives you fellows are to admit such a defeat. However, I've taken the matter into my own hands now."

"Yours?"

"Yes! I've engaged two of the most skillful men in the Secret Service to run down this smuggler. I refer to Old and Young King Brady."

"Indeed!" sneered the inspector, whose pride was wounded. "I'm sure if we can't find that smuggler, they can't."

"They can't, eh?" grimly demanded the Collector. "Well, you'll find out whether they can or not, Andrew Gibson, for they'll be here presently to take your work right out of your hands. Do you hear me?"

With glum looks the inspectors glanced at each other.

It was a bitter pill for them to swallow, to have an outsider come in to do the work they found themselves unable to cope with.

Finally Gibson affected a mocking laugh, and said, derisively:

"What can a Secret Service man do in a Custom House case, if we men, educated for it, can't finish a job we find too hard for us?"

"They'll find the smuggler I'm after," replied the Collector, banging his fist on the desk to emphasize his remark. "I've got every faith in that remarkable man and boy. They are the most skillful detectives in the profession. There's nothing they can't do in their own line, and you'll find it out soon."

"On police and criminal cases——"

"On *any* work!" roared the Collector, excitedly.

"They must be marvels, indeed!" sneered Gibson.

"So they are, sir—so they are."

"I'd like to see these wonders!"

Just then two men in uniform standing apart from the rest, advanced.

They wore the costume of boarding officers, the dark-blue uniforms being garnished with brass buttons and on their heads were caps with bands across the front bearing the word in gilt letters, "Inspector."

One of these men was tall and muscular, with a bushy black beard, deep gray eyes and a heavy mass of dark-brown hair.

His companion looked like a mere boy, with a handsome face, a pair of keen eyes and a dashing, aggressive air that showed he was of a bold, intrepid character. He walked right up to the inspector.

"So you want to see the Bradys, do you?" he asked Gibson, quietly.

"Yes, I would," asserted the inspector, glaring at him in surprise.

"Then look, for we are the Bradys!" exclaimed the boy.

He took off his cap and his companion stripped off a wig and false beard.

Every one in the room glanced at them in amazement.

No one suspected their identity before.

Old King Brady was now seen to have white hair and a clean-shaven face, in which a daring, determined character was shown.

Even the Collector was astonished.

When he recovered his composure, a smile crossed his face, and he rose and warmly shook hands with the pair, saying:

"Well, this is an agreeable surprise."

Old King Brady smiled, took a chew of tobacco and replied:

"You got our chief to assign us on this case and requested us to be here at two o'clock, and here we are."

"Ready for work?"

"Yes, sir. Instruct us."

"Well, all I can tell you is that this country is being flooded with precious stones upon which no duty is being paid, and I want you to find the party who is doing the crooked work."

"Have you any clews upon which we can work?"

"None, whatever. You'll have to get them yourselves from the importers in John street, Broadway and Maiden Lane. They may give you some points."

"We shall follow your suggestion."

The two detectives started for the door, then paused.

Harry Brady, the boy, then said:

"Mr. Gibson has some doubts about our ability to work for the Custom House. Since he has flung defiance at us, we'll accept his challenge."

"How? growled the inspector, in ugly tones.

"Well, we'll meet you officers and the Collector on board the steamer Campania, of the Cunard line, in one hour, when she reaches her pier from Quarantine. If we don't show up more smugglers than you do, we'll give up this assignment."

"I'll go you!" eagerly exclaimed the jealous inspector.

"And I'll be there to see that you get fair play," grimly said the Collector.

The Bradys silently bowed and withdrew.

When they reached the street, Old King Brady laughed and said:

"They're all jealous of us. But we'll show them a trick or two, Harry."

"They'll be a surprised lot," laughed the boy. "We have them beaten already."

They headed for the jewelry district and called upon several of the most prominent importers and lapidaries, from whom they gained some very valuable information. The last importer they spoke to said:

"Paul La Croix, a French-Canadian, was just in here with his daughter, trying to sell us some smuggled diamonds. See—there he goes now."

He pointed out the window at a tall, thin, stylishly-clad man of forty in light trousers, a black frock coat and high hat.

The detectives observed that he now did not have his daughter with him.

From where they were, they could see that La Croix had a thin, sallow face, a long, sharp nose and a closely-trimmed dark moustache.

He turned into Broadway and disappeared in the crowd.

"Who is he?" asked Old King Brady, of the dealer in precious stones.

"A mystery. No one knows. He makes many trips between New York and Havre to smuggle diamonds which he sells here. Every jeweler in the Lane knows him. Some deal with him."

"Where does he live?"

"At the Fifth Avenue Hotel."

"Thank you."

And a moment later the detectives were gone.

Reaching Broadway they hurried ahead intending to find La Croix and arrest him with contraband diamonds in his possession.

But the man disappeared and they found no trace of him.

The Bradys gave up the hunt, temporarily, for they were determined to find the man again.

They crossed the city, going to the west side.

People who saw the pair paid no heed to them now, for they had made some changes in their apparel, in a sheltering doorway, and by turning their coats inside out, pocketing their uniform hats and putting on soft felt hats, they transformed their appearance.

They now looked like ordinary citizens.

Each one adjusted a false moustache and a wig to hide his identity.

They had their clothing so made that they could change to several characters with but little trouble.

This fact was well known to most of the crooks at large, and they feared the Bradys more than any other detetectives on the force.

Although they bore the same name, there was no relationship between them, for Harry was merely an apt pupil the old detective had chanced to meet, and was educating in his profession.

As a team, they made themselves famous.

When they drew near the Cunard steamship dock, Old King Brady carried his handkerchief in his hand as a signal.

A man was on the lookout and ran up to him.

Handing the detective a letter he exclaimed:

"I followed your order, Mr. Brady and went down to Quarantine to-day with the port doctor. He took me aboard the Campania, and I found out a great deal. It's all written in that letter. I wrote it coming up on the Custom House tug."

"Has the steamer reached her dock yet?"

"She's swinging in now. I beat her up on the tug."

"Very well. You may go."

The spotter hastened away and the detectives eagerly read his letter.

It was full of valuable information for which they sent the man and having read the letter they hastened to the pier.

The big trans-Atlantic steamer was just tying up to her dock and the detectives saw the Collector and his inspectors standing on the pier waiting for the passengers to land.

CHAPTER II.

NINE SMUGGLERS.

A scene of great animation and excitement was soon transpiring on the pier.

Passengers were swarming down the gangplank of the big steamer, crowds of friends were waiting to greet them, porters and waiters were landing the baggage on the dock and stevedores were preparing to discharge the cargo.

The two Bradys took up a favorable position and calling the purser of the steamer, they induced him to point out several people whose names they mentioned.

These people were the ones whom they had spotted as smugglers.

Presently the owners of the baggage began opening their trunks and valises so the inspectors could examine their effects.

While this was going on the Bradys joined the Collector and spoke to him. He was startled to discover their identity and remarked:

"Well, you certainly have the faculty of hiding your identity in the most complete manner. Have you found any smugglers yet?"

"Several," replied Harry, quickly.

"Indeed! Who are they?"

"We'll show you when your men get through."

They chatted together until the inspection was finished and all the luggage had been marked and received the pasters to show they were passed.

"Now call your men and get their report, sir," said Harry.

The Collector did as he was requested.

Out of several hundred passengers only a lace shawl had been captured.

"Is that all you managed to find that was dutiable?" asked Harry, in surprise, as the searchers gathered round them.

They recognized him by his voice and Gibson growled sarcastically:

"Do you think you can do any better?"

"Oh, my—yes."

"Well, I'd like to see you do it."

"So we shall. Let us begin with Mrs. Harvey. Open her trunk again."

Despite the lady's protests this was done.

Pointing at the tray, Harry said, coolly:

"Pick up that cake of toilet soap, cut it in two and you'll find a very valuable gentleman's ruby ring and scarf pin buried inside of it."

Gibson complied with a poor grace.

As Harry said, he disclosed the articles mentioned.

"My!" said the lady, innocently, "I wonder how they got there?"

"Madam," replied Harry, politely, "you put them there yourself. As a lady don't wear such things and you've been traveling alone, it's clear you were trying to smuggle those things. Seize them, Gibson, and they'll be appraised in the Custom House. If the lady then wishes to pay the full duty charged on them she can get back her ornaments."

The Collector burst out laughing.

"Any more?" he asked Old King Brady.

"Yes. See that short fat man? He is Mr. Jacobs, a stock broker. I guess we'll have to pull off the gentleman's left boot. Hey, Mr. Jacobs!"

"Vell?" growled the fat broker, glancing at the detective in some surprise.

"Sit down on your trunk, please," said Old King Brady.

"Vot for?"

"I'll show you in a moment."

The broker sat down and Harry seized him and held him there.

At the same moment Old King Brady grabbed him by the left foot, gave it a tug and the struggling man gave a yell, and demanded, excitedly, as the boot slipped off and remained in the detective's hand:

"Py shiminey, vot yer mean py dot outrages alretty?"

"We think you are cheating the government," replied Old King Brady.

"Vot? Me? You vas grazy!"

"Am I?" blandly asked Old King Brady.

"Sure you are! Vot mein boot vas got mit it ter do?"

"I'll show you, my innocent friend," grimly replied the old detective, as he drew out his pocket knife.

With the large blade he removed the first layer of leather from the heel and showed that the heel was hollow.

Lying within this neat little opening was a small paper

package which the detective drew out. Opening the paper he showed its contents.

It consisted of five magnificent diamonds.

The broker gave a gasp of horror and Old King Brady said to him sweetly:

"You forgot to put these on the manifest, Mr. Jacobs, didn't you?"

"*Och, Gott!*" groaned the unlucky broker, in deep anguish of spirit, "I vas ruint vunct. Vot vill I do? Vot vill I do?"

"Pay the duty and redeem them from the Custom House," replied the detective, and the gems were seized on the spot.

All the inspectors looked envious of the two detectives.

The Collector regarded them with a cold glance and finally asked:

"Why didn't you find these things?"

"Didn't know they had 'em," sheepishly replied Gibson.

"We ain't half through yet," said Harry at this juncture.

"What else have you discovered?" demanded the Collector, curiously.

"Several hundred yards of fine point lace."

"Where is it?"

"In a false bottom under Miss Daisy Linden's trunk. See—there she stands—that handsome big actress there. Do you think she's as fat as she looks? Well, just notice how big around her body is, and how thin her arms and neck are. If you'll get one of the lady inspectors to examine her privately, you'll find she's got several valuable oil paintings wrapped around her body, under her clothes."

The woman made a great fuss when they insisted upon rummaging in her trunk a second time and reluctantly opened it again.

Harry threw everything out and the woman shrieked, scolded and protested. But when the boy opened the false bottom of the trunk and withdrew the lace he mentioned, she fainted.

When the actress came to, she found that a lady inspector had disrobed her in a stateroom on the steamer and taken five very costly paintings away, which she was smuggling under her clothes.

By the time the Bradys finished, they had nine smugglers exposed, and fully quarter of a million dollars' worth of valuables were seized.

The Collector had been watching these proceedings with deep interest.

When his own men reached him, he said to them:

"I'm ashamed of you. Here you let two absolutely green men step in and do the work you've been at for years, much better than you do it yourselves."

"Well," grimly admitted Gibson, "they've kept their boast and beaten us badly, I'm sorry to say. I don't need to wish them luck for they've got either a large amount of it, or else they had some inside information."

"Your latter surmise is the correct one," said Harry. "We sent a man down the bay to meet the steamer. People who are going to smuggle anything rarely take pains to conceal their contraband goods till they are nearing port. We know something about the matter, you see. Moreover, we know would-be smugglers who don't make a profession of it are very careless, talkative about what they are going to smuggle, and apt to give themselves away. By sending a good, smart spotter ahead we learned all about the people we've exposed."

"That game may work very nicely with amateurs. But it would not go with a professional smuggler by any means."

"I quite agree with you," assented Harry.

"Well," said the Collector, "I'm quite satisfied with your performance, Mr. Brady, and am convinced that you are the very men to run down the big smuggler I am so anxious to see arrested."

"We'll do our best," said Old King Brady.

The Collector and the inspectors then went away.

As they were leaving the pier, the quick, keen eyes of Harry observed a young girl on the steamer acting in a mysterious manner.

She was standing in the gangway, peering out one of the port holes and sharply watching the departing officials.

Every time one of them chanced to glance back, she suddenly dodged down behind the bulwark out of sight.

She was a beautiful girl of about sixteen, handsomely clad in a short dress and zouave waist of fine silk, while a stylish big Gainsborough hat with black ostrich plumes crowned her short, yellow, curly hair.

Her skin was as white as milk and she had a pair of big brown eyes, a pretty little Grecian nose and rosebud lips.

Young King Brady was charmed with her beauty, yet his suspicions of her actions were aroused to the fever point.

He touched his partner on the arm and pointed at her.

"See there!" he exclaimed. "What can she be up to?"

"We'd better keep an eye on her, Harry," returned the old detective, after a careful survey. "It looks to me as if she were up to some trick. She wouldn't be watching those inspectors' departure that way unless it was of vital importance to her."

"But surely she can't be so silly as to think there are no officers left here. Everyone knows that a couple remain constantly on the watch in their office at the entrance to the dock."

"Ha! What's that? She's waving her handkerchief to that man who is coming out on the pier from West street."

Young King Brady gazed keenly at the person in question and suddenly recognizing him he exclaimed in excited tones:

"Why, it's Paul La Croix, the diamond smuggler!"

"So it is, by thunder!"

"And this beautiful girl must be his daughter, for she greatly resembles him."

"Harry, I believe that pair are up to some crooked work!"

"We can find out by watching them."

La Croix now went aboard the steamer and joined the girl in the gangway.

CHAPTER III.

CAUGHT IN AN ELEVATOR.

The Bradys felt convinced that the smuggler and his daughter were working some scheme to take some valuables ashore, duty free.

Closely watching the pair they saw them enter the cabin.

Following them in, the Bradys observed the pair gliding swiftly down a passage, out on which opened the doors of several staterooms.

La Croix and his daughter entered one of these rooms.

Rushing forward, the Bradys listened outside the partition and heard the man ask:

"Did you geet eet, Clara?"

"Yes, papa," replied the girl in a low, pleasant tone of voice. "After I left you on Maiden Lane, I came right here and mingled with the throng waiting to meet the various passengers. As soon as the gangplank was down, I slipped aboard and met the steward. He had the parcel and gave it to me."

"Open eet so we can distribute ze jewelry about our pairsons. Zen we geet ze sings ashore ver' easy, an' no wong weel see ze package bulge out our clothing. *Mon Dieu*, but I vas ver'—vot you call—ze—ze—worried."

The crackling of paper was heard.

For a few moments afterward there ensued a deep silence.

Old King Brady silently beckoned to Harry and they retreated a few paces.

"I'm going right in after La Croix," he whispered.

"We've got him dead to rights," replied the boy.

"Are you prepared for a fight?"

"Oh, yes. I've got a powerful persuader in my hip pocket."

"Then come on with me."

He strode forward and pushed the stateroom door open.

It opened inward and as the room was very small, it pushed La Croix against the two bunks and wrung the startled cry from his lips:

"Look out, Clara!"

The girl glared at the detectives and demanded:

"What do you want in here?"

"That man!" said Harry, pointing at her father.

"What for?"

"Smuggling!"

"He isn't!"

"We'll search him and see."

The Bradys grasped the excited Frenchman.

His clothing in the region of his stomach was bulging suspiciously and Old King Brady slapped the spot and demanded:

"What have you got there?"

"Nosing!" protested La Croix. "Zees ees an outrage, sair!"

"Oh, I don't know!" laughed Harry.

"Clara!" roared the man. "Go tell ze captaine, quick, to come 'ere."

The girl slipped out the door and vanished.

Left alone with the man, the detectives laughed and Harry said:

"Unbutton your coat and vest."

"*Sacre!* For why?" growled La Croix.

"We want to see what you've got stuffed in there."

"Gentlemen, you wrong me!"

"Bosh! Open up quick, or we'll do it for you."

La Croix reluctantly opened his vest and a package dropped out.

He then was of normal size.

"This is what we are after!" laughed Harry, picking up the parcel.

"But, Monsieur, eet ees only a worthless——"

"Silence, sir!"

And Harry opened the mysterious parcel.

It was filled with sawdust.

The man laughed, shrugged his shoulders, and asked:

"Vell, sair, you ees satisfied?"

There was a look of disgust on Harry's face and he cried:

"He has cleverly duped us and the girl got away with the valuables."

Old King Brady was furious.

"Confound her!" he roared. "Come—search this man thoroughly, and if he has not got any contraband stuff, we'll search the ship and arrest the girl."

Harry turned La Croix's pockets inside out.

Nothing was found upon his person.

Then they searched the room.

Still nothing came to light and Harry said:

"He has nothing with him."

"Very well. The girl has, then."

"Now, Monsieur, I hope you see zat you wrong me?" said La Croix.

Old King Brady gave him a peculiar look, shook his finger at the Frenchman and replied in angry tones:

"We know you, La Croix. You are the worst smuggler in this port. It won't be long before we run you in for your crooked work."

"Ah—how you can say zat?" innocently asked the man.

"We have no time to discuss the matter now, for we are very anxious to nab your daughter Clara," said the old detective. "But you will meet us again very soon. Then look out!"

They hastened out of the stateroom.

Once outside Harry whispered hastily:

"You go ahead and I'll fool him."

He thereupon slipped into an adjoining room.

Old King Brady knew at once what the boy wanted to do, and he left the cabin and began to search the ship for the girl.

La Croix was peering cautiously from the room he was in and seeing the old detective disappearing out the door, he emerged.

Watching Old King Brady to see that his own actions were not observed, the smuggler finally left the steamer with Harry at his heels in a change of appearance which even his keen eyes failed to penetrate.

Old King Brady saw them depart.

He transformed his own appearance.

Both he and Harry now had assumed their natural looks.

There was a big white felt hat on the old detective's head, his frock coat of dark-blue was buttoned up to the neck, around which there now was a standing collar and an old-fashioned stock and on his hands were cotton gloves.

The boy's suit of brown plaid, and a bicycle cap on his head, were much different from the reverse side of his clothing and the other hat he had worn.

In the street Harry saw the man hail a cab and get in.

He saw his partner and beckoned to him.

When they met, Harry asked eagerly:

"Did you find the girl?"

"No. She must have hurried from the steamer."

"Well, La Croix is bound to meet her now."

"Of course."

"Our plan is to keep him shadowed."

"See if we can't get a cab, too."

They pursued the carriage on foot as far as Eighth avenue before they encountered a public hack and got in.

Instructing the driver to pursue the other vehicle, they were carried up to Fourteenth street, across town to Broadway and thence up to Twenty-third street.

La Croix's vehicle paused before the Fifth Avenue Hotel and he alighted.

"We were not misinformed about his address," commented Harry.

"No. He is probably going in there to meet the girl."

"Let's get out here at the Arch so as not to attract his attention."

"Very well. Be careful now."

They dismissed the cab and hurried into the hotel.

La Croix had disappeared from view and the detectives hastened to the office and said to the clerk:

"Got a party here named La Croix?"

"Yes, sir. They're in room 678. Wish to send up your name?"

"No," replied Old King Brady, with a smile, as he exhibited his badge.

"Oh," said the clerk, detective, eh?"

"We're after La Croix. He's a crook."

"He is? What has he done?"

"Smuggler."

"I see. How about his wife and daughter?"

"They must be in his game too."

"Going to pull them in?"

"Probably. Is he in his room?"

"He just went up the stairs."

"I wish we could reach his apartments ahead of him."

"So you can by going up in the elevator. It's on the top floor."

"We'll try it."

They hastened over to the elevators and found that the only one down was one which had no conductor in it. As they did not wish to lose time, they both got in, shut the door and pulled the wire cable.

Up they glided, story after story, without seeing him ascending the stairs.

He had gone up in an elevator from the floor above.

Above on the beams over the elevator shaft La Croix was crouching with a big hatchet in his hand, as he peered down at the people ascending in the cars.

He had detected them in pursuit and expecting trouble, he was waiting to give the detectives a warm reception. He evidently recognized them without their disguises.

As he caught view of his pursuers coming up in the car, he picked up the hatchet he had found lying on the beam.

Raising it above his head, he brought it down upon the cable by which the car was suspended, with all his strength.

The shock caused the Bradys to look up and they saw what he was doing.

Bang! went the keen blade upon the cable again where it crossed the wheel.

The weight of the car caused the wire rope to part where he cut it, and the elevator's ascent was checked.

It began to fall with the detectives in it.

CHAPTER IV.

THE CLEW IN THE BASIN.

A cry of alarm escaped Old King Brady when he saw the Frenchman.

"Harry," he gasped, "he is trying to kill us."

"There goes the cable!" muttered the boy, and a cold chill darted through him as he heard the ominous snap of the parting strands.

"The safety-clutch may save us, Harry."

"No! It don't work," groaned the boy as the car shot down.

A sickening sensation passed through the pair as the falling car went plunging down at lightning speed.

They expected to get dashed to death at the bottom as they went flying down past the different floors, and heard a fiendish chuckle from the Frenchman above their heads.

Like rats in a trap, the two detectives were held so they could do nothing to aid themselves.

All they could do was to wait for the final crash, and visions of the wrecked car and their bodies crushed to a pulp flashed across their minds.

The desperation of their situation was appalling.

The speed of their fall took their breath away and both instinctively grasped the sides of the car and clung to it tenaciously.

Down three stories they plunged.

Then there suddenly sounded a sharp "click."

The car paused, slid a few feet, then came to a sudden stop.

At the last moment the clutches flew out and tightened on the pilot rods, holding the falling car in midair.

The sudden stopping hurled the detectives to the floor,

but they quickly scrambled to their feet, overjoyed at their salvation.

For an instant neither could speak.

To be so suddenly snatched from the very jaws of death was such a strain upon their nerves that they could hardly stand it.

Old King Brady was the first to recover, and glancing upward he saw that their enemy had disappeared from the beam overhead.

"By thunder!" he exclaimed. "La Croix is baffled!"

"I never expected such good luck," replied Harry, delightedly.

"The car is holding, all right."

"Yes, but how are we to get out of it?"

They were caught midway between the second and third floors.

But the parting of the cable had been detected by the engineer and the conductor of an ascending car in the next shaft as the falling elevator flew down past him, and help was coming.

As the news spread, people flocked out in the hall, filled with dread lest the two officers had been killed.

They peered down the shafts through the grill work and when some saw the car, a shout of relief went up, and a man yelled at the Bradys:

"Were you hurt?"

"No. We are all right, so far."

"Wait, and we'll have the car lowered."

Up came men with ropes, and the end of a line was passed down from the floor above the car and Old King Brady made it fast.

When the danger of the car falling was obviated, another gang secured the cut cable, passed it over the drum, brought it down to the roof of the car and spliced it to the piece remaining there.

The elevator was then lowered to the ground floor and opening the door the detectives passed out, none the worse for their adventure.

A crowd of anxious people surrounded them, but they quickly avoided them by dodging into another car and saying to the conductor:

"Top floor—quick!"

Bang! went the gate and up they shot.

Reaching the upper story the detectives made a rush for the room La Croix had been occupying and found it empty.

"The birds have flown!" muttered Old King Brady in disgust.

"No wonder. We were caged up in the elevator so long they had ample time."

"They may have left some clew behind. Let us search the room."

This was done, and in the slop basin they found a letter torn up in small pieces.

Harry carefully gathered up the fragments and put them in his pocketbook.

"It's written in French," he commented, "but it may be of some use. I'll put the pieces together and we'll have it translated."

They failed to find anything else and went downstairs.

Returning to the clerk, they asked if La Croix had been seen.

"He did not come out this way," replied the man, shaking his head.

"Sure?"

"Positive!"

"Well, he and his family are gone."

"Ain't they up in their room?"

"No."

"That's queer."

"Not at all. You heard how the elevator fell with us?"

"Yes."

"Well, La Croix saw us and cut the cable."

"Good Lord! Tried to kill you?"

"Exactly. That's why they fled."

"What a villain that fellow must be."

"Is there any other exit from here?"

"Yes, indeed. I'll have a boy show you."

He rang a hand-bell and a uniformed boy approached, to whom he gave an order and the Bradys were escorted away.

By questioning the help they soon found that the smuggler, his wife and his daughter had left the hotel by another exit.

A policeman in the street had seen them hire a cab and drive away through Broadway at a rapid pace.

Unable to learn anything else, the detectives went home. They had very comfortable apartments and spent the day there piecing out the torn letter so it could be read.

On the following day they had it translated, and read the following startling piece of information:

"Paris, France, May 19.

"My dear La Croix: In reply to yours of the 5th inst., I beg to say that I can easily meet your daughter at Havre, if she comes over on the Champagne. I shall then take her to Amsterdam, Holland, and procure the fifty packages of diamonds. She can then assume a fictitious name and take passage on the steamer Labrador, to Canada. You can meet her in Montreal, and the stones can be taken across the border at Niagara Falls, as you suggest. Should you follow this plan, wire me at once, and I shall so arrange matters that the American spies for the Customs officials who are on the lookout here shall know knothing about the transaction. Everything depends upon keeping this a secret from them, or they will cable back to the U. S. inspectors to keep a watch for Clara when she returns to Canada——"

The letter ended abruptly here, for the rest was missing.

But there was enough to expose the whole plan of smuggling a huge amount of diamonds into the United States.

The Bradys were astonished and Harry said at once:

"This letter proves that La Croix must be the gigantic smuggler whom the Customs department want run down."

"No question about it," replied Old King Brady. "And as we have the details of a scheme he intends to operate, we had better make preparations to nip the plan in the bud, or else to capture the girl smuggler when she makes her attempt to beat the Custom House."

"Are you aware that the steamer Champagne sails for Havre to-day?"

"Does she?" muttered Old King Brady, glancing at his watch. "Well, we'll barely have time to reach her if we go at once. Get a cab and we'll see if we can catch her before she departs."

"Even if we miss her," said Harry, consolingly, "we will be pretty sure to see La Croix on the pier, seeing his daughter off."

"I don't want to arrest him in that case," said Old King Brady, "for if the girl gets away, we'll have to keep the man watched in order to let him lead us to his daughter when she returns. As she's pretty sure to have all those diamonds with her, we can nab them with evidence on their persons, of their smuggling enterprise."

Harry nodded and they hurried out together.

A hack was engaged and they rode over to the French Trans-Atlantic Company's pier on the North river.

By the time the cab reached the dock, however, the steamship's mooring lines had been cast off, the gangplank was down and the vessel was being pulled out into the stream.

The detectives were disappointed.

Eagerly scanning the throng of passengers on the upper deck, they suddenly caught view of Clara La Croix.

The girl was standing in the stern waving her handkerchief and shouting to a stylishly-dressed middle-aged woman on the stringpiece:

"Good-by, mamma!"

"Farewell, Clara—be very careful of yourself, my child!" replied the woman, as she waved her handkerchief back at the girl.

Harry nudged Old King Brady.

"There's her mother," he muttered, "but La Croix has not shown up. He fears arrest now, as he knows we are after him."

"So much the better," replied the old detective, drily. "This woman won't know us. It will therefore be all the easier to follow her undetected."

The steamship soon went down the river and the friends and relatives of the departing passengers began to leave the pier.

Mrs. La Croix was one of the last to go. She did not know that the Bradys were close behind her.

CHAPTER V.

AT A VILLAIN'S MERCY.

The smuggler's wife leisurely left the pier, crossed the street and went in the direction of Sixth avenue, on foot.

It did not seem to occur to her that she might be followed, for she never once glanced back in the direction she came from.

Old King Brady and his partner did not know much about the woman.

Whether she was actually concerned in La Croix's smuggling games or not, they had not the faintest idea.

She was a fine-looking woman, tall and stately, with brown hair, blue eyes and handsome features. But she seldom laughed.

Hers was one of those set, inscrutable faces, hard to read, for she seldom showed the emotions preying upon her mind.

"She don't seem to fear detection," commented Harry, as they walked along. "She hasn't made the slightest effort to conceal her actions."

"Well," replied the old detective, as he thoughtfully took a fresh quid of tobacco, "you must not forget that the woman isn't aware of the fact that we are on her trail."

"She certainly must be interested in her husband's crooked work or she would not see her daughter off to Europe in this manner. In fact, if she were not so greatly interested, I doubt if she would allow her child to make such a long, dangerous trip alone."

"Your reasoning is very sensible," commented Old King Brady, "but you must recollect that the girl smuggler is very smart. She is used to danger. This may not be her first voyage abroad alone. In fact, she has probably been making many trips to the other side, bringing back jewels to be smuggled ashore."

"Judging by what that letter said," remarked Harry, "the man and his wife are likely to go to Canada now and wait there for the girl's return with that large consignment of precious stones. We shall be obliged to follow them there. We can't arrest them now on suspicion, nor can we pull La Croix in for trying to murder us in the Fifth Avenue Hotel elevator. If we do, it will interfere with our capturing the girl when she returns with those jewels."

"I'm sorry to say your view of the matter is correct, Harry."

"There goes the woman up Sixth avenue. She's a good walker. It looks to me as if she were heading for the French district in the neighborhood of Third street. Queer she didn't ride."

They tracked her to West Broadway.

Here she suddenly turned into the hall of a very old house across the front of which hung the sign of an artificial flower maker.

Old King Brady passed into the hall after her and Harry remained on guard at the door.

Going up a flight of stairs, the woman knocked at a door and when it was opened, she passed into a room, closing the door after her.

The detective glided over to the door and listened.

Voices were heard inside, a man crying out eagerly:

"Well, Lena, ees ze child gone?"

"Yes, Paul," Mrs. La Croix replied, in said tones. "The Champagne just departed with our daughter. We shall not see her for a month."

"Ah, but when she return we make ze largest stake of our lives."

"I wish this risky business was ended, Paul. I'm getting

sick of it. We do not lead the peaceful lives of other people. It is a constant excitement and fear of police interference."

"Do not complain, Lena. Zees ees ze last treep ze child make. Eef eet ees wong success, we make so much dollaires zat we can retiaire an' leeve ze life of ease for ze rest of our days, by gar!"

He laughed and the woman replied, resignedly:

"Well, I hope your dream will come true, Paul."

"Take zees seat an' 'ave your suppair, my dear. You need ze rest, for to-night we leave New York by rail for Canada, for I have sold all ze stones I had, an' mail my draft to Paris."

Old King Brady smiled and muttered:

"I'm glad you've told me your business, old fellow."

The shadows of twilight had fallen by this time and the hall was getting dark.

Hearing some one coming downstairs from an upper floor, the old detective retreated along the hall and crouched back in a doorway.

He pressed himself back flat against the door hoping the person who was coming would pass him in the gloom without observing his presence.

Unfortunately the door behind him was not shut tight.

As he pressed his back against it, it flew inward all of a sudden and pitching over backward, the detective fell sprawling upon the floor of a small room adjoining the one occupied by La Croix and his wife.

He heard the Frenchman utter a startled cry.

Like a tiger he sprang into the room and saw the detective.

"*Parbleu!*" he hissed, a look of rage and hate upon his dark face. "Ze secret police. Watching me, eh? I show you, Monsieur."

He seized an iron bar standing in the corner and as the old detective was upon the point of scrambling to his feet, he dealt the officer a fearful blow that knocked him senseless.

He just had time to bang the door shut to prevent the person who was coming from upstairs from seeing what was going on.

Just then his wife rushed in.

"What is the matter, Paul?" she demanded.

"Old King Brady!" he replied, pointing at the old detective excitedly.

"Ah;" was her cool reply. "He has found our refuge, eh?"

"Yes. An' probable he has been listen to our talk."

"That is very dangerous for us, Paul."

"Not since I 'ave him at my mercy. *Sacriste!* When I geet through wiz heem now, he not weel trouble us again een wong hurry."

Fearing the detective might recover he got a piece of rope and bound and gagged Old King Brady.

When this was done an idea suddenly flashed across his mind, and he bounded to his feet and exclaimed, hoarsely:

"Where ees ze othair?"

"I don't understand you," his wife replied.

"Young King Brady."

"Do they always travel together?"

"Sairtainly."

"Then the boy must be lurking near here."

"Wait. I find heem eef I can."

He hastened from the room and made a search of the hall. Then he quietly passed downstairs and there caught view of the young detective keeping guard outside the street door.

The Frenchman was greatly excited.

He retreated into the hall and went upstairs again, muttering:

"I must geet zat boy een my powair just as queek as possible. So long as ze Bradys ees on my track, I may go to ze preeson at any moment. It makes me nairvous, by gar!"

He took up a position at the head of the stairs, wondering how he could get the best of the detectives.

Convinced that they knew all about his smuggling business and would arrest him at the first opportunity, it made him so desperate that he would not have hesitated to kill both of them.

He had not been standing at the head of the stairs long before he saw Harry glide into the hall as quietly as a shadow.

The boy was becoming impatient over his partner's long absence and made up his mind to find him.

Searching the lower hall, he failed to see anything of Old King Brady and then cautiously made his way upstairs.

The Frenchman saw him coming.

He slipped into the room where the old detective lay.

Raising his finger to his wife, he hissed:

"Hush! He coming up ze stair! Put out ze light—hurry!"

Keeping the door open on a crack when darkness fell upon the room, he peered out and listened intently.

It was too dark to see anything.

But he heard the young detective's soft footfalls passing the door and he stepped out into the hall behind Harry.

Slight as the noise was which he made, the boy heard him and turned around. striving to pierce the gloom with his sight.

La Croix had the boy located.

He suddenly sprang forward with both hands extended, struck against the boy, clutched him by the throat and knocked him over backward.

A stifled cry escaped Harry.

He was knocked down and struck the floor with a crash.

As his head went back, with the Frenchman's grip on his windpipe, his skull banged against the door-casing.

He was stunned.

"Lena! Lena!" roared La Croix.

"What is it, Paul?" asked the woman, appearing in the doorway.

"Breeng a light—queek!" he panted.

She struck a match and he saw that Harry was senseless.

With a look of evil triumph on his dark face, the man seized the boy, dragged him into the room and his wife locked the door.

La Croix bound and gagged Harry.

"Got zem both!" he chuckled.

"What are you going to do with them, Paul?" demanded his wife.

"Do wiz zem? Put zem out of ze way, my dear. Dispose of zem so effectually zat we not weel be trouble wiz zem again."

The woman met his evil glance and shuddered.

She saw what murderous thoughts were filling his mind.

CHAPTER VI.

TWO MEN IN A BOX.

On the following morning Paul La Croix went upstairs to the man who made artificial flowers and said to him:

"Monsieur Reynard, to-day ve go avay to Europe. I 'ave some sings een ze rooms ve occupy zat I weesh to send to a friend een Sacramento. To do so, I must 'ave wong beeg packing case. I see an empty wong standing over zere near ze hatchway. Can I buy him from you?"

"I'll make you a present of the big case, and be glad to get rid of it, as it takes up valuable space," replied Mr. Reynard, pleasantly. "Come, I'll help you to get it downstairs to your floor by means of the fall."

He opened the hatchway while La Croix was profusely thanking him, put a sling around the box and lowered it.

La Croix pulled the box into his front room through a door in the partition which surrounded the hatchway.

This done and Reynard out of the way, the smuggler turned to his wife, pointed at the box and asked her, with a grim smile:

"You know what zat ees for, my dear?"

"No. I have no idea. What?"

"To pack ze detectives in."

"What for?"

"So I can ship zem away."

"Won't it kill them?"

"I don't know," he replied, indifferently, shrugging his shoulders.

"Well," she remarked, after a moment's reflection, "it will give us time to get away to Canada without them knowing our destination."

"*Ma foi!* Zat ees my object."

He was provided with a hammer and some nails, and taking the lid off the box, he saw that it was amply big to hold the detectives' bodies.

Some of the joints were shrunk open, he noticed, which would admit air for the officers to breathe. This would keep them alive some time if they were not killed some other way in transit.

He did not care much about that, however.

Calling his wife to aid him, he went into the next room where the two bound and gagged detectives laid upon the floor side by side.

Neither could move or speak.

They were wondering what their fate was to be.

It filled them with chagrin to reflect that this Frenchman had alone overpowered them without the slightest trouble.

La Croix seized Old King Brady first and dragged him into the next room.

"Now, Lena," he remarked, "help me to leeft him in ze box."

He took the detective by the head and she grasped his ankles and they quickly dropped their prisoner in the case.

Harry was served the same way.

There was just room enough to hold them.

When La Croix nailed on the lid, they realized what he intended to do with them and it made them feel very downhearted.

"Going to ship us away," thought Old King Brady.

La Croix then borrowed Reynard's brush and marking pot and they heard him chuckle and say to his wife:

"I weel direct ze box to wong fictitious address in Sacramento, California. By ze time ze secret police arrive zere, *par Dieu,* zey weel be zez dead mans!"

He then addressed the case and went after a truckman.

This done, between them they lowered the case through the hatchway into the street, and it was banged with a hook, turned over and over and pushed up a pair of rungs on the truck.

The Bradys were badly bumped and bruised.

But being gagged they had to suffer in silence.

Finally the truck was driven away with them, and reaching the Erie freight depot, the driver got a receipt for the box and dumped it off his truck.

The shock upon the imprisoned detectives was awful.

They heard the driver say:

"Collect de charges. Dat box goes via Buffalo, don't it?"

"Yes," replied the freight agent.

"Well, yer'd better handle it wid care, as I tink it's got artificial flowers in it, an' yer might smash de stuffins out o' dem."

"Mighty heavy artificial flowers," growled the agent.

Then the truck drove away.

The detectives laid in the freight building for some time, and the interior of the box became hot and stifling.

Fortunately the box stood as they were lying on their sides.

About noontime their troubles began again, for the freight handlers got hold of the box to send it over the river to Jersey with other freight. The detectives were tumbled and slammed about roughly, at one moment resting on their heads, at another on their faces, then they were picked up by a hand-truck and banged upon their backs on the boat. For a while they had a rest.

No one heard the groans of pain they uttered as they were bumped, bruised and cut, and they were carried over the river.

Here the rough handling began again until they were laden on a freight car due to go out that night.

The box now rested so that they were standing up.

It was such a painful attitude in those cramped quarters that they were in misery, for they were face to face, with their bodies bent over on account of the box being too short for the length of their bodies.

Both had made the most desperate efforts to get rid of their bonds and gags, but found it impossible to do so.

Some hours later they felt the train get in motion and knew they were on their way to Buffalo.

The time dragged very slowly.

Hour after hour passed by and the night passed and another day came.

Hunger and thirst were now added to the miseries they already endured and the strain they were under brought them to the verge of fainting.

Toward noontime the train paused at a way station to take on some freight and the box in which the detectives were packed was thrown over to make room for it.

As it struck the floor, Old King Brady struck his face forcibly against the side of the box and made his nose bleed.

He gave a deep groan and one of the freight handlers heard it.

"Good Lor'!" he exclaimed in startled tones, as he glared around. "What's that? Sounded like a man's voice."

Another groan from the old detective attracted his attention to the packing case, and he saw a tiny stream of blood trickling out of it through one of the cracks, upon the floor.

A thrill of horror darted through the man.

He began to suspect a corpse was in the box, and visions of a dreadful murder mystery floated through his mind.

"Hey, Tom! Hey, Bill! Come here, quick!" he yelled at his companions.

"What's the matter?"

"What do you want?"

"Bring a hammer here!"

"Did you bust open a box?"

"No. But I'm going to."

"What for?"

"I heard a man groaning in that—ha! Hear it?"

A third groan from Old King Brady reached their ears and seeing the blood, they quickly realized that there was some one in the case.

Procuring a hammer, they pulled off the lid.

The two detectives were revealed.

Harry was senseless.

Cries of astonishment escaped the men, and observing that the pair were still alive, they pulled them out of the box and laid them on the floor.

Removing the gags and bonds, the trainmen brought water and bathed the bruised and swollen faces of the detectives.

This treatment revived Harry.

Both were very weak, and they ached all over.

"Give us a drink," Old King Brady implored.

When this was done they asked for something to eat.

The trainmen got some food at the station and a big crowd gathered round when the news spread.

After eating and drinking and rubbing their legs and arms, the Bradys recovered rapidly and told who they were and what befell them.

In a short time they were able to walk.

"Are you going back to New York to arrest the rascal who did this?" asked the man who discovered them.

"No, indeed!" replied Harry, quickly. "We wouldn't find them there if we did. They are probably on their way to Canada now."

"Going after them?"

"Yes."

"Then you'd better stay with us until we arrive in Buffalo and you won't have so far to go to reach Montreal."

"We'll do that," said Old King Brady. "But don't let on about our escape. If the newspapers get hold of the story and publish it, our enemy may learn how we baffled his design and he will be on his guard against an attack from us."

"I'll keep mum, Mr. Brady. We'll reach Buffalo to-night and you can then attend properly to your injuries."

The train then moved on, and the detectives finally reached their destination and put up in a hotel, where a physician attended to their injuries.

CHAPTER VII.

A MYSTERIOUS WOMAN IN BLACK.

"Old King Brady, your life is in danger."

"From what?"

"The man your are persecuting."

"You mean Paul La Croix, I presume?"

"I do. Go back to New York at once."

"Madam, I shall do nothing of the kind."

"Then you must suffer for your obstinacy."

"I am prepared for anything, madam."

"Remember, I have given you fair warning. You cannot arrest La Croix on Canadian soil for smuggling."

And the veiled woman in deep mourning, who accosted the old detective in a dark street in Toronto, turned as if to walk away.

This happened several weeks after the Bradys reached Buffalo.

They had been vainly searching for La Croix and his wife.

On the night in question, Old King Brady had gone out from his hotel alone, when the woman in mourning met him in the street.

The light of a street lamp fell upon them.

She gave a slight start and began to follow him.

When he discovered this and turned around, asking why she was dogging his footsteps, she gave the above recorded answer.

By her mentioning his name, he realized that she knew him, and he at once suspected she was La Croix's wife.

He resolved to fathom the mystery of her identity.

Seizing her arm, he exclaimed:

"Hold on a moment."

"Well?" she asked, pausing obediently.

"I want to know who you are that takes such a deep interest in my welfare. I want to know who it is that knows me—who knows all about the private business which has brought me to this city. Speak out. Who are you?"

"Your friend," replied the mysterious unknown.

"What is your name?" he persisted.

"I must decline to tell you."

"But I won't take a refusal. You must speak."

"No. Allow me to retain my incognito. It were best for us both."

Old King Brady was determined to know her, however, and he seized her long crepe veil and attempted to remove it from her face.

A subdued cry of anger escaped her.

"Let that be!" she exclaimed, imperiously.

"Madam, I must see who you are!" he persisted.

"Is this the gratitude you show for the favor I have done you?"

"You have aroused my curiosity."

"Stand back, sir. Don't you dare lay a hand on me again.

"Why," he laughed, "is it dangerous?"

"Very!"

"How?"

She drew a slender dagger from the folds of her dark dress, and as the lamplight glanced upon the blade, it flashed as she drew it back.

Old King Brady was startled.

He did not expect to see anything like this.

Raising the dagger, the mysterious woman hissed:

"If you attempt to penetrate my identity, I shall stab you!"

There was a ring of intense earnestness to her voice, and it froze the smile that rose to the old detective's face.

He regarded her with a puzzled look.

It now began to dawn upon his mind that she was not Mrs. La Croix after all. The voice was different. She was shorter and stouter than the smuggler's wife. Her actions were different.

To gain time to form a different tactic he exclaimed:

"How can you be a friend of mine if you are going to stab me?"

"I am bound to keep my identity a secret," she replied, firmly.

"What object have you in befriending me?"

"You are a brave man and a dutiful officer. I know you are only following up this case because you were ordered to do so. I therefore don't wish to see you perish."

"How do you know I'm doomed to get killed?"

"Because I heard your enemies plot your destruction."

"In that case they know we are here on their trail?"

"Yes. Every move you make is being keenly watched by spies."

"Our enemies must be well-disguised and keep well under cover."

"You haven't thus far detected them, have you?"

"No," admitted Old King Brady.

"Then that shows how secure they are. A number of times they have been as close to you as I am. Yet you did not know it. By this you can realize how easy it would be for them to attack you unexpectedly, kill you, and escape."

"Even that thought won't scare me off the case."

"You are very obstinate and persevering."

"Those two elements will yet make me win this fight."

"Foolish man. Don't delude yourself. Your enemies are very powerful people. They will beat you in the end."

"I don't agree with your idea."

"Is my warning in vain?"

"Entirely so."

The veiled woman sighed and bowed her head in thought. Finally she strode away, saying in impatient tones:

"Very well. Since I can't dissuade you from your set purpose, I shall not bother myself any further about the matter."

She seemed to be very angry at the old detective.

He strode after her.

"Wait a moment longer!" he exclaimed.

"No. I have no more to say," she replied, sharply. "Don't attempt to follow me. If you do, it will be as much as your life is worth."

"Humbug!" he replied.

"So you doubt me, eh? Well, look behind you."

He glanced over his shoulder and caught view of the shadowy figures of several men lurking about the trees lining the street.

Old King Brady was astonished.

She evidently had a body-guard of watchful men.

"Who are those people?" he demanded.

"My friends," she replied, quietly. "If they saw you attack or follow me, they would put a sudden end to your career at long range."

"By firing?"

"Yes."

"Let me walk as far as the corner with you."

"Very well, Mr. Brady. I have no objection to that."

The journey was made in utter silence, and the old detective noticed that the shadowy men were following them.

When they reached the corner, Old King Brady glanced around, looking for Harry, who agreed to meet him there.

The boy was nowhere in sight.

Old King Brady then coughed and dropped his handkerchief as a signal.

For a moment there was no notice paid to it, but presently he heard a distant hissing sound of singular penetration.

It was an answer to his signal and meant that he was seen and understood.

With a satisfied feeling the old detective now said to the veiled woman:

"I shall leave you here. Don't think I am ungrateful for your kindness. On the contrary, I appreciate it very much. But my duty compels me to pay no heed to your valuable warning. I must run down my quarry. Good-night, madam."

"Good-night, sir."

He tipped his hat and strode away to the Walker House, where he was staying.

She stood watching him until he was several blocks distant and then gave vent to a low, peculiar whistle.

Instantly four men came gliding from the shadows, and grouped around her, as she started to walk away.

She was heading for the railroad depot.

When she was gone, Harry Brady slid down from the dense foliage of a nearby tree where he had been a hidden watcher.

The boy had seen the woman and her body-guard, and knew that his partner wanted him to shadow her from that point.

Accordingly he glided along after them.

Dodging from tree to tree, slinking along in the densest shadows and never exposing himself for an instant in a ray of light which would betray him, Harry dogged them to the railroad station.

He saw them purchase tickets and board a train.

Gliding over to the ticket office he asked the agent:

"Where did those five people buy tickets for?"

"Montreal," replied the man, "on the Grand Trunk road."

"Thank you," said Harry, politely.

And the boy ran behind a freight car to shelter him from the gaze of the passengers in the waiting train.

Finding an opening between two of the cars he peered through.

Directly opposite him sat the woman in black, with two of her male companions in the seat ahead and two behind her.

She was close to the window.

Just then she drew her veil aside and Harry saw her face.

A startled cry escaped the boy.

"By jove!" he gasped. "She's Clara La Croix, the girl smuggler!"

And so she was!

CHAPTER VIII.

GAINING A FEW POINTS.

Young King Brady, of course, knew nothing about the dialogue which passed between his partner and the girl. But he felt pretty confident that Old King Brady did not know who the girl was.

Without the slightest hesitation Harry made his way unseen to the rear car, and boarded the train just as it pulled out of the station.

The boy wore a bicycle suit and a false beard.

He felt pretty sure he would not be known in this outfit, and passing inside the car, he took a seat.

The distance between Toronto and Montreal was about 350 miles along the Lake Ontario and the St. Lawrence river.

"I don't believe La Croix or his wife are in Toronto," the boy muttered, "for we've gone over the city with a fine-toothed comb, and failed to find the slightest sign of them. They must be either in Montreal or Quebec, for the girl is going to the former place. Miss Clara made a quick trip. She could not have been here long from Holland. And I presume she is laden with those diamonds she went after. La Croix is now doubtless scheming to smuggle them over the border into the United States. We've got to watch these people closely now. That Frenchman is a desperate man. We have seen that he would not stop at murder to attain his purposes. When I reach Montreal, I must telegraph Old King Brady to come on and meet me. He will be wondering what has become of me now."

When the conductor came through, Harry paid his fare in cash.

A short time afterward one of the girl's male companions made a trip from one end of the train to the other.

He sharply eyed every passenger on the cars and favored Harry with a particularly keen and searching stare.

It made the boy imagine for an instant that his identity was known, but he never flinched.

The man passed on, however, without making any remark.

It took fifteen hours to make the run, and it was three o'clock on the following afternoon before the train pulled into Montreal.

Shadowing the girl smuggler and her companions, Harry saw them go to a hotel, where the men left her.

While they went down to the Dominion Line dock, the girl passed into the hotel and Harry saw her go upstairs.

The hotel clerk, a dudish young fellow, was staring after her when Harry approached him and said:

"Deuced pretty girl that."

"Very," assented the clerk. "A widow, too!"

"Rather young to be a widow, don't you think?"

"Yes, indeed."

"What's her name?"

"Mrs. Marie P. Savoy."

"Been here long?"

"A week."

"Alone?"

"She came in on the steamer Dominion from Havre alone, but her mother and father soon joined her here. She went down to Toronto a few days ago leaving the old folks here. She's just returned."

"I see. I'd like to get acquainted with her."

"You may if you stop here."

"That's what I'm going to do. Give me a good room."

"Very well, sir. Got any baggage?"

"None, whatever. I came from Niagara in a hurry."

"You can have No. 37. That's right next to the one occupied by the beautiful young widow. Perhaps it may lead to your becoming acquainted with her as you wish."

"I hope so," laughed Harry, who was delighted at his good luck. "Got a telegraph station here?"

"No. But there's one across the street."

Harry went out and telegraphed to Old King Brady to

come and meet him in Montreal and then went to his room.

While washing, he heard the hum of voices in Clara La Croix's room, and gliding over to the wall, pressed his ear against the partition.

It was a hollow wall and nearly every word was quite audible.

The first thing he heard was a man's voice which he did not recognize, but presumed was La Croix, asking:

"Well, how did you make out in Toronto, Clara?"

"All right," the girl replied. "I found your four spies there. They report that the Custom House inspectors at Niagara Falls are on the alert. There has been a shaking up of the department. The Collector of the Port of New York is dissatisfied with the amount of smuggling that is being carried on, and made it very hot for everybody."

"That ees bad for us."

"Very. We'll either have to keep shady a while or play a trick on them to pass the diamonds I brought over from Holland. As there are $250,000 worth of the gems, you can't afford to have them seized for duty and run chances on going to prison for the job, papa."

"That ees a fact. It would ruin me. I'll have to think of some—vat you call—plan to beat ze Custom House."

"I've got some bad news for you, too."

"Vat ees zat?" asked La Croix, nervously.

"The Bradys are in Toronto looking for you."

The smuggler started as if he were stung and turned deathly pale.

A look of blank dismay settled upon his sallow face, his dark eyes sparkled angrily and he exclaimed:

"*Parbleu!* I thought zey was done for!"

"You told me how you had shipped them in a box."

"Zen zey have escape, eh?"

"So it seems. One of your men discovered them. Before I came here, I met Old King Brady in the street and warned him of the danger of following you up. He refused to quit."

"Zat man ees a demon! I weel keel heem yet!" raved La Croix.

"Look out he don't kill you," replied his daughter.

"What wiz him deed you do?"

"Left him in Toronto."

"An' he not know we ees here?"

"No. I'm sure he don't."

"But eet puzzle me to know how he learn we ees in Canada."

"He may have had some method of finding out those things."

"I wondair how from ze box zey escape?"

"I'm sure I don't know."

"Where ees ze four men?"

"Gone down to the steamship dock for my trunk."

"Zen zey come back here soon, eh?"

"Yes. I presumed you wished to consult with them and therefore ordered them to report here to you."

"So I do. Ve must vatch for ze detectives ver' sharp now."

"Where is mother?"

"Een my room."

"I'll go in and see her. I'm going to get rid of these uncomfortable widow's weeds. They were all very well as a disguise in which to travel in Europe and come back here, but I am heartily sick of wearing them. They make me feel so old."

"Suit yourself, my dear."

The girl then left her room and as there was no more to hear, Harry resumed his ablutions and put on his false beard again.

He kept a strict watch upon the smuggler all that day and saw La Croix hold a meeting with his spies in his own room.

The boy failed to overhear what they had to say, but that did not worry him, as long as he had his quarry under observation.

On the following afternoon an old farmer with a homespun suit, an old felt hat, and gray whiskers, arrived at the hotel.

Harry was standing in the lobby when he came in and recognized him at once as Old King Brady, but made no sign.

The old detective recognized the boy at the same moment, and calling for a room, he seized his carpet bag and umbrella, and followed the bell-boy upstairs.

Harry considered it safest to keep apart from his partner in public, and for that reason failed to speak to him.

When he afterward learned which room Old King Brady occupied, he quietly went up there and was admitted.

In whispers they explained to each other all that transpired and the old detective was delighted over the boy's success.

"So the mysterious woman in black was the girl smuggler, eh?" asked the old detective. "Well, I'm surprised."

"Her warning you, shows that she has some regard for us and don't wish to see us come to grief," replied Harry, sentimentally.

"On the other hand, it may have been a diplomatic move on her part to bluff us off until they smuggle that big consignment of diamonds over the border," replied Old King Brady, practically.

"Well, she didn't succeed."

"By no means."

"Have you formed any plan of action?"

"Only one."

"And that is?"

"To catch them smuggling those diamonds and arrest them with the evidence in their possession, which will send them to prison for many years," replied Old King Brady.

CHAPTER IX.

CROSSING THE BORDER.

As La Croix's party did not seem to be in any hurry to leave Montreal, the Bradys had plenty of time to arrange their plans.

On the following day they went to the telegraph office and sent two messages, the first being couched in the following terms:

"Collector of Port, N. Y.: Swear out warrant for arrest of Clara La Croix, charge of smuggling, and mail at once to International, Niagara Falls. Brady."

The second was addressed to the Customs department at Suspension Bridge, saying:

"Keep watch for La Croix, wife and daughter with four spies. Are going to attempt to pass $250,000 worth of diamonds."

As La Croix was well known, details were useless.

The Bradys watched their quarry closely.

Knowing they had those diamonds with them, and that they would very likely play a sharp trick to evade the inspectors, the Bradys were very careful.

Scarcely a move made by the family escaped them.

It soon became apparent to the detectives that an important move was soon to be made, for the four spies were in frequent consultation with the Frenchman and his family.

"They are evidently arranging a plan of action," Harry commented, as he and his partner traced the men to La Croix's room for the fourth time.

"I wish there was some way of getting a clew to their design," Old King Brady replied, in wistful tones. "We are completely in the dark."

"That's a sheer impossibility," Harry answered. "They are taking the most extraordinary care not to let anyone hear a word they are saying or see a thing they are doing. I've tried several times, and failed."

"We've got a sharp gang to deal with, my boy. And the worst of it is that $250,000 worth of diamonds makes such a small package that they won't have the slightest trouble to conceal it."

"As they are not likely to allow so valuable a parcel to leave their hands, by arresting the whole gang the moment they reach the American side, we are likely to find the jewels on the person of one or the other."

"And I quite agree with that plan," said Harry. "In fact, it's the only safe method of securing them for a certainty."

"Have you noticed whether they made friends with any outsiders here?"

"No, they haven't. They keep strictly aloof from everybody. I made an attempt to speak to each one of the party in a friendly way at the table, but they gave me such a cold reception, I had to withdraw in a hurry."

That day, La Croix and his party left Montreal.

Boarding a train for Toronto, they went away.

The Bradys were on the same train.

Once more their disguises were changed, for they did not want the smugglers to see them in Toronto in the same characters, as it might arouse their suspicions.

They were now rigged out as two regular army soldiers, and pretended to be sightseeing, as most Americans are up in that region.

La Croix and his party only remained a day in Toronto.

The detectives now discovered that two of the spies had disappeared and a swift search was made to find them.

Harry did the investigating.

He finally discovered that one of them had gone to get married, and the other acted as best man at the ceremony.

The spy married a pretty French-Canadian girl.

His companion returned to La Croix's party and the bride and groom started off on a short wedding trip.

Young King Brady dropped them.

"They'll be so busy spooning and lally-gagging that he won't have any time to attend to this smuggling game," thought the boy detective, as he went back to his partner to report the occurrence.

Old King Brady was watching the Frenchman's party.

Next day the smugglers boarded the cars for Niagara, and the Bradys felt that their work would soon be at an end.

As the Custom House officers of Niagara had been specially warned against these people, they made a very careful search of their baggage and persons.

Every one underwent a most rigid examination.

Not a thing or place was overlookd in which there was the faintest chance of concealing precious stones.

But despite the keenness of the scrutiny—despite the extraordinary watchfulness—despite every care—not a diamond was found.

The Bradys looked on eagerly.

Each one expected a remarkable disclosure.

But when they saw the officers baffled, it worried them.

They could not understand this want of success, except by thinking that the La Croix party were playing some deep, shrewd game.

The Frenchman laughed sardonically at the officers and said:

"Ah, Messieurs, zis ees ze time I fool you! *Comprong?*"

"If any of your party have anything contraband," grimly answered the officer, in disappointed tones, "you must have swallowed it."

"Zen why you not examine us wiz ze X-ray?" chuckled La Croix.

"I'd like to take you at your invitation, you are such a slippery customer," growled the officer, who had had some experience with him before.

The party were permitted to go.

They headed for the International hotel and as the Bradys had already arranged to go there, they followed the Frenchman's party.

Upon the arrival of the officers, a legal envelope was handed to Old King Brady, and he opened it and withdrew a warrant for Clara La Croix.

"No need of this, yet," he grumbled, holding it up.

"We may want it very soon," replied Harry. "They had the diamonds, and if they've eluded our vigilance, or given them to anyone else to smuggle over, they'll have to get the jewels away from the smuggler and that will be the time for us to grab them."

Several days passed by, during which La Croix's three spies returned to Canada, as they were then of no further service.

The day after they had gone, the fourth spy, who had got married, suddenly came over from Canada with his bride, and the detectives saw them go to the hotel where the La Croix party was stopping.

With their suspicions aroused, the Bradys watched them.

They went up to the clerk, sent their card to La Croix's room, and Clara presently came down and greeted them warmly.

"Papa is shaving," she remarked. "Can't you come to my room? I'll try to entertain you until he is disengaged."

She had abandoned her widow's weeds and resumed her wonted attire in which she looked very young and charming.

The bride smiled, patted her on the head and said:

"I like you. Nothing would please me better."

The moment she assented, the Bradys hastened upstairs.

Clara's room was open and they entered and glanced around.

It was a magnificently-furnished apartment and the trunk she brought over from France stood in the middle of the room.

At one side was a closet.

The Bradys dodged into it and closed the door.

No sooner were they concealed when Clara and her two guests came in and at her invitation, seated themselves.

"Well?" said the girl smuggler, in eager tones, "how did you make out?"

"Fine," laughed the spy, producing a package from his pocket. "We kept the diamonds and remained in Canada, spending our honeymoon. When we started for the American side, my wife had the package of diamonds fastened under the lining of her skirt. No one suspected us, of course. The officers only made a careless examination of our satchel and valise. We had no trouble whatever."

"How lucky!"

"Is there any use for us to remain here to see your father? We are in a hurry, and can come back in the course of an hour."

"That will do."

"We will go, then."

And they left the room.

A few moments later there came a knock at the door.

"Come in," cried the girl.

Her mother entered the room.

"Where are the bridal couple, Clara?" she asked, glancing around.

"Just gone. They'll return in an hour."

"Did they leave the package of diamonds?"

"Yes. And here it is."

Another knock came at the door.

"Hide the parcel!" gasped Mrs. La Croix, nervously.

The girl thrust it in her pocket.

"Enter!" she cried.

The door opened and a hall-boy came in.

"Did you ring, Miss La Croix?" he asked.

"Yes," she replied. "I want you to do something for me."

Rising to her feet she drew the boy aside and held a whispered talk with him for several moments.

In the course of their conversation he said to her.

"I saw two men enter this room just before you came in with that lady and gentleman, and they didn't go out again, either."

The girl looked startled.

She spoke to him rapidly a moment, and he started for the door.

Before he could depart, however, the closet door flew open with a bang and the Bradys sprang from their place of concealment.

"Hold on, there!" cried Harry. "Let no one leave this room!"

The hall-boy paused, an alarmed look on his face.

CHAPTER X.

SERVING THE WARRANT.

Mrs. La Croix and her daughter were possessed of good nerves, for the dramatic entrance of the Bradys did not seem to startle them in the least.

They glanced coolly at the detectives and Mrs. La Croix asked, haughtily:

"Who are these men?"

"Detectives, madam," replied Old King Brady, politely.

"Indeed! What were you sneaking in that closet for?"

"To learn the true inwardness of your gigantic smuggling scheme."

"You must be mad."

"No, indeed. We are quite sane, I assure you."

"What do you mean by our smuggling?"

"Simply this: We know all about your daughter's trip to Holland and we've been watching her since she landed at Montreal."

"Oh," said the lady, icily, "you have, eh?"

"Yes, we have."

"Well, what do you want, now?"

"Madam," said Old King Brady, "here is a warrant for the arrest of your daughter. The charge is smuggling!"

Calmly taking the document, the lady read it.

Harry opened the door and let the hall-boy go.

The young detective did not want the boy to hear all that transpired and the hall-boy hastened away.

Rushing to Paul La Croix's room, he pounded on the door, entered and found the smuggler shaving himself.

"There's two detectives in your daughter's room!" he gasped.

"*Sacre!*" roared La Croix in startled tones.

"They've got a warrant for your daughter's arrest."

"Who zey are?" groaned La Croix.

"The Bradys."

"We are lost!"

"Your daughter slipped me this package and told me to give it to you."

He handed over the parcel of diamonds, and with a glad cry, La Croix eagerly seized it and thrust it in the bosom of his shirt.

"Here—five dollaire for you!" he panted, giving the boy a bill. "Keep ze still tongue about our affairs. Now go!"

The boy shot out of the room and the man wrote a note and left it on the bureau.

La Croix hastily dressed and rushed out of the hotel.

He was fearfully excited.

Reaching the street, he called a cab, doubled the driver's fare and was driven furiously to the railroad depot.

Here he caught a departing train.

Meantime, the Bradys imagined they had Clara La Croix with the package of diamonds in her possession.

Harry placed his hand on the girl smuggler's arm.

"I hate to do it, Miss," said he, half apologetically, "but you are my prisoner."

She took her arrest with exasperating coolness.

Smiling up at him, she said in low, sweet tones:

"I'm charged with smuggling, ain't I?"

"Yes."

"What?"

"About $250,000 worth of diamonds."

"How ridiculous!"

"No, it isn't. We've got all the facts."

"Please name them."

"You went to Amsterdam and came back on the Dominion with the jewels I mentioned. In Toronto you gave them to one of your father's spies who got married. Your party crossed the border and were searched. Of course, no jewels were found on you. A short time ago the spy and his bride followed you; they smuggled the diamonds over the Suspension Bridge for you. A few minutes ago they were here and delivered the package to you. You've got it now, so hand it over."

"I haven't got any package of diamonds," protested the girl.

"Now, don't try to lie out of it. We've got the evidence against you which you can't deny. Be sensible and save yourself further trouble by handing over the gems. If you don't we'll take them by force."

"I am telling you the truth."

"Further concealment is useless."

"Then search us and convince yourself."

Harry accepted her offer and failed to find the stones.

While he was so employed, Old King Brady searched her mother with equal non-success, and a surprised look spread over their faces.

"The girl hasn't got them!" exclaimed Harry, in disgust.

"Nor has her mother," added Old King Brady.

"They must have hidden them."

"Search the room."

"Don't move, ladies, or we'll handcuff you."

"No need of that ignominy," said the girl.

They made a thorough and painstaking search of the place, but failed to meet with any success and finally gave it up.

The diamonds remained missing.

Both were greatly puzzled.

Suddenly an idea occurred to Harry and he cried:

"The hall-boy!"

"What about him?" asked his partner.

"He may have carried off the parcel."

"See!"

"You guard them."

"All right."

Harry rushed out of the room.

Finding the boy down in the office, Harry seized him.

"Where did you put the package that girl gave you?" he roared.

The boy turned pale with fright, and a panic seized him as he suddenly thought his share in the matter was known.

With bulging eyes and chattering teeth, he gasped:

"For mercy's sake don't arrest me, and I'll tell you, sir."

"Well? Speak out—quick!"

"The young lady told me to give it to her father."

"And you did?"

"Yes, sir."

"Where was he?"

"In his room."

"Is he there yet?"

"I don't know."

Harry rushed upstairs again.

Pushing open the door of Paul La Croix's room he entered.

None of the man's possessions was disturbed, but Harry caught view of the note he had written and placed on his bureau.

The boy picked it up and read the following lines:

"Monsieur Brady: By the time you get this letter I will be far away. You are duped. Do as you please with my innocent wife and daughter. You can prove nothing against them. An outsider did the smuggling. That lets us out. I defy you. Do your worst. La Croix."

Young King Brady smiled at the note.

"The raving of a madman!" he muttered scornfully. "If he imagines he has beaten us, we will soon relieve him of that notion."

He carried the note to Old King Brady and exclaimed:

"La Croix has escaped with the diamonds."

"How did he get them?" asked the old detective, curiously.

"Clara sent them to him by the hall-boy."

"As I feared!"

"We can't convict these women."

"No. Release them."

"Ladies, you are free."

"Thank you," said Clara, with a pleasant smile.

"Go your way. We can't secure anything but revenge by prosecuting you, and that isn't what we are after. I must say, though, Mrs. La Croix, that was an inhuman thing for you and your husband to do, boxing us up and shipping us to California. We are more merciful to you when it lies in our power to put you in prison."

The woman's face reddened with shame.

She hung her head, but made no reply.

Old King Brady then said to Harry in hurried tones:

"Come. We must get on La Croix's trail. We'll run him down if it takes a year to do it!"

They rushed from the room.

Harry, however, paused outside the door and listened.

The woman and her daughter uttered a merry peal of laughter.

"Good for papa!" cried the girl. "He'll save the gems yet."

"Those detectives have gone on a wild goose chase," contemptuously replied her mother. "Paul will outwit them. To-morrow you and I will go back to New York, and put up at the Waldorf. When your father has safely disposed of those gems he will go there to look for us. It's a rendezvous we had arranged beforehand in case trouble came up."

Harry nodded and smiled.

"Glad you've posted me," he muttered. "I won't lose sight of you two charming creatures. It wasn't good policy to pull you in without the diamonds if you only knew it, and that's the only reason you are at liberty now. We'll play with you as a cat plays with a mouse."

And he walked away from the door feeling well satisfied with the shape the case was taking.

CHAPTER XI.

SUBDUING A TARTAR.

Old King Brady had gone ahead in an effort to find out what had become of Paul La Croix.

Reaching the street he accosted a man at the door with the question:

"Did you see a thin man with a black moustache, a high hat, and frock coat come out of here in a hurry a few moments ago?"

"Yes, sir. He got in a cab and rode away."

"Did you notice the sort of cab it was?"

"I did. Do you know Pork Chops, the negro hackman?"

"Oh, yes."

"Well, it was his rig."

"Which way did they go?"

"In the direction of the railroad depot."

Thanking his informant, the old detective hastened away convinced that the fugitive was going out of Niagara by rail.

When he reached the depot he described La Croix and asked where he had gone.

"That's none of your business," growled the surly ticket agent.

"Oh, isn't it?" queried the detective, blandly.

"No!" shouted the man, "and I'll not tell you."

"It wouldn't hurt you to be polite and accommodating, would it?"

"I ain't here to keep inquisitive people posted about our passengers."

"That's a fact," assented Old King Brady, "but I have an urgent reason for wishing to know where that man went."

"I don't care anything about your private reasons. If you don't want to buy a ticket, get away from that window and don't annoy me."

"Very well," meekly answered the detective.

He thereupon stepped through the door into the agent's office, and the man scowled, and glared at him and roared:

"What in thunder do you want in here, anyway?"

"I've come in to arrest you," quietly answered the old detective, as he showed his badge. "I'm a detective, as you can plainly see, and the man I inquired about is a fugitive smuggler. As you are aiding him to escape, by withholding the information I want, you must be an accessory of his. As such, you'll have to go to jail!"

The man wilted.

All his lordly, overbearing manners vanished.

Turning as pale as death and trembling like an aspen, he gasped tremulously:

"For pity's sake don't lock me up. I didn't know the circumstances."

"You're an unmannerly dog."

"I know it, sir. I'm sorry if I offended you."

"Promise me to act more civilly in future."

"Yes. Yes. Certainly I shall."

"Then I'll let you go. Let this be a lesson to you. Now, where did he go?"

"He bought a ticket to New York."

"Why didn't you save all this bother by saying so in the first place?"

"I—I—I don't know," stammered the fellow in subdued tones.

Giving him a look of contempt, Old King Brady purchased a ticket for New York, and said in angry tones:

"For two pins I'd notify the company what a brute you are, and have a gentleman put here in pour place."

And with this rebuke he departed.

He went to a telegraph office and flashed a message to the authorities of various stations along the line to New York, asking them to hold La Croix if they caught him on the cars.

He had to wait an hour for a train to Buffalo, and sent Harry a message telling where he was going.

Finally he was carried away in his train.

The old detective stopped off at every station to which he telegraphed, but in every instance he received the same answer, that nothing was seen of a man answering La Croix's description.

That set the detective thinking.

"La Croix was probably keen-witted enough to suspect that we would find his trail and pursue him. In order to conceal his identity he has doubtless disguised himself and thus passed through unrecognized. He has got to dispose of that big lot of diamonds yet. Carrying such a huge amount will of course attract a great deal of attention. Therefore it should be an easy matter to find out where he is operating when he reaches New York."

On the following day Old King Brady reached the city.

He instituted inquiries about La Croix at once in the jewelry district, but no one seemed to have seen him yet.

That did not worry Old King Brady.

He was too astute a man to be discouraged by a trifling rebuff.

"The villain is keeping shady," was the conclusion he arrived at. "He is going to let the fuss blow over before he exposes his stock. Very foxy, no doubt, but I'm bound to land on him sooner or later."

He did not relax his hunt.

Nor did he let on to the authorities that he was in town again.

He believed in the golden principle of keeping his business to himself until it became absolutely necessary to disclose it.

Two days later Harry joined him at their joint lodgings.

Young King Brady told how he had tracked Mrs. La Croix and her daughter to swell apartments in the luxurious Waldorf.

Here the pair had taken up their abode under the fictitious name of Mrs. Marie P. Savoy and daughter.

The Bradys conjectured that it would not take them long to let La Croix know of their whereabouts.

They therefore carefully shadowed the big hotel.

Nearly a week passed by and one rainy night while Harry was on watch, under an umbrella, across the street from the hotel, he saw a hansom cab dash up to the door, and a man looking like La Croix alighted and hastily made his way into the building on the Thirty-fourth street side.

"La Croix, as sure as fate!" the boy muttered, hastily crossing the street.

He was heading for the glass portico, when he happened to glance into the spacious dining-room and saw the girl smuggler at supper.

Young King Brady paused and watched her.

Presently a waiter approached her with a card on a salver.

She glanced at it, said something to the man, and while he hastened away, she resumed her supper in a leisurely manner.

There were many fashionable guests in the room.

In a few moments Harry saw her father approach her smilingly, and sit down at the same table with her.

"Now is my time to nab him!" muttered Harry.

He ran into the hotel without ceremony, and making his way to the door of the dining-room, he paid no heed to the servants who offered to take his hat, mackintosh and umbrella.

In he dashed, his queer actions causing the guests to look up at him in astonishment, and he headed for La Croix.

The Frenchman had a big carving knife in his hand with which he was going to cut a steak instead of allowing the waiter to do it.

Harry's hand fell upon his shoulder.

"La Croix, you are my prisoner!" he exclaimed.

A hoarse cry escaped the smuggler and he became excited as he noticed that most every one in the room overheard the remark.

Clara gave a suppressed shriek and sprang to her feet.

Quick to recover his composure the Frenchman put on his eyeglasses, stared at Harry coolly from head to foot, and exclaimed:

"Young man, haf you not mek a meestake?"

"No, indeed!" replied the boy, resolutely. "You are my man all right."

"Why, sair, I don't know you. I nevair saw you before een my life."

"Come—come. You can't cheek it out that way, La Croix."

"Monsieur, please let go my arm or I have ze vatairs throw you out of here!"

Harry's patience became exhausted.

He did not intend to mince matters, so he said:

"You stop your humbug and come with me, or I'll pull you out of here by the neck, do you understand me?"

He took a firm grip on his man with one hand and drew a pair of handcuffs out of his pocket with the other.

Seeing he could not brave the matter out, and fearing lest the boy would attempt to handcuff him, the Frenchman wrenched himself free.

"You geet avay!" he hissed.

"Not without you!" retorted Harry, pluckily.

And he rushed forward to grasp the villain again.

By this time La Croix had become frantic with desperation.

Seeing the boy coming, he drew back the big carving knife with a quick motion and aimed a blow at the boy, shouting in the meantime:

"Zen take zat!"

The deadly blade leaped toward Harry's breast.

He tried to avoid it by leaping back, but was too late.

The knife struck him and the point pierced his side.

A sudden cry of agony escaped Young King Brady, and he flung up his hands and pitched over upon the floor.

Nearly every one in the room having had their attention attracted toward the pair had witnessed the tragedy.

Men turned pale and leaped to their feet, women shrieked and fainted, and some of the bolder waiters rushed at the Frenchman to disarm and capture him.

La Croix brandished the knife.

"I keel ze fairst man who touch me!" he yelled.

Dashing out of the room, he rushed upstairs and flourished the knife at his pursuers. He swore at every step and threatened to run the blade into the first man who got within his reach.

That cowed the crowd and he disappeared on the floor above.

CHAPTER XII.

RUN TO COVER.

There was a scene of furious excitement in the hotel dining-room, and during the confusion, Clara La Croix made her escape.

Among the guests who had been dining was a physician who ran to Harry's aid and made a rapid examination of his wound.

To the many anxious, pale-faced spectators who gathered round, he said:

"Don't be alarmed. It's a mere flesh wound and will soon heal up."

"Isn't he dead?" demanded a gentleman in a dress-suit, anxiously.

"No. Simply fainted from the shock on his system."

"He's evidently a detective."

"Yes, sir, and his assailant is a criminal. Waiter, get me some water—a sponge—bandages, and some linament. I'll bandage this wound and stop the bleeding."

While the doctor was busy working over the unconscious boy, the hotel detective and a policeman came running in and got the details.

They hastened away and scoured the hotel in quest of La Croix.

That worthy had gone to his wife's room.

Garbed in one of her bonnets, veils and dresses, he descended in the elevator and swiftly got away from the Waldorf, undetected.

His wife and daughter followed as rapidly as possible.

Meantime Harry recovered.

The doctor brought him home in a carriage.

Old King Brady was at home and got the particulars.

His rage knew no bounds when Harry explained all, after the doctor's departure, and he cried bitterly:

"That villain has caused us more trouble than any other criminal we ever attempted to run down. I'll even matters up with him. Had you not retreated just when you did, that knife would surely have killed you."

"I'll be laid up a few days, the doctor said," replied Harry, "but I'll soon get over it. If I ever meet La Croix again, I won't have any mercy on him. He's a bad man."

The boy then went to bed.

A week afterward, Old King Brady met Harry at police headquarters, and the boy saw by the look of triumph on his face that he had good news.

"How are you feeling to-day?" he asked the boy.

"Fine. My wound don't bother me at all."

"I've been working hard, Harry."

"So I imagine, as I haven't seen anything of you since yesterday."

"La Croix's four spies have arrived in town."

"What! Come from Canada?"

"Yes. I saw them going up Broadway in a bunch, to-day."

"Why didn't you arrest them?"

"Couldn't. Had my hands full at the time."

"Of what?"

"Mrs. La Croix."

"Did you catch her?"

"Yes. Shopping in Twenty-third street."

"Good enough."

"She's locked up now. I've changed my plans."

"How?"

"Well, I think we've made a great mistake in allowing those women their liberty, hoping they would lead us to Paul La Croix's hiding place. My new plan is this: To yank every one of them in, the moment we catch them."

Harry pondered over the proposition a few moments.

As a fact, he did not fancy such a summary proceeding. He firmly believed that using the different members of the gang as a bait to trap the others was the most efficient method of acting.

However, Old King Brady was getting impatient over the slow progress they were making to arrest the smugglers. His plan would show a quick result. That's what he wanted.

The boy, therefore, did not contradict him.

"Any way you say," he replied, presently.

"I'm following out my idea now," said the old detective, as he took a chew of tobacco. "The moment I saw Mrs. La Croix, I grabbed her."

"She protested, of course?"

"Vigorously. But I locked her up just the same."

"Couldn't you get any information out of her about the rest?"

"No. She wouldn't say a word."

"Acts like an old offender."

"Exactly. Her husband and daughter must be somewhere about the city. I suppose La Croix sent for the spies. He may have use for them, else they wouldn't be here. I only hope he hasn't disposed of any of those stones yet."

"And I've sent a warning to all jewelers, pawnbrokers and dealers in gems, not to handle La Croix's gems under penalty of the law. I've offered them a reward for the smuggler's arrest. The villain is bound to keep shady now. He must know the danger he is in. He's a very foxy Frenchman," said Harry.

"I wish I could find out where the woman lives."

"Nothing easier," said Harry.

"Don't you fool yourself. She won't confess."

"I don't expect she will."

"Then how am I to find out?"

"You said she was shopping in Twenty-third street?"

"I caught her coming out of Sterns' store."

"What's more likely than that she made some purchases and ordered the things sent home?"

Old King Brady's face brightened.

He had not thought of her leaving her address.

"Your idea is all right!" he exclaimed.

"Of course it is. It only has one drawback."

"And what's that?"

"She may have given a fictitious name."

"True. But she favors the name of Marie Savoy."

"It wouldn't do any harm to try asking for it."

"Come with me and see what we can do."

They left headquarters and hastened to the big dry goods store.

Going to the delivery department they asked the head clerk if he had anything on his books to be delivered to either Mrs. La Croix or Savoy.

A short search of the record elicited this response:

"I've got twenty yards of dress goods to be delivered to Mrs. M. P. Savoy."

"Bought a couple of hours ago?" asked Old King Brady.

"About that."

"Where are you going to deliver it?"

"At No. 160 Bleecker street."

"That's all."

"Anything wrong about it?"

"No. It's paid for, ain't it?"

"Yes."

"What time are you going to deliver the parcel?"

"Our wagon ought to reach there about five o'clock."

Old King Brady thanked him and they departed, leaving the clerk looking very much mystified over their peculiar actions.

The Bradys went to the Bleecker street address and saw that it was one of a row of old-fashioned brick houses with green blinds.

There was an ornamental iron stoop in front, and a furnished room sign hanging in one of the windows.

"Shall we go in?" asked Harry, hesitatingly.

"No. Wait for the wagon. We can then see who comes to the door. I presume they only have furnished rooms here."

"It's a poor neighborhood."

"So much the better for their purpose, perhaps."

They entered a saloon on the corner and took up a position where they could watch the house over the window screen.

They had not been there long before Harry caught view of two familiar figures coming down the street and called his partner's attention to them.

"Here comes two of La Croix's spies!" he exclaimed.

"Yes, and they are going into the house," muttered Old King Brady.

"That clinches our doubts. He surely must live there."

"No doubt of it. It's a strange servant admitting them. She's a mulatto."

The men disappeared in the house.

An hour passed by uneventfully.

Then Sterns' wagon came along and Old King Brady said hastily:

"When that driver rings, we must force our way in."

"Hurry up, then!"

Running across the street they arrived just in time to go up the stoop with the driver, and when he rang, the colored girl answered the bell.

"Mrs. Savoy live here?" demanded the driver, who had a bundle.

"Yes," replied the girl. "Parcel for her?"

"Here it is."

He handed it over and went away.

"Is the lady in?" Old King Brady asked the girl.

"No, sir. But her daughter is."

"We'd like to see her on important business."

"Come inside, if you please."

She ushered them into the parlor and asked:

"What name?"

"The Bradys."

"Wait here, sir."

She left the room and they silently followed her.

Pushing open the door of the back parlor the girl said:

"Miss Savoy—the Bradys——"

"At your service!" added Harry.

And they strode into the room where Clara La Croix sat.

CHAPTER XIII.

A HUMAN SHIELD.

It was a beautifully furnished bedroom and the girl smuggler sat by the window reading a novel when the detectives rushed in at her.

She was a cool, level-headed girl, and seemed to possess a remarkable set of nerves for she did not look at all startled by their entrance.

Meeting the detectives' look with a cool stare, she asked, quietly:

"Well, gentlemen, what can I do for you?"

Then seeing the astonished servant lingering at the door, she added:

"You may go, Hattie."

The servant closed the door and vanished.

Old King Brady strode over to her and exclaimed:

"We want those smuggled diamonds."

"Really, you are provoking. I have no smuggled diamonds."

"But you know where they are!"

"Do I?"

"Yes. You fooled us once, very cleverly, by passing them to the hotel hall-boy, but you shan't do so again, I can tell you."

She laughed as if enjoying a good joke.

"Well," she said, finally, "evasions are useless I see."

"Perfectly!"

"Do you want me to be frank with you?"

"My dear young lady, lies ain't going to do you any earthly good."

"The gems you are after are in my father's possession."

"We know that much already."

"To get them you must first get him."

"That's manifest."

"As for smuggling them onto American soil, none of us did that."

"But you caused one of your spies to do so for you."

"Admitted."

"And you have them now."

"So we have."

"That makes you as guilty as if you did the work of smuggling yourself."

"So I presume. We connived the trick, for our own benefit, to cheat the Custom House. We ain't denying that. In fact, it's going to be a big thing for us. Now, we don't wish to be pestered with your persecutions any longer."

"I don't see how you can help yourself."

"We do."

"How?"

"Name your price to quit."

"You mean to bribe us off, eh?"

"That's about the size of it."

"We are not to be bought."

"Humbug! I never knew a Custom House officer to refuse."

"We ain't of that stamp, young lady."

She looked at him incredulously a moment, and saw by the stern look in his deep gray eyes that he meant what he said.

It seemed to unnerve her for a moment.

She reflected and finally asked:

"Are you determined?"

"Absolutely!"

"You are bound to hound us?"

"We are, until we gain our point."

"This is astonishing."

"Are you aware that we have your mother in jail?"

A look of alarm swept over her face, the color fled from her cheeks and she slowly rose to her feet and asked in strained tones:

"What! My mother in prison?"

"Yes, and you are going to join her in a few moments."

"Mr. Brady, you are very much mistaken."

"Why am I?"

"I'll show you, sir."

She gave utterance to a cough. It was a signal. Instantly the door of an ante-room flew open. In the opening stood four men. They were the spies.

Each one was armed with a revolver.

These weapons were aimed at the Bradys and the girl laughed outright when she saw the involuntary expressions of astonishment that swept over their features.

"Quite a surprise, isn't it?" she asked in grim tones.

"We are in a trap!" Harry muttered.

"That's the situation!" said the girl, quietly. "If you move hand or foot, you'll get shot. Those men never miss their mark. At such short range they could kill you even if they were not expert shots."

The Bradys saw the force of her reasoning.

In a word, they were helpless.

Neither attempted to draw a weapon in self-defense.

To do so would be to seal their doom.

An awkward silence ensued.

Old King Brady finally asked in gruff tones:

"Well, what are you going to do about it?"

"Make prisoners of you and hold you until we have disposed of the diamonds," quickly replied Clara.

The detectives looked disgusted.

"Shall we resist?" muttered Harry, desperately.

"No. It would be folly to attempt it," his partner replied.

Old King Brady was not so fiery and impetuous as the boy; he was more slow, deliberate and cool in the face of danger.

He saw that the smugglers had concluded to throw off the mask and make no further pretenses.

That meant bitter warfare.

He had no plan to suggest, and the girl exclaimed:

"Come in and bind them, Jean."

One of the men entered.

He was the man who had done the smuggling.

Walking over to the detectives, he said to them in low tones:

"If you resist, my friends will fire."

"We don't intend to," replied Old King Brady.

"Then I'll relieve you of your own handcuffs to secure you."

He felt in the old detective's pocket, brought out the steel bracelets and snapped them on the detective.

Young King Brady was very restless.

To submit without a fight was more than he could bear.

His obstinacy suddenly got the best of his good judgment, and he made up his mind to give them a tussle.

Leaping beside the girl he seized her, swung her around between himself and the other men and cried:

"If you fire, you'll hit this girl!"

Clara gave a shriek.

"Harry!" roared Old King Brady in some dismay.

The men in the doorway dared not fire.

Jean, fearing an attack, plunged across the room intending to get out of danger in the hall.

"Let me go!" gasped the girl.

"Give up my advantage? Never!" panted the boy, a reckless, daring light gleaming in his eyes.

He was close to the open window.

At a glance he saw a way to escape.

Unaided, he could not expect to arrest these men and the girl, for Old King Brady was rendered powerless.

The yard was only eight feet below.

"Can you jump out the window?" he asked his partner.

"They'll fire if I budge."

This remark was certainly true.

While Harry had the advantage of using the girl as a shield, the four Canadians held the old detective at their mercy.

Harry drew his pistol.

The girl began to struggle to get free.

"Keep still!" said the boy in threatening tones. "If any harm befalls my partner, I'll put a bullet in you, young woman!"

The terrible earnestness of his voice alarmed her.

"You wouldn't injure a lady, would you?" she asked, appealing to his manhood. "No gentleman would do that."

"You are only a criminal," he replied coldly, "and as it's a case of our lives or yours, I wouldn't hesitate to shoot you to save ourselves."

Detectives are not sentimental.

On the contrary, their work makes them harsh.

Harry wanted to scare the girl and he succeeded well, for she remained passive, and burst into tears.

The boy quickly saw his advantage and cried:

"Now, if any of your gang attempts to injure us, I'll kill you!"

As he spoke, he placed the muzzle of his pistol against her head, turned her around and backed over to Old King Brady.

"Come!" he whispered. "We'll use her as a shield and back over to the door. They'll bitterly rue it if they fire!"

The four spies looked desperate and one of them spoke to the girl in French as the detectives retreated, holding her between them and their enemies. The girl replied in English, saying:

"Never mind me. We must not let them escape. Tackle them."

Obeying her, they rushed toward the officers.

Harry aimed his pistol at them and fired twice.

"Go for the door!" he yelled.

And hurling the girl against the four Canadians, he and his partner rushed out into the hall. The door was locked.

CHAPTER XIV.

ON HARLEM BRIDGE.

"Upstairs with you!" gasped Harry. "We can't get out the front door."

Old King Brady saw that the girl had collided with the four smugglers and they all fell in a heap upon the parlor floor.

The detective rushed up the stairs.

On the top landing Old King Brady panted:

"Unlock these handcuffs!"

Harry obeyed in an instant.

Just then the gang came rushing from the parlor, and were about to ascend the stairs when Harry opened fire on them.

Bang! Bang! Bang! went three shots.

He was a dead shot and could have killed those desperadoes had he been inclined to. But he merely shot to wound them.

The yells of pain that followed showed how true his aim was.

Two of the Canadians were hit.

A stampede among them ensued.

Back to the parlor they rushed, swearing and groaning, and the detectives laughed at them, for the tables were now turned.

The Bradys had the advantage.

At the head of those stairs they could have held an army at bay.

Old King Brady got his handcuffs from his wrists, put them in his pocket and withdrew his own revolver.

"By thunder!" he muttered. "I'm glad you made that dash, Harry."

"We would now be helpless prisoners if I hadn't."

Just then several lodgers stuck their heads out of the doors of their rooms, alarmed at the shots and yells.

Seeing the two armed detectives, they shouted with alarm, withdrew into the rooms, banged their doors shut and some rushed to the windows, flung them open and screamed:

"Murder! Murder! Help! Police!"

The cries startled the neighborhood.

For a moment everyone was in an uproar. A big crowd gathered before the house and several policemen came running to the scene from different directions, looking for trouble.

A suspicious silence ensued down on the parlor floor.

"Do you suppose they've skipped?" asked Harry.

"I'm going to venture down and see," replied his partner.

They dashed down the stairs, holding their pistols in readiness for use, and ran into the parlor.

It was empty.

Passing back into Clara's room, they found it vacant.

"Gone!" exclaimed Harry.

"Not by the front," replied his partner. "The door and windows are locked."

"Let's try the basement."

Down they ran, nervous over the disappearance of the smugglers and in the dining-room found the mulatto girl Hattie.

She sat in terror, with her face buried in her hands, and when she saw them rush in with drawn pistols, she shrieked:

"Oh, don't kill me! Don't kill me!"

"Where did that Savoy girl and the four men go?" sternly asked Old King Brady, glancing around the room.

"Out the back door."

"Into the yard?"

"Yes, sir."

The police began pounding on the front doors just as the Bradys rushed out into the rear yard.

Just as they emerged, Harry saw the figure of Jean disappearing over the back fence and pointing at it, he cried excitedly:

"There they go!"

"After them!" roared Old King Brady.

They rushed across the yard.

Over the fence they climbed like a couple of cats, and leaping into the yard of an adjoining tenement, they ran for the hall.

Blood spots on the flags left a plain trail.

The wounded men had dropped it in their flight, and

the detectives easily traced the stains through the hall into the street.

Hearing wild yells, they saw a baker's wagon dashing along at a furious gallop, and saw Clara and her friends in it.

The owner of the wagon was racing out of his store.

A small boy had told him that a gang had stolen his horse and wagon and it was his yells the detectives heard.

He was a fat German and he paused in the middle of the street, wildly waving his arms and crying in despairing tones:

"*Ach Gott!* I vos robbed! Dey shtole mein horse und vagon!"

The Bradys started off on a run after the vehicle.

Block after block was covered until the wagon, far in advance of the detectives, swung around the corner into West Broadway.

Here, panting and foam-covered, the horse was reined in.

The fugitives alighted.

"We are going to lose them now," groaned Old King Brady.

"I don't see why," returned Harry, breathlessly.

"Don't you see they're going for the elevated?"

"Oh, gee, so they are!"

The five rushed up the stairs on the downtown side, just as a train pulled into the station.

After them ran the Bradys, hoping fervently that they would miss the train. But they were doomed to disappointment.

When the detectives reached the platform, the train was steaming away and they saw their enemies in the last car.

"That's the end of them!" said Old King Brady.

"Can't we have them headed off by telephoning down to the Battery station?" eagerly asked the boy.

"Might try."

Down the street they went and as there was a public telephone near by, they sent the message down.

Then they took the next train down.

The train on which the fugitives stopped was yet at the Battery station and they found the gateman of the last car and Harry asked him:

"Did you notice where the four men in black, and a hatless girl of sixteen who got on at the Bleecker street station alighted?"

"Oh, yes. I remember them. They only rode one station and got off at Grand street."

This reply gave the Bradys a shock.

"We are baffled!" exclaimed Old King Brady in disgust.

"They're a shrewd set," Harry added.

They spoke to the stationmaster too, but he said they had not come down to the Battery and repeated what the gateman said.

The Bradys rode back to Grand street.

Here they made careful and endless inquiries.

All the information they could get came from the boy who had the news-stand on the corner.

He had seen the fugitives.

They had boarded a Grand street car going eastward.

He did not notice the number of the car, but thought the officers would find it down at the ferry.

Hiring a cab they were driven fast.

Reaching the ferry, several blue cars were found.

Inquiry among the conductors followed, and they presently discovered the one on whose car Clara and the spies had ridden.

He informed them that the fugitives alighted at the Bowery with transfer tickets on the uptown side.

Back went the Bradys to the Bowery.

"If we stick to their trail long enough," commented Harry, "we may finally locate them. But it's going to be a hard job."

"We'll beat the car they're in by taking the elevated," said the old detective as he dismissed the cab. "Up at the stables we may learn which car passed Grand street quarter of an hour ago."

"It's worth while trying."

So up they went.

When they reached the stable, they were disgusted to find that the cars which passed the corner of Grand and the Bowery about the time the smugglers boarded one, were all gone ten minutes before.

But one more course was open to the detectives.

That was to proceed to Harlem bridge on the elevated and make another effort to head off the fugitives at the terminal of the road.

Once more they started.

Each defeat whetted their appetite more to capture the fugitives.

The elevated cars passed many of the surface cars, and when the 129th street station was reached, they went down to the street.

Just as they were about to start for the surface cars, to begin making inquiries, Harry glanced over at the Harlem bridge.

To his surprise and joy he saw Clara and the four spies hurrying over the structure on foot.

"There they are at last!" he cried, pointing at the party.

Old King Brady was startled.

He saw them the next moment.

"Come on!" he cried.

Off on a run they went, and passed out on the bridge.

The fugitives were half way over the structure and two of the men who were wounded in the legs were limping painfully.

Rushing up behind them noiselessly, Harry and his partner each grasped a man by the neck.

CHAPTER XV.

PUMPING A PRISONER.

"Gentlemen, you are our prisoners!" cried Harry.

The bursting of a bomb could not have startled the smugglers more.

With cries of affright, they glanced around and seeing who was attacking them, they were more startled than ever.

The detectives had grasped the wounded men.

Seeing their peril, the two uninjured Canadians rushed to the rescue.

With one accord, the detectives hurled their prisoners to the planks of the bridge and sprang forward eagerly to meet their foes.

The next moment the smugglers drew their pistols.

Before they could fire a shot, the detectives let their fists fly, and in a moment more a terrific fight was going on.

During the fracas Clara escaped.

Bang! went Old King Brady's powerful fist against the jaw of one of the villains, and it knocked the man flat on his back.

He was stunned.

As he fell close to the wounded man whom Harry had flung down, the old officer whipped out his handcuffs and linked the pair together.

Harry had kicked the pistol out of his opponent's hand.

The man now had to depend upon his fists.

Both he and Young King Brady met with a crash and were punching each other furiously when the old detective arose.

It was Jean, the one who had smuggled the diamonds over the border, and Harry was delighted over the discovery.

The young detective was a scientific boxer.

He warded off several heavy swings and gave Jean an upper cut on the mouth that split his lips open.

The man recoiled, but Harry followed him up like a bull dog.

He received a painful blow in the stomach, and caught Jean's foot as he aimed a swinging kick at the boy.

Harry clung to the man's ankle.

Giving it a jerk, he upset the Canadian's balance and Jean fell with a crash, and rolled over.

He was just going to rise when the boy pounced on him, and a fierce struggle began for the mastery.

Old King Brady would have gone to his pupil's aid had not the other wounded man drawn a pistol and opened fire on him.

A bullet whistled past the old detective's head.

He sprang at the man just as he was about to fire a second shot and grasping him by the wrist, turned the pistol aside.

The ball was spent harmlessly in the air.

Jabbering in French, the man made an effort to wrench the weapon free, but Old King Brady was too quick for him.

He brought down his fist on the rascal's arm.

The force of that blow was awful.

It numbed the arm and the pistol fell from his nerveless fingers.

The next moment Old King Brady's fist caught him on the nose, almost smashing that organ flat, and as the Canadian bit the dust, the detective landed on top of him like a tiger seizing its prey.

"I've got you now!" exclaimed the old detective, fiercely.

"Mercy!" groaned the man.

"Roll over."

"Yes—yes."

"Place your hands behind your back."

"Yes."

"Now keep still, or I'll strangle you."

Old King Brady tied the man with his handkerchief and rose.

By the time he got upon his feet, Harry had overpowered Jean and had the bracelets on his wrists.

"Victory!" chuckled the boy.

"Four," said the old detective. "That ain't a bad haul!"

"But the girl has escaped."

"Never mind, Harry. We are well paid for our work."

The shots, noise, fight and general excitement, had brought a crowd rushing to the spot. There was a policeman among them.

But they arrived too late to be of any assistance.

Rushing up to the Bradys officiously, the panting policeman asked:

"What's the matter here?"

"Nothing," replied Harry.

"Do you call that nothing?" asked the policeman, grabbing the boy.

"Here—you!" exclaimed Old King Brady, showing his badge. "Let go that detective and ring up the wagon so we can run in these prisoners. Step lively now, and don't try to be too smart."

"Detective?" asked the policeman.

Harry showed his badge.

The policeman wilted, and the crowd laughed at him.

Without a word he hurried away to order the patrol wagon.

It soon arrived.

The prisoners were lifted aboard and accompanied by the Bradys, were driven to the nearest police station.

Formal complaints were entered against the four Canadians and when they were locked up, the detectives departed.

In the street Harry said to his partner:

"After all, we haven't accomplished such a lot."

"Why not?" demanded Old King Brady, in surprise.

"Because we've only got Mrs. La Croix and the four spies."

"Well, ain't they valuable?"

"Of course. But they are of the least consequence in this case. We don't know where the diamonds are, and both La Croix and his daughter are yet at large."

"Oh, we'll find them before long. As for the diamonds, why, La Croix can't offer them to any big dealer in this city, Boston, Philadelphia, or Chicago, but what we will be informed of the fact."

"He hasn't made any effort to dispose of them yet, then."

"No. We would have heard of it, if he had."

"There are plenty of unscrupulous people who would buy them in small lots, and thus he'd gradually get rid of the whole lot."

"That ain't La Croix's game. He expects to save $35,000 duty on those gems, besides about $15,000 profit which he expects to make. He's got to do his work quick to gain his money. With a stake of $50,000 to work for, he's going to give us a hard fight."

"Of course. Can't you put the screws on the prisoners?"

"Make them confess?"

"One of the bunch might squeal."

"Perhaps, if we give them the Third Degree."

"Try it. They must know where the Frenchman and his daughter are."

"I shall. It's our only chance to locate the diamonds."

They went home and laid out a plan.

Before the prisoners were brought to court next morning, the Bradys appeared at the police station and had a talk with the captain.

He fell in with their views and said:

"You are at liberty to pump the prisoners here, if you can."

Accompanied by the doorkeeper, the detectives went back to the cell occupied by Jean.

The man was nervously pacing to and fro and glanced at the detectives with an ugly scowl, when they entered.

Pausing before them he demanded:

"Have you come to gloat over my misery?"

"No. We are not so cruel. All we want is some information."

"What about, Old King Brady?"

"The smuggled diamonds."

"And if I refuse?"

"We'll arrest your bride!"

The man turned pale, for the detective had touched his weakest point.

Grasping Old King Brady's arm, he said in appealing tones:

"Don't do that. She is innocent. Why drag her into my trouble?"

"She was with you when the diamonds were smuggled."

"True. But she didn't know anything about it. She didn't have anything to do with the work. I alone am the guilty party."

"That don't make any difference to us. If you don't make a clean breast of the matter, I'll pull her in. That settles it!"

The Canadian pondered a few moments.

Then he said with a sigh:

"Well, I may as well tell you La Croix has got them. You'd find it out anyway, the way you are following up this case."

"Of course I will. And what's more, we know he's got them. But what I want to know most of all, is, where is La Croix?"

"At the Astor House."

"Under what name?"

"His wife's maiden name: Savoy."

"Does Clara know it?"

"Certainly."

"Are any of the diamonds sold yet?"

"Not that I know. But they will be."

"When?"

"To-day."

"He has found a purchaser for the lot?"

"Exactly. They are to meet in the Astor House to-day at twelve and end the sale."

Old King Brady glanced hastily at his watch.

It was then half-past eleven and to reach the Astor House would take three-quarters of an hour!

CHAPTER XVI.

THE CAPTURE OF LA CROIX.

Leaving the prisoner's cell, the Bradys hastened from the police station and hastily getting aboard a City Hall train on the elevated road, they went downtown.

"As it takes about three-quarters of an hour to get down to the bridge," said Harry, in anxious tones, "I'm afraid we will reach the Astor House too late to prevent the consummation of that diamond sale."

"Well, that depends upon how long it is going to take La Croix and his customer to arrive at a bargian," said Old King Brady, quietly.

He was not very nervous over the matter.

Taking a chew of plug tobacco, he settled back comfortably in his seat, drew a newspaper from his pocket and began to read the news.

Harry watched him restlessly.

The boy was very impatient.

"I can't understand how you can take it so cool," he muttered.

"What's the good of fuming and fretting? It isn't going to hurry us, is it?"

"No. But La Croix may beat us."

"Keep cool. The more you worry, the warmer you'll get."

That ride downtown was torture to Young King Brady, and there wasn't a minute he did not have his watch in his hand and kept counting the minutes as they slipped by.

It was with a deep sense of relief that he saw the train stop at the bridge and he was the first one off the cars.

"Quarter past twelve," he growled, feverishly, "and it will take us five or ten minutes longer to reach the hotel."

"Have patience——" began Old King Brady.

"Can't do it. Let's run, or I'll get wild!"

They made rapid time down Park Row and crossing past the post-office, they hastened into the hotel.

Going to the desk, they asked the clerk:

"Is Mr. Savoy here?"

"Yes. Room 76. Name, please."

"He's a friend. We wish to surprise him. Is he in?"

"Oh, yes. I'll send a boy up with you."

"Anyone call on him to-day?"

"Not a soul."

"Not a soul?" blankly asked Harry.

"Except yourselves," laughed the clerk.

Old King Brady burst into a hearty peal of laughter, but not at what the clerk said, for he was laughing at Harry for being so impatient.

The boy drew a deep breath and wiped the sweat from his forehead.

"Thank fortune, we're in time!" he muttered.

"You've had all your stewing for nothing."

"I'm mighty glad of it. His customer must be late."

"All the better for us. This experience will teach you a good lesson in our profession—namely, never to get excited."

"I'll try to profit by it," said Harry, quietly.

Just then a boy came running up and the clerk said:

"Show these gentlemen up to 76—Mr. Savoy's room."

Just as they were about to follow the boy, a tall, thin man, without whiskers, came along and seeing the Bradys, gave a slight start.

The Bradys got a good look at him before he turned his back to them and Harry clutched his companion's arm and whispered:

"By jove, that's Andrew Gibson, the Custom House inspector, in disguise."

"Yes," assented Old King Brady, nodding, "I recognized him. He knew us, too, I could tell at a glance. That man hates us. I wonder what he is doing here. Can he be after La Croix, too?"

Harry was startled at the very suggestion.

"He knows La Croix is a professional smuggler," he remarked, "and I wouldn't be surprised if he got on to the man living here. He may be trying to nab him as we are doing."

"He won't cheat us out of our prey this way, Harry."

Just then they heard the inspector say to the clerk:

"Send up my card to Mr. Savoy. He expects me. I was to meet him at twelve o'clock on some business, but was detained."

The Bradys darted startled glances at each other.

Gibson's remark exposed his hand.

He was the supposed jeweler with whom La Croix had been negotiating to sell the contraband diamonds.

The Bradys had arrived just in time to prevent this man from cheating them out of their legitimate prey.

Had they been delayed a few minutes longer Gibson would have had La Croix under arrest and the smuggled diamonds in his possession.

After all their arduous work, he would have stepped in at the last moment and gained the credit for the arrest.

It made the Bradys shiver to think of it.

Harry said to the hall-boy:

"Go ahead, as fast as you can!"

They hastened upstairs while the hotel clerk was writing Gibson's name on a card, and the boy knocked at the door of No. 76.

"Who ees zat?" demanded La Croix's voice from within.

"Boy, sir."

"Ah! An' vat you vant?"

"Gentlemen to see you, sir."

"Yes. I expect him. Wait, I open ze door."

"Go!" whispered Harry to the boy.

The little fellow ran downstairs.

La Croix unlocked the door and stuck out his head.

"Come in, Meestair Geebson——" he began.

And the Bradys interrupted him by rushing against the door; it hit La Croix on the shoulder, sending him reeling back into the room, and he gave a yell as the detectives dashed in.

"*Par Dieu!*" Ze detectives!" he screamed.

Then he began to yell, swear, and rave in French, as he scrambled to his feet, and the officers made a rush for him.

"Ze Bradys! Ze Bradys!" he shrieked.

At first they imagined these cries were due to his excitement. But when he backed up against a door opening into an adjoining room with his arms stretched out, they saw through his purpose.

"Harry!"

"Well?"

"He's warning some one in the next room."

"I'll see!"

The boy dashed out into the hall.

Old King Brady had his pistol in his hand.

Taking aim at the man's head, he roared in stern tones:

"Drop on your knees!"

"Oh, don't fiair!" yelled La Croix, obeying.

"Raise your hands!"

"Sairtainly, Monsieur."

"Now don't budge, or——"

He made a threatening gesture with the pistol at the wild-eyed Frenchman, from whose face all vestige of color had fled.

"No! No!" gasped La Croix, imploringly.

Reaching his side, the detective handcuffed him.

Just then a boy knocked at the hall door.

"Who's there?" cried the old detective.

"Boy, sir."

"What do you want?"

"Mr. Gibson wants to see you, sir."

"Send him up."

"Yes, sir."

Just then the door between the two rooms was flung open and Harry strode through with a puzzled look upon his face.

"No one in here," he announced.

A pleased smile crossed La Croix's face.

Observing it, Old King Brady exclaimed:

"Your daughter was in that room, wasn't she?"

"She was," admitted La Croix, "but she hear ze attack and escape."

"You warned her by yelling our names?"

"I deed, Monsieur."

"Confound you! Where are those diamonds?"

"Clara has got zem."

"Don't lie."

"Sairch ze place an' you see."

The Bradys complied, but failed to find the missing diamonds.

"I'll go after her!" cried Harry, hastily, and he rushed out.

A few moments after he had gone, Gibson came in, and a look of mingled surprise, rage and jealousy crossed his face when he saw the situation of affairs.

"How are you, Gibson?" laughed Old King Brady. "I've got La Croix!"

"You've cheated me!" snarled the inspector, furiously.

"Bless your heart, you've got the matter twisted. It was you interfering with our game. We've been after this man two months. And you ain't going to skim the cream off our hard work, I can tell you."

"You lie, Brady——"

An angry light sparkled in the old detective's eyes at this insult and he doubled up his fist, strode over to the inspector and struck him in the face.

"Don't you dare insult me, you cur!" he exclaimed.

Gibson reeled back swearing, and seeing the old detective coming at him again, he rushed from the room shouting wildly:

"I'll pay you off for that blow!"

CHAPTER XVII.

RECOVERING THE DIAMONDS.

When Harry ran from La Croix's room, he passed Andrew Gibson in the hall, and smiled when he thought of the man's coming surprise.

Racing downstairs, the boy made inquiries at the different entrances to the hotel, for information about the girl smuggler.

A man had seen her go out the Vesey street door.

As he was interested in her pretty face, he watched her a few moments and had seen her go hurrying over to Broadway.

She had kept on the west side of the street and was evidently going downtown on foot in the dense crowd thronging the street.

With this meagre clew to follow, Harry hurried away.

"She had the gems," he muttered. "Perhaps she had an idea of selling them quick to raise money to aid her parents, both of whom she now knows are in trouble. She's a wise girl, and must certainly know that she would be helpless to aid them without money. Money will give her power. It's possible, therefore, that she's heading for the jewelry district, which is near by. As the street is crowded with vehicles and she'd have to cross to reach Maiden Lane or John street, she must have gone over under the protection of a policeman. He would remember her and might post me. I'll try all the big cops from here down to Wall street, if necessary."

Harry knew that the largest part of the time of these officers was spent at escorting people across the crowded street.

He therefore began with the policeman at Fulton street, giving him an accurate description of Clara, but the officer had not seen her.

On the corner of Dey street he met with the same result.

At Cortlandt street he gained a clew.

The officer there had piloted a girl over who answered her description and said she had gone down the Lane on the north side.

Harry hastened down the great jewelry center.

He scrutinized every one he met.

As a general rule, excepting girls who are employed in the business houses of the downtown section of the city, but few females frequent the side streets.

In fact, so few pass through these streets, that when they do, they are noticed by the numerous boys and business men thereabouts.

Harry was relying upon this curious, but true fact, to gain some news of the girl he was pursuing.

He therefore did not hesitate to ask everyone with whom he came in contact if they had seen such a girl as Clara was.

In some cases he received a negative answer, while in others, not a few people admitted they had noticed her.

According to the latter information, he traced her to Nassau street, and an Italian apple vender with a pushcart near the corner, said he had seen her turn the corner and proceed toward John street.

Following up this clew, Harry met a man standing near the window of a haberdasher's store who asserted that he had seen such a person go through John street toward Broadway.

He averred that she had gone into a building near the corner and pointed out the place to the young detective

When Harry reached the building in question, he paused and studied the business men's signs in the doorway.

One in particular attracted his attention, worded this way:

"Cliquot & Co., Diamonds, Second Floor Front."

A curious smile flitted over the young detective's face and he passed into the narrow hall and ascended the stairs muttering:

"I wonder if she's in there?"

In the upper hall he saw the name of the dealer in precious stones, painted on the ground-glass window.

Harry opened the door and strode in.

He found himself in a small office containing two huge Herring safes, guarded with burglar alarm cabinets. A long table covered with blue cloth served as a counter. Near the front windows was a bookkeeper working at his desk. At the rear a small compartment was partitioned off to serve as a private office.

A fat little Frenchman was behind the counter, but Harry did not see any signs of Clara La Croix.

A feeling of disappointment overcame him.

The salesman bowed, looked at him inquiringly, and asked politely:

"Well, sir, what can I do for you to-day?"

"Is Mr. Cliquot in?" asked Harry, in low tones.

The salesman smiled and shook his head.

"No," he replied. "He is dead."

"Dead? But the name on your sign——"

"Is only kept as a firm name. His partner is in."

"Are you the gentleman?"

"No. His name is Decker. But he is engaged at present."

"I wish to see him personally."

"Won't you sit down?"

"Thank you. I am in a great hurry."

"In that case, perhaps I can arrange an interview."

"I won't detain him a minute."

The clerk passed into the little private office, and Harry heard the low hum of voices. Then the proprietor said:

"Send him in."

The salesman reappeared, nodded, smiled and said:

"Go right in, sir, through that door in the partition."

Harry pushed the door open.

It was a small room containing a desk at which sat a bald-headed, little, old man with a mass of diamonds spread before him on the desk.

He had a magnifying glass in his eye, a pair of tweezers in his hand, and a small delicate scale in front of him.

Evidently he had been weighing and sizing up the stones.

In a chair beside him sat Clara La Croix!

As Harry stepped forward with a smile on his face, their glances met.

She half started from her chair, uttering a smothered cry of intense dismay, and her face turned as pale as death.

"Young King Brady!" she gasped, faintly.

"Clara, I've run you down at last!"

She fairly groaned.

Her defeat was hard to bear.

"This is terrible!" she muttered.

Harry pointed at the diamonds in front of the astonished dealer.

"Ain't those the smuggled diamonds?" he asked.

Before she could reply, Mr. Decker sprang to his feet, crying in alarm:

"Good heavens! Are these smuggled diamonds?"

"Yes," replied Harry, with a nod.

"No wonder she wanted to sell them so cheap!"

"Mr. Decker, I am a Custom House officer."

"Ah!"

"This girl is a smuggler."

"I see!"

"We've been on her trail since she brought those gems from Holland to Canada, and thence over the border without paying duty on them."

"The little wretch!"

"Are you a party to this deal?"

"No, indeed!" emphatically replied the dealer. "I'm a victim. She came in a while ago and said her father died, leaving a stock of diamonds to her as he had been an importer. As she offered to sell them very cheap, I was selecting a lot to buy, when you came in."

"I believe you, sir."

"I am a respectable business man."

"Oh, there can't be any doubt of that. This girl is developing into one of the most expert crooks in the country. For her own good it's a blessing that I've caught her before she gets any worse."

"That's a fact."

"Kindly gather up those gems in a package for me."

"Certainly. I'm glad you arrived in time to save me from buying goods of this kind. I have no desire to do any crooked business."

He made a package of the diamonds.

Harry then turned his attention to Clara who was weeping bitterly and said to her in low tones:

"There's no use playing the baby act. We've got your father, mother and the four spies. You and the diamonds are the last of the bunch."

"But I don't want to go to prison," she sobbed.

"I can't help that. You've broken the law and now you have got to take the consequence of your evildoing."

"Can't you let me go?"

"No."

"I'll give you all those diamonds if you do."

"My dear girl, I'm going to take them anyway."

"But I mean for keeps. They're worth $250,000."

"I wouldn't let you go for ten times that amount."

"Very well," she replied, despairingly, "take me."

"If you'll go along peacefully I won't handcuff you and I'll take you in a cab so people won't be staring."

"You are very kind. I'll do anything you ask."

Harry took the diamonds from Mr. Decker and ranging himself alongside of the girl he led her down to the street.

A cab was procured and they drove away.

CHAPTER XVIII.

CONCLUSION.

After Andrew Gibson rushed from the room in the Astor House, Old King Brady walked over to Paul La Croix and asked him:

"Were you going to sell him your diamonds?"

"Yes, sair," admitted the terrified prisoner, "but, by gar, I deed not know zat he was wong Custom House inspectair."

"Well, that's exactly what he was."

"Hark! What eez zat?"

"Gibson in the hall, yelling bloody murder."

"Ze man ees crazy!"

Old King Brady was puzzled by the defeated inspector's actions. But he soon was destined to learn what the man meant by it.

His yells brought up a policeman at the head of a crowd.

"What's the fuss about?" demanded the patrolman.

"See this badge?" demanded Gibson.

"Yes. You're a Custom House officer."

"That's what I am. I'm after a smuggler."

"Well, what of it?"

"He's in that room. Just as I was going to arrest him a friend of his rushed in, armed with a gun and gave me a punch in the eye."

"I see he did."

"Well, I want you to arrest that fellow, so I can take in the smuggler."

"Very well. Come and point him out to me."

Gibson rushed to the door and flung it open.

Striking a dramatic attitude and pointing at Old King Brady, he shouted in ferocious tones:

"There stands the man. Arrest him!"

Old King Brady was astonished to hear this, and bristling up with just indignation, he demanded:

"Of what does this man accuse me?"

"Interfering with an officer in the discharge of his duty."

Instantly comprehending Gibson's game, the old detective burst out laughing, and finally asked:

"How did I interfere with him?"

"He was arresting yonder man, he says."

"Lock him up, officer!" shouted the inspector. "Lock him up!"

The policeman took a firmer grip on his club and made a rush at Old King Brady, whom he grasped by the collar.

"You're my prisoner!" he exclaimed. "If you resist, I'll club you!"

While this was going on, Gibson grabed La Croix and dragged him over to the door, exclaiming:

"You come with me!"

He designed to arrest the man and get the credit for it, while Old King Brady was fighting with the policeman.

But his plot was doomed to dismal failure.

Old King Brady flung back the lapel of his vest, and exclaimed:

"Do you know I'm Old King Brady, the Secret Service detective?"

"What!" gasped the policeman, glaring at his badge.

"If you don't believe it, you can come to the station when I pull in my prisoner. That fellow is a Custom House inspector all right, but he's sailing under false colors. We were both after the same man, as I am working for the Custom House. I caught the man, and now he wants to take the glory of the capture. See through his game?"

The policeman did.

He released the detective.

Then he made a rush at the spiteful inspector, and poking and jabbing him with his club, he put Gibson out of the hotel.

The inspector finding himself baffled, departed in a fury for the whole crowd was laughing and jeering at him, and one of the spectators threatened to report his meanness to the Collector.

Old King Brady now seized La Croix.

Accompanied by the policeman he went to the Church street station and there met Harry, who had just brought in Clara.

The prisoners were put in cells and the Bradys departed.

Going straight to the Custom House, they were ushered into the Collector's room and gave him the details of their work from start to finish.

When Harry handed over the seized diamonds he was delighted, and praised the pair in the most glowing terms for their efficient work.

He declared that they had broken up the most dangerous gang of smugglers who ever infested the United States, and expressed his regret that he was unable to keep them permanently on his staff.

Gibson, he declared, would be dismissed in disgrace.

The detectives then went to Secret Service headquarters and reported to their own chief, saying their work for the Custom House was finished.

Soon after that the trial and conviction of the La Croixs and their accomplices took place.

It is safe to assume that they got the extreme penalty of the law upon the evidence furnished by the Bradys.

When they were disposed of, the Secret Service detectives returned to their regular duties on the force.

It was not long after that, when one of the most startling events in their lives occurred. This happened when they were detailed upon a Secret Service case. The adventures they met with were of the most thrilling description. Their lives were threatened by dangers, and they did some of the most marvellous work ever known in the department. But want of space here prohibits our giving the details in this story. We have reserved it for a new tale which will be issued in our next number.

THE END.

Read "THE BRADYS AND THE RUNAWAY BOYS; OR, SHADOWING THE CIRCUS SHARPERS," which will be the next number (80) of "Secret Service."

MORRISON'S SENSATIONAL SERIES

Copyrighted 1882 by JOHN W. MORRISON. [Entered at the Post Office, New York, as second class matter.] July 1, 1882.

Vol. I. No. 46.} $2.50 per Year. JOHN W. MORRISON, Publisher, 13 and 15 Vandewater St., N.Y. 6 Months $1.25. {Price 5 Cents.

FRANK JAMES ON THE TRAIL.

A wild cheer broke over the death-scene, and a dozen men, well-armed and mounted, appeared upon the spot.

FRANK JAMES ON THE TRAIL.

CHAPTER I.

"Halloo!"

Rat-a-tat-tat! rat-a-tat!

"What in the name of the fiend do you want?"

"Open the door, Jack Maguire,"

"Who to?"

"Tom Moore."

"All serene."

The above conversation took place on a dark night quite recently in an out-of-the-way place in the state of Texas.

A farm house nestled calmly in a small valley.

All was darkness. No sign of life, except the occasional neighing of a horse, or bleating of a sheep.

It was nearly eleven o'clock and the good folks in those parts had not imbibed the city habit of turning night into day.

In fact their habits might have been formed because of the old adage:

"Early to bed and early to rise,
Makes a man healthy, wealthy and wise."

But if you asked them, they would tell you that night was from sunset to sunrise, and that was the time to sleep.

Of course even in that peaceful Texan district there were some who wanted longer days and shorter nights, and who swore by the Irish national bard that:

"The best of all ways to lengthen our days,
Is to steal a few hours from the night, my boys."

Tom Moore was one of those roving blades who seemed as though their never required the same amount of sleep that others took.

Tom had ridden across country five miles or so to see his friend, Jack Maguire, who had been in bed close upon three hours.

Jack was a farmer.

He was also sheriff and still further was a most important man. To be chairman of the Republican County Committee, was something to be proud of; to be elected sheriff without opposition placed another feather in the cap of honest Jack, but the position he valued most and thought the best was that of captain of the "Emergency Committee of vigilants."

What a name!

What objects that committee had!

As the "Emergency Committee of Vigilants." may perhaps have something to do with our story, we may say, that it was founded by Jack Maguire.

Its objects were of a twofold character. In cases of emergency, such as a fire or flood, the Maguire Association stood ready to lend a helping hand. If a horse was stolen, chicken roosts robbed, or a child kidnapped, then the vigilants headed by Captain Jack Maguire would put on their war paint, start in pursuit of the offender, and it was even chances whether the man who was captured was handed over to Maguire, the sheriff, to be dealt with according to Texan law, or whether Captain Maguire, the vigilant, would on the having a rope fastened, one end in a slipping noose round his neck and the other end over the branch of a tree.

In short, Maguire was not only sheriff, but was the Judge Lynch of the district as well.

We have left Tom Moore out in the cold—no, we beg pardon it's never cold in Texas—that is if we believe the glowing statements made by authority of the state legislature when inviting settlers to purchase land in the southern Paradise. Tom Moore had got off his horse, and was anxiously waiting for his friend to open the door.

Jack Maguire was in no hurry to go down stairs, but at last he opened the door, and in a half-sleepy manner invited Tom Moore inside.

That night rover gladly availed himself of the opportunity and invitation.

"Now what in the name of the fiend do you want at this unearthly hour?" asked Jack.

"Fetch out the whisky bottle my boy and I'll tell you."

Jack knew his friend of old and was convinced that it was best to obey.

"Hot or cold?" asked Jack.

"Well," drawled out Moore, "if it came to a question of likes, I should say—hot."

"All serene, my hearty, there's a fire in the range and some water in the kettle, so it won't be long before you can have your likes."

"That's good," said Moore. "Now, Jack, let's have one of those cigars for which Sheriff Maguire is so famous."

The box of cigars was produced, cigars chosen and lighted, the whisky teemed in the goblets, a taste of lemon and a lump of sugar added, and then—steaming hot water poured on the mixture, the grateful fragrance of which ascended and mingled with the tobacco smoke.

"Jack, would you like to share twenty thousand dollars with me?" asked Tom Moore, breaking the five minutes silence abruptly.

Jack turned round in his chair and faced his visitor, anxiously wondering whether he was entertaining a madman in his house.

After satisfying himself that Moore was perfectly cool, he exclaimed:

"What?"

"My dear boy," calmly replied Moore, "don't get excited, but if I can tell you where you can get twenty thousand dollars, which I could have all to myself, will you give me half?"

"Of course I will!" said the astonished Maguire mental'y hoping that Mrs. Maguire was dressing and about to come down so that she might be a witness if Moore assaulted his host.

"You agree to give me half?"

"You bet I will."

"Well, then, to come to business. Frank James and two of his masked band are within five miles of us."

"By jiminy, where?"

"You know where Will Branigan lives?"

"Well, Frank is at his house."
"By thunder, you don't say so."
"Yes, I do."
"Will Brannigan would never harbor Frank James," said Jack Maguire.
"Not if he knew who he was."
"How did you find out about Frank?"
"I had to call on Will, and I heard two men talking——"
"And you listened?" asked Jack.
"Yes."
"Well, go on. Man alive, I'm all on fire to know what you heard."

It was evident Jack Maguire, sheriff and captain of the Emergency Committee of Vigilants, was getting excited.

"Don't flurry yourself," coolly remarked Moore, "and I'll tell you all I heard."

Tom then repeated the conversation to which he had been an unknown listener, and Jack became convinced that one of the men was the veritable outlaw.

"The other man was Will Brannigan?" asked Jack.
"No, you fool. Brannigan was a-bed, the other was Bill Polk, who is Frank James' right hand man."
"Do you think I should call out the vigilants?"
"Yes."
"Are the masked outlaws well-armed and equipped?"
"I reckon so."
"To-morrow I'll get together a dozen men and go over to Brannigan's, and it may be a fortune to us."
"Yes," said the calculating Tom Moore. "The rewards sum up pretty big, don't they?"
"Rather," said Sheriff Maguire, looking at a small memorandum book. "Texas offers twenty thousand, Missouri, ten thousand, Minnesota, five thousand, and Kansas, five thousand."
"Or a grand total of?" asked Moore.
"Forty thousand dollars," replied Jack, "and the best of it is that it will all be paid on satisfactory proof that Frank James is dead or in jail."
"Bravo, Jack! Give each of your vigilants a cool thousand, and we should have twenty thousand a-piece."
"Yes, but we had better not build too much on capturing Frank. He is cunning as a serpent, and as slippery as an eel."
"Well, I guess I'll go now," said Tom.
"No, I hear Mrs. Maguire coming down stairs, and I know she has got a bed ready for you, so hitch up your horse in the stable, and make a night of it here," said hospitable Maguire.

The worthies spent a jolly time, and built many a *chateau d'Espagne* before they retired to bed to catch a few hours' repose.

CHAPTER II.

Will Brannigan was a broad-shouldered, tall, sturdy Irishman

He had left his native land because he had joined the Fenian movement, and was "wanted" by the police.

He believed in dear, old Ireland, and was one of those men of whom the peasantry are constantly singing as being:

"Dear Ireland's strength.
Her truest strength is still
The rough and ready, roving boys,
Like Rory of the Hill."

Will Brannigan had met Frank James and his brother Jesse soon after he had arrived from the old world.

Will had a kindly liking for the outlaw brothers, and often helped them out of their difficulties, but would never join their band or share the plunder.

"No, Frank," Brannigan would say, "no Brannigan was ever 'wanted' for anything but political offences, and I'm not going to join you."

"Well, Will," answered Frank, "you're a good fellow, and I will never ask you again to unite your fortunes with ours."

"Remember, Frank, where I live, and if I can ever help you or your brother, rely on me," answered the warm-hearted Celt.

It was in this man's house that Tom Moore had fancied he had discovered the outlaw Nemesis.

Whilst Captain Jack Maguire was hunting up his

"Who was that fellow who was over here yesterday?" asked Frank.
"An old pal called Tom Moore," was Brannigan's answer
"Is he safe?"
"No, not if he recognized you."
"Well, I guess he did," answered Frank.
"I feel sure of it," remarked Bill Polk.
"Then you will have to get ready for attack, for Moore would sell his God if he could," solemnly assured Brannigan.

Bill Polk had been wounded in the shoulder a few days previously, and he hoped he was going to have a few days' rest.

"We've got to move," said Frank.
"Yes, I'm ready," was Polk's reply.
"Do you feel strong enough?"
"Don't worry about me," said Polk.

The horses were brought out and saddled. Polk was helped to mount.

"Good-bye, Brannigan," called out Frank, as he commenced his journey.

"Halt!" came from a voice in the rear.

Frank James did not heed it.

"Halt!"

"Ride on, Polk, and I will cover your retreat," said generous hearted Frank James.

"Not if I know it," was the reply.
"Crack!"
"Bang!"
"Crack!"

A volley of pistol and rifle shots whistled above their heads.

Frank slackened his speed for a moment.

Then drew his surest revolver and examined it.

"Crack!"

The report rang out almost as loud as a rifle shot.

The smoke gradually rose and lifted the veil from their eyes and a riderless horse was seen.

"Crack!"
"Crack!"
"By God, I'm hit!" said Frank.
"For mercy's sake where?" asked Polk.
"One of my spurs taken off, I guess," and Frank laughed heartily to think it was no worse.
"Crack!"
"Crack!"

The bullets whizzed and rattled, the reports clanged and clacked, and, as Frank jestingly said, seemed to play a death waltz.

"Men," cried Jack Maguire, "I'll give two thousand to he man who can kill that villain, Frank James."

"Come on," retorted Frank, "I'll give a leaden tonic to the one who first comes."

"Crack!"

Bill Polk had fired but not at the vigilants.

"What did you fire that way for?" hurriedly asked Frank.

"Because the scoundrel informer Tom Moore was sneaking there."

"Crack!"

Another one of Captain Maguires Emergency Committee of Vigilants had bitten the dust. On the pursuers came. Frank shouted back to them:

"Not a man of you will live if you continue the pursuit."

Frank halted, and then, with the speed of lightning, fired six shots at the enemy.

Two more of the vigilants were rendered powerles

"Crack!"
"Whiz-z!"
"Bang! Crack!"

A perfect storm of bullets seemed to be falling.

Frank James had often declared he bore a charmed life and it seemed so. Not a shot but was aimed at him, and yet he was unharmed. The vigilants screamed and yelled and roared. One by one they fell, wounded, many never to rise again from their grassy bed.

Frank and Bill rode on, their horses showing no signs of fatigue. The bullets whistled over their heads. Frank James returned them with interest, and he, with his companion, rode on, gradually gaining the advantage. They came to a narrow pass. At the far end they saw a man evidently waiting for them. As they neared him, he called out:

"Halt! Who are you?"

The man had raised his revolver and took aim.

"Crack!"

"Crack!"

It was a duel. The man had fired. So had Frank James. Frank and his pal rode on, there was no one to stop them, for, in the duel Frank's shot had taken effect, whilst his would-be-captor had shot wide of the mark.

For hours the pursuit was continued, but at last rest was at hand. They had ridden over a hundred miles without rest, and they needed it badly.

No pursuers were to be seen, and Frank James determined to rest for a few hours—days if need be.

Tom Morris's dead body was found in the wood.

He had died, a victim to his greed and love of money.

Captain Jack Maguire had lost seven of his men and he was shot in the wrist, temporarily disabling his left hand.

"Curse the fellow," he muttered, as he rode back home, "the devil does take good care of his own."

CHAPTER III.

A few days later Frank was alone. He had sent his faithful companion on an expedition of trust and caution.

Frank was making for the house of a Scotch settler named McVittie with whom he had left his favorite horse "Stonewall."

Walking along, Frank met and walked with a shepherd and it was fortunate that he did so. The man was one of McVittie's helps and considered the boss of great importance because he had recently been elected a justice of the peace.

"The boss will have lively times here shortly," said the help.

"Why?" asked Frank.

"Because he is making preparations for the capture of a great criminal."

"Indeed; who is it?"

"Why, Frank James the outlaw."

"Oh, that's it, is it! How do you know that Frank James is in the neighborhood?"

"Well, you know, he left his horse 'Stonewall' with the boss, and it's too good a bit of horseflesh to lose."

"Yes?"

"Now, isn't it likely that Mr. James will want the horse back?"

"Yes, I should say so."

"That's what the boss thinks, and so he is determined to have the reward, and has gone to tell the police to be in readiness to catch Frank."

"Oh, the scoundrel!" muttered Frank to himself, as he walked on.

Instead of going straight up to the farm, he concealed himself in a belt of timber and waited for the approach of nightfall.

He noticed M'Vittie ride up, and remarked with disgust that the old fellow was mounted on no less a steed than Stonewall himself.

"Jee-rusalem!" mentally ejaculated Frank. "You'll never cross such a piece of stuff as that again, my bloomer. You'll sell Frank James, will you? I'll teach you a lesson that will last you longer than a plate of porridge for your breakfast, you Scotch hound! Wait till I'm on your track, Mr. M'Vittie."

Evening gradually came on, the men on the home station came in, the horses were turned into the paddock, and preparations for supper made.

Frank had brought some provisions with him, so this last operation did not tantalize him as it might otherwise have done.

At last, as darkness came on, all signs of human life about the station began to disappear.

The men had withdrawn into their huts, which were close to the main dwelling inhabited by M'Vittie.

People who have to be out by sunrise are not usually given to sit up late, and in a very short time the gleams of light that had shown through the cracks in the closed shutters faded away.

Still Frank resolved to be cautious.

He knew that the soundest slumber is that which comes after midnight, and had made up his mind not to approach the farm till that hour.

He therefore sat patiently under a tree speculating as to what means he could employ to get M'Vittie into his power, and running over all the various punishments his ingenuity could devise as best fitted for that venerable hypocrite.

Mentally he vowed that the first task he would set about would be vengeance on the Scotchman.

Night had fallen calm and placid, and the sky was gemmed with a multitude of stars.

"I think it's safe to make a move now," thought Frank; "it must be past midnight."

Rising, he took up the saddle and stealthily approached the farm.

"If there are any dogs prowling around there may be a bit of a muss," he meditated; and with a view of meeting this emergency, he looked to his knife.

A few minutes brought him to the paddock.

Here he paused for a short time to reconnoitre.

A strong temptation stole over him to knock at M'Vittie's house and shoot the old ruffian as he appeared at the door.

It was necessary, however, to secure Stonewall in order to carry out this scheme.

Accordingly he proceeded to the paddock.

The night was a clear and brilliant one, and he had no difficulty in making out his horse amongst the others.

The next question was how to catch him.

He could not expect that the animal would come to his call, any more than a bird would wait to have salt put on its tail.

A sieve full of oats might have proved handy though.

However, the task proved an easier one than he had anticipated when he slipped the bar and entered the paddock.

Stonewall was evidently in the habit of being ridden, and had been turned out with a trail rope attached to him, to facilitate catching.

Frank profited by this to effect his capture.

"Steady, old man, steady," he whispered, as he laid his hand on Stonewall's mane.

With rapid dexterity he saddled and bridled the animal.

"By Jove!" he exclaimed, as he noted certain marks on the horse's withers; "so that herring-gutted old skeleton of a split-shingle couldn't ride you without getting you saddle-galled, whilst I, big and heavy as I am, never scraped an inch off your skin, my beauty. Never mind, old man, it's the last time anyone will throw a leg over you but Frank James."

As he spoke, Frank led the horse out of the paddock, the slip-bar of which he purposely omitted to replace after he had done so.

"If the old devil's beasts have strayed away a few miles by morning, why so much the better," was his reflection, as he hoisted himself into the saddle and marked with satisfaction that, owing to the exercise to which he had been put, Stonewall was in capital condition.

Again he debated whether he should ride up to the old fellow's door, and try to lure him forth so as to shoot him down.

No, that would be letting him off too easy.

He would make the Scotch traitor suffer in such a way that he should remember his act of treachery.

CHAPTER IV.

Mr. M'Vittie's slumbers were not destined to be prolonged to a very late hour that night.

Just after daybreak he was aroused by hearing someone pounding away at the door of his dwelling.

"Ech, wha's there?" was his response.

"Get up, gov'nor; there's a blessed fine go," was the answer, in the voice of his overseer.

"Andrew, my mon," was his reply; "how often must I tell ye to lay aside the profane and unguidly habit o' blasphemin' which is a sair abomination baith in the sight o' the Lord, and in the lugs o' a decent douce mon like mysel'."

"Confound it all, it's enough to make an angel swear. Some fool or other has left the slip panel open, and every one of the horses are out of the paddock."

"D——" began M'Vittie; but he checked himself just in time, with a gulp that almost made him bite his tongue off.

"Ech, now," he ejaculated as soon as he had got his breath; "but this is sair tidings, sair tidings; it's eneuch to drive a decent body clean daft, to have to deal wi' sic' a pack o' blaitherin' boobies as I hae around' me. Let me see wha's the gowk that has done this."

Hurrying on his garments he sallied forth, and soon a general muster of the men took place.

On being interrogated, each and all stoutly declares that the slip rail had been in its place when they had last set eyes on it.

Further cross-examination showed that three of the hands who had been the last to leave the paddock had done so in company, and that, according to their united testimony, the rail had been carefully replaced by one of them.

"Ye must one and all start awa' at aince in search o' the beasties."

The men started on their expedition, but in a few minutes returned to say that the tracks showed that a man had been to the field and saddled Stonewall and rode away.

M'Vittie determined to join in the chase, the consciousness coming over him that he had been outwitted by Frank James.

He more than ever itched to possess the reward, and swore that Frank, the outlaw, should fall a victim to his treachery.

On the next afternoon, after joining in the search, the Scotchman found himself in a narrow ravine.

To the right and left rose ridges of brown stone.

Suddenly the report of a pistol shot rang out from behind a rock.

Struck by the bullet, M'Vittie's horse staggered and dropped in its tracks as dead as a canned lobster.

M'Vittie was thrown over his horse's head and fell on his own.

The shock with which his skull came in contact with the rocks was so sharp a one that he lost all consciousness for a time.

When he recovered, it was several minutes before he could exactly realize the state of affairs.

At length consciousness returned.

He found himself lying on his back, with his head aching most horribly.

Drawing a long breath he endeavored to rise.

He could not do so.

His limbs refused to move.

He fell asleep again.

Then when he woke his senses seemed clearer.

Again he attempted to move.

Still he could not rise.

What was the matter?

Full consciousness returned, and he found that he was tightly secured.

His arms were tied to his sides.

His legs secured at the ankles.

This was past all comprehension.

The Scotchman was a hardshell Baptist, but he swore like a trooper and cursed like a Colorado miner.

Who could have done it?

And what motive could anyone have in securing him?

An hour so it seemed to him, but in reality only half an hour passed and the Scotchman almost became convinced that he was dreaming an unpleasant dream, when he turned his eyes round and then saw a man sitting quietly on a rock smoking a cigar and watching him.

"Oh, Heaven!" gasped M'Vittie.

The man was Frank James.

"Well, Mr. M'Vittie," he repeated, "how do you find yourself?"

For a moment M'Vittie's senses seemed on the point of leaving him from mingled fear and astonishment.

He managed, however, to pull himself together again.

"What, Frank James!" he ejaculated. "Ech, mon, but this is a strange meetin'. Sakes alive, what garred ye shoot the puir beastie and lap me in bonds like a sucklin' babe in its swaddlin' claithes?"

"Can't you guess?" said Frank.

"De'il a bit, mon; de'il a bit, unless ye tuik me for anither. But joost loosen these tows ye have cast about me if it's a bit crack ye're wushin for."

"You didn't think to meet me hereabouts, eh?"

"Na, I didna, I didna even ken that ye were bock ag'in in the state, and it's little I thocht to foregather wi' ye in sic a fashion."

Frank looked at him for a little time in silence.

"What brought you here, M'Vittie?"

"'Deed, it was joost a wee bit service I was doin' yer animel, Frank. Ye ken the browny beastie, it's Stonewall ye ca'd him, that ye left in my care sinsyne?"

"Yes."

"Weel, some hellicate loon has stolen him fra' the farm, and I was trackin' the villain. Sae if ye'll undo the bonds we'll just set out after him together. But I misdoubt me. Surely if ye have been lurkin' here ye must have seen him pass, the reevin' rogue."

"I've only seen one rogue to-day," said Frank with a grim earnestness; "and he's about as black-hearted a traitor as ever broke bread or swallowed porridge."

"What dy'e mean?" asked M'Vittiee, who, for all his coolness, began to grow terribly uneasy.

At that moment the neigh of a horse sounded from behind the angle of the ravine.

"Why, 'tis the neigh of the beastie himself," said M'Vittie, somewhat reassured. "Ah, I'd ken it amangst a thousand. I see how it is. Ye came across the reiver, who was walkin' off wi' him."

"No," shouted Frank, throwing off all disguise; "but I have come across the scoundrel who was going to use him as bait to draw me into the hands of the traps, and by —— I'm not going to leave go of him in a hurry, now I've got him. You didn't expect to drop on an old friend so soon again, did you? you blood-thirsty Scotch whelp! ain't you glad? You look it."

And James burst into a loud laugh. The terror of his quondam associate would have been ludicrous if it had not been despairing.

"Out with it, old man. Why have you taken such a fancy to Frank James, that you must track him like a spy? Yes, like a spy! D'ye hear—a spy? and you know, Mac, how Frank pays spies—eh? You've mistaken me."

"Fac or neath, I thocht it was some roving thief that had lifted your bonnie beast, my lad; and I was just——"

"Yes, I know, you were just seeing if you could see whether James was handy to fill a cellar or jail. I know ye, Andy. I'm fly to it all, and your little game too, But you haven't won the trick yet, my laddie. No, you've got a little performance to go through before them cards turn up trumps. Just get up and follow me."

"What do you want me to get up for—I may as well be where I am when I have no horse."

"Why, you don't think I'd be so cruel as to let you lie out here until the crows picked your liver out?" laughed Frank James. "Oh, dear, no, Mac, I mean to provide a lodging for you *for life.*"

"What the deil are ye at, mon?" said M'Vittie, looking rather anxiously at Frank James, but still ignorant that his enemy was aware of his treacherous intentions.

"Up, you sneaking hound; you shall never lap my blood. D'ye think I'm not fly to your police jabberings; do you think I don't know your game for the reward? You've come for it, and my government oath, you'll have something that will show such vermin as you are what it is to meddle with the James brothers.

"I know your little game. I know how you plotted to keep the horse till I came for it, so as to hand me over to the traps. I know all about your meeting the police at the out-station. The man who stole the horse you talk of! Why, the man who stole the horse was me, and as I stood by your blooming shanty, I felt a devilish mind to put a light to the roof, and shoot you down as you came out, like the dog you are."

He paused for a moment, half choked with fury.

Then he resumed in more solemn tones.

"Only I'm very glad I didn't, for then I should have lost the chance of teaching you the very pretty little lesson of how Frank James repays treachery, which I mean to do before you're an hour older."

"But, Frank——" began M'Vittie, feebly.

"Stow it!" thundered the bushranger. "Don't try any of your gibberish with me. I ain't been very particular in my life about knocking a fellow on the head if he stood in my way, but if I did a trifle more, I never put a pal's life in my pocket and drunk out his heart's blood in the nearest saloon. No; the James boys never sold a pal or sneaked a swag. Frank always went straight at his work, whether it was a man or a bank. No; he'd stand or fall like a man, not like a cur that would bite you in your sleep, and sell your wisen to the rope as he would a bale of wool or a cask of tallow."

Thoroughly alarmed, Andrew tremulously cried:

"I dinna ken what ye are bletherin' aboot me betrayin' ye, it's a'together a mistake on your pairt. I'm yer friend, an'

I can prove it. Let me gang and I'll gie ye any sum in reason ye could name."

"There's only one thing I mean to take from you," replied Frank James.

"And what's that?"

"Every drop of blood in your body, and every ounce of meat on your bones."

As he spoke, Frank stooped over the prostrate figure of the settler, and hoisted it to its feet.

Then throwing it on his shoulder, he carried it to the spot beyond the angle where Stonewall was tethered. The Scotchman roared loud and long, hoping, but in vain, to attract succor. A few minutes later, and M'Vittie was balancing like a sack across the saddle of the gallant animal, which Frank took by the bridle. Andrew threw himself off the animal, and fell on his face, and lay there howling and imploring for mercy, and asking wildly what Frank James was going to do.

"If you don't lie quiet in the saddle, I'm hanged if I don't drag you by this tether-rope to the lodging I'm going to give you for the night, at all events."

Groan upon groan flowed from M'Vittie's throat. He realized his prospects, and he knew his man; he also knew his man knew him. White despair enshrouded his face, the features of which were working with dread. He ceased to plead, for hope had fled. Frank threw him again across the saddle, face downward, like a sack, saying:

"Tumble again, and you'll know more of the stones than you ever yet felt."

After traveling for half an hour, they arrived at the foot of a small, isolated peak, on the flat summit of which was a solitary tree, forming a conspicuous landmark. Here Frank halted, and laughed and chuckled, while his eyes gleamed revenge. He removed M'Vittie—whose sufferings, mental and physical, had reduced him to almost a state of imbecility—from the back of Stonewall. Placing him on his own shoulder, he commenced the ascent of the peak, which was not very high, merely prominent.

The ground led very gradually up to it, and Stonewall had carried the burden up to the foot of the rock.

At length they reached the summit of the peak, which formed a small plateau.

Frank threw himself down, utter exhausted, by the side of M'Vittie, whom bruises and terror had by this time reduced to a condition of almost imbecility.

The plateau was about eight or ten feet square, and from its summit an extensive view could be obtained. The tree rooted in it was a small but strong one.

As soon as he had recoveged himself, Frank rose and lifted M'Vittie to his feet. He placed the squatter against the tree and lashed him to it securely. A look of frozen terror spread over the squatter's face. He turned his eyes to Frank James, his blue lips parted, and in a husky whisper he gasped out:

"What is it ye mean to do wi' me?"

Without vouchsafing him any reply, the outlaw drew his knife.

"For mercy's sake, for pity's sake spare me; I'm no fit to dee. I'm a miserable sinner," screamed M'Vittie.

Still in silence Frank raised his knife, but instead of plunging it into M'Vittie's breast as he had anticipated, he deliberately set to work to cut away every shred of clothing the unhappy man wore, taking care at the same time not to sever his bonds.

When this was completed, and M'Vittie stood as naked as Adam before the fall, Frank returned his knife to its sheath, and said:

"I told you I meant to have every drop of blood from your body, and every ounce of flesh from your bones. I give the first to the insects and the last to the birds."

"For God's sake," yelled M'Vittie, who began to realize the awful fate awaiting him, "put your knife into me."

"No," answered Frank, "my knife for a man who fights me, and not for a sneak who wanted to earn my blood-money like you."

"Help, mercy, mercy, help, murder," yelled the settler, almost mad with fear.

"It's no use howling, M'Vittie, there's not a living soul within fifty miles of us."

The squatter made a desperate effort to free himself.

He tugged at his bonds till they buried themselves in his flesh, and then heedless of the agony he inflicted on himself he endeavored to snap them by a series of jerks.

At length he paused, exhausted and bleeding from a dozen places where they had cut through his skin.

"You won't get loose, those fastenings would hold a couple of working bullocks."

"Ye coward, ye faust-hearted coward, I spit at ye, ye dare na snub me, ye dare na," howled M'Vittie, in the hope of taunting the outlaw into using his knife.

"That cove won't fight," replied Frank, calmly.

"Kill me in mercy, mon, it's the only thing I ask o' ye, if ye've got a human heart in ye, kill me."

With his eyes protruding from his head, and his hair standing on end, M'Vittie forced this frantic appearl from between his lips, from which blood and froth were running down to his chest, that panted and heaved with his recent exertions and his present terror.

"No," answered Frank. "Good-bye. I mean to leave you as a warning to others not to play tricks on the James Boys."

With these words he turned away and began to descend the peak heedless of the wild string of prayers, blasphemies, curses and entreaties that pealed forth from the lips of the doomed wretch at its summit.

As he descended, the sounds grew fainter and fainter.

On reaching the bottom he looked up.

The figure of M'Vittie lashed to the tree trunk was plainly visible against the sky, across which clouds that indicated a storm were floating.

Frank fancied he could discern it struggling to get loose.

After gazing at it for some time he mounted Stonewall and rode onward.

As he did so one last, wild, despairing yell reached his ears.

Before nightfall a terrible storm of wind and rain broke over the mountains.

This weather lasted for several days and its effects extended over a large area.

When, after waiting a week without hearing anything of M'Vittie, his overseer made an attempt to track him, the faintest hope of doing so had vanished.

It was not until several weeks had passed that a man in search of adventure climbed the rock and beheld a sight to freeze the blood in his veins.

There was the body, or what remained of it, of M'Vittie. Eagles and other birds of prey had taken huge pieces of flesh away. And all sorts of loathsome insects were crawling over the rotting remains.

It was a terrible vengeance, and one which Jesse James would have scorned, but Frank was more cold-blooded and cruel, and woe be to those who fall a victim to the vengeance of this saturnine man.

CHAPTER V.

Mount Tabor Valley was the name of a beautiful glade in Texas.

A pretty rippling brook meandered gracefully through its grassy dells.

Ripple, ripple, the brook went on, unceasing, singing its ditty:

> "Men may come, and men may go,
> But I go on forever."

In this valley, by the side of the clear, crystal sheen of the brook, two men were to meet and settle their differences by a duel to the death.

The sun was dipping far below the horizon when Captain Morris and his friend rode down the glade.

"Our friends have not arrived yet, it seems," said Captain Morris.

"No, nor will they," said his companion.

"Why do you doubt?"

"Because Frank James is not fond enough of death to court it in this fashion."

"It is the boast of the outlaw that he never broke his word," replied Captain Morris.

A quarrel had taken place between Captain Morris, a settler, holding a good social position in the state, and Frank James, the notorious outlaw.

Strange as it seems, yet 'tis true, that as the quarrel became bitter, a feeling of hatred grew up in the hearts of each, and the death of one was declared necessary.

Frank challenged Captain Morris to a duel, and the gallant captain accepted the challenge, and all preliminaries were arranged.

"It will soon be too hot," remarked Morris, as he waited for the other contestant.

"Ah, here he comes," rejoined his companion.

Two horsemen were seen galloping down the hill.

"This is stupid work," said Tom Nash, who acted as second for Frank James.

"Yes, but we have naught to do with that."

"Let us get it over as soon as possible."

"Agreed."

"My man wishes to wear a mask, as he has no idea who may see him, and you know that he has reasons for not wanting to be recognized."

"Yes, if he gains the victory——"

"If?" queried Nash. "Why, my dear sir, of course he will."

"Well, we shall see."

The preliminaries were arranged, the ground marked off, and the duellists ready.

"Stop!" cried Captain Morris. "What freak is it to fight in a mask?"

"My man fights in a mask or not at all," said Nash.

"Then I won't fight," rejoined Morris.

"I thought so. You are too great a coward."

"Liar!" yelled Morris. "I will fight."

The two principals took their places at twenty paces apart. They were to fire at the word four.

"One!" said Nash.

"Two!" came from the second accompanying Captain Morris.

"Three!"

"Four!"

"Crack!"

One report rang out on the clear silence of the night.

Captain Morris held a smoking pistol. His antagonist had not fired.

"Heavens, he is lost!" gasped Captain Morris' friend.

The captain folded his arms, and stood waiting for death.

"Shoot, Frank James, and end this farce," called out Captain Morris.

"No," answered Frank, "the duel is over"

"I demand another shot," cried Morris.

"Very well."

The pistols were loaded, the paces counted, and the seconds began to count.

"One!"

"Two!"

"Three!"

"Four?"

Again only a single shot resounded.

The masked duelist fell to the ground.

Nash uttered a fierce cry.

Captain Morris hurried forward, but before he reached the fallen duelist, a clatter of horses' hoofs was heard, and looking round they saw to their utter amazement and alarm Frank James and Bill Polk riding to the rendezvous.

Who was the masked duelist?

Frank James, who is this masked man whom I have shot?"

"I don't know," answered James, as he leaped from his horse and went to the side of the one who had taken his place in the sad duel.

Captain Morris and his friend pressed forward to see the wounded, if not killed antagonist.

The mask was torn away, and then a wild, piercing cry fell from the lips of all.

"Great Heavens! What do I see?" ejaculated Captain Morris.

"My God! Nash what is the meaning of this?" asked Frank James.

What was the meaning of this wild emotion?

Why these frantic exclamations?

Who was this masked duelist lying there in the stiffness of death that should cause strong men to weep tears of bitter agony, and make them dumb with astonishment?

It was a woman!

Strongly built, she had availed herself of her appearance and the darkness of the evening to personate the notorious outlaw, Frank James.

Who could it be?

Was there in the whole of the United States a woman so devoted, so loving and so courageous, that she would offer her life in place of a man for whose body so large a reward was offered?

"Yes! There was one!"

And that one, whose love was so matchless was——

Annie Ralston James.

The wife of the outlaw. The sharer of his troubles, the partner of his joys.

Mrs. James had returned from an expedition on which she had gone for her husband, and accidentally heard that her dear Frank was to fight a duel.

She had also heard that Captain Morris was a famous shot, and had vowed that he would kill her husband, by fair or foul means.

A letter, which Annie had written, calling Frank away to aid her out of some supposed difficulty, had the desired effect of delaying her husband.

Whilst he was away, she told her old retainer, Nash, what she intended doing.

Swore him to secrecy.

Dressed herself in male attire.

Masked.

And now was lying dead.

"Oh! my darling, my beautiful wife, my pet, to think you lie here murdered by that villain," sobbed Frank James. And then turning to Captain Morris he said: "You scoundrel, where is your manliness to fight with and kill a woman?"

"How did I know that a woman had taken you place?" asked Morris.

"You should have insisted on the mask being removed."

Morris explained the request he had made and the taunt that he was a coward.

"How did I know that you hadn't turned coward and sent one of your minions to fight me," sneered Morris.

Frank James jumped forward and would have made an end of Captain Morris had it not been for a groan which he heard.

"She's not dead!" cried out Nash.

"Thank Heaven!" exclaimed Frank, as he forgot all about the sneering captain and took his place by the side of his wife.

Captain Morris and his friend seized this opportunity to leave the scene.

They were glad to get away with their lives.

Annie Ralston James raised herself slightly.

"Frank!"

"Annie!"

And then the wounded woman sank back again in her swoon. Frank poured a little brandy from his flask into her mouth and she quickly revived. It was found that the bullet had only inflicted a flesh wound on her shoulder, and that the force of the blow had stunned her.

In a very few minutes she was her own lively self again.

Glad to think that Frank had escaped, she gloried in her exploit.

CHAPTER VI.

Captain Morris went away from Tabor Valley haboring thoughts of vengeance.

He had intended to kill Frank James, and had prepared a ruse by means of which he would succeed.

The excitement of waiting and then having to fight a masked duellist unnerved him and he forgot all about the foul play he intended. On his way, he however conferred with his friend Blair, and together they resolved to gather together a number of their friends and never rest until the whole of the Frank James' party was exterminated. The next day fortune favored them somewhat.

Bill Polk had gone some distance to obtain some liniment for Annie James' wound.

As he was returning he found himself surrounded, and before he had time to make any serious resistance—even if it would have been of any avail—he found himself bound hand and foot.

Captain Morris and his friend, Joshua Blair, took charge of the proceedings of a mock trial, and Bill Polk found himself adjudged guilty of being an outlaw and was sentenced to death.

A rope was ready, and a slip-knot made at one end. A branch of a tree convenient was to be the gallows.

"Now, boys," said Captain Morris, "before we string up the prisoner, I want to say a few words."

"Bravo for Morris!"

"Bully boy, forever!" shouted his men.

"This man, by name William Polk, is one of Frank

James' band of outlaws who call themselves the Death Avengers. Polk is Frank's head man. We have vowed to shoot, hang or drown every man of the avengers——"

"We have."

"That's so."

"Just the ticket."

"Well, boys, we are agreed on that. Now I propose we pardon this fellow——"

"What?"

"Never!"

"Listen to me and then make your remarks," continued Captain Morris. "There is a large reward offered for Frank James. It would make you all comfortable. Now we will pardon this fellow, on condition he tells us where Frank James can be found. We will then go and see if his information is correct. If so, we nab James and let this man go free. If not, why we hang Polk, and do our best to find Frank James. What say you boys?"

"I think the Captain's idea a good one," said Blair.

"So do I."

"And me."

"Begorra, I think so too," said another.

"Very well, we are all agreed," said Captain Morris.

Poor Bill Polk had been standing all the time firmly bound, with the fatal noose round his neck, the other end of the rope dangling over the branch of the tree.

Not a pleasant predicament. Hempen rope never did make a good necktie.

No one wants to try one.

Bill Polk was no exception to the rule.

By treachery to the outlaw chief he could save his life. By truth, honor and fidelity, he would, perhaps, save Frank James but his own life would be gone.

These thoughts passed through his mind as he stood there and listened to the speech of Captain Morris and the interruptions of the men.

He felt he must say something. At last he opened his mouth:

"Captain Morris and devils generally," not a very polite way to commence a speech, you will say, but wait, reader, until you get a rope round your neck and expect to feel its tightening embrace every minute and we guess you will be no more choice in your language than was Bill Polk. "You want to catch Frank James," he continued.

"Yes."

"Yes."

"That's just the ticket."

"Well, in thirty or forty years time Mr. James will be dead, and then if you go to the graveyard you can have his body if it is any good to you."

"Where is Frank James?" asked Captain Morris.

"In safety," was the reply.

"Do you know where he is?"

"Yes."

"Bravo."

"Excellent."

The vigilants or murderers, whatever you please to call them, exulted at Bill Polk's reply; their hands itched for the reward, and some even began to imagine how they would spend their share.

"Where is he?" asked Captain Morris.

"Where you can't find him."

"Will you tell us?"

"No," answered Polk.

"He wants to make better terms" whispered Joshua Blair, and then, speaking aloud, he said: "Polk, if you will take us to the place where Frank James is hidden, we will save your life and give you a thousand dollars out of the reward."

"Very generous," sneered Polk. "Now listen to me, you devils. I'm trussed like a turkey at a Thanksgiving dinner, and I get a rope round my throat to keep me upright. I know you can easily kill me if you like, but I tell you that if I had a thousand lives you could take them all before I would turn traitor and peach on the best man that I ever served under."

"Do you mean it?" asked Blair.

"Yes. I am no lying hound of a traitor."

"Then you shall die."

"All right, go ahead," coolly replied Bill Polk.

Blair stepped forward, and, with the aid of another man, began to draw at the rope which was to pull Bill Polk up in the air until he was dead.

A crackling of leaves was heard, and then the earth seemed to quake as though an army was riding over it. A wild cheer broke over the death-scene, and a dozen well armed, appeared upon the spot.

"Long live Frank James."

"Death to the vigilants."

"To hell with Captain Morris," shouted the men, as they rode up to Judge Lynch's gallows.

The most astonished person was Bill Polk.

He had felt the rope tightening, and had nearly lost consciousness, when he felt his thongs give way before the keen edge of a knife, and realized that he was a free man.

The Morris party of vigilants leaped to their horses and rode quickly away.

They were too discomfited to offer any resistance.

Bill Polk was glad that he had been no traitor, and warmly thanked Frank James for liberating him from death.

It appeared that Will Brannigan had heard that Morris was going to waylay Bill Polk, and Brannigan thought it a friendly act to inform Frank James.

The outlaw chief wasted no time in getting his men together and starting in search of his lieutenant.

We have seen that he arrived only just in time to save Polk's life.

CHAPTER VII.

Bill Polk, when at home, lived with his mother, an aged lady, who had a small farm left her by her husband, and which her son tilled and cared for until he had joined the outlaws. Since then his career had prevented him working at home as he had done formerly.

Joshua Blair determined that Bill Polk should be captured.

He had so humiliated the band by his escape, and the outlaws were so evidently powerful that every victory they gained made resistance or an attempt to capture them still more difficult.

The large rewards offered for the capture of Frank James had let loose some of the vilest creatures that ever lived.

They were ready to commit any crime in order to find their way to the capture of Frank James.

When will governments learn that two crimes will never make justice?

Blood money!

Ay, what crimes have been committed, what desolation caused by the offer of rewards for the apprehension of criminals.

Blood money!

Aye, for the desire to obtain it innocent men have been imprisoned, and many ascended the gallows steps, their lives and liberties being sworn away by the perjurers' love of gold.

Innocent women have been left husbandless, their homes destroyed, their children made outcasts.

Girls have been forced into lives of shame and ignominy, and murder itself committed in the craving to obtain blood money.

Governments offering such large rewards, put temptations in the way of thousands of weak and criminal men.

It was so in the case of the James boys.

Hundreds of men left their business, in city and country, and gave themselves up to hunting the outlaws.

The hope of getting the reward was the actuating motive.

Out of these many a dozen became criminals of quite as black, and perhaps worse, dye than Frank and Jesse James.

Joshua Blair had neglected his farm, allowing it to go to ruin, and had become so absorbed in outlaw hunting that he committed crimes every day, and excused himself with the plea that the crimes were necessary.

He gathered round him six of the most brutal men he could trust, and confided to them that he was going to find Bill Polk and Frank James both at one time.

The proceedings were novel.

He would find Polk's mother, and compel her to tell her son's whereabouts. To find Bill, was to find Frank James. Joshua's eyes danced with delight at the thought of a task so easy.

* * * * * * *

"Does Mrs. Polk live here?"

"Yes, massa."

That lady came to the door when she heard someone ask her negro boy as to her whereabouts.

"I am Mrs. Polk," she said.

"Mother of Bill Polk?" asked Joshua Blair, for it was he.

"Yes. Is he well?"

"Nay, ma'am, that's what we want to know. We called to see him."

"He is not here."

"Well, where is he?"

"I don't know," answered Mrs. Polk.

"What! not know where Bill is?"

"I do not, indeed."

"Then I don't believe you," said Josh.

"It's the truth, sir."

"Well, we shall see. Here, boys, lend a hand, and we will find out whether this old woman knows where Bill Polk is."

Mrs. Polk was dragged outside, and by Blair's orders taken to a tree and lashed securely to it.

"Oh, heaven! What are you doing? Don't murder me," cried the poor, old woman.

"Tell us where Bill is then," said Josh.

"I—I don't know."

"I'll soon compel you to know, said Josh Blair.

Blair's companions were picked men. He knew full well that it required villain of the lowest order—brutes—to assault a woman, and he had picked his men accordingly, low, despised creatures, whom he had plied with poor whisky, that even their low, unfeeling natures might not relent at the last minute. The two ruffians dragged the half-fainting woman to a small cottonwood, to which they bound her, facing the trunk. The four remaining men sat glaring upon the scene in drunken glee. At this stage of the proceedings Joshua Blair produced a heavy driver's whip, and advanced to the side of the bound woman.

"Now, then, old lady, speak out, if you would save yourself from a good hiding."

"Heaven be merciful!" gasped the widow; "I can tell you nothing."

There was a sudden whiz, and the heavy lash cut a long welt across the shoulders of the poor woman.

"Perhaps that'll open your lips!" sneered the brutal Blair. "I've no mercy, you'll find, so speak out and tell me where Bill Polk hides himself."

"Mercy!" gasped Mrs. Polk.

Whiz came the lash. Once more a welt was raised on the back of the helpless victim, which was followed by a scream of agony that ought to have melted hearts of stone. A loud laugh came from the drunken horsemen.

"How the old hag yells. This hyar's wuth a farm, Josh," cried one of the men. "Give her the lash good. Consarn her mug, she's as bad as her cub."

Blair, insane with liquor himself, rained a dozen blows upon the swollen back of his victim, amidst the jeers and brutal laughter of his villainous confederates. The thin dress was cut to shreds, exposing the bare back of the helpless woman, which was now one mass of blood. Her cries grew fainter each minute. No longer did she beg for mercy. Her gray head, dabbled with gore, fell forward against the tree, while a gray pallor touched the wrinkled face.

"Hold up, boss," cried one of the men, at last, "don't kill the woman, Josh."

"Curse the jade! she's no better than her son."

Again the inhuman villain rained heavy blows upon the bleeding back, blows which cut no more to the soul of the poor victim. Heaven had been merciful to the wretched prisoner. The brutal villain's fury was expended at last.

"Cut her loose, boys," growled Joshua Blair. "I guess she'll speak now. It takes me to manage ugly females."

"I guess she won't speak, boss," said one of the men, as he cut the cords that bound Mrs. Polk, and laid her on the grass.

"Won't, eh? We'll see," and the inhuman wretch staggered forward and bent over the silent form on the grass.

"Eh, what's this? Playing possum, I guess."

"No," said one of the men, in an awed voice, "the old woman is dead!"

"Dead!" ejaculated Blair, starting back with a shudder. "No, no, that can't be. Wake up, old woman. Lord a mercy! I did not mean to—to kill yer."

The drunken brute grasped the woman's shoulder, and shook her sharply.

"No use, boss, she's dead as a hammer."

This fact forced itself upon the brain of Joshua Blair at last. The effect was to sober him utterly. He saw the avenging arm of the murdered woman's son upraised to strike him down, saw the dark visage of Nemesis scowling upon him, and with a wild cry he turned and reeled from the spot, white and trembling with mortal fear. With no little difficulty did the inhuman scoundrel regain his saddle.

"Boys," said Blair, in a husky voice, "let's get out of this."

"And leave that woman there?"

"Yes, yes, come on. They'll find her there. No one will suspect us, unless—unless we have been seen here."

The villain struck his horse a sharp blow and galloped rapidly away from the scene of the murder, followed by his heartless companions.

It was a cowardly and infamous deed, one long to be remembered in the annals of the state.

The sun, now low in the heavens, hid his face under the clouds, as if to hide the horrors of the awful scene.

In single file the murderers dashed down the forest-road, never once looking behind to see if they were followed.

A tall form stood watching the band as they passed a little knoll some forty rods from the Polk farm.

Unseen by them, the man sent his eagle glances over the faces of the seven.

"Wonder what new deviltry is in the wind now. Joshua Blair and his gang have not been here for nothing," muttered Brannigan, as he entered the road and hastened toward the widow's cabin.

Scarcely had the infamous gang passed from sight of the scene of the murder, when a black face peered from a clump of bushes near at hand.

Presently the body of a negro followed, and the black boy, Pompey, crept forward and stood over the form of his murdered mistress.

The slave had heard the thunder of approaching horsemen, and secreted himself, being naturally timid.

From his concealment, he had witnessed the whole scene, and trembling with terror, had crouched down close to the earth, until the murderous gang had taken their departure.

Pompey threw himself down beside his murdered mistress and was howling in true African style when Brannigan appeared suddenly upon the scene.

"Mercy sabe us, good massa," cried the negro, rolling his eyes upward and falling at the feet of the new comer.

"Let up," said Brannigan sternly. "I will not harm you if you behave yourself."

"Deed an 'deed, massa, an' I'll 'have."

Brannigan stood gazing down upon the white face of the murdered woman, not a muscle of his countenance moving, a grim, gray look settling over his rugged countenance.

Silent and motionless he stood for some minutes. The horrors of the situation were too great for words just then.

"Pompey, who perpetrated this crime?"

He had found his voice at last.

"Heaben sabe us, massa, 'twas that mean t'ief, Josh Blair."

"He had six companions?"

"Yes, massa."

Brannigan drew forth a small flat book, together with a pencil. With slow, calm deliberation he jotted down seven names.

"I know them, every one," he muttered. "I saw each face, seven in all, with Joshua Blair in the van. This will prove a dear job for you, gentlemen, a dear job, indeed."

Silence fell over the scene then.

Bending down the man raised the bruised and bleeding victim of Blair's inhuman cruelty and bore her into the house. On a lounge in the little front room the hunter placed his burden, then he ordered Pompey, who had followed him, to bring water.

The negro complied and Brannigan proceeded to wash the blood from the lacerated back of the dead woman.

After this was done, he threw a light shawl over the silent form and then turned to Pompey.

"You will remain here and watch until I return."

"Golly, massa, I darsent. I—them murderin' raskils may come back——"

"No danger of that, blackskin," returned Brannigan. "The work they came to do is finished, and not one of them will dare show himself here again. You must remain until I bring help."

Brannigan grasped his rifle and was about to depart, when a light, quick step fell on his ear a shadow darkened the doorway, and a tall man crossed the threshold of the shadowed home.

"Mother; where is she?" questioned the eager voice of Bill Polk. "I can stop but a minute. I know the danger, yet I must see her once more. Why do you look so strange, Will? What has happened? Where is my mother?"

With averted face the man pointed to the couch, then, with a groan, passed from the room.

When Bill Polk came out of the room where was laid the corpse of his mother, he was a changed man.

Every bit of good in his nature was obliterated.

He staggered toward Brannigan and then grasped the door-casing and drew himself upright.

"Aye!" exclaimed Polk, with flaming eyes and rigid form, "for me there is but one object in life now. They have proclaimed me an outlaw, I will earn the title in good truth.

"The State of Texas shall shudder when the name of Bill Polk is spoken. The land shall fatten on the blood of the infamous scoundrels who have slaughtered my blessed mother, and wrenched the last spark of human feeling from my bosom.

"Revenge! Aye, ample and bitter shall it be! until, for every drop of my sainted mother's blood, a thousand shall redden the soil of Texas.

"Captain Morris, this is your work, the work of your minions, and I here and now, before Heaven, hold you to strict accountability for this red ruin, this treacherous, devilish murder."

Brannigan shuddered at the fierce invective, the wild, vengeful look that accompanied the words of the hunted outlaw.

He could well understand the feeling that prompted the wild words, nor did Brannigan doubt the determination of the speaker to carry them into execution.

The shadows of night fell over the clearing ere Bill Polk and his friend left the spot.

In the deepening shadows the two men stood beside a new-made grave in which lay buried everything that made life dear to one of them.

"Your hand, Brannigan," said Bill Polk, in a low, husky voice.

Two hands were clasped over the fresh mound.

"Standing here, under the blue arch of heaven, I swear to avenge my murdered parent," said Bill Polk, in low, steady tones. Seven lives for the one—seven! Aye, and then my reckoning will come with Captain Morris, for he is not guiltless."

"I will help you to fulfill the oath to the uttermost," said Brannigan, as their clasped hands fell apart.

CHAPTER VIII.

When Bill Polk returned to the outlaw's camp he was accompanied by Will Brannigan.

"Frank, my boy," said Brannigan, "I am outlawed as well as you, for I have sworn to help exterminate men who murder innocent women."

"I am on the track of those who killed my brother,' said Frank, "and then I, too, will follow Morris and his deputy, Josh Blair, to the death.'

"Thanks, James," said Bill; "I knew I could count on you.

"We have a journey before us, and I propose we start at once," said Frank James. "I want to get into Missouri as soon as possible."

The next day a dozen men, all well seated on the best of horseflesh, were cantering along the road leading away from Texas, and into the delightful scenery of southern Arkansas.

Accompanying the twelve men, was one lady.

She was the wife of Frank James, and determined to go with him and share his new trials and dangers.

When the party arrived at Toxarkana, Frank persuaded his wife to take the cars to St. Louis, where he promised to join her as early as possible.

Poor Annie did not like the idea of leaving Frank, but he promised that he would use extra care, and would not enter into any more danger than possible. This had to suffice, and the faithful wife who had forsaken friends, home and society for the sake of her outlaw husband, journeyed with far more comfort on the luxurious palace cars on the St. Louis and Southern railroad, than she could possibly have done on horseback. When she had left, Frank told his pals that it would be just as well to get a little money before they proceeded any further. All agreed with this proposition, and it was resolved that the coach running across county should be the first means resorted to.

* * * * * * *

The stage coach left Toxarkana well loaded with passengers. All kinds and conditions of men were there. Yankees from New England, greasers from Mexico, and even miners from Arizona. Never before had the coach taken such a valuable load.

By some means Frank James had managed in the city to obtain information of the names and property to be carried. The coach driver smelt a rat, and prepared accordingly.

Turning to his passengers after they were a good many miles on the road, he said:

"Shouldn't wonder if we met some road agents, so take advice. Those of yer thet want to save yer watches, put 'em in yer boot-top, and manage to conceal yer small change, and d—n it, do it right quick——"

"Whoa-ho!" he continued; this time addressing his horses. "What's up wi' yer? Now, then, yer brutes."

The horses plunged and reared, and then stopped.

"Now, then, you outsiders, up with your hands," shouted a voice from the brush.

A dozen rifles were seen pointed at the coach, and the passengers thought it was better to obey.

"Now you insiders. throw out your irons, there's six of you got them."

Two revolvers were thrown out of the coach.

"Come, no nonsense, let's have some more or we will make a sieve of the coach with our bullets."

At last all had thrown out their revolvers, and the road agents, who were headed by Frank James in person, rode up to the coach and took possession of money and watches which hitherto had belonged to the passengers in that coach.

"Frank James, by the eternal " exclaimed one of the passengers.

"Yes, that is my name," incautiously replied the outlaw.

The coach dashed away with the passengers' pockets lighter than before, and Frank James felt that his acknowledgement of his identity would lead to trouble.

The whole country was soon in a state of terror and alarm. These atrocious crimes, attributed by public opinion to one man, caused a universal feeling of dread, and people asked themselves—what next? The police were urged by the government to find the miscreant, but his cunning was too great.

Besides, in these days there is such extent of bush that, with a population scattered about sympathizing with crime, he had many accomplices.

Still Frank, on this occasion, determined to be quiet for a little while.

Frank, in the district where he had concealed himself with his associates, had made himself a rough hut. It was so situated that anyone could be seen at a quarter of a mile off, when he could get into accessible hiding-places. But his comrades were always ready to give him warning.

The time fixed on for the attack on Pine Bluff, as the spot was called, rapidly approached. Frank made an appointment with his men at a point six miles from the place. It was a very wooded spot on the bank of a small river. It was in the center of a number of sheep runs, and was accounted a rather populated place.

Frank James had provided himself with a mask and wore a wig of gray hair. No one who did not know him would have for one moment believed in the deception. One young man had gone forward as scout, and when they got within a short distance from the spot, came and told them that the coast was clear. In a few minutes more twelve heavily armed men surrounded the bank, Frank and five others alighting and entering.

The bank was a quiet, private-looking house, and, with the exception of the word "bank," might be taken for the village doctor's residence.

A few loiterers are always at the cottage doors; and the post office is always full of gossips. The arrival of anyone is an event. His appearance and business is soon ferreted out, and form interesting topics of discussion for days. The locality is generally characterized by a stagnant calm, and generally remains in profound repose.

About mid-day several horsemen were seen quietly riding down Market street, smoking short pipes, and quietly regarding the inhabitants.

They passed the bank and approached the police station, where two of the mounted force were also engaged in the arduous duty of "blowing a cloud." Suddenly pulling up in front of the officers they presented their revolvers at their heads, desired them to remain still, sent Jack Marsh inside for the arms desired the men to retire inside the station, and left one of their gang to mount guard over the prisoners. This operation was performed very quietly, and the horses' head turned toward the bank

Frank, Bill Polk and Nash dismounted at the door. Frank entered first, and, presenting a piece of paper which the clerk took for a check, suddenly drew his six-shooter—an operation imitated by his assistants—and swore, if the astonished clerk did not deliver up his cash and the keys of the safe, his passage from this world would be more speedy than he would desire. The manager at this moment came out from the inner office, upon which Bill Polk pointed his revolver at the midriff of the electrified banker, and desired him to "look sharp and cash up" without delay.

Binding the clerk and the manager and placing them in different rooms, the doors of which they locked, the band rode off quietly with their booty.

Of course, in a short time the victims made known the robbery, when the consternation was at fever height.

"It's James; no one but Frank James would chance it," was the universal cry.

The police, who had also been similarly locked up, looked very small and very vexed.

The instant they were gone the terrified wife and daughter of the cashier appeared and liberated the two unfortunate men, one of whom, the clerk, rode off to the police station, where he learned how the occupants of that building had been treated.

Returning to the rendezvous the plunder was divided and the band separated.

Frank James appointing a time and place for their next meeting.

CHAPTER IX.

Frank James felt it to be safer for the band to travel singly especially after the affair at Pine Bluff.

He had not gone very far on his lonely way when he found himself a prisoner.

He had been seized from behind and thrown from his horse.

Cool and collected, Frank knew that he was not well known in Arkansas. He had hopes, therefore, to evade the law even though he was now a prisoner.

He, with the greatest *sang froid*, asked what they meant by arresting a respectable farmer in that manner. He was told that a number of sheep had been stolen, and from the description they imagined he was one of the thieves.

"You are wrong, as I can easily prove," said Frank.

"Well, in the morning we shall produce our witnesses to identify you."

"All serene."

Frank was taken to a small country police station and placed in a cell for the night.

"Twelve" struck from the station clock and Frank slept soundly.

"One," and the men on watch reported the prisoner sleeping.

"Two," the same report.

The captain in charge gave orders that the prisoner need not be longer watched, as he evidently intended to have a good night's rest.

"Three" struck, but Frank James did not hear it.

He had quietly loosened the bars across his cell window, lowered himself out, found his horse, and bade adieu to his hospitable friends.

Very unceremonious, but, perhaps, more pleasant for Frank than if he had remained for identification next day.

He rode on about three miles, and then, finding a house where he was told a friend resided, he knocked.

The door was opened after a long while, during which time Frank was in anxious suspense.

When the door showed a light on Frank's face, the host stepped quickly back and asked:

"Who are you, and what do you want?"

"Avenger and——"

"Come in," said the man, evidently understanding the password.

Frank entered, and found, as he had been told, a good friend of Jesse James in the owner of the house.

Frank told him of his escape, and both agreed that it would be safer to resume his journey at once.

A pleasant hour was spent at the farm-house and Frank promised to pay his hospitable host another visit soon.

After a hearty meal, Frank thanked the man for his hospitality, and once more started on his road. He was in high spirits, had a good horse, and congratulated himself on his wonderful escape from prison. A few hours ago he had never expected to breathe the air of freedom, and he laughed to himself as he thought over the way he had outwitted the police and jailers. Not one feeling of regret or remorse entered his mind. The outrages and crimes he had committed were, he considered, matters to exult over rather than regret. The law had no terror for him; he was brave and feared nothing, and openly declared that he cared neither for God nor man. Frank, of course, expected to be pursued, and knew there was every chance of being captured. But he had been in so many dangers and desperate situations that he did not despair of eluding his pursuers, in fact, he had begun to believe that he was protected by Providence, forgetting that a man's crimes are not always punished swiftly, and justice if slow is nearly always sure.

The daring recklessness of the man often saved him, when a more timid man would have been lost.

He had not proceeded far on his road along the rough highway, when he was startled to hear horses' hoofs behind him.

As they came nearer and nearer, Frank James glanced round as if seeking a hiding-place, but after a moment's hesitation decided to face it out whatever the danger might be.

Without once glancing back he continued to advance, although he felt curious enough to know what the horsemen were.

At last they came up with him, and Frank James saw that they were two young policemen evidently in pursuit of himself.

They pulled in their horses to give them breath, for they had been hardly ridden, judging by appearance.

"Good-morning," said James, as he too reined in, with a pleasant smile, as if highly delighted at the prospect of company for a few minutes. "You seem in a rare hurry. Going in search of sheep-stealers, I suppose?"

"We are going after bigger game than that," replied one of the policemen, "we are looking after Frank James, the train robber."

"Frank James!" repeated our hero. "I heard he was safe in prison. You don't mean to say he has escaped?" This in a horrified tone. "He ought to have been shot when first captured. The news you have just imparted to me will fill hundreds of people with alarm and dread."

"Yes," replied the young policeman who had spoken before and was evidently a more communicative man than the other; "but if I am not mistaken we shall soon capture him."

"You think so?" casually remarked Frank.

"Yes," the other replied. "I am certain."

"He is very cunning and clever, from what I hear," responded Frank James, "and, if what I hear is true, two men would stand a very poor chance with him. He can fight like the devil, and the knife and the pistol are weapons which he knows how to use better than any man in the country."

"We know all about that," cried the policeman, rather angrily, for his pride was hurt at Frank's insinuation that they were no match for the notorious outlaw; "but we have no reason to be afraid if we come across him. We are well-armed and well-mounted, and besides have the feeling that we are in the right. Frank James fights with a rope round his neck. He is the biggest scoundrel that ever lived, and must be hunted down like a rat. The highwaymen in the old days were saints to the man who has made his name the terror of the west."

"If every man got his deserts, few would go unpunished," said Frank, with a laugh, turning away his face to hide the look of rage that disfigured every feature.

For one moment he felt inclined to draw his pistol from his belt and shoot the policeman through the head, but he conquered the impulse, reflecting that it would do no good.

These two policemen might not be by themselves; others might be following close behind. If Frank James was a bad man, he was not a fool. No one could accuse him of that. Besides, he was afraid that the report of his pistol might attract attention.

Nothing in his manner evinced that he had any hostile feelings against his companions.

He spoke craftily of his own escape, trying to find out how much they knew, and keeping a keen watch upon them without appearing to do so.

The police seemed in no hurry to part company with him, and presently Frank fancied he saw them exchange significant glances as much as to say, "This is our man."

But not a muscle in his face betrayed the conviction that was in his mind, that they had discovered his identity.

He talked and laughed pleasantly enough, and wished them every success in their undertaking.

"If I were you I should not like the job," he said, presently, "but perhaps after all folks exaggerate about Frank James' power and pluck."

"We do not underrate his powers," said the policeman, significantly, and then, as if by accident, he pulled his rein, and Frank found himself between the two horsemen.

"The rascal will not surrender without a desperate struggle," observed James, with a look of menace in his eyes.

He saw that they were rapidly approaching a police-station and there was no time to be lost, and suddenly pulling out a short, black pipe, asked one of his would-be captors in a nonchalent way for a light.

"Oh, I'll get you one close by," was the reply, as off No. 1 went to the police-station, which just hove in sight, to get more than the light required.

No sooner had he disappeared than Frank, drawing a pistol from his pocket, swore he would scatter No. 2's brains if he did not at once dismount.

The persuasive eloquence of the muzzle of the pistol had the desired effect, and down jumped the lad (for he was nothing more), and allowed Frank James to take hold of the bridle.

"Good-bye, my friend," he coolly said. "The prison isn't made, or the traps born, that are a match for Frank James."

With a loud laugh, he rode rapidly away, leading the trooper's horse with him, to "keep him," as he said, "in good company."

When No. 2 arrived at the police-station, great was the chagrin and rage at the success of the *ruse*. The police, on hearing of his escape, rose with loud yells of anger and disappointment, and, mounting their horses, started in pursuit.

They were not only eager to reap the great reward, but they now had a personal grievance against Frank James, and wanted to be revenged upon him for the success of his "dodge."

In fact, they were cruelly mortified.

Frank, now perfectly calm and self-possessed, urged forward his horses as he heard the shouts of his pursuers behind him.

He necessarily rode blindly along the first path that presented itself.

It was a race for life and liberty once more, and all caused by his own folly.

The policemen fired more than once, but the bullets whizzed over Frank's head, and he gave a shout of derisive and laughing defiance as his horse dashed forward at hot and headlong speed.

The men, as can be easily imagined, did not spare their steeds, and Frank James, hearing another shout of triumph, looked back and saw that his pursuers were gaining upon him.

He resolved to keep the second horse with him, and change steeds when his weight began to tell upon that he rode.

He made up his mind instantly that if they came much nearer he would turn and fight.

A sinister light gleamed in his eye as he listened to the yells and oaths of the enraged men.

His position was desperate indeed, but he did not despair; he never did—the secret of success.

He was flying along at full speed, without following any particular direction, when he glanced ahead, and a smothered cry escaped from his lips.

Just in his path, just before him, was a wide gully, cutting off his retreat, and he must turn and face the policemen, or take this awful, this terrible leap.

In an instant his mind was made up.

There was only one thing to be done. He would not attempt the leap.

The pace had been a killing one.

His horse was distressed, and those of his followers were not much less so.

He resolved, as he said, to "burst the lot," and so pressed his animal still more with spur and hand.

He had the satisfaction of gaining on his pursuers.

He saw they were flagging, and that the men were somewhat done up from excitement.

He avoided the leap, and turned sharply toward the shrub, and for a few minutes was hidden from view.

He rapidly changed horses, and mounting the led one, felt he now really had the foot of the field.

The time occupied in the change had allowed his enemies to gain on him, and a loud howl of delight pealed from their lips as they thought they had him at last.

They were quickly deceived, for they now felt he was leaving them at every stride.

Seeing further pursuit useless, they moderated their pace, upon which Frank likewise "drew it milder," and, mocking his friends with what the French call a *pied-a-nez*, begged them to go and get the reward and drink his health.

"Never saw such a thing in all my life," said the first policeman.

"Faith, and it bates Bannager Biddy," replied the second, who was an Irishman, "and Biddy bates me."

And they rode away.

Frank gave a deep sigh of relief, and laughed mockingly as he continued on his way.

At present, at least, he was out of danger—but for how long?

He did not allow his horse to relax his pace, but rode hard till night came on, looking back every now and then to convince himself that he was not being followed, until it was too dark for him to see any object distinctly, when he allowed his steed to take it easy.

He had entered the wild scrub, and was slowly moving through the long grass, when he suddenly saw a faint light in the distance, and knew that he was nearing some habitation.

CHAPTER X.

Frank James hesitated, but only for a moment, as to whether he should crave hospitality at the house where he saw the light burning.

He was weary, and his horse needed rest, and so he thought that it would be as well to get an hour's rest, even if he had to obtain it in the way that he had often been compelled to in times past, viz: at the revolver's muzzle.

He rode up to the door and knocked loudly. The door was opened by a lady, who asked:

"Who's there?"

Instead of answering, Frank, who had dismounted, quietly walked into the house.

A brusque-looking gentleman was sitting near the stove, whilst two ladies were clearing the supper things away.

The gentleman, Captain Cathcart, rose to his feet, and was perhaps about to try and turn the intruder out, when he was stopped by Frank, exclaiming:

"Keep your seat, sir, please!"

Captain Carhart indignantly inquired the object of his visit and the meaning of his conduct. The stranger coolly replied:

"I want my supper."

The indignant host responded that, while their latch-string always hung on the outside, and their cheer was free to all, yet to such intrusive guests as he there was no welcome and no supper. There were a town and hotels four miles distant, and he could betake himself thither as abruptly as he had invaded his house.

"Did you hear what I said? I want my supper," calmly replied the stranger.

"We do not keep a hotel, and our supper is long over," said Captain Carhcart.

With the same ironical coolness, the unbidden guest said: "Did you understand me? I want my supper."

With that the captain made a demonstration as if to arise, and others of the household group began to manifest alarm and indignation, but the imperturbable stranger commanded:

"Keep your seats. Do not any of you attempt to leave the room."

A sort of revelation flashed over the captain's mind. He kept his seat and photographed the stranger on his vision.

About his waist was a broad belt, and from beneath the skirts of his coat ominously peeped the muzzles of two large revolvers. The captain fumbled at his watch and chain in a futile effort to release them from their receptacles and transfer them to a safer hiding-place, for he had begun to realize that he was confronting a desperado and robber instead of the drunken man he had at first supposed him to be.

The unbidden guest explained that he had ridden hard and far and had eaten but little for twenty-four hours, and that while he regretted to alarm or put to inconvenience the family, he was compelled to satisfy the hunger of himself and horse. He inquired if there was negro about the premises, and upon being told that there was, he demanded that one of the ladies send him in.

The demand was complied with, and the frightened darkey approached and received orders to go to the stile take his horse to the barn, feed him, remain with him until he had finished eating, bridle and saddle him and return him to the stile.

The negro immediately obeyed orders and the ladies in the meantime prepared supper. The captain was required to remain with his mysterious guest. He soon made friends with the children, chatted with them pleasantly, and courteously apologized to his astonished host for his conduct.

He said he was an outlaw and was being pursued, and that he knew not who were friends or enemies, and that he could trust nobody. therefore his reasons for requiring those who could give an alarm or do him an injury, to remain under his guardianship.

He chatted with the captain about war incidents, and was well posted on all events of recent occurrence, but he did not disclose his name or identity, where he was from or whither he was going.

Supper was announced, and then he required all the household to repair with him to the dining-room and remain with him till he had finished.

When they returned to the sitting-room, he asked one of the ladies to play and sing.

His request was complied with, and the young daughter of the captain sang, with exqisite grace, Claribel's pretty song, "Five o'clock in the morning."

Frank thanked her with all the airs of a gentleman, and then when she rose from her seat, he took his place at the piano, and, playing his own accompaniment, sang in a rich, baritone voice:

THE OUTLAW'S SONG.

Our fire on the turf, and our tent 'neath a tree—
Carousing by moonlight, how merry are we?
Let the lord boast his castle, the baron his hall,
But the house of the outlaw is widest of all.
We may shout o'er our cups, and laugh loud as we will,
Till echo rings back from wood, welkin and hill;
No joys seem to us like the joys that are lent
To the wanderer's life and the outlaw's tent.

Much crime and some folly may fall to our lot;
We have sins, but pray, where is the one who has not?
We are rogues, arrant rogues; yet remember! 'tis rare
We take but from those who are able to spare.
You may tell us of deeds justly branded with shame,
But if rich ones heard truth, you could tell them the same;
There's many a king would have less to repent,
If his throne was as pure as the outlaw's tent.

Pant ye for beauty? Oh, where would ye seek
Such bloom as is found on the tawny one's cheek?
Our limbs, that go bounding in freedom and health,
Are worth all your pale faces and coffers of wealth.
There are none to control us, we rest or we roam,
Our will is our law, and the world is our home;
E'en Jove would repine at his lot if he spent
A night of wild glee in the outlaw's tent.

The party thanked the bold outlaw for his excellent song.

Frank then said he would like two hours' sleep. He was shown to an up-stairs room, requiring his host, with lighted lamp, to precede him. He gave peremptory instructions for nobody to leave the house, and at the expiration of the two hours to arouse him by calling him from below, and not by any means attempt to come up stairs. He threw himself, clothed, upon the bed, his revolvers behind him.

The captain returned to the family room and began to talk with bated breath about the mysterious events of the evening. But in a few moments the stranger came down stairs and announced that he could not sleep above, it was too high from the ground, and requested to lie upon the floor of the room in which they were seated. A pair of blankets and pillow were provided, and soon the man was restlessly sleeping.

At the appointed time he was aroused. He summoned the darkey, learned that his horse was in waiting, gave the darkey a dollar, and proffered pay for the trouble he had given the family, but this was declined. He, however, filled the children's hands with coins.

He apologized to the ladies for his intrusion and thanked them for all their kindness.

He then said:

"If it is any interest to you to know who I am I will tell you. My name is Frank James."

Guess, if you can, the astonishment on every face.

"But he was a nice man," said one of the young ladies.

However nice he was, Captain Cathcart was glad to see his visitor jump on his horse and ride away.

The events which followed caused Captain Cathcart oftentimes to talk of Frank James' visit as he passed through Arkansas to avenge his brother's death.

CHAPTER XI.

Frank James arrived in Missouri, and, the better to carry out his schemes of vengeance, determined to lull the authorities to sleep.

At St. Louis, Frank James staid at the same hotel on May 27th last as did Sheriff Timberlake and Marshall Craig.

Frank knew of their whereabouts, but they did not recognize him. The bold outlaw next paid a visit to Kansas City, and there commenced his lullaby to the governor and the other officials of the state.

What he did and how he did it can best be told by an interview the authorities had with Frank's lawyer.

R. J. Haire, a Kansas City lawyer, who has ever since the killing of Jesse appeared to speak with authority on things connected with the Jameses, says he speaks by the card when he says:

"Governor Crittenden has given a written promise for the pardon of Frank if he shall surrender within a certain period, and that the document is in the possession of Frank, to whom it was forwarded."

"Why did Timberlake and Craig come to St. Louis if they had nothing to do with the matter?" I asked.

"They got wind of the proceedings and came here to capture Frank. They were not only accompanied by several detectives, but also by Dick Little. In brief, they knew I was in communication with Frank and they expected to get a clew from my actions. I trust they are satisfied."

"Do you find it easy to reach Frank?"

"It is the most difficult thing I ever undertook. Since the killing of Jesse he has almost melted in total obscurity. On some days I am enabled to communicate with him in a few hours, and the next thing I know it requires several days. He is restless and always moving, so that it is almost impossible to hasten the negotiations."

"Would you show me the letter addressed to Frank by Governor Crittenden?"

"No, sir, because I did not say it was in my possession; and wherever it may be it is a solemn secret not to be divulged until the proper time arrives. I presume it is no violation of confidence to say that such a letter is in existence and in the possession of Frank James' friends."

"Are Frank's friend's desirous that he should accept the amnesty?"

"Most assuredly, and they are bringing every argument to bear to have him surrender. This is the critical moment —the turning point in Frank's life. If he should accept, the reformation will be complete, but if the negotiations are not satisfactorily concluded I predict he will proceed to the bush and rush headlong on till his death occurs. That is one great reason why I am particularly anxious to secure his surrender. He never before came so near settlement as now, and it will be a matter for deep regret and concern if he should refuse."

"Does Crittenden feel kindly disposed toward Frank?"

"He evidently desires to extend the utmost clemency, for in his letter he uses this sentence: 'Let us join in the noble effort to reform this man and restore him to a peaceful and honorable citizenship.' To my mind the governor intends to break up the remainder of the gang by peaceful means, and will use all lawful means in that direction."

All this from the recognized attorney of the James family seems confirmed by the sudden appearance of Mrs. Frank James at Independence, Mo., her former home, from nobody seems to know exactly where, and her announcement that she has come home to stay. She refuses to say where Frank is or to talk about him at all.

Mrs. Zerelda Samuels, mother of the notorious James boys, accompanied by her daughter-in-law, Mrs. Frank James, was at the residence of Colonel Sam Ralston, near Independence, and left on the morning of May 30th in company with Sheriff Timberlake for Jefferson City. The result or object of last night's visit cannot be learned just now, but the impression is very strong there that Frank is in the neighborhood and that he met his mother last night. Mrs. Frank James has been indisposed since her arrival, being worn out by the long journey. She treats her old friends with extreme cordiality, but refuses positively to go out or meet strangers. The people will anxiously await the result of Mrs. Samuels' visit to Governor Crittenden. Notwithstanding all this it is difficult to see what terms the governor can offer that Frank could accept. It is altogether improbable that he will be so foolish as to give himself up even if the governor were willing to enter into any agreement with him. If he made a settlement with Missouri, which secured him amnesty after trial, Minnesota, Texas, Kentucky, Tennessee, Arkansas and other states would be to hear from—not to speak of the United States government, which would want him for robbing mails.

I then went off to see the governor, and found him as pert as you please.

He evidently had Frank James on the brain, for the moment we mentioned the outlaw's name, the excellent governor put his hand in the direction of his hip pocket.

I immediately disarmed him by telling him that we were only a special envoy from Mr. J. W. Morrison, the publisher of the most authentic accounts of the James boys' career.

That pleased his excellency and he said he was ready to answer questions.

In response to questions the governor said that he was surprised at the way some of the papers were publishing accounts concerning the matter; that he has not offered a pardon to Frank James through Mr. Haire or any other person. A pardon could not be granted before conviction and he makes no rash promises. He has never received a line from Mr. Haire in regard to pardon or other form of executive clemency in behalf of the outlaw. He has not by word or otherwise, made a proposition to the governors of other states, asking them to join him in extending clemency to James. The governor also states that Frank James has never applied to him for clemency or pardon; that when he desires a pardon it is presumable he will apply for it after a conviction for some of his crimes. Then he certainly would have the same right as others to ask such clemency.

When asked what course he would pursue should a pardon for Frank James be applied for, his excellency, replied:

"That is my business, and when such application is made I shall act as I please, regardless of importunities or curses; and I wish to state also, that Mr. Haire, provided he is correctly reported by the sensational papers, is doing much unnecessary and loose talk concerning the matter, and pursuing an injudicious course. A noted bandit may have cause to pray for deliverance from such a friend, and further, that the words attributed to me by Haire, in an interview with a reporter of a St. Louis evening newspaper, 'Let us join in the noble effort to reform this man and restore him to a peaceful and honorable citizenship,' were never used by me to Mr. Haire, or anyone else. But suppose I had used them, is it not better to secure and reform them than to forever condemn and punish? As the executive of this state, I will pursue such a course as will, in my estimation, secure the enforcement of the law, and give full security and protection to life and property in the manner which to me seems wisest, and leave my administration to be judged by the result, fully believing that the people in their sober second thought will measure my administration more by results than by the profusion of unmerited abuse poured upon it by an inimical and venal press. Nor will I be checked in that course by the ravings of a few sensational editors, whose patriotism is alone measured by the number of their papers daily sold."

CHAPTER XII.
A DARING MOVE.

We have seen the deep ruse made use of by the outlaw and his friends, now let us go to the outlaws' retreat and we shall see some old faces.

* * * * * * *

"By Jove, Jim, I didn't know you," said Frank, as he entered a cabin on the mountain side.

Before the outlaw stood an old man. His body was bent apparently with age, his long white hair hung on his shoulders, and as he leaned on his strong cane, one would…

Frank James recognized in the old man, his companion in many a raid—Jim Cummins.

Now the said Jim was only about thirty-eight, so the disguise was for an object.

"I have been paying my respects to the bank," said Jim, resuming his natural voice.

"With what prospect?"

"Three of us can do the trick," answered Jim.

"What gain?" asked Frank.

"Should imagine about ten thousand dollars," responded Jim.

"Then let us arrange for to-morrow."

"What about horses?" asked one of the men who had listened to the conversation.

"We shall want six," said Frank, interrogatively.

"Yes."

"Farmer Jones has three, and——"

"Mrs. Byrne two more," interrupted Jim Cummins.

"That will do then," said Frank, "for I know where I can put my hand on the fastest mare in Missouri."

Arrangements were then made for each of the five men to meet Frank at two o'clock the following day.

* * * * * * *

The little town of Brookfield, in Linn county, was minding its own business on Tuesday, June 6, 1882.

Brookfield claims to have about fifteen hundred inhabitants.

It is a peaceable, law-abiding town.

At half past three on the day above noted, the quiet of the people was rudely broken, and some of the older people listened, rubbed their eyes to see if they were really awake, then looked at the calendar.

"For it seems like war times," said an old man.

Crack! crack! crack!

A regular fusilade of pistol shots were heard in the street. The more daring inhabitants looked out of their houses and saw six men well mounted.

They were all masked.

One had long, white hair, and seemed quite a patriarch. The others were strongly-built, daring men.

All were armed with pistols. A revolver in each hand, the men guiding their horses by the bridles held in their teeth.

Crack! crack!

Every man kept firing as rapidly as he could as he rode up the street.

The people were terrorized.

The bank was reached, and then the old gentleman and three others entered the building.

The remaining two, holding the horses, and firing an occasional shot as any inhabitant put his head outside the door of his residence.

Inside the bank there were only the cashier and the daughter of the president.

The party of masked men entered, and the aged one took off his mask, and walked up to the counter.

"I have come, you see, to open an account," he said.

"You—you—are the gentleman who called the other day?" stammered out the cashier.

"Yes," answered Jim Cummins.

Frank and Tom Malloy then walked round the counter, whilst Jim and his friend covered the pretty girl and the cashier with their revolvers.

Frank and Tom quickly emptied the cash drawers and safe, and then as quickly as they had rode into the town, they left the bank, mounted their horses, and rode away to the mountains.

"Like old times, eh, Jim?" exclaimed Frank James.

"Yes, and the money will be useful," responded Jim Cummins.

"Aye, so it will, for we have a big work before us. Never shall I rest until my brother is avenged."

The party counted up the spoils and found that they had bagged nearly twelve thousand dollars.

The next day the cables flashed the intelligence to every city that Frank James is not dead.

No, nor do we expect he will die until he has made his name a greater terror than it is even now.

Frank James and Jim Cummins rode away to Independence, where doubtless they will stay until they can develop some new and daring enterprise.

Some of the bank robbers were captured a day or two afterward, but the daring leader is still at large.

NEW NICK CARTER WEEKLY

Issued Weekly. By subscription $2.50 per year. Entered as Second-class Matter at the N. Y. Post Office, by STREET & SMITH, *79-89 Seventh Ave., N. Y.*

No. 465 NEW YORK, NOVEMBER 25, 1905. **Price, Five Cents**

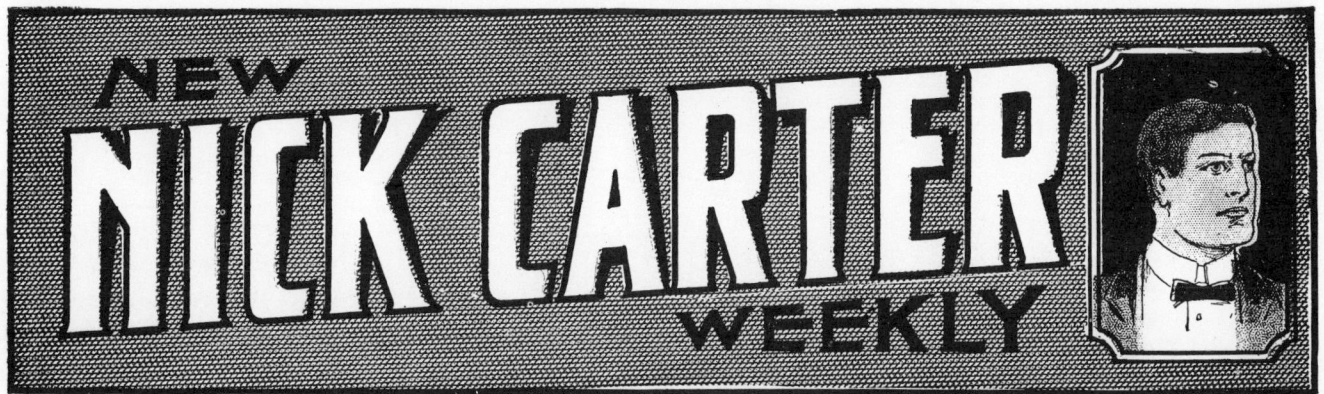

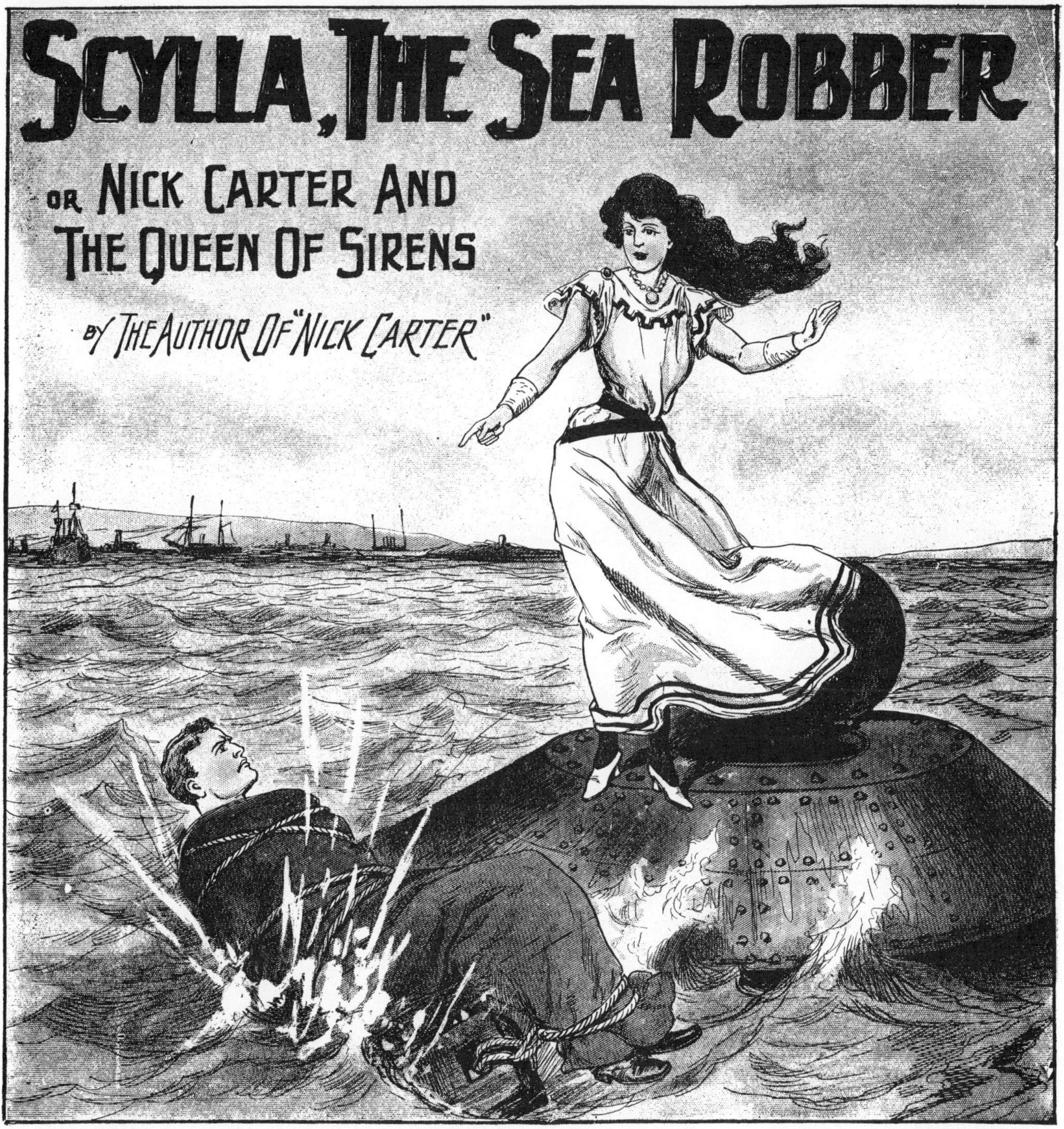

The last thing he saw as he disappeared were the eyes of Scylla, the Siren, gazing with a strange expression into his own.

NEW NICK CARTER WEEKLY

Issued Weekly. By Subscription $2.50 per year. Entered as Second-class Matter at the N. Y. Post Office, by STREET & SMITH, 79-89 Seventh Avenue, N. Y. Entered according to Act of Congress in the year 1905, in the Office of the Librarian of Congress, Washington, D. C.

No. 465. NEW YORK, November 25, 1905. Price Five Cents.

Scylla, the Sea Robber;

OR,

Nick Carter and the Queen of Sirens.

Edited by CHICKERING CARTER.

CHAPTER I.

SCYLLA, THE SEA ROBBER.

"I tell you, Nick, it is the most astounding thing I ever stacked up against."

"And yet," replied the detective, leaning back in his chair and relighting his cigar, "we have encountered some rather unusual adventures during the course of our experience, inspector."

"Oh, I'll admit all that; but here is a mystery that would puzzle the devil himself."

"Don't forget that I am still in the dark. You haven't told me about it yet."

The inspector selected a fresh cigar from the box on the table, and studied it with great care; then, instead of replying directly to the question, he asked another.

"How long have you been away from home this time, Nick?"

"It was seven months to a day, and almost to an hour, when I arrived at the Grand Central Station last night."

"A great deal can happen in seven months."

"Yes; or in seven days—or seven hours for that matter."

"But, in seven months, a man will get almost as much out of the running of affairs in the city of New York as if he had never lived here at all."

"I will grant you that. There is not a city in the world like New York in that particular. One may be absent from Paris two or three years, and from London almost a lifetime, and returning, find that very few changes have taken place; but let an old rounder stay out of New York for a few months, and he finds on his return a city that is in parts almost new, and a lot of people whom he has never known occupying his old haunts."

"That's as sure as you live."

"But what has all this to do with the case you have brought to me this morning, inspector?"

"Why, it strikes me as rather remarkable that you have heard nothing of Scylla the Siren, notwithstanding the fact that you have been absent so long a time, that is all."

"Scylla the Siren, eh? That has rather a mythological sound, hasn't it?"

"It is more than a sound; it is a condition as well."

"You don't say! Do you mean that this Scylla is a myth; eh?"

"No; I don't mean that. Not by a long shot."

"Don't you think that you have whetted my appetite for information sufficiently by this time? Or do you propose to keep me in the dark indefinitely? You must remember that not only have I been absent from the city myself, but that every one of my assistants has been with me, and that I am absolutely in the dark as to what has occurred here in New York during the last seven months."

"But, great Scott, man, there have been columns about it in the papers!"

"One doesn't find the New York *Herald* on the breakfast table in Japan, where I have been, you know," said Nick.

"Quite true. Then you have absolutely heard nothing about Scylla the Siren; eh?"

"I have heard something about her since I returned, but nothing till then, and nothing definite since."

"Tell me what you have heard; it will make my story somewhat easier," said the inspector.

"In a word, then, I have been told that there is a new kind of a pirate infesting New York harbor; that incoming and outgoing steamships are robbed indiscriminately; that a big liner—an ocean greyhound—is as easy a mark for the robberies as a tramp steamer lying at anchor in the bay; that the victims are inevitably taken by surprise and the robbery is consummated, and the robbers escape, before there is an opportunity to offer defense; and—in a word—that the robbers escape as mysteriously as they appear, leaving no trace behind, either as to how they came aboard the vessel, or how the escape from it is made."

"Well, that will do very well for a starter. Let me give you a case in point."

"That is exactly what I wish you would do."

"One week ago to-day, at half-past ten o'clock in the morning, the steamship *Jupiter*, of the Planet Line, was steaming down the bay, having just started on her voyage eastward. She was exactly in the Narrows when the purser retired for a moment to his office, in pursuit of his duty.

"The purser's name is Conley. He had just taken his seat at his desk, and believed himself to be alone in the office—he had closed the door when he entered it, and the door is latched by a spring lock—when he heard the voice of a woman proceeding from directly behind his chair.

"He wheeled his chair suddenly, too surprised at the interruption to stop to consider what he was doing, and found himself gazing into the muzzle of an exceedingly ugly-looking .44 Colt."

"I've never happened to notice that end of a revolver when it did not look ugly, have you, inspector?" asked the detective.

"Can't say I have. But to proceed."

"Yes; go ahead."

"Behind the revolver was a woman—or a girl; anyhow, a female. Conley says she looked like a chorus girl who had just stepped off the stage. She wore some sort of a robe which trailed from her shoulders to her feet, and only half concealed the fact that there were tights underneath it. Tights, and a skirt, mind you, not unlike —according to Conley's description—some of the bathing suits one sees at Ocean Grove at this season of the year."

"Humph!" remarked the detective, smiling, "go on, Steve. You are getting interesting."

"Her whole costume was a sort of blending of light blue and gray, and there were spangles all over it, such as one sees on the costumes of mermaids in the side shows and museums."

"I see. Well?"

"There was a half mask of the same description over the upper part of her face, and she stood with the robe I have mentioned, draped over her left arm, so that it would not impede her movements if she should have to move quickly—and all the time the revolver was looking at him straight between the eyes."

"Rather an interesting *tableau*, that," said Nick. "I almost wish that I might have been in Conley's place."

"Well, he would have been mighty glad if you had been, for I can assure you that he did not enjoy it at all."

"What happened next?"

"I have already told you that he was startled by hearing the voice of a woman proceeding from directly behind him. What he heard was this:

"'Mr. Conley?' said the voice, precisely as if a passenger had entered the room and merely wished to speak to him; and then he wheeled his chair to find himself looking into the muzzle of the pistol."

"Precisely. Well?"

"'Where the devil did you come from?' he exclaimed, when he saw the woman in the strange costume; and——"

"Wait a moment. Had this man Conley never heard of the visitations of Scylla the Siren?"

"Sure he had. But, like all others, he took no stock in the stories."

"Took no stock in them? I thought it was generally accepted that her visitations were facts."

"So it is—all save the apparently supernatural part of them. I will wager now that if you will go aboard any one of the steamships in the harbor and question the officers, they will, every one of them, tell you that 'if Scylla comes aboard my ship, she won't get away.' Well, that is the way Conley felt about it. He had never taken any stock in the stories, and he did not feel in the least afraid of an encounter with the pirate—for that is what she is, you know—least of all did he expect to see her in person."

"Well, go ahead with the story."

"'Where the devil did you come from?' he demanded.

"'From the bottom of the sea,' she replied.

"'What do you want here?' he asked, then.

"For reply, Conley says she smiled at him and pointed toward the safe. Then, to make a long story short, she commanded him to open the safe, in which, by the way, there was one hundred and fifty thousand dollars in gold."

"In bullion, or in coin?" asked the detective.

"In coin. Done up in packages of fifty double eagles each. Now, the remarkable thing about what happened then was that she produced from under her robe a lot of oiled-silk bags, each of which was capable of containing five of the packages.

"At the point of her pistol she compelled Conley to fill each of the bags with the gold, and these were connected, one with another, by a stout cord of hemp. Do you begin to understand?"

"I am following your recital as closely as I can."

"When the filled bags were tied together so that the whole hundred and fifty thousand had been taken from the safe, she compelled Conley to thrust them, one by one, through the porthole of his cabin."

"And drop them into the sea?" asked the detective.

"Exactly. You see, the hemp cord connected the bags containing the gold at a distance of three or four feet apart. To the last of the bags was a much longer piece of cord, and to the end of that was a round, bladder-like float. The whole business was pitched into the sea somewhere between the Narrows and Sandy Hook. Conley could not tell exactly where it was, for he had no guide to go by save his recollection of the time that might have elapsed after he went to his cabin."

"I see."

"When the stuff was pitched into the sea, the woman suddenly raised her left hand from beneath the folds of her robe, and pointed a second weapon at him. This she fired; but it was not the same sort of a weapon as the other. It contained a liquid."

"A liquid? What was it?"

"Conley hasn't an idea. It smarted his eyes and he was on the point of crying out when he got a clip on the back of his head which knocked him out."

"Well? What next?"

"Nothing next."

"Eh? Is that all?"

"That is the end of the story. When Conley came to his senses, he was lying on his back on the floor of his cabin. The safe where the gold was kept was open. The port through which he had been forced to thrust the gold was also open. He was alone.

"He jumped to his feet and looked into the safe, thinking that he might be mistaken, but the gold was gone, all right. Then he rushed on deck, and straight to the captain, to whom he told his story.

"Now, Nick, of course there are several details connected with this and other stories of the same kind, which I have not yet explained, but that is the gist of the story. The woman had disappeared. Conley's story was not believed by the captain at first, but, at his earnest request, he was sent back to New York by the pilot boat, and he came to me with his story."

"And you believed it, eh?"

"I had to believe it. It is so precisely like others I have heard that all the world is beginning to believe them now, although it is only since this robbery and one other that credence has been placed in them. Before that, they were considered too fishy; but I have made up my mind that Conley told the truth, and that there is much more in the 'Scylla the Siren' tales than we have any idea of. Besides, I have a man waiting outside who will tell you a strange tale about her. Shall I have him come in now?"

"Yes. By all means. Let's have him in at once."

CHAPTER II.

A WEIRD AND WONDERFUL TALE.

The man who entered the room at the request of the inspector was a typical sea dog; a sea captain of the old school, who explained in a few characteristic phrases that he was in command of the tramp steamer *Phryne*, of Glasgow, now lying at anchor off Liberty Island.

"I'm Capt. Bob Staples," he said, accepting a chair and placing one of his feet upon another. "I've been in command of the *Phryne* ever since she was la'nched, but I've never seen no sich doin's as I've come here to tell you about since I've followed the sea, and that has been for more'n forty year, man an' boy. I've heard tell about Scylla and Charybdis, an' I've seen some rocks in my time off the coast of Greece that they call by that name, but I never s'posed that Scylla was a real live mortal until I ran afoul of her here in the waters of New York Bay."

"Then you have been afoul of her, have you, captain?" asked the detective.

"Yes, sir, I have; leastwise, of the gal wot they calls by that name; an' I s'pose it's as good a name as another when you come to describe a woman."

"What did she look like, captain?"

"Well, sir, I ain't much good at describin' things, but I remember the days when I used to go to see the 'Black Crook' at the old Niblo's Theater when I happened to be in this port, an' you kin rate me as a 'foremasthand if

I'm lyin' when I tell you that she looks jest as if she had stepped down out of that air play-actin' piece."

He paused long enough to stow away in his jaws a huge wad of fine cut, and then he continued:

"When she came aboard of the *Phryne* I was sittin' in my cabin goin' over a lot of figgers that I had to do, and figgers an' me don't get on very well together, so they was a-botherin' me like sixty. When I wasn't a-figgerin' I was swearin', because I couldn't seem to make 'em come right, nohow; and I had give orders that I wasn't to be interrupted on any account.

"First thing I knowed, somebody said, right in my weather ear, 'Hullo, Cap'n Bob!'

"Well, I wheeled around mighty quick, and reached for something to throw at whoever it was who had come in uninvited; but I didn't reach fur, 'cos there was a gun that made me think of the old-fashioned blunderbusses you read about, a-starin' me right in the face, and it warn't more'n three feet from my nose, either; and then I spied the 'Black Crook' gal a-standin' abaft of it, an' I knowed that it was up to me to sit still.

"'Hullo yourself!' says I, 'what in he—— Beg parding, I didn't notice that you was a woman—what in hullabaloo do you want?'

"Well, sir, she only grinned at me, showin' her purty teeth under the edge of the mask, and with her eyes a-gleamin' through the holes of it, like two stars in the southern heavens. I s'pose you know that stars are a heap brighter below the line than they are hereabouts."

"Yes; I have heard that," admitted the detective. "Go on with your story, captain, for it is very interesting. But first tell me when this happened?"

"Well, sir, as near as my reckonin' 'll show, it was the night following the same day that the purser aboard the *Jupiter* was held up."

"What happened next, captain?"

"I jest watched her till she quit grinnin' an' I never said another word; but arter a little she says, says she, 'Cap'n, ain't ye goin' ter arsk me to have a seat?'

"'Well, miss,' says I, 'seein' as how you ain't got any too many clothes on ye, I thought ye might feel a leetle delicate about settin' down'; but Lord bless you, sir, she only larfed fit to kill, an' she warped up alongside of an armchair that was on t'other side of the table from me, and says she, settin' on the arm of it, says she:

"'Cap'n, I understand that you have got a few casks of fine old Madeira wine in your cargo.'

"'I hev,' says I.

"'I want one of 'em,' says she. 'Would you oblige me by heavin' one of 'em overboard?'

"'Doin' what?' says I. 'Heave one of them casks of wine overboard? Not by a damsite, savin' your presence, miss.'

"Well, sir, that air smile died outen her face jest exactly as mebby you've seen the sun git behind a cloud, 'fore now, as though somebody had spanked it fur its mother; an' the hull outfit o' stars in the southern heavens weren't a binnacle light alongside o' the way them eyes o' her'n spit fire at me as she says, quiet-like:

"'Cap'n, this here gun o' mine is sorter tender about the tackle, an' it's likely to drag its doggoned anchor at a'most any minute. Now, if you'll be real obligin', you'll touch that air bell at your elbow after I have stepped behind this here curtain, and when your steward shows up, you'll tell him to call the third mate, as is on deck at this blessed minit, an' you'll order that him and the mate is to heave that air cask o' wine wot you've got stowed away in the pantry for your own private use, but which you ain't had broached yet—you'll order the steward and the mate to roll that air cask out on the deck and heave it overboard.'

"I expect that my jaw sorter dropped, 'cos she larfed ag'in, jest es if there war suthin' funny about it, and says she:

"'Cap'n, if either of 'em look surprised, you kin tell 'em that you've climbed up onto the water waggin and are sort of ashamed that you stole that air cask.'

"'I didn't steal it,' says I. 'The owners——'

"But she wouldn't let me say no more, an' I knowed by the glint in her eyes through the holes in her mask that she meant it when she said she was in a hurry.

"She stepped behind the curtain and I rang for the steward and gave the order.

"He looked as if he had a fit when he heard the order, but he knowed me well enough to do as I said without waitin' to arsk questions; and, arter a little, back he comes with the report that it was done; and he looked so fidgety that I asked him wot was the matter, and says he:

"'Cap'n, there was a long boat alongside, lying just out there in the dark, and she laid fast to the cask and towed it away the minnit it struck the water.'

"I thought I heerd a chuckle from behind the curtain, but I wasn't sure; anyhow it made me mad, and so I roared at the steward:

"'What d'ye take me fur? D'ye think I'm a cussed lubber to chuck a cask o' good wine adrift without knowin' that there would be somebody there to pick it up?' And then I made as if I was goin' to heave the inkstand at him, and he lit out.

"Well, sir, Miss Scylla slips her moorings behind the curtain and sails into the cabin again, larfin' to beat the band, and says she:

"'Cap'n, that was well done. I'm very much obleeged to ye,' says she. 'Good-night!'

"Out she goes, with that, through the cabin door jest as if she owned the hull darned vessel; but she hadn't more'n got hull down in the offing afore I was after her under a full head of steam, and with every sail set.

"But bless ye! I might as well ha' tried to follow one

o' Mother Cary's chickens, fur I didn't see a thing when I landed on deck. I heard suthin', though. It war a splash in the water, and I made sure that she had dodged overboard, so I ups with a life-preserver and chucks it into the water and then I dove over arter her.

"It was a hot night and I didn't have any too many clothes on myself—jest a shirt and trousers and a pair o' Chinese sandals, which I kicked off."

The captain stopped abruptly at this point and spat out the tobacco. At the same time he bristled up as if something had angered him, and he rested his eyes fiercely upon the detective; so fiercely that Nick wondered what had happened to anger the man, and would have been disturbed, had he not caught a gleam of amusement in the eyes of the inspector, who was seated a little distance from them, at what the captain would have described as the weather beam.

So Nick kept silent, and waited.

"Cap'n Carter," said the sailor, presently, speaking very slowly, as if he were deeply in earnest, "I now come to a part of my yarn which most people are dodgasted mean enough to say as how they don't believe it. I refused to tell it to you, when the inspector here arsked me to do it, but when he assured me that you would believe every word I told you as bein' the gospel truth, I agreed to cast loose my jaw tackle fur your benefit. But I want to tell you right here, if you don't believe wot I'm goin' to tell you, I'll jest jibe around and scud off to leeward. Somehow I ain't never accustomed myself to bein' called a liar."

"I hope, captain, that you will continue your story to the end and tell me all that happened," said the detective.

"An' you'll believe me if I assure you that what I say to you is the gospel truth?"

"Certainly."

"Well, sir, then here goes. I ain't got no call to lie to you, an' I'm only tellin' you what actually occurred to me. If so be as you're surprised, you can jest figger on how flabbergasted I was."

"All right. I will do that."

"Well, I dove into the sea arter that air young woman. Mebby I ain't told you yet that the time was mighty close to eight bells in the night watch, which is what you call midnight ashore, an' it was darker'n a pocket comin' out of the cabin onto the deck so suddin-like.

"I struck the water headfirst, of course, and as the *Phryne* is only in ballast 'ceptin' a few casks of wine, she stands rather high outen the water. So you see it was some considerable distance from her deck to the water.

"I thought I seed the Scylla gal a-glistenin' in the water afore I dove, but I wasn't dead certain. However, I wasn't a mite in doubt about it soon arter I struck the water, 'cos in less'n a holy minit from that time I was convinced that I had struck a hull school of 'em."

"A what?"

"A shoal of 'em; a school o' mermaids, mebby. I couldn't exactly count 'em jest then, but I'll take my oath that there were more than six or seven of 'em right around me, and they was a-swimmin' and a-divin' jest like so many porpusses; an' they was all spangled and riggled out jest like that air one wot came into my cabin arter the cask o' wine.

"Well, sir, one of 'em grabbed one of my feet, and another grabbed another foot, and they got all around me, an' I'll take my oath that they was covered with phosphorus or suthin' like it to make 'em shine, for you'd ha' thought that there was a dynamo or suthin' like it down there, and that the hull outfit war connected with it by wires.

"Fur jest about a minit I tried to fight 'em off, an' then I seed it warn't any sort o' use, so I gives up an' let them do with me as they pleased, an' the result was that they clustered around me, larfin' to beat the band, one of 'em on one side and another on t'other side, an' two more abaft at my caudle fins, an' two more ahead, like pilot fishes steerin' a bloomin' shark to its prey; an' there I was, not knowin' any more'n the Ancient Mariner did where I was headed fur."

"You weren't under the water all this time, were you?" asked Nick, trying hard not to laugh outright.

"No, I warn't," replied the captain, suspiciously. "I ain't no fish. Once I made fur to sing out, thinkin' that the watch aboard the *Phryne* would hear me, but one o' them mermaid women put her fingers to her lips to signify that silence war the rule, and at the same time she showed me one o' them doggoned pistols shinin' through the water, and I kept still.

"Well, sir, believe me 'r not, we swam around in this way fur about a quarter of an hour, when suddenly a long boat, like sich as a whaler uses, loomed up alongside of us, an' I war dragged aboard of it quicker'n you could say 'Scat.'

"An' that ain't all, either. There war more of them air gals aboard that boat, and I had one glimpse of 'em afore they spliced a bit o' sail over my peepers so's I couldn't see no more.

"One of 'em told me to keep still an' I wouldn't be hurt, and then I could feel that the boat was bein' pulled somewhere.

"Purty soon they stopped; then they h'isted me outen the boat, an' I war passed from hand to hand till I was let down into suthin'; an' then my hands war placed onto some sort of a ship's riggin' like a rope ladder, an' I was told to go below—which I did.

"Say, that war the funniest goin' below I ever tried, fur I felt all the time jest as if I were aboard of a small boat in a gale o' wind the way the thing bobbed around. Once I made shift to reach out, thinkin' that I could touch the bulkhead somewhere and so get an ijee of my whereabouts, but I got a clip across the knuckles which made me satisfied to cling to the riggin'.

"I can't tell you how far down we went in this way, but it was some considerable distance before we touched solid deck ag'in; an' it wasn't any too solid at that.

"I'm a-watchin' you, Cap'n Carter, jest to see if you're believin' all I'm a-tellin' you, an' I kin see that it's purty hard to swalley. All the same, it's true."

"Go ahead, captain."

"Well, sir, we took a walk arter that, and a long walk, too. It was sort of uphill all the way, and was slimy and soft under foot as if we were steppin' in mud most of the way; and arter a while we comes to another ladder an' I war told to climb—which I did.

"I should say that 't war about the distance from the main deck to the crosstrees of an ordinary ship, where I climbed up, an' arter we had come out into a sort of cabin, a chair was shoved under me an' I war told to sit down.

"I could hear a lot of giggling and a-larfin' around me fur some time arter that, fur all the world as if a gals' boardin' school had broken loose; an' there was a rustlin' of things like women's apparel around me, too; and then, of a suddin, the bandage was taken from my eyes and I'm blest if I didn't find myself in the doggondest place that ever a mortal man has visited since the days of Aladdin's lamp.

"Now, you hear me, mister, an' don't you dare to say I'm a liar. Did you ever read about the feller they call Monte Cristo? And about the cavern he had on an island, somewhere? Well, I was in a cavern jest like that one. There were rocks all around me, with little port an' starboard lights—that is to say, little red and green lights—stuck into the cracks; an' there war rugs a foot thick scattered over the floor; an' there war couches an' chairs an' a lot o' sich things everywhere around me, an' larst, but not least, so help me, I war in the presence of thirteen female women. Now, what d'ye think of that? Hey?"

"I should have thought it rather astonishing," replied the detective.

"Astonishin'! Huh!"

"What did they look like, captain?"

"They looked jest like any other women might look, dressed out to kill, with black half masks over their bloomin' faces, and all a-gigglin' an' a-larfin' at the same time.

"One of 'em—an' I knowed it war the one who had visited me in my own cabin—said as how I war the honored guest of the occasion, an' they would have a glass o' grog in my honor. I noticed then that they had the cask o' wine they had taken from the *Phryne*, jacked up like a keg o' beer, an' they broached it an' passed around the licker for fair.

"They had a pianer in the cavern, an' arter a little, one of 'em went to it, an' arter that there was playin' and singin' to beat a symphony orchestra; an' all the while they kept a-fillin' that air glass o' mine an' a-holdin' it under my old nose.

"Well, sir, I don't remember much arter that. I woke up arter a while—I suppose it must ha' been hours arterward—an' I war stretched on my bunk in my own berth with the steward an' the mate a-standin' over me.

"I'd ha' thought it war all a blessed dream if it warn't fur the fact that the steward an' the mate both swear that I war brought alongside in a long boat an' h'isted on deck with tackle; the people as brought me sayin' as how I'd got drunk ashore.

"That's my yarn, an' I'll fight the lubber as dares to say I'm a liar."

CHAPTER III.

THE QUEEN OF THE SIRENS.

The detective looked at the inspector, and the inspector looked at the detective.

To have laughed at that moment would have been fatal, for the captain was shifting his eyes from one to the other of them in an angry stare, prepared to explode with wrath at the first sign of unbelief that he discovered.

With heroic effort both the inspector and the detective preserved an appearance of becoming gravity; and, after a moment, the detective said:

"Captain, how do you account for this wonderful experience?"

"I don't account for it. I can't. I'm glad you take it serious, for most people don't."

"I would like to ask you some questions about it, captain."

"Ask me anything you like, sir."

"All right; but I wish to impress you with the fact that if some of my questions seem offensive, or suggest that I have not believed your story, you must overlook them, for I only wish to get at the whole truth."

"Heave ahead, sir. I reckon I can stand all you'll send, now that I know that you don't put me down as a cussed liar."

"You say that the people who returned you to the *Phryne* reported that you had got drunk while ashore?"

"Ay, ay."

"Were those people men or women?"

"The steward and the mate said as how they were women."

"So that bears out your tale, doesn't it?"

"Ay, ay."

"Did the steward or the mate question them?"

"They didn't have no time to do it. As soon as I was h'isted aboard the *Phryne*, they pulled away in the dark an' disappeared."

"What time was it when you woke up to consciousness?"

"About seven bells—that is, about half-past three in the morning."

"And how long had you been back in your own cabin at that time?"

"Half an hour, the mate said."

"So you were returned to your own ship about three o'clock."

"Some'eres thereabouts."

"When you went overboard, you say that you were dressed in shirt, trousers and slippers. Now, when you woke up, was your clothing wet?"

"Well, 't war moist; but, you see, I had other togs on over the old ones. The gals had rigged me out from main truck to kelson in the uniform of a captain of the navy. They had put the togs on over my wet clothes, an' the mate said as how he didn't know me from Adam when he first seed me over the side, in the long boat. I had the hull outfit, from the cap to the spats over my shoes."

"And what about that cask of wine? Had it really disappeared from the pantry?"

"It had."

"And did the steward and the third mate remember the fact that they had heaved it overboard at your order?"

"They did; and they do."

"What did they have to say about it?"

"Well, it's their private opinion—although neither of them dares to put it in words, fur they both know mighty well that I'd trice 'em up for it if they did—but, all the same, it's their private opinion that the hull thing war a leetle game that I had fixed up with some of them air gals, to send the cask ashore somewhere, and then to go there an' git drunk. You know neither of 'em seed any woman come aboard the *Phryne* afore I gave the order about the cask. The hull thing makes me out a bloomin' liar, whichever way I head, so about all that I can do is to luff up and ride out the gale, head on. That's my way o' puttin' it, but it about explains the sitooation."

"How does it happen that only the steward and the third mate are cognizant of all this affair?"

"'Cos the steward and the third mate comes mighty near to bein' all the crew I've got at the present time. I'm mighty short-handed. Most of my men deserted when we struck New York, an' I've been lyin' by waiting to sign on a new crew. There's the chief engineer an' one of his assistants aboard, but they were asleep at the time; an'——"

"I understand. You seemed to enjoy yourself while you were in the cabin of the mermaids, captain."

"Well, wouldn't you? There war thirteen purty girls——"

"Were they pretty, captain?"

"Cap'n Carter, if you kin jedge a woman by the way she stands on her two feet, by the way she carries her sails when she walks, by the cut of her figgerhead an' her manner o' comin' up into the wind, so to speak, by the red of her lips and the gleam of her white an' even teeth between 'em, by the sparklin' of her eyes through the holes of a mask which jest hides enough to make ye want to see more, by the archin' of her instep and the coils of hair atop of her head, by the music in her voice an' the sunshine in her manners, why, then, the hull thirteen war purty, an' don't you forgit it!"

"That is a very comprehensive answer. Were they also young?"

"If ye kin jedge that by the way they danced, and sang and larfed, and swalleyed their red wine, they war more'n seven, an' less'n seventy."

"And I suppose you have told me all that you know about them; eh?"

"Every blessed thing."

"Did you hear any names used among them while you were in the cavern?"

"Lots of 'em. There was Rose, an' Cora, an' Jane, an' Pansy, an'——"

"Did you hear the name of the one who interrupted you when you were busy with your figures in your own cabin?"

"Ay, ay; she was the one they called Cora. She was the queen bee, too. When she sneezed, the hull ship's company coughed, so to speak."

"Now, about the cavern."

"Ay, ay."

"How big was it?"

"Well, I should say that it was thirty or forty feet, either way."

"What articles did you notice inside the cavern, save those you have already mentioned?"

"There was a lot of truck there that looked as if it had come off some ship, or ships; but, fur the most part, I think the plunder was stowed away some'eres else, 'cos there was a passage or two a-leadin' off from the room I was in."

"Have you any idea where the cavern is located?"

"Jest about as much as you have."

"But when you were hauled into the long boat from the water, couldn't you tell which direction the boat was headed after that?"

"No, sir. I had lost my bearin's, teetotally; but if I war to guess at it, I should say it war south'ard."

"About how much time elapsed after you were taken into the boat before you were lifted out of it and told to climb down the rope ladder?"

"I couldn't tell that, either. I was listenin' to the talk around me all the time; but I should say that it war some'eres near an hour."

"And the thing you were made to climb into; what was that like?"

"Well, it was damp and musty, and it rocked and tumbled around as I climbed down. I ain't got no idea about that part of it. It was a different sort of a craft from any that I ever shipped aboard of afore. All I know is that when I got to the bottom it warn't easy to breathe."

"And after that you walked a long distance through mud and slime, you say?"

"Yes; but I don't know how fur it was."

"And then you climbed up about the distance from a deck to a masthead of an ordinary ship?"

"Precisely."

"And found yourself in the cavern you have described?"

"Ay, ay; when they took the bandage from my eyes. You see they was some time about that, fur they all took time to put on different clothes afore they let me see 'em ag'in."

"You are sure, I suppose, that you were in a cavern surrounded by rocks, and not inside the hull of an old ship; eh?"

"Cap'n Carter, I've followed the sea, man an' boy, fur forty year, and I know a ship's hull when I sees one. That warn't no hull; it was a cavern, with the rocks a-stickin' out all over the place and with port and starboard lights all around. Now an' then there was a masthead light—a white one, you know—too; but, for the most part, they was red and green."

"Captain, that cavern was doubtless somewhere along the shore of Staten Island; eh?"

"Well, I about figgered it like that, sir."

"Have you seen or heard anything of your strange visitor since that night?"

Capt. Bob Staples did not immediately reply.

Instead, he turned his eyes, with a quizzical expression, toward the inspector, and it was not until Nick repeated the question that he answered at all.

"Well, sir," he said, then, "to tell you the truth, I have, although I have told the inspector differently. He asked me that question, and I said 'No,' but the truth is, I have."

"Tell me about it," said the detective. "When was it?"

"Night before last, Cap'n Carter."

"Where?"

"In the cabin of my ship."

"The same young woman?"

"Ay, ay."

"And did she appear just as suddenly and just as mysteriously?"

"Precisely."

"Tell me about it."

"There ain't much more to tell than that. I was settin' there doin' nothin' in perticlar, when I got a hail from behind the curtain where she hid the fust time she came aboard—the time when she made me send out fur the steward, you remember?"

"Yes."

"Well, that was where she hailed me from."

"Did she have the gun with her this time?"

"Sure thing."

"And what did she want? Another cask of wine?"

"Nope. She just came to make a call; leastwise that is what she said about it, and seein' as how she didn't take nothin' away with her, I reckon she spoke the truth about it."

"Was she dressed the same?"

"Precisely."

"What did she have to say to you?"

"Well, the first I knowed that she was there, I got the hail.

"'Evenin', capting,' says she; an' then she stepped out afore me, an' I could see by the stretchin' of her lips an' by the sparkle in her eyes that she was larfin. Say, Cap'n Carter, you arsked me a little while ago if she was purty, an' now I want to tell you suthin' about it. You see, I couldn't ketch a glimpse of any part of her face, 'ceptin' that part of it as shows under the mask, but I'll take my oath that there ain't a purtier woman this side of the angels that kin hold a candle to her.

"She had that flowin', robelike thing a-hangin' from her shoulders almost to her heels, jest like you see 'em in play actin'; an' a short skirt of sky-blue, all covered with spangles like I've seen the sun a-shinin' on icebergs that reflected the blue of the heavens; and mebby they was long stockin's, 'r tights, 'r whatever you've a mind to call 'em under the skirt, and they was blue, too, and likewise covered with the spangles; and there was a crownlike thing, set with gems, around her temples and agin' her hair—black hair it was, too—and a short jacket, like Spanish bullfighters wear; and she stood there fur all the world es if she had jest stepped down outen a picture. I jest ketched my breath, and waited; that's wot I done."

CHAPTER IV.

THE DETECTIVE'S BOLD DECISION.

"Arter I'd waited a minit 'r so," continued the captain, "she took a step 'r two toward me, an' she says to me, says she, 'Can I come in, cap'n?' says she, jest like silver bells a-chimin' away off in the distance; an' I says to her, 'It strikes me kinder es if you war in already, ain't ye?' says I.

"Then she larfed, and she seated herself agin' the arm of the chair, same as she'd done afore, if you'll remember, and she says:

"'Did you have a head on ye when ye woke up the next mornin' arter our spree?' says she.

"'I did,' says I; an' then I arsked her wot it was that

she put into that grog, 'cos I knowed that no straight-out Madeira wine that was ever made would ha' served me like that.

"'Oh,' says she, 'we jest wanted to have a little lark with you, and when you dived overboard arter us we had to do something with you, and so we took you to the tunnel.'"

"Wait," said the detective. "Did she make use of that word, 'tunnel'?"

"Ay, ay; for sure."

"Go ahead, captain. What happened next?"

"'Well,' says I to her, 'that was all very nice of you to take me out and give me sich a rousin' good time 'thout any expense on my part, but it was kind o' low-down mean to up an' put drugs into my licker so's I couldn't say "Good-night" to ye when I came away.'

"She shrugged her shoulders; an' then, changin' the subject, she says:

"'Cap'n, I've heer'd es how you've been to the inspector in New York an' told him all about that leetle affair of ours. Is that so?'

"'Precisely,' says I.

"'What did you do that fur?' says she.

"'Bekuz I war arsked,' says I.

"'I s'pose he thought that you was a bloomin' old liar,' says she, at that; leastwise, them ain't the precise words she used, but they had that meanin' all the same; an' I said that she was dead right about it; and you ought to have heard her larf.

"'What did you come here fur this time?' says I. 'Another one o' them air casks?'

"'Yes,' says she! 'but I'm goin' to arsk you to give it to me this time. I shan't make ye go fur to call the steward an' the mate to help ye with it, but I'll jest leave it to your own good nature; an',' says she, 'if you do want to give me another cask of it, in remembrance of your spree the other night, ye kin jest heave it overboard yerself arter I've gone, an' nobody but you an' me need know a word about it. What d'ye say, cap'n?'

"Well, sir, what could I say? I jest turned it over in my mind for a minit 'r two an' then I says to her, says I, 'Miss Scylla,' says I——

"'Hello, there,' says she, 'where did you git that name?'

"'From the inspector,' says I; and then you should have heard her larf.

"'I'll tell you wot I'll do, Miss Cora,' says I, 'if you like that air name better'n the other one;' an' I saw her lips twitch in a half smile.

"'Wot'll you do?' says she.

"'If you like that air wine so well,' says I, 'I'll put two of them casks overboard fur you an' your young lady friends, instead o' one; only I want you to know that I'm half owner in the *Phryne,* an' that them casks o' wine is mine to give away as I see fit. I shipped 'em as a private venture of my own,' says I, 'an' if you want a couple of 'em, why, you shall have 'em—but on one condition,' says I.

"'Wot's the condition?' says she.

"'That arter you git 'em, an' have 'em all stowed away in your cavern, you'll come arter me some night an' take me there ag'in fur another spree like the last one. I had such a good time,' says I, 'that I'd like to play a repeater,' I says to her.

"At that she larfed. Then she seemed to think it over; an' bimeby she says, says she:

"'Mebby so.'

"'Is it a go?' says I.

"'Mebby so,' says she, ag'in. 'I'll think about it.'

"'Decide now,' says I, 'an' in less'n no time arter you're gone, overboard goes two casks of that air wine.'

"Well, sir, she throwed back her head and larfed and larfed; an' then all of a sudden she stopped in the midst of it an' arsked:

"'Which one of us be you in love with, cap'n?'

"'You!' says I, bold as the devil; an' that time I thought she'd have hy-steer-icks fur sure; but she ketched herself, an' she says, says she:

"'It's a bargain, cap'n.'

"'Precisely,' says I. 'When'll you come arter me?'

"'Oh, in a day 'r two, 'r three,' says she.

"'Wot's the matter with to-night?' says I.

"'Can't be did,' says she.

"'Then wot's the matter with to-morrer night?' says I.

"'That'll do,' says she."

"Then you are expecting to see her again this very night," said the detective.

"I be," was the quiet rejoinder.

"That is splendid!" exclaimed Nick. "I'll go aboard with you when you return to your ship, and——"

"Wot's that?"

"I was saying that I would go back with you when you return——"

"You'll excuse me, Cap'n Carter, but I'm hanged if you will!"

"Eh? You don't want me?"

"Not by a long sight, sir. Say, wot d'ye take me fur, anyway? D'ye think that I'm goin' to make a date with a young woman an' then up an' give her away like that? I ain't built in jest that air way, sir, I ain't. I'll come around an' tell you all about the affair to-morrer, if she shows up an' keeps her engagement, but I ain't a-goin' to help no perlice officers to git on that young woman's track, not if I can help it, an' I think I can. She ain't done me no larstin' harm as I knows on, an' she's mighty welcome to the wine, which I chucked overboard accordin' to agreement. No, sirree! I'm a-goin' to send my steward, and the mate, and the chief engineer and his assistant, and every son of a sea cook aboard my ship— I'm a-goin' to send the hull b'ilin' of 'em ashore to-night when I git back to the *Phryne*, and I'm a-goin' to keep watch alone, fur the comin' of that air gal, and if any landlubber, 'r perlice officer, 'r any other person comes within rifle shot of that air ship without first havin' permission, he'll git a bullet into him as sure as my name is Staples, and don't you forget it!"

"But, captain, she is a sea robber—a pirate—a thief."

"I don't care if she's the devil himself, which ain't likely, seein' as how she's a woman; it's all one to me. I ain't goin' to take no part in her undoin'; you hear me!"

"All right," said Nick. "We will drop that part of it. It was very kind of you to come here and tell us all you have told."

"Well, I had agreed to come here to-day to meet you, an' tell you all about it, an' I'm a man as always lives up to my agreements, so here I be; but I reckon as how my contract is about filled now, an' if you don't mind, I'll be goin'."

"Did you make any especial arrangements with her about to-night?" asked Nick, tentatively.

"Nothin' more'n that I agreed to do precisely as I done afore."

"You mean about diving into the water? Eh?"

"Well, she allowed that that warn't necessary this time, seein' as how I was to send all my men ashore an' would be on the *Phryne* all alone."

"How is it going to be managed this time?"

"Why, she said that they'd row up alongside in their boat and hail me, and when I answered an' said that all was clear aboard the *Phryne*, two on 'em would come aboard and bind up my eyes, so's I couldn't see and then they'd take me away. See?"

"Yes," replied the detective, thoughtfully. "I see. It will be quite an experience, won't it, captain?"

"You betcher life."

"You will have something to tell the next time I see you."

"Mebby so, if we do see each other ag'in; and I think I orter tell. It depends——"

The detective looked at his watch and then started to his feet in pretended consternation.

"Well, well!" he exclaimed. "You have been so interesting, captain, that you made me forget something that I had to attend to. Will you wait here just a minute before you go? I won't be absent more than five or ten minutes at the most—and it is only half-past two o'clock now."

"I don't know as I have got anything more to wait fur, Cap'n Carter; but howsumever——"

"Oh, yes, wait. I won't be long."

"All right. But understand that you ain't goin' to coddle me into takin' you aboard the *Phryne* with me. I wouldn't do that fur a thousand dollars, nohow."

"Oh, I won't ask you again to do that. I know how you feel about it. You will wait here for me, won't you?"

"Yes; if you ain't gone too long a time."

There was no opportunity for Nick to cast more than one quick, but meaning, glance at the inspector, but the latter readily understood from the detective's manner that Nick had some idea up his sleeve which he was on the point of putting into execution.

And as a matter of fact, the detective went no further than the outer office, where he seated himself at a desk and wrote rapidly for several moments.

When he had completed what he had to say, he placed the message in an envelope and sealed it, after which he addressed it to the inspector, marked it important and called to one of the regular office men to carry it inside.

And this is what the inspector read when he opened the letter:

"It is plain that Staples won't permit anybody to remain aboard the *Phryne* with him to-night, and so Staples must be detained somehow, while I take his place and represent him in that interesting episode which is likely to occur, for I tell you truthfully that as impossible and unreal as the whole story sounds, I believe it—that is, the greater part of it. I am convinced that the captain is thoroughly in earnest in all he says.

"I have taken his measure so thoroughly that I am convinced that I can make up sufficiently like him to carry out the part, but the important thing is that I do not wish him ever to have an idea that I was instrumental in detaining him. You see, therefore, that you must take the onus of this thing on your own shoulders—if you are willing to do it.

"My scheme is this: Keep him there with you half an hour or more, and at the end of that time I will send in another note which you can show to him after you read it. I will say in the note that I am called away on an important matter and cannot return to your office just now, and I will ask you to apologize to the captain for me, for keeping him waiting; and in the meantime you will have fixed up some scheme by which he can be detained ashore until to-morrow morning. I know that I can trust you to do that.

"He must not be permitted to return to his ship; and when you have arranged things so that he cannot do so, please telephone to me at my house. I will be awaiting the message.

"Then, to-night, when Scylla the Siren calls for him aboard his ship, she will find that she has me to entertain, instead of Capt. Staples, although I do not intend that she will be made aware of that interesting fact until after I have been introduced into that wondrous cavern, and have made the acquaintance of her twelve interesting friends."

Nick did not await a reply from the inspector after

sending the note in to him, but left headquarters at once, returning immediately to his own home, where, after writing the second note that he had agreed to send to the inspector, he busied himself with his preparations for the adventures of the coming night.

He realized that it was no small thing that he had undertaken to do, for he was thoroughly aware that a woman who was smart enough and fearless enough to act the part of Scylla the Siren would be a difficult person to deceive.

But the game was thoroughly worth the candle, and he was determined to carry it through.

And so he proceeded with his preparations as calmly as if he were not actually taking his life in his hands and literally putting his head into the lion's jaws.

CHAPTER V.

THE START OF A DESPERATE ADVENTURE.

The detective had perhaps never before in his life undertaken a disguise that was so difficult as this one.

In build, the captain was rather squat and thickset; his complexion had been tanned to a reddish brown and the skin on his face and hands resembled sole leather, more than anything else—and sole leather that had somehow been seamed and fluted into furrows and frills, not unlike the waves of the ocean where he had passed the greater part of his life.

A heavy shock of iron-gray hair, worn in unkempt profusion upon a massive head, and whiskers of the same hue, worn underneath his chin, while the face itself was clean shaven, made up his general appearance.

His brawny hands were knotted and seamed with use, and his arms suggested the capstan bars which were a part and parcel with his early training.

When it is asserted that the detective passed the entire day that remained to him in his preparation of this disguise, the reader can readily understand how difficult he found it; he who, as a rule, found half an hour sufficient time for the most complicated of his make-ups.

But when the disguise was completed, and Nick Carter looked in the mirror at himself after having put on the finishing touches, he was satisfied.

Not only had he been successful in producing an exact representation of the captain, but he had done it so thoroughly that he believed that he could even dive into the water if necessary, without in any way interfering with the make-up.

In a word, he had made use of a new preparation of pigment that he had lately invented, which was waterproof; it was, in a sense, not unlike varnish, and he had only to apply it after the general make-up had been put on, to render it impervious, at least for a time, to the action of water.

The wig and the whiskers were fastened on in the same manner, and the detective had no fear but that he could face the world defying anybody to penetrate the fact that he was wearing a make-up at all.

It was just at the moment when the disguise was complete that his telephone rang, and, replying to it, he discovered that the inspector was at the other end of the wire.

"Well," said Nick. "What luck?"

"When I left the captain half an hour ago at my own house," replied the inspector, "he was snoring to beat the fog horn off Hatteras. He is blissfully unconscious that he has been detained, and to-morrow, when he wakes up, he will find nobody to blame but himself."

"Are you sure that he won't wake up before to-morrow?" asked the detective.

"Absolutely positive."

"Then I can go ahead with my plans, eh?"

"I don't know any reason why you cannot do so."

"Where are you now?"

"At the office."

"Will you remain there till I come down?"

"Sure. And, say——"

"Well?"

"That steward he talked to us about is here."

"Eh? Is that so? Where is he?"

"In the reception room. He has asked for the captain half a dozen times, and seems to be worried about him. Shall I send him away, or keep him?"

"Keep him, by all means. I will be there inside half an hour. What have you said to the steward about the captain?"

"Why, without exactly saying so, I have managed to give him the idea that the old chap has taken a little too much and has been sleeping it off in my office. I told him that I would let the captain know, as soon as I could, that his steward was waiting for him."

"Good. Do you know the steward's name?"

"Sure. The captain calls him Pete; and, by the way, Pete says that the mate, whose name is Corker, is waiting for them at the Bishop's Tavern, down on the corner."

"Good again! It could not be better. I'll be there as soon as I can get there, now. I will come in by the back entrance and go directly to your private door. Leave it on the latch for me, will you? I might have to step through that door mighty quick."

"All right."

The detective lost no time in leaving his house after that, and in the course of less than half an hour he stepped into the inspector's private office.

"Well, by Jove!" exclaimed the inspector, when he saw him. "Say, Nick, if it were not for the fact that I know the captain to be safely at my own house I'm blowed if you wouldn't have fooled even me. How did you manage to copy the clothes so well?"

"I studied everything about the old chap with great

care before I left this office," replied Nick; "and I remembered that I happened to have an old suit among my disguises that was almost precisely like the one the captain wore. Only I had nothing to match the huge watch-chain, and——"

"And the seal ring, eh? Well, I thought of them both, and I took the liberty of borrowing them for the occasion. Here they are."

"With these in my possession," said the detective, "I think the disguise is about as complete as it can be made."

"You are right, it is. There is only one real danger now."

"What is that?"

"You might say or do something, or leave something unsaid or undone, in the presence of Pete and Corker, to betray you."

"I have thought of that. I will pretend to be just stupid full, you know. I think I can get around all the difficulties in that way."

"Sure thing. Say, Nick, do you take full stock in that yarn of the captain's?"

"Yes; pretty nearly so. I think that he told what he honestly believed to be the whole truth."

"Then I wish you would tell me how you account for it all."

"For all of what?"

"That yarn. The cavern in the rocks, which must be out somewhere in the middle of the bay. The girls in the 'Black Crook' costumes, and all that. Eh?"

"You think it is rather fishy, do you?"

"I certainly do."

"Well, suppose we begin at the cavern?"

"Yes."

"Do you remember that once he referred to it as the tunnel? Or rather that he quoted the woman as having done so?"

"Yes."

"Don't you also remember that, somewhere in the early eighties, the Baltimore and Ohio Railroad began the building of a huge tunnel from the mainland to Staten Island, with the intention of making the grand terminal of their railway on the island?"

"Yes, I do."

"I was a youngster at that time, but I remember visiting the work on that tunnel once in company with my father, and that I was greatly interested in it. Just why the work was ultimately abandoned I do not know, but I do know that a great deal of it was accomplished before the project was finally given up."

"Do you mean——"

"Wait; I will tell you what I mean."

"Go ahead."

"Engineers did not know as much about caissons and that sort of work in those days as they do now, and I suppose the undertaking was abandoned because it was found to be next to impossible of practical completion. At all events it was abandoned."

"Well."

"When it was decided to give it up, as much as possible of what had been already done was destroyed."

"I see."

"Much of the tunnel was filled up—but I do not think that all of it was filled."

"Humph! I begin to understand."

"Now, when I visited that tunnel, I remember that there was one place, some distance back from the shore of the kill where the contractors encountered a pocket of sand which they had to dig out in entirety, and the result was that, when it was removed, a huge chamber was left, almost in the middle of a solid mass of rocks."

"And you believe that chamber to be the cavern described by the old man?"

"I am almost certain of it."

"And you know where to find it?"

"Ah! There is where you have me, for that is just what I do not know."

"But——"

"I know approximately where it is located, but how to find it is quite another matter."

"How so?"

"Because, as I have already told you, a great part of the old tunnel was filled in. All the approaches to it were concealed. Indeed, it was supposed by everybody that the whole thing had been filled up, else the price of property would have depreciated right around that point, for nobody wishes to live over an abandoned tunnel."

"That is right, too."

"But you and I both know that a lot of contractors would not be too particular about carrying out such a contract. If they could fill such a place sufficiently so that nobody would ever find out that less than half of the real work had been done, that would be exactly the method they would use, thereby saving many thousand dollars and rendering their profits accordingly larger; don't you see?"

"Sure."

"Well, the captain's story has convinced me that there is a great deal of that tunnel which was never filled up; that the chamber in the rocks which I have described is the cavern of the captain's story; that these sea robbers have somehow found their way to it, and that they have managed to create another means of entrance from the water.

"Now, Steve, I don't know how to get to that place without blasting through a lot of rock, which would consume months in knocking them to pieces; but there is one entrance at least, and without doubt there is more than one. I don't know how to get into the place, but I'll bet that once I am inside of it I will know how to get out."

"And that is why you propose to let the women take you there and——"

"Precisely, as the captain would say."

"Nick, do you believe that part of the story? About the women, I mean? Do you believe that they are all women?"

"The old captain looks to me like a man who knows a woman when he sees one," said the detective, with a smile.

"Yes; but it seems preposterous that a lot of women could conceive and carry out such a scheme as this one."

"Women are doing a lot of things lately, Steve. They are making lawyers, doctors, ministers and detectives of themselves, and I don't see why they should not undertake the profession of expert sea robbers as well. do you?"

"N-no; I guess not."

"Women never do things by halves. A woman goes the whole hog or none. If one is brave, she is braver than the bravest. However, there is no use in that sort of argument at the present moment."

"No."

"The point is that I am satisfied that the captain's story is, in the main, true; that I think I know, approximately, at least, where the mysterious cavern he tells about is located; that the captain had an engagement with Scylla the Siren for to-night, and that now I am prepared to keep that engagement in his place."

"I wish I might go with you, Nick."

"So do I; but this is an adventure which I must undertake alone, or not at all, so send out for the steward and I'll begin."

CHAPTER VI.

SCYLLA, THE BEAUTIFUL.

The inspector went to the outer room and presently returned with the steward, and at a glance the detective saw that he would have little or no difficulty in imposing upon this man, who had himself, during the time he was waiting for his master, looked into the bottom of more than one glass of grog.

He saluted awkwardly when he entered the room, and stood waiting for the man, whom he supposed to be his captain, to speak.

"Throw me a heavin' line, there, you lubber!" roared Nick, rising from the chair in which he had been stretched almost at full length, and lurching toward the steward as if nothing could save him from falling. "Give me your flipper. This is a rough sea, and a choppy one at that, Pete."

He placed one hand solemnly on the shoulder of the steward, and allowed himself to be led through the door, without so much as deigning a backward glance at the inspector, who stood near his own desk, smiling broadly.

Nick accompanied the steward out of the building and along the street toward the tavern that the inspector had indicated; but at the entrance to it he paused, and, clinging fast to the railing that led to the stairs, he exclaimed:

"Avast, there, Pete. Can't you see that I've got to put a reef in this 'ere sail o' mine afore I da'st to come about on the other tack? Pipe the mate up from below an' we'll be headin' away fur the *Phryne*. There's grog enough in my own cabin fur all I'll want more to-night."

He clung to the rail while Pete descended the stairs, presently reappearing, accompanied by a low-browed, fierce-looking sailor of the old-fashioned type, who pulled his forelock respectfully when he encountered his captain—or, the man whom he thought to be his captain.

"Mr. Corker, you're drunk," said Nick, thickly, still clinging to the rail.

"Ay, ay, sir; an' by the same token, so are you, sir," was the reply.

Nick pretended to think the answer funny, for he chuckled audibly; and after a moment he said:

"Pete, you take the wheel an' be skipper for a leetle while. This head sea is a leetle too much for my old eyes, an' I don't know my bearin's among all these new lights. Haul a leetle mite more into the wind, Pete, 'r by the Lord Harry we'll ship a sea that'll carry me overboard in the wash. That's right. Warp up alongside an' throw out your grapplin' hooks, 'r I'll swamp right alongside o' ye afore I know it. Phwhew! but that air grog wot them perlice fellers throw into ye is strong, all right.

"Avast, there!" he added, when a few moments later Pete sought to signal to a car. "I ain't goin' aboard no craft o' that kind in this gale, an' don't you forgit it. Sing out to one o' them air two-wheeled dories with the ports in the bows instead of on the beams, so's we kin see where we're goin'."

A hansom was called and the three piled into it together, after Pete had given directions that they be taken to Pier A, North River, which is near Castle Garden.

When they left the cab it was at once apparent to Pete and the mate that the motion of the vehicle had lulled their master to sleep, for it was as much as their united efforts could accomplish to waken him and afterward to lead him to the boat.

But they finally succeeded in tumbling him into the stern in any old way, and then the two men manned the oars and presently they shot out upon the waters of the bay, headed toward the *Phryne*.

Nick observed, through his half-closed lids, that although the two men had been drinking deeply, they were well able to row the boat, and so he permitted it to appear that he was sleeping peacefully, and he did not rouse himself until they were alongside their own ship.

Here, he managed to render it no easy matter for them to sling him aboard the vessel, after which they conducted him to his cabin, where he flung himself into a chair, and ordered Pete to bring him a bottle of grog instantly, on pain of being hurled into the sea if he was too long about it.

Then, while he poured out a tumbler brimming full of the liquor, he blurted out:

"Didn't I tell you lubbers that you could all have a night ashore to-night, Pete? I have forgotten whether I said to-night, 'r some other night."

"Ay, ay, sir. You said to-night."

"Well, then, why don't you go? Hey?"

"I thought——"

"Git out o' here, the hull b'ilin' lot of ye!"

"Are we to go, sir? All of us?"

"Every mother's son of you! Git out. What time is it?"

"Six bells, sir."

"Well, you can all have till seven bells o' the mornin' watch. That'll be half-past seven o'clock ashore, where they don't strike no bells, so you look out fur it Pete, If ye ain't aboard here afore eight bells——"

"We'll be here, sir."

"Then git out. I can manage the old ship to-night myself; an' besides, I'm expectin' company."

"Ay, ay, sir; that's what you said. Mebby you'd like to have me here to wait on ye."

For reply Nick reached forward and seized a book from the table which he hurled at the steward's head, and that worthy, with a broad grin on his face, fled through the companion way to the deck.

Nick rose from his chair and followed far enough to hear what was said between the steward and the mate.

"He ain't as bad as usual," said Pete, to his companion. "He'll be all right, and he does remember wot he said about our goin' ashore fur the night."

"Then we kin cast off at oncet, eh?" said the mate.

"Sure. Call the others, and we'll be gone afore he changes his mind."

They lost no time after that, and before it was fairly dark, the detective had the satisfaction of knowing that he was entirely alone aboard the *Phryne*.

It was with a feeling of intense satisfaction that he returned to the cabin, then, prepared to await with patience the coming of Scylla the Siren.

It was not yet eight o'clock in the evening, and he knew that there was little likelihood that the female sea robber would put in an appearance much before midnight; nor did he have a doubt but that the vessel had been watched by one of her crew throughout the afternoon and evening, in order to make it positive that the old sea dog had not laid a trap for his expected visitors.

The masthead and anchor lights had been put out by the mate before he left the vessel. There was literally nothing for the detective to do save to eat the lunch which the steward had been thoughtful enough to prepare for him before taking his departure, so having done that, he made himself comfortable in the cabin, and having discovered a book that he had not seen before, he soon forgot the flight of time in reading.

And thus the hours passed, one after another.

Twice he went on deck and looked off over the waters of the bay, but he saw nothing there to interest him particularly, and believing that the playing of his part consisted in his remaining in the cabin until he was hailed, he gave himself up to the enjoyment of the book.

There was nobody left aboard the ship to strike the bells and thus to warn him of the flight of time, and midnight came before he was aware of it.

It had just occurred to him that the hour must be getting late, and that it was almost time to expect his callers, when he was startled so that he almost leaped to his feet by the sound of a voice which spoke softly to him, almost directly into his ear—and it was the voice of a woman; there was no mistaking that fact.

"Good-evening, captain," it said; and as the detective started and half turned, he found that the captain's description of the incidents had been quite true.

A woman, apparently young, and undoubtedly beautiful beneath the half mask she wore, stood before him, near the curtain that hung between the cabin and the companion way which led to the berths abaft of it.

And her costume? The captain had but faintly described it, or she had gotten herself up with unusual care for the occasion.

Her jet-black hair and clear, white brow were partly concealed by a crown-shaped headdress that was studded with jewels. A half mask concealed the upper part of her face to the tip of her nose, but below it he could see that the chin was perfect in mold and contour, that her lips were red and smiling, and that her teeth were wonderfully white and even.

A jacket, shaped like the bullfighter's jacket, of Spain, enveloped her shoulders and bust. It was fastened together at the bottom, was sea-blue in color and literally blazed with gems.

Below this, to her knees, hung a skirt of the same color and texture; and this also was ablaze with decorations—the captain had described them as spangles, but Nick perceived that the effect was produced by cleverly interwoven strips of mica, which reflected every glint of light that touched them.

Below the skirt the shapely limbs of the young woman were encased in stockings, or tights, whereof the general color effect was blue, as in the case of the other garments, but here, again, a glistening, scalelike effect had been accomplished by the use of mica, until, as she stood there before him in the glare of the cabin lights, she seemed literally to be on fire, while the smile on her lips and the glow of her dark eyes through the holes in the mask, produced an effect on the detective which he never quite forgot as long as he lived.

The long, narrow cape—the captain had called it a robe—of thin, gauzy substance, which clung to her shoulders at the back, she had caught up in her left hand, and she did appear, as the captain had said, as if she had stepped down out of a mediæval painting.

"Blast my eyes!" exclaimed Nick, in well-simulated imitation of the captain's voice and manner, as well as language, "if you don't beat all the way you appear before a feller so suddin. Say, miss, it war a-gittin' so bloomin' late that I had begun to fear that you warn't goin' to hail."

The woman laughed lightly, and half seated herself gingerly against the arm of a chair near her, throwing one foot carelessly across it.

"Tell me about your visit to New York to-day," she said, lightly; but Nick could see that her lips had tightened over her teeth, and that she was very much in earnest in asking the question.

"What about it?" he asked.

"You were a long time at police headquarters, weren't you?" she asked.

"Yes; some considerable time."

"And what did you find to talk about during all that time?"

"Mostly about you," replied the detective, boldly, for he saw that the movements of the captain had been spied upon, and he realized that it would not do to carry his attempts at deception too far lest she suspect something.

"I suppose that much," she said, slowly. "Now, if you please, I will hear what you—and the men who were with you—had to say about me."

"Well, I s'pose I done most of the talkin'."

"I suppose you did. And you had two good listeners, did you not?"

"Yep. They war purty good, considerin'."

"Considering what?"

"Considerin' that I didn't go there intendin' to tell 'em any more than I wanted to."

"Did you, for instance, tell them about your engagement for to-night?"

"Well, I ain't quite such a jack as all that, miss."

"Did the inspector and Nick Carter believe all that you did tell them about me, or did they think that you were lying?"

"The inspector and—who?"

"Nick Carter."

"Was that the other feller's name?"

"Yes; weren't you introduced?"

"Sure; but I don't think I caught the name; leastwise, I didn't remember it."

"Well, the other man was Nick Carter. The great Nick Carter. Have you never heard of him?"

"Can't say as I have, miss."

"You certainly are behind the times. Nick Carter would feel greatly offended if he supposed that you had never heard of him."

"Well, he'd have to git over it, then, for I ain't never heard about him, as I knows on."

"Did those two men believe all that you told them about me?" she repeated.

"To tell ye th' truth, I don't think they did," replied Nick, leering at her in a confidential smile that was inimitable.

"Nick Carter left you there for some time alone with the inspector, didn't he?" was her next question.

"Yes; he was called away or suthin'; I don't know what it was."

"And a little while after that you went out with the inspector and entered a carriage."

The detective was startled by this question, for he felt that it might portend that the inspector and the captain had been shadowed from headquarters, and that it was known to the woman before him that the captain was at that very moment drugged and asleep at the house of the inspector, while the man to whom she was talking was a fraud.

However, he determined to play the game out to the end, no matter what happened; and so, to her last question, he nonchalantly replied.

"Sure."

"Where did you go in the carriage?" she asked.

"To the inspector's house."

"What for?"

"Bekus he arsked me to."

"Why?"

"Said as how he had some new kind of grog up there that he wanted to blow me to."

"And I suppose he did 'blow' you, and that you drank a lot of it; eh?"

"I believe as how I tucked away my share, miss."

"And got yourself drunk, eh?"

"Precisely."

"And talked a whole lot more after that. It was then, I suppose, that you gave away the whole thing about what you thought of doing to-night, was it not?"

"Say, miss, I ain't no liar, whatever else you've a mind to call me. Jest now I said that I ain't told nobody about that leetle date of ourn, an' I meant wot I said, so help me."

"Well, what did the inspector want with you? You can take my word for it that he did not take you to his house for nothing. He isn't built that way. What's more, the other one—Nick Carter—didn't leave you alone with him without having some game in his mind that he wanted played on you, or wanted to play on you himself. Now, what was it all?"

"Miss Cora, s'help me, you kin search me from main truck to kelson. I give it up."

"How long were you at the house of the inspector?"

"I'll be blowed if I know. It was quite a while, but there warn't nobody strikin' bells up in that locality and I didn't keep no account of the time."

"You mean that you were too drunk to remember, don't you?"

"Not by a jugful, I don't; but these 'ere questions o' yourn bother me, an'——"

"Possibly I will bother you more than you think before we part to-night," she interrupted him, meaningly.

CHAPTER VII.
NICK CARTER'S STRANGEST EXPERIENCE.

The detective began to experience an uneasy sensation before the searching gaze of those black eyes which bored into him through the holes in the half mask, and the still more searching questions the woman asked.

He wondered how much she did know; and how nearly he ought, for the sake of entire safety, to approach the truth in answering her.

But there was only one thing to do under the circumstances, and that was to reply as best he could, and to trust to luck to carry him through.

"But," he thought to himself, "suppose that one of her people followed the inspector and the captain, when they drove uptown; suppose it is known to her that the captain did not return to headquarters with the inspector; suppose it is known to her that, when I left the central office, I went straight to my own house, and that it was Capt. Staples who mysteriously came out of that house later on. Suppose, in a word, that she is already aware of the fact that I am Nick Carter? Whew! In that case I am certainly walking into a nice fix."

But he made no remark aloud, and he did not permit the perturbation he felt to find expression on his features.

"Did you come away from the inspector's house with him?" was the next question she fired at him, and for an instant Nick was dazed by it, for he did not know exactly how he should reply; but after a pause that was imperceptible to her, he answered:

"No."

"Why not?" she asked.

"Well, I reckon I war takin' a nap when he left the house."

"When did you leave it?"

"When I woke up."

"Did you leave the house alone?"

"Nope. The other feller came there arter me."

"What other fellow? Whom do you mean?"

"The other one. The one who was at the central office with the inspector when I went there to see him."

"Do you mean Nick Carter?"

"I s'pose I do, if that is his name."

"Where did you go with him when he went to the inspector's house after you?"

"Say, miss, be I bein' cross-examined fur any perticlar reason? Bekus if I be, ye might es well spit out wot it is ye want to know all at once, an' I'll answer it ef I kin. It'll save a hull lot o' time, I'm thinkin'."

"Where did you go with Nick Carter when you left the inspector's house with him?" she asked, calmly, and as if she had not heard his protest at all.

"Hanged if I know. We got into a four-wheeled craft and tacked down half a dozen streets, till finally we moored fur a minit in front of a house where he got out and left me. Arter that we got under weigh ag'in, an' afore I knowed it we were at perlice headquarters ag'in, an' I was talkin' with the inspector once more. Pete—my steward—was there, an' Corker—my third mate—was takin' on cargo over at a corner saloon. A leetle arter that we slipped our cable an' set sail fur the *Phryne*. Pete, he took the tiller, 'cos I couldn't see to steer in good shape, an' when we got aboard here he reminded me that I had promised all hands a night ashore, so I lets 'em all go, an' then I takes a book an' tries to keep from droppin' asleep by readin', 'r purtendin' to read, which is the same thing, if readin' comes es hard to you as it does to me; an' then, afore I knows it, I hear you pipin' all hands to th' quarter-deck; an' so help me that's all I knows about the hull bloody thing, an' wot's more, it's all I'm goin' ter try to say about it, too."

"That was rather a long speech for you to make, captain," she said, smiling.

"Well, it war very much to the point, fur it's wot I mean; an' ef you're goin' to take me on that air experdition of yourn to-night I think we'd better be mannin' the halyards; hey?"

"So you still think that you would like to visit us again, do you?" she asked.

"Betcher life I do; but say, don't put nothin' into my drink to-night, will ye?"

"Possibly not. We will see about that. It may be necessary, when the time comes to bring you back to the ship."

"Not by a long shot. There ain't a soul here to interfere with you. There ain't nobody to arsk any questions of you when you bring me back; an' if you're afraid I'll see anything, all you've got to do is to——"

"Oh, I shall know very well, indeed, what to do."

"Huh! I shouldn't wonder if you would. Say, miss!"

"Well?"

"I wish you'd let me see yer hull beautiful face, will ye?"

"Possibly; a little later."

"Say, by thunder! Ye won't furgit that air half promise, will ye?"

"No."

"Now, wot d'ye want me to do afore we start? Fur I s'pose we are a-goin' to start, ain't we, Miss Scylla?"

"Yes, at once. Stand up where you are, in front of your chair. That is right. Now put your hands behind you."

Nick obeyed, and rather to his surprise, for he had not heard a sound in the cabin behind him, his hands were suddenly seized in a viselike grip, and stout cords were bound around his wrists instantly.

But he was careful to make no sound or motion of protest.

When his wrists had been firmly bound together a bandage was placed over his eyes by the same unseen hands, and the last thing he saw was the beautiful half face of the woman who stood in front of him, and there was a smile on her lips which he thought, in that instant, had taken upon itself rather a sardonic expression.

Again he felt that sensation of uneasiness, as if he were walking into some kind of trouble, and as if all would not be as smooth sailing with this girl-woman before him as he had anticipated.

And now he heard her voice again, talking rapidly to some person who stood behind him; and it was greatly to his astonishment that he could not understand what was said.

It must be remembered that Nick Carter speaks almost every known language, as well as many that are comparatively unknown; and now to hear one spoken without his having the least idea what it was, or what the words implied, was certainly a new one on him.

It was soft and musical, and flowed along as glibly as the Spanish tongue when spoken by a woman, and yet he could detect no familiar sound to it.

There was a rapid interchange of sentences between the two women—one behind him and the one who had all the time been in front of him, and then a hand grasped his arm, and he felt himself led none too gently toward the companion way.

"If ye want another cask of that wine," he said, "all ye've got to do is to send some of your folks arter it—that is, if ye know where to find it. You're es welcome es the flowers that bloom in the spring, tra, la."

There was no reply until after they had reached the deck and crossed it to the starboard side; but then a voice whispered in his ear:

"You are not to speak again, or to make a sound of any kind, until permission is given you. Do you understand that?"

"Ye say it purty middlin' plain," replied Nick.

There was silence after that, and presently he felt a rope passed under his arms and drawn tightly around his body; after that came the creaking of block and tackle, and he was hoisted from the deck, swung out over the side and then lowered into a small boat which was lying beside the ship.

There, he felt ready hands seize hold of him, and in another moment additional cords were drawn tightly around his ankles, and he was placed at full length upon some tarpaulin in the bottom of the boat.

Almost instantly it was pulled away from proximity to the *Phryne,* but after proceeding only a short distance the rowers rested on their oars and appeared to wait for something.

He wished then that he could see, but the bandage over his eyes had been well placed, and the fact that his hands were tied behind him effectually prevented him from doing anything to loosen it.

He figured that they were not more than a hundred yards from the vessel, and as he listened he could hear strange sounds proceeding from the deck of the *Phryne,* as if heavy objects were being moved about it, and he smiled to himself when he understood what those sounds meant.

"They are looting the ship from stem to stern," he thought to himself. "That is why I am tied up in this manner. They have determined to take everything of value from the ship on this trip. The opportunity is too good a one to be lost. Won't the old captain be wild when he knows about it? But still, I have not myself to blame, for if I had not interfered he would have been here alone, and would have been served in the same way."

It seemed to him, lying there, bound as he was, that the time they consumed in looting the ship was almost interminable; but after an hour or more had passed he felt that the boat he was in was moving again, and he knew that the oars had been silently dipped into the water, in obedience to some order as silently given.

After that, the motion was steadily forward, but other than the ripple of the water against the boat as it shot forward there was no sound whatever.

The people in the boat, whoever they were, remained utterly silent.

Nick had no idea who they were nor how many there might be, although he knew by the shape of the hull against which he was lying, save for the piece of tarpaulin beneath him, that the craft was a very small one, and that, therefore, there could not be many rowers at the oars.

He longed to ask a question or two, and to do something to induce his captors to talk, but he deemed it best, for many reasons, to stick to the agreement he had made, so he did not open his mouth.

But he tried to reckon the time that passed after they began to row, as well as he was able to do so, and also to decide something about the direction they followed through the water; but he speedily discovered that this latter task was an impossible one.

With the former, however, it was different.

Nobody spoke to him, and he was prohibited from addressing anyone himself, so there was nothing to prevent him from counting.

He timed the count, as well as he could, to seconds, and when at last their goal was reached, while they were lifting him from the boat into something else—and he could not for the moment get any idea of what it might be, only that he knew positively it was not another boat—he divided the product of his counting by sixty, and the dividend again by sixty, so that by the time he was out of the boat he already had the time fairly well computed in minutes.

There were eighty of them—an hour and twenty minutes.

At the rate they had been rowing through the water—and Nick knew that there had been two pairs of oars—he figured that they must have covered five or six miles, or less; and he knew that such a distance would be in keeping with his ideas about the old tunnel of the Baltimore and Ohio Railroad.

But he speedily forgot all sense of computation in the new developments that were taking place.

Before he was hoisted from the bottom of the boat the ropes were cast off from his ankles and wrists, and then he was told to stand upright.

He did so, and then strong arms seized him—and he marveled at the strength of these women, for he knew that they were women—he was raised bodily in the air, and passed into other hands that seemed to have been outstretched to receive him.

From these he was passed on to others, and then he felt himself thrust against a dangling rope ladder which he was ordered, in a low tone, to seize upon and to descend.

Then for the first time he realized what the captain had meant when he said that the craft he went down through was like a ship in a rough sea, for it rolled and pitched with him in a manner that gave him a feeling of nausea despite the fact that he had never been seasick in his life; and he muttered to himself:

"Of all the strange places I was ever in, this is the strangest."

CHAPTER VIII.

THE SPIDER AND THE FLY.

All the time that he was descending the ladder he knew that there was a person on it, beneath him, and another just above him; and they went down and down until it seemed to Nick that they must be approaching the bottom of the sea.

At last they did touch bottom—a bottom that was covered with slime and damp.

But the detective was given no time to conjecture where he might be, for immediately he was hustled forward.

He heard the clanging of iron against iron. He heard the swinging of a heavy door upon rusty hinges. He felt a rush of colder and somewhat purer air against his face. That was all.

Then he was pushed forward again, unceremoniously, and he felt that although he was walking through a wet and slimy place, where there was quite a deposit of mud, that, nevertheless, his feet trod upon a bottom that was circular in form, and that beneath the mud there was a very hard substance.

"It is certainly the tunnel," he thought, "though how we could possibly enter it from the sea is more than I can determine now."

Once he reached out one of his arms in an effort to touch the sides of the gallery with his hands, but he received a sharp blow upon his wrist which made him wince, and he did not deem it wise to repeat the effort.

All this time not a word was uttered.

He might as well have been in the company of a lot of ghosts for all the sound they made.

So surprised was he by what was taking place that he forgot to count his steps in order to reckon the distance, or the time, but he knew that they had traveled a considerable distance when at last they came to a halt and there ensued a second of clanging of iron against iron, more opening of doors, and then the ascent of a long spiral staircase.

It was up and up and up, until he was assured that the ascent here was much greater than the descent at the other end of the tunnel; and then they passed through another set of doors into a place where the air was at last pure and sweet, and which he correctly guessed was the cavern of the captain's story.

Still all was silence around him.

Hands seized upon him a second time, and he was led away through the room, another door was opened, another corridor or gallery was traversed, after which still another door was opened and he was thrust through it.

Then the touch of the hands left him.

An instant later he heard the sound of a closing door behind him and he had the feeling that he was alone.

He spoke aloud, but received no reply.

He tried it a second time, only to be met by utter silence as before.

Then he raised his hands and tore the bandage from his eyes, but he might as well have left it there, for he was in darkness so absolute that he could see nothing at all.

For a moment he stood there, undecided what to do.

Then he reached out with his hands, and when they touched nothing he took two or three cautious steps forward.

In this manner he walked from side to side of his prison until he discovered that he was in an apartment that was not more than twelve feet square; that one side of it was circular as if it were the side of the old tunnel, and that the remaining three sides were square and firm, and formed of heavy planking.

"Humph!" he thought. "This is evidently a room that has been constructed here for this very purpose."

He regretted that he had not his electric light with him, but in making up for his disguise as the captain he had deemed it wise to leave all his usual paraphernalia at home, so that in case he was searched nothing would be found on him to lend suspicion to the people he was up against.

The consequence was that he was not only deprived of the use of his light, but that he was also without the little weapons that he ordinarily carried in his sleeves.

In fact, he was unarmed, save for his strong muscles and terrible fists, and he smiled grimly to himself when he thought of the utter absurdity of attempting to use them against women.

"I wonder what they are up to, anyhow?" he mused, half aloud. "This isn't at all the way in which they treated the old captain, and it certainly is not what he was led to expect at their hands to-night."

But there was no way to get a reply to his question, so, perceiving that the floor was dry and that some sort of a rug covered it, he felt around still further, until at last he found a couch, two chairs and a table.

He stretched himself upon the couch then, and gave himself up to awaiting developments.

But the minutes lengthened themselves into hours, and still nobody came near him, and he heard not a sound.

When he thought that the time must be long past daylight, he removed the crystal from his watch—or rather, it was the captain's watch—and felt of the hands, discovering in that way that it was past four o'clock.

After another interval which he thought must have been several hours, he felt of the hands again to discover, to his surprise, that it was only a little past five.

And so, hour after hour, at almost regular intervals, he resorted to the hands of the watch to ascertain the time, and thus marked almost every hour as it passed.

And there were many of them; very many of them.

The night waned into morning, and the morning deepened to midday; and it was not until long after two o'clock in the afternoon that he detected any sound at all.

But then he did hear something.

It was some person at his door, and presently, when it was thrown open, a gleam of light entered the room, almost blinding him for an instant.

"Say, miss," he exclaimed, before his visitor could speak, "air ye goin' to starve a mate to death, an' never once offer him a drop to drink? I didn't call fur no sich treatment es this 'ere, 'r I'll be dod-gasted ef I'd ha' come a step."

It was a merry laugh that replied to him, and a half-masked woman, dressed as a woman should be, appeared in the doorway.

Nick knew at once that it was not the same woman who had visited him in the cabin of the ship, and he waited for her to speak.

"We quite forgot all about you," she said.

"Forgot me! Huh! That ain't fair, miss. If you'd ha' been as hungry an' dry as I be, you'd never have forgotten, I kin tell you that."

"Never mind, captain. We will make up for it now. You shall have all you want to eat and drink; you shall have your fill."

"Thank goodness fur that; an' say! Ye can't begin to sarve it any too quick, miss."

"You shall be fed and watered at once, captain."

"Watered? Who the h—ullabaloo said anything about water? Hey?"

"Well, wine, then. How will that do?"

"That's better. Say! I'm dryer'n an ol' jawbone, I am."

"Follow me, captain. Have you any idea what time it is?"

"No; but I reckon it must be about six bells next week."

The woman laughed merrily at this.

"As a matter of fact," she said, "it is late in the afternoon of what you would have called to-morrow when we brought you here."

"Is that so? What in thunder——"

"You are going to ask what has happened to the *Phryne* during that time, I suppose?"

"I suppose I was."

"Well, I can tell you that she is there at her anchorage all right. Your men have returned to her, and finding things not exactly as they expected to, they have reported the matter to the harbor police, and now the deck of your ship is swarming with officers who are chiefly engaged in looking over the sides to find the holes in the water where the thieves who visited her last night have disappeared."

"You don't say so! Well, say, there warn't any thieves aboard that craft last night that I didn't arsk to be there, and I'd thank the perlece if they'd stay away."

"Perhaps you don't know what happened to your vessel after you left her last night," said the girl, tentatively.

"Mebby I don't. Suppose you tell me, miss."

"It was looted from stem to stern."

"Was—what?"

"Looted. Stripped of everything of value."

"You don't tell me. Who done it? Hey?"

"Why, we did, of course. You don't suppose that we intended to let it go past, do you?"

"Let what go past?"

"The chance; the opportunity; the occasion."

"When'd you do it? Is that why you clean forgot me an' left me to starve and thirst?"

She laughed merrily again by way of reply; and at the same moment they stepped through into the main room of the cavern; the same room that the old captain had so graphically described.

If Nick Carter had expected to be astonished he had certainly been correct in the surmise, for if the captain's tale had, in a measure, prepared him for what he now encountered it had by no means been adequate to the real existing conditions.

The room—if it may be designated by that name, was circular in form and dome shaped at the top.

It was quite large, too, and what was still more interesting, the detective perfectly remembered it as the one he had long ago visited in company with his father, as he had explained to the inspector.

There was nothing wonderful about it when viewed from the standpoint of an engineer.

It was merely a cavity in the rocks which had formerly been filled with sand, and in the course of the excavations for the building of the tunnel it had been emptied, leaving the spacious chamber.

But if it had actually been fashioned by the hand of man it could not have been better adapted for the uses to which it had now been put.

Here and there along the sides, wherever the rocks jutted out sufficiently to form a shelf, a light had been placed, and as the captain had said, they were red and green and white, and the blended glow from all of them lent a strange and somewhat weird aspect to the place.

Next, there were the draperies which hung from the walls, and the rugs which covered the floor, as the captain had graphically described, a foot deep. And he had not been so far wrong at that, for they had been piled one upon another, possibly to keep out the natural dampness of the place.

And the couches and chairs scattered about the place, all evidently taken from ships at one time and another, gave it a cozy and homelike, yet half barbarous appearance which was particularly attractive.

But all this was as nothing compared to the general scene which met the eyes of the detective when he was conducted into the place.

It was evident to him at once that the company assembled there was awaiting him, and for an instant he felt as if he had suddenly been introduced into the saloon of some princess of the blood, as an ambassador from a foreign court.

There was not a man present save himself.

But there were women. Young women, evidently, all of them.

It is true that it was impossible to determine their ages from their appearance, since each and every one of them had her features concealed by the same form of half mask that he had noticed before; but if one were to judge from the figures and manners of the occupants of the room it was plain to be seen that they were little more than girls, after all.

But a still greater surprise than all this awaited him.

As he advanced into the room the one who was called Scylla rose in her place and bowed profoundly to him; and at the same time, in a mocking voice, she said:

"Welcome to the cavern of Scylla the Siren, Mr. Nicholas Carter."

CHAPTER IX.

IN THE CAVERN OF THE SEA ROBBERS.

The instant his own name was uttered, Nick Carter realized that he had gotten himself into a fix from which it would be no easy matter to escape.

But he did not permit a muscle of his face to depict the surprise he felt.

Instead, he stopped still in the middle of the room, and returning the bow, said in his own natural tones:

"Madam, permit me to compliment you upon your cleverness."

There was a general laugh around the room in response to this; and then Scylla said:

"You must have taken infinite pains in the manufacture of that disguise you are wearing, Mr. Carter. It is almost perfect."

"I did; I assure you I did," replied Nick. "But why do you qualify your compliment?"

"I said it was almost perfect."

"Exactly; and all the time I believed it to be quite perfect."

"Well," she said, and her eyes sparkled with humor through the holes of her mask, "you see it is not quite perfect, for the reason that I took good care to know where Capt. Staples went and what he did, as well as all that he did, when he went ashore yesterday. To have rendered your disguise perfect you should have provided against my obtaining all that information."

"Yes; I realize that now. In fact, I have realized it almost since the instant you came to me in the cabin of the *Phryne*."

"Then I wonder that you permitted yourself to be enticed here in the manner you did."

"You see," said Nick, in a tone that was half apologetic, "I was not sure; and then, again, you were so charming."

She laughed again at this; and a ripple of laughter went the round of the group—for there were twelve others of them there, as the captain had said.

"I wish I might entreat you to remove your mask," continued Nick, with scarcely a pause in his remarks.

Without a word of remonstrance she raised one hand and deftly took the mask from her face, standing there before him in the full revelation of her almost matchless beauty—for that she was a superbly beautiful woman was apparent at a glance.

It could not be said that she was dressed in the height of fashion unless one placed a period of time against that statement; indeed, it seemed to Nick almost as if he were in attendance upon a costume party, for there were no two of the women dressed alike.

Scylla herself was a reproduction of a Greek maiden—of another Parthenia, in fact; and among the others there were costumes representing almost every emphasized epoch in history, and in mythology as well.

But it was upon the queen of this assemblage that the eyes of the detective were fixed.

She had known well what manner of costume would become her best, and she had adopted it.

As she stood there before him, her lips parted in a half smile, her white teeth gleaming between them, her black, sloelike eyes sparkling with ill-concealed amusement, and with her beautiful and stately figure poised in an attitude of perfect, if unstudied, grace, she seemed the embodiment of personified beauty.

Nick had expected that she would at least demur to his request that she remove her mask, if she did not altogether refuse to do so, and he was agreeably surprised when, without the least hesitation, she did as he had asked.

He argued rather ill for it, too.

He could see in the act one of two things, neither of which argued in favor of his own safety.

The act assured him that these women had no fear that he would escape from them, or they believed that by reason of their charm, and their sex, they could prevail upon him to be merciful.

He could not believe that a lot of women—of beautiful women, too—would actually murder him in cold blood, and yet he was forced to admit to himself that some of the most heartless criminals he had ever encountered had been women.

And here was a group of them, banded together in crime.

Here was the mystic number of thirteen of them, professedly pirates of the sea, and therefore, perforce, robbers and possibly murderers as well, who had sought a retreat that was so cleverly hidden that it would defy discovery; and he was absolutely in their power.

True, he stood there before them, with his hands free, and every faculty on the alert; but he was unarmed.

But even had he been bristling with weapons, he realized that he could not have made use of them to fight his way out.

A man cannot fight a woman; a man will not fight a woman.

He may, on occasion, overpower her and force her to conform to his ideas of right, but he cannot engage in a combat against her as he would do against a man.

It might be said that all this passed through the brain of the detective in that instant which intervened between his request that Scylla remove her mask and the actual act on her part, and he caught his breath when her startling beauty was revealed to him so suddenly.

"You are beautiful—very beautiful," he said.

She smiled, and replied:

"The remark is not original. I have been told that before—by others."

"I have no doubt of it. The remark may not of itself be original, but it would not require much of a stretch of the imagination to say that you are the type of original beauty."

"You are almost as neat at turning compliments, Nick Carter, as you are in the matter of disguises," she said.

"Better, madam; there is no flaw in my remark; there was, in my disguise."

She laughed gleefully at that.

"I have removed my mask at your request," she said; "will you not wash away that hideous disguise to please me?"

"Certainly; if you have some alcohol, some cocoa butter, and a more fitting costume than this one, that I may adopt after I have made the old captain disappear."

"We have everything that you require," she replied. "Indeed, I anticipated this moment. If you will follow me, you will find everything that you require—here."

She stepped back and drew aside a curtain as she spoke, and Nick passed beyond it into a small room that had been curtained off from the larger one.

It was lighted brilliantly, and arranged around it Nick discovered everything that he required for the change he was to make, while across a chair rested a costume which needed only a glance to tell him that it represented the character of Sardanapalus.

Left to himself, he at once busied himself in making the changes, washing the pigments from his face, hands and arms, and removing the gray hair and whiskers which had so perfectly represented the old captain, but which had proven so utterly useless.

He was occupied all of half an hour in this manner, after which he donned the costume that had been provided for him; but he took care to place the cast-off garments that he had worn as the captain where he could find them again if it should happen that he required them, for he well knew that it was doubtless a part of their scheme that he could not go out from that cavern in the costume of a Sardanapalus without being subject to arrest as a lunatic, before he traveled a mile.

But when he returned to the larger room he was transformed.

Every vestige of the disguise had been removed, and his handsome face shone with the excitement of the adventure as he stepped out before his strange hostesses; nor could anything have been more becoming than the costume they had provided for him, for it set off the lines of his manly figure to perfection.

If he had been surprised when the queen of the sea robbers unmasked before him, it was her turn to evince astonishment; but she showed it merely by a deeper flush which suffused her beautiful face; as for the others, they were still masked, as Nick had first seen them.

He bowed low to them all with mock ceremoniousness.

"Will not the other ladies permit me to see their faces also?" he asked.

As if they had been only awaiting the request, twelve hands were raised to twelve masks, as with one motion, and they were removed; and the detective gazed upon them in amazement.

He had expected that among so many there would be at least one who could not lay claim to surpassing beauty; but here were thirteen young women before him, each more beautiful than any other one—if such a paradox were possible.

For a moment he was almost speechless, and then, with a sigh, he said:

"Years ago, when I was a boy, I read the story of the 'Roc's Egg,' and of the forty beautiful maidens who dwelt alone in a palace. I feel now as if I had stepped down into that scene in person."

"But here are only thirteen instead of forty," said Scylla the Siren.

"Ay; but all the beauty of the forty has been condensed into the thirteen," he retorted.

"You think, then, that you have fallen into good hands?" she asked.

"I know at least that I have fallen into fair hands."

"And do you not regard yourself as standing in danger, Mr. Carter?"

"Frankly, I never was in such imminent peril in my life. Being somewhat of a stoic, I might resist the fascinations of one; but of thirteen——"

"I am afraid that you are not entirely sincere."

"Heaven grant that I am not, for then I should surely fall a victim before you."

"You are incorrigible."

"I am also hungry, madam."

A peal of laughter replied to this sally, for they had quite forgotten that he had not been fed for hours, and, forthwith, cold chicken, some salad, wine, etc., were placed before him and he was bidden to eat and drink.

While he was thus engaged, Scylla waited upon him in person, and if we might have looked in upon the scene at that moment it might well have been thought to represent anything but what it really did.

"What disposition shall we make of you, Mr. Carter?" Scylla asked, when the detective's appetite was partly appeased.

"I might reply to that," he said, smiling, "if I were the sultan of Turkey, or at the head of the Mormon church."

She affected not to notice his reply, but continued:

"You are aware, of course, that we can never permit you to go free from this place without at least exacting a pledge of secrecy from you."

"Something of that sort has occurred to me, I will admit," he said.

"And are you prepared to make such a pledge?"

"You see," he replied, poising his fork as the leader of an orchestra might have used a baton, "I am for the moment literally between Scylla and Charybdis. I——"

"The time for facetiousness has passed, Mr. Carter. I am speaking in deadly earnest."

"Indeed?"

"Yes. Are you prepared to make us such a pledge?"

"Suppose I should say 'No'; what then?"

"It would be bad for you."

"May I ask in what manner it would be bad for me?"

"You would at once place yourself in imminent peril."

"Peril of what?"

"Of death, Mr. Carter."

"Do you mean that you would kill me?"

"I mean that you can never leave this tunnel alive without first having made the pledge I have demanded."

"Would you murder me?"

"That is an ugly word."

"But it has a clear meaning. There is no other word to express what I mean."

"You can never leave this place alive unless you swear a solemn oath never to reveal what you have seen here, what you know of us, or what you suspect concerning the locality of this place, and the business that I and my friends here follow."

"Then, if I refuse to take the oath, you will put me to death; eh? Is that it?"

"We cannot keep you here. That is evident. You cannot leave the place alive. You may draw your own conclusions."

Nick smiled into her eyes as he said, slowly:

"Death at the hands of one so beautiful as you might be a new form of ecstasy, Madame Scylla the Siren."

CHAPTER X.

THE DETECTIVE'S TERRIBLE PERIL.

The detective could see that the woman was in deadly earnest.

He could discern, moreover, that she was troubled; as if the necessity which the presence of the detective put upon her was not a welcome one by any means.

"You give me the choice between death and dishonor," he said, quietly.

"Do you regard it as stultifying your honor to refuse to betray a woman? Or, rather, thirteen women?" she asked, calmly.

"I must reply to that question by asking another," he said.

"Well, what is it?"

"Do you not think that you voluntarily put yourself outside the pale of womanhood, in so far as it can lay claim to the protection of man, when you adopt a profession such as you have done?"

"That is neither here nor there," she replied.

"Oh, yes it is. Very much here and there, both."

"I must still insist upon an answer to my question."

"Then I must reply that to me you are only sea robbers here. I can recognize no sex in the performance of my duty."

"And you consider that duty to be to hound me and my friends to prison, do you?"

"I consider it my duty to place all malefactors beyond the power to commit further trespass upon the laws of the land, when it is in my power to do so," he said.

"You have said that I am beautiful, Mr. Carter."

"And I have no hesitation in repeating that statement, madam."

"Would you condemn my beauty to a prison cell?"

"If it were necessary in the pursuit of my calling—yes."

"And, likewise, these twelve friends and followers of mine?"

"Likewise all of them."

"You would not take an oath to blot out from your recollection all the experiences you have met with since yesterday?"

"I could not."

"If we release you, and permit you to go from here free, do I understand that you will at once begin a campaign against us?"

"Such would be my plain duty."

"That is not the question. The question is would you do so?"

"I most certainly would do so."

"Then, Nick Carter, you must die."

"It is not the first time, or the only time when that remark has been made to me, madam, and frequently it has been said under much more trying circumstances than this."

"But it has never been said to you with more deadly earnestness, sir."

"I will grant that you mean it. What then?"

"What then? There can be but one thing after that?"

"And that is——"

"You might call it the fulfillment of the prophecy."

"You will put me to death?"

"Yes."

"How?"

"Does it matter how, Mr. Carter?"

"Ay," he said, laughing into her troubled eyes—for they were troubled, and he saw it; and for reasons of his own he thought it wise at this moment to anger her if possible, since through anger only did he believe that he could induce her to talk more plainly of her intentions.

"Ay," he repeated, "you might smother me with kisses; that would be an ecstatic death. Or you and your twelve friends might take turns at the execution, and the ecstasy would then be twelvefold greater."

She looked at him a moment without replying; and then, quite calmly, she said:

"Mr. Carter, if I did not know that you do not mean that remark as it sounds, you would have accomplished your purpose in making it, and I would be angry. As it is, you have only needlessly hurt me."

"Then I will beg your pardon. There are moments when you make me forget what you are, and I remember only that you are a young and a beautiful woman; and there are other moments when I cannot help recalling the fact that you are—or profess to be—a siren, a sea robber, a criminal and a thief."

She flushed angrily, but he went on, imperturbably:

"Those are harsh words, doubtless, but they are true ones. A thief is a thief, despite the costume or the sex; and this assemblage here is nothing more nor less than a gang of thieves, is it not?"

"Have your way if you will."

"It is more than that, madam. It is a gang of thieves

which is about to resolve itself into a gang of murderers. There are no two ways about that, are there?"

While this dialogue was taking place the remaining twelve of the women had grouped themselves behind their queen, and Nick found it rather a difficult task to retain his composure with thirteen pairs of eyes fixed intently upon his face, and each pair with a different expression.

He could read hate in some of them; in others, sadness; in others, regret; and collectively they represented the whole gamut of emotions.

But not in one pair of eyes among them all did he discover the requisite friendly glance which could be relied upon to undertake to free him from his peril.

And it was at this point in their conversation that Scylla rose from the chair she had occupied opposite him, and, turning to the others, drew them aside.

Nick, perceiving that they were about to discuss him, and doubtless also the manner in which he would be put to death, pretended to attack again the food that had been placed before him.

But it was only pretense.

He knew that the time had come for him to act if, indeed, he acted at all, to save himself from the consequences of the danger in which he stood.

He had kept his eyes busy while he talked with Scylla, but, although he had looked everywhere, he had been unable to decide where the beautiful sea robbers kept their weapons.

That there were plenty of them in the cavern, he did not doubt; and at last he fixed upon a huge sea chest, inlaid with gold and silver, that stood at one side of the apartment, as being the repository for them.

Now, as they drew aside and conversed together in low tones, of which he could catch no word at all, and while he pretended again to be interested only in the food and drink that had been placed before him, he was in reality gathering himself for a leap toward that chest.

He calculated to a nicety the instant when he made the spring, and he figured that if he was only correct in his conjecture, and the chest were not locked, that he would soon be in a position at least to defy these strange, if beautiful, women.

And then he made the leap.

With a sudden move he threw the chair to the floor behind him, and sprang toward the chest.

He reached it even as they turned toward him, and he threw the lid back as Scylla herself started forward to intercept him.

He had been right.

One glance inside convinced him of that, for it was half filled with a collection of pistols and swords, rapiers and cutlasses.

He seized two of the weapons; a long, slender, gleaming rapier in his right hand, and a business-like-looking revolver in his left hand.

He did not know whether it was loaded or not, and he did not much care, for he had no idea of making use of the firearm for more than intimidation.

It was the rapier upon which he depended, for he was master of the art of its use, and he knew that with it in his hand he could play with the women, and drive them into one corner of the cavern without inflicting any injury upon any of them which would be worthy of the name.

But he had to do with women who were vastly different from any that he had ever met before.

He remembered, for that moment, only that they were women; but now he was speedily to discover that they were more—that they were what he had called them—criminals; and that they were desperate and fearless.

When Scylla perceived that the detective had succeeded in possessing himself of the weapons, she laughed aloud, and, with a bound, returned to her place beside her followers.

Then she uttered a sharp command, and the result was that in that instant each one of them raised her right hand, and Nick found that he was looking into the muzzles of thirteen revolvers.

He had not expected them to be so fully prepared, but he laughed aloud when he saw how ready they were to meet him halfway.

"Drop those weapons instantly!" said Scylla, coldly, to him; but he only laughed at her, standing on his guard with the rapier firmly grasped in his right hand.

"Put down those weapons!" she repeated.

"I will not," replied Nick. "What do you suppose I possessed myself of them for?"

"Not to use against women, Nick Carter. I think that I know you too well for that."

"You have ceased to be women in my estimation, now. You are only thieves and murderers."

"Beware, Nick Carter! You may wag that tongue of yours too freely."

Nick smiled at her derisively.

"I repeat," he said; "you are only thieves and murderers."

"Put down those weapons."

"I will not."

"Then I shall give the order to fire."

"Do so. It will be as easy a death as any other; but I also think that I know you too well for that. You have selected some choicer method of putting me out of the way than by the use of bullets."

She smiled at him in derision.

"Even if we were all unarmed; even if there were no impediment in your way, you could not escape from this cavern,' said Scylla. "You could never find your way out of it."

"That remains to be seen," replied the detective. "I have found my way out of worse places than this before now."

"Will you drop those weapons?"

"No."

"Are you determined to die?"

"You seem to be determined to kill me. Why don't you do it?"

"Nick Carter, listen to me. It goes very much against us to put you to death. That is the matter we were discussing just now when you interrupted us."

"I suppose I should consider that a very kind act on your part; eh?"

"You have but to take that oath I asked you to do, and you will be set free."

"But that is out of the question."

"Why do you force us to this act?"

"I might reply by asking you why you brought me here?"

"To force you to take the oath."

"And that you will never succeed in doing."

"Is that your last answer?"

"Yes. It is."

"You have thought well over the consequences?"

"Oh, yes; but I am tired of discussing it with you."

"You do not think that I will dare to kill you, perhaps?"

"I think you would dare almost anything, Scylla."

"For the last time, do you refuse to take the oath?"

"I do," he replied.

"Fire!" she said, wheeling and facing her followers; and the twelve revolvers blazed out upon him with a detonation that was deafening.

CHAPTER XI.

THE EXECUTION OF THE SENTENCE.

The detective had not expected the sudden order to fire.

In reality, he believed that the attitude of Scylla was more of a bluff than anything else, and in this idea he was presently to find that he was correct, although in a different manner than he had anticipated.

If he had expected the women to fire so soon, he could have done nothing to escape the effect of the bullets—had there been bullets in the cartridges.

But as it happened there were none there.

The twelve revolvers that had been leveled at him, and that had been fired almost in his face, were loaded with blank cartridges, placed there for that especial purpose—to intimidate him.

But if they were not loaded, they had almost as much an effect upon the detective as if they were.

The women, when they fired the revolvers, were not more than ten feet away from him, and the twelve weapons, being exploded at once almost in his face, sending sheets of flame toward him as they did, created a shock which was in a sense almost as startling as the impact of bullets against his body might have been.

He was thrown down, flat on his back, as if he had been hit by a club, and in that instant, although he was actually unharmed, he felt as if every hair on his head had been burned off, and as if the drums of his ears had burst.

But if he was not prepared for what actually occurred, the women were.

The instant they fired their revolvers, they leaped forward, and the detective was no sooner on his back where he had fallen than a blanket was thrown over him, and it seemed to him as if the entire twelve of his assailants piled themselves on top of him at once.

Struggle he did, but his efforts were as fruitless as if he had been held down by so many giants.

The blanket that had been thrown over him impeded the use of his arms and legs and he was practically helpless in their hands.

Nor did it take them long to bind him so that he was rendered entirely so.

Considering the fact that they were women, they were possessed of prodigious strength, and presently, when they drew away from him, he had been triced up in a manner that would have excited the envy of Capt. Staples himself.

They placed him, then, none too gently in the chair he had lately occupied; and then, once more, they grouped themselves at the other side of the table in the positions they had occupied while he was engaged in consuming his luncheon.

"You perceive," said Scylla, coldly, "that women can act when the occasion arises to do so, Nick Carter."

"I will have to admit that you are right about that."

"You are now a helpless prisoner."

"Isn't that the condition that has existed since you brought me here?" he asked.

"Yes. Shall I ask you again if you will take the oath we require of you?"

"It is unnecessary. The reply would be the same."

Scylla turned and motioned silently to one of her companions, who disengaged herself from the group; but she returned after a moment with a bandage in her hands, which, without preamble, she proceeded at once to bind tightly over the eyes of the detective.

"Am I not to have the honor of witnessing the manner of my death?" asked the detective.

"Not even that; but you will know soon enough how it is to be consummated."

"Am I to be drawn and quartered? Shot to death? Stabbed? Choked? Smothered? Bled? Or what is your barbarous notions of such enterprises?"

"You are to be drowned," she said, coldly.

Nick felt that a shudder passed through him, although he did not permit it to manifest itself to them.

"Drowned?" he repeated after her.

"Yes."

"I have heard that drowning is not an unpleasant experience, after the first swallow of water."

"You shall have an opportunity to make certain about that presently."

"Drowned, eh? In the bay?"

"Yes."

"When?"

"Now."

Again she signaled to her followers, and now several of them approached him.

They raised him from the chair in their arms. Others brought a rude sort of a stretcher forward from one corner of the room and the detective was placed upon it.

He could see nothing, of course, but he presently felt that they raised him from the floor and that a solemn march was begun toward one end of the cavern—the end, he thought, by which he had first been brought into the place.

Again he heard the iron doors open before them.

Again he was taken through a short corridor, and then he was lifted from the stretcher by two of the women, and carried down the winding, spiral stairway to the bottom.

That reached, the stretcher was again brought into use, and he knew by the odor of the place as they proceeded that they were once more traversing that tunnel where the mud and slime still covered the bottom of it.

He could not doubt now that they had meant what they said.

He recalled the strange method by which they had entered the place; from a boat into something that rocked and swayed with their weight when they entered it, and he wondered what sort of a place or contrivance it could be.

"At least," he thought, as they proceeded, "they will find it difficult to carry me to the top of that rope ladder, and, if I refuse to climb, it may place them at some inconvenience."

But nothing of the kind occurred.

When they arrived at the end of the tunnel and the last iron doors had been opened and they had passed through them, the stretcher was set down for a moment, and then he felt that a rope was being passed under his arms.

Presently he knew that some of them were mounting the ladder, and after a little he felt the rope tighten against his body, and then he was lifted into the air and borne swiftly upward.

"Humph!" he thought. "They got around that difficulty without much trouble. I wonder now what will happen next?"

Again he felt that he was inside the swaying, moving, rocking thing which defied all his imagination to guess what it might be, and again he had that experience of indefinite seasickness that he had felt before.

Then, suddenly, a light broke upon his reasoning powers.

It came to him when he heard what sounded like the opening of an iron hatch above his head.

"By all the powers!" he thought to himself, "I believe on my word that we are inside a huge government buoy.

A buoy which these people have somehow managed to connect with the old tunnel. It seems impossible, but it must be true. It is the only way in which this strange experience can be explained."

But he was not given time for further conjecture.

The cold voice of Scylla the Siren broke in upon his reflections.

"Do you know where you are?" she asked.

"I should imagine that I am inside a big buoy which I know is located near——"

"You know altogether too much, Nick Carter."

"Yes. I suppose so; for your good, you mean."

He felt that some article was being tied to his legs; but she continued to talk while it was being done.

"There is a hundred pound of iron fast to your feet now," she said.

"I perceive that you have fastened something to me."

"In a moment we shall drop you into the water. It is forty feet deep here."

"That should be sufficient, I think."

"You will keep guard, hereafter, at the base of this shaft."

"A silent guard, eh?"

"A dead guard."

"Will you not do me the favor to take the bandage from my eyes before you cast me into the water, in order that I may have one more look at your face, Scylla?"

Without replying in words, she tore the bandage from his eyes, and he saw in that instant that she was alone with him; that her companions had disappeared.

The next, he felt himself sliding toward the brink.

He could offer no resistance whatever, for he was firmly bound.

Then there came a sudden lurch. He slipped from the buoy and glided downward into the sea, while the waters closed over him.

And the last that he saw as he disappeared were the eyes of Scylla the Siren gazing, with a strange expression, into his own.

CHAPTER XII.

A DARING RESCUE.

The detective had in a measure prepared himself for the ordeal.

He had drawn in a full breath of air, and his lungs were well filled when he was so suddenly precipitated into the water.

As he felt himself going down, down, down into the depths, he sought with all his strength to tear his hands loose from the cords which held them, and so to free himself from the terrible weight that was dragging him down.

But the effort was utterly futile.

Strive as he might, he could accomplish nothing whatever, and as he descended and the pressure of the water became heavier against him, he gave himself up for lost.

The descent was, of course, rapid, with the hundred pounds of iron fastened to his feet, and he touched the bottom much sooner than he expected, if indeed the depth was as great as he had been told.

All the time he kept his eyes open, looking upward at the light he was leaving; for it was yet daylight outside, and he could see through the water as it closed over his head that the sun was shining brightly.

And then he saw something more.

He saw a flash of glistening color cleave the waters over him.

For one instant he believed that it was the belly of a shark that had witnessed the execution and was about to play a part in it.

But he knew that no shark could be arrayed in such resplendent colors.

The thing, whatever it was, came nearer. Indeed it seemed to approach with the rapidity of a fish, and then he saw that it was a human being.

More; it was a woman.

Still more, it was a woman arrayed as he had first seen Scylla in the cabin of the ship *Phryne*.

Was it Scylla? He could not answer that, though, in the imperfect light that was afforded him. He only knew that it was a woman; that it was one of the women he had seen in the cavern in the cliffs; that for some reason she was swimming toward him.

For what purpose?

He could not answer that, either.

Doubtless it was to make sure that he did not escape from the bonds that held him, to rise to the surface and to menace the safety of the thirteen women of the cavern.

All this happened during a few seconds; but nevertheless he felt that he was rapidly arriving at a point where he could not hold his breath longer, and when he must permit his mouth to open and the water to rush in and strangle him.

Then the form of the woman, arrayed in the glistening scales of her costume, glided directly to him.

He felt that she touched him.

More, he could feel that she was engaged in doing something that was foreign to what he had expected, for her hand glided along his body until suddenly he felt the weight leave his legs as if by magic, and instantly his body shot upward again toward the surface.

Even as it did so, the woman again used her knife, and this time she severed the cords that held his wrists, and in that instant he was free indeed.

He made a motion to strike out with his hands, but he felt that she was pulling him, and with a heroic effort he determined to hold his breath a little longer, even if his lungs should burst, and he followed her.

The rapidity with which all this happened must be taken into account in order to understand how it could have occurred, for it was only a second or two after that when he found that he was at the surface of the water, clinging to the sides of the buoy, and that his rescuer was beside him.

That draught of sweet air that he took in then was delicious; but he managed to gasp:

"You are Scylla, and you have saved me!"

She made no reply in words, but she motioned to him to follow her, and then she swam around to the opposite side of the buoy.

In a moment more they were upon it.

In another she had made use of a key that was fastened around her neck by a small gold chain, and in the next, she had unlocked the trapdoor in the buoy.

He clung to the sides of the place, looking down into the depths of the shaft at the rope ladder that had so deeply mystified him; and when he turned again toward his companion, to question her, she had disappeared.

He rubbed his eyes and looked again, but she was gone; and he was clinging there to the buoy, with the way open to him to the cavern of the sea robbers.

But he had no thought of that in that instant. It was of Scylla that he thought, if indeed the woman were Scylla, which he now doubted, although the resemblance between them was strong.

He released his hold upon the buoy and permitted himself to sink again into the water, but, although he looked and searched in every direction, he could discover no sign of his mysterious rescuer.

After a little he turned his attention again to the trapdoor in the buoy, and he saw that the key to it was still in the lock, and that the woman had wrenched it free from the chain in order to leave it there.

Her reason for doing so was obvious.

He closed the door again and locked it, and then, being thoroughly rested from his terrifying experience, he permitted himself to glide back again into the water, after which he struck out for the shore.

* * * * * * *

It was midnight when Nick Carter returned again to that floating buoy, but this time he was differently dressed, and there were a dozen men with him in the boat that took him there.

The night was not a dark one, and it was not difficult to find the buoy; nor to enter it when it was once found.

The detective led the way down the ladder.

The iron doors at the foot of the shaft, which he had heard opened when he was conducted there, were not locked, and he had no difficulty in opening them, and thus, followed by the men who were with him, he made his way along the gallery, through the remaining doors, and up the spiral staircase to the top.

At the last door, before entering the cavern room where he had met with such a strange experience, he paused long enough to give the last directions to his men, and then suddenly he thrust the door open and appeared upon the threshold.

The sea robbers—the twelve beautiful women, for he noticed in the first glance that one of them was absent—were seated around the table, evidently at dinner.

The surprise was complete.

It is true that they leaped to their feet, but only to confront Nick and his men, and to realize that resistance was useless.

"You see," said Nick to Scylla, for it was she who stood first in front of him, "that, in spite of all, I have returned."

"Yes," she replied, scornfully, "aided by a traitor. You see there are only twelve of us now. The thirteenth—my sister—proved a traitor. We should have been gone from here in an hour, Nick Carter."

"And you *will* be gone from here in an hour," he replied, grimly.

THE END.

The next title will be "The Beautiful Pirate of Oyster Bay; or, Nick Carter's Strangest Adventure."

Vol. I. Single Number. BEADLE AND ADAMS, PUBLISHERS, No. 98 WILLIAM STREET, NEW YORK. Price, 5 Cents. No. 1

Deadwood Dick,
THE PRINCE OF THE ROAD;
OR,
THE BLACK RIDER of the BLACK HILLS.

BY EDWARD L. WHEELER.

CHAPTER I.
FEARLESS FRANK TO THE RESCUE.

ON the plains, midway between Cheyenne and the Black Hills, a train had halted for a noonday feed. Not a railway train, mind you, but a line of those white-covered vehicles drawn by strong-limbed mules, which are most properly styled "prairie schooners."

There were four wagons of this type, and they had been drawn in a circle about a camp-fire, over which was roasting a savory haunch of venison. Around the camp-fire were grouped half a score of men, all rough, bearded, and grizzled, with one exception. This being a youth whose age one could have safely put at twenty, so perfectly developed of physique and intelligent of facial appearance was he. There was something about him that was not handsome, and yet you would have been puzzled to tell what it was, for his countenance was strikingly handsome, and surely no form in the crowd was more noticeable for its grace, symmetry, and proportionate development. It would have taken a scholar to have studied out the secret.

He was of about medium stature, and as straight and square-shouldered as an athlete. His complexion was nut-brown, from long exposure to the sun; hair of hue of the raven's wing, and hanging in long, straight strands adown his back; eyes black and piercing as an eagle's; features well molded, with a firm, resolute mouth and prominent chin. He was an interesting specimen of young, healthy manhood, and, even though a youth in years, was one that could command respect, if not admiration, wheresoever he might choose to go.

One remarkable item about his personal appearance, apt to strike the beholder as being exceedingly strange and eccentric, was his costume—buckskin throughout, and that dyed to the brightest scarlet hue.

On being asked the cause of his odd freak of dress, when he had joined the train a few miles out from Cheyenne, the youth had laughingly replied:

"Why, you see, it is to attract buffers, if we should meet any, out on the plains 'twixt this and the Hills."

He gave his name as Fearless Frank, and said he was aiming for the Hills; that if the party in question would furnish him a place among them, he would extend to them his assistance as a hunter, guide, or whatever, until the destination was reached.

Seeing that he was well armed, and judging from external appearances that he would prove a valuable accessory, the miners were nothing loth in accepting his services.

Of the others grouped about the camp-fire only one is specially noticeable, for, as Mark Twain remarks, "the average of gold-diggers look alike." This person was a little, deformed old man; humpbacked, bow-legged, and white-haired, with cross eyes, a large mouth, a big head, set upon a slim, crane-like neck; blue eyes, and an immense brown beard, that flowed downward half-way to the belt about his waist, which contained a small arsenal of knives and revolvers. He hobbled about with a heavy crutch constantly under his left arm, and was certainly a pitiable sight to behold.

He too had joined the caravan after it had quitted Cheyenne, his advent taking place about an hour subsequent to that of Fearless Frank. His name he asserted was Nix—Geoffrey Walsingham Nix—and where he came from, and what he sought in the Black Hills, was simply a matter of conjecture among the miners, as he refused to talk on the subject of his past, present or future.

The train was under the command of an irascible old plainsman who had served out his apprenticeship in the Kansas border war, and whose name was Charity Joe, which, considering his avaricious disposition, was the wrong handle on the wrong man. Charity was the least of all old Joe's redeeming characteristics; charity was the very thing he did not recognize, yet some wag had facetiously branded him Charity Joe, and the appellation had clung to him ever since. He was well advanced in years, yet withal a good trailer and an expert guide, as the success of his many late expeditions into the Black Hills had evidenced.

Those who had heard of Joe's skill as a guide, intrusted themselves in his care, for, while the stages were stopped more or less on each trip, Charity Joe's train invariably went through all safe and sound. This was partly owing to his acquaintance with various bands of Indians, who were the chief cause of annoyance on the trip.

So far we see the train toward the land of gold, without their having seen sight or sound of hostile red-skins, and Charity is just chuckling over his usual good luck:

"I tell ye what, fellers, we've hed a fa'r sort uv a shake, so fur, an' no mistake 'bout it. Barrin' thar ain't no Sittin' Bulls layin' in wait fer us, behead yander, in ther mounts, I'm of ther candid opinion we'll get through wi'out scrapin' a ha'r."

"I hope so," said Fearless Frank, rolling over on the grass and gazing at the guide, thoughtfully, "but I doubt it. It seems to me that one hears of more butchering, lately, than there was a month ago—all on account of the influx of ruffianly characters into the Black Hills!"

"Not all owing to that, chippy," interposed "General" Nix, as he had immediately been christened by the miners—"not all owing to that. Thar's them gol danged copper-colored guests uv ther government—they're kickin' up three pints uv the'r rumpus, more or less—consider'bly less of more than more o' less. Take a passel uv them barbarities an' shet 'em up inter a prison for three or thirteen yeers, an' ye'd see w'at an impression et'd make, now. Thar'd be siveral less massycrees a week, an' ye wouldn't see a rufyan onc't a month W'y, gentlefellows, thar'd never yar been a ruffian, ef et hedn't been fer ther cussed Injun tribe—not one! Ther infarnal critters ar' ther instigators uv more deviltry nor a cat wi' nine tails."

"Yes, we will admit that the reds are not of saintly origin," said Fearless Frank, with a quiet smile. "In fact I know of several who are far from being angels, myself. There is old Sitting Bull, for instance, and Lone Lion, Rain-in-the-Face, and Horse-with-the-Red-Eye, and so forth, and so forth!"

"Exactly. Every one o' 'em's a danged descendant o' ther old Satan, hisself."

"Layin' aside ther Injun subjeck," said Charity Joe, forking into the roasted venison, "I move thet we take up a silent debate on the

Ha! ha! ha! isn't that rich, now? Ha! ha! ha! arrest Deadwood Dick if you can!

pecooliarities uv a deer's hind legs; so heer goes!"

He cut out a huge slice with his bowie, sprinkled it over with salt, and began to devour it by very large mouthfuls. All hands proceeded to follow his example, and the noonday meal was dispatched in silence. After each man had fully satisfied his appetite and the mules and Fearless Frank's horse had grazed until they were full as ticks, the order was given to hitch up, which was speedily done, and the caravan was soon in motion, toiling along like a diminutive serpent across the plain.

The afternoon was a mild, sunny one in early autumn, with a refreshing breeze perfumed with the delicate scent of after-harvest flowers wafting down from the cool regions of the Northwest, where lay the new El Dorado—the land of gold.

Fearless Frank bestrode a noble bay steed of fire and nerve, while old General Nix rode an extra mule that he had purchased of Charity Joe. The remainder of the company rode in the wagons or "hoofed it," as best suited their mood—walking sometimes being preferable to the rumbling and jolting of the heavy vehicles.

Steadily along through the afternoon sunlight the train wended its way, the teamsters alternately singing and cursing their mules, as they jogged along. Fearless Frank and the "General" rode several hundred yards in advance, both apparently engrossed in deepest thought, for neither spoke until, toward the close of the afternoon, Charity Joe called their attention to a series of low, faint cries brought down upon their nearing by the stiff northerly wind.

"'Pears to me as how them sound sorter human like," said the old guide, trotting along beside the young man's horse, as he made known the discovery. "Jes' listen, now, an' see if ye ain't uv ther same opinion!"

The youth did listen, and at the same time swept the plain with his eagle eyes, in search of the object from which the cries emanated. But nothing of animal life was visible in any direction beyond the train, and more was the mystery, since the cries sounded but a little way off.

"They *are* human cries!" exclaimed Fearless Frank, excitedly, "and come from some one in distress. Boys, we must investigate this matter."

"You can investigate all ye want," grunted Charity Joe, "but I hain't a-goin' ter stop ther train till dusk, squawk or no squawk. I jedge we won't get inter their Hills any too soon, as it ar'."

"You're an old fool!" retorted Frank, contemptuously. "I wouldn't be as mean as you for all the gold in the Black Hills country, say nothin' about that in California and Colorado."

He turned his horse's head toward the north, and rode away, followed, to the wonder of all, by the "General."

"Ha! ha!" laughed Charity Joe, grimly, "I wish you success."

"You needn't; I do not want any of your wishes. I'm going to search for the person who makes them cries, an' ef you don't want to wait, why go to the deuce with your old train!"

"There ye err," shouted the guide; "I'm goin' ter Deadwood, instead uv ter the deuce."

"*Maybe* you will go to Deadwood, and then, again, maybe ye won't," answered back Fearless Frank.

"More or less!" chimed in the general—"consider'bly more of less than less of more. Look out thet ther allies uv Sittin' Bull don't git ther *dead wood* on ye."

On marched the train—steadily on over the level, sandy plain, and Fearless Frank and his strange companion turned their attention to the cries that had been the means of separating them from the train. They had ceased now, altogether, and the two men were at a loss what to do.

"Guv a whoop, like a Government Injun," suggested "General" Nix; "an' thet'll let tner critter know thet we be friends a-comin'. Par'ps she'm g'in out ontirely, a-thinkin' as no one war a-comin' ter her resky!"

"She, you say?"

"Yas, she; fer I calkylate 'twern't no *he* as made them squawks. Sing out like a bellerin' bull, now, an' et ar' more or less likely—consider'bly more of less 'n less of more—that she will respond!"

Fearless Frank laughed, and forming his hands into a trumpet he gave vent to a loud, ear-splitting "hello!" that made the prairies ring.

"Great whale uv Joner!" gasped the "General," holding his hands toward the region of his organs of hearing. "Holy Mother o' Mercy! don't do et ag'in, b'yee—don' do et; ye've smashed my tinpanam all inter flinders! Good heaven! ye hev got a bugle wus nor enny steam tooter frum heer tew Lowell."

"Hark!" said the youth, bending forward in a listening attitude.

The next instant silence prevailed, and the twain anxiously listened. Wafted down across the plain came in faint piteous accents the repetition of the cry they had first heard, only it was now much fainter. Evidently whoever was in distress, was weakening rapidly. Soon the cries would be inaudible.

"It's straight ahead!" exclaimed Fearless Frank, at last. "Come along, and we'll soon see what the matter is!"

He put the spurs to his spirited animal, and the next instant was dashing wildly off over the sunlit plain. Bent on emulation, the "General" also used his heels with considerable vim, but alas! what dependence can be placed on a mule? The animal bolted, with a vicious nip back at the offending rider's legs, and refused to budge an inch.

On—on dashed the fearless youth, mounted on his noble steed, his eyes bent forward, in a sharp scrutiny of the plain ahead, his mind filled with wonder that the cries were now growing more distinct, and yet not a first glimpse could he obtain of the source whence they emanated.

On—on—on; then suddenly he reins his steed back upon its haunches, just in time to avert a frightful plunge into one of those remarkable freaks of nature—the blind canal, or, in other words, a channel valley washed out by heavy rains. These the tourist will frequently encounter in the regions contiguous to the Black Hills.

Below him yawned an abrupt channel, a score or more of feet in depth, at the bottom of which was a dense chaparral thicket. The little valley thus nestled in the earth was about forty rods in width, and one would never have dreamed it existed, unless they chanced to ride to the brink, above.

Fearless Frank took in the situation at a glance, and not hearing the cries, he rightly conjectured that the one in distress had again become exhausted. That that person was in the thicket below seemed more than probable, and he immediately resolved to descend in search. Slipping from his saddle, he stepped forward to the very edge of the precipice and looked over. The next second the ground crumbled beneath his feet, and he was precipitated headlong into the valley. Fortunately he received no serious injuries, and in a moment was on his feet again, all right.

"A miss is as good as a mile," he muttered, brushing the dirt from his clothing. "Now, then, we will find out the secret of the racket in this thicket."

Glancing up to the brink above to see that his horse was standing quietly, he parted the shrubbery, and entered the thicket.

It required considerable pushing and tugging to get through the dense undergrowth, but at last his efforts were rewarded, and he stood in a small break or glade.

Stood there, to behold a sight that made the blood boil in his veins. Securely bound with her face toward a stake, was a young girl—a maiden of perhaps seventeen summers, whom, at a single glance, one might surmise was remarkably pretty.

She was stripped to the waist, and upon her snow-white back were numerous welts from which trickled diminutive rivulets of crimson. Her head was dropped against the stake to which she was bound, and she was evidently insensible.

With a cry of astonishment and indignation Fearless Frank leaped forward to sever her bonds, when like so many grim phantoms there filed out of the chaparral, and circled around him, a score of hideously painted savages. One glance at the portly leader satisfied Frank as to his identity. It was the fiend incarnate—Sitting Bull!

CHAPTER II.

DEADWOOD DICK, THE ROAD-AGENT.

"**$500 Reward:** For the apprehension and arrest of a notorious young desperado who hails to the name of Deadwood Dick. His present whereabouts are somewhat contiguous to the Black Hills. For further information, and so forth, apply immediately to HUGH VANSEVERE,

"At Metropolitan Saloon, Deadwood City."

Thus read a notice posted up against a big pine tree, three miles above Custer City, on the banks of French creek. It was a large placard tacked up in plain view of all passers-by who took the route north through Custer gulch in order to reach the infant city of the Northwest—Deadwood.

Deadwood! the scene of the most astonishing bustle and activity, this year (1877.) The place where men are literally made rich and poor in one day and night. Prior to 1877 the Black Hills have been for a greater part undeveloped, but now, what a change! In Deadwood districts every foot of available ground has been "claimed" and staked out; the population has increased from fifteen to more than twenty-five hundred souls.

The streets are swarming with constantly arriving new-comers; the stores and saloons are literally crammed at all hours; dance-houses and can-can dens exist; hundreds of eager, expectant, and hopeful miners are working in the mines, and the harvest reaped by them is not at all discouraging. All along the gulch are strung a profusion of cabins, tents and shanties, making Deadwood in reality a town of a dozen miles in length, though some enterprising individual has paired off a couple more infant cities above Deadwood proper, named respectively Elizabeth City and Ten Strike. The quartz formation in these neighborhoods is something extraordinary, and from late reports, under vigorous and earnest development are yielding beyond the most sanguine expectation.

The placer mines west of Camp Crook are being opened to very satisfactory results, and, in fact, from Custer City in the south, to Deadwood in the north, all is the scene of abundant enthusiasm and excitement.

A horseman riding north through Custer gulch, noticed the placard so prominently posted for public inspection, and with a low whistle, expressive of astonishment, wheeled his horse out of the stage road, and rode over to the foot of the tree in question, and ran his eyes over the few irregularly-written lines traced upon the notice.

He was a youth of an age somewhere between sixteen and twenty, trim and compactly built, with a preponderance of muscular development and animal spirits; broad and deep of chest, with square, iron-cast shoulders; limbs small yet like bars of steel, and with a grace of position in the saddle rarely equaled; he made a fine picture for an artist's brush or a poet's pen.

Only one thing marred the captivating beauty of the picture.

His form was clothed in a tight-fitting habit of buck-skin, which was colored a jetty black, and presented a striking contrast to anything one sees as a garment in the wild far West. And this was not all, either. A broad black hat was slouched down over his eyes; he wore a thick black vail over the upper portion of his face, through the eye-holes of which there gleamed a pair of orbs of piercing intensity, and his hands, large and knotted, were hidden in a pair of kid gloves of a light color.

The "Black Rider" he might have been justly termed, for his thoroughbred steed was as black as coal, but we have not seen fit to call him such—his name is Deadwood Dick, and let that suffice for the present.

It was just at the edge of evening that he stopped before, and proceeded to read, the placard posted upon the tree in one of the loneliest portions of Custer's gulch.

Above and on either side rose to a stupendous hight the tree-fringed mountains in all their majestic grandeur.

In front and behind, running nearly north and south, lay the deep, dark chasm—a rift between mighty walls—Custer's gulch.

And over all began to hover the cloak of night, for the sun had already imparted its dying kiss on the mountain craters, and below, the gloom was thickening with rapid strides.

Slowly, over and over, Deadwood Dick, outlaw, road-agent and outcast, read the notice, and then a wild sardonic laugh burst from beneath his mask—a terrible, blood-curdling laugh, that made even the powerful animal he bestrode start and prick up its ears.

"Five hundred dollars reward for the apprehension and arrest of a notorious young desperado who hails to the name of Deadwood Dick! Ha! ha! ha! isn't that rich, now? Ha! ha! ha! *arrest* Deadwood Dick! Why, 'pon my word it is a sight for sore eyes. I was not aware that I had attained such a desperate notoriety as that document implies. They will make me out a murderer before they get through, I expect. Can't let me alone—everlastingly they must be punching after me, as if I was some obnoxious pestilence on the face of the earth. Never mind, though—let 'em keep on! Let them just continue their hounding game, and see which comes up on top when the bag's shook. If more than one of 'em don't get their fingers burned when they snatch Deadwood Dick bald-headed, why I'm a Spring creek sucker, that's all. Maybe I don't know who foots the bill in this reward business; oh, no; maybe I can't ride down to Deadwood and frighten three kind o' ideas out of this Mr. Hugh Vansevere, whoever he may be. Ha! ha! the fool that h'isted that notice didn't *know* Deadwood Dick, or he would never have placed his life in jeopardy by performing an act so uninteresting to the party in question. Hugh Vansevere; let me see—I don't think I've got that registered in my collection of appellatives. Perhaps he is a new tool in the employ of the old mechanic."

Darker and thicker grew the night shadows. The after-harvest moon rose up to a sufficient hight to send a silvery bolt of powerful light down into the silent gulch; like an image carved out of the night the horse and rider stood before the placard, motionless, silent.

The head of Deadwood Dick was bent, and he was buried in a deep reverie. A reverie that engrossed his whole attention for a long, long while; then the impatient pawing of his horse aroused him, and he sat once more erect in his saddle.

A last time his eyes wandered over the notice on the tree—a last time his terrible laugh made the mountains ring, and he guided his horse back into the rough, uneven stage-road, and galloped off up the gulch.

"I will go and see what this Hugh Vansevere looks like!" he said, applying the spurs to his horse. "I'll be dashed if I want him to be so numerous with my name, especially with five hundred dollars affixed thereto, as a reward."

Midnight.

Camp Crook, nestling down in one of the wildest gulch pockets of the Black Hills region—basking and sleeping in the flood of moonlight that emanates from the glowing ball up afar in heaven's blue vault, is suddenly and rudely aroused from her dreams.

There is a wild clatter of hoofs, a chorus of strange and varied voices swelling out in a wild mountain song, and up through the very heart of the diminutive city, where the gold-fever has dropped a few sanguine souls, dash a cavalcade of masked horsemen, attired in the picturesque garb of the mountaineer, and mounted on animals of superior speed and endurance.

At their head, looking weird and wonderful in his suit of black, rides he whom all have heard of—he whom some have seen, and he whom no one dare raise a hand against, in single combat—Deadwood Dick, Road-Agent Prince, and the one person whose name is in everybody's mouth.

Straight on through the single northerly street of the infant village ride the dauntless band, making weirdly beautiful music with their rollicking song, some of the voices being cultivated, and clear as the clarion note.

A few miners, wakened from their repose, jump out of bed, come to the door, and stare at the receding cavalcade in a dazed sort of way. Others, thinking that the noise is all resulting from an Indian attack, seize rifles or revolvers, as the case may be, and blaze away out of windows and loopholes at whatever may be in the way to receive their bullets.

But the road-agents only pause a moment in their song to send back a wild, sarcastic laugh; then they resume it, and merrily dash along up the gulch, the ringing of iron-shod hoofs beating a strange tattoo to the sound of the music.

Sleepily the miners crawl back to their respective

couches; the moon smiles down on mother earth, and nature once more fans itself to sleep with the breath of a fragrant breeze.

Deadwood—magic city of the West!

Not dead, nor even sleeping, is this headquarters of the Black Hills population at midnight, twenty-four hours subsequent to the rush of the daring road-agents through Camp Crook.

Deadwood is just as lively and hilarious a place during the interval between sunset and sunrise as during the day. Saloons, dance-houses, and gambling dens keep open all night, and stores do not close until a late hour. At one, two and three o'clock in the morning the streets present as lively an appearance as at any period earlier in the evening. Fighting, shooting, stabbing and hideous swearing are features of the night; singing, drinking, dancing and gambling another.

Nightly the majority of the miners come in from such claims as are within a radius of from six to ten miles, and seldom is it that they go away without their "load." To be sure, there are some men in Deadwood who do not drink, but they are so few and scattering as to seem almost entirely a nonentity.

It was midnight, and Deadwood lay basking in a flood of mellow moonlight that cast long shadows from the pine forest on the peaks, and glinted upon the rapid, muddy waters of Whitewood creek, which rumbles noisily by the infant metropolis on its wild journey toward the south.

All the saloons and dance-houses are in full blast; shouts and maudlin yells rend the air. In front of one insignificant board, "ten-by-twenty," an old wretch is singing out lustily:

"Right this way ye cum, pilgrims, ter ther great Black Hills Thee'ter; only costs ye four bits ter go in an' see ther tender sex, already a-kickin' in their striped stockin's; only four bits, recollect, ter see ther greatest show on earth, so heer's yer straight chance!"

But, why the use of yelling? Already the shanty is packed, and judging from the thundering screeches and clapping of hands, the entertainment is such as suits the depraved tastes of the ruffianly "bums" who have paid their "four bits," and gone in.

But look!

Madly out of Deadwood gulch, the abode of thousands of lurking shadows, dashes a horseman.

Straight through the main street of the noisy metropolis he spurs, with hat off, and hair blowing backward in a jetty cloud.

On, on, followed by the eyes of scores curious to know the meaning of his haste—on, and at last he halts in front of a large board shanty, over whose doorway is the illuminated canvas sign: Metropolitan Saloon, by Tom Young.

Evidently his approach is heard, for instantly out of the "Metropolitan" there swarms a crowd of miners, gamblers and bummers to see "what the row is."

"Is there a man among you, gentlemen, who bears the name of Hugh Vansevere?" asks the rider, who from his midnight dress we may judge is no other than Deadwood Dick.

"That is my handle, pilgrim!" and a tall, rough-looking customer of the Minnesotian order steps forward. "What mought yer lay be ag'in me?"

"A *sure* lay!" hisses the masked road-agent, sternly. "You are advertising for one Deadwood Dick, and he has come to pay you his respects!"

The next instant there is a flash, a pistol report, a fall and a groan, the clattering of iron-shod hoofs, and then, ere anyone scarcely dreams of it, *Deadwood Dick is gone!*

CHAPTER III.

THE "CATTYMOUNT"—A QUARREL AND ITS RESULTS.

THE "Metropolitan" saloon in Deadwood, one week subsequent to the events last narrated, was the scene of a larger "jamboree" than for many weeks before.

It was Saturday night, and up from the mines of Gold Run, Bobtail, Poor Man's Pocket, and Spearfish, and down from the Deadwood in miniature, Crook City, poured a swarm of rugged, grisly gold-diggers, the blear-eyed, used-up-looking "pilgrim," and the inevitable wary sharp, ever on the alert for a new buck to fleece.

The "Metropolitan" was then, as now, the headquarters of the Black Hills metropolis for arriving trains and stages, and as a natural consequence received a goodly share of the public patronage.

A well-stocked bar of liquors in Deadwood was *non est*, yet the saloon in question boasted the best to be had. Every bar has its clerk at a pair of tiny scales, and he is ever kept more than busy weighing out the shining dust that the toiling miner has obtained by the sweat of his brow. And if the deft-fingered clerk cannot put six ounces of dust in his own pouch of a night, it clearly shows that he is not long in the business.

Saturday night!

The saloon is full to overflowing—full of brawny, rough, and grisly men; full of ribald songs and maudlin curses; full of foul atmospheres, impregnated with the fumes of vile whisky, and worse tobacco, and full of sights and scenes, exciting and repulsive.

As we enter and work our way toward the center of the apartment, our attention is attracted by a coarse, brutal "tough," evidently just fresh in from the diggings; who, mounted on the summit of an empty whisky cask, is exhorting in rough language, and in the tones of a bellowing bull, to an audience of admiring miners assembled at his feet, which, by the way, are not of the most diminutive pattern imaginable. We will listen:

"Feller coots and liquidarians, behold before ye a lineal descendant uv Cain and Abel. Ye'll reckolect, ef ye've ever bin ter camp-meetin', that Abel got knocked out o' time by his cuzzin Cain, all becawse Abel war misproperly named, and warn't *able* when the crysis arriv ter defen' himsel' in an able manner.

"Hed he bin 'heeled' wi' a shipment uv Black Hills sixes, thet would hev en*abled* him to distinguish hisself fer superyer *ability*. Now, as I sed before, I'm a lineal descendant uv ther notorious Ain and Cable, and I've lit down hyar among ye ter explain a few p'ints 'bout true blessedness and true cussedness.

"Oh! brethern, I tell ye I'm a snorter, I am, when I git a-goin'—a wild screechin' cattymount, right down frum ther sublime spheres up Starkey—ar' a regular epizootic uv religyun, sent down frum clouddum and scattered permiscously ter ther forty winds uv ther earth."

We pass the "cattymount," and presently come to a table at which a young and handsome "pilgrim," and a ferret-eyed sharp are engaged at cards. The first mentioned is a tall, robust fellow, somewhere in the neighborhood of twenty-three years of age, with clear-cut features, dark lustrous eyes, and teeth of pearly whiteness. His hair is long and curling, and a soft brown mustache, waxed at the ends, is almost perfection itself.

Evidently he is of quick temperament, for he handles the cards with a swift, nervous dexterity that surprises even the professional sharp himself, who is a black, swarthy-looking customer, with "villain" plainly written in every lineament of his countenance; his eyes, hair, and a tremendous mustache that he occasionally strokes, are of a jetty black; did you ever notice it?—dark hair and complexion predominate among the gambling fraternity.

Perhaps this is owing to the condition of the souls of some of these characters.

The professional sharp in our case was no exception to the rule. He was attired in the hight of fashion, and the diamond cluster, inevitably to be found there, was on his shirt front; a jewel of wonderful size and brilliancy.

"Ah! curse the luck!" exclaimed the sharp, slapping down the cards; "you have won again, pilgrim, and I am five hundred out. By the gods, your luck is something astonishing!"

"*Luck!*" laughed the other, coolly; "well, no. I do not call it luck, for I never have luck. We'll call it chance!"

"Just as you say," growled the gambler, bringing forth a new pack. "Chance and luck are then twin companions. Will you continue longer, Mr.—"

"Redburn," finished the pilgrim.

"Ah! yes—Mr. Redburn, will you continue?"

"I will play as long as there is anything to play for," again finished Mr. R., twisting the waxed ends of his mustache calmly. "Maybe you have got your fill, eh?"

"No; I'll play all night to win back what I have lost."

A youth, attired in buck-skin, and apparently a couple of years younger than Redburn, came sauntering along at this juncture, and seeing an unoccupied chair at one end of the table (for Redburn and the gambler sat at the sides, facing each other), he took possession of it forthwith.

"Hello!" and the sharp swore roundly. "Who told *you* to mix in your lip, pilgrim?"

"Nobody, as I know of. Thought I'd squat right here, and watch your *sleeves!*" was the significant retort, and the youth laid a cocked six-shooter on the table in front of him.

"Go on, gentlemen; don't let me be the means of spoiling your fun."

The gambler uttered a curse, and dealt out the pasteboards.

The youth was watching him intently, with his sharp black eyes.

He was of medium hight, straight as an arrow, and clad in a loose-fitting costume. A broad sombrero was set jauntily upon the left side of his head, the hair of which had been cut close down to the scalp. His face—a pleasant, handsome, youthful face—was devoid of hirsute covering, he having evidently been recently handled by the barber.

The game between Mr. Redburn and the gambler progressed; the eyes of he whom we have just described were on the card sharp constantly.

The cards went down on the table in vigorous slaps, and at last Mr. Pilgrim Redburn raked in the stakes.

"Thunder 'n' Moses!" ejaculated the sharp, pulling out his watch—an elegant affair, of pure gold, and studded with diamonds—and laying it forcibly down upon the table.

"There! what will you plank on that!"

Redburn took up the time-piece, turned it over and over in his hands, opened and shut it, gave a glance at the works, and then handed it over to the youth, whom he instinctively felt was his friend. Redburn had come from the East to dig gold, and therefore was a stranger in Deadwood.

"What is its money value?" he asked, familiarizing his tone. "Good, I suppose."

"Yes, perfectly good, and cheap at two hundred," was the unhesitating reply. "Do you lack funds, stranger?"

"Oh! no. I am three hundred ahead of this cuss yet, and—"

"You'd better quit where you are!" said the other, decisively. "You'll lose the next round, mark my word."

"Ha! ha!" laughed Redburn, who had begun to show symptoms of recklessness. "I'll take my chances. Here, you gamin, I'll cover the watch with two hundred dollars."

Without more ado the stakes were planked, the cards dealt, and the game began.

The youth, whom we will call Ned Harris, was not idle.

He took the revolvers from the table, changed his position so that his face was just in the opposite direction of what it had been, and commenced to pare his finger nails. The fingers were as white and soft as any girl's. In his hand he also held a strangely-angled little box, the sides of which were mirror-glass. Looking at his finger-nails he also looked into the mirror, which gave a complete view of the card-sharp, as he sat at the table.

Swiftly progressed the game, and no one could fail to see how it was going by watching the cunning light in the gambler's eye. At last the game-card went down, and next instant, after the sharp had raked in his stakes, a cocked revolver in either hand of Ned Harris covered the hearts of the two players.

"Hello!" gasped Redburn, quailing under the gaze of a cold steel tube—"what's the row, now?"

"Draw your revolver!" commanded Harris, sternly, having an eye on the card-sharp at the same time. "Come! don't be all night about it!"

Redburn obeyed; he had no other choice.

"Cock it and cover your man!"

"Who do you mean?"

"The cuss under my left-hand aim."

Again the "pilgrim" felt that he could not afford to do otherwise than obey.

So he took "squint" at the gambler's left breast after which Harris withdrew the siege of his left weapon, although he still covered the young Easterner the same. Quietly he moved around to where the card-sharp sat, white and trembling.

"Gentlemen!" he yelled, in a clear, ringing voice, "will some of you step this way a moment?"

A crowd gathered around in a moment: then the youth resumed:

"Feller-citizens, all of you know how to play cards, no doubt. What is the penalty of cheating, out here in the Hills?"

For a few seconds the room was wrapt in silence; then a chorus of voices gave answer, using a single word:

"Death!"

"Exactly," said Harris, calmly. "When a sharp hides cards in Chinaman fashion up his sleeve, I reckon that's what you call cheatin', don't you?"

"That's the size of it," assented each bystander, grimly.

Ned Harris pressed his pistol-muzzle against the gambler's forehead, inserted his fingers in each of the capacious sleeves, and a moment later laid several high cards upon the table.

A murmur of incredulity went through the crowd of spectators. Even "pilgrim" Redburn was astonished.

After removing the cards, Ned Harris turned and leveled his revolver at the head of the young man from the East.

"Your name?" he said, briefly, "is—"

"Harry Redburn."

"Very well. Harry Redburn, that gambler under cover of your pistol is guilty of a crime, punishable in the Black Hills by death. As you are his victim—or, rather, were to be—it only remains for you to aim straight and rid your country of an A No. 1 dead-beat and swindler!"

"Oh! no!" gasped Redburn, horrified at the thought of taking the life of a fellow-creature—"I cannot, I cannot!"

"You *can!*" said Harris, sternly; "go on—*you must salt that card-sharp, or I'll certainly salt you!*"

A deathlike silence followed.

"*One!*" said Harris, after a moment.

Redburn grew very pale, but not paler was he than the card-sharp just opposite. Redburn was no coward; neither was he accustomed to the desperate character of the population of the Hills. Should he shoot the tricky wretch before him, he knew he should be always calling himself a murderer. On the contrary, in the natural laws of Deadwood, such a murder would be classed justice.

"*Two!*" said Ned Harris, drawing his pistol-hammer back to full cock. "Come, pilgrim, are you going to shoot?"

Another silence; only the low breathing of the spectators could be heard.

"*Three!*"

Redburn raised his pistol and fired—blindly and carelessly, not knowing or caring whither went the compulsory death-dealing bullet.

There was a heavy fall, a groan of pain, as the gambler dropped over on the floor; then for the space of a few seconds all was the wildest confusion throughout the mammoth saloon.

Revolvers were in every hand, knives flashed in the glare of the lamplight, curses and threats were in scores of mouths, while some of the vast surging crowd cheered lustily.

At the table Harry Redburn still sat, as motionless as a statue, the revolver still held in his hand, his face white, his eyes staring.

There he remained, the center of general attraction, with a hundred pair of blazing eyes leveled at him from every side.

"Come!" said Ned Harris, in a low tone, tapping him on the shoulder—"come, pardner; let's git out of this, for times will be brisk soon. You've wounded one of the biggest card-devils in the Hills, and he'll be rearin' pretty quick. Look! d'ye see that feller comin' yonder, who was preachin' from on top of the barrel, a bit ago? Well, that is Catamount Cass, an' he's a pard of Chet Diamond, the feller you salted, an' them fellers behind him are his gang. Come! follow me, Henry, and I'll nose our way out of here."

Redburn signified his readiness, and with a cocked six-shooter in either hand Ned Harris led the way.

CHAPTER IV.

SAD ANITA—THE MINE LOCATER—TROUBLE.

STRAIGHT toward the door of the saloon he marched, the muzzles of the grim sixes clearing a path him; for Ned Harris had become notorious in Deadwood for his coolness, courage and audacity. It had been said of him that he would "just es lief shute a man as ter look at 'im," and perhaps the speaker was not far from right.

Anyway, he led off through the savage-faced audience with a composure that was remarkable, and, strange to say, not a hand was raised to stop him until he came face to face with Catamount Cass and his gang; here was where the youth had expected molestation and hindrance, if anywhere.

Catamount Cass was a rough, illiterate "tough" of the mountain species, and possessed more brute courage than the general run of his type of men, and a bull-dog determination that made him all the more dangerous as an enemy.

Harry Redburn kept close at Ned Harris' heels, a cocked "six" in either hand ready for any emergency.

It took but a few moments before the two parties met, the "Cattymount" throwing out his foot to block the path.

"Hello!" roared the "tough," folding his huge knotty arms across his partially bared breast; "ho! ho! whoa up thar, pilgrims! Don' ye go ter bein' so fast. Fo'kes 'harn't so much in a hurry now-'days as they uster war. Ter be sure ther Lord manyfactered this futstool in seven days; sumtimes I think he did, an' then, ag'in, my geological ijees convince me he didn't."

"What has that to do with us?" demanded Ned, sternly. "I opine ye'd better spread, some of you, if you don't want me to run a canyon through your midst. Preach to some other pilgrim than me; I'm in a hurry!"

"Haw! haw! Yas, I obsarve ye be; but if ye're my meat, an' I think prob'ble ye be, I ain't a-goin' fer ter let yer off so nice and easy. P'arps ye kin tell who fired the popgun, a minnit ago, w'at basted my ole pard?"

"I shall not take trouble to tell!" replied Ned, fingering the trigger of his left six uneasily. "Ef you want to know who salted Chet Diamond, the worst blackleg, trickster and card-player in Dakota, all you've got to do is to go and ask him!"

"Hold!" cried Harry Redburn, stepping out from behind Harris; "I'll hide behind no man's shoulder. *I* salted the gambler—if you call shooting salting—and I'm not afraid to repeat the action by salting a dozen more just of his particular style."

Ned Harris was surprised.

He had set Redburn down as a faint-hearted, dubious-couraged counter-jumper from the East; he saw now that there was something of him, after all.

"Come on, young man!" and the young miner stepped forward a pace; "are you with me?"

"To the ears!" replied Harris, grimly.

The next instant the twain leaped forward and broke the barrier, and mid the crack of pistol-shots and shouts of rage, they cleared the saloon. Once outside, Ned Harris led the way.

"Come along!" he said, dodging along the shadowy side of the street; "we'll have o scratch gravel, for them up-range 'toughs' will follow us, I reckon. They're a game gang, and 'hain't the most desirable kind of enemies one could wish for. I'll take you over to my coop, and you can lay low there until this jamboree blows over. You'll have to promise me one thing, however, ere I can admit you as a member of my household."

"Certainly. What is it?" and Harry Redburn redoubled his efforts in order to keep alongside his swift-footed guide.

"Promise me that you will divulge nothing, no matter what you may see or hear. Also that, should you fall in love with one who is a member of my family, you will forbear and not speak of love to her."

"It is a woman, then?"

"Yes—a young lady."

"I will promise;—how can I afford to do otherwise, under the existing circumstances. But, tell me, why did you force me to shoot that gambler?"

"He was a rascal, and cheated you."

"I know; but I did not want his life; I am averse to bloodshed."

"So I perceived, and that made me all the more determined you should salivate him. You'll find before you're in the Hills long that it won't do to take lip or lead from any one. A green pilgrim is the first to get salted; I illustrated how to serve 'em!"

Redburn's eyes sparkled. He was just beginning to see into the different phases of this wild exciting life.

"Good!" he exclaimed, warmly. "I have much to thank you for. Did I kill that card-sharp?"

"No; you simply perforated him in the right side. This way."

They had been running straight up the main street. Now they turned a corner and darted down one that was dark and deserted.

A moment later a trim boyish figure stepped before them, from out of the shadow of a new frame building; a hand of creamy whiteness was laid upon the arm of Ned Harris.

"This way, pilgrims," said a low musical voice, and at the same instant a gust of wind lifted the jaunty sombrero from the speaker's head, revealing a most wonderful wealth of long glossy hair; "the 'toughs' are after you, and you cannot find a better place to coop than in here." The soft hand drew Ned Harris inside the building, which was finished, but unoccupied, and Redburn followed, nothing loth to get into a place of safety. So far, Deadwood had not impressed him favorably as being the most peaceable city within the scope of a continent.

Into an inner room of the building they went, and the door was closed behind them. The apartment was small and smelled of green lumber. A table and a few chairs comprised the furniture; a dark lantern burned suspended from the ceiling by a wire. Redburn eyed the strange youth as he and Harris were handed seats.

Of medium hight and symmetrically built; dressed in a carefully tanned costume of buck-skin, the vest being fringed with the fur of the mink; wearing a jaunty Spanish sombrero; boots on the dainty feet of patent leather, with tops reaching to the knees; a face slightly sun-burned, yet showing the traces of beauty that even excessive dissipation could not obliterate; eyes black and piercing; mouth firm, resolute, and devoid of sensual expression; hair of raven color and of remarkable length;—such was the picture of the youth as beheld by Redburn and Harris.

"You can remain here till you think it will be safe to again venture forth, gentlemen," and a smile—evidently a stranger there—broke out about the speaker's lips. "Good-evening!" "Good-evening!" nodded Harris, with a quizzical stare. The next moment the youth was gone.

"Who was that chap?" asked Redburn, not a little bewildered.

"That?—why that's Calamity Jane!"

"Calamity Jane? *What* a name."

"Yes, she's an odd one. Can ride like the wind, shoot like a sharp-shooter, and swear like a trooper. Is here, there and everywhere, seemingly all at one time. Owns this coop and two or three other lots in Deadwood; a herding ranch at Laramie, an interest in a paying placer claim near Elizabeth City, and the Lord only knows how much more."

"But it is not a *woman?*"

"Reckon 'tain't nothin' else."

"God forbid that a child of mine should ever become so debased and—"

"Hold! there are yet a few redeeming qualities about her. She was *ruined*—" and here a shade dark as a thunder-cloud passed over Ned Harris' face—"and set adrift upon the world, homeless and friendless; yet she has bravely fought her way through the storm, without asking anybody's assistance. True, she may not now have a heart; that was trampled upon, years ago, but her character has not suffered blemish since the day a foul wretch stole away her honor!"

"What is her real name?"

"I do not know; few in Deadwood do. It is said, however, that she comes of a Virginia City, Nevada, family of respectability and intelligence."

At this juncture there was a great hubbub outside, and instinctively the twain drew their revolvers, expecting that Catamount Cass and his toughs had discovered their retreat, and were about to make an attack. But soon the gang were heard to tramp away, making the night hideous with their hoarse yells.

"They'll pay a visit to every shanty in Deadwood," said Harris, with a grim smile, "and if they don't find us, which they won't, they'll h'ist more than a barrel of bug-juice over their defeat. Come, let's be going."

They left the building and once more emerged onto the darkened street, Ned taking the lead.

"Follow me, now," he said, tightening his belt, "and we'll get home before sunrise, after all."

He struck out up the gulch, or, rather, down it, for his course lay southward. Redburn followed, and in fifteen minutes the lights of Deadwood—magic city of the wilderness—were left behind. Harris led the way along the rugged mountain stage-road, that, after leaving Deadwood on its way to Camp Crook and Custer City in the south, runs alternately through deep, dark canyons and gorges, with an ease and rapidity that showed him to be well acquainted with the route. About three miles below Deadwood he struck a trail through a transverse canyon running north-west, through which flowed a small stream, known as Brown's creek. The bottom was level and smooth, and a brisk walk of a half-hour brought them to where a horse was tied to an alder sapling.

"You mount and ride on ahead until you come to the end of the canyon," said Harris, untying the horse. "I will follow on after you, and be there almost as soon as you."

Redburn would have offered some objections, but the other motioned for him to mount and be off, so he concluded it best to obey.

The animal was a fiery one, and soon carried him out of sight of Ned, whom he left standing in the yellow moonlight. Sooner than he expected the gorge came to an abrupt termination in the face of a stupendous wall of rock, and nothing remained to do but wait for young Harris.

He soon came, trotting leisurely up, only a trifle flushed in countenance.

"This way!" he said, and seizing the animal by the bit he led horse and rider into a black, gaping fissure in one side of the canyon, that had hitherto escaped Redburn's notice. It was a large, narrow, subterranean passage, barely large enough to admit the horse and rider. Redburn soon was forced to dismount and bring up the rear.

"How far do we journey in this shape?" he demanded, after what seemed to him a long while.

"No further," replied Ned, and the next instant they emerged into a small, circular pocket in the midst of the mountains—one of those beauteous flower-strewn valleys which are often found in the Black Hills.

This "pocket," as they are called, consisted of perhaps fifty acres, walled in on every side by rugged mountains as steep, and steeper, in some places, than a house-roof. On the western side Brown's creek had its source, and leaped merrily down from ledge to ledge into the valley, across which it flowed, sinking into the earth on the eastern side, only to bubble up again, in the canyon, with renewed strength.

The valley was one vast, indiscriminate bed of wild, fragrant flowers, whose volume of perfume was almost sickening when first greeting the nostrils. Every color and variety imaginable was here, all in the most perfect bloom. In the center of the valley stood a log-cabin, overgrown with clinging vines. There was a light in the window, and Harris pointed toward it, as, with young Redburn, he emerged from the fissure.

"There's my coop, pilgrim. There you will be safe for a time, at least." He unsaddled the horse and set it free to graze.

Then they set off down across the slope, arriving at the cabin in due time.

The door was open; a young woman, sweet, yet sad-faced, was seated upon the steps, fast asleep.

Redburn gave an involuntary cry of incredulity and admiration as his eyes rested upon the picture—upon the pure, sweet face, surrounded by a wealth of golden, glossy hair, and the sylph-like form, so perfect in every contour. But a charge of silence from Harris, made him mute.

The young man knelt by the side of the sleeping girl and imprinted a kiss upon the fresh, unpolluted lips, which caused the sleeping beauty to smile in her dreams.

A moment later, however, she opened her eyes and sprung to her feet with a startled scream.

"Oh, Ned!" she gasped, trembling, as she saw him, "how you frightened me. I had a dream—oh, such a sweet dream! and I thought *he* came and kissed—"

Suddenly did she stop as, for the first time, her penetrating blue eyes rested upon Harry Blackburn.

A moment she gazed at him as in a sort of fascination; then, with a low cry, began to retreat, growing deathly pale. Ned Harris stepped quickly forward and supported her on his arm.

"Be calm, Anita," he said, in a gentle, reassuring tone. "This is a young gentleman whom I have brought here to our home for a few days until it will be safe for him to be seen in Deadwood. Mr. Redburn, I make you acquainted with Anita."

A courteous bow from Redburn, a slight inclination of Anita's head, and the introduction was made. A moment later the three entered the cabin, a model of neatness and primitive luxury.

"How is it that you are up so early, dear?" young Harris asked, as he unbuckled his belt and hung it upon a peg in the wall. "You are rarely as spry, eh?"

"Indeed! I have not been to bed at all," replied the girl, a weary smile wreathing her lips. "I was nervous, and feared something was going to happen, so I staid up."

"Your old plea—the presentiment of coming danger, I suppose," and the youth laughed, gayly. "But, you need not fear. No one will invade our little Paradise, right away. What is your opinion of it, Redburn?"

"I should say not. I think this little mountain retreat is without equal," replied Harry, with enthusiasm. "The only wonder is, how did you ever stumble into such a delightful place."

"Of that I will perhaps tell you, another time," said Harris, musingly.

Day soon dawned over the mountains, and the early morning sunlight fell with charming effect into the little "pocket," with its countless thousands of odorous flowers, and the little ivy-clad cabin nestling down among them all.

Sweet, sad-faced Anita prepared a sumptuous morning repast out of antelope-steak and the eggs of wild birds, with dainty side dishes of late summer berries, and a large luscious melon which had been grown on a cultivated patch, contiguous to the cabin.

Both Harris and his guest did ample justice to the meal, for they had neither eaten anything since the preceding noon. When they had finished, Ned arose from the table, saying: "Pardner, I shall leave you here for a few days, during which time I shall probably be mostly away on business. Make yourself at home and see that Anita is properly protected; I will return in a week at the furthest;—perhaps in a day or two."

He took down his rifle and belt from the wall, buckled on the latter, and half an hour later left the "pocket." That was a day of days to Harry Redburn. He rambled about the picturesque little valley, romped on the luxuriant grass and gathered wild flowers, alternately. At night he sat in the cabin door and listened to the cries of the night birds and the incessant hooting of the mountain owls (which by the way, are very abundant throughout the Black Hills.)

All efforts to engage Anita in conversation proved fruitless.

On the following day both were considerably astonished to perceive that there was a stranger in their Paradise;—a bow-legged, hump-backed, grisly little old fellow, who walked with a staff. He approached the cabin, and Redburn went out to find who he was.

"Gude-mornin'!" nodded General Nix, (for it was he) with a grin. "I jes' kim over inter this deestrict ter prospect fer gold. Don' seem ter recognize yer unkle, eh? boy; I'm Nix Walsingham Nix, Esquire, geological surveyor an' mine-locater. I've located more nor forty thousan' mines in my day, more or less—ginerally a consider'ble more of less than less of more. I perdict frum ther geological formation o' this nest an' a dream I hed last night, thet thar's sum uv ther biggest veins right in this yere valley as ye'll find in ther Hills!"

"Humph! no gold here," replied Redburn, who had already learned from study and experience how to guess a fat strike. "It is out of the channel."

"No; et's right in the channel."

"Well, I'll not dispute you. How did you get into the valley?"

"Through ther pass," and the General chuckled approvingly. "See'd a feller kim down ther canyon, yesterday, so I nosed about ter find whar he kim from, that's how I got here; 'sides, I hed a dream about this place."

"Indeed!" Redburn was puzzled how to act under the circumstances. Just then there came a piercing scream from the direction of the cabin.

What could it mean? Was Nix an enemy, and was some one else of his gang attacking Anita?

Certainly she *was* in trouble!

CHAPTER V.

SITTING BULL—THE FAIR CAPTIVE.

FEARLESS FRANK stepped back aghast, as he saw the inhuman chief of the Sioux—the cruel, grim-faced warrior, Sitting Bull; shrunk back, and laid his hand upon the butt of a revolver.

"Ha!" he articulated, "is that you, chief? You, and at such work as this?" there was stern reproach in the youth's tone, and certain it is that the Sioux warrior heard the words spoken.

"My friend, Scarlet Boy, is keen with the tongue," he said, frowning. "Let him put shackles upon it, before it leaps over the bounds of reason."

"I see no reason why I should not speak in behalf of yon suffering girl!" retorted the youth, fearlessly, "on whom you have been inflicting one of the most inhuman tortures Indian cunning could conceive. For shame, chief, that you should ever assent to such an act—lower yourself to the grade of a dog by such a dastard deed. For shame, I say!"

Instantly the form of the great warrior straightened up like an arrow, and his painted hand flew toward the pistols in his belt.

But the succeeding second he seemed to change his intention; his hand went out toward the youth in greeting:

"The Scarlet Boy is right," he said, with as much graveness as a red-skin can conceive. "Sitting Bull listens to his words as he would to those of a brother. Scarlet Boy is no stranger in the land of the Sioux; he is the friend of the great chief and his warriors. Once when the storm-gods were at war over the pine forests and picture rocks of the Hills; when the Great Spirit was sending fiery messengers down in vivid streaks from the skies, the Big Chief cast a thunderbolt in playfulness at the feet of Sitting Bull. The shock of the hand of the Great Spirit did not escape me; for hours I lay like one slain in battle. My warriors were in consternation; they ran hither and thither in affright, calling on the Manitou to preserve their chief. You came, Scarlet Boy, in the midst of all the panic;—came, and though then but a stripling, you applied simple remedies that restored Sitting Bull to the arms of his warriors.*

"From that hour Sitting Bull was your friend—is your friend, now, and will be as long as the red-men exist as a tribe."

"Thank you, chief;" and Fearless Frank grasped the Indian's hand and wrung it warmly. "I believe you mean all you say. But I am surprised to find you engaged at such work as this. I have been told that Sitting Bull made war only on warriors—not on women."

An ugly frown darkened the savage's face—a frown wherein was depicted a number of slumbering passions.

"The pale-face girl is the last survivor of a train that the warriors of Sitting Bull attacked in Red Canyon. Sitting Bull lost many warriors; yon pale squaw shot down full a half-score before she could be captured; she belongs to the warriors of Sitting Bull, and not to the great chief himself."

"Yet you have the power to free her—to yield her up to me. Consider, chief; are you not enough my friend that you can afford to give me the pale-face girl? Surely, she has been tortured sufficiently to satisfy your braves' thirst for vengeance."

Sitting Bull was silent.

"What will the Scarlet Boy do with the fair maiden of his tribe?"

"Bear her to a place of safety, chief, and care for her until I can find her friends—probably she has friends in the East."

"It shall be as he says. Sitting Bull will withdraw his braves and Scarlet Boy can have the red-man's prize."

A friendly hand-shake between the youth and the Sioux chieftain, a word from the latter to the grim painted warriors, and the next instant the glade was cleared of the savages.

Fearless Frank then hastened to approach the insensible captive, and, with a couple sweeps of his knife, cut the bonds that held her to the torture-stake. Gently he laid her on the grass, and arranged about her half-nude form the garments Sitting Bull's warriors had torn off, and soon he had the satisfaction of seeing her once more clothed properly. It still remained for him to restore her to consciousness, and this promised to be no easy task, for she was in a dead swoon. She was even more beautiful of face and figure than one would have imagined at a first glance. Of a delicate blonde complexion, with pink-tinged cheeks, she made a very pretty picture, her face framed as it was in a wild disheveled cloud of auburn hair.

A hatful of cold water from a neighboring spring dashed into her upturned face; a continued chafing of the pure white soft hands; then there was a convulsive twitching of the features, a low moan, and the eyes opened and darted a glance of affright into the face of the Scarlet Boy.

"Fear not, miss;" and the youth gently supported her to a sitting posture. "I am a friend, and your cruel captors have vamosed. Lucky I came along just as I did, or it's likely they'd have killed you."

"Oh! sir, how can I ever thank you for rescuing me from those merciless fiends!" and the maiden gave him a grateful glance. "They whipped me, terribly!"

"I know, lady—all because you defended yourself in Red Canyon."

"I suppose so: but how did you find out so much, and, also, effect my release from the savages?"

Fearless Frank leaned up against the tree which had been used as the torture-stake, and related what is already known to the reader.

When he had finished, the rescued captive seized his hand between both her own, and thanked him warmly.

"Had it not been for you, sir, no one but our God knows what would have been my fate. Oh! sir, what can I do, more than to thank you a thousand times, to repay you for the great service you have rendered me?"

"Nothing, lady; nothing that I think of at present. Was it not my duty, while I had the power, to free you from the hands of those barbarians? Certainly it was, and I deserve no thanks. But tell me, what is your name, and were your friends all killed in the train from which you were taken?"

"I had no friends, sir, save a lady whose acquaintance I made on the journey out from Cheyenne. As to my name—you can call me Miss Terry."

"Mystery!" in blank amazement.

"Yes;" with a gay laugh—"Mystery, if you choose. My name is Alice Terry."

"Oh!" and the youth began to brighten. "Miss Terry, to be sure; Mystery! ha! ha! good joke. I shall call you the latter. Have you friends and relatives East?"

"No. I came West to meet my father, who is somewhere in the Black Hills."

"Do you know at what place?"

"I do not."

"I fear it will be a hard matter to find him, then. The Hills now have a floating population of about twenty-five thousand souls. Your father would be one to find out of that lot."

A faint smile came over the girl's face. "I should know papa among fifty thousand, if necessary;" she said, "although I have not seen him for years."

She failed to mention how many, or what peculiarities she would recognize him by. Was he blind, deaf or dumb?

Fearless Frank glanced around him, and saw that a path rugged and steep led up to the prairie above.

"Come," he said, offering his arm, "we will get up to the plains and go."

"Where to?" asked Miss Terry, rising with an effort. The welts across her back were swollen and painful.

"Deadwood is my destination. I can deviate my course, however, if it will accommodate you."

"Oh! no; you must not inconvenience yourself on my account. I am of little or no consequence, you know."

She leaned upon his arm, and they ascended the path to the plain above.

Frank's horse was grazing near by where the scarlet youth had taken his unceremonious tumble.

Off to the north-west a cloud of dust rose heavenward, and he rightly conjectured that it hid from view the chieftain, Sitting Bull, and his warriors.

His thoughts reverting to his companion, "General" Nix, and the train of Charity Joe, he glanced toward where he had last seen them.

Neither were to be seen, now. Probably Nix had rejoined the train, and it was out of eye-shot behind a swell in the plains.

"Were you looking for some one?" Alice asked, looking into her rescuer's face.

"Yes, I was with a train when I first heard your cries; I left the boys, and came to investigate. I guess they have gone on without me."

"How mean of them! Will we have to make the journey to the Hills alone?"

"Yes, unless we should providentially fall in with a train or be overtaken by a stage."

"Are you not afraid?"

"My cognomen is Fearless Frank, lady; you can draw conclusions from that."

He went and caught the horse, arranged a blanket in the saddle so that she could ride side-fashion, and assisted her to mount.

The sun was touching the lips of the horizon with a golden kiss; more time than Frank had supposed had elapsed since he left the train.

Far off toward the east shadows were hugging close behind the last lingering rays of sunlight; a couple of coyotes were sneaking into view a few rods away; birds were winging homeward; a perfume-laden breeze swept down from the Black Hills, and fanned the pink cheeks of Alice Terry into a vivid glow.

"We cannot go far," said Frank, thoughtfully, "before darkness will overtake us. Perhaps we had better remain in the canal, here, where there is both grass and water. In the morning we will take a fresh start."

The plan was adopted; they camped in the break, or "canal," near where Alice had been tortured.

Out of his saddle-bags Frank brought forth crackers, biscuit and dried venison; these, with clear sparkling water from the spring in the chaparral, made a meal good enough for anybody.

The night was warm; no fire was needed.

A blanket spread on the grass served as a resting-place for Alice; the strange youth in scarlet lay with his head resting against the side of his horse. The least movement of the animal, he said, would arouse him; he was keen of scent and quick to detect danger—meaning the horse.

The night passed away without incident; as early as four o'clock—when it is daylight on the plains—Fearless Frank was astir.

He found the rivulet flowing from the spring to abound with trout, and caught and dressed the morning meal.

Alice was awake by the time breakfast was ready. She bathed her face and hands in the stream, combed her long auburn hair through her fingers, and looked sweeter than on the previous night—at least, so thought Fearless Frank.

"The day promises to be delightful, does it not?" she remarked, as she seated herself to partake of the repast.

"Exactly. Autumn months are ever enjoyable in the West."

The meal dispatched, no delay was made in leaving the place.

Fearless Frank strode along beside his horse and its fair rider, chatting pleasantly, and at the same time making a close observation of his surroundings. He knew he was in parts frequented by both red and white savages, and it would do no harm to keep on one's guard.

They traveled all day and reached Sage creek at sunset.

Here they remained over night, taking an early start on the succeeding morning.

That day they made good progress, in consequence of Frank's purchase of a horse at Sage creek from some friendly Crow Indians, and darkness overtook them at the mouth of Red Canyon, where they went into camp.

By steady pushing they reached Rapid creek the next night, for no halt was made at Custer City, and for the first time since leaving the torture-ground, camped with a miner's family. As yet no cabins or shanties had been erected here, canvas tents serving in the stead; to-day there are between fifty and a hundred wooden structures.

Alice was charmed with the wild grandeur of the mountain scenery—with the countless acres of blossoms and flowering shrubs—with the romantic and picturesque surroundings in general, and was very emphatic in her praises.

One day of rest was taken at Rapid Creek; then the twain pushed on, and when night again overtook them, they rode into the bustling, noisy, homely metropolis—Deadwood, magic city of the North-west.

CHAPTER VI.

ONLY A SNAKE—LOCATING A MINE.

HARRY REDBURN hurried off toward the cabin, which was some steps away. In Anita's scream there were both terror and affright.

Walsingham Nix, the hump-backed, bow-legged explorer and prospecter hobbled after him, using his staff for support.

He had heard the scream, but years' experience among the "gals" taught him that a feminine shriek rarely, if ever, meant anything.

Redburn arrived at the cabin in a few flying bounds, and leaped into the kitchen.

There, crouched upon the floor in one corner, all in a little heap, pale, trembling and terrified, was Anita. Before her, squirming along over the sand-scrubbed floor, evidently disabled by a blow, was an enormous black-snake.

It was creeping away instead of toward Anita, leaving a faint trail of crimson in its wake; yet the young girl's face was blanched with fear.

"You screamed at that?" demanded Redburn, pointing to the coiling serpent.

"Ugh! yes; it is horrible."

"But, it is harmless. See: some one has given it a blow across the back, and it is disabled for harm."

Anita looked up into his handsome face, wonderingly.

"I guv et a rap across the spinal column, w'en I kim into the valley," said General Nix, thrusting his head in at the door, a ludicrous grin elongating his grisly features. "'Twar a-goin' ter guv me a yard or so uv et's tongue, more or less—consider'bly less of more than more of less—so I jest salivated it across ther back, kerwhack!"

Anita screamed again as she saw the General, he was so rough and homely.

"Who are you?" she managed to articulate as Redburn assisted her to rise from the floor. "What are you doing here, where you were not invited?"

There was a degree of haughtiness in her tone that Redburn did not dream she possessed.

The "General" rubbed the end of his nose, chuckled audibly, then laughed, outright.

"I opine this ar' a free country, ain't it, marm, more or less? W'en a feller kerflummuxes rite down onter a payin' streek I opine he's goin' ter roost thar till he gits reddy to vamoose, ain't he?"

"But, sir, my brother was the first to discover this spot and build us a home here, and he claims that all belongs to him."

"He do? more or less—consider'bly less of more than more uv less, eh? Yas, I kno' yer brother—leastways I hev seen him an' heerd heeps about him. Letters uv his name spell Ned Harris, not?"

"Yes, sir; but how can you know him? Few do, in Deadwood."

"Nevyer mind thet, my puss. Ole Walsingham Nix do kno' a few things yet, ef he ar' a hard old nut fer w'ich thar is not cra'kin'."

Anita looked at Redburn, doubtfully.

"Brother would be very angry if he were to return and find this man here. What would you advise?"

"I am of the opinion that he will have to vacate," replied Harry, decidedly.

"*Nix* cum-a-rouse!" disagreed the old prospecter. "I'm hayr, an' thar's no yearthly use o' denyin' *that*. Barrin' ye ar' a right peart-lookin' kid, stranger, allow me ter speculate thet it would take a dozen, more or less—consider'bly less uv more than more o' less—ter put me out."

Redburn laughed heartily. The old fellow's bravado amused him. Anita however, was silent: she did

*A fact.

dependence in her protector to arrange matters satisfactorily.

"That savors strongly of rebellion," Redburn observed, sitting down upon a lounge that stood hard by. "Besides, you have an advantage; I would not attack you; you are old and unfitted for combat; deformed and unable to do battle."

"Exactly!" the "General" confidently announced.

"What good can come of your remaining here?" demanded Anita.

"Sit down, marm, sit down, an' I'll perceed ter divest myself uv w'at little infermation I've got stored up in my noddle. Ye see, mum, my name's Walsingham Nix, at yer sarvice—Walsingham bein' my great, great grandad's fronticepiece, while Nix war ther hind-wheeler, like nor w'at a he-mule ar' w'en hitched ter a 'schooner.' Ther Nix family were a great one, bet yer false teeth; originated about ther time Joner swallered the whale, down nigh Long Branch, and 've bin handed down frum time ter time till ye behold in me ther last survivin' pilgrim frum ther ancestral block. Thar was one remarkable pecooliarity about ther Nix family, frum root ter stump, an' thet war, they war nevyer known ter refuse a gift or an advantageous offer; in this respeck they bore a striking resemblance ter the immortell G'orge Washington. G'orge war innercent; he ked never tell a lie. So war our family; they never hed it in their hearts to say *Nix* to an offer uv a good feed or a decoction o' brandy.

"It war a disease—a hereditary affection uv ther hull combined system. The terrible malady attacked me w'en I war an infant prodigy, an' I've nevyer yit see'd thet time when I c'u'd resist the temptation an' coldly say 'nix' w'en a brother pilgrim volunteered ter make a liberal dispensation uv grub, terbarker, or bug-juice. Nix ar' a word thet causes sorrer an' suffering ter scores 'n' scores o' people, more or less—ginerally more uv less than less o' more—an' tharfore I nevyer feel it my duty, as a Christyun, ter set a bad example w'ich others may foller."

Redburn glanced toward Anita, a quizzical expression upon his genial face.

"I fail to see how that has any reference as to the cause of your stay among us," he observed, amused at the quaint lingo of the prospecter.

"Sart'in not, sart'in not! I had just begun ter git thar. I've only bin gi'in' ye a geological ijee uv ther Nix family's formation; I'll now perceed to illustrate more clearly, thru' veins an' channels hitherto unexplored, endin' up wi' a reg'lar hoss-car proposal."

Then the old fellow proceeded with a rambling "yarn," giving more guesses than actual information and continued on in this strain:

"So thar *war* gold. I went ter work an' swallered a pill o' opium, w'ich made me sleep, an' while I war snoozin' I dreampt about ther perzact place whar thet gold war secreted. It war in a little pocket beneath the bed of a spring frum which flowed a little creeklet.

"Next mornin', bright an' early, I shouldered pick, shuvyel an' pan, an' went for thet identical spring. To-day thet pocket, havin' been traced into a rich vein, is payin' as big or bigger nor any claim on Spring creek."*

Both Redburn and Anita were unconsciously becoming interested.

"And do you think there is gold here, in this flower-strewn pocket-valley?"

"I don't think it—I know it. I hed a dreem et war hayr in big quantities, so I h'isted my carcass this direction. Ter-nite I'll hev ernuther nighthoss, an' thet'll tell me precisely where ther strike ar'."

Redburn drummed a tattoo on the arm of the lounge with his fingers; he was reflecting on what he had heard.

"You are willing to make terms, I suppose," he said, after a while, glancing at Anita to see if he was right. "You are aware, I believe, that we still hold possession above any one else."

"True enuff. Ye war first ter diskiver this place; ye orter hev yer say about it."

"Well, then, perhaps we can come to a bargain. You can state your prices for locating and opening up this mine, and we will consider."

"Wal, let me see. Ef the mine proves to be ekal ter the one thet I located on Spring creek, I'll rake in a third fer my share uv the divys. Ef 'tain't good's I expect, I'll take a quarter."

Redburn turned to Anita.

"From what little experience I have had, I think it is a fair offer. What is your view of the matter, and do you believe your brother will be satisfied?"

"Oh! yes, sir. It will surprise and please him, to return and find his Paradise has been turned into a gold-mine."

"All right; then, we will go ahead and get things in shape. We will have to get tools, though, before we can accomplish much of anything."

"My brother has a miner's outfit here," said Anita.

"That will save you a trip to Deadwood, for the present."

And so it was all satisfactorily arranged. During the remainder of the day the old "General" and Redburn wandered about through the flower-meadows of the pocket, here and there examining a little soil; now chipping rock among the rugged foothills, then "feeling" in the bed of the creek. But, not a sign of anything like gold was to be found, and when night called them to shelter, Redburn was pretty thoroughly convinced that Nix was an enormous "sell," and that he could put all the gold they would find in his eye. The "General," however, was confident of success, and told many doubtful yarns of former discoveries and exploits.

Anita prepared an evening meal that was both tempting and sumptuous, and all satisfied their appetites, after which Harry took down the guitar, suspended from the wall, tuned it up, and sung in a clear mellow voice a number of ballads, to which the "General," much to the surprise of both Redburn and Anita, lent a rich deep bass—a voice of superior culture.

The closing piece was a weird melody—the lament of a heart that was broken, love-blasted—and was rendered in a style worthy of a professional vocalist. The last mournful strains filled the cabin just as the last lingering rays of sunlight disappeared from the mountain top, and shadows came creeping down the rugged walls of rock to concentrate in the Flower Pocket, as Anita had named her valley home. Redburn rose from his seat at the window, and reached the instrument to its accustomed shelf, darting a glance toward sad Anita, a moment later. To his surprise he perceived that her head was bowed upon her arm that lay along the window-ledge—that she was weeping, softly, to herself.

Acting the gentlemanly part, the young miner motioned for Nix to follow him, and they both retired to the outside of the cabin to lounge on the grass and smoke, and thus Anita was left alone with her grief and such troubles as were the causes thereof.

Certain it was that she had a secret, but what it was Redburn could not guess.

About ten o'clock he and Nix re-entered the cabin and went to bed in a room allotted to them, off from the little parlor. Both went to sleep at once, and it was well along toward morning when Redburn was aroused by being rudely shaken by "General" Nix, who was up and dressed, and held a torch in his hand.

"Come! come!" he said in a husky whisper, and a glance convinced Harry that he was still asleep, although his eyes were wide open and staring.

Without a word the young man leaped from bed, donned his garments, and the old man then led the way out of the cabin.

In passing through the kitchen, Redburn saw that Anita was up and waiting.

"Come!" he said, seizing a hatchet and stake, "we are about to discover the gold-mine, and our fortunes;" with a merry laugh.

Then both followed in the wake of the sleep walker, and were led to near the center of the valley, which was but a few steps in the rear of the cabin. Here was a bed of sand washed there from an overflow of the stream, and at this the "General" pointed, as he came to a halt.

"There! *there* is the gold—millions of it deep down—twenty or thirty feet—in sand—easy to get! dig! DIG! DIG!"

Redburn marked the spot by driving the stake in the ground.

It now only remained to dig in the soil to verify the truth of the old man's fancy.

CHAPTER VII.

DEADWOOD DICK ON THE ROAD.

RUMBLING noisily through the black canyon road to Deadwood, at an hour long past midnight, came the stage from Cheyenne, loaded down with passengers, and full five hours late, on account of a broken shaft, which had to be replaced on the road. There were six plunging, snarling horses attached, whom the veteran Jehu on the box, managed with the skill of a circusman, and all the time the crack! snap! of his long-lashed gad made the night resound as like so many pistol reports.

The road was through a wild tortuous canyon, fringed with tall spectral pines, which occasionally admitted a bar of ghostly moonlight across the rough road over which the stage tore with wild recklessness.

Inside, the vehicle was crammed full to its utmost capacity, and therefrom emanated the strong fumes of whisky and tobacco smoke, and stronger language, over the delay and the terrible jolting of the conveyance.

In addition to those penned up inside, there were two passengers positioned on top, in the rear of the driver, where they clung to the trunk railings to keep from being jostled off.

One was an elderly man, tall in stature and noticeably portly, with a florid countenance, cold gray eyes, and hair and beard of brown, freely mixed with silvery threads. He was elegantly attired, his costume being of the finest cloth and of the very latest cut; boots patent leathers, and hat glossy as a mirror; diamonds gleamed and sparkled on his immaculate shirt-bosom, on his fingers and from the seal of a heavy gold chain across his vest front.

The other personage was a counterpart of the first in every particular, save that while one was more than a semi-centenarian in years, the other was barely twenty. The same faultless elegance in dress, the same elaborate display of jewels, and the same haughty, aristocratic bearing produced in one was mirrored in the other.

They were father and son.

"Confound such a road!" growled the younger man, as the stage bounced him about like a rubber ball. "For my part I wish I had remained at home, instead of coming out into this outlandish region. It is perfectly awful."

"Y-y-y-e-s!" chattered the elder between the jolts and jerks—"it is not what it should be, that's true. But have patience; ere long we will reach our destination, and—"

"Get shot like poor Vansevere did!" sneered the other. "I tell you, governor, this is a desperate game you are playing."

The old man smiled, grimly.

"Desperate or not, we must carry it through to the end. Vansevere was not the right kind of a man to set after the young scamp."

"How do you mean?"

"He was too rash—entirely too rash. Deadwood Dick is a daring whelp, and Vansevere's open offer of a reward for his apprehension only put the young tiger on his guard, and he will be more wary and watchful in the future."

This in a positive tone.

"Yes; he will be harder to trap than a fox who has lost a foot between jaws of steel. He will be revengeful, too!"

"Bah! I fear him not, old as I am. He is but a boy in years, you remember, and will be easily managed."

"I hope so; I don't want my brains blown out, at least."

The stage rumbled on; the Jehu cursed and lashed his horses; the canyon grew deeper, narrower and darker, the grade slightly descending.

The moon seemed resting on the summit of a peak, hundreds of feet above, and staring down in surprise at the noisy stage.

Alexander Filmore (the elder passenger) succeeded in steadying himself long enough to ignite the end of a cigar in the bowl of Jehu's grimy pipe; then he watched the trees that flitted by. Clarence, his son, had smoked incessantly since leaving Camp Crook, and now threw away his half-used cheroot, and listened to the sighing of the spectral pines.

"The girl—what about her?" he asked, after some moments had elapsed.

"She will be as much in the way as the boy will."

"She? Well, we'll attend to her after we git him out of the way. He is the worst obstacle in our path, at present. Maybe when you see the girl you will take a fancy to her."

"Pish! I want no petticoats clinging to me—much less an ignorant backwoods clodhopper. She is probably a fit mate for an Indian chief."

"You are too rough on the tender sex, boy," and the elder Filmore gave vent to a disconnected laugh. "You must remember that your mother was a woman."

"Was she?" Clarence bit the end of his waxed mustache, and mused over his sire's startling announcement. "*You* recollect that I never saw her."

"D'ye carry poppin'-jays, pilgrims?" demanded Jehu, turning so suddenly upon the two passengers as to frighten them out of their wits.

"Popping-jays?" echoed Filmore, senior.

"Yas—shutin'-irons—revolvers—patent perforatin' masheens."

"Yes, we are armed, if that is what you mean."

On dashed the stage through the echoing canyon—on plunged the snorting horses, excited to greater efforts by the frequent application of the cracking lash. The pines grew thicker, and the moonlight less often darted its rays down athwart the road.

"Hey!" yelled a rough voice from within the stage, "w'at d'ye drive so fast fer? Ye've jonced the senses clean out uv a score o' us."

"Go to blazes!" shouts back Jehu, giving an extra crack to his whip. "Who'n the name o' John Rodgers ar' drivin' this omnybust, pilgrim?—you or I?"

"You'll floor a hoss ef ye don' mind sharp!"

"Who'n thunder wants ye to pay fer et, ef I do?" rings back, tauntingly. "Reckon w'en Bill McGucken can't drive ther thru-ter-Deadwood stage as gude as ther average, he'll suspend bizness, or hire *you* ter steer in his place."

On, on rumbles the stage, down through a lower grade of the canyon, where no moonlight penetrates, and all is of Stygian darkness.

The two passengers on top of the stage shiver with dread, and even old Bill McGucken peers around him, a trifle suspiciously.

It is a wild spot, with the mountains rising on each side of the road to a stupendous hight, the towering pines moaning their sad, eternal requiem; the roar of the great wheels over the hardpan bottom; the snorting of the fractious lead-horses; the curses and the cracking of Jehu's whip; the ring of iron-shod hoofs—it is a place and moment conducive to fear, mute wonder, admiration.

"*Halt!*"

High above all other sounds now rings this cry, borne toward the advancing stage from the impenetrable space of gloom ahead, brought down in clear commanding tone wherein there is neither fear nor hesitation.

That one word has marvelous effect. It brings a gripe of iron into the hands of Jehu, and he jerks his snorting steeds back upon their haunches; it is instrumental in stopping the stage. (Who ever knew a Black Hills driver to offer to press on when challenged to halt in a wild dismal place?)

It sends a thrill of lonely horror through the veins of those to whose ears the cry is borne; it causes hands to fly to the butts of weapons, and hearts to beat faster.

"Halt!" Again the cry rings forth, reverberating in a hundred dissimilar echoes up the rugged mountain side.

The horses quiet down; Jehu sits like a carved statue on his box; the silence becomes painful to those within the stage—those who are trembling in a fever of excitement, and peering from the open windows with revolvers cocked for instant use.

The moon suddenly thrusts her golden head over the pinnacle of a hoary peak a thousand feet above, and lights up the gorge with a ghastly distinctness that enables the watchers to behold a black horseman blocking the path a few rods ahead.

"Silence! Listen!" Two words this time, in the same clear, commanding voice. A pause of a moment; then the stillness is broken by the ominous click! click! of a score of rifles; this alone announces that the stage is "covered."

Then the lone horseman rides leisurely down toward the stage, and Jehu recognizes him. It is Deadwood Dick, Prince of the Road!

Mounted upon his midnight steed, and clad in the weird suit of black, he makes an imposing spectacle.

* A fact.

as he comes fearlessly up. Well may he be bold and fearless, for no one dares to raise a hand against him, when the glistening barrels of twelve rifles protruding from each thicket that fringes the road threaten those within and without the stage.

Close up to the side of the coach rides the daring young outlaw, his piercing orbs peering out from the eye-holes in his black mask, one hand clasping the bridle-reins the other a nickel-plated seven-shooter drawn back at full cock.

"You do well to stop, Bill McGucken!" the road-agent, observes, reining in his steed. "I expected you hours ago, on time."

"Twarn't my fault, yer honor!" replies Jehu, meek as a lamb under the gaze of the other's pop-gun. "Ye see, we broke a pole this side o' Custer City, an' that set us behind several p'ints o' ther compass."

"What have you aboard to-night worth examining?"

"Nothin', yer honor. Only a stageful uv passengers, this trip."

"Bah! you are getting poor. Get down from off the box, there!"

The driver trembled, and hesitated.

"Get down!" again commanded the road-agent, leveling his revolver, "before I drop you."

In terror McGucken made haste to scramble to the ground, where he stood with his teeth chattering and knees knocking together in a manner pitiable to see.

"Ha, ha, ha!" That wild laugh of Deadwood Dick's made the welkin ring out a wierd chorus. "Bill McGucken, you should join the regular army, you are so brave. Ha, ha, ha!"

And the laugh was taken up by the road-knights, concealed in the thicket, and swelled into a wild, boisterous shout.

Poor McGucken trembled in his boots in abject terror, while those inside the coach were pretty well scared.

"Driver!" said the Prince of the Road, coolly, after the laugh, "go you to the passengers who grace this rickety shebang and take up a collection. You needn't cum to me wi' less'n five hundred ef ye don't want me to salt ye!"

Bowing humble obeisance, McGucken took off his hat, and made for the stage door.

"Gentlemen!" he plead, "there is need o' yer dutchin' out yer dudads right liberal ef ye've enny purtic'lar anticypation an' desire ter git ter Deadwood ter-night. Dick, the Road-Agent, are law an' gospel heerabouts, I spec'late!"

"Durned a cent 'll I fork!" growled one old fellow, loud enough to be heard. "I ain't afeerd o' all the robber Dicks from here ter Jerusalum."

But when he saw the muzzle of the young road-agent's revolver gazing in through the window, he suddenly changed his mind, and laid a plethoric pocketbook into McGucken's already well-filled hat.

The time occupied in making the collection was short, and in a few moments the Jehu handed up his battered "plug" to the Prince of the Road for inspection.

Coolly Deadwood Dick went over the treasure, as if it were all rightfully his own; then he chucked hat and all into one of his saddle-bags, after which he turned his attention toward the stage. As he did so he saw for the first time the two passengers on top, and as he gazed at them a gleam of fire shot into his eyes and his hands nervously griped at his weapon.

"Alexander Filmore, you here!" he ejaculated, his voice betraying his surprise.

"Yes," replied the elder Filmore, coldly—"here to shoot you, you dastardly dog," and quickly raising a pistol, he took rapid and deadly aim, and fired.

CHAPTER VIII.

NOT YET!

With a groan Deadwood Dick fell to the ground, blood spurting from a wound in his breast. The bullet of the elder Filmore had indeed struck home.

Loud then were the cries of rage and vengeance, as a score of masked men poured out from the thickets, and surrounded the stage.

"Shoot the accursed nigger!" cried one. "He's killed our leader, an' by all the saints in ther calendur he shall pay the penalty!"

"No! no!" yelled another, "we'll do no such a thing. He shall swing in mid-air!"

"Hey!" cried a third, rising from the side of the prostrate road-agent, "don' ye be so fast, boys. The capt'in still lives. He is not seriously wounded, even!"

A loud huzza went up from the score of throats, that caused a thousand echoing reverberations along the mountain side.

"Better let ther capt'in say what we shall do wi' yon cuss o' creashun!" suggested one who was apparently a leading spirit; "it's *his* funeral, ain't it?"

"Yas, yas, it's his funeral!"

"Then let him do ther undertakin'."

Robber Dick was accordingly supported to a sitting posture, and the blood that flowed freely from his wound was stanched. In the operation his mask became loosened and slipped to the ground, but so quickly did he snatch it up and replace it, that no one caught even a glimpse of his face.

In the meantime Clarence Filmore had discharged every load in his two six-shooters into the air. He had an object in doing this; he thought that the reports of fire-arms would reach Deadwood (which was only a short mile distant, around the bend), and arouse the military, who would come to his rescue.

Dick's wound dressed, he stood once more upon his feet, and glared up at the two men on the box. They were plainly revealed in the ghostly moonlight, and their features easily studied.

"Alexander Filmore!" the young road-agent said, a terrible depth of meaning in his voice, that the cowering wretch could but understand.

"Alexander Filmore, you have at last come out and shown your true colors. What a treacherous, double-dyed villain you are! Better so; better that you should take the matter into your own hands and face the music, than to employ *tools*, as you have done heretofore. I can fight a dozen enemies face to face better than one or two lurking in the bushes."

The elder Filmore uttered a savage curse.

"You triumph *now!*" he growled, biting his nether lip in vexation; "but it will not always be thus."

"Eh? think not? I think I shall have to *adopt* you for awhile. Boys, haul down the two, and bind them securely."

Accordingly, a rush was made upon the stage, and the two outside passengers. Down they were hauled, head over heels, and quickly secured by strong cords about the wrists and ankles.

This done, Deadwood Dick turned to Bill McGucken, who had ventured to clamber to the seat of the coach.

"Drive on, you cowardly lout—drive on. We've done with you for the present. But, remember, not a word of this to the population of Deadwood, if you intend to ever make another trip over this route. Now, go!"

Jehu needed not the second invitation. He never was tardy in getting out of the way of danger; so he picked up the reins, gave an extra hard crack of the long whip, and away rolled the jolting stage through the black canyon, disappearing a moment later around the bend, beyond which lay Deadwood —magic city of the wilderness.

Then, out from the thicket the road-agents led their horses; the two prisoners were secured in the saddles in front of two brawny outlaws, and without delay the cavalcade moved down the gorge, weirdly illuminated by the mellow rays of the soaring moon.

Clarence Filmore had hoped that the report of his pistol-shots would reach Deadwood. If so, his wishes were fulfilled. The reports reached the barracks above Deadwood just as a horseman galloped up the hill—Major R——, just in from a carouse down at the "Met."

"Halloo!" he shouted, loudly. "To horse! there is trouble in the gorge. The Sioux, under Sitting Bull, are upon us!"

As the major's word was law at the barracks, in very short order the garrison was aroused, and headed by the major in person, a cavalcade of sleepy soldiers swept down the gorge toward the place whence had come the firing.

Wildly around the abrupt bend they dashed with yells of anticipated victory; then there was a frightful collision between the incoming stage and the outgoing cavalry; the shrieks and screams of horses, the curses and yells of wounded men; and a general pandemonium ensued.

The coach, passengers, horses and all was upset, and went rolling down a steep embankment.

Major R—— was precipitated headlong over the embankment, and in his downward flight probably saw more than one soaring comet. He struck head-first in a muddy run, and a sorrier-looking officer of the U. S. A. was never before seen in the Black Hills as he emerged from his bath, than the major. His ridiculous appearance went so far as to stay the general torrent of blasphemy and turn it into a channel of boisterous laughter.

No delay was made in putting things ship-shape again, and ere morning dawned Deadwood beheld the returned soldiers and wrecked stage with its sullen passengers within its precincts.

Dick and his men rode rapidly down the canyon, the two prisoners bringing up the rear under the escort of two masked guards.

These guards were brothers and Spanish-Mexicans at that.

The elder Filmore, a keen student of character, was not long in making out these Spaniards' true character, nor did their greedy glances toward his and his son's diamonds escape him.

"We want to get free!" he at last whispered, when none of those ahead were glancing back. "You will each receive a cool five hundred apiece if you will set us at liberty."

The two road-agents exchanged glances.

"It's a bargain!" returned one. "Stop your horses, and let the others go on!"

The main party were at this juncture riding swiftly down a steep grade.

The four horses were quietly reined in, and when the others were out of hearing, their noses were turned back up the canyon in the direction of Deadwood.

"This will be an unhealthy job for us!" said one of the brothers, "should we ever meet Dick again."

"Fear him not!" replied Alexander Filmore, with an oath. "If he ever crosses your path shoot him down like a dog, and I'll give you a thousand dollars for the work. The sooner he dies the better I'll be suited."

He spoke in a tone of strongest hate—deepest rancor.

CHAPTER IX.

AT THE "MET."

A few nights subsequent to the events related in our last chapter, it becomes our duty to again visit the notorious "Metropolitan" saloon of Deadwood, to see what is going on there.

As usual everything around the place and in it is literally "red hot." The bars are constantly crowded, the gaming-tables are never empty, and the floor is so full of surging humanity that the dance, formerly a chief attraction, has necessarily been suspended.

The influx of "pilgrims" into the Black Hills for the last few days has been something more than wonderful, every stage coming in overcharged with feverish passengers, and from two to a dozen trains arriving daily.

Of course Deadwood receives a larger share of all this immigration—nothing is more natural, for the young metropolis of the hills is *the* miner's rendezvous, being in the center of the best yielding locates.

Every person in Deadwood can tell you where the "Met" is, as it is general head-quarters.

We mount the mud-splashed steps and disappear behind the screen that stands in front of the door. Then the merry clink of glasses, snatches of ribald song, and loud curses from the polluted lips of some wretch who has lost heavily at the gaming-table, reach our hearing, while our gaze wanders over as motley a crowd as it has ever been our fortune to behold.

Men from the States—lawyers, doctors, speculators, adventurers, pilgrims, and dead-beats; men from the western side of the Missouri; grisly miners from Colorado; hunters and trappers from Idaho and Wyoming; card sharps from Denver and Fr'isco; pickpockets from St. Joe and bummers from Omaha —all are here, each one a part of a strange and on the whole a very undesirable community.

Although the dance has been suspended, that does not necessitate the discharge of the brazen-faced girls, and they may yet be seen here with the rest mingling freely among the crowd.

Seated at a table in a somewhat retired corner, were two persons engaged at cards. One was a beardless youth attired in buck-skin, and armed with knife and pistols; the other a big, burly tough from the upper chain—grisly, bloated and repulsive. He, too, was nothing short of a walking arsenal, and it was plain to see that he was a desperate character.

The game was poker. The youth had won three straight games and now laid down the cards that ended the fourth in his favor.

"You're flaxed ag'in, pardner!" he said, with a light laugh, as he raked in the stakes. "This takes your all, eh?"

"Every darned bit!" said the "Cattymount"—for it was he—with an oath. "You've peeled me to ther hide, an' no mistake. Salivated me' way out o' time, sure's thar ar' modesty in a bar-girl's tongue!"

The youth laughed. "You are not in luck to-night. Maybe your luck will return, if you keep on. Haven't you another V?"

"Nary another!"

"Where's your pard, that got salted the other night?"

"Who—Chet Diamond? Wal, hee's around heer, sum'ars, but I can't borry none off o' him. No; I've gotter quit straight off."

"I'll lend you ten to begin on," said the youth, and he laid an X in the ruffian's hands. "There, now, go ahead with your funeral. It's your deal."

The cards were dealt, and the game played, resulting in the favor of the "Cattymount." Another and another was played, and the tough won every time. Still the youth kept on, a quiet smile resting on his pleasant features, a twinkle in his coal-black eye. The youth, dear reader, you have met before.

He is not he, but instead—Calamity Jane. On goes the game, the burly "tough" winning all the time, his pile of tens steadily increasing in hight.

"Talk about Joner an' the ark, an' Noar an' ther whale!" he cries, slapping another X onto the pile with great enthusiasm; "I hed a grate, grate muther-in-law w'at played keerds wi' Noar inside o' thet eyedentical whale's stummick—played poker wi' w'alebones fer pokers. They were afterward landed at Plymouth rock, or sum uther big rock, an' fit together, side by side, in the rebellyuns."

"Indeed!"—with an amused laugh—"then you must have descended from a long line of respected ancestors."

"Auntsisters? Wa'al, I jest about reckon I do. I hev got ther blood o' Cain and Abel in my veins, boyee, an' ef I ken't raise the biggest kind o' Cane 'tain't because I ain't *able*—oh! no. Pace anuther-pilgrim?"

"I reckon. How much have ye got piled up thar in that heap!"

"Squar' ninety tens, my huckleberry, an' all won fa'r, you bet."

"Then it's the first time you ever won anything fair, Cass Diamond!" exclaimed a voice close at hand, and the two players looked up to see Ned Harris standing near by, with his hands clasped across his breast.

Calamity Jane nodded, indifferently. She had seen the young miner on several occasions; once she had been rendered an invaluable service when he rescued her from a brawl in which a dozen toughs had attacked her.

"Cattymount" Cass, brother of Chet Diamond, the Deadwood card-king, recognized him also, and with an oath, sprung to his feet.

"By all the Celestyals!" he ejaculated, jerking forth a six-shooter—"by all the roarin', screechin', shriekin', yowlin', squawkin,' ring-tailed, flat-futted cattymounts thet ever did ther forest aisles o' old Alaska traverse! *you* here, ye infernal smooth-faced varmint? *You* heer, arter all ye've did to ride ther cittyzens o' Deadwood inter rebellyun, ye leetle pigminian deputy uv ther devil? Hurra! hurra! boys; let's string him up ter ther nearest sapling!"

"Ha! ha!" laughed Harris, coolly, "hear the coward squeal for his pard's assistance. Dassen't stand on his own leather fer fear of gettin' salted fer all he's worth."

"You're a liar!" roared the "Cattymount," spreading himself about promiscuously, but the two words had scarcely left his lips when a blow from the fist of Ned Harris reached him under the left eye, and he went sprawling on the ground in a heap.

"Here! here!" roared a stranger, rushing in upon the scene, and hurling the crowd aside with a dexterity something wonderful. "What is the meaning of all this? Who knocked Cass Diamond down?"

"I had that honor!" coolly remarked Ned Harris, stepping boldly up and confronting the Deadwood card-king, for it was the notorious Chet Diamond who had asked the question. "I smacked him in the gob, Chet Diamond, for calling me a liar, and am ready to accommodate a few more, if there are any who wish to prefer the same charge!"

"Bully, Ned! and here's what will back you!" cried Calamity Jane, leaping to the miner's side, a cocked six in either white, shapely hand; "so sail in, pilgrims!"

Diamond cowered back, and swore furiously. The wound in his breast was yet sore and rankling, and he knew he owed it to the cool and calculating young miner whose name was an omen of terror among the "toughs" of Deadwood.

"Come on, you black-hearted ace thief!" shouted Calamity Jane, thrusting the muzzle of one of her plated revolvers forcibly under the gambler's prominent nose—"come on! slide in if you are after squar' up-an'-down fun. We'll greet you, best we know how, an' not charge you anything, either. See! I've got a couple full hands o' sixes—every one's a trump! Ain't ye got no aces hid up yer sleeves?"

The card sharp still cursed furiously, and backed away. He dare not reach for a weapon lest the dare-devil girl or young Harris (who now held a cocked pill-box in each hand), "should salt him on a full fly."

"Ha! ha! ha!" and the laugh of Calamity rung wildly through the great saloon—"Ha! ha! ha! here's a go! Who wants to buy a clipped-winged sharp?"

"Sold out right cheap!" added Ned, facetiously. "Clear the track and we'll take him out and boost him to a limb."

At this juncture some half a dozen of the gambler's gang came rushing up, headed by Catamount Cass, who had recovered from the effects of the blow from Harris' fist.

"At them! at 'em!" roared the "screechin' catty mount frum up nor'." "Rip, dig an' gouge 'em. Ho! ho! we'll see now who'll swing, *we* will! We'll larn who'll display his agility in mid-air, we will. At 'em, b'yees, at 'em. We'll hang 'em like they do hoss-thieves down at Cheyenne!"

Then followed a pitched battle in the bar-room of the "Metropolitan" saloon, such as probably never occurred there before, and never has since.

Revolvers flashed on every hand, knives clashed in deadly conflict; yells, wild, savage, and awful made a perfect pandemonium, to which was added a second edition in the shape of oaths, curses, and groans. Crack! whiz! bang! the bullets flew about like hailstones, and men fell to the reeking floor each terrible moment.

The two friends were not alone in the affray.

No sooner had Catamount Cass and his gang of "toughs" showed fight, than a company of miners sprung to Harris' side, and showed their willingness to fight it out on the square line.

Therefore, once the first shot was fired, it needed not a word to pitch the battle.

Fiercely waged the contest—now hand to hand—and loud rose the savage yells on the still night air.

One by one men fell on either side, their life-blood crimsoning the floor, their dying groans unheeded in the fearful melee.

Still unharmed, and fighting among the first, we see Ned Harris and his remarkable companion, Calamity Jane; both are black, and scarcely recognizable in the cloud of smoke that fills the bar-room. Harris is wounded in a dozen places and weak from loss of blood; yet he stands up bravely and fights mechanically.

Calamity Jane if she is wounded shows it not, but faces the music with as little apparent fear as any of those around her.

On wages the battle, even as furiously as in its beginning; the last shot has been fired; it is now knife to knife, and face to face.

Full as many of one side as the other have fallen, and lay strewn about under foot, unthought of, uncared for in the excitement of the desperate moment. Gallons of blood have made the floor slippery and reeking, so that it is difficult to retain one's footing.

At the head of the ruffians the Diamond brothers* still hold sway, fighting like madmen in their endeavors to win a victory. They cannot do less, for to back off in this critical moment means sure death to the weakening party.

But hark! what are these sounds?

The thunder of hoofs is heard outside; the rattle of musketry and sabers, and the next instant a company of soldiery, headed by Major R——, ride straight up into the saloon, firing right and left.

"Come!" cried Calamity Jane, grasping Harris by the arm, and pulling him toward a side door, "it's time for us to slope now. It's every man for himself."

And only under her guidance was Ned able to escape, and save being killed and captured with the rest.

About noon of the succeeding day, two persons on horseback were coming along the north gulch leading into Deadwood, at an easy canter. They were the fearless Scarlet Boy, or as he is better known, Fearless Frank, and his lovely protege, Miss Terry. They had been for a morning ride over to a neighboring claim, and were just returning.

* Living characters.

Since their arrival in Deadwood the youth had devoted a part of his time in a search for Alice's father, but all to no avail. None of the citizens of Deadwood or its surroundings had ever heard of such a person as Captain Walter Terry.

The young couple had become fast friends from their association, and Alice was improving in looks every day she stayed in the mountains.

"I feel hungry," observed Frank, as they rode along. "This life in the hills gives me a keen appetite. How is it with you, lady?"

"The same as with you, I guess. But look! Yonder comes a horseman toward us!"

It was even so. A horseman was galloping up the gulch—no other than our young friend, Ned Harris.

As the two parties approach, the faces of each of the youths grow deadly pale; there comes into their eyes an ominous glitter; their hands each clasp the butt of a revolver, and they gradually draw rein.

That they are enemies of old—that the fire of rancor burns in their hearts, and that this meeting is unexpected, is plain to see.

Now, that they have met, probably for the first time in months or years, it remains not to be doubted but a settlement must come between them—that their hate must result in satisfaction, whether in blood or not.

CHAPTER X.

THE DUEL AND ITS RESULT.

BELLIGERENT were the glances exchanged between the two, as they sat there facing each other, each with a hand closed over the butt of a pistol; each as motionless as a carved statue.

Alice Terry had grown pale, too. She saw that friend and protector and the stranger were enemies, —that this meeting though purely accidental was not to end without trouble. Her lips grew set, her eyes flashed, and she reined her horse closer to that of the Scarlet Boy.

Ned Harris let a faint smile, of contempt and pity combined, come into relief on his lips, as he saw this action. Better ten male enemies than one female, he thought; but, then, women must not stand in the way, now. No! nothing must block the path intervening between enmity and vengeance.

Harris was, if anything, the coolest of the three; but, after all, why should he not be? He had spent several years in society that seemed callous to fear, —that knew not what it was to be a Christian; where the utmost coolness was necessary to the preservation of life; where bravery was all, and education a dead letter. Fearless Frank, too, had seen all phases of rough western life, probably, but his temperament was more nervous and excitable, his passions tenfold harder to restrain. Still, he managed to exercise a cool exterior now, that equaled that of his opposite—his hated enemy. Mystery, as Frank habitually called the girl, did not offer to conceal her feelings. It was but natural that she should side with him to whom she owed her life, and the glances of scorn and indignation she shot at the young miner might have driven another man than him into a retreat.

Fearless Frank made no motion toward speech; he was determined that the young miner should open the quarrel, if a quarrel it was to be. But beneath his firm-set lips were clenched two rows of teeth, tightly, fiercely; while every nerve in the youth's body was drawn to its utmost tension.

Harris was wonderfully calm and at ease; only a gray pallor on his handsome face and a menacing fire in his piercing eyes told that he was in the least agitated.

"Justin McKenzie!"

Sternly rung out the words on the clear mountain air. Ned Harris had spoken, and the grayish pallor deepened on his countenance while the fire of rancor burned with stronger gleam in his eagle eye.

The effect on the scarlet youth was scarcely noticeable, more than that the lips grew more rigid and compressed, and the right hand clutched the pistol-butt more tightly. But no answer to the other's summons.

"Justin McKenzie!" again said the young miner, calmly, "do you recognize me?"

The Scarlet Boy bows his head slowly, his eyes watchful lest the other shall catch the drop on him.

"Justin McKenzie, you *do* recognize me, even after the elapse of two long weary years, during which I have sought for you faithfully, but failed to find you until this hour. We have at last met, and the time for settlement between you and me, Justin McKenzie, has arrived. Here in this out-of-the-way gorge, we will settle the grudge I hold against you—we will see who shall live and who shall die!"

Alice Terry uttered a terrified cry.

"Oh! no! no! you must not fight—you *must* not. It is bad—oh! so awful wicked!"

"Excuse me, lady, but you will have no voice in this matter;" and the miner's tone grew a trifle more severe. "Knew you the bitter wrong done me by this young devil with the smooth face and oily tongue—if you knew what a righteous cause I have to defend, you would say 'let the battle proceed.' I am not one to thirst for the blood of my fellow-men, but I *am* one that is ever ready to raise my hand and strike in the defense of women!"

Alice Terry secretly admired the stalwart young miner for this gallant speech.

Fearless Frank, his face paler than before, an expression of remorse combined with anguish about his countenance, and moisture standing in either eye, assumed his quasi-erect attitude as he answered:

"Edward Harris, if you will listen, I will say all I have to say in a very few words. You hate me because of a wrong I did you and yours, and you want my life for the forfeit. I shall not hinder you longer in your purpose. For two long years you have trailed and tracked me with the determination of a bloodhound, and I have evaded you, not that I was at all afraid of you, but because I did not wish to make you a murderer. I have come across your path at last; here let us settle, as you have said. See! I fold my arms across my breast. Take out your pistol, aim steadily, and fire twice at my breast. I have heard enough concerning your skill as a marksman to feel confident that you can kill me in two shots!"

Ned Harris flushed, angrily. He was surprised at the cool indifference and recklessness of the youth; he was angered that McKenzie should think *him* mean enough to take such a preposterous advantage.

"You are a fool!" he sneered, biting his lip with vexation. "Do you calculate I am a *murderer?*"

"I have no proof that you are or that you are *not!*" replied Fearless Frank, controlling his temper by a master effort. "You remember I have not kept a watch upon your actions."

"Be that as it may, I would be an accursed dog to take advantage of your insulting proposal. You must fight me the same as I shall fight you!"

"No, Ned Harris, I will do nothing of the kind. It is I who have wronged you and yours; you must take the offensive; I will play a silent hand."

"You refuse to fight me?"

"I *do* refuse to fight you, but do *not* refuse to give you satisfaction for what wrong you have suffered. Take my life, if you choose; it is yours. Take it, or forever after this consider our debt of hatred canceled, and let us be—"

"Friends? Never, Justin McKenzie, *never!* You forget the stain dyed by your hand that will never wash out!"

"No! no! God knows I do not forget!" and the youth's voice was hoarse with anguish. "Could it be undone, I would gladly undo the deed. But, tell me, Harris, about *her*. Does she still live?"

"*Live?* We-l-l, yes, if you can call staying living. Life is but a blank; better she had died ere she ever met you!"

"You speak truly; better she had died ere she met me."

Unconsciously the two had ridden closer to each other; had they forgotten themselves in recalling the past?

"She lives—may live on her lonely life for years to come," Harris resumed, thoughtfully, "but her life will be merely endurance."

"Will you tell me where—where I can go in secret and take but one look at her? If you will do this, I will agree to meet you and give you your chance for satis—"

"No!" thundered Harris, growing suddenly furious, "*no!* a thousand times! I'd sooner see her in the burning depths of the bottomless pit than have you get within a hundred miles of her with your contaminating presence. She is safely hidden away, and that forever, from the companionship of our sex. So let her be till death claims her!"

"You are too hard on her!"

"And not hard enough on you, base villain that your are! Who is this young lady you have in your company—another of your victims?"

"Hold! Edward Harris; enough of your vile insinuations. This lady is one whom I rescued from Sitting Bull, the Sioux, and I am helping her to hunt a father who she says is somewhere in the Black Hills. Your language should at least be respectful!"

The rebuke stung young Harris to the quick, but he reined in his passion in a moment, and doffed his hat.

"Pardon me, miss, pardon me. It was ungentlemanly for me to speak as I did, but I was surprised at seeing one of your sex in company with this accomplished scamp, Justin McKenzie."

"My presence with him is, as he said, for the purpose of finding my father. He rescued me from the Indians, and has volunteered his services, for which I am very thankful. So far, sir, he has acted in a courteous and gentlemanly manner toward me!" said Alice Terry. "What he may have been heretofore concerns me not, as you must know."

"He is always that—smooth-tongued, until he has lured his victim to ruin!" retorted Ned, bitterly. "Beware of him, lady, for he is a rattlesnake in the disguise of a bright-winged butterfly."

Fearless Frank grew livid at this last thrust. Forbearance is virtue, sometimes, but not always. In his case the Scarlet Boy felt that he could bear the taunts of the miner no longer.

"You are a liar and a dastard!" he cried, fiercely. "Come on if you wish satisfaction, and I'll give it to you!"

"I am ready, always, sir. I challenged you first; you have the choice!" retorted Ned, as cool as ever, while his enemy was all trembling with excitement.

"Pistols, at fifty yards; to be fired until one or the other is dead!" was the prompt decision.

"Good! Young lady, you will necessarily have to act as second for both of us. If I drop, leave my body where I fall, and it will be picked up by friends. If he falls, I will ride on to Deadwood, and send you out help to carry him in."

Without delay the distance was guessed at, and each of the young men rode to position. Miss Terry, the beautiful second, took her place at one side of the gulch, midway between the antagonists, and when all was in readiness she counted:

"One!"

The right hands of the two youths were raised on a level, and the gleaming barrel of a pistol shone from each.

"Two!"

There was a sharp click! click! as the hammers of the weapons were pulled back at full cock. Each click meant danger or death.

Harris was very white; so was Fearless Frank, but not so much so as the young woman who was to give the signal.

"Three! *Fire!*" cried Alice, quickly; then, there was a flash, the report of two pistols, and Ned Harris fell to the ground without a groan.

McKenzie ran to his side, and bent over him.

"Poor fellow!" he murmured, rising, a few moments later—"poor Ned. *He is dead!*"

It was Harris' request to be left where he fell. Accordingly he was laid on the grass by the roadside, his horse tethered near by, and then, accompanied by Alice, Justin McKenzie set out to Deadwood.

CHAPTER XI.

THE POCKET GULCH MINES—INVADERS OF THEM.

We see fit to change the scene once more back to the pocket gulch—the home of the sweet, sad-faced Anita. The date is one month later—one long, eventful month since Justin McKenzie shot down Ned Harris under the noonday sun, a short distance above Deadwood.

Returning to the Flower Pocket by the route to the rugged transverse gulch, and thence through the gaping fissure, we find before us a scene—not of slumbering beauty, but of active industry and labor, such as was not here when we last looked into the flower-strewn paradise of the Hills.

The flowers are for the most part still intact, though occasionally you will come across a spot where the hand of man hath blighted their growth.

Where stood the little vine-wreathed cabin now may be seen a larger and more commodious log structure, which is but a continuation of the original.

A busy scene greets our gaze all around. Men are hurrying here and there through the valley—men not of the paleface race, but of the red race; men, clad only to the waist, with remarkable muscular developments, and fleetness of foot.

Over the little creek which dashes far adown from pine-dressed mountain peaks, and trails its shining waters through the flowering land, is built another structure—of logs, strongly and carefully erected, and thatched by a master hand with bark and grass. From the roof projects a small smoke-stack, from which emanates a steady cloud of smoke, curling lazily upward toward heaven's blue vault, and inside is heard the grinding, crushing rumble of ponderous machinery, and we rightly conjecture that it is a crusher in full operation. Across from the northern side of the gulch comes a steady string of mules in line, each pulling behind him a jack-sled (or, what is better known to the general reader as a stone-boat) heavily laden with huge quartz rocks. These are dumped in front of one of the large doorways of the crusher, and the "empties" return mechanically and disappear within a gaping fissure in the very mountain side—a sort of tunnel, which the hand of man, aided by that great and stronger arm—powder—has burrowed and blasted out.

All this is under the immediate management of the swarthy-skinned red-men, whose faces declare them to be a remnant of the once great Ute tribe—now utilized to a better occupation than in the dark and bloody days of the past.

Near the crusher building is a large, stoutly-constructed windlass, worked by mule power, and every few moments there comes up to the surface from the depths of a shaft, a bucketful of rock and sand, which is dumped into a push-car, and from thence transferred to the line of sluice-boxes in the stream, where more half-clothed Utes are busily engaged in sifting golden particles from the rich sand.

What a transformation is all this since we left the Flower Pocket a little over a month ago! Now, everywhere within those majestic mountain-locked walls is bustle and excitement; then, the valley was sleeping away the calm, perfume-laden autumnal days, unconscious of the mines of wealth lying nestling in its bosom, and content and happy in its quietude and the adornments of nature's beauties.

Now, shouts, ringing halloos, angry curses at the obstinate mules, the rumbling of ponderous machinery, the clink of picks and reports of frequent blasts, the deadened sound of escaping steam, the barking of dogs, the whining of horses—all these sounds are now to be heard.

Then, the valley was peacefully at rest; the birds chimed in their exquisite music to the Æolian harp-like music of the breeze through the branches of the mountain pines; the waters pouring adown from the stupendous peaks created an everlasting song of love and constancy; bees and humming-birds drank delicious draughts from the blushing lips of a million nodding flowers; the sun was more hazy and drowsy-looking; everything had an appearance of ethereal peace and happiness.

But, like a drama on the stage, a grand transformation had taken place; a beautiful dream had been changed into stern reality; quietude and slumber had fled at the bold approach of bustling industry and life. And all this transformation is due to whom?

The noonday sun shone down on all the busy scene with a glance of warmth and affection, and particularly did its rays center about two men, who, standing on the southern side of the valley, up in among the rugged foothills, were watching the living panorama with the keenest interest.

They were Harry Redburn and the queer old humpbacked, bow-legged little locater, "General" Walsingham Nix.

Redburn was now looking nearly as rough, unkempt and grizzled as any veteran miner, and for a fact, he actually had not waxed the ends of his fine mustache for over a week. But there was more of a healthy glow upon his face, a robustness about his form, and a light of satisfaction in his eye which told that the rough miner's life agreed with him exceedingly well.

The old "General" was all dirt, life and animation, and as full of his eccentricities as ever. He was a character seldom met with—ever full of a quaint humor and sociability, but never known to get mad, no matter how great the provocation might be.

His chance strike upon the spot where lay the gold of Flower Pocket imbedded—if it could be called a chance, considering his dream—was the prelude to the opening up of one of the richest mining districts south of Deadwood.

We left them after Harry had driven a stake to mark the place which the somnambulist had pointed out as indicating the concealed mine.

On the succeeding day the two men set to work, and dug long and desperately to uncover the treasure, and after three days of incessant toil they were rewarded with success. A rich vein of gold, or, rather, a deposit of the valuable metal was found, it being formed in a deep, natural pocket and mixed alternately with sand and rock.

During the remaining four days of that week the two lucky miners took out enough gold to evidence their supposition that they had struck one of the richest fields in all the Black Hills country. Indeed, it seemed that there was no end to the depth of sand in the shaft, and as long as the sand held out the gold was likely to.

When, just in the flush of their early triumph, the old humpback was visited by another somnambulistic fit, and this time he discovered gold deep in the northern mountain side, and prophesied that the quartz rock which could be mined therefrom would more than repay the cost and trouble of opening up the vein and of transporting machinery to the gulch.

We need not go into detail of what followed; suffice it to say that immediate arrangements were made and executed toward developing this as yet unknown territory.

While Redburn set to work with two Ute Indians (transported to the gulch from Deadwood, under oath of secrecy by the "General") to blast into the mountain-side, and get at the gold-bearing quartz, the old locater in person set out for Cheyenne on the secret mission of procuring a portable crusher, boiler and engine, and such other implements as would be needed, and getting them safely into the gulch unknown to the roving population of the Hills country. And most wonderful to relate, he succeeded.

Two weeks after his departure, he returned with the machinery and two score of Ute Indians, whom he had sworn into his service, for, as a Ute rarely breaks his word, they were likely to prove valuable accessories to the plans of our two friends. Redburn had in the meantime blasted in until he came upon the quartz rock. Here he had to stop until the arrival of the machinery. He however busied himself in enlarging the cabin and building a curb to the shaft, which occupied his time until at last the "General" and his army returned.*

Now, we see these two successful men standing and gazing at the result of their joint labors, each financially happy; each growing rich as the day rolls away.

The miners are in a prosperous condition, and everything moves off with that ease and order that speaks of shrewd management and constant attention to business.

The gold taken from the shaft is much finer than that extracted from the quartz.

The quartz yielded about eighteen dollars to the ton, which the "General" declared to be as well as "a feller c'u'd expect, considerin' things, more or less!"

Therefore, it will be seen by those who have any knowledge whatever of gold mining that, after paying off the expenses, our friends were not doing so badly, after all.

"Yes, yes!" the "General" was remarking, as he gazed at the string of mules that alternately issued from and re-entered the fissure on the opposite side of the valley; "yes, yes, boyee, things ar' workin' as I like ter see 'em at last. The shaft 'll more'n pay expenses if she holds her head 'bove water, as I opine she will, an' w'at ar' squeezed out uv the quartz ar' cleer 'intment fer us."

"True; the shaft is more than paying off the hands," replied Redburn, seating himself upon a bowlder, and staring vacantly at the dense column of smoke ejected from the smoke-stack in the roof of the crusher building.

"I was looking up accounts last evening, and after deducting what you paid for the machinery, and what wages are due the Utes, we have about a thousand dollars clear of all, to be divided between three of us."

"Exactly. Now, that's w'at I call fair to middling. Of course thar'll be more or less expense, heerafter, but et'll be a consider'ble less o' more than more o' less. Another munth 'll tell a larger finanshell tale, I opine."

"Right again, unless something happens more than we think for now. If we get through another month, however, without being nosed out, why we may consider ourselves all-fired lucky."

"Jes' so! Jes' so! but we'll hev ter take our chances. One natteral advantage, we kin shute 'em as fast as they come—"

"Ho!" Redburn interrupted, suddenly, leaping to his feet; "they say the devil's couriers are ever around when you are talking of them. Look! invaders already."

He pointed toward the east, where the passage led out of the valley into the gorge beyond.

Out of this passage two persons on horseback had just issued, and now they came to a halt, evidently surprised at the scene which lay spread out before them.

No sooner did the "General" clap his eyes on the pair than he uttered a cry of astonishment, mingled with joy.

"It's thet scarlet chap, Fearless Frank!" he announced, hopping about like a pig on a hot griddle; "w'at I war tellin' ye about; the same cuss w'at desarted Charity Joe's train, ter look fer sum critter w'at war screechin' fer help. I went wi' the lad fer a ways, but my jackass happened to be more or less indispositioned—consider'bly more o' less than less o' more—an' so I made up my mind not ter continny on his route. Ther last I see'd o' the lad he disappeared over sum kind o' a precypice, an' calkylatin' as how he war done fer, I rej'ined Charity Joseph, an' kim on."

"He has a female in his company!" said Redburn, watching the new-comer keenly.

"Yas, 'peers to me he has, an' et's more or less likely that et's the same critter he went to resky w'en he left Charity Joe's train!"

"What about him? We do not want him here; to let him return to Deadwood after what he has seen would be certain death to our interests."

"Yas, thar's more or less truth in them words o' yours, b'yee—consider'bly more o' less than less o' more. He ken't go back now, nohow we kin fix et. He's a right peart sort o' a kid, an' I think ef we was ter guv him a job, or talk reeson'ble ter him, thet he'd consent to do the squar' thing by us."

Redburn frowned.

"He'll have to remain for a certain time, whether he wants to or not," he muttered, more savage than usual. It looked to him as if this was to be the signal of a general invasion. "Come! let's go and see what we can do."

They left the foothills, clambered down into the valley and worked their way toward where Fearless Frank and his companion sat in waiting.

As they did so, headed by a figure in black, who wore a mask as did all the rest, a band of horsemen rode out of the fissure into the valley. One glance and we recognize Deadwood Dick, Prince of the Road, and his band of road-agents!

CHAPTER XII

MAKING TERMS ALL AROUND.

Old General Nix was the first to discover the new invasion.

"Gorra'mighty!" he ejaculated, flourishing his staff about excitedly, "d'ye mind them same w'at's tuk et inter the'r heads to invade our sancty sanctorum, up yander? Howly saints frum ther cullender! We shall be built up inter an entire city 'twixt this an' sunset, ef ther population sect becum enny more numersome. Thar's a full fifty o' them sharks, more or less—consider'bly more o' less than less o' more—an' ef we hain't got ter hold a full hand in order to clean 'em out, why, ye can call me a cross-eyed, hair-lipped hyeeny, that's all."

Redburn uttered an ejaculation as he saw the swarm of invaders that was perhaps more forcible than polite.

He did not like the looks of things at all. If Ned Harris were only here, he thought, he could throw the responsibility all off on his shoulders. But he was not; neither had he been seen or heard of since he had quitted the valley over a month ago. Where he was staying all this time was a problem that no one could solve—no one among our three friends.

The "General" had made inquiries in Deadwood, but elicited no information concerning the young miner. He had dropped entirely out of the magic city's notice, and might be dead or dying in some foreign clime, for all they knew. Anita worried and grew sadder each day at his non-return; it seemed to her that he was in distress, or worse, perhaps—dead. He had never stayed away so long before, she said, always returning from his trips every few days. What, then, could now be the reason of his prolonged absence?

Redburn foresaw trouble in the intrusion of the road-agents and Fearless Frank, although he knew not the character or calling of the former, and he resolved to make one bold stroke in defense of the mines.

"Go to the quartz mines as quickly as you can!" he said, addressing Nix, "and call every man to his arms. Then rally them out here, where I will be waiting with the remainder of our forces, and we will see what can be done. If it is to be a fight for our rights, a desperate fight it shall be."

The "General" hurried off with as much alacrity as was possible, with him, toward the quartz mine, while Redburn likewise made haste to visit the shaft and collect together his handful of men.

He passed the cabin on the way, and, seeing Anita seated in the doorway, he came to a momentary halt.

"You had better go inside and lock the doors and windows behind you," he said, advisingly. "There are invaders in the gulch, and we must try and effect a settlement with them; so it is not desirable that they should see you."

"You are not going to fight them?"

"Yes, if they will not come to reasonable terms which I shall name. Why?"

"Oh! don't fight. You will get killed."

"Humph! what of that? Who would care if I were killed?"

"I would, for one, Mr. Redburn."

The miner's heart gave a great bound, and he gazed into the pure white face of the girl, passionately. Was it possible that she had in her heart anything akin to love, for *him?* Already he had conceived a passing fancy for her, which might ripen into love, in time.

"Thanks!" he said, catching up her hand and pressing it to his lips. "Those words, few as they are, make me happy, Miss Anita. But, stop! I must away. Go inside, and keep shady until you see me again;" and so saying he hurried on.

---

* This crusher is said to have been the first introduced into the Black Hills.

In ten minutes' time two score of brawny, half-dressed Utes were rallied in the valley, and Redburn was at their head, accompanied by the "General."

"I will now go forward and hold parley," said Harry, as he wrapped a kerchief about the muzzle of his rifle-barrel. "If you see me fall, you can calculate that it's about time for you to sling in a chunk of your lip."

He had fallen into the habit of talking in an illiterate fashion, since his association with the "General."

"All right," assented the old locater; "ef they try ter salt ye, jes' giv' a squawk, an' we'll cum a-tearin' down ter yer resky at ther rate o' forty hours a mile, more or less—consider'bly more o' less than less o' more."

Redburn buckled his belt a hole tighter, looked to his two revolvers, and set out on his mission.

The road-agents had, in the mean time, circled off to the right of the fissure, and formed into a compact body, where they halted and watched the rallying of the savages in the valley.

Fearless Frank and his lovely companion remained where they had first halted, awaiting developments. They had stumbled into Paradise and were both surprised and bewildered.

Redburn approached them first. He was at loss how to open the confab, but the Scarlet Boy saved him the trouble.

"I presume I see in you one of the representatives of this concern," he said, doffing his hat, and showing his pearly teeth in a little smile, as the miner came up.

"You do," replied Redburn, bowing stiffly. "I am an owner or partner in this mining enterprise, which, until your sudden advent, has been a secret to the outside world."

"I believe you, pilgrim; for, though I am pretty thoroughly acquainted with the topography of the Black Hills country, I had not the least idea that such an enterprise existed in this part of the territory."

"No, I dare say not. But how is it that we are indebted to you for this intrusion?—for such we feel justified in calling it, under the existing circumstances."

"I did not intend to intrude, sir, nor do I now. In riding through the mountains we accidentally stumbled into the fissure passage that leads to this gulch, and as there was nothing to hinder us, we came on through."

"True; I should have posted a strong guard n the pass. You have a female companion, I perceive: not your wife?"

"Oh, no! nor my sister, either. This is Miss Terry—an estimable young lady, who has come to the Black Hills in search of her father. Your name is—"

"Redburn—Harry Redburn; and yours, I am told, is Fearless Frank."

"Yes, that is the title I sail under. But how do you know aught of me?"

"I was told your name by a partner of mine. Now, then, concerning the present matter; what do you propose to do?"

"To do? Why, turn back, I suppose; I see nothing else to do."

Redburn leaned on his rifle and considered.

"Do you belong to that other crowd?"

"No, indeed;" Frank's face flushed, half angrily. "I thank my stars I am not quite so low down as that, yet. Do you know them? That's Deadwood Dick, the Prince of the Road, and his band of outlaws!"

"What—is it possible? The same gang whom the Pioneer is making such a splurge over, every week."

"The same. That fellow clad in black is Deadwood Dick, the leader."

"Humph! He in black; you in scarlet. Two contrasting colors."

"That is so. I had not thought of it before. But no significance is attached thereto."

"Perhaps not. Have you the least idea what brought them here?"

"The road-agents? I reckon I do. The military has been chasing them for the last two days. Probably they have come here for protection."

"Maybe so; or for plunder. Give me your decision, and I will go and see what they want."

"There is nothing for me to decide more than to take the back track."

Redburn shook his head, decidedly.

"You cannot go back!" he said, using positiveness in his argument; "that is, not for a while. You'd have all Deadwood down on us in a jiffy. I'll give you work in the shaft, at three dollars a day. You can accept that offer, or submit to confinement until I see fit to set you at liberty."

"And my companion, here—?"

"I will place under the charge of Miss Anita for the present, where she will receive hospitable treatment."

Fearless Frank started as though he had been struck a violent blow; his face grew very white; his eyes dilated; he trembled in every joint.

"Anita!" he gasped—"Anita!"

"I believe that is what I said!" Redburn could not understand the youth's agitation. He knew that the sister of Ned Harris had a secret; was this Fearless Frank in any way connected with it, and if so, how? "Do you know her?"

"Her other name is—"

"Harris—Anita Harris, in full. Do you know her, or aught of her?"

"I—I—I did, once!" was the slow reply. "Where is she; I want to see her?"

Redburn took a moment to consider.

Would it be best to permit a meeting between the two until he should be able to learn something more definite concerning the secret? If Ned Harris were here would he sanction such a meeting? No! something told the young miner that he would not;

something warned him that it could result in no good to allow the scarlet youth an interview with sad, sweet-faced Anita.

"You cannot see her!" he at last said, decidedly. "There is a reason why you two should never meet again, and if you remain in the gulch, as you will be obliged to, for the present, you must give me your word of honor that you will not go near yonder cabin."

Fearless Frank had expected this; therefore he was not surprised. Neither did Redburn know how close he had shied his stone at the real truth.

"I promise," McKenzie said, after a moment's deliberation, "on my honor, that I will not approach the cabin, providing you will furnish me my meals and lodgings elsewhere. If Anita comes to me, what then?"

"I will see that she does not," Redburn answered, positively. Gradually he was assuming full control of things, in the absence of Harris, himself. "Miss Terry, you may ride down to yonder cabin, and tell Anita I sent you. Pilgrim, you can come along with me."

"No; I will accompany Alice as far as where your forces are stationed," said Frank, and then they rode down the slope, Redburn turning toward where the road-agents sat upon their horses in a compact body, with Deadwood Dick at their head.

As the miner drew nigh and came to a standstill, the Prince of the road rode forward to his side.

"Well—?" he said, interrogatively, his voice heavy yet pleasant; "I suppose you desire to know what bizness we've got in your cornfield, eh, stranger?"

"That's about the dimensions of it, yes," replied Redburn, at once conceiving a liking for the young road-agent, in whom he thought he saw a true gentleman, in the disguise of a devil. "I came over to learn the object you have in view, in invading our little valley, if you have no objections in telling."

"Certainly not. As you may have guessed already, we are a band of road-agents, whose field of action we have lately confined to the Black Hills country. I have the honor of being the leader, and you have doubtless heard of me—Deadwood Dick, the 'Road-Agent Prince,' as the Pioneer persists in terming me. Just at present, things are rather sultry in the immediate vicinity of Deadwood, so far as we are concerned, and we sought this locality to escape a small army of the Deadwood military, who have been nosing around after us for the past week."

"Well—?"

"Well, we happened to see a man and woman come this way, and believing that it must lead to somewhere or other, we followed, and here we are, out of the reach of the blue-coats, but, I take it, in the way of a party of secret miners. Is it not so?"

"No, not necessarily so, unless you put yourselves in the way. You wish to remain quartered here for the present?"

"If not contrary to your wishes, we should like to, yes."

"I have no objections to offer, providing you will agree to two points."

"And what are they, may I ask?"

"These. That you will camp at the mouth of the passage, and thus keep out any other intruders that may come; second, that you will keep your men to this side of the valley, and not interfere with any of our laborers."

"To which I eagerly agree. You shall experience no inconvenience from our presence here; you furnish us a haven of safety from the pursuing soldiers; we in return will extend you our aid in repelling a host of fortune-seekers who may any moment come down this way in swarms."

"Very well; that settles it, then. You keep your promise, and all will go well."

The two shook hands; then Redburn turned and strode back to dismiss his forces, while Dick and his men took up their position at the place where the fissure opened into the gulch. Here they made preparations to camp. Redburn, while returning to his men, heard a shout of joy, and looking up, saw, to his surprise, that the old "General" and Alice Terry were locked in each other's arms, in a loving embrace.

CHAPTER XIII.
AT THE CABIN.

What did it mean?

Had the old hump-backed, bow-legged mine-locater gone crazy, or was he purposely insulting the beautiful maiden? Fearless Frank stood aside, apparently offering no objections to the hugging, and the Indians did likewise.

At least Miss Terry made no serious attempts to free herself from the "General's" bear-like embrace.

A few bounds brought Redburn to the spot, panting, breathless, perspiring. "What is the meaning of this disgraceful scene?" he demanded, angrily.

"Disgraceful!" The old "General" set Miss Terry down on her feet, after giving her a resounding smack, and turned to stare at the young miner, in astonishment. "Disgraceful!! Waal, young man, ter tell the solid Old Testament truth, more or less—consider'bly less o' more 'n more o' less—I admire yer cheek, hard an' unblushin' as et ar'. Ye call my givin' this pretty piece o' feminine gander a squar', fatherly sort o' a hug, disgraceful, do ye? Think et's all out o' ther bounds o' propriety, do ye?"

"I look at it in that light, yes," Redburn replied.

"Haw! haw! haw!" and the General shook his fat sides with immoderate laughter. "Why, pilgrim-tender-fut, this 'ere hundred an' twenty-six pounds o' feminine gender b'longs to me—ter yours, truly, Walsingham Nix—an' I have a parfec' individual right ter hug an' kiss her as much as I please, wi'out brookin' enny interference frum you. Alice, dear, this ar' Harry Redburn, gineral' sup'intendent o' ther Flower Pocket gold-mines, an' 'bout as fair spe-

cimen as they make, nowadays. Mr. Redburn, I'll formally present you to Miss Alice Terry, my darter!"

Redburn colored, and was not a little disconcerted on account of his blunder; but he rallied in a moment, and acknowledged the introduction with becoming grace and dignity.

"You must excuse my interference," he said, earnestly. "I saw the old 'General' here taking liberties that no stranger should take, and knowing nothing of the relationship existing between you, I was naturally inclined to think that he was either drunk or crazy; therefore I deemed it necessary to investigate. No offense, I hope."

"Of course not," and Alice smiled one of her sweetest smiles. "You did perfectly right and are deserving of no censure, whatever."

After a few moments of desultory conversation, Redburn took the "General" to one side, and spoke on the subject of Fearless Frank and Anita Harris—of his action in the matter, and so forth. Nix—or Terry, as the latter was evidently his real name—heartily coincided with his views, and both agreed that it was best not to let the Scarlet Boy come within range of Anita, or, at least, not till Ned Harris should return, when he could do as he chose.

Accordingly it was decided that Fearless Frank should be set to work in the quartz mine, that being the furthest from the cabin, and he could eat and sleep either in the mine or in the crusher building, whichever he liked best.

After settling this point the two men rejoined the others, and Frank was apprised of their decision. He made no remarks upon it, but it was plain to see that he was anything but satisfied. His wild spirit yearned for constant freedom.

The Utes were dismissed and sent back to their work; the "General" strolled off with McKenzie toward the quartz mine; it devolved upon Redburn to escort Alice to the cabin, which he did with pleasure, and gave her an introduction to sweet, sad-faced Anita, who awaited their coming in the open doorway.

The two girls greeted each other with warmth; it was apparent that they would become fast friends when they learned more of each other.

As for Redburn, he was secretly enamored with the "General's" pretty daughter; she was beautiful, and evidently accomplished, and her progenitor was financially well-to-do. What then was lacking to make her a fitting mate for any man? Redburn pondered deeply on this subject, as he left the girls together, and went out to see to his duties in the mines.

He found Terry and Fearless Frank in the quartz mine, looking at the swarthy-skinned miners; examining new projected slopes; suggesting easier methods for working out different lumps of gold-bearing rock. While the former's knowledge of practical mining was extended, the latter's was limited.

"I think thet thar ar' bigger prospects yet, in further," the old locater was saying. "I ain't much varsed on jeeological an' toppygraffical formation, myself, ye see; but then, it kinder 'peers to me thet this quartz vein ar' a-goin' to hold out f_r a consider'ble time yet."

"Doubtless. More straight digging an' less slopes I should think would be practicable," McKenzie observed.

"I don't see it!" said Redburn, joining them. "Sloping and transversing discovers new veins, while line work soon plays out. I think things are working in excellent order at present"

They all made a tour of the mine which had been dug a considerable distance into the mountain. The quartz was ordinarily productive, and being rather loosely thrown together was blasted down without any extra trouble. After a short consultation, Redburn and the "General" concluded to place Frank over the Utes as superintendent and mine-boss, as they saw that he was not used to digging, blasting or any of the rough work connected with the mine, although he was clear-headed and inventive.

When tendered the position it was gratefully accepted by him, he expressing it his intention to work for the interest of his employers as long as he should stay in the gulch.

Night at last fell over the Flower Pocket gold-mines, and work ceased.

The Utes procured their own food—mainly consisting of fish from the little creek and deer and mountain birds that could be brought down at almost any hour from the neighboring crags—and slept in the open air. Redburn had McKenzie a comfortable bed made in the crusher-house, and sent him out a meal fit for a prince.

As yet, Anita knew nothing of the scarlet youth's identity;—scarcely knew, in fact, that he was in the valley.

At the cabin, the evening meal was dispatched with a general expression of cheerfulness about the board. Anita seemed less downcast than usual, and the vivacious Alice made life and merriment for all. She was witty where wit was proper, and sensible in an unusual degree.

Redburn was infatuated with her. He watched her with an expression of fondness in his eyes; he admired her every gesture and action; he saw something new to admire in her, each moment he was in her society.

When the evening meal was cleared away, he took down the guitar, and sung several ballads, the old "General" accompanying him with his rich deep bass, and Alice with her clear birdlike alto; and the sweet melody of the trio's voices called forth round after round of rapturous applause from the road-agents camped upon the slope, and from the Utes who were lounging here and there among the flower-beds of the valley. But of the lot, Deadwood Dick was the only one bold enough to approach the cabin.

He came sauntering along and halted on the threshold, nodding to the occupants of the little apartment with a nonchalance which was not assumed.

"Good-evening!" he said, tipping his sombrero, but taking care not to let the mask slip from his face. "I hope mine is not an intrusion. Hearing music, I was loth to stay away, for I am a great lover of music;—it is the one passion that appeals to my better nature."

He seated himself on the little stone step, and motioned for Redburn to proceed.

One of those inside the cabin had been strangely affected at the sight of Dick, and that person was Anita. She turned deathly pale, her eyes assumed an expression of affright, and she trembled violently, as she first saw him. The Prince of the Road, however, if he saw her, noticed not her agitation; in fact, he took not the second glance at her while he remained at the cabin. His eyes were almost constantly fastening upon the lovely face and form of Alice.

Thinking it best to humor one who might become either a powerful enemy or an influential friend, Redburn accordingly struck up a lively air, *a la banjo*, and in exact imitation of a minstrel, rendered "Gwine to Get a Home, Bymeby." And the thunders of *encore* that came from the outside listeners, showed how surely he had touched upon a pleasant chord. He followed that with several modern seriocomic songs, all of which were received well and heartily applauded.

"That recalls memories of good old times," said the road-agent, as he leaned back against the door-sill, and gazed at the mountains, grand, majestic, stupendous, and the starlit sky, azure, calm and serene. "Recalls the days of early boyhood, that were gay, pure, and happy. Ah! ho!"

He heaved a deep sigh, and his head dropped upon his breast.

A deathlike silence pervaded the cabin; that one heartfelt sigh aroused a sensation of pity in each of the four hearts that beat within the cabin walls.

That the road-agent was a gentleman in disguise, was not to be gainsayed; all felt that, despite his outlawed calling, he was deserving of a place among them, in his better moods.

As if to accord with his mood, Alice began a sweet birdlike song, full of tender pathos, and of quieting sympathy.

It was a quaint Scottish melody,—rich in its honeyed meaning, sweetly weird and pitiful; wonderfully soothing and nourishing to a weeping spirit.

Clear and flute-like the maiden's cultured voice swelled out on the still night air, and the mountain echoes caught up the strains and lent a wild peculiar accompaniment.

Deadwood Dick listened, with his head still bowed, and his hands clasped about one knee;—listened in a kind of fascination, until the last reverberations of the song had died out in a wailing echo; then he sprung abruptly to his feet, drew one hand wearily across the masked brow; raised his sombrero with a deft movement, and bowed himself out—out into the night, where the moon and stars looked down at him, perhaps with more lenience than on some.

Alice Terry rose from her seat, crossed over to the door, and gazed after the straight handsome form, until it had mingled with the other road-agents, who had camped upon the slope. Then she turned about, and sat down on the couch beside Anita.

"You are still, dear," she said, stroking the other's long, unconfined hair. "Are you lonely? If not why don't you say something?"

"I have nothing to say," replied Anita, a sad, sweet smile playing over her features. "I have been too much taken up with the music to think of talking."

"But, you are seldom talkative."

"So brother used to tell me. He said I had lost my heart, and tongue."

Redburn was drumming on the window-casing with his fingers;—a sort of lonely tattoo it was.

"You seemed to be much interested in the outlaw, Miss Terry," he observed, as if by chance the thought had just occurred to him, when, in reality, he was downright jealous. "Had you two ever met—"

"Certainly not, sir," and Alice flashed him an inquiring glance. "Why do you ask?"

"Oh! for no reason, in particular, only I fancied that song was meant especially for him."

Redburn, afterward, would have given a hundred dollars to have recalled those words, for the haughty, half-indignant look Alice gave him instantly showed him he was on the wrong track.

If he wished to court her favor, it must be in a different way, and he must not again give her a glimpse of his jealous nature.

"You spoke of a brother," said Alice, turning to Anita. "Does he live here with you?"

"Yes, when not away on business. He has now been absent for over a month."

"Indeed! Is he as sweet, sad, and silent as yourself?"

"Oh! no; Ned is unlike me; he is buoyant, cheerful, pleasant."

"Ned! What is his full name, dear?"

"Edward Harris."

Alice grew suddenly pale and speechless, as she remembered the handsome young miner whom Fearless Frank had slain in the duel, just outside of Deadwood. This, then, was his sister; and evidently she as yet knew nothing of his sad fate.

"Do you know aught concerning Edward Harris?" Redburn asked, seeing her agitation. Alice considered a moment.

"I do," she answered, at last. "This Fearless Frank, whom I came nere with, had a duel with a man, just above Deadwood, whose name was Edward Harris!"

"My God;—and his fate—?"

"He was instantly killed, and left lying where he dropped!"

There was a scream of agony, just here, and a heavy fall.

Anita had fainted!

CHAPTER XIV.

THE TRANSIENT TRIUMPH.

REDBURN sprung from his seat, ran over to her side, and raised her tenderly in his arms.

"Poor thing!" he murmured, gazing into her pale, still face, "the shock was too much for her. No wonder she fainted." He laid her on the couch, and kept off the others who crowded around.

"Bring cold water!" he ordered, "and I will soon have her out of this fit."

Alice hastened to obey, and Anita's face and hands were bathed in the cooling liquid until she began to show signs of returning consciousness.

"You may now give me the particulars of the affair," Redburn said, rising and closing the door, for a chilly breeze was sweeping into the cabin.

Alice proceeded to comply with his request by narrating what had occurred and, as nearly as possible, what had been said. When she had concluded, he gazed down for several moments thoughtfully into the face of Anita. There was much yet that was beyond his powers of comprehension—a knotty problem for which he saw no immediate solution.

"What do you think about it, "General'?" he asked, turning to the mine-locater. "Have we sufficient evidence to hang this devil in scarlet?"

"Hardly, boyee, hardly. 'Peers ter me, 'cordin' to ther gal's tell, thet thar war a fair shake all around, an' as duelin' ar' more or less ther fashun 'round these parts,—considera'bly more o' less 'n less o' more—et ain't law-fell ter yank a critter up by ther throat!"

"I know it is not, according to the customs of this country of the Black Hills; but, look at it. That fellow, who I am satisfied is a black-hearted knave, has not only taken the life of poor Harris, but, very probably, has given his sister her death-blow. The question is: should he go unpunished in the face of all this evidence?"

"Yes. Let him go; *I* will be the one to punish him!"

It was Anita who spoke. She had partly arisen on the couch; her face was streaked with water and slightly haggard; her hair blew unconfined about her neck and shoulders; her eyes blazed with a wild, almost savage fire.

"Let him go!" she repeated, more of fierceness in her voice than Redburn had ever heard there, before. "He shall not escape my vengeance. Oh, my poor, poor dead brother!"

She flung herself back upon the couch, and gave herself up to a wild, passionate, uncontrollable outburst of tears and sobs—the wailings of a sorrowing heart. For a long time she continued to weep and sob violently; then came a lull, during which she fell asleep, from exhaustion—a deep sleep. Redburn and Alice then carried her into an adjoining room, where she was left under the latter's skillful care. Awhile later the cabin was wrapped in silence.

When morning sunlight next peeped down into the Flower Pocket, it found everything generally astir. Anita was up and pursuing her household duties, but she was calm, now, even sadder than before, making a strange contrast to blithe, gaysome Alice, who flitted about, here and there, like some bright-winged butterfly surrounded by a halo of perpetual sunshine.

Unknown to any one save themselves, two men were within the valley of the Flower Pocket gold-mines—there on business, and that business meant bloodshed. They were secreted in among the foot-hills on the western side of the flowering paradise, at a point where they were not observed, and at the same time were the observers of all that was going on in front of them.

How came they here, when the hand of Deadwood Dick guarded the only accessible entrance there was to the valley? The answer was: they came secretly through the pass on the night preceding the arrival of the road-agents, and had been lying in close concealment ever since.

The one was an elderly man of portly figure, and the other a young, dandyish fellow, evidently the elder's son, for they resembled each other in every feature. We make no difficulty in recognizing them as the same precious pair whom Outlaw Dick captured from the stage, only to lose them again through the treachery of two of his own band.

Both looked considerably the worse for wear, and the gaunt, hungry expression on their features, as the morning sunlight shone down upon them, declared in a language more adequate than words, that they were beginning to suffer the first pangs of starvation.

"We cannot hold out at this rate much longer!" the elder Filmore cried, as he watched the bustle in the valley below. "I'm as empty as a collapsed balloon, and what's more, we're in no prospects of immediate relief."

Filmore, the younger, groaned aloud in agony of spirit.

"Curse the Black Hills and all who have been fools enough to inhabit them, anyhow!" he growled, savagely; "just let me get back in the land of civilization again, and you can bet your bottom dollar I'll know enough to stay there."

"Bah! this little rough experience will do you good. If we only had a square meal or two and a basket of sherry, I should feel quite at home. Nothing but a fair prospect of increasing our individual finances would ever have lured me into this outlandish place. But money, you know, is the root of all—"

"Evil!" broke in the other, "and after three months' wild-goose-chase you are just as destitute of the desired root as you were at first."

"True, but we have at least discovered one of the shrubs at the bottom of which grows the root!"

"You refer to Deadwood Dick?"

"I do. He is here in the valley, and he must never leave it alive. While we have the chance we must strike the blow that will forever silence his tongue."

"Yes; but what about the girl? She will be just as much in the way, if not a good deal more so."

"We can manage her all right when the proper time arrives. Dick is our game, now."

"He may prove altogether too much game. But, now that we are counting eggs, how much of the 'lay' is to be mine, when this boy and girl are finished?" he queried.

"How much? Well, that depends upon circumstances. The girl *may* fall to you."

"The girl? Bah! I'd rather be excused."

The day passed without incident in the mines. The work went steadily on, the sounds of the crusher making strange music for the mountain echoes to mock.

Occasionally the crack of a rifle announced that either a road-agent or a Ute miner had risked a shot at a mountain sheep, bird, or deer. Generally their aim was attended with success, though sometimes they were unable to procure the slaughtered game.

Redburn, on account of his clear-headedness and business tact, had full charge of both mines, the "General" working under him in the shaft, and Fearless Frank in the quartz mine.

When questioned about his duel with Harris by Redburn, McKenzie had very little to say; he seemed pained when approached on the subject; would answer no questions concerning the past; was reserved and at times singularly haughty.

During the day Anita and Alice took a stroll through the valley, but the latter had been warned, and fought shy of the quartz mine; so there was no encounter between Anita and Fearless Frank.

Deadwood Dick joined them as they were returning to the cabin, loaded down with flowers—flowers of almost every color and perfume.

"This is a beautiful day," he remarked, pulling up a daisy, as he walked gracefully along. "One rarely sees so many beauties centered in one little valley like this—beautiful landscape and mountain scenery, beautiful flowers beneath smiling skies, and lovely women, the chief center of attraction among all."

"Indeed!" and Alice gave him a coquettish smile, "you are flattering, sir road-agent. You, at least, are not beautiful, in that horrible black suit and villainous mask. You remind me of a picture I have seen somewhere of the devil in disguise; all that is lacking is the horns, tail and cloven-foot."

Dick broke out into a burst of laughter—it was one of those wild, terrible laughs of his, so peculiar to hear from one who was evidently young in years.

Both of the girls were terrified, and would have fled had he not detained them.

"Ha, ha!" he said, stepping in front of them, "do not be frightened; don't go, ladies. That's only the way I express my amusement at anything."

"Then, for mercy's sake, don't get amused again," said Alice, deprecatingly. "Why, dear me, I thought the Old Nick and all his couriers had pounced down upon us."

"Well, how do you know but what he has? *I* may be his Satanic majesty, or one of his envoys."

"I hardly think so; you are too much an earthly being for that. Come, now, take off that detestable mask and let me see what you look like."

"No, indeed! I would not remove this mask, except on conditions, for all the gold yon toiling miners are finding, which, I am satisfied, is no small amount."

"You spoke of conditions. What are they?"

"Some time, perhaps, I will tell you, lady, but not now. See! my men are signaling to me, and I must go. Adieu, ladies;" and in another moment he had wheeled, and was striding back toward camp.

In their concealment the two Filmores witnessed this meeting between Dick and the two girls.

"So there are females here, eh?" grunted the elder, musingly. "From observation I should say that Prince Dick was a comparative stranger here."

"That is my opinion," groaned Clarence, his thoughts reverting to his empty stomach. "Did you hear that laugh a moment ago? It was more like the screech of a lunatic than anything else."

"Yes; he is a young tiger. There is no doubt of that in my mind."

"And we shall have to keep on the alert to take him. He came to the cabin last night. If he does to-night we can mount him!"

Before night the elder Filmore succeeded in capturing a wild goose that had strayed down with the stream from somewhere above. This was killed, dressed and half cooked by a brushwood fire which they hazarded in a fissure in the hillside wherein they had hidden. This fowl they almost ravenously devoured, and thus thoroughly satisfied their appetites. They now felt a great deal better, ready for the work in hand—of capturing and slaying the dare-devil Deadwood Dick.

As soon as it was dark they crept, like the prowling wolves they were, down into the valley, and positioned themselves midway between the cabin and the road-agent's camp, but several yards apart, with a lasso held above the grass between them, to serve as a "trip-up."

The sky had become overcast with dense black clouds, and the gloom in the valley was quite impenetrable. From their concealment the two Filmores could hear Redburn, Alice and the "General" singing up at the cabin, and it told them to be on their guard, as Dick might now come along at any moment.

Slowly the minutes dragged by, and both were growing impatient, when the firm tread of "the Prince" was heard swiftly approaching. Quickly the lasso was drawn taut. Dick, not dreaming of the trap, came boldly along, tripped, and went sprawling to the ground. The next instant his enemies were on him, each with a long murderous knife in hand.

CHAPTER XV.

TO THE RESCUE!

THE suddenness of the onslaught prevented Deadwood Dick from raising a hand to defend himself, and the two strong men piling their combined weights upon him, had the effect to render him utterly helpless. He would have yelled to apprise his comrades of his fate, but Alexander Filmore, ready for the emergency, quickly thrust a cob of wood into his mouth, and bound it there with strong strings.

The young road-agent was a prisoner.

"Ha! ha!" leered the elder Filmore, peering down into the masked face—"ha! ha! my young eaglet; so I have you at last, have I? After repeated efforts to get you in my power, I have at last been rewarded with success, eh? Ha! ha! the terrible scourge of the Black Hills lies here at my feet, mine to do with as I shall see fit."

"Shall we settle him, and leave him lying here, where his gang can find him?" interrupted the younger Filmore, who, now that his blood was up, cared little what he did. "You give him one jab, and I will guarantee to finish him with the second!"

"No! no! boy; you are too hasty. Before we silence him, forever, we must ascertain, if possible, where the girl is."

"But, he'll never tell us."

"We have that yet to find out. It is my opinion that we can bring him to terms, somehow. Take hold, and we will carry him back to our hole in the hill."

Deadwood Dick was accordingly seized by the neck and heels, and borne swiftly and silently toward the western side of the gulch, up among the foothills, into the rift, where the plotters had lain concealed since their arrival. Here he was placed upon the ground in a sitting posture, and his two enemies crouched on either side of him, like beasts ready to spring upon their prey.

Below in the valley, the Utes had kindled one solitary fire, and this with a starlike gleam of light from the cabin window, was the only sign of life to be seen through the night's black shroud. The trio in the foothills were evidently quite alone.

Alexander Filmore broke the silence.

"Well, my gay Deadwood Dick, Prince of the Road, I suppose you wish to have the matter over with, as soon as possible"

The road-agent nodded.

"Better let him loose in the jaws," suggested Filmore the younger; "or how else shall we get from him what we must know? Take out his gag. I'll hold my six against his pulsometer. If he squawks, I'll silence him, sure as there is virtue in powder and ball!"

The elder, after some deliberation, acquiesced, and Dick was placed in possession of his speaking power, while the muzzle of young Filmore's revolver pressed against his breast, warned him to silence and obedience.

"Now," said the elder Filmore, "just you keep mum. If you try any trickery, it will only hasten your destruction, which is inevitable!"

Deadwood Dick gave a little laugh.

"You talk as if you were going to do something toward making me the center of funeralistic attraction."

"You'll find out, soon enough, young man. I have not pursued you so long, all for nothing, you may rest assured. Your death will be the only event that can atone for all the trouble you have given me, in the past."

"*Is* that so? Well, you seem to hold all the *trump* cards, and I reckon you ought to win, though I can't see into your inordinate thirst for *diamonds*, when *spades* will eventually triumph. Had I a *full hand* of *clubs*, I am not so sure but what I could *raise* you, *knaves* though you are!"

"I think not; when kings win, the game is virtually up. We hold altogether to high cards for you, at present, and *beg* as you may, we shall not *pass* you."

"Don't be too sure of it. The best trout often slips from the hook, when you are sanguine that you have at last been immoderately successful. But, enough of this cheap talk. Go on and say your say, in as few words as possible, for I am in a hurry."

Both Filmore, Sr., and Filmore, Jr., laughed at this—it sounded so ridiculously funny to hear a helpless prisoner talk of being in a hurry.

"Business must be pressing!" leered the elder, savagely. "Don't be at all scared. We'll start you humming along the road to Jordan soon enough, if that's what you want. First, however, we desire you to inform us where we can find the girl, as we wish to make a clean sweep, while we are about it."

"Do you bathe your face in alum-water?" abruptly asked the road-agent, staring at his captor, quizzically. "Do you?"

"Bathe in *alum*-water? Certainly not, sir. Why do you ask?"

"Because the hardness of you cheek is highly suggestive of the use of some similar application."

Alexander Filmore stared at his son a moment, at loss to comprehend; but, as it began to dawn upon him that he was the butt of a hard hit, he uttered a frightful curse.

"My cheek and your character bear a close resemblance, then!" he retorted, hotly. "Again I ask you, will you tell me where the girl is?"

"No! you must take me for an ornery mule, or some other kind of an animal, if you think I would deliver her into *your* clutches. No! no! my scheming knaves, I will not. Kill me if you like, but it will not accomplish your villainous ends. She has all of the papers, and can not only put herself forward at the right time, but can have you arrested for my murder!"

"Bah! we can find her, as we have found you; so we will not trifle. Clarence, get ready; and when I count one—two—three—pull the trigger, and I'll finish him with my knife!"

"All right; go ahead; I'm ready!" replied the dutiful son.

Fearless Frank sat upon a bowlder in the mouth of the quartz mine, listening to the strains of music that floated up to him from the cabin out in the valley, and puffing moodily away at a grimy old pipe he had purchased, together with some tobacco, from one of the Utes, with whom he worked.

He had not gone down to the crusher-house for his supper; he did not feel hungry, and was more contented here, in the mouth of the mine, where he could command a view of all that was going on in the valley. With his pipe for a companion he was as happy as he could be, deprived as he was from association with the others of his color, who had barred him out in the cold.

Once or twice during the day, on coming from within, to get a breath of pure air, he had caught a glimpse of Anita as she flitted about the cabin engaged at her household duties, and the yearning expression that unconsciously stole into his dark eyes, spoke of a passion within his heart, that, though it might be slumbering, was not extinct—was there all the same, in all its strength and ardor. Had he been granted the privilege of meeting her, he might have displaced the barrier that rose between them; but now, nothing remained for him but to toil away until Redburn should see fit to send him away, back into the world from which he came.

Would he want to go, when that time came? Hardly, he thought, as he sat there and gazed into the quiet vale below him, so beautiful even in darkness. There was no reason why he should go back again adrift upon the bustling world.

He had no relatives—no claims that pointed him to go thither; he was as free and unfettered as the wildest mountain eagle. He had no one to say where he should and where he should not go; he liked one place equally as well as another, providing there was plenty of provender and work within easy range; he had never thought of settling down, until now, when he had come to the Flower Pocket valley, and caught a glimpse of Anita—Anita whom he had not seen for years; on whom he had brought censure, reproach and—

A step among the rocks close at hand startled him from a reverie into which he had fallen, and caused him to spill the tobacco from his pipe.

A slight trim figure stood a few yards away, and he perceived that two extended hands clasped objects, whose glistening surface suggested that they were "sixes" or "sevens."

"Silence!" came in a clear, authoritative voice. "One word more than I ask you, and I'll blow your brains out. Now, what's your name?"

"Justin McKenzie's my name. Fearless Frank generally answers me the purpose of a nom de plume," was the reply.

"Very good," and the stranger drew near enough for the Scarlet Boy to perceive that he was clad in buck-skin; well armed; wore a Spanish sombrero, and hair long, down over the square shoulders. "I'm Calamity Jane."

If McKenzie uttered an ejaculation of surprise, it was not to be wondered at, for he had heard many stories, in Deadwood, concerning the "dare-devil gal dressed up in men's toggery."

"Calamity Jane?" he echoed, picking up his pipe. "Where in the world did *you* come from, and how did you get here, and what do you want, and—"

"One at a time, please. I came from Deadwood with Road-Agent Dick's party—unknown to them, understand you. That answers two questions. The third is, I want to be around when there's any fun going on; and it's lucky I'm here now. I guess Dick has just got layed out by two fellows in the valley below here, and they've slid off with him over among the foot-hills yonder. I want you to stub along after me, and lend the voices of your sixes, if need be. I'm going to set him at liberty!"

"I'm at your service," Frank quickly replied. Excitement was one of his passions; adventure was another.

"Are you well heeled?"

"I reckon. Always make it a point to be prepared for wild beasts and the like, you know."

"A good idea. Well, if you are ready, we'll slide. I don't want them toughs to get the drop on Dick if I can help it."

"Who are they?"

"Who—the toughs?"

"Yes; they that took the road-agent."

"I don't know 'm. Guess they're tender-foots—some former enemies of his, without doubt. They propose to quiz a secret about some girl out of him, and then knife him. We'll have to hurry or they'll get their work in ahead of us."

They left the mouth of the mine, and skurried down into the valley, through the dense shroud of gloom.

Calamity Jane led the way; she was both fleet of foot and cautious.

Let us look down on the foot-hill camp, and the two Filmores who are stationed on either side of their prisoner.

The younger presses the muzzle of his revolver against Deadwood Dick's heart; the elder holds a long gleaming knife upheld in his right hand.

"One!" he counts, savagely.

"Two!"—after a momentary pause. Another lapse of time, and then—

"Hold! gentlemen; that will do!" cries a clear ringing voice; and Calamity Jane and McKenzie, stepping out of the darkness, with four gleaming "sixes" in hand, confirm the pleasant assertion!

CHAPTER XVI.

THE ROAD-AGENT'S MERCY—CONCLUSION.

NEVERTHELESS, the gleaming blade of Alexander Filmore descended, and was buried in the fleshy part of Deadwood Dick's neck, making a wound, painful but not necessarily dangerous.

"You vile varmint," cried Calamity Jane, pulling the hammer of one of her revolvers back to full cock; "you cursed fool; don't you know that thet only seals yer own miserable fate?"

She took deliberate aim, but Dick interrupted her.

"Don't shoot, Jennie!" he gasped, the blood spurting from his wound; "this ain't none o' your funeral. Give three shrill whistles for my men, and they'll take care o' these hounds until I'm able to attend to 'em. Take me to the cab—"

He could not finish the sentence; a sickening stream of blood gushed from his mouth, and he fell back upon the ground insensible.

Fearless Frank gave the three shrill whistles, while Calamity Jane covered the two cowering wretches with her revolvers.

The distress signal was answered by a yell, and in a few seconds five road-agents came bounding up.

"Seize these two cusses, and guard 'em well!" Calamity said, grimly. "They are a precious pair, and in a few days, no doubt, you'll have the pleasure of attending their funerals. Your captain is wounded, but not dangerously, I hope. We will take him to the cabin, where there are light and skillful hands to dress his wounds. When he wants you, we will let you know. Be sure and guard these knaves well, now."

The men growled an assent, and after binding the captives' arms, hustled them off toward camp, in double quick time, muttering threats of vengeance. Fearless Frank and Calamity then carefully raised the stricken road-agent, and bore him to the cabin, where he was laid upon the couch. Of course, all was now excitement.

Redburn and Alice set to work to dress the bleeding wound, with Jane and the "General" looking on to see that nothing was left undone. Fearless Frank stood apart from the rest, his arms folded across his breast, a grave, half-doubtful expression upon his handsome, sun-browned features.

Anita was not in the room at the time, but she came in a moment later, and stood gazing about her in wondering surprise. Then, her eyes rested upon Fearless Frank for the first, and she grew deathly white; she trembled in every limb; a half-frightened, half-pitiful look came into her eyes.

The young man in scarlet was similarly affected. His cheeks blanched; his lips became firmly compressed; a mastering expression fell from his dark magnetic orbs.

There they stood, face to face, a picture of doubt; of indifferent respect, of opposite strong passions, subdued to control by a heavy hand

None of the others noticed them; they were alone, confronting each other; trying to read the other's thoughts; the one penitent and craving forgiveness, the other cold almost to sternness, and yet not unwilling to forgive and forget.

Deadwood Dick's wound was quickly and skillfully dressed; it was not dangerous, but was so exceedingly painful that the pangs soon brought him back to consciousness.

The moment he opened his eyes he saw Fearless Frank and Anita—perceived their position toward each other, and that it would require only a single word to bridge the chasm between them. A hard look came into his eyes as they gazed through the holes in the mask, then he gazed at Alice—sweet piquant Alice—and the hardness melted like snow before the spring sunshine.

"Thank God it was no deeper," he said, sitting upright, and rubbing the tips of his black-gloved fingers over the patches that covered the gash. "Although deucedly bothersome, it is not of much account."

To the surprise of all he sprung to his feet, and strode to the door. Here he stopped, and looked around for a few moments, sniffing at the cool mountain breeze, as a dog would. A single cedar tree stood by the cabin, its branches, bare and naked, stretching out like huge arms above the doorway. And it was at these the road-agent gazed, a savage gleam in his piercing black eyes.

After a few careful observations, he turned his face within the cabin.

"Justin McKenzie," he said, gazing at the young man, steadily, "I want you to do me a service. Go to my camp, and say to my men that I desire their presence here, together with the two prisoners, and a couple of stout lariats, with nooses at the end of them. Hurry, now!"

Fearless Frank started a trifle, for he seemed to recognize the voice; but the next instant he bowed assent, and left the cabin. When he was gone, Dick turned to Redburn.

"Have you a glass of water handy, Cap? This jab in the gullet makes me somewhat thirsty," he said.

Redburn nodded, and procured the drink; then a strange silence pervaded the cabin—a silence that no one seemed willing to break.

At last the tramp of many feet was heard, and

a moment later the road-agents, with Fearless Frank at their head, reached the doorway, where they halted. The moment Deadwood Dick came forward, there was a wild, deafening cheer.

"Hurra! hurra! Deadwood Dick, Prince of the Road, still lives. Three long hearty cheers, lads, and a hummer!" cried Fearless Frank, and then the mountain echoes reverberated with a thousand discordant yells of hurrah.

The young road-agent responded with a nod, and then said:

"The prisoners; have you them there?"

"Here they are, Cap!" cried a score of voices, and the two Filmores were trotted out to the front, with ropes already about their necks. "Shall we h'ist 'em?"

"Not jest yet, boys; I have a few words to say, first."

Then turning half-about in the doorway, Deadwood Dick continued:

"Ladies and gentlemen, a little tragedy is about to take place here soon, and it becomes necessary that I should say a few words explaining what cause I have for hanging these two wretches whom you see here.

"Therefore, I will tell you a short story, and you will see that my cause is just, as we look at these things here in this delectable country of the Black Hills. To begin with:

"My name is, to you, *Edward Harris!*" and here the road-agent flung aside the black mask, revealing the smiling face of the young card-sharp. "I have another—my family name—but I do not use it, preferring Harris to it. Anita, yonder, is my sister.

"Several years ago, when we were children, living in one of the Eastern States, we were made orphans by the death of our parents, who were drowned while driving upon a frozen lake in company with my uncle, Alexander Filmore, and his son, Clarence—those are the parties yonder, and as God is my judge, I believe they are answerable for the death of our father and mother.

"Alexander Filmore was appointed guardian over us, and executor of our property, which amounted to somewhere in the neighborhood of fifty thousand dollars, my father having been for years extensively engaged in speculation, at which he was most always successful.

"From the day of their death we began to receive the most tyrannical treatment. We were whipped, kicked about, and kept in a half-starved condition. Twice when we were in bed, and, as he supposed, asleep, Alexander Filmore came to us and attempted to assassinate us, but my watchfulness was a match for his villainy, and we escaped death at his hands.

"Finding that this kind of life was unbearable, I appealed to our neighbors and even to the courts for protection, but my enemy was a man of great influence, and after many vain attempts, I found that I could not obtain a hearing; that nothing remained for me to do but to fight my own way. And I did fight it.

"Out of my father's safe I purloined a sum of money sufficient to defray our expenses for a while, and then, taking Anita with me, I fled from the home of my youth. I came first to Fort Laramie, where I spent a year in the service of a fur-trader.

"My guardian, during that year, sent three men out to kill me, but they had the tables turned on them, and their bones lay bleaching even now on Laramie plains.

"During that year my sister met a gay, dashing young ranger, who hailed to the name of Justin McKenzie, and of course she fell in love with him. That was natural, as he was handsome, suave and gallant, and, more than all, reported tolerably well to-do.

"I made inquiries, and found that there was nothing against his moral character, so I made no objections to his paying his attentions to Anita.

"But one day a great surprise came.

"On returning from a buffalo-hunt of several days' duration I found my home deserted, and a letter from Anita stating that she had gone with McKenzie to Cheyenne to live; they were not married yet, but would be, soon.

"That aroused the hellish part of my passionate nature. I believed that McKenzie was leading her a life of dishonor, and it made my blood boil to even think of it. Death, I swore, should be his reward for this infidelity, and mounting my horse I set out in hot haste for Cheyenne.

"But I arrived there too late to accomplish my mission of vengeance.

"I found Anita and took her back to my home, a sad and sorrowing maiden; McKenzie I could not find; he had heard of my coming, and fled to escape my avenging hand. But over the head of my weeping sister, I swore a fearful oath of vengeance, and I have it yet to keep. I believe there had been some kind of a sham marriage; Anita would never speak on the subject, so I had to guess at the terrible truth.

"And there's where you made an accursed mess of the whole affair!" cried McKenzie, stepping into the cabin, and leading Anita forward, by the hand. "Before God and man *I acknowledge Anita Harris to be my legally wedded wife.* Listen, Edward Harris, and I will explain. That day that you came to Cheyenne in pursuit of me, I'll acknowledge I committed an error—one that has caused me much trouble since. The case was this:

"I was the nearest of kin to a rich old fur-trader, who proposed to leave me all his property at his death; but he was a desperate woman-hater, and bound me to a promise that I would never marry.

"Tempted by the lust for gold, I yielded, and he drew up a will in my favor. This was before I met Anita here.

"When we went to Cheyenne, the old man was lying at the point of death; so I told Anita that we would not be married for a few days, until we saw how matters were going to shape. If he died, we would be married secretly, and she would return to your roof until I could get possession of my inheritance, when we would go to some other part of the country to live. If he recovered, I would marry her anyway, and let the old man go to Tophet with his money-bags. I see now how I was in the wrong.

"Well, that very day, before your arrival, the old man himself pounced down upon us, and cursed me up hill and down, for my treachery, and forthwith struck me out from his will. I immediately sent for a chaplain, and was married to Anita. I then went up to see the old man and find if I could not effect a compromise with him.

"He told me if I would go with him before Anita and swear that she was not legally my wife, and that I would never live with her, he would again alter his will in my favor.

"Knowing that that would make no difference, so far as the law was concerned, I sent Anita a note apprising her of what was coming, and stating that she had best return to you until the old man should die, when I would come for her. Subsequently I went before her in company with the old man and swore as I had promised to do, and when I departed she was weeping bitterly, but I naturally supposed it was sham grief. A month later, on his death-bed, the old trader showed me the letter I had sent her, and I realized that not only was my little game up, but that I had cheated myself out of a love that was true. I was left entirely out of the will, and ever since I have bitterly cursed the day that tempted me to try to win gold and love at the same time. Here, Edward Harris," and the young man drew a packet of papers from inside his pocket, "are two certificates of my marriage, one for Anita, and one for myself. You see now, that, although mine has been a grievous error, no dishonor is coupled with your sister's name."

Ned Harris took one of the documents and glanced over it, the expression on his face softening. A moment later he turned and grasped McKenzie's hand.

"God bless you, old boy!" he said, huskily. "I am the one who has erred, and if you have it in your heart to forgive me, try and do so. I do not expect much quarter in this world, you know. There is Anita; take her, if she will come to you, and may God shower his eternal blessings upon you both!"

McKenzie turned around with open arms, and Anita flew to his embrace with a low glad cry. There was not a dry eye in the room.

There was an impatient surging of the crowd outside; Dick saw that his men were longing for the sport ahead; so he resumed his story:

"There is not much more to add," he said, after a moment's thought. "I fled into the Black Hills when the first whispers of gold got afloat, and chancing upon this valley, I built us a home here, wherein to live away the rest of our lives.

"In time I organized the band of men you see around me, and took to the road. Of this my sister knew nothing. The Hills have been my haunt ever since, and during all this time yon scheming knaves"—pointing to the prisoners—"have been constantly sending out men to murder me. The last tool, Hugh Vansevere by name, boldly posted up reward papers in the most frequented routes, and he went the same way as his predecessors. Seeing that nothing could be accomplished through aids, my enemies have at last come out to superintend my butchery in person; and but for the timely interference of Calamity Jane and Justin McKenzie, a short time since, I should have ere this been numbered with the dead. Now, I am inclined to be merciful to only those who have been merciful to me; therefore, I have decided that Alexander and Clarence Filmore shall pay the penalty of hanging, for their attempted crimes. Boys, *string 'em up!*"

So saying, Deadwood Dick stepped without the cabin, and closed the door behind him.

Redburn also shut down and curtained the windows, to keep out the horrible sight and sounds.

But, for all this, those inside could not help but hear the pleading cries of the doomed wretches, the tramp of heavy feet, the hushed babble of voices, and at last the terrible shout of, "Heave 'o! up they go!" which signaled the commencement of the victims' journey into mid-air.

Then there was a long blank pause; not a sound was heard, not a voice spoke, nor a foot moved. This silence was speedily broken, however, by two heavy falls, followed almost immediately by the tramp of feet.

Not till all was again quiet did Redburn venture to open the door and look out. All was dark and still. The road-agents had gone, and left no sign of their work behind.

When morning dawned, they were seen to have recamped on the eastern slope, where the smoke of their camp-fires rose in graceful white columns through the clear transparent atmosphere.

During the day Dick met Alice Terry, as she was gathering flowers, a short distance from the cabin.

"Alice—Miss Terry," he said, gravely, "I have come to ask you to be my wife. I love you, and want you for my own darling. Be mine, Alice, and I will mend my ways, and settle down to an honest, straightforward life."

The beautiful girl looked up pityingly.

"No," she said, shaking her head, her tone kind and respectful, "I cannot love you, and never can be your wife, Mr. Harris."

"You love another?" he interrogated.

She did not answer, but the tell-tale blush that suffused her cheek did, for her.

"It is Redburn!" he said, positively. "Very well; give him my congratulations. See, Alice;" here the young road-agent took the crape mask from his bosom; "I now resume the wearing of this mask. Your refusal has decided my future. A merry road-agent I have been, and a merry road-agent I shall die. Now, good-by forever."

On the following morning it was discovered that the road-agents and their daring leader, together with the no less heroic Calamity Jane, had left the valley—gone; whither, no one knew.

About a month later, one day when Calamity Jane was watering her horse at the stream, two miles above Deadwood, the road-agent chief rode out of the chaparral and joined her.

He was still masked, well armed, and looking every inch a Prince of the Road.

"Jennie," he said, reining in his steed, "I am lonely and want a companion to keep me company through life. You have no one but yourself; our spirits and general temperament agree. Will you marry me and become my queen?"

"No!" said the girl, haughtily, sternly. "I have had all the *man* I care for. We can be friends, Dick; more we can never be!"

"Very well, Jennie; I rec'on it is destined that I shall live single. At any rate, I'll never take a refusal from another woman. Yes, gal, we'll be friends, if nothing more."

There is little more to add.

We might write at length, but choose a few words to end this o'er true romance of life in the Black Hills.

McKenzie and Anita were remarried in Deadwood, and at the same time Redburn led Alice Terry to the altar, which consummation the "General" avowed was "more or less of a good thing—consider'bly less o' more 'n' more o' less."

Through eastern lawyers, a settlement of the Harris affairs was effected, the whole of the property being turned over to Anita, thereby placing her and Fearless Frank above want for a lifetime.

Therefore they gave up their interest in the Flower Pocket mines to Redburn and the "General."

Calamity Jane is still in the Hills.

And grim and uncommunicative, there roams through the country of gold a youth in black, at the head of a bold lawless gang of road-riders, who, from his unequaled daring, has won and rightly deserves the name—Deadwood Dick, Prince of the Road.

THE END.

Edward L. Wheeler's

Deadwood Dick Novels

IN

Beadle's Half-Dime Library.

1. Deadwood Dick; or, The Black Rider of the Black Hills.
20. The Double Daggers; or, Deadwood Dick's Defiance.
28. Buffalo Ben; or, Deadwood Dick in Disguise.
35. Wild Ivan, the Boy Claude Duval; or, The Brotherhood of Death.
42. The Phantom Miner; or, Deadwood Dick's Bonanza.
49. Omaha Oll; or, Deadwood Dick in Danger.
75. Deadwood Dick's Eagles; or, The Pards of Flood Bar.
73. Deadwood Dick on Deck; or, Calamity Jane, the Heroine of Whoop-Up.
77. Corduroy Charlie; or, The Last Act of Deadwood Dick.
100. Deadwood Dick in Leadville; or, A Strange Stroke for Liberty.
104. Deadwood Dick's Device; or, The Sign of the Double Cross.
109. Deadwood Dick as Detective.
121. Cinnamon Chip, the Girl Sport; or, The Golden Idol of Mount Rosa.
129. Deadwood Dick's Double; or, The Ghost of Gorgon's Gulch.
138. Blonde Bill; or, Deadwood Dick's Home Base.
149. A Game of Gold; or, Deadwood Dick's Big Strike.
156. Deadwood Dick of Deadwood; or, The Picked Party.
195. Deadwood Dick's Dream; or, The Rivals of the Road.
201. The Black Hills Jezebel; or, Deadwood Dick's Ward.
205. Deadwood Dick's Doom; or, Calamity Jane's Last Adventure.
217. Captain Crack-Shot, the Girl Brigand; or, Gypsy Jack from Jimtown.
221. Sugar Coated Sam; or, The Black Gowns of Grim Gulch.

The above are for sale by all newsdealers, five cents a copy, or sent by mail on receipt of six cents each.

BEADLE AND ADAMS, PUBLISHERS,
98 William street, New York.

A NEW FIELD! WITHOUT A RIVAL! JUST THE THING! TRUTH STRANGER THAN FICTION!

Beadle's Boy's Library of Sport, Story and Adventure

$2.50 a year. Entered at the Post Office at New York, N.Y., as Second Class Mail Matter. Copyrighted in 1881 by BEADLE AND ADAMS. December 14, 1881.

Vol. I.   Single Number.   PUBLISHED WEEKLY BY BEADLE AND ADAMS, No. 98 WILLIAM STREET, NEW YORK.   Price, Five Cents.   No. 1.

Adventures of BUFFALO BILL FROM BOYHOOD TO MANHOOD.
Deeds of Daring and Romantic Incidents in the Life of Wm. F. Cody, the Monarch of Bordermen.

BY COLONEL PRENTISS INGRAHAM.

MADDENED WITH FRIGHT, THE BULL BOUNDED INTO THE AIR, SNORTED WILDLY, GORED THOSE IN ADVANCE, AND SOON LED THE HERD.

Adventures of Buffalo Bill

From Boyhood to Manhood.

Deeds of Daring, Scenes of Thrilling Peril, and Romantic Incidents in the Early Life of W. F. Cody, the Monarch of Bordermen.

BY COLONEL PRENTISS INGRAHAM.

CHAPTER I.
PROLOGUE.

THAT Truth is, by far, stranger than Fiction, the lessons of our daily lives teach us who dwell in the marts of civilization, and therefore we cannot wonder that those who live in scenes where the rifle, revolver and knife are in constant use, to protect and take life, can strange tales tell of thrilling perils met and subdued, and romantic incidents occurring that are far removed from the stern realities of existence.

The land of America is full of romance, and tales that stir the blood can be told over and over again of bold Privateers and reckless Buccaneers who have swept along the coasts; of fierce naval battles, sea chases, daring smugglers; and on shore of brave deeds in the saddle and afoot; of red trails followed to the bitter end and savage encounters in forest wilds.

And it is beyond the pale of civilization I find the hero of these pages which tell of thrilling adventures, fierce combats, deadly feuds and wild rides, that, one and all, are true to the letter, as hundreds now living can testify.

Who has not heard the name of Buffalo Bill—a magic name, seemingly, to every boy's heart?

And yet in the uttermost parts of the earth it is known among men.

A child of the prairie, as it were, Buffalo Bill will go down to history as one of America's strange heroes who has loved the trackless wilds, rolling plains and mountain solitudes of our land, far more than the bustle and turmoil, the busy life and joys of our cities, and who has stood as a barrier between civilization and savagery, risking his own life to save the lives of others.

Glancing back over the past, we recall a few names that have stood out in the boldest relief in frontier history, and they are Daniel Boone, Davy Crockett, Kit Carson and W. F. Cody—the last named being Buffalo Bill, the King of Bordermen.

Knowing the man well, having seen him amid the greatest dangers, shared with him his blanket and his camp-fire's warmth, I feel entitled to write of him as a hero of heroes, and in the following pages sketch his remarkable career from boyhood to manhood.

Born in the State of Iowa in 1843, his father being one of the bold pioneers to that part of the West, Buffalo Bill, or Will Cody, was inured to scenes of hardship and danger ere he reached his tenth year, and being a precocious youth, his adventurous spirit led him into all sorts of deeds of mischief and daring, which well served to lay the foundation for the later acts of his life.

CHAPTER II.
A CAPTURE OF OUTLAWS.

WHEN Will was but nine years of age his first thrilling adventure occurred, and it gave the boy a name for pluck and nerve that went with him to Kansas, where his father removed with his family shortly after the incident which I will now relate.

The circumstance to which I refer, and that made a boy hero of him in the eyes of the neighbors for miles around where his parents t, showed the wonderful nerve that has never since deserted him, but rather has increased with his years.

The country school which he attended was some five miles from his father's house and he was wont to ride there each morning and back in the afternoon upon a wiry, vicious little mustang that every one had prognosticated would some day be the death of him.

Living a few miles from the Cody ranch was a poor settler who had a son two years Billy's senior, who also attended the same school, but whose parents were too poor to spare him a horse from the farm to ride.

This boy was Billy's chum, and as they shared together their noonday meal, the pony was also shared, for the boy rode behind my hero to and from school, being called for each morning and dropped off near his cabin on the return trip.

Owing to the lawlessness of the country Mr. Cody allowed his son to go armed, knowing that he fully understood the use of weapons, and his pistol Billy always hung up with his hat upon reaching the log cabin, where, figuratively speaking, the young idea was taught to shoot.

The weapon was a revolver, a Colt's, which at that time was not in common use, and Billy prized it above his books and pony even and always kept it in perfect order.

One day Rascal, his pony, pulled up the lariat pin which held him out upon the prairie and scampered for home, and Billy and Davie Dunn, his chum, were forced to "hoof it," as the western slang goes, home.

A storm was coming on, and to escape it the boys turned off the main trail and took refuge in a log cabin which was said to be haunted by the ghosts of its former occupants; at least they had been all mysteriously murdered there one night and were buried in the shadow of the cabin, and people gave the place a wide berth.

It was situated back in a piece of heavy timber and looked dismal enough, but Billy proposed that they should go there, more out of sheer bravado to show he was not afraid than to escape a ducking, for which he and Davie Dunn really little cared.

The boys reached the cabin, climbed in an open window and stood looking out at the approaching storm.

"Kansas crickets! but look there, Davie!"

The words came from Buffalo Billy and he was pointing out toward the trail.

There four horsemen were seen coming toward the cabin at a rapid gallop.

"Who be they, Billy?" asked Davie.

"They are some of them horse-thieves, Davie, that have been playing the mischief of late about here, and we'd better dust."

"But they'll see us go out."

"That's so! Let us coon up into the loft, for they'll only wait till the storm blows over, for they are coming here for shelter."

Up to the loft of the cabin, through a trap-door, the boys went quickly and laid quietly down, peering through the cracks in the boards. The four horsemen dashed up, hastily unsaddled their horses and lariated them out, and bounded into the cabin through the window, just as the storm broke with fury upon forest and plain.

As still as mice the boys lay, but they quickly looked toward each other, for the conversation of the men below, one of whom was kindling a fire in the broad chimney, told them that, if discovered, their lives would be the forfeit.

In fact, they were four of a band of outlaws that had been infesting the country of late, stealing horses, and in some cases taking life and robbing the cabins of the settlers, and one of them said plainly:

"Pards, when I was last in this old ranch it was six years ago, when we came to rob Foster Beal who lived here; he showed fight, shot two of the boys, and we wiped the whole family out; but now let us get away with what grub we've got, and then plan what is best to do to-night. As for myself, I say strike old Cody's ranch, for he's got dust."

The boys were greatly alarmed at this, but, putting his mouth close to Davie Dunn's ear, Billy Cody whispered:

"Davie, you see that shutter in the end of the roof?"

"Yes, Billy," was the trembling reply.

"Well, you slip out of there, drop to the ground and make for your home and tell your father who is here."

"And you, Billy?"

"I'll just keep here, and if these fellows attempt to go I'll shoot 'em."

"But you can't, Billy."

"I've got my revolver, Davie and you bet I'll use it! Go, but don't make a fuss, and get your father to come on with the settlers as soon as you can, for I won't be happy till you get back."

Davie Dunn was trembling considerably; but he arose noiselessly, crossed to the window at the end of the roof, and which was but a small aperture, closed by a wooden shutter, which he cautiously opened. The noise he made was drowned by the pelting rain and furious wind, and the robbers went on chatting together, while Davie slipped out and dropped to the ground.

But ere he had been gone half an hour the outlaws were ready to start, the rain having ceased in a measure, and night was coming on to hide their red deeds."

"Hold on, boys, for I've got ye all covered. He's a dead man who moves."

Billy had crept to the trap, and in his hoarsest tones, had spoken, while the men sprung to their feet at his words, and glancing upward saw the threatening revolver.

One attempted to draw a weapon, but the boy's forefinger touched the trigger, and the outlaw fell dead at the flash, shot straight through the heart!

This served as a warning to the others, and they stood like statues, while one said:

"Pard, who is yer?"

But Billy feared to again trust his voice and answered not a word. He lay there, his revolver just visible over the edge of the boards, and covering the hearts of the three men crouching back into the corner, but full in the light from the flickering fire, while almost at their feet lay their dead comrade.

Again and again they spoke to Billy, but he gave no reply.

Then they threatened to make it warm for him, and one suggested that they make a break for the door.

But, each one seemed to feel that the revolver covered him, and none would make the attempt, for they had ocular demonstration before them of the deadly aim of the eye behind the weapon.

To poor little Billy, and I suppose to the men too, it seemed as if ages were passing away, in the hour and a quarter that Davie Dunn was gone, for he had bounded upon one of the outlaws' horses and ridden away like the wind.

But, at last, Billy heard a stern voice say:—

"Boys, you is our meat."

At the same time several pistols were thrust into the window, and in came the door, burst open with a terrific crash that was music to Billy's ears; while in dashed a dozen bold settlers, led by farmer Dunn.

The three outlaws were not only captured, but, being recognized as old offenders, were swung up to a tree, while Billy and Davie became indeed boy heroes, and the former especially was voted the lion of the log cabin school, for had he not "killed his man?"

CHAPTER III.
BILLY'S FIRST DUEL.

NEAR where Billy's father settled in Kansas, dwelt a farmer who had a son and daughter, the former being fourteen, and the latter eighteen.

As is often the case with boys, Billy fell in love with Nannie Vannor, which was the young lady's name, although she at eighteen was just seven years older than he was.

But she had been over to call on the Cody girls with her brother, and a deep attachment at once sprung up between the boys, and Billy became the devoted slave of Nannie, making her a horse-hair bridle for her pony, gathering her wild flowers whenever he went over to the Vennor farm, and in fact being as devoted in his attentions as a young man of twenty-one could have been.

But Nannie had another lover, in fact a score of them from among the neighboring young settlers, but one in particular who bid fair to be Billy's most dangerous rival. This one was a dashing young fellow from Leavenworth, with a handsome face and fine form, and who always had plenty of money.

Folks said he was very dissipated, was a gambler, and his name had been connected several times with some very serious affairs that had occurred in the town.

But then he had a winning manner, sung well, and Nannie's beaux had to all admit that he was every inch the man, and one they cared not to anger.

From the first Billy Cody hated him, and did not pretend to hide the fact; but it seemed the boy's intuitive reading of human nature, as much as his jealousy on account of Nannie Vennor.

One day Billy was seated by the side of a small stream fishing.

The bank was behind him, rising some eight feet, and he had ensconced himself upon a log that had been drifting down the stream in a freshet, and lodged there.

Back from him, bordering the little creek ran the trail to the nearest town, and along this rode two persons.

The quick ear of the boy heard hoof-falls, and glancing quickly over the bank he saw three horsemen approaching, and one of these he recognized as Hugh Hall his rival.

Just back of Billy was a grove of cottonwood trees, and here the men halted for a short rest in the shade, and all they said distinctly reached the boy's ears.

"I tell you, pards," said Hugh Hall, "I cannot longer delay then, so if old Vennor refuses to let me have Nannie I'll just take her."

"The best way, Hugh; but what about the wife that's now on your trail?" asked one.

"What care I for her, after I have run off with Nannie?"

"But she'll blow on you to old man Vennor."

"I do not care. I'll deny it to Nannie, say the woman is crazy, and one by one the family will drop off until she only remains, and then she'll get the property."

"You are sure it's coming to 'em, Hugh?" asked one.

"I am so sure that I drew up the will of Vennor's brother four years ago, when I was practicing law in Chicago."

"He may have changed his mind."

"Nonsense; he died shortly after, and the will says if Richard Vennor was not found, and the fortune turned over to him, within five years after Robert Vennor's death, the fortune was to go to charity."

"Now I kept the secret dark, came out to look up Richard Vennor, and having found him, shall marry his daughter and get all!"

"Your wife will give you trouble."

"I wish you to get rid of her then, and I'll pay well for it."

"We'll do the job, and help you all we can," said one, and the second one of the pair whom Billy did not recognize, echoed his comrade's sentiments.

"Well, Hugh, we found Lucy was trailing you, and hearing you was about to strike it rich, concluded we'd come and post you for old friendship's sake."

"And I'll pay you for it; but we must not be seen together, so I'll wait here while you ride on to Leavenworth, and in an hour I'll follow you."

This agreement seemed satisfactory, and two horsemen rode away, after a few more words, while Hugh Hall threw himself down upon the grass to rest.

For awhile Billy Cody was very nervous at what he had heard; but he soon grew calm, and having waited until he knew the two men were more than a mile away, he cautiously stood up upon the log and glanced over the bank.

Hugh Hall was fast asleep, and his horse was feeding near.

Noiselessly Billy drew himself upon the bank and approached the man, his faithful revolver held in his hand.

"I wonder if it would be wrong if I killed him, when he is such a villain?" he muttered.

"Yes, I won't do it; but I'll make him go straight to Mr. Vennor and I'll tell him all I heard.

"Here, Hugh Hall, farmer Vennor wants to see you."

The man sprung to his feet, his hand upon his revolver.

But Billy had taken the precaution to get behind a tree, and had the drop on his rival.

"Oh, it's you, you accursed imp of Satan," cried the man angrily.

"Yes, it's me, and I want you to go to Mr. Vennor, for I'm going to tell him all I heard you say," said the boy boldly.

Hugh Hall knew Billy's reputation as a fearless boy and a sure shot, and he saw that he was in great danger; but he said quietly:

"Well, I was going to the farmer's and we'll ride together."

"No, I'll ride and you'll walk, for I came down the stream fishing to-day, and haven't got my pony."

As quick as a flash the man then drew his pistol, and firing, the bullet cut the bark off the tree just above the boy's head.

Instantly however Billy returned the shot, and the revolver of Hugh Hall fell from his hand, for his arm was broken; but he picked it up quickly and leveled it with his left, and two shots came together.

Billy's hat was turned half round on his head, showing how true was the aim of his foe, while his bullet found a target in the body of Hugh Hall.

With a groan he sunk upon the ground, and springing to his side, Billy found him gasping fearfully for breath.

"I am sorry, Hugh Hall, but you made me do it," he said sorrowfully.

But the man did not reply, and running to the horse feeding near, he sprung into the saddle and dashed away like the wind.

Straight to farmer Vennor's he went and told him all, and mounting in hot haste they rode back to the grove of cottonwoods.

Hugh Hall still lay where he had fallen; but he was dead, greatly to Billy's sorrow, who had hoped he would not die.

Then, while farmer Vennor remained by the body, Billy went for the nearest neighbors, and ere nightfall Hugh Hall was buried, and his two allies in crime were captured in Leavenworth, and given warning to leave Kansas forever, which they were glad to do, for they had not expected such mercy at the hands of the enraged farmers.

But before they left they confessed that Billy's story was a true one, and told where the wife of Hugh Hall could be found, and once again did the boy become a hero, even in the eyes of the bravest men, and the settlers gave him the name of Boss Boy Billy, while Nannie Vennor, now a mother of grown sons, each Christmas time sends him a little souvenir, to show him that she has not forgotten her boy lover who fought his first duel to save her from a villain.

CHAPTER IV.
SHOOTING FOR A PRIZE.

While Mr. Cody was an Indian trader at Salt Creek Valley in Kansas, Billy laid the foundation for his knowledge of the red-skin character, and which served him so well in after years and won him a name as scout and hunter that no one else has ever surpassed.

For days at a time Billy would be in the Indian villages, and often he would go with the warriors on their buffalo and game hunts, and now and then would join a friendly band in a war trail against hostiles.

Another favorite resort of Billy's was Fort Leavenworth, where his handsome face, fearlessness and manly nature made him a great favorite with both officers and men.

On one occasion while at the fort a large Government herd of horses, lately brought up from Texas, where they had been captured wild on the prairies, stampeded, and could not be retaken.

Once or twice Billy had come into the fort with a pony of the fugitive herd which he had captured, and the quartermaster said to him:

"Billy, if that herd remains much longer free, they will be harder to take than real wild horses, so go to work and I'll give you a reward of ten dollars for every one you bring in, for the Government authorizes me to make that offer."

This was just to Billy's taste, and he went at once home and spent a couple of days preparing for the work before him, and from which his mother and sisters tried to dissuade him; but the boy saw in it a bonanza and would not give it up.

His own pony, Rascal, he knew, was not fast enough for the work ahead, so he determined to get a better mount, and rode over to the fort to see a sergeant who had an animal not equaled for speed on the plains.

Rascal, some sixty dollars, a rifle, and some well-tanned skins were offered for the sergeant's horse and refused, and in despair Billy knew not what to do, for he had gotten to the end of his personal fortune.

"Sergeant," he suddenly cried, as a bright idea seized him.

"Well, Billy?"

"They say you are the crack shot in the fort."

"I am too, Billy."

"Well, I'll tell you what I'll do to win your horse, Little Grey. I'll put up all I have offered you against your animal and shoot for them."

"Why, Billy, I don't want to win your pony and money."

"And I don't want you to; but I'll shoot with you for your horse against mine and all else I have offered."

The sergeant was a grasping man, and confident of his powers, at last assented, and the match was to take place at once.

But the officers learning of it were determined Billy should have fair play, and a day was set a week off, and the boy was told to practice regularly with both pistol and rifle, for the terms were ten off-hand shots with the latter at fifty and one hundred yards, and six shots standing with the revolver at fifteen paces and six from horseback, and riding at full speed by the target.

Billy at once set to work to practice, though he had confidence in his unerring aim, and upon the day of trial came to the fort with a smiling face.

Nearly everybody in the fort went out to see the match, and the sergeant was called first to toe the mark.

He raised his rifle and his five shots at fifty yards were quickly fired.

Billy gave a low whistle, but toed the scratch promptly, and his five shots were truer than the sergeant's, and a wild cheer broke from one and all.

At one hundred yards the sergeant's shooting was better than the boy's; and so it was with the pistol shooting, for when standing the sergeant's shots were best, and in riding full speed by the target, Billy's were the truest, and it was called a tie.

"How shall we shoot it off, Billy?" asked the sergeant, who seemed somewhat

Billy made no reply, but went to his haversack and took from it an apple, and going up to his pony placed him in position, the rein over the horn of the saddle.

The apple he then put on the head of the pony, directly between his ears, and, stepping back while all present closely watched him, he threw forward his pistol and fired.

The apple flew into fragments and a wild burst of applause came from all sides, while Billy said quietly:

"I've got another apple, sergeant, for you to try the same on Little Grey."

"I'll not run the risk, Billy, of killing him, so give in; but I'll win him back from you sometime," said the sergeant.

"Any time, sergeant, I'm willing to shoot," replied the boy, and with a happy heart he mounted his prize and set off for home.

CHAPTER V.

WILD HORSE HUNTING.

For several days after Billy Cody got his prize he did nothing but train the animal to his use and was delighted to find that Little Grey would follow him like a dog wherever he went.

Having all arranged now for his wild horse hunting, he set out one day from home to be gone a week or more, he told his mother, and with the promise that he would bring her a small fortune soon.

He had already discovered the feeding grounds of the herd, and thither he went at once, arriving in the vicinity shortly before dark.

As he had expected, he found the herd, nearly five hundred in number, but he kept out of sight of them, as it was so near dark, and camped until morning, when he found they had gone up the valley for some miles.

Cautiously he followed them, and getting near unobserved at last made a dash upon them.

Into their midst he went and a good horse was picked out and lariated in the twinkling of an eye and quickly hoppled and turned loose.

Then another and another, until Billy felt that he had done a pretty good day's work.

He had discovered two things, however, and that was that Little Grey seemed more than a match for any of the herd with one exception, and that one was a large, gaunt-bodied black stallion, that appeared to drop him behind without much effort.

"I've got to have him," said Billy, as he returned to his hoppled prizes and began to drive them toward the fort.

It was a long and tedious work, but the boy was not impatient and reached the fort at last and received his reward, which he at once carried to his mother and received her warm congratulations upon his first success.

Back to the herd's haunts went Billy, and again he camped for the night, but was aroused at dawn by a sound that he at first thought was distant thunder.

But his ears soon were undeceived as he sprung to his feet, well knowing that it was the herd of wild horses.

Instantly Billy formed his plan of action and mounting Little Grey rode into a thicket near by, which wholly concealed him from view.

Here he waited, for he knew that the herd was coming to the river to drink, and a cry of delight burst from his lips as he beheld the black stallion in the lead.

"It is the horse the settlers call Sable Satan and that belonged to a horse-thief, father told me, who was shot from his back one night.

"Well, if I can catch him I'll be in luck, and I'll try it, though they say he is awful vicious. Be quiet, Grey, or you'll spoil all."

On came the large drove at a trot directly for the river, and a beautiful sight it was as they moved forward in solid mass, with flowing mane and tail and the rising sun glancing upon every variety of color.

The leader was a perfect beauty, black as ink, with glossy hide and long mane and tail—the equine king of the herd.

With his reins well in hand, his lariat ready, and full of excitement, Billy waited for the horses to reach the stream, which they entered to quench their thirst.

As every head was lowered and the nostrils driven deep into the cool waters, out of the thicket dashed the Boy Horse-Hunter, and the clattering hoofs startled the drove, and in confusion and fright they turned to fly.

Straight as an arrow went the boy toward the black stallion, which attempted to dash by with the mass.

But with an unerring hand the lariat was thrown, the coil settled down over the haughty head, a tremendous jerk followed, and Sable Satan was thrown to the ground.

With an exultant cry Billy sprung from his saddle, and quickly formed a "bow-stall"* which, when properly made, is more effective than a severe curb bit—and placed it upon the animal that was choked beyond the power of resistance.

Loosening the lariat around his neck Billy sprung upon the prostrate animal, which, with a wild snort bounded to his feet, and with prodigious leaps started on after the flying herd, his daring young rider firmly seated upon his back.

Finding he could not unseat Billy by bounding, he came to a sudden halt, and then reared wildly; but with catlike tenacity the boy clung to him, and then Sable Satan mad with rage and fright, attempted to tear him from his back with his gleaming teeth.

A severe jerk on the bow-stall however thwarted this, and with a maddened cry the splendid prairie king bounded on once more after the flying herd, a call to Little Grey from Billy causing him to follow at a swift run.

With a speed that was marvelous Sable Satan flew on, directly into the drove, the daring young rider still clinging to him, determined to dare any danger to keep the animal whose capture had baffled the very best horsemen of the plains.

Sweeping through the herd, as though they were stationary, so great was his speed, the black stallion soon left them far behind, and glancing back Billy saw that Little Grey had not cared to venture into the midst of the wild band and was galloping away over the prairies.

Not knowing who might pick him up, and having his rifle, ammunition and provisions strapped to his saddle, he determined to go on after Little Grey, and at once a fierce fight began between the boy and his horse.

But the boy proved the master, and after a severe struggle the black stallion was subdued, and guided by the bow-stall was in full chase of Little Grey, while Sable Satan's former subjects were flying away northward without their leader.

When in chase of Little Grey, Billy soon discovered the remarkable speed of his new capture, for he overhauled his former pet with ease, and now thoroughly broken in, the saddle and bridle were transferred to the black's back, and exultant over his success the boy rode on to the fort, where large sums were offered him for the famous stallion.

But Billy refused each tempting offer, and on Sable Satan set out to capture more of the herd, and which he readily succeeded in doing; but as the Government offer of ten dollars for the fugitive animals became known, there were a number of men starting on the trail of the wild mustangs and though Billy got the lion's share, he did not quite realize the expected fortune, but was content with the few hundreds he made, and the ownership of Sable Satan and Little Grey, the two fastest horses on the Kansas prairies.

---

* A bow-stall " is formed by taking a turn with a rope or lariat between the nostrils and eyes of a horse, and passing one end over the head, back of the ears and tied on the opposite side. A second noose is then made around the jaws and from this the reins lead back toward the rider, who can then thoroughly manage the animal.—THE AUTHOR.

CHAPTER VI.

SAVING A FATHER'S LIFE.

While in Kansas Mr. Cody became interested in the affairs of the State and joined the Free State party, and while making a speech on one occasion was deliberately attacked and severely wounded.

He however recovered sufficiently to work on his farm again, but was constantly harassed by his old foes, who on several occasions visited his home with the intention of hanging him.

On one occasion, when in town, Billy learned of an attack to be made upon his father, and mounting Sable Satan rode with all speed out to the farm.

He was recognized and hotly pursued; but he got home in time to warn his father who took Little Grey and made his escape.

The horsemen, a score in number, came to the farm, and finding Mr. Cody gone, the leader struck Billy a severe blow and when he departed carried with him Sable Satan.

This almost broke the boy's heart; but he declared he would some day regain his horse, and for weeks he tried to do so, but without success.

One night two horsemen came to the Cody farm and again asked for the farmer, but were told by Mrs. Cody that he was away.

They would not take her word for it; but thoroughly searched the house, after which they forced Billy's sisters to get them some supper.

While they were eating Billy and his father returned, and warned by one of the girls, Mr. Cody went up-stairs to bed, for he was quite ill, and suffering from the wound he had received.

But Billy went into the kitchen and saw there the very man who had struck him the severe blow; and who had taken Sable Satan on his last visit.

"Well, boy, that's a good horse I got from you," he said, with a rude laugh.

"Yes, he's too good for such a wretch as you are," was the fearless reply.

"No lip, boy, or I'll give you a licking you'll remember. By the way, where's that old father of yours?" said the man.

Billy made no reply but walked out of the kitchen, to be soon after followed by his sister Mary who said anxiously:

"Oh, Will, they say father must have come with you, and they intend to search the house again."

"Then I'll go up and tell father," whispered Billy, and up-stairs he went.

He found his father asleep, and his mother was seated near him and told Billy he had a high fever.

"Then don't wake him, and I'll not let them come up here," said Billy, and he went out of the room and took his place at the stairs.

A moment after the two men, both with pistols in their hands, came out of the kitchen and started to come up-stairs.

"Stop, Luke Craig, for you can't come up here," said the boy.

With a hoarse laugh the man sprung up the steps to fall back as a pistol flashed in his face and roll back to the bottom, knocking his companion down too.

But the latter quickly sprung to his feet and dashed out of the house to where their horses were hitched.

His horse was a white one, and his comrade's was Sable Satan, and to the latter he ran.

But up went the window and in a loud voice Billy cried:

"I've got my rifle on you, and I'll fire if you take my horse."

The man evidently believed that he would from what he had seen, and mounting his own horse dashed swiftly away in the dark, while Billy returned to the one he had shot.

He found him badly wounded, but not fatally, and putting him in his father's buggy, drove him to the nearest doctor, at whose house he remained for months before he was well again.

CHAPTER VII.
LOVE AND RIVALRY.

FINDING that Billy was becoming far more accomplished as a rider and shot, than in his books, Mrs. Cody determined to send him to a small school that was only a few miles away.

Billy, though feeling himself quite a man, yielded to his mother's wishes and attended the school, which was presided over by a cross-grained Dominie that used the birch with right good earnest and seeming delight.

Of course Billy's love of mischief got him many a whipping; but for these he did not seem to care until there suddenly appeared in the school another pupil in the shape of a young miss just entering her teens.

The name of this young lady was Mollie Hyatt, and she was the daughter of a well-to-do settler who had lately arrived, and was as pretty as a picture.

Billy's handsome face and dark eyes won her young heart, and the love-match was going smoothly along until a rival appeared in the field in the shape of a youth two years the junior of young Cody, and larger and stronger.

These virtues on the part of Master Steve Gobel, with his growing love of Mollie, made him very assuming, and he forced his company upon the little maid, and had things pretty much his own way, as all the boys seemed afraid of him.

As for Billy he let him have his own way for awhile, and then determined not to stand it any longer he sought Steve Gobel for a settlement of the affair, the result of which was, the teacher hearing them quarreling and coming out took the word of young Cody's rival about it, and gave my hero a severe whipping before the whole school.

Since his meeting Mollie Hyatt Billy had been a most exemplary youth, never having had a single whipping, and this cut him to the heart so deeply that he did not seem to feel the pain of the rod.

And it made him treasure up revenge against Steve Gobel, who was laughing at him during the castigation.

The next day Billy built for Mollie a pretty little arbor on the bank of the creek, and all admired it greatly excepting Steve Gobel, who, as soon as it was finished pulled it down.

Poor Mollie began to cry over her loss, and infuriated at beholding her sorrow, Billy rushed upon his rival and a fierce fight at once began between them.

Finding that he was no match for the bully in brute strength, and suffering under his severe blows, Billy drew from his pocket his knife, opened the blade with his teeth, and drove it into the side of his foe, who cried out in wild alarm.

Springing to his feet, amid the frightened cries of the children, Billy rushed to his pony, drew up the lariat pin, and springing upon his back, rode away across the prairie like the wind.

Coming in sight of a wagon-train bound for the West, he rode up to it and recognizing the wagon-master as an old friend of his father, he told him what had occurred, and that he feared he had killed Steve Gobel.

"Served him right, Billy, and we'll just go into camp, take the boys along, and go over and clean out the house o' l'arnin'," was the blunt reply of the wagon-master.

But this Billy would not hear to, and the wagon-master said:

"Well, my boy, I'm bound with the train to Fort Kearney, so come along with me, and I'll make a man of you."

"But what will my mother think of me?"

"Oh! I'll send a man back with word to her, while you stay, for I won't give you up to that boy's friends."

And thus it was settled; a man rode back to the Cody farm, and the following day he overtook the train again, and Billy's heart was made glad by a letter from his mother telling him that Steve Gobel was not badly wounded, but that under the circumstances he had better go on with the wagon-master and remain away until the anger of the Gobel family cooled down.

Thus, as a Boy Bullwhacker, Billy made his first trip across the plains, and months after, upon his return home, found that the Gobels had forgiven the past, and that Mary Hyatt had, little coquette that she was, found another beau.

But shortly after his return his father died, and having to aid in the support of his mother and sisters, Billy accepted a position as herder for a drove of Government cattle to be driven to the Army of General Albert Sydney Johnson, that was marching against the Mormons at Salt Lake.

CHAPTER VIII.
KILLING HIS FIRST INDIAN.

WHEN the train and beef-herd, with which Billy Cody had gone, arrived in the vicinity of old Fort Kearney their first serious adventure occurred, and for a while the boy thought of his mother's prediction, that he "would be killed or captured by Indians."

Not expecting an attack from red-skins in that vicinity, the party had camped for dinner, and most of them were enjoying a *siesta* under the wagons, Billy being among the latter number, while but three men were on duty as herders.

But suddenly they were aroused by shots, wild yells, and rapid hoof-falls, and down upon them dashed a band of mounted warriors, while others had killed the three guards and the cattle were stampeding in every direction. But the train hands quickly sprung to their feet, rallied promptly for the fight, and met the advancing red-skins with a volley from their Mississippi yagers, which were loaded with ball and buck-shot, and checked their advance.

Knowing that they could not hold out there the train-master called out:

"Boys, make a run for the river, and the banks will protect us."

All started, when Billy called out:

"Don't let us leave these wounded boys."

They turned at his word, to find that two of their number had been wounded, one seriously in the side and the other in the leg.

Raising them in their arms they started at a run for the bank, ere the Indians had rallied from the fire that met them, and reached it in safety, though the man who had been shot in the side was dead ere they got there.

A short consultation was then held, and it was decided to make their way back to Fort Kearney, by wading in the river and keeping the bank as a breast work.

A raft of poles was constructed for the wounded man, and the party started down the stream, protected by the bank, and keeping the Indians at bay with their guns, for they followed them up closely.

As night came on, utterly worn out with wading and walking, Billy dropped behind the others; but trudged manfully along until he was suddenly startled by a dark object coming down over the bank.

It was moonlight, and he saw the plumed head and buckskin-clad form of an Indian, who, in peering over the bank to reconnoiter had lost his balance, or the earth had given way, and sent him down into the stream.

He caught sight of Billy as he was sliding down, and gave a wild war-whoop, which was answered by a shot from the boy's rifle, for though taken wholly by surprise he did not lose his presence of mind.

Hearing the war-whoop and the shot, and at the same time missing Billy, the men came running back and found him dragging the red-skin along in the stream after him.

"It's my Injun, boys," he cried exultantly.

"It are fer a fact, an' I'll show yer how ter take his scalp," replied Frank McCarthy the train-master, and he skillfully cut off the scalp-lock and handed it to Billy, adding:

"Thar, thet is yer first scalp, boy, an' I'm willin' ter swear it won't be yer last, for Billy, you is ther boss boy I ever see."

Billy thanked McCarthy for the gory trophy, gave a slight shudder as he took it, and said significantly:

"I ain't so tired as I was, and I guess I'll keep up with you all now, for if the bank hadn't caved in that Injun would have had me."

At daylight they came in sight of Kearney, and after a volley or two at the Indians still dogging their steps, made for the fort and reached it in safety.

The commanding officer at once sent out a force in pursuit of the red-skins; but they neither found them or the cattle they had driven off.

After a short stay at Fort Kearney Billy returned with a train to Leavenworth, where the papers dubbed him the "Boy Indian-Killer," and made a hero of him for his exploit on the South Platte.

CHAPTER IX.
WINNING A NAME.

WHEN Billy returned home, after his first Indian-killing expedition, he carried with him the pay of a bullwhacker, and all of it he placed in his mother's hands, for the death of Mr. Cody had left the family in indigent circumstances.

Finding that she could not keep Billy at home when he had found out that by his exertions, boy though he was, he could support the family, Mrs. Cody gave a reluctant consent for him to make another trip to the far West under an old and experienced wagon-master named Lew Simpson, and who had taken a great fancy to the youthful Indian-fighter.

Bill was accordingly enlisted as an "extra," which meant that he was to receive full pay and be on hand ready to take the place of any one of the train that was killed, wounded, or got sick.

The wagon train pulled out of Leavenworth, all heavily freighted, each one carrying about six thousand pounds weight, and each also drawn by four yoke of oxen under charge of a driver, or "bullwhacker."

The train consisted of twenty-five wagons, under Lew Simpson, then an assistant wagon-master, next Billy, the "extra," a night herder, a cavallard driver, whose duty was driving the loose and lame cattle, and the bullwhacker for each team.

All were armed with *yagers* and Colt's revolvers, and each man had a horse along, Billy's being Sable Satan, still as good as the day he captured him, and a piece of equine property all envied the boy the possession of; in fact there were several of the men who swore they would yet have the horse.

"I guess not, pards; the boy caught that horse wild on the prairies, and the man that lays hands on him settles with me."

The speaker was J. B. Hickok, known to the world as "Wild Bill," and upon that trail he and William F. Cody for the first time met.

Wild Bill was assistant wagon-master on that trip, and all knew him so well that the idea of possessing Sable Satan by unfair means was at once given up and Billy felt secure in his treasure, for such the horse was, as his equal for speed and bottom had not been found on the plains.

As an "extra hand" Billy had nothing to do while the bullwhackers kept in good health, and no Indians were met with, so became the hunter of the train, keeping it well supplied with fresh meats and wild fowl.

It was upon one of these hunts that Billy won the name of Buffalo Billy, though afterward it was shortened by dropping the y after proving himself the champion buffalo-killer on the plains.

Dismounting from Sable Satan to cut up an

antelope he had shot, he was suddenly startled by seeing his horse bound away over the prairie.

Springing to his feet he at once discovered the cause, for over a distant roll of the prairie a herd of thousands of buffaloes were coming at terrific speed.

One chance of escape alone presented itself and that was a lone cottonwood tree standing some few hundred yards distant.

In all the prairie around not another tree was visible, and Billy had noticed this lone sentinel as he was creeping up for a shot at the antelope.

At full speed he rushed for the tree and hastily climbed it, securing a safe seat amid its branches, while yet the herd was some distance away.

But glancing back over the huge drove to his horse he beheld a band of mounted warriors in full chase.

The center of the herd was headed directly for the tree, and the Indians were so following that they must come directly under it.

If discovered Billy knew well what his fate would be. The Indians would give up buffalo meat for a human scalp.

These thoughts flashed through the boy's mind, and he at once decided what he would do.

To remain, was certain death at the hands of the red-skins.

To leave, as he intended, by the means of a buffalo was a fearful risk.

But he would take it; and accordingly strapped his rifle upon his back, picked out his buffalo, a huge bull, and swinging quickly from a limb, watched his chance and dropped down upon the back of his choice.

Clutching the long, shaggy mane he clung for dear life, at the same time holding himself on with his spurs.

Maddened with fright the bull bounded into the air, snorted wildly, gored those in the advance and soon led the herd.

Billy kept his seat nobly, a grim smile upon his face, and occasionally glanced backward at the herd and the pursuing Indians.

And straight for camp went the herd, until discovered by the train men, who started out in force to head them off.

But pell-mell into camp they went, stampeding the oxen and horses and frightening the men, and Billy began to feel that he must keep on his racer clear to the hills.

But the animal was tired out now and had dropped to the rear of the herd, and Wild Bill, seeing his young friend, raised his rifle and dropped the buffalo bull just as he was running out of camp.

From that day the boy was known as Buffalo Billy.

CHAPTER X.

CAPTURED BY DANITES.

WITH the usual adventures incident to a trip across the plains, an occasional fight with Indians, and several grand hunts, the train at last arrived near Green River in the Rocky Mountains.

Billy, Lew Simpson and another of the train had dropped back during the afternoon for a hunt, and upon drawing near the place where they were to encamp, were surprised to discover a band of horsemen coming toward them, whom they observed, however, to be white men.

Suspecting no harm from those of their own race, they rode forward, and, as they met, were startled to hear:

"Up with your hands! You are dead men if you resist!"

"Who are you?" asked Lew Simpson, angrily.

"Joe Smith, the Danite," was the calm reply of that leader.

"If I had known you were that accursed scoundrel I'd have shot you," growled Lew Simpson.

"Am awful glad you did not know it; but come, you are my prisoners, and your train is in my power," was the reply, and upon arriving at camp they found that it was but too true, for the boys had not suspected danger from men they had believed a party of United States cavalry.

The Danite leader, Joe Smith, then ordered all that could be packed on horses to be taken and the wagons set on fire, and told the train men to set out on foot for Fort Bridger, saying:

"You can reach there, but I guess Albert Sydney Johnson and his troops will never get the supplies."

The train was burned, all but one wagon, which carried supplies for the men, and armed only with their revolvers, they were ordered away by the Danites.

But Buffalo Billy was not one to see his splendid horse go without remonstrance, and, as begging did no good, offered to take him upon any terms he could get him on.

"Boy, ain't you the one who killed Hugh Hall in Kansas some time ago?" asked the man who had Billy's horse.

"I am."

"Well, I owe you one, for he was my pard, and you got me run out of the country by your work, so I'm willing to be even by keeping your horse."

"I'll fight you for him," said Billy, fiercely.

"What with, boy, fists or knives?"

"You are a fool to talk that way, for you weigh double what I do; but I'll fight you for the horse with rifle or pistol."

The train men tried to dissuade Billy from this determination, for they saw the Danite was anxious to take him at his word, and to kill him; but he had made the offer and the Mormon urged it on, and the arrangements were made to fight with pistols at fifty paces, walking on each other and firing until one fell.

They at once took their stands and Joe Smith gave the word, saying in a low tone before doing so:

"He's a boy in years; but he must be got rid of."

At the word the Danite advanced at a rapid walk firing; but Buffalo Billy stood still, and waited until he had received four shots, all coming dangerously near, when he suddenly threw his revolver to a level and drew trigger.

At the flash the man fell, shot in the leg, and the duel ended.

But the Danites would not give up the horse, saying that a wounded man could not continue the fight, and as Billy had not killed his foe, the animal could not be claimed by them.

Wild Bill and Lew Simpson roundly cursed Joe Smith and his Danites for a set of thieves, while Billy said sadly:

"Good-by, Sable, old fellow, good-by."

As he spoke he went up to his splendid horse, that stood saddled near, and throwing himself upon his back, with a defiant yell, bounded away like an arrow from the bow.

The Danites opened a perfect fusilade of pistol-shots upon the boy, but they flew harmlessly by him, and a number mounted and gave pursuit in hot haste.

But Sable Satan left them far behind and they gave up the chase, while Billy hung about until the train-men came along, and joined them, receiving from one and all the highest praise for his daring escape.

Some days after the disconsolate train-men reached Fort Bridger, to find that other trains than theirs had been robbed by the Danites.

CHAPTER XI.

A HOT INDIAN FIGHT.

As it was late in the fall Lew Simpson and his men were compelled to winter at the fort, where there were a number of troops and train employees of Russell, Majors and Waddell, who were formed into military companies, officered by wagon-masters.

As Wild Bill was placed in command of the battalion of train-men, he made Buffalo Billy an *aide-de camp* and the boy devoted himself assiduously to the duties devolving upon him, and before the long and tedious winter passed was forced to experience hardships of the severest kind, as the garrison had to live on mule meat, and haul wood from the distant mountains themselves, their animals having been served up as food.

In the spring Simpson started east with a train, and Buffalo Bill accompanied him as hunter for the men, his well known marksmanship and skill in securing game readily getting for him that position.

One day Lew Simpson and an "extra hand" accompanied him on one of his hunting expeditions, and to their surprise they came upon a band of Indians coming out of a canyon not far from them.

They were out on the prairie, and knowing that they could not escape on their mules, Simpson and the extra told Billy to ride off on Sable Satan and save himself.

But this the boy would not do, saying that he would remain with them.

"Then your horse must go with our mules," said Simpson.

"All right, Lew," said Billy, though the tears came into his eyes.

Telling them to dismount, just as they came to a buffalo wallow, Lew Simpson said:

"Now, give 'em a shot just back of the ears."

The shots were fired, Billy shutting his eyes as he pulled the trigger, and Sable Satan and the two mules dropped dead in their tracks.

In an instant they were dragged into position, so as to form a triangular fort, and getting into the wallow, with their knives the three threw up the dirt as rapidly as possible to make their position safer.

By this time the Indians, some half hundred in number, were rushing upon them with wildest yells.

But crouching down in their little fort of flesh and dirt, Lew Simpson and his man and boy comrade leveled their rifles over the bodies of the slain animals, and, as the howling red-skins came within sixty yards, fired together.

Down went three Indians, and while Lew Simpson reloaded the yagers Billy and George Woods fired with their revolvers with such right good will the Indians were checked in their advance and turned to retreat out of range, followed by three more shots from the yagers.

Five Indians and four ponies were the result of this fight, and it gave the holders of the triangular fort confidence in themselves.

But the Indians did not give up the attack, but circled around and around the fort, firing upon the defenders with their arrows, and slightly wounding all three of them, while the bodies of the mules and horse were literally filled with shafts.

After a few rides around their pale-face foes, the Indians suddenly charged again, coming from every quarter, and forcing the whites to each defend the space in his front.

With demoniacal yells they came on once more, and once more the yagers opened, and then were thrown aside for the rapidly firing revolvers which did fearful execution.

Glancing toward Billy Lew Simpson saw that he was perfectly cool and had a revolver in each hand, although his shirt was saturated with blood from the arrow wound in his shoulder.

Unable to understand, or stand the hot fire of the revolvers, they again broke, when within twenty yards of the fort and rode off rapidly out of range.

"You got three that time, Billy," cried Lew Simpson gleefully, as he saw a trio of redskins scattered along in the front of the boy.

Billy smiled grimly and reloaded his weapons, after which Lew Simpson dressed the wounds of his comrades, who returned a like favor for him.

But the Indians had by no means gone, for they had gone into camp in a circle around their foes, but well out of range of the fearful Mississippi yagers.

The three defenders in the mean time improved their opportunity to strengthen their fort with dirt and dig a deeper space within, while they also lunched upon their scanty supply of food.

"They'll starve us out if they can't take us by charging," said Simpson.

"They can't starve me as long as your mule holds out, Lew, for I won't eat poor Sable; it would choke me," replied Billy.

"Well, mule meat's good," said Woods.

"Yes, when there ain't anything else to eat, but I prefer buff'ler or Injun," was Billy's response.

"We may have to eat Injun yet," laughed Lew Simpson.

All made a wry face at this supposition and again prepared to meet a charge, for the red-skins were coming down in column.

But again they were checked with loss, and Billy's shot brought down the chief.

Darkness coming on, the Indians formed in line as though to ride away, when Lew Simpson said:

"They must take us for durned fools not to know that they won't leave their dead unburied, and that they think they can draw us out. No, here is where we live until the boys from the train come to look us up."

During the night the Indians, finding their foes would not leave their fort, set the grass on fire to burn them out.

But it was too scanty to burn well and only made a smoke, under cover of which they once more advanced, to be once more driven back.

With the morning they showed that their intention was to starve them out for they went into a regular camp in a circle upon the prairie.

But during the afternoon a party of horsemen appeared in sight, and the three hungry, suffering, half-starved defenders gave a yell of delight, which the red-skins answered with howls of disappointed rage as they hastily mounted their ponies and fled.

The train-men soon came up and were wild in their enthusiasm over the brave defense made, while the fort came in for general praise, although one and all deeply regretted Sable Satan's sad end, though his death had served a good purpose.

CHAPTER XII.

BOY TRAPPERS' ADVENTURES.

It was a proud day for Buffalo Billy when he returned home and was welcomed by his mother and sisters, to whom he gave all of his earnings, which were considerable, as his pay had been liberal.

The neighborhood, hearing from members of the train of Billy's exploits, for he was very close-mouthed about what he had done, made a hero of him, and many a pretty girl of seventeen regretted that the boy was not a man grown, to have him for a lover.

But Billy's restless nature would not allow him to remain idle at home, so he joined a party of trappers who were going to trap the streams of the Laramie and Chugwater for otter, beaver and other animals possessing valuable fur, as well as to shoot wolves for their pelts.

This expedition did not prove very profitable, and not wishing to return home without enough furs to bring a fair sum, Buffalo Billy joined a young man, only a few years his senior, by the name of Dave Harrington, and the two started off for the Republican.

Their outfit consisted of a wagon and yoke of oxen, for the transportation of their supplies and pelts, and they began trapping in the vicinity of Junction City, Kansas, and went up the Republican to Prairie Dog creek, where they found plenty of beaver.

While catching a large number of beavers, one day they returned to camp to find one of their oxen had fallen over a precipice and killed himself, and they were left without a team.

But the Boy Trappers, for Dave Harrington was not eighteen, determined to trap on through the winter, and in the spring one of them would go for a team to haul back their wagon.

Ill fortune seemed however to dog their steps as trappers, for one day, while chasing elk, Buffalo Billy fell and broke his leg, and Dave Harrington had to carry him to camp.

Here was a sad predicament, for the nearest settlement was one hundred miles distant.

But Dave set the leg as skillfully as he could, built a "dug-out," for the wounded boy to live in, filled it with wood and provisions, and then set out to procure a yoke of oxen and sled to return for billy and their pelts.

The "dug-out," was a hole in the side of a bank, covered with poles, grass and sod, and with a fire-place in one end, and a bunk near it, was by no means uncomfortable; but the prospect of remaining there for a month alone, for it would take Harrington that time to go and return through the deep snow, was by no means a pleasant prospect for a boy under fourteen, and with a broken leg.

Dave started the following morning on foot, and Billy was left alone, helpless, and in the solitude of the mountain wilds.

To throw wood on the fire was a painful effort for him, and to move so as to cook his food was torture, and boys of his age can well feel for him in distress and loneliness.

But Buffalo Billy was made of stern stuff, and knew not what fear was; but who can picture the thoughts that were constantly in his young brain, when the winds were sweeping through the pines at night, the wolves were howling about his door, and the sleet and snow was almost continually falling.

It were enough to drive a strong man mad, let alone a boy.

But he stood it bravely, each day however counting with longing heart the hours that went so slowly by, and hoping for his comrade's return.

"Perhaps he has been frozen to death."

That was his thought one day about Harrington.

The next it was:

"I wonder if he has not lost his way?"

Again it was:

"I fear the Indians may have killed him."

When Dave had been gone about two weeks, Buffalo Billy was startled one day from a sound nap, to see an Indian standing by his side.

He was in full war-paint and feathers, which showed he was on the war-path, and Billy felt that it was all over with him.

Speaking to him in Sioux, which the boy understood, he asked:

"What pale-face boy do here?"

"My leg is broken."

"What for come here?"

"To get furs."

"This red-skin country?"

This laconic assertion Billy could not contradict, so he wisely held his peace.

"Let see leg," came next.

Billy showed him the bandaged limb, which was broken between the knee and ankle.

Just then another Indian entered whom Billy recognized, as having seen before, and whom he knew to be the great Sioux Chief, Rain-in-the-Face.

Billy called him by name, and he kept back the warriors, who were about to end the boy's life then and there.

"Boy pale-face know chief?" asked Rain-in-the-Face.

"Yes, I saw you at Fort Laramie, and gave you a knife," said Billy with hope in his heart.

"Ugh! chief don't forget; have knife here," and he showed a knife which he had doubtless often used upon the scalps of pale-faces.

"What pale-face boy do here?"

Billy told him.

"Where friend?"

"Gone after team."

"When come back?"

Billy was afraid to tell him the truth, so said:

"In two moons."

"Long time."

"Yes; but do your young men intend to kill me?"

"Me have talk and see."

The Indians then held a council together, and Billy could see that the chances were against him; but old Rain-in-the-Face triumphed in the end, and said:

"As pale-face boy is only pappoose, my young men not kill him."

Billy had often longed to be a man; but now he was happy that he was a boy, and answered:

"Yes, I am only a little pappoose."

"Him heap bad pappoose, me remember," said Rain-in-the-Face, recalling some of the jokes the boy played at Fort Laramie.

The Indians then unsaddled their ponies and camped at the dug-out for two days, and when they left they carried with them the sugar and coffee, Billy's rifle and one revolver, and most of the ammunition, besides what cooking utensils they needed.

Then old Rain-in-the-Face bade the boy good-by, and they rode off without poor Billy's blessing following them.

Hardly had they gone before a severe snow-storm sprung up, and it was hard indeed for the crippled boy to get wood enough to build a fire, for the red-skins had put it out before leaving.

The wolves, seemingly understanding how helpless the boy was, scratched at the door, and ran over the roof of the dug-out, at the same time howling viciously; but Billy frightened them off with an occasional shot, and resigned himself to his lonely fate.

But at last a month passed away, and with its end appeared brave Dave Harrington.

He had passed through innumerable dangers, but had at last come back in safety, and brought with him an ox-team.

Never in his life had Buffalo Billy felt the joy of that moment, and, though not a boy given to showing his feelings, he burst into tears of delight.

As it was impossible to at once return, on account of the very great depth of the snow, Dave told Billy they would wait until spring, as he had plenty of provisions, and that fur animals were plenty.

As soon as the snow began to melt Dave got his traps in, collected his pelts, which numbered a thousand, and putting them on the wagon, so as to serve as a bed for Billy, started his oxen homeward.

After twelve days they reached the ranch where Dave had purchased the oxen, paid in furs for the team, and started on to Junction City. Arriving there they sold their team, wagon and furs, the latter bringing them about two hundred and fifty dollars, a handsome sum for each when divided, and which made Billy's heart glad to take home with him, for it paid off a mortgage on his mother's farm.

CHAPTER XII.

BUFFALO BILLY STRIKES IT RICH.

It was months before Billy obtained perfect use of his broken leg and was able to throw his crutches aside; but when he did do so it was with a glad heart, for once more he longed to be upon the plains.

Hearing of a rich discovery of gold in Colorado, he joined a party of miners that were bound there, and, reaching the mining camps, staked out a claim and began work.

He was the youngest person in the mines, in fact the only boy there, and with many he was a great favorite; but there were a few men there who sought to impose upon him on account of his youth.

This treatment Buffalo Billy was not the person to stand, and the result was one of his foes struck him one night without the slightest cause.

The result was a general row, for Billy's friends at once backed him in resenting the blow, and, though the fracas lasted but a few minutes, there were several burials next day as the result.

Of course this made Billy more disliked by those who, without reason, had become his foes, and to add to their dislike, he one day struck a rich vein that promised to pan out well in ore.

A few days he toiled in his lead, laying up considerable sums by his work, and one morning, as he went to his mine, he found it occupied by two rough-looking men whom he did not remember to have ever seen before.

"Well, pards, I guess you're up the wrong tree," he said, pleasantly.

"I guesses not; this are our lead," said one, rudely.

"How do you make that out?"

"We staked it months ago, and was called away, and now we has returned to it."

"Well, I believe you both to be lying, and until you prove it's your claim you can't have it," was the bold reply.

"Who's goin' ter say no?"

"I am."

"You!"

"Yes."

"Who is you?"

"I am named William Frederick Cody."

"You has handle enough."

"I have more than that."

"Waal."

"I'm called Buffalo Billy."

"We has heer'd o' you as a chap as has too much cheek fer one so young."

"Then if you know me you will understand that though I am but a boy I won't let you walk away with my claim."

"Get out, boy."

Billy obeyed; that is he went down to the camps and consulted his friends about what was best for him to do.

"We'll go up and call in their chips, Billy," was the universal decision.

"No, let us find out if the claim is theirs," said Billy.

"Find out nothin'; they has no right to it and 'tain't justice."

So up to the mine they went, and Billy's friends recognized the two claimants of the mine as two worthless fellows who had been in the valley months before, but who had no claim upon the boy's property

"You must git!"

That was the decision; but just then others came up who sided with the desperadoes and things looked very scary for awhile, for half the crowd swore that the mine had belonged to the two claimants to it and that Billy ought to give it up.

But these were the men who disliked Billy and his party, as they were the honest miners, and who were willing to side with his foes.

"Ef ther boy wants ther mine he will hev to fight fer it," said one.

"He will fight for it and so will we!" cried one of Billy's friends.

All this time Billy had remained silent; but now he saw that his friends were in deadly earnest, and to prevent a general fight and much loss of life he said:

"The mine I own legally and I'll fight for it if that will settle it, but I don't want to have to fight both of you."

"Oh, but you must though," said one.

"If I must, I'll do it."

"But you shall not, Billy. These two devils only want to murder you so they can get the mine, and they sha'n't do it."

This was said by Billy's best pard and the others who liked the boy backed him up in his words, and pistols were drawn on both sides and the slightest act now all knew would cause trouble.

"If they'll fight me with revolvers and separately I'll be willing," said Billy, hastily, anxious to avert the trouble.

"Waal, we'll do that, so sail in," said one.

"No, not this way, you accursed coward, but go off there, stand with your back to the boy, as he will to you, and twenty paces apart, and at a word wheel and fire," cried Billy's friend.

This seemed fair and all agreed to it, and the man and the boy were placed in position, Billy pale but calm.

The other side won the word to wheel and fire, and though the man tried to aid his friend in giving it, Buffalo Billy was too quick for him and fired a second in advance of his adversary.

But that second was enough, for the bullet went straight to the heart of the one at which it was aimed, while his shot flew wild.

A yell burst from Billy's friends as they rushed forward while his foes were bringing up their other man.

But just then a stranger rode up, and leveling a pistol at the second claimant for the mine said sternly:

"Dick Malone, my gallows-bird, I arrest you in the name of the law."

The stranger was a United States detective, and the one he arrested an escaped convict.

This ended the fight for the mine; but after a few days' longer work in it Billy found that the vein panned out badly, and selling out his interest in it returned to his home once more, convinced that mining was not his forte, though he certainly had dug out enough of the yellow ore to prove to his mother that he had not been idle.

CHAPTER XIV.

THE YOUNG GUIDE.

THE next time that Buffalo Billy left home it was in the capacity of assistant guide to a train of emigrants that were going to the far West to settle.

In Leavenworth one night he met in a common assembling room for all classes of men, a man who was Train Boss, or captain, and who was going to the West to raise cattle and also to farm.

His train, consisting of some thirty families, was encamped out of town resting and fitting up for the renewal of the march, and he had come into Leavenworth to secure a competent guide, the one who had been acting as such having been taken very ill.

He had just secured the services of a young man who professed to know the country well though he was a stranger in Leavenworth, and fearing an accident might deprive him of his services too, the captain was looking around for an assistant when he came upon Billy.

He liked the boy from the first, but feared, on account of his youth, that he might not be competent for the position, until assured by several teamsters that he was fully so, and consequently he engaged Billy at a fair salary.

The chief guide, who called himself Roy Velvet, Billy had never met, until the morning the train rolled out of camp on its way westward, and from the very first he did not like him.

He was a handsome, but dissipated looking young man, dressed like a dandy, was more than thoroughly armed, and rode a superb bay mare.

He smiled when Captain Luke Denham, the Train Boss, introduced Billy as an assistant guide, and said sneeringly:

"I guess he won't be of much use ten miles away from Leavenworth, captain."

Billy made no reply, but kept up considerable thinking, and set to work at his duties.

For some days the train went on finely, and all felt the new guide knew his business; but then there came some stormy days, it was hard traveling, several times the train had to make a dry camp, and once they were attacked by Indians, until some of the old teamsters felt confident that Roy Velvet had lost the way.

Yet on they plodded until at last the nature of the country was such that it was difficult for the train to travel, while, to add to their discomfort and fears, a large band of Indians were hovering near them.

"Well, Velvet, where will you find a camping place to-night?" asked Captain Denham, riding forward and joining the guide.

"Oh! I'll find a good place, and only a short distance ahead; after that the country will be all right for traveling," was the quiet answer.

"I don't believe it, for it has not that look."

"Then ask the assistant guide," was the stern reply.

"I would, but he is not with the train, and has not been seen since last night."

"Perhaps he got out of sight of the train and couldn't find his way back," sneered the guide.

"Oh no! that boy knows what he is about, and I'll trust him for it."

"Well, yonder is the camp," and Roy Velvet pointed to a little meadow not far distant, through which ran a deep stream, and beyond and overshadowing it, was a range of bold hills.

"It's a pleasant spot indeed, and I guess we'll halt a day or two," said the captain, and he gave orders for the train to encamp.

But suddenly up dashed Billy Cody, mounted upon a large horse no one had ever seen him ride before, and it was evident that he had been riding hard.

"Captain Denham, don't camp there, sir, for you place yourself at the mercy of the renegades and Indians that are dogging your trail," he said hastily.

"I am the guide, boy, and have selected the camp," sternly answered Roy Velvet.

"And you are my prisoner, Roy Velvet," and quicker than a flash the revolver of Buffalo Billy covered his heart.

Roy Velvet turned very pale, but said:

"Are you mad, boy?"

"No."

"Billy, what is the matter?" asked Captain Denham, while the teamsters and settlers gathered quickly around.

"Tie that man and I will tell you."

"But, Billy—"

"Tie him, captain, or I shall shoot him, for I know who and what he is," cried Billy, and his manner, his charge against the chief guide, his mysterious absence from the train for eighteen hours, and his return upon a strange horse, proved to all that he did know something detrimental to Roy Velvet.

"Speak, Billy, and if you know aught against this man, tell us," said the captain.

"Disarm him then for he is a tricky devil."

"Captain Denham, will you permit that boy to cover me with his revolver and hurl insult upon me?" cried the guide.

"As you will not do as I ask I will do it myself," and Billy rode up to the guide, still holding his cocked revolver upon him, and deliberately took from his belt his revolvers and knife.

"You are so sly, so soft in your cunning, Velvet, that I'll be on the safe side," said Billy with a smile, as he felt over the man for another weapon.

"Ah! I'll take this Derringer from your breast pocket," and out he drew the concealed weapon.

"Now, captain, I'll introduce to you Red Reid, the Renegade Chief."

All were astonished at this charge made by Billy against the guide, for Red Reid was one of the vilest road-agents that infested the overland trails to the West, and had robbed and murdered many a train of emigrants, and of Government supplies.

He was known also to be in league with the red-skins, and had them for allies, when his own force of renegades was not large enough to make a successful attack.

"He lies! I am not that monster," shouted the guide as white as a corpse.

"I do not lie, sir; from the first I did not like you, and knowing that you were going off the regular trail west I watched you.

"I have seen you, at night, slip out of camp and meet Indians, and last night I followed the one you met.

"I overtook him on the prairies, after a hard chase, and he shot my horse; but I shot him and found he was a white man in Indian disguise, and more, before he died he recognized me, for he was once my father's friend, but went to the bad.

"He told me who and what you were, and when he died to-day I mounted his horse and came on after the train, for I knew you were going to lead them here to attack this very night with your band that is not far away."

The story of Billy made a deep impression upon the train people, and the result was that Roy Velvet was seized, bound, and hanged to a tree within fifteen minutes, and the boy who had saved them from death was made chief guide.

At once he led them out of the dangerous locality where they could be ambushed and attacked, and the truth of the charge against Roy Velvet was sustained by the attack of the supposed Indians upon their camp; for, when driven off and the dead examined, a number of white men were found in the red paint and dress of Indian warriors.

Without difficulty Buffalo Billy led the train on to its destination, proving himself thereby a perfect guide, and after a short stop in the new settlement, he returned with a Government train bound East, and again was warmly welcomed "home again."

CHAPTER XV.
THE PONY EXPRESS RIDER.

ONE day when he had ridden into Leavenworth Buffalo Billy met his old friend, Wild Bill, who was fitting out a train with supplies for the Overland Stage Company, and he was at once persuaded to join him in the trip West going as assistant wagon-master.

Putting a man on his mother's farm to take care of it, for as a farmer Billy was not a success, he bade his mother and sisters farewell and once more was on his way toward the land of the setting sun.

Having been at home for several months, for his mother not being in the enjoyment of good health he hated to leave her, Billy had been attending school, and had been a hard student, while in the eyes of his fellow pupils, girls and boys alike, he was a hero of heroes.

On his trip West with Wild Bill he had carried his books, and often in camp he had whiled away the time in studying, until he was asked if he was reading for a lawyer or a preacher.

But when well away from civilization his books were cast aside for his rifle, and he was constantly in the saddle supplying the train with game.

Without any particular adventures the train arrived in due season at Atchison, and there so much was said about Pony Riding on the Overland that Buffalo Billy decided to volunteer as a rider.

Resigning his position with the train, Mr. Russell gave him a warm letter to Alf Slade, a noted personage on the frontier, and to him Billy went.

Slade was then stage agent for the Julesberg and Rocky Ridge Division, with his headquarters at Horseshoe, nearly forty miles west of Fort Laramie, and there Billy found him and presented his letter.

Slade read the letter, looked Billy carefully over, and said:

"I would like to oblige you, my boy, but you are too young, the work kills strong men in a short time."

"Give me a trial, sir, please, for I think I can pull through," said Billy.

"But are you used to hard riding and a life of danger?"

"Yes, sir, I've seen hard work, young as I am."

"I see now that Russell says you are Buffalo Billy," and Slade glanced again at the letter.

"Yes, sir, that's what my pards call me."

"I have heard of you, and you can become a pony rider; if you break down you can give it up."

The very next day Billy was set to work on the trail from Red Buttes on the North Platte, to Three Crossings on the Sweet Water, a distance of seventy-six miles.

It was a very long piece of road, but Billy did not weaken, and ere long became known as the Boss Pony Rider.

One day he arrived at the end of his road to find that the rider who should have gone out on the trip with his mail, had been killed in a fight, so he at once volunteered for the run to Rocky Ridge, a distance of eighty-five miles, and arrived at the station even ahead of time.

Without rest he turned back and reached Red Buttes on time, making the extraordinary run of *three hundred and twenty-two* miles without rest, and at an average speed of fifteen miles an hour.

This remarkable feat won for him a presentation of a purse of gold from the company, and a fame for pluck and endurance that placed him as the chief of the Pony Riders.

CHAPTER XVI.
A RIDE FOR LIFE.

ONE day, after Buffalo Billy had been a few months Pony Riding, a party of Indians ambushed him near Horse Creek.

He however, as did his horse, miraculously escaped their foes, dashed through them and went on like the wind.

But the red-skins gave hot chase, firing as they ran, yet still without effect.

Billy was well mounted and had not felt fear of them until he saw two of the Indians rapidly drawing ahead of the other, and gaining upon him.

He urged his horse on at full speed with lash and spur, but still the red-skins gained.

Then he saw that they too were splendidly mounted, not on ponies, but large American horses which they had doubtlessly captured from the cavalry.

Nearer and nearer came the Indians, and on Billy pressed at full speed.

Throwing a glance over his shoulder he saw that one of the red-skins, whose feathers proved him to be a chief, was gaining on his comrade, and yet seemed not to be urging the large roan he rode.

"I want that horse, and I want that Injun," muttered Billy, and he quietly took his revolver from his belt.

Nearer and nearer came the chief, and Billy felt his own horse wavering, and knew he was forced beyond his powers of endurance, and fearing he might fall with him, determined to act at once.

Dragging the animal he rode to a sudden halt, and reining him back upon his haunches, he suddenly wheeled in his saddle and fired.

The Indian saw his sudden and unexpected movement, and was taken so wholly off his guard that he had no time to fire, and ere he could raise his pistol, a bullet went crashing through his brain.

He fell back on his horse, that dashed straight on, and was then thrown to the ground, while the rein of the animal was seized by Billy with a force that checked his mad flight.

It was an easy thing for the Pony Rider to spring upon the back of the roan and get away; but he would not give up his own saddle and the mail bags which were attached to it, and, dismounting, he was hastily making the transfer from his own to the red skin's horse when up dashed the second Indian, and firing as he came, sent a bullet through the cap of the youth, knocking it from his head.

The two horses he held began to both pull back in alarm, and for an instant things looked very dismal for the brave Pony Rider; but a second shot from the warrior missed the boy and killed his horse, and this relieved him of that trouble, and instantly he drew his revolver and fired.

Down from his horse fell the red skin, but only wounded, and as he still clutched his pistol, Billy was forced to give him another shot, which quieted him forever, just as the band of Indians came in sight.

But the presence of mind for which he was noted did not desert the Pony Rider, and he quickly cut loose his saddle from his dead horse, sprung with it in his hand upon the back of the roan and dashed away once more just as the shots of his foes began to patter around him.

The Indians, however, kept the chase up, and Billy dashed up to the station to find that the stock-tender lay dead and scalped in front of his cabin and the stock had been driven off.

But without an instant's delay the Pony Rider urged the splendid roan he had captured on once more and arrived in safety at Ploutz Station *ahead of time*, and made known what had happened back on the overland trail, and added new laurels to his name.

CHAPTER XVII.
THE BOY STAGE DRIVER OF THE OVERLAND.

AFTER six months longer of Pony Riding over the dangerous trail of seventy-six miles, ridden by day and night in all kinds of weather, Buffalo Billy met with an adventure that was the cause of his again finding another occupation.

The Indians had become very troublesome as fall came on and a number of pony-riders had been killed and stations burned along the route until there were few who cared to take the risks.

The stage coaches also were often attacked, and on one occasion the driver and two passengers were killed and several others were wounded.

But Billy did not flinch from his long, lonely and desperate rides, and seemed to even take pleasure in taking the fearful chances against death which he was forced to do on every ride out and in.

One day as he sped along like the wind he saw ahead of him the stage coach going at full speed and no one on the box.

At once he knew there was trouble, and as he drew nearer he discovered some Indians dash out of a ravine and give chase.

As he heard the clatter of hoofs behind him he looked around and saw a dozen red-skins coming in pursuit, and felt confident that he must have dashed by an ambush they were preparing for him, by suddenly changing his course and riding *around* instead of *through* a canyon.

The stage coach was now in the open prairie, and dashing along the trail as fast as the horses could go, while the Indians in close pursuit numbered but three.

Billy was well mounted upon a sorrel mare, and urging her with the spur he soon came in range of the red-skin furthest in the rear and hastily fired.

Down went the pony, and the Indian was thrown with such violence that he was evidently stunned, as he lay where he had fallen.

Another shot wounded one of the remaining Indians, and they hastily sped away to the right oblique in flight, while Billy dashed on to the side of the coach.

There were five passengers within, and two of them were women, and all were terribly frightened, though evidently not knowing that their driver lay dead upon the box, the reins still grasped in his nerveless hands.

Riding near, Billy seized his mail bags and dextrously got from his saddle to the stage, and the next instant he held the reins in his firm gripe.

He knew well that Ted Remus, the driver, had carried out a box of gold, and was determined to save it for the company if in his power.

His horse, relieved of his weight and trained to run the trail, kept right on ahead, and he, skillfully handling the reins, for he was a fine driver, drove on at the topmost speed of the six animals drawing the coach.

Behind him came the Indians, steadily gaining; but Billy plied the silk in a style that made his team fairly fly, and they soon reached the hills.

Here the red-skins again gained, for the road was not good and in many places very dangerous.

But once over the ridge, and just as the Indians were near enough to fill the back of the coach with arrows, Billy made his team jump ahead once more, and at breakneck speed they rushed down the steep road, the vehicle swaying wildly, and the passengers within not knowing whether they would be dashed to pieces, or scalped by the Indians, or which death would be the most to be desired.

But Billy, in spite of his lightning driving, managed his team well, and after a fierce run of half an hour rolled up to the door of the station in a style that made the agent and the lookers on stare.

But he saved the box and the lives of the passengers, and several days after was transferred from the Pony Rider line to stage driving on the Overland, a position he seemed to like.

CHAPTER XVIII.

A CLEVER DISGUISE.

WHILE riding Pony Express the road on Buffalo Billy's run became infested with road-agents, who were wont to halt every rider they could catch, and also rob the stages.

The chief of these outlaws was noted as a man of gallantry, for he never robbed a woman, no matter what the value of her personal effects might be.

Ladies with valuable diamonds in their ears, and rings that were worth a small fortune, were always spared by this man, who became known by his forbearance to the fair sex as the "Cavalier."

Poor men were also exempt from being robbed by the Cavalier; that is if he really thought a man was poor and not "playing possum," to get off from paying the toll demanded.

In halting a stage the driver was never robbed, but Government and the Company's moneys were always taken, and well-to-do travelers had to pay liberally.

Pony Express Riders were never robbed of their pocket money, but the mail was invariably searched for money.

Once only had Buffalo Billy been halted by the Cavalier, though the other riders had frequently been brought to a halt and made to pony up.

That once Billy had shown fight, had tried to run by, and his horse had been shot; but he slightly wounded the Cavalier in the arm, and for it he was told if he ever attempted resistance again he would be promptly killed.

This did not trouble the young Rider in the least, but he made up his mind that he would not be caught; and after that the road-agents found it impossible to bring him to a halt, and his mails always went through in perfect safety.

At last it became rumored that Buffalo Billy had been removed to another part of the road, and that as no riders could be found to take his long night rides, a daughter of one of the stock-tenders had volunteered for it, and the company, knowing her ability as a rider, accepted her services until another could be found.

The first night on the run she arrived at the other end on time, though she reported that she had been halted by the Cavalier and four of his men.

The road-agent seemed greatly surprised that a woman, in fact a young and very pretty girl, should be riding the road, but she made known the circumstances, and he told her she should always go through unmolested by him and his men.

But he made the mails, carried by the other riders, and the stage-coach passengers, suffer for his leniency to the Girl Rider, and the Government and both the express and stage companies offered a large reward for the capture of himself and men alive.

This seemed to do no good, although a number of attempts were made to capture him, which signally failed, and the reward was increased and added "dead or alive."

All this time the Girl Rider often met the Cavalier in her rides, and when the moonlight nights came on, he would often, as she was flying along, dash out from some thicket, and ride with her ten or fifteen miles.

The more he saw of her the more he seemed to admire her, and his times of joining her increased, and he seemed to so enjoy his rides with her, that he would, when she went into a station to change horses, make a circuit around it, and joining her beyond, continue on for another dozen miles, for he rode a fleet steed, and one of great bottom.

One night as they thus sped along he told the Girl Pony Rider that he had learned to love her, tho' he had never seen her face in the daylight, and that he had accumulated a large sum, for he had a treasure hiding-place in the mountains, and, if she only would love him in return and fly with him, he would be the happiest of men, and give up his evil life.

The maiden promised to think of it, said it was so sudden and unexpected, that she had never loved before, and did not even then know her own heart, and with this she dashed on her way like the wind.

The next night the Cavalier again met her, and again renewed his vows of love, and she told him she had thought of it, and would stand by him until death parted them.

The Cavalier went into ecstasies over this, and an evening was appointed when they should leave the country together, which was a night on which the Girl Rider knew she was to carry quite a sum of money in huge bills to the paymaster of the company at the other end of the line.

The night in question came round, and the cavalier road-agent, as he had promised, had relays of fresh horses every twenty miles until they should have gone two hundred, which would put them beyond pursuit; in fact the company would not discover for twenty-four hours just what had happened, the outlaw and maiden both believed, so considered themselves safe.

At the hour he had agreed to meet the maiden, the Cavalier was on hand at the timber, mounted on his finest horse, dressed in his best, and carrying a couple of large saddle-bags loaded with treasure, consisting of his lion's share of the robberies, and which included watches, jewelry, gold, silver and paper money.

The maiden asked him to dismount and arrange her saddle-girths, and as he was stooping, she threw down the rein of his horse which she was holding, and to which she had attached something, and away he started in a run, for the violent motion had frightened him; but he soon came to a halt.

Rising to his feet the Cavalier suddenly felt the cold muzzle of a revolver pressed against his head, and heard the words:

"You are my prisoner; resist and I will kill you; up with your arms!"

He tried to laugh it off as a joke, but she was in deadly earnest, and he soon found it out.

Leaning over she took the weapons of the road-agent from his belt, and told him to move on ahead.

He could but obey, for he knew she would kill him if he did not.

A mile up the trail and the stock-tender's station came in sight, and in the moonlight they both saw a crowd of men awaiting them there.

Once more the Cavalier begged for his release; but she was determined, and marched him straight up to the crowd.

"Well, Billy, you've got him," cried a voice as they approached.

"I most certainly have, and if you'll look after him I'll go and fetch his horse, for I've got a hook fastened to his rein and he can't go far."

"Billy!" cried the road-agent.

"Yes, I am Buffalo Billy, and I assumed this disguise to catch you and I've done it.

"Do you love me now, pard?"

The road-agent foamed and swore; but it was no use; he had been caught, was taken to the town, tried, found guilty of murdering and robbing and ended his life on the gallows, and Buffalo Billy got the reward for his capture, and a medal from the company, and he certainly deserved all that he recieved for his daring exploit in the guise of a young girl, and a pretty one too, the boys said he made, for he had no mustache then, his complexion was perfect, though bronzed, and his waist was as small as a woman's, while in the saddle his hight did not show.

As to the Cavalier, Billy said he deserved his name, and certainly talked love like an adept at the art, and his lovemaking, like many another man's, led him to ruin and death.

CHAPTER XIX.

THE DESPERADOES' DEN.

SHORTLY after this adventure of the rescue of the stage coach, the Indians became so bad along the line that the Pony Express and stages had to be stopped for awhile on account of the large number of horses run off.

This caused a number of the employees of the Overland to be idle, and they at once formed a company to go in search of the missing stock, and also to punish the red-skins.

Of this company Wild Bill, who had been driving stage, was elected the commander, and, as they were all a brave set of men, it was expected they would render a good account of themselves.

Of course Buffalo Billy went along, by years the youngest of the party, but second to none for courage and skill in prairie craft.

They first struck the Indians in force on the Overland trail, and defeating them with heavy loss, pursued them to the Powder River, and then down that stream to the vicinity of where old Fort Reno now stands.

Pushing them hard the whites had several engagements with them, and each one of the company performed some deed of valor, but none were more conspicuous for daring deeds than was Buffalo Billy.

Permitting them no rest the whites drove the Indians into their village, and although they were outnumbered four to one, captured all of the company's stock as well as the ponies of the red-skins.

Having been so successful Wild Bill gave the order to return, and the Indians had been too badly worsted to follow, and they reached Sweetwater Bridge in safety, and without the loss of an animal they had retaken or captured.

The stages and Pony Express at once began to run again on time, and Buffalo Billy was transferred to another part of the line, to drive through a mountainous district.

But anxious to return home, after his long absence, he resigned his position, determined to take advantage of a train going east, and in which he could get a position as assistant baggage-master on the homeward-bound trip, which would pay him for a couple of months' service, thereby giving him a larger sum to carry to his family.

As it would be several days before the train started, Buffalo Billy determined to enjoy a bear-hunt, and mounting his favorite horse, the roan he had captured from the Indian chief, he set out for the foot-hills of Laramie Peak.

After a day of pleasure, in which he had shot considerable game, such as deer, antelope and sage hens, but not a bear, he camped for the night in a pretty nook upon one of the mountain streams.

Hardly had he fastened his roan and begun to build a fire, by which to cook his supper, when he was startled by the neigh of a horse up in the mountains.

Instantly he sprung to his horse, and, by his hand over his nostrils, prevented him from giving an answering whinny, while he stood in silence listening, for he knew that he might rather expect to see a foe there than a friend.

As the neigh was once more repeated, Buffalo Billy resaddled his horse, hitched him so that he could be easily unfastened, and, with his rifle started cautiously on foot up the stream.

He had not gone far when in a little glen he beheld nearly half a hundred horses grazing and lariated out.

This was a surprise to him, and he was most cautious indeed, for he was convinced that they belonged to some prowling band of Indians.

Presently, up the mountain further, he caught sight of a sudden light, and his keen eye detected that a man's form had momentarily appeared and then all was darkness once more.

On he went in the direction of the light, going as noiselessly as a panther creeping upon its prey, until presently he dimly discovered the outline of a small cabin, built back against the precipitous side of an overhanging hill.

Hearing voices, and recognizing that they were white men, he stepped boldly forward and knocked at the door.

Instantly there followed a dead silence within, and again he knocked.

"Who is there?" asked a gruff voice.

"A pard."

"Come in, pard."

Billy obeyed.

But instantly he regretted it, for his eyes fell upon a dozen villainous-looking fellows, several of whom he recognized as having seen loafing at the Overland stations, and who were considered all that was bad.

"Who are you?" asked one who appeared to be the leader.

"I am Bill Cody, a stage driver on the Overland, and I came up here on a bear-hunt."

"You're a healthy looking stage driver, you are, when you are nothing more than a boy."

"Yes, Bob, he tells ther truth, fer I hes seen him handle ther ribbons, and he does it prime too; he are the Pony Rider who they calls Buff'ler Billy," said another of the gang.

"Ther devil yer say: waal, I has heerd o' him as a greased terror, an' he looks it; but who's with yer, young pard?"

"I am alone."

"It hain't likely."

"But I am."

"Yer must be durned fond o' b'ar-meat ter come up here alone."

"I am."

"Waal, did yer get yer b'ar?"

"No."

"Whar's yer critter?"

"My horse is down the mountain."

"I'll go arter him," said one suspiciously; but Billy answered quickly:

"Oh, no, I'll not trouble you; but if I can leave my rifle here, I'll go after him."

"All right, pard; but I guesses two of us better go with yer fer comp'ny, as we loves ter be sociable."

Buffalo Billy well knew now that he was in a nest of horse-thieves and desperadoes; but he dared not show his suspicions, as he felt assured they would kill him without the slightest compunction.

So he said pleasantly:

"Well, come along, for it is pleasanter to have company, and I'll stay with you to-night if you'll let me."

"Oh, yes, we'll let yer stay, fer we is awful social in our notions. Here Ben, you and Tabor go with my young pard and bring his horse up to the corral."

The two assigned for this duty were the very worst looking of the band, as far as villainous faces went; but Buffalo Billy's quick brain had already formed a plan of escape, and he was determined to carry it out.

Down the hill they went until they came to the horse, and both eyed his fine points, as dimly seen in the darkness, with considerable pleasure, while one muttered:

"The Cap will be sure to fancy him."

"There is a string of game that might come in well for supper," said Billy, as he pointed to a dark object on the ground.

"They will, fer sure," was the eager answer, and the man stooped to pick up the game when Billy suddenly dealt him a blow that felled him to the earth.

At the same time he wheeled upon the other, who already had his hand upon his revolver, and before he could fire, his own finger touched the trigger, and the desperado fell.

Bounding into his saddle he turned his horse down the mountain side, just as the door of the cabin was thrown open and he saw the band streaming out from their den, alarmed by the shot.

In hot pursuit they rushed down the mountain side, and for a short while gained upon Billy, for he dared not urge his horse rapidly down the steep hillside.

But once in the valley and the roan bounded forward at a swift pace, and not a moment too soon, for the revolver shots began to rattle, and the bullets to fly uncomfortably near.

On, at a swift gait the roan went, and though Billy heard the clatter of hoofs in chase, he had no fear, as he well knew the speed of the animal he rode.

After a few miles' pursuit the desperadoes gave up the chase and returned toward the mountains, while Buffalo Billy urged the roan on, and a couple of hours before dawn he reached the station, roused the men, and in fifteen minutes two score horsemen were on the way to the mountains, led by the boy, though Alf Slade himself went in command of the company.

But though they found the dug-out, and the grave of the man Billy had killed, the birds had flown, leaving one of their number in his last resting place to mark the visit of the youth to the desperadoes' den.

CHAPTER XX.

A MAD RIDE.

BACK to his home in Kansas went Buffalo Billy, to cheer the heart of his mother and sisters by his presence, and win their admiration by his rapid growth into a handsome manly youth.

To please those who so dearly loved him he again attended school for a couple of months; but with the first wagon-train bound west he went as hunter, and arriving in the vicinity of the Overland again sought service as a stage-driver, and was gladly accepted and welcomed back.

He had been driving but a short time after his return, when he carried east on one trip a coach load of English tourists, whose baggage loaded down the stage.

Although he was driving at the average regulation speed, to make time at each station, the Englishmen were growling all the time at the slow pace they were going and urging Billy to push ahead.

Billy said nothing, other than that he was driving according to orders, and which was, by the way, by no means a slow gait, and then listened to their growling in silence, while they were anathematizing everything in America, as is often the case with foreigners who come to this country.

Billy heard their remarks about the "bloody 'eathen in Hamerica," "the greatness of hall things hin Hingland," "slow horses," "bad drivers," and all such talk, and drove calmly on into Horseshoe.

There the horses were changed, and the six hitched to the coach were wild Pony Express animals that had been only partially broken in as a stage team, which Billy delighted in driving.

As they were being hitched up Buffalo Billy smiled grimly, and said:

"I'll show those gents that we know how to drive in this country," and those who knew him could see the twinkle of deviltry in his eyes.

At last, the Englishmen, having dined, took their seats, Billy gave the order to let the animals go, and they started off at a rapid pace.

But Billy reined them down until they reached the top of the hill, and then, with a wild yell, that suddenly silenced the grumbling of the Englishmen, he let the six horses bound forward, while with utter recklessness he threw the reins upon their backs.

Frightened, maddened by the lash he laid upon them, they went down the mountain at a terrific speed, the coach swaying wildly to and fro, and the Englishmen nearly frightened out of their wits.

Glancing out of the windows and up at Billy they called to him to stop for the sake of Heaven.

But he only laughed, and tearing the large lamps from the coach threw them at the leaders, the blows, and the jingling of glass frightening them fearfully.

"For God's sake stop, driver!"

"He is mad!"

"We'll all be killed!"

"Stop! stop!"

Such was the chorus of cries that came from the coach, and in reply was heard the calm response:

"Don't get excited, gents; but sit still and see how we stage it in the Rocky Mountains."

Then, to add still greater terror to the flying team and the frightened passengers, Billy drew his revolver from his belt and began to fire it in the air.

As the station came in sight, the man on duty saw the mad speed of the horses and threw open the stable doors, and in they dashed dragging the stage after them, and tearing off the top, but not hurting Billy, who had crouched down low in the boot.

The passengers were not so lucky, however, for the sudden shock of halt sent them forward in a heap and the arm of one of them was broken, while the others were more or less bruised.

A canvas top was tacked on, the coach was run out, and a fresh team hitched up, and Billy sung out:

"All aboard, gents!"

But he went on with an empty coach, for the Englishmen preferred to wait over for another driver, and one of them was heard to remark that he would rather go in a hearse than in a stage with such a madman holding the reins.

But far and wide Billy's mad ride was laughed at, and he recieved no reprimand from the company, though he richly deserved it.

CHAPTER XXI.

WINNING A REWARD.

DRIVING over the trail through the Rocky Mountains, the drivers were constantly annoyed by road-agents, whose daring robberies made it most dangerous for a coach to pass over the line.

If the driver did not obey their stern command: "Halt! up with your hands!" he was certain to be killed, and the passenger within who offered the slightest resistance to being robbed, was sure to have his life end just there.

So dangerous had it become to drive the

mountain passes, as several drivers had been shot, the company found it difficult to get men to carry the stages through, and offered double wages to any one who had the courage to drive over the road-agents dominions.

Buffalo Billy at once volunteered for the perilous work, and his first trip through he met with no resistance.

The next he was halted, and promptly obeying the order to throw up his hands, he was not molested, though the gold-box was taken from the coach, and all the passengers were robbed.

After this it was almost a daily occurrence for the road-agents to rob a stage-coach, and the Overland Company offered a reward of five thousand dollars for the capture of their chief and the band.

One day Billy drove away from the station with a coach full of women, not a single man having the pluck to go, and promptly, at their favorite place, the road-agents appeared.

"Halt! up with your hands!"

With military promptitude Buffalo Billy obeyed, and putting on the California brakes, he drew his horses to a stand-still.

"Well, what have you got to-day that's worthy our picking, my Boy Driver?" said the road-agent leader approaching the coach.

"Only women, and I beg you not to be brute enough to scare 'em," said Billy.

"Oh! they must pay toll; and they generally have good watches; but what is it, a woman's rights meeting, or a Seminary broke loose?"

"Ask 'em," was the quiet reply, and as the leader of the road-agents, closely followed by his half-dozen men, all in masks, rode up to the stage door, Billy suddenly drew his revolver and with the flash the chief fell dead.

"Out, boys!" yelled Billy, and the stage doors flew open, dresses and bonnets were cast aside, and nine splendid fellows began a rapid fire upon the amazed road-agents.

One or two managed to escape; but that was all, for after four of their number had fallen, the balance were glad enough to cry for quarter, which was shown them only until a rope could be thrown over the limb of a tree and they drawn up to expiate their crimes by hanging.

It was Billy's little plot, and he got the larger part of the reward, and the credit of ridding the country of a daring band of desperate men.

Shortly after this bold act, hearing of the continued failing health of his mother, Buffalo Billy, like the dutiful son he was, once more resigned his position as stage-driver, and returned to Kansas, arriving there a few months after the breaking out of the civil war in 1861.

CHAPTER XXII.

THE BOY SOLDIER.

AFTER a very short stay at home Buffalo Billy began to show signs of uneasiness, for he was too near Leavenworth, then an important military post, not to get the soldier's fever for battles and marches.

He soon discovered that a company of cavalry was being raised to do service in Missouri, and he at once enlisted and went as a guard to a Government train bound to Springfield, Missouri, and after that he was made a dispatch runner to the different forts, and met with many thrilling adventures while in that capacity.

From this duty Buffalo Billy was sent as guide and scout to the Ninth Kansas Regiment which was ordered into the Kiowa and Comanche country, and it did good service there, and the young soldier added new laurels to his name.

The second year of the war Billy became one of the famous "Red Legged Scouts," formed of the most noted rangers of Kansas.

While a member of this daring band he was sent to guide a train to Denver, but upon arriving there, learning of the severe illness of his mother, he at once set off for home, going the entire distance alone and making wonderful time through a country infested with dangers.

To his joy, he found his mother still living, yet failing rapidly, and soon after his arrival she breathed her last and Buffalo Billy had lost his best, truest friend, and the sad event cast a gloom over the life of the young soldier.

As one of his sisters had married some time before, her husband took charge of the farm, while Billy returned to the army and was sent into Mississippi and Tennessee with his command.

But Billy did not relish military duty, for he had become too well accustomed to the free life of the plains, and, resigning his position as scout, started upon his return to the prairies.

But while on the way he came in sight of a pleasant farm-house, from which came a cry of help in the voice of a woman.

Billy saw five horses hitched to a fence on the other side of the house; but this array of numbers did not deter him when a woman called for aid, and dismounting quickly he bounded upon the piazza, and was just running into the door when a man came out into the hall and fired at him, but fortunately missed him.

Bill instantly returned the fire, and his quick, unerring aim sent a bullet into the man's brain.

At the shots a wilder cry came from within for help and two men dashed out into the hall, and, seeing Billy, three pistols flashed together.

But Billy was unhurt, and one of his foes fell dead, while springing upon the other he gave him a stunning blow with his revolver that put him out of the fight, and then bounded into the room to discover an elderly lady and a lovely young girl threatened by two huge ruffians, who were holding their pistols to their heads to try and force from them the hiding-place of their money and valuables.

Seeing Billy, they both turned upon him, and a fierce fight ensued, which quickly ended in the killing of both ruffians by the brave young soldier, who seemed to bear a charmed life, for he was unhurt, though he had slain four men in a desperate combat and wounded a fifth.

Just then into the room dashed three men, and their weapons were leveled at Buffalo Billy, and right then and there his days would have ended had it not been for the courage and presence of mind of the lovely young girl, who threw herself forward upon his breast, to the youth's great surprise, and cried out:

"Father! Brothers! don't fire, for this man is our friend."

The old man and his sons quickly lowered their rifles, while the former said:

"A friend in blue uniform, while we wear the gray?"

"I am a Union soldier, sir, I admit, and I was going by your home, heard a cry for help, and found your wife and daughter, as I suppose them to be, at the mercy of five ruffians, and I was fortunate enough to serve them.

"But I will not be made prisoner, gentlemen."

Billy's hands were on his revolvers and he looked squarely in the faces of those in his front, and they could see that he was a man who meant what he said.

"My dear sir, I am a Confederate, I admit, and this is my home; but I am not the one to do a mean action toward a Union soldier, and especially one who has just served me so well in killing these men, whom I recognize as jay-hawkers, who prey on either side, and own no allegiance to North or South.

"Here is my hand, sir, and I will protect you while in our lines."

Billy grasped the hand of the farmer, and then those of his sons, and all thanked him warmly for the service he had done them.

But Billy was surprised to find he was within the Confederate lines, and found by inquiring that he had taken the wrong road a few miles back.

The farmer was the captain of a neighborhood military company, and it was his custom to come home with his sons whenever he had opportunity, and arriving just as the fight ended he saw a man in gray uniform lying dead in the hall, and beholding Billy in the blue, had an idea that the Northern soldiers were on a raid, had been met by some of his men, and he certainly would have killed the young scout but for the timely act of his lovely daughter, Louise.

And it was this very circumstance, the meeting with Louise Frederici, the Missouri farmer's daughter, that caused Buffalo Billy to decide to remain in the army, and not to return to the plains, for when stationed in or near St. Louis, he could often see the pretty dark-eyed girl who had stolen his heart away.

Before the war ended Buffalo Billy returned to Kansas, but he carried with him the heart of Louise Frederici, and the promise that she would one day be his wife.

After a short visit to his sisters he again became a stage-driver, and it was by making a desperate drive down a mountain side to escape a band of road-agents that he won the well-deserved title of the Prince of the Reins.

CHAPTER XXIII.

IN FETTERS.

ALL the time that Buffalo Bill was driving stage his thoughts were turning to dark-eyed pretty Louise Frederici in her pleasant Missouri home, and at last he became so love-sick that he determined to pay her a visit and ask her to marry him at once.

He was no longer a boy in size, but a tall, elegantly-formed man, though his years had not yet reached twenty-one.

He had saved up some money, and off to Missouri he started, and his strangely-handsome face, superb form and comely manners were admired wherever he went, and people wondered who he was, little dreaming they were gazing upon a man who had been a hero since his eighth year.

He soon won Louise over to his way of thinking, by promising he would settle down, and they were married at farmer Frederici's home and started on their way, by a Missouri steamer, to Kansas.

Arriving at Leavenworth, Buffalo Bill and his bride received a royal welcome from his old friends, and they were escorted to their new home, where for awhile the young husband did "settle down."

But at last, finding he could make more money on the plains, and that being to his liking, he left his wife with his sisters and once more started for the far West, this time as a Government scout at Fort Ellsworth.

CHAPTER XXIV.

SEEING SERVICE.

IT was while in the capacity of scout at Fort Harker and Fort Hayes that Buffalo Bill added to his fame as an Indian-fighter, scout and guide, for almost daily he met with thrilling adventures, while his knowledge of the country enabled him to guide commands from post to post with the greatest of ease and without following a trail, but by taking a straight course across prairie or hill-land.

While in the vicinity of Hayes City Buffalo Bill had a narrow escape from capture, with a party that was under his guidance; in fact death would very suddenly have followed the capture of all.

A party of officers and their wives, well mounted and armed, were determined not to go with the slow wagon-train from one fort to the other, and accordingly Buffalo Bill was engaged to guide them.

He made known to them the great dangers of the trip, but they being determined, the party started, some dozen in all.

For awhile all went well, but then Buffalo Bill discovered signs of Indians, and hardly had the discovery been made when a large force, over two hundred in number, came in sight and gave chase.

Of course the party were terribly alarmed, and regretted their coming without an escort of soldiers.

But Buffalo Bill said quietly:

"You are all well mounted, so ride straight on, and don't push too fast, or get separated."

"And you, Cody?" asked an officer.

"Oh, I'll be along somewhere; but I've got a new gun, a sixteen-shooter, and I want to try just what it will do."

The Indians were now not more than half a mile away and coming on at full speed, with wild yells and whoops, confident of making a splendid capture.

Directing the officers what course to take, Buffalo Bill saw them start off at full speed while he remained quietly seated upon his splendid horse Brigham, a steed that equaled Sable Satan for speed and endurance.

It was evident that the red-skins were surprised at beholding a single horseman standing so calmly in their path, and awaiting their coming, and the party in flight looked back in great alarm as they saw that Buffalo Bill did not move, appearing like a bronze statue of horse and rider.

"What could it mean?"

"Was he mad?"

And many more were the comments made by the party, while the Indians were equally as inquisitive upon the subject.

Nearer and nearer came the rushing band, for what had two hundred mounted warriors to fear from one man?

Nearer and nearer, until presently Buffalo Bill was seen to raise his rifle, and a perfect stream of fire seemed to flow out of the muzzle, while the shots came in rapid succession.

It was a Winchester repeating rifle, and Buffalo Bill had been testing it thoroughly.

And the result was such that the Indians drew rein, for down in the dust had gone several of their number, while half a dozen ponies had been killed by the shots; in fact, fired into the crowded mass of men and horses, nearly every discharge had done harm.

With a wild, defiant war-cry, Buffalo Bill wheeled and rode away, loading his matchless rifle as he ran.

It did not take long for Brigham to overtake the horses in advance, and warm congratulations followed, for the officers and ladies had seen the daring scout check the entire band of red-skins.

But though temporarily stunned by the effects of the shots, for the Indians had not seen repeating rifles in those days, they soon rallied and came on once more at full speed.

And again did the scout drop behind and await their coming, to once more administer upon the amazed warriors a check that made them more cautious, for they kept out of range.

Yet they kept up the chase all day, and only drew off when the fort came in view, and the party arrived in safety in its walls.

CHAPTER XXV.

CAPTURING A HERD OF PONIES.

While at the fort the colonel in command complained at the non-arrival of a drove of Government horses, as he was anxious to make a raid into the Indian country, and Buffalo Bill volunteered to go and hurry the cattle on.

He had been gone but a few hours from the fort when he crossed a trail which he knew to have been made by a large Indian village on the move.

Cautiously he followed it, and just at sunset came in sight of the camp, pitched at the head of a valley, and saw below a large herd of horses grazing.

To return to the fort for aid he knew would take too long, so he determined to make an attempt to capture the herd himself, and, with his field-glass carefully reconnoitered the surroundings as long as it was light.

He saw that the nature of the valley was such that the herd could only escape by two ways, one through the Indian village and the other at the lower end, where he had observed four warriors placed as a guard and herders.

"That is my quartette," he said to himself, and mounting Brigham he began to make his way around to the lower end of the valley.

After an hour's ride he gained the desired point, and then set down to work.

Carrying with him in case of need a complete Indian costume, he was not long in rigging himself up in it and painting his face.

Then he left Brigham in a canyon near by and cautiously approached the entrance to the valley, which was not more than two hundred yards wide at this point.

Peering through the darkness he saw the four dark objects, about equal distances apart, which he knew were the ponies of the four warriors on guard, and that they were lying down near in the grass he felt confident.

Getting past the line of herders he boldly advanced toward the one nearest the hill on the left, and knew he would be taken for some chief coming from the village and accordingly not dreaded.

It was just as he had expected: the Indian herder saw him coming directly from the village, as he believed and did not even rise from the grass as Buffalo Bill drew near.

With a word in Sioux Buffalo Bill advanced and suddenly threw himself upon the prostrate warrior.

There was a short struggle, but no cry, as the scout's hand grasped the red-skin's throat, and then all was still, the Indian pony lariated near, not even stopping his grazing.

Throwing the red-skin's blanket over his body, Buffalo Bill moved away a few paces to where the pony stood, and called to the next herder in the Sioux tongue to come to him.

The unsuspecting warrior obeyed, and the next instant found himself in a gripe of iron and a knife blade piercing his heart.

"This is red work, but it is man to man and in a few days the whole band would make a strike upon the settlements," muttered the scout, as he moved slowly toward the position his enemy had left at his call.

As he reached the spot he saw the third warrior standing on his post and boldly walked up to him, when again the same short, fierce, silent fight followed and Buffalo Bill arose from the ground a victor.

The fourth, and only remaining guard he knew was over under the shadow of the hill, and thither he went.

Arriving near he did not see him, and looking around suddenly discovered him asleep at the foot of a tree.

"I'd like to let you sleep, Mr. Red-skin, but you'd wake up at the wrong time, so you must follow your comrades to the happy hunting-grounds," he muttered, as he bent over and seized the throat of the Indian in his powerful gripe.

The warrior was almost a giant in size, and he made a fierce fight for his life.

But the iron hold on his throat did not relax, and at last his efforts ceased and his grasp upon the scout, which had been so great he could not use his knife, weakened and there was no more show of resistance.

Then not an instant did Buffalo Bill tarry, but went up the valley, rounded up the herd of horses and quickly drove them away from the village, in which he knew slept half a thousand warriors.

Slowly he moved the large brute mass, and they went toward the mouth of the valley and were soon out upon the prairie.

Then mounting Brigham he urged them on until out of hearing of the camp, when he headed them for the fort.

It was a hard drive and taxed both Brigham and his rider fearfully; but at last the herd was driven to a good grazing place a few miles from the fort and Buffalo Bill left them and rode rapidly on, and just at dawn reported his valuable capture and that the same horses could be used in an attack upon the Indian camp.

The colonel at once acted upon his suggestion; the cavalrymen who had no horses, loaded with their saddles, bridles and arms, went at a quick march to the grazing place of the horses, and ere the day was three hours old three hundred men were mounted and on the trail for the red-skin village, while the remainder of the ponies were driven to the fort.

Deprived of the greater part of their horses, the red-skins could march but slowly; but they were in full retreat when Buffalo Bill led the command in sight of them, and though the dismounted warriors fought bravely, they were severely whipped and all their village equipage captured or destroyed, while instead of attacking the white settlements as they had intended, they were glad enough to beg for relief.

This gallant act made the name of Buffalo Bill, or Pa-e-has-ka (Long Hair), as they called him, known to every Indian on the north-west border, and they regarded him with the greatest terror, while it made him an idol among the soldiers.

CHAPTER XXV

THE CHAMPION OF THE PLAINS.

As Buffalo Bill was known to be the most successful hunter on the prairies, shortly after his capture of the herd of Indian ponies he received an offer from the Kansas Pacific Railroad Company to keep their workmen supplied with meat, and the terms allowed him were so generous that he felt he owed it to his family, for he had become the father of a lovely little daughter, Arta, born in Leavenworth, to accept the proposition, and did so.

The employees of the road numbered some twelve hundred, and Buffalo Bill's duty was to supply them with fresh meat, a most arduous task, and a dangerous one, for the Indians were constantly upon the war-path.

But he undertook the work, and it was but a very short while before his fame as a buffalo-killer equaled his reputation as an Indian-fighter, and often on a hunt for the shaggy brutes, he had to fight the red savages who constantly sought his life.

It was during his service for the Kansas Pacific that he was rechristened Buffalo Bill, and he certainly deserved the renewal of his name, as in one season he killed the enormous number of *four thousand eight hundred and twenty buffaloes*, a feat never before, or since equaled.

And during this time, in the perils he met with, and his numerous hair-breadth escapes, in conflict with red-skins, horse-thieves and desperadoes, it is estimated that over a score of human beings fell before his unerring rifle and revolvers, while, he still bearing a charmed life, received only a few slight wound

CHAPTER XXVII.

THE CHAMPION.

Some time after his great feat of killing buffalo for the Kansas Pacific, Buffalo Bill was challenged by Billy Comstock, another famous buffalo-hunter, and a scout and Indian interpreter, to a match at killing the shaggy wild animals.

Those who knew Comstock and had seen him among a herd of buffalo, and had heard of Buffalo Bill's exploits, were most desirous of making a match between the two to discover which was the best "killer."

On the other side, those who knew Buffalo Bill and had seen him at work at the buffaloes, were willing to bet high that he would prove the champion.

As the men were not only willing, but anxious to meet, it was not difficult for them to do so, and all preliminaries were satisfactorily arranged to all parties concerned.

The men were to, of course, hunt on horseback, and to begin at a certain hour in the morning and keep it up for eight hours, a large herd having just been found and its locality marked for the day of the sport.

The stakes were made five hundred dollars a side, and there were numbers, both ladies and gentlemen, out on horseback to see the sport.

The herd having been located early the next morning, the two hunters left for the field, and the large crowd followed at a distance.

The counters, those chosen to follow each hunter and count his killed, followed close behind Bill and Comstock, who rode side by side, chatting in a most friendly way until the herd was sighted.

Buffalo Bill was mounted upon Brigham, a noted buffalo horse, and he was armed with a breech-loading Springfield rifle, and a weapon which had sent many a red-skin to the happy hunting-grounds.

Comstock was also splendidly mounted, and carried his favorite buffalo repeating rifle, and both men felt confident of victory.

Reaching the herd, the two hunters, followed by their counters, well mounted also, dashed into a herd, and it quickly divided, giving each one an opportunity to show his skill, as though the buffaloes themselves sympathized with the match and were willing to do all in their power to forward it.

In his first run Buffalo Bill killed thirty-eight, while in the same length of time Billy Comstock dropped twenty-three, which gave the former the advantage thus far.

A rest was then called for both horses and men, and once more they started out for the second run, a small herd appearing opportunely in sight.

In this run Buffalo Bill's tally was eighteen to Comstock's fourteen, and another halt was made for rest and refreshments.

When called to the scratch for the third run, Buffalo Bill, knowing he had the best buffalo horse in the country, stripped him of saddle and bridle and sprung upon his bare back.

A third herd was looked up, and the two killers began their work with a will, and buffalo Bill sailed to the front with thirteen, which gave him a list of sixty-nine to Comstock's forty-six.

The third run closed the match, and Buffalo Bill was proclaimed the winner and the champion buffalo-killer of the prairies.

CHAPTER XXVIII.

A GAME FOR LIFE AND DEATH.

HAVING concluded his engagement with the Kansas Pacific Railroad, Buffalo Bill once more became a Government scout, and it was while serving on the far border that he won the hatred of a notorious band of desperadoes whom he had several times thwarted in their intended crimes.

Hearing that they had said they would kill him at sight, he boldly rode into the town where they had their haunts, and, true to their word, two of them came out and attacked him.

At the first shot Bill was wounded in the right arm, which destroyed his aim, and, ere he could draw a revolver with his left hand, his horse fell dead beneath him, pinning him to the ground.

Instantly his foes rushed upon him to complete their work, when, rising on his wounded arm, he leveled his revolver with his left hand and shot them down as they were almost upon him.

An army officer who witnessed the affray was so much pleased with the nerve of Buffalo Bill that he presented him with a splendid horse, one of a pair he had just received from the East, and having had his wound dressed the scout rode back to camp delighted with his present.

But the leader of the desperado band still swore to kill Buffalo Bill, and to pick a quarrel with him one night in a saloon, boldly dared him to play him a game of cards.

"Yes, you accursed thief and murderer, I'll play you a game of cards if you will let me name the stakes," said Buffalo Bill.

"All right, name what you please, so you play," was the answer, and the crowd gathered eagerly around, confident that there would be trouble.

"I'll name life and death as the stakes," said Buffalo Bill.

"What do you mean?"

"I mean that if you win the game I'll stand ten paces away and give you a shot at me; if I win, you are to give me a shot at you."

The desperado did not like this arrangement, but having challenged Buffalo Bill to play, and given him the choice of the stakes, he dared not back down, and said:

"All right, let us begin."

"Mind you, no cheating, for I shall shoot you the moment I catch you at it."

"Two can play at that game, Buffalo Bill," said the desperado, and seating themselves at the table the game was begun, each man having his revolver lying by his side.

Buffalo Bill was calm and smiling, for he had confidence in his universal good luck to win.

The desperado was pale and stern, and played warily, for he saw the eye of his foe watching him like a hawk.

Once Bill dropped his hand upon his revolver and his adversary attempted to do the same; but the scout was too quick for him and merely said:

"Beware, for if I catch you cheating, I will kill you."

"Who's cheating, Buffalo Bill?"

"You were about to make an attempt to do so; but I warn you," was the calm reply.

Then, in breathless silence the game went on, and Buffalo Bill won.

Instantly the desperado seized his revolver, but he felt against his head the cold muzzle of a weapon, and heard the stern tones:

"Bent, I guess I'll save Buffalo Bill from killing you, by hanging you to the nearest tree."

The speaker was Wild Bill, who had stood behind the chair of the desperado.

All knew him, and that he was an officer of the law, and would keep his word.

Buffalo Bill said nothing, and the crime-stained wretch was dragged out of the saloon, a rope put around his neck, and he was hanged for his many red deeds, thereby escaping death at the hands of the scout.

CHAPTER XXIX.

BILL'S STORY OF HIS BECOMING AN ACTOR.

As Buffalo Bill in the past few years has become known as an actor, and appears as such with his Dramatic Combination, during the winter months, when he is not on the plains, it will not be by any means uninteresting to my readers to learn how he came to go upon the stage, and the story I give in his own words, in relating his experience to a reporter who had called upon him for some jottings regarding his life.

He said:

"It was in the fall of '71, that General Sheridan came to the plains with a party of gentlemen for the purpose of engaging in a buffalo-hunt, to extend from Fort McPherson, Nebraska, to Fort Hayes, Kansas, on the Kansas Pacific Railroad, a distance of 228 miles, through the finest hunting country in the world. In the party were James Gordon Bennett of the New York *Herald*, Lawrence and Leonard Jerome, Carl Livingstone, S. G. Heckshire, General Fitzhugh of Pittsburg, General Anson Stager of the Western Union Telegraph Company, and other noted gentlemen. I guided the party, and when the hunt was finished, I received an invitation from them to go to New York and make them a visit, as they wanted to show me the East, as I had shown them the West. I was then Chief of Scouts in the Department of the Platte. And in January, 1872, just after the Grand Duke Alexis's hunt, which, by the way, I organized, I got a leave of absence, and for the first time in my life found myself east of the Mississippi river.

"Stopping at Chicago two days, where I was the guest of General Sheridan, I proceeded to New York, where I was shown the 'elephant.' During my visit I attended the performance at the Bowery Theater, in company with Colonel E. Z. C. Judson (Ned Buntline), and witnessed a dramatization of Judson's story, entitled 'Buffalo Bill, King of Border Men.' The part of 'Buffalo Bill' was impersonated by J. B. Studley, an excellent actor, and I must say the fellow looked like me, as his make-up was a perfect picture of myself. I had not watched myself very long before the audience discovered that the original Buffalo Bill was in the private box, and they commenced cheering, which stopped the performance, and they would not cease until I had shown myself and spoken a few words.

"At that time I had no idea of going on the stage, such a thought having never entered my head. But some enterprising managers, believing there was money in me, offered me as high as $1,000 per week to go on the stage I told them I would rather face 1,000 Indians than attempt to open my mouth before all those people. I returned to my duties as a scout, and during the summer of 1872 Ned Buntline was constantly writing to me to come East and go on the stage, offering large inducements. As scouting business was a little dull, I concluded to try it for awhile, and started East in company with Texas Jack. Met Buntline in Chicago with a company ready to support me.

"We were to open in Chicago in Nixon's Amphitheater on December 16th, 1872. I arrived in Chicago December 12th, 1872. We were driven to the theater, where I was introduced to Jim Nixon, who said, 'Mr. Buntline, give me your drama, as I am ready to cast your piece, and we have no time to lose, if you are to open Monday, and these men who have never been on the stage will require several rehearsals.' Buntline surprised us all by saying that he had not written the drama yet, but would do so at once. Mr. Nixon said, 'No drama! and this is Thursday. Well, I will cancel your date.' But Buntline was not to be balked in this way, and asked Nixon what he would rent the theater one week for. 'One thousand dollars,' said Nixon. 'It's my theater,' said Buntline, making out a check for the amount. He rushed to the hotel, secured the services of several clerks to copy the parts, and in four hours had written 'The Scouts of the Prairie.' He handed Texas Jack and I our parts, told us to commit them to memory and report next morning for rehearsal. I looked at Jack's and then at my part. Jack looked at me and said, 'Bill, how long will it take you to commit your part?' 'About seven years, if I have good luck.' Buntline said, 'Go to work.' I studied hard, and next morning recited the lines, cues and all, to Buntline. Buntline said, 'You must not recite cues; they are for you to speak from—the last words of the persons who speak before you.' I said, 'Cues be d—d; I never heard of anything but a billiard cue.'

"Well, night came. The house was packed. Up went the curtain. Buntline appeared as Cale Durg, an old Trapper, and at a certain time Jack and I were to come on. But we were a little late, and when I made my appearance, facing 3,000 people, among them General Sheridan and a number of army officers, it broke me all up and I could not remember a word. All that saved me was my answer to a question put by Buntline. He asked, 'What detained you?' I told him I had been on a hunt with Milligan. You see Milligan was a prominent Chicago gentleman who had been hunting with me a short time before on the plains, and had been chased by the Indians, and the papers had been full of his hunt for some time; Buntline saw that I was 'up a stump,' for I had forgotten my lines, and he told me to tell him about the hunt. I told the story in a very funny way, and it took like wild-fire with the audience.

"While I was telling the story, Buntline had whispered to the stage manager that when I got through with my story to send on the Indians. Presently Buntline sung out: 'The Indians are upon us.' Now this was 'pie' for Jack and I, and we went at those bogus Indians red hot until we had killed the last one and the curtain went down amid a most tremendous applause, while the audience went wild. The other actors never got a chance to appear in the first act. Buntline said, 'Go ahead with the second act, it's going splendid.' I think that during the entire performance, neither Jack nor myself spoke a line of our original parts. But the next morning the press said it was the best show ever given in Chicago, as it was so bad it was good, and they could not see what Buntline was doing all the time if it took him four hours to write that drama.

"Our business was immense all that season, and if we had been managed properly we would have each made a small fortune. As it was I came out $10,000 ahead. In June, 1873, I returned to the plains, came East again in the fall, this time my own manager. I got a company, took the noted 'Wild Bill' with me, but could not do much with him as he was not an easy man to handle, and would insist on shooting the supers in the legs with powder, just to see them jump. He left a few months later and returned to the plains. He was killed in August, 1876, in Deadwood.

"In the summer of 1876 I was Chief of Scouts under General Carr, afterward with General Crook and General Terry.

"On the 17th of July I killed Yellow Hand, a noted Cheyenne chief, and took the first scalp for Custer. I returned to the stage in October, 1876, and during the season of 1876 and 1879 I cleared $38,000. I have generally been successful financially on the stage. I am now in the cattle business in Nebraska, to which place I will return as soon as the season is over, providing nothing serious occurs to call me home earlier."

CHAPTER XXX.

THE YELLOW HAND DUEL.

As Buffalo Bill, in the foregoing chapter speaks of his killing Yellow Hand, the celebrated Cheyenne chief, who was greatly feared by his own people, and a terror to the whites, I will give an account of that tragic duel between a white man and two Indians, for another chief also rode down and attacked the noted scout, after his red comrade had fallen.

When the Indian war of 1876 broke out Buffalo Bill at once closed his dramatic season, and started post haste for the West, having received a telegram from General E. A. Carr asking for his services as scout in the coming campaign.

He joined the command at Fort D. A. Russell, where the famous Fifth Cavalry Regiment was then in camp, and arriving received a boisterous welcome from his old comrades, who felt that, with Buffalo Bill as Chief of Scouts, they would surely have warm work with the Indians.

The Fifth Cavalry was at once ordered to operate in scouting the country on the South Fork of the Cheyenne and to the foot of the Black Hills, and it was while driving the Indians before them that the news came of Custer's fatal fight with Sitting Bull on the Little Big Horn.

General Merritt, who had superseded Carr in command marched at once to the Big Horn country, and while *en route* there came news of a large force of warriors moving down to join Sitting Bull.

Instantly five hundred picked men of the Fifth started back by forced marches, and Buffalo Bill, splendidly mounted, kept on ahead of the command a couple of miles.

Discovering the Indians, he at the same time beheld two horsemen whom he saw to be whites, riding along unconscious of the presence of foes.

He knew that they must be scouts bearing dispatches, and at once determined to save them for they were riding in a direction down one valley that would bring them directly upon the red-skins, who had already seen them, and had sent a force of thirty warriors out to intercept them.

Instantly Buffalo Bill dashed over the ridge of the hill that concealed him from the view of the Cheyennes, and rode directly toward the band going to attack the two white horsemen.

They halted suddenly at sight of him, but, seeing that he was alone, they started for him with wild yells.

But still he kept on directly toward them, until within range, when he opened upon them with his matchless Evans rifle, a thirty-four-shot repeater, and a hot fight began, for they returned the fire.

This was just what Buffalo Bill wanted, for the firing alarmed the horsemen and placed them on their guard, and he knew that the Indian volleys would be heard at the command and hasten them forward.

Having dropped a couple of red-skins and several ponies, Buffalo Bill wheeled to the rightabout, dashed up to the top of a hill, and, signaling to the two whites to follow him, headed for the command at full speed.

As he had anticipated, the two men were scouts with important dispatches for General Merritt, and Bill's bold act had not only saved their lives, but also the dispatches, and the result of it was that the Fifth Cavalry went at once into line of battle, while the Cheyennes also formed for battle, though evidently surprised at being headed off at that point.

But they saw that they were double the force of the whites, and were determined upon a fight, and their chiefs reconnoitered carefully their foes' strength and position.

Buffalo Bill also volunteered to go out and get a closer look at them, to see what they were up to, and General Merritt told him to do so, but not to venture too near and expose himself.

As he left the line two Indian horsemen also rode out from among their comrades, and one was some lengths in front of the other.

At a glance Buffalo Bill saw that the two were full chiefs, and they had not advanced far toward each other when he discovered that he was the especial object of their attention.

But though one halted, the other came on, and the scout and the chief came within a hundred yards of each other.

Then the Indian cried out in his own tongue:
"I know Pa-e-has-ka the Great White Hunter and want to fight him."

"Then come on, you red devil, and have it out," shouted back Buffalo Bill, and forgetting General Merritt's orders not to expose himself, and to the horror of the regiment, every man of whom saw him, as well as did the Indians, he dashed at full speed toward the chief, who likewise, with a wild yell rode toward him.

Together both fired, the chief with his rifle, and Buffalo Bill with his revolver, and down dropped both horses.

Buffalo Bill nimbly caught on his feet, while the Indian was pinned by one leg under his horse, and with his war-cry the scout rushed upon him.

As he advanced the chief succeeded in releasing his leg from beneath his horse and again fired, as did Buffalo Bill, and both of them with revolvers.

The Indian's bullet cut a slight gash in Bill's arm, while his struck the red-skin in the leg, and the next instant sprung upon him with his knife, which both had drawn.

The hand-to-hand fight was hardly five seconds in duration, and Buffalo Bill had driven his knife into the broad red breast, and then tore from his head the scalp and feather war-bonnet, and waving it over his head, shouted in ringing tones:

"Bravo! the first scalp to avenge Custer!"

A shout of warning from the cavalry caused him to turn quickly and he beheld the second chief riding down upon him at full speed.

But Bill turned upon him, and a shot from his revolver got him another scalp.

But hardly had he stooped to tear it from the skull, when the Indians, with wildest yells, charged upon him.

They were nearer to him than was the regiment, and it looked bad for Buffalo Bill; but the gallant Fifth charged in splendid style, met the Indians in a savage fight, and then began to drive them in wild confusion, and pushed them back into the Agency a sorely whipped body of Cheyennes, and grieving over heavy losses.

Upon reaching the Agency Buffalo Bill learned that the two Indians he had killed in the duel were Yellow Hand and Red Knife, and Cut Nose, the father of the former swore some day to have the scout's scalp.

But Buffalo Bill laughed lightly at this threat, evidently believing the old adage that "A threatened man is long lived."

CHAPTER XXXI.

CONCLUSION.

HAVING gone over many of the thrilling scenes in the life of W. F. Cody, Buffalo Bill, from boyhood to manhood, and shown what indomitable pluck he possesses, and the pinnacle of fame he has reached unaided, and by his own exertions and will, I can only now say that much remains to be told of his riper years, from the time he stepped across the threshold from youth to man's estate, for since then his life has been one long series of perilous adventures which, though tinged with romance, and seeming fiction, will go down to posterity as true border history of this most remarkable man, the truly called King of Prairiemen.

THE END.

Half-Dime Singer's Library

1 WHOA, EMMA! and 59 other Songs.
2 CAPTAIN CUFF and 57 other Songs.
3 THE GAINSBORO' HAT and 62 other Songs.
4 JOHNNY MORGAN and 60 other Songs.
5 I'LL STRIKE YOU WITH A FEATHER and 62 others.
6 GEORGE THE CHARMER and 56 other Songs.
7 THE BELLE OF ROCKAWAY and 52 other Songs.
8 YOUNG FELLAH, YOU'RE TOO FRESH and 60 others.
9 SHY YOUNG GIRL and 65 other Songs.
10 I'M THE GOVERNOR'S ONLY SON and 58 other Songs.
11 MY FAN and 65 other Songs.
12 COMIN' THRO' THE RYE and 55 other Songs.
13 THE ROLLICKING IRISHMAN and 59 other Songs.
14 OLD DOG TRAY and 62 other Songs.
15 WHOA, CHARLIE and 59 other Songs.
16 IN THIS WHEAT BY AND BY and 62 other Songs.
17 NANCY LEE and 58 other Songs.
18 I'M THE BOY THAT'S BOUND TO BLAZE and 57 others.
19 THE TWO ORPHANS and 59 other Songs.
20 WHAT ARE THE WILD WAVES SAYING, SISTER? and 59 other Songs.
21 INDIGNANT POLLY WOG and 59 other Songs.
22 THE OLD ARM-CHAIR and 58 other Songs.
23 ON CONEY ISLAND BEACH and 58 other Songs.
24 OLD SIMON, THE HOT-CORN MAN and 60 others.
25 I'M IN LOVE and 56 other Songs.
26 PARADE OF THE GUARDS and 56 other Songs.
27 YO, HEAVE, HO! and 60 other Songs.
28 'TWILL NEVER DO TO GIB IT UP SO and 60 others.
29 BLUE BONNETS OVER THE BORDER and 54 others.
30 THE MERRY LAUGHING MAN and 56 other Songs.
31 SWEET FORGET-ME-NOT and 55 other Songs.
32 LEETLE BABY MINE and 53 other Songs.
33 DE BANJO AM DE INSTRUMENT FOR ME and 53 others.
34 TAFFY and 50 other Songs.
35 JUST TO PLEASE THE BOYS and 52 other Songs.
36 SKATING ON ONE IN THE GUTTER and 52 others.
37 KOLORED KRANKS and 59 other Songs.
38 NIL DESPERANDUM and 53 other Songs.
39 THE GIRL I LEFT BEHIND ME and 50 other Songs.
40 'TIS BUT A LITTLE FADED FLOWER and 50 others.
41 PRETTY WHILHELMINA and 60 other Songs.
42 DANCING IN THE BARN and 63 other Songs.
43 H. M. S. PINAFORE, COMPLETE, and 17 other Songs.

Sold everywhere by Newsdealers, at five cents per copy, or sent post-paid, to any address, on receipt of *Six cents* per number.

BEADLE AND ADAMS, PUBLISHERS,
98 WILLIAM STREET, NEW YORK.

FOURTH EDITION.

$2.50 a year. Entered at the Post Office at New York, N. Y., at Second Class Mail Rates. Copyrighted in 1882 by BEADLE AND ADAMS. October 8, 1882.

Vol. XI. | Single Number. | PUBLISHED WEEKLY BY BEADLE AND ADAMS, No. 98 WILLIAM STREET, NEW YORK. | Price, 5 Cents. | No. 271.

THE HUGE HUNTER; or, THE STEAM MAN OF THE PRAIRIES.

BY EDWARD S. ELLIS.

AUTHOR OF "THE BOY MINERS," "SETH JONES," "BILL BIDDON," ETC., ETC., ETC.

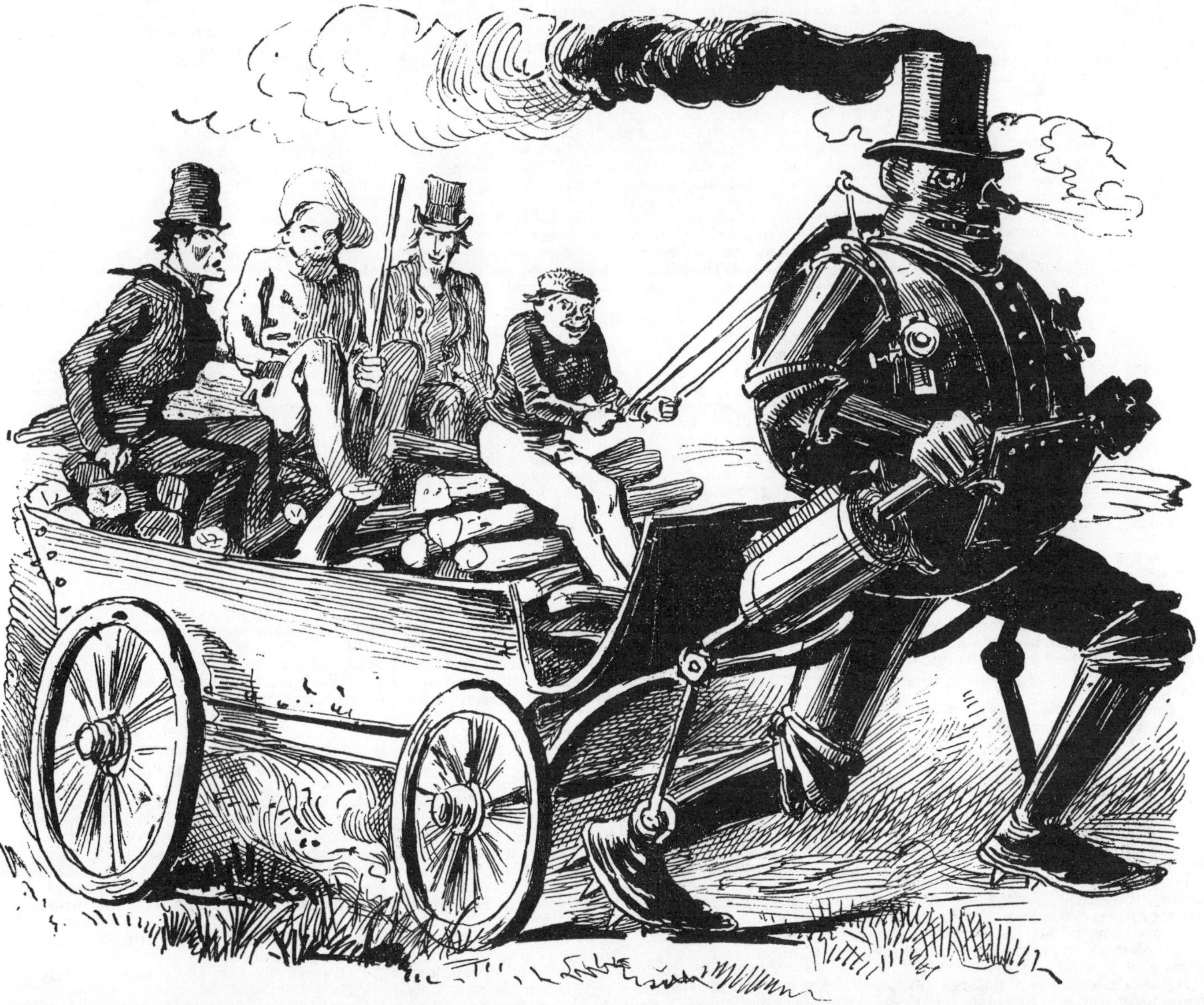

"BEGORRAH, BUT IT'S THE OULD DIVIL, HITCHED TO HIS THROTTIN' WAGING, WID HIS OULD WIFE HOWLDING THE REINS!" EXCLAIMED MICKEY.

The Huge Hunter;

OR,

The Steam Man of the Prairies.

BY EDWARD S. ELLIS,

AUTHOR OF "THE HALF-BLOOD," "THE HUNTED HUNTER," "THE BOY MINERS," ETC.

CHAPTER I.

THE TERROR OF THE PRAIRIES.

"HOWLY vargin! what is that?" exclaimed Mickey McSquizzle, with something like horrified amazement.

"By the Jumping Jehosiphat, naow if that don't beat all natur'!"

"It's the divil, broke loose, wid full steam on!"

There was good cause for these exclamations upon the part of the Yankee and Irishman, as they stood on the margin of Wolf Ravine, and gazed off over the prairie. Several miles to the north, something like a gigantic man could be seen approaching, apparently at a rapid gait for a few seconds, when it slackened its speed, until it scarcely moved.

Occasionally it changed its course, so that it went nearly at right angles. At such times, its colossal proportions were brought out in full relief, looking like some Titan as it took its giant strides over the prairie.

The distance was too great to scrutinize the phenomenon closely; but they could see that a black volume of smoke issued either from its mouth or the top of its head, while it was drawing behind it a sort of carriage, in which a single man was seated, who appeared to control the movements of the extraordinary being in front of him.

No wonder that something like superstitious awe filled the breasts of the two men who had ceased hunting for gold, for a few minutes, to view the singular apparition; for such a thing had scarcely been dreamed of at that day, by the most imaginative philosophers; much less had it ever entered the head of these two men on the western prairies.

"Begorrah, but it's the ould divil, hitched to his throttin' waging, wid his ould wife howlding the reins!" exclaimed Mickey, who had scarcely removed his eyes from the singular object.

"That there critter in the wagon is a man," said Hopkins, looking as intently in the same direction. "It seems to me," he added, a moment later, "that there's somebody else a-sitting alongside of him, either a dog or a boy. Wal, naow, *ain't* that queer?"

"Begorrah! begorrah! do ye hear that? What shall we do?"

At that instant, a shriek like that of some agonized giant came home to them across the plains, and both looked around, as if about to flee in terror; but the curiosity of the Yankee restrained him. His practical eye saw that whatever it might be, it was a human contrivance, and there could be nothing supernatural about it.

"Look!"

Just after giving its ear-splitting screech, it turned straight toward the two men, and with the black smoke rapidly puffing from the top of its head, came tearing along at a tremendous rate.

Mickey manifested some nervousness, but he was restrained by the coolness of Ethan, who kept his position with his eye fixed keenly upon it.

Coming at such a railroad speed, it was not long in passing the intervening space. It was yet several hundred yards distant, when Ethan Hopkins gave Mickey a ringing slap upon the shoulder.

"Jerusalem! who do ye s'pose naow, that man is, sitting in the carriage and holding the reins?"

"Worrah, worrah! why do yez ax me, whin I'm so frightened entirely that I don't know who I am myself?"

"*It's Baldy.*"

"Git out!" replied the Irishman, but added the next moment, "am I shlaping or dhraming? It's Baldy or his ghost."

It certainly was no ghost, judging from the manner in which it acted; for he sat with his hat cocked on one side, a pipe in his mouth, and the two reins in his hands, just as the skillful driver controls the mettlesome horses and keeps them well in hand.

He was seated upon a large pile of wood, while near nestled a little bump-backed, bright-eyed boy, whose eyes sparkled with delight at the performance of the strange machine.

The speed of the steam man gradually slackened, until it came opposite the men, when it came to a dead halt, and the grinning "Baldy," as he was called, (from his having lost his scalp several years before, by the Indians), tipped his hat and said:

"Glad to see you hain't gone under yit. How'd you git along while I was gone?"

But the men were hardly able to answer any questions yet, until they had learned something more about the strange creation before them. Mickey shied away, as the timid steed does at first sight of the locomotive, observing which, the boy (at a suggestion from Baldy), gave a string in his hand a twitch, whereupon the nose of the wonderful thing threw out a jet of steam with the sharp screech of the locomotive whistle. Mickey sprung a half dozen feet backward, and would have run off at full speed down the ravine, had not Ethan Hopkins caught his arm.

"What's the matter, Mickey, naow? Hain't you ever heard anything like a locomotive whistle?"

"Worrah, worrah, now, but is that the way the crather blows its nose? It must have a beautiful voice when it shnores at night."

Perhaps at this point a description of the singular mechanism should be given. It was about ten feet in hight, measuring to the top of the "stove-pipe hat," which was fashioned after the common order of felt coverings, with a broad brim, all painted a shiny black. The face was made of iron, painted a black color, with a pair of fearful eyes, and a tremendous grinning mouth. A whistle-like contrivance was made to answer for the nose. The steam chest proper and boiler, were where the chest in a human being is generally supposed to be, extending also into a large knapsack arrangement over the shoulders and back. A pair of arms, like projections, held the shafts, and the broad flat feet were covered with sharp spikes, as though he were the monarch of base-ball players. The legs were quite long, and the step was natural, except when running, at which time, the bolt uprightness in the figure showed different from a human being.

In the knapsack were the valves, by which the steam or water was examined. In front was a painted imitation of a vest, in which a door opened to receive the fuel, which, together with the water, was carried in the wagon, a pipe running along the shaft and connecting with the boiler.

The lines which the driver held controlled the course of the steam man; thus, by pulling the strap on the right, a deflection was caused which turned it in that direction, and the same acted on the other side. A small rod, which ran along the right shaft, let out or shut off the steam, as was desired, while a cord, running along the left, controlled the whistle at the nose.

The legs of this extraordinary mechanism were fully a yard apart, so as to avoid the danger of its upsetting, and at the same time, there was given more room for the play of the delicate machinery within. Long, sharp, spike-like projections adorned tho so es of the immense feet, so that there was little danger of its slipping, while the length of the legs showed that, under favorable circumstances, the steam man must be capable of very great speed.

After Ethan Hopkins had somewhat familiarized himself with the external appearance of this piece of mechanism, he ventured upon a more critical examination.

The door being opened in front, showed a mass of glowing coals lying in the capacious abdomen of the giant; the hissing valves in the knapsack made themselves apparent, and the top of the hat or smoke-stack had a sieve-like arrangement, such as is frequently seen on the locomotive.

There were other little conveniences in the way of creating a draft, and of shutting it off when too great, which could scarcely be understood without a scrutiny of the figure itself.

The steam man was a frightful looking object, being painted of a glossy black, with a pair of white stripes down its legs, and with a face which was intended to be of a flesh color, but which was really a fearful red.

To give the machinery an abundance of room, the steam man was exceedingly corpulent, swelling out to aldermanic proportions, which, after all, was little out of harmony with its immense hight.

The wagon dragged behind was an ordinary four-wheeled vehicle, with springs, and very strong wheels, a framework being arranged, so that when necessary it could be securely covered. To guard against the danger of upsetting it was very broad, with low wheels, which it may be safely said were made to "hum" when the gentleman got fairly under way.

Such is a brief and imperfect description of this wonderful steam man, as it appeared on its first visit to the Western prairies.

CHAPTER II.

"HANDLE ME GENTLY."

WHEN Ethan Hopkins had surveyed the steam man fully, he drew a long sigh and exclaimed:

"Wal, naow, that's too bad!"

"What's that?" inquired Bicknell, who had been not a little amused at his open-mouthed amazement.

"Do you know I've been thinking of that thing for ten years, ever since I went through Colt's pistol factory in Hartford, when I was a youngster?"

"Did you ever think of any plan?"

"I never got it quite right, but I intended to do it after we got through digging for gold. The thing was just taking shape in my head. See here, naow, ain't you going to give a fellow a ride?"

"Jis' what I wanted; shall I run it for you?"

"No, I see how it works; them 'ere thingumbobs and gimcracks do it all."

"Johnny, hyar, will tell yer 'bout it."

The little humpback sprung nimbly down, and ran around the man, explaining as well as he could in a few moments the manner of controlling its movements. The Yankee felt some sensitiveness in being instructed by such a tiny specimen, and springing into the wagon, exclaimed:

"Git eout! tryin' to teach yer uncle! I knowed how the thing would work before you were born!"

Perching himself on the top of the wood which was heaped up in the wagon, the enthusiastic New Englander carefully looked over the prairie to see that the way was clear, and was about to "let on steam," when he turned toward the Irishman.

"Come, Mickey, git up here."

"Arrah now, but I never learnt to ride the divil when I was home in the ould country," replied the Irishman, backing away.

But both Ethan and Baldy united in their persuasions, and finally Mickey consented, although with great trepidation. He timidly climbed upon the wagon and took his seat beside the Yankee, looking very much as a man may be supposed to look who mounts the hearse to attend his own funeral.

"When yer wants to start, jist pull that 'ere gimcrack!" said Baldy, pointing to the crook in the rod upon which his hand rested.

"Git eout, naow! do you think you're goin' to teach me that has teached school fur five years in Connecticut?"

There were some peculiarities about the steam man which made him a rather unwieldy contrivance. He had a way of starting with a jerk, unless great skill was used in letting on steam; and his stoppage was equally sudden, from the same cause.

When the Irishman and Yankee had fairly ensconced themselves on their perch, the latter looked carefully round to make sure that no one was in the way, and then he turned the valve, which let on a full head of steam.

For a second the monster did not stir. The steam had not fairly taken "hold" yet; then he raised one immense spiked foot and held it suspended in air.

"That's a great contrivance, ain't it?" exclaimed Ethan, contemptuously.

"Can't do nothin' more than lift his foot? Wait till you see more! he's goin' to dance and skip like a lamb, or outrun any locomotive you ever sot eyes on!"

"Bad luck to the loikes of yees, why don't yees go on?" exclaimed the irate Irishman, as he leaned forward and addressed the obdurate machine. "Are yees tryin' to fool us, bad luck to yees—"

At this instant, the feet of the steam man began rising and falling with lightning like rapidity, the wagon being jerked forward with such sudden swiftness, that both Ethan and Mickey turned back summersets, rolling heels over head off the vehicle to the ground, while the monster went puffing over the prairie, and at a terrific rate. Baldy was about to start in pursuit of it, when Johnny, the deformed boy, restrained him.

"It won't run far; the steam is nearly out."

"Be jabers! but me head is caved in!" exclaimed the Irishman, rising to his feet, rubbing his head, and looking at his hand to see whether there was blood upon it.

"Jerusalem! I thought she had upset or bu'sted her b'iler!" said the Yankee, looking around him with a bewildered air.

The two spectators were laughing furiously, and they could scarcely stand the trick which had been played upon them.

"Let your old machine go to blazes!" muttered Ethan. "If it acts that way, I don't want nothin' to do with it."

In the mean time the steamer had gone rattling over the prairie, until about a quarter of a mile distant, when it rapidly slackened, and as quickly halted.

"What's the matter wid it now?" asked Mickey; "has it got the cramps and gi'n out?"

"The steam is used up!" replied the dwarf, as he hurried after it; "we can soon start it again!"

All four made all haste toward the stationary figure; but the light frame and superior activity of little Johnny brought him to it considerably in advance of the others. Emptying a lot of wood from the wagon, he was busily engaged in throwing it into his stomach when the other two came up. His eyes sparkled, as he said:

"Jump up there, and I'll give you all a ride!"

The three clambered up and took their seats with great care, Mickey and Ethan especially clinging as if their life depended on it.

Johnny threw in the fuel until the black smoke poured in a stream from the hat. Before leaving it, he opened two smaller doors, at the knees, which allowed the superfluous cinders and ashes to fall out. The water in the boiler was then examined, and found all right. Johnny mounted in his place, and took charge.

"Now we are ready! hold fast!"

"Begorrah, if I goes I takes the wagon wid me," replied Mickey, as he closed his teeth and hung on like death.

The engineer managed the monster with rare skill, letting on a full head of steam, and just as it made a move shutting it off, and letting it on almost immediately, and then shutting off and admitting it again, until it began moving at a moderate pace, which, however, rapidly increased until it was going fully thirty miles an hour.

Nothing could be more pleasant than this ride of a mile over the prairie. The plain was quite level, and despite the extraordinary speed attained, the wagon glided almost as smoothly as if running upon a railroad. Although the air was still, the velocity created a stiff breeze about the ears of the four seated on the top of the wood.

The hight of the steam man's head carried the smoke and cinders clear of those behind, while the wonderful machinery within, worked with a marvelous exactness, such as was a source of continued amazement to all except the little fellow who had himself constructed the extraordinary mechanism. The click of the joints as they obeyed their motive power was scarcely audible, and, when once started, there was no unevenness at all in its progress.

When the party had ridden about a half-mile, Johnny described a large circle, and finally came back to the starting, checking the progress with the same skill that he had started it. He immediately sprung down, examined the fire, and several points of the man, when finding everything right, he opened his knee-caps and let cinders and ashes drop out.

"How kin yeou dew that?" inquired Ethan Hopkins, peering over his shoulder.

"What's to hinder?"

"How kin he work his legs, if they're holler that way and let the fire down 'em?"

"They ain't hollow. Don't you see they are very large, and there is plenty of room for the *leg-rods*, besides leaving a place for the draft and ashes?"

"Wal, I swan, if that ain't rather *queer*. And you made it all out of your head naow?" asked the Yankee, looking at the diminutive inventor before him.

"No, I had to use a good deal of iron," was the reply of the youngster, with a quizzical smile.

mean you got up the thing yourself?"

Yes, sir," was the quiet but proud reply of the boy.

"Jingo and Jerusalem! but your daddy must be fond of you!" exclaimed the enthusiastic New Englander, scanning him admiringly from head to foot.

"I haven't any father."

"Your mother then?"

"I don't know about that."

"Say, you, can't yer tell a feller 'bout it?"

"Not now; I haven't time."

As the steam horse was to rest for the present, he was "put up." The engineer opened several cavities in his legs and breast, and different parts of his body, and examined the machinery, carefully oiling the various portions, and when he had completed, he drew a large oil skin from the wagon, which, being spread out, covered both it and the steam man himself.

CHAPTER III.

A GENIUS.

Having progressed thus far in our story, or properly having begun in the middle, it is now necessary that we should turn back to the proper starting point.

Several years since a widow woman resided in the outskirts of St. Louis, whose name was Brainerd. Her husband had been a mechanic, noted for his ingenuity, but was killed some five years before by the explosion of a steam boiler. He left behind him a son, hump-backed, dwarfed, but with an amiable disposition that made him a favorite with all with whom he came in contact.

If nature afflicts in one direction she frequently makes amends in another direction, and this dwarf, small and misshapen as he was, was gifted with a most wonderful mind. His mechanical ingenuity bordered on the marvelous. When he went to school, he was a general favorite with teachers and pupils. The former loved him for his sweetness of disposition, and his remarkable proficiency in all studies, while the latter based their affection chiefly upon the fact that he never refused to assist any of them at their tasks, while with the pocket-knife which he carried he constructed toys which were their delight. Some of these were so curious and amusing that, had they been secured by letters patent, they would have brought a competency to him and his widowed mother.

But Johnny never thought of patenting them, although the principal support of himself and mother came from one or two patents, which his father had secured upon inventions, not near the equal of his.

There seemed no limit to his inventive powers. He made a locomotive and then a steamboat, perfect in every part, even to the minutest, using nothing but his knife, hammer, and a small chisel. He constructed a clock with his jack-knife, which kept perfect time, and the articles which he made were wonderfully stared at at fairs, and in show windows, while Johnny modestly pegged away at some new idea. He became a master of the art of telegraphy without assistance from any one, using merely a common school philosophy with which to acquire the alphabet. He then made a couple of batteries, ran a line from his window to a neighbor's, insulating it by means of the necks of some bottles, taught the other boy the alphabet, and thus they amused themselves sending messages back and forth.

Thus matters progressed until he was fifteen years of age, when he came home one day, and lay down on the settee by his mother, and gave a great sigh.

"What is the matter?" she inquired.

"I want to make something."

"Why, then, don't you make it?"

"Because I don't know what it shall be; I've fixed up everything I can think of."

"And you are like Alexander, sighing for more worlds to conquer. Is that it?"

"Not exactly, for there is plenty for one to do, if I could only find out what it is."

"Have you ever made a balloon?"

The boy laughed.

"You were asking for the cat the other day, and wondering what had become of her. I didn't tell you that the last I saw of her was through the telescope, she being about two miles up in the clouds, and going about fifty miles an hour."

"I thought you looked as though you knew something about her," replied the mother, trying to speak reprovingly, and yet smiling in spite of herself.

"Can't you tell me something to make?" finally asked the boy.

"Yes; there is something I have often thought of, and wonder why it was not made long ago; but you are not smart enough to do it, Johnny."

"Maybe not; but tell me what it is."

"*It is a man that shall go by steam!*"

The boy lay still several minutes without speaking a word and then sprung up.

"By George! I'll do it!"

And he started out of the room, and was not seen again until night. His mother felt no anxiety. She was pleased; for, when her boy was at work, he was happy, and she knew that he had enough now, to keep him engaged for months to come.

So it proved. He spent several weeks in thought, before he made the first effort toward constructing his greatest success of all. He then enlarged his workshop, and so arranged it, that he would not be in danger of being seen by any curious eyes. He wanted no disturbance while engaged upon this scheme.

From a neighboring foundry, whose proprietor took great interest in the boy, he secured all that he needed. He was allowed full liberty to make what castings he chose, and to construct whatever he wished. And so he began his work.

The great point was to obtain the peculiar motion of a man walking. This secured, the man himself could be easily made, and dressed up in any style required. Finally the boy believed that he had hit upon the true scheme.

So he plied harder than ever, scarcely pausing to take his meals. Finally he got the machine together, fired up, and with feelings somewhat akin to those of Sir Isaac Newton, when demonstrating the truth or falsity of some of his greatest discoveries, he watched the result.

Soon the legs began moving up and down, but never a step did they advance! The power was there, sufficient to run a saw-mill, every thing seemed to work, but the thing *wouldn't go!*

The boy was not ready to despair. He seated himself on the bench beside the machine, and keeping up a moderate supply of steam, throwing in bits of wood, and letting in water, when necessary, he carefully watched the movement for several hours.

Occasionally, Johnny walked slowly back and forth, and with his eyes upon the "stately stepping," endeavored to discover the precise nature of that which was lacking in his machine.

At length it came to him. He saw from the first that it was not merely required that the steam man should lift up its feet and put them down again, but there must be a powerful forward impulse at the same moment. This was the single remaining difficulty to be overcome. It required two weeks before Johnny Brainerd succeeded. But it all came clear and unmistakable at last, and in this simple manner:—

(Ah! but we cannot be so unjust to the plodding genius as to divulge his secret. Our readers must be content to await the time when the young man sees fit to reveal it himself.)

When the rough figure was fairly in working order, the inventor removed everything from around it, so that it stood alone in the center of his shop. Then he carefully let on steam.

Before he could shut it off, the steam man walked clean through the side of his shop, and fetched up against the corner of the house, with a violence that shook it to its foundation. In considerable trepidation, the youngster dashed forward, shut off steam, and turned it round. As it was too cumbersome for him to manage in any other way, he very cautiously let on steam again, and persuaded it to walk back into the shop, passing through the same orifice through which it had emerged, and came very nigh going out on the opposite side again.

The great thing was now accomplished, and the boy devoted himself to bringing it as near perfection as possible. The principal thing to be feared was its getting out of order, since the slightest disarrangement would be sufficient to stop the progress of the man.

Johnny therefore made it of gigantic size, the body and limbs being no more than "Shells," used as a sort of screen to conceal the working of the engine. This was carefully painted in the manner mentioned in another place, and the machinery was made as strong and durable as it was possible for it to be. It was so constructed as to withstand the severe jolting to which it necessarily would be subjected, and finally was brought as nearly perfect as it was possible to bring a thing not possessing human intelligence.

By suspending the machine so that its feet were clear of the floor, Johnny Brainerd ascertained that under favorable circumstances it could run very nearly sixty miles an hour. It could easily do that, and draw a car behind it on the railroad, while on a common road it could make thirty miles, the highest rate at which he believed it possible for a wagon to be drawn upon land with any degree of safety.

It was the boy's intention to run it twenty miles an hour, while where everything was safe, he would demonstrate the power of his invention by occasionally making nearly double that.

As it was, he rightly calculated that when it came forth, it would make a great sensation throughout the entire United States.

CHAPTER IV.
THE TRAPPER AND THE ARTISAN.

"HELLO, younker! what in thunder yer tryin' to make?"

Johnny Brainerd paused and looked up, not a little startled by the strange voice and the rather singular figure which stood before him. It was a hunter in half civilized costume, his pants tucked into his immense boot-tops, with revolvers and rifles at his waist, and a general negligent air, which showed that he was at home in whatever part of the world he chose to wander.

He stood with his hand in his pocket, chewing his quid, and complacently viewing the operations of the boy, who was not a little surprised to understand how he obtained entrance into his shop.

"Stopped at the house to ax whar old Washoe Pete keeps his hotel," replied the stranger, rightly surmising the query which was agitating him, "and I cotched a glimpse of yer old machine. Thought I'd come in and see what in blazes it war. Looks to me like a man that's gwine to run by steam."

"That's just what it is," replied the boy, seeing there was no use in attempting to conceal the truth from the man.

"Will it do it?"

"Yes, sir."

"Don't think you mean to lie, younker, but I don't believe any sich stuff as that."

"It don't make any difference to me whether you believe me or not," was the quiet reply of the boy; "but if you will come inside and shut the door, and let me fasten it, so that there will be no danger of our being disturbed, I will soon show you."

These two personages, so unlike in almost every respect, had taken quite a fancy to each other. The strong, hardy, bronzed trapper, powerful in all that goes to make up the physical man, looked upon the pale, sweet-faced boy, with his misshapen body, as an affectionate father would look upon an afflicted child.

On the other hand, the brusque, outspoken manner of the hunter pleased the appreciative mind of the boy, who saw much to admire, both in his appearance and manner.

"I don't s'pose yer know me," said the stranger, as he stepped inside and allowed the boy to secure the door behind him.

"I never saw you before."

"I am Baldy Bicknell—though I ginerally go by the name of 'Baldy.'"

"That's rather an odd name."

"Yas; that's the reason."

As he spoke, the stranger removed his hat and displayed his clean-shaven pate.

"Yer don't understand that, eh? That 'ere means I had my ha'r lifted ten years ago. The Sioux war the skunks that done it. After they tuk my top-knot off, it had grow'd on ag'in and that's why they call me Baldy."

In the mean time the door had been closed, and all secured. The hat of the steam man emptied its smoke and steam into a section of stove-pipe, which led into the chimney, so that no suspicion of anything unusual could disturb the passers-by in the street.

"You see it won't do to let him walk here, for when I tried it first, he went straight through the side of the house; but you can tell by the way in which he moves his legs, whether he is able to walk or not."

"That's the way we ginerally gits the p'ints of an animal," returned Baldy, with great complaisance, as he seated himself upon a bench to watch the performance.

It required the boy but a short time to generate a sufficient quantity of steam to set the legs going at a terrific rate, varying the proceedings by letting some of the vapor through the whistle which composed the steam man's nose.

Baldy Bicknell stood for some minutes with a surprise too great to allow him to speak. Wonderful as was the mechanism, yet the boy who had constructed it was still more worthy of wonder. When the steam had given out, the hunter placed his big hand upon the head of the little fellow, and said:

"You'se a mighty smart chap, that be you. Did anybody help you make that?"

"No; I believe not."

"What'll you take for it?"

"I never thought of selling it."

"Wal, think of it now."

"What do you want to do with it?"

"Thar's three of us goin' out to hunt fur gold, and that's jist the thing to keep the Injins back an' scart. I've been out thar afore, and know what's the matter with the darned skunks. So, tell me how much money will buy it."

"I would rather not sell it," said Johnny, after a few minutes' further thought. "It has taken me a great while to finish it, and I would rather not part with it, for the present, at least."

"But, skin me, younker, I want to buy it! I'll give you a thousand dollars fur it, slap down."

Although much less than the machine was really worth, yet it was a large offer, and the boy hesitated for a moment. But it was only for a moment, when he decidedly shook his head.

"I wish you wouldn't ask me, for I don't want to sell it, until I have had it some time. Besides, it isn't finished yet."

"It ain't?" exclaimed Baldy, in surprise. "Why, it works—what more do you want?"

"I've got to make a wagon to run behind it."

"That's it, eh? I thought you war goin' to ride on its back. How much will it draw?"

"As much as four horses, and as fast as they can run."

The hunter was half wild with excitement. The boy's delight was never equal to one-half of his.

"Skulp me ag'in, ef that don't beat all! It's jest the thing for the West; we'll walk through the Injins in the tallest kind of style, and skear 'em beautiful. How long afore you'll have it done?"

"It will take a month longer, at least."

Baldy stood a few minutes in thought.

"See here, younker—we're on our way to the 'diggin's,' and spect to be thar all summer. Ef the red-skins git any ways troublesome, I'm comin' back arter this y'ar covey. Ef yer don't want to sell him, yer needn't. Ef I bought him, it ain't likely I'd run him long afore I'd bu'st his b'iler, or blow my own head off."

"Just what I thought when you were trying to persuade me to sell it," interrupted the boy. "Then, if he got the cramp in any of his legs, I wouldn't know how to ile it up ag'in, and thar we'd be."

"I am glad to see you take such a sensible view of it," smiled Johnny.

"So, I'm goin' on West, as I said, with two fools besides myself, and we're goin' to stay thar till yer get this old thing finished; and then I'm comin' after you to take a ride out thar."

"That would suit me very well," replied the boy, his face lighting up with more pleasure than he had shown. "I would be very glad to make a trip on the prairies."

"Wal, look fur me in about six weeks."

And with this parting, the hunter was let out the door, and disappeared, while Johnny resumed his work.

That day saw the steam man completed, so far as it was possible. He was painted up, and every improvement made that the extraordinarily keen mind of the boy could suggest. When he stood one side, and witnessed the noiseless but powerful workings of the enormous legs, he could not see that anything more could be desired.

It now remained for him to complete the wagon, and he began at once.

It would have been a much easier matter for him to have secured an ordinary carriage or wagon, and alter it to suit himself; but this was not in accordance with the genius of the boy. No contrivance could really suit him unless he made it himself. He had his own ideas, which no one else could work out to his satisfaction.

It is unnecessary to say that the vehicle was made very strong and durable.

This was the first great requisite. In some respects it resembled the ordinary express wagons, except that it was considerably smaller.

It had heavy springs, and a canvas covering, with sufficient, as we have shown in another place, to cover the man also, when necessary. This was arranged to carry the wood, a reserve of water, and the necessary tools to repair it, when any portion of the machinery should become disarranged.

English coal could be carried to last for two days, and enough wood to keep steam going for twenty-four hours. When the reserve tank in the bottom of the wagon was also filled, the water would last nearly as long.

When these contingencies were all provided against, the six weeks mentioned by the hunter were gone, and Jonny Brainerd found himself rather longing for his presence again.

CHAPTER V.
ON THE YELLOWSTONE.

BALDY BICKNELL was a hunter and trapper who, at the time we bring him to the notice of the reader, had spent something over ten years among the mountains and prairies of the West.

He was a brave, skillful hunter, who had been engaged in many desperate affrays with the red-skins, and who, in addition to the loss of the hair upon the crown of his head, bore many other mementos on his person of the wild and dangerous life that he had led.

Like most of his class, he was a restless being, constantly flitting back and forth between the frontier towns and the western wilds. He never went further east than St. Louis, while his wanderings, on more than one occasion, had led him beyond the Rocky Mountains.

One autumn he reached the Yellowstone, near the head of navigation, just as a small trading propeller was descending the stream. As much from the novelty of the thing, as anything else, he rode on board, with his horse, with the intention of completing his journey east by water.

On board the steamer he first met Ethan Hopkins and Mickey McSquizzle, who had spent ten years in California, in a vain hunt for gold, and were now returning to their homes, thoroughly disgusted with the country, its inhabitants and mineral resources.

Baldy was attracted to them by their peculiarities of manner; but it is not probable that anything further would have resulted from this accidental meeting, but for a most startling and unforeseen occurrence.

While still in the upper waters of the Yellowstone, the steamer exploded her boiler, making a complete wreck of the boat and its contents. The hunter, with the others, was thrown into the water, but was so bruised and injured that he found it impossible to swim, and he would assuredly have been drowned but for the timely assistance of his two acquaintances.

Neither the Yankee nor Irishman were hurt in the least, and both falling near the trapper, they instantly perceived his helplessness and came to his rescue. Both were excellent swimmers, and had no difficulty in saving him.

"Do ye rist aisy!" said Mickey, as he saw the hunter's face contorted with pain, as he vainly struggled in the water, "and it's ourselves that'll take the good care of yees jist."

"Stop yer confounded floundering," admonished Hopkins; "it won't do no good, and there ain't no necessity for it."

One of them took the arm upon one side, and the other the same upon the opposite side, and struck out for the shore. The poor trapper realized his dire extremity, and remained motionless while they towed him along.

"Aisy jist—aisy now!" admonished Mickey: "ye're in a bad fix; but by the blessin' of Heaven we'll do the fair thing wid yees. We understand the science of swimmin', and—"

At that moment some drowning wretch caught the foot of the Irishman, and he was instantly drawn under water, out of sight.

Neither Hopkins nor Baldy lost presence of mind in this fearful moment, but continued their progress toward shore, as though nothing of the kind had happened.

As for the Irishman, his situation for the time was exceedingly critical. The man who had clutched his foot did so with the grasp of a drowning man; in their struggle both went to the bottom of the river together. Here, by a furious effort, Mickey shook him free, and coming to the surface, struck out again for the suffering hunter.

"It is sorry I am that I was compelled to leave yees behind," he muttered, glancing over his shoulder in search of the poor fellow from whom he had just freed himself; "but yees are past helpin', and so it's meself that must attend to the poor gentleman ahead."

Striking powerfully out, he soon came beside his friends again and took the drooping arm of Baldy Bicknell.

"Be yees sufferin' to a great extent?" inquired the kind-hearted Irishman, looking at the white face of the silent hunter.

"Got a purty good whack over the back," he replied, between his compressed lips, as he forced back all expression of pain.

"Ye'll be aisier when we fotch ye to the land, as me uncle observed whin he hauled the big fish ashore that was thrashing his line to pieces jist."

"Twon't take you long to git over it," added Hopkins, anxious to give his grain of consolation; "you look, now, like quite a healthy young man."

The current was quite rapid, and it was no light labor to tow the helpless hunter ashore; but the two friends succeeded, and at length drew him out upon the land and stretched him upon the sward.

The exertion of keeping their charge afloat, and breasting the current at the same time, carried them a considerable distance down-stream, and they landed perhaps an eighth of a mile below where the main body of shivering wretches were congregated.

"Do yees feel aisy?" inquired Mickey, when the hunter had been laid upon the grass, beneath some overhanging bushes.

"Yes—I'll soon git over it—but woofh! that ar war a whack of the biggest kind I got. It has made me powerful weak."

"What might it have been naow!" inquired Hopkins.

"Can't say—fust thing I know'd, I didn't know nothin'—remember suthin' took me back the head, and the next thing I kerwholloped in the water."

The three men had lost everything except what was on their bodies when the catastrophe occurred. Their horses were gone, and they hadn't a gun between them; nothing but two revolvers, and about a half-dozen charges for each.

Of the twenty odd who were upon the steam-er at the time of the explosion, nearly one-half were killed; they sinking to the bottom almost as suddenly as the wrecked steamer, of which not a single trace now remained.

The survivors made their way to land, reach-ing it a short distance below their starting-point, and here they assembled, to commiserate with each other upon their hapless lot and de-termine how they were to reach home.

Our three friends had remained upon shore about half an hour, the two waiting for the third to recover, when the latter raised himself upon his elbow in the attitude of listening. At the same time he waved his hand for the others to hold their peace.

A moment later he said:

"*I hear Injins!*"

"Begorrah! where bees the same?" demanded Mickey, starting to his feet, while Ethan gazed alarmedly about.

"Jist take a squint up the river, and tell me ef they ain't pitchin' into the poor critters thar."

Through the sheltering trees and under-growth, which partly protected them, the two men gazed up-stream. To their horror, they saw fully fifty Indians massacring the survivors of the wreck—whooping, screeching and yell-ing like demons, while their poor victims were vainly endeavoring to escape them.

"Begorrah, now, but that looks bad!" ex-claimed the Irishman. "Be the same towken, what is it that we can do?"

"Jerusalem! they'll be sure to pay us a visit —I'll be gummed if they won't," added the Yankee, in some trepidation, as he cowered down again by the side of the hunter, and said to him in a lower voice:

"The worst of it is, we haven't got a gun atwixt us. Of course we shall stick by you if we have to lose our heads fur it. But don't you think they'll pay us a visit?"

"Like 'nough!" was the indifferent reply of the hunter, as he laid his head back again, as if tired of listening to the tumult.

"Can't we do anything to get you out of danger?"

"Can't see that you kin; you two fellers have done me a good turn in gittin' me ashore—so jist leave me yere, and it don't make no differ-ence about me one way or t'other. Ef I hear 'em comin' I'll jist roll into the water and go under in that style."

"May the Howly Vargin niver smile upon us if we desart you in this extremity," was the re-ply of the fervent-hearted Irishman.

"And by the jumpin' jingo! if we was con-sarnedly mean enough to do it, there ain't no need of it."

As the Yankee spoke, he ran down to the river, and walking out a short distance, caught a log drifting by and drew it in.

"Naow, Mr. Baldy, or Mr. Bicknell, as you call yourself, we'll all three git hold of that and float down the river till we git beyond fear of the savages."

The plan was a good one, and the hunter so expressed himself. With some help he man-aged to crawl to the river bank, where one arm was placed over the log, in such a manner that he could easily float, without any danger of sink-ing.

"Keep as close to shore as you kin," he said, as they were about shoving off.

"We can go faster in the middle," said Hop-kins.

"But the reds'll see us, and it'll be all up then."

This was the warning of prudence, and it was heeded.

CHAPTER VI.
THE MINERS.

It was late in the afternoon when the explo-sion occurred, and it was just beginning to grow dark when the three friends began drift-ing down the Yellowstone.

This fact was greatly in their favor, although there remained an hour or two of great danger, in case the Indians made any search for them. In case of discovery, there was hardly an earth-ly chance for escape.

The log or raft, as it might be termed, had floated very quietly down-stream for about half an hour, when the wonderfully acute ears of the trapper detected danger.

"Thar be some of the skunks that are creep-in' 'long shore," said he; "you'd better run in under this yar tree and hold fast awhile."

The warning was heeded. Just below them, the luxuriant branches of an oak, dipped in the current, formed an impenetrable screen. As the log, guided thither, floated beneath this, Mickey and Ethan both caught hold of the branches and held themselves motionless.

"Now wait till it's dark, and then thar'll be no fear of the varmints," added the trapper.

"'Sh! I haars sumfin'!" whispered the Irish-man.

"What is it?" asked Ethan.

"How does I know till yees kaaps still?"

"It's the reds goin' long the banks," said the trapper.

The words were yet in his mouth, when the voice of one Indian was heard calling to another. Neither Mickey nor Ethan had the remotest idea of the meaning of the words uttered, but the trapper told them that they were inquiring of each other whether anything had been dis-covered of more fugitives. The answer being in the negative, our friends considered their present position safe.

When it was fairly dark, and nothing more was seen or heard of the Indians, the raft was permitted to float free, and they drifted with the current. They kept the river until day-light, when, having been in the water so long, they concluded it best to land and rest them-selves. By the aid of their revolvers they suc-ceeded in kindling a fire, the warmth of which proved exceedingly grateful to all.

They would have had a very rough time had they not encountered a party of hunters who accompanied them to St. Louis, where the trap-per had friends, and where, also, he had a good sum of money in the bank.

Here Baldy remained all winter, before he entirely recovered from the hurt which he re-ceived during the explosion and sinking of the steamer. When the Irishman and Yankee were about to depart, he asked them where they were going.

"I'm goin' hum in Connecticut and goin' to work on the farm, and that's where I'm goin' to stay. I was a fool ever to leave it for this confounded place. I could live decent out there, and that's more than I can do in this blamed country."

"And I shall go back to work on the Erie railroad, at thirty-siven cents a day and boord myself," replied the Irishman.

"If yer were sartin of findin' all the gold yer want, would yer go back to Californy?"

"Arrah, now, what are yees talkin' about?" asked McSquizzle, somewhat impatiently. "What is the good of talkin'?"

"I didn't ax yer to fool with yer," replied the trapper—"thar's a place that I know away out West, that I call Wolf Ravine, whar thar's 'nough gold to make both of yer richer than yer ever war afore, and then leave some for yer children."

"Jerusalem! but you're a lucky dog!" ex-claimed Ethan Hopkins, not daring to hope that he would reveal the place. "Why don't you dig it up naow, yourself?"

"I only found it a month ago, and I made a purty good haul of it, as it was. When that old hoss of mine went down with the steamer, he carried a powerful heft of gold with him, and if anybody finds his carcass, it'll be the most vallyable one they ever come across."

"Jingo! if I'd know'd that, I'd taken a hunt for him myself."

"Howsumever, that's neither yar nor thar. You both done me a good turn when I got into trouble on the river, and I made up my mind to do what I could toward payin' it back the first chance I got. I didn't say nothin' of it when we war on our way, 'cause I was afeard it would make you too crazy to go back ag'in; but if you'll come back this way next spring I'll make the trip with you."

"Why not go naow?" eagerly inquired Hop-kins.

"It's too late in the season. I don't want to be thar when thar's too much snow onto the ground, and then I must stay yar till I git well over that whack I got on the boat."

It is hardly necessary to say that the offer of the kind-hearted trapper was accepted with the utmost enthusiasm. Mickey and Ethan were more anxious to go out upon the prairies than they had been a year and a half before, when they started so full of life and hope for that vast wilderness, and had come back with such discouragement and disgust.

It was arranged that as soon as the succeed-ing spring had fairly set in, they would set out on their return for St. Louis, where the trapper would meet and accompany them to the won-derful gold region of which he had spoken.

Before continuing their journey homeward, Baldy presented each with a complete outfit, paid their passage to their homes, and gave them a snug sum over. Like the Indian, he never could forget a kindness shown him, nor do too great a favor to those who had so signally benefited him.

So the separation took place again; and, on the following spring Mickey and Ethan ap-peared in St. Louis, where they had no diffi-culty in finding their old friend, the trapper.

He had recovered entirely from his prostrat-ing blow, and was expecting them, anxious and glad to join in the promised search for gold. As the fair weather had really begun, there was no time lost in unnecessary delay. The purse of Baldy Bicknell was deep, and he had not the common habit of intoxication, which takes so much substance from a man. He purchased a horse and accouterments for each of his friends; and, before they started westward, saw that nothing at all was lacking in their outfit.

Three weeks later the men drew rein in a sort of valley, very deep but not very wide. It was on the edge of an immense prairie, while a river of considerable size flowed by the rear, and by a curious circuit found its way into the lower portion of the ravine, dashing and roar-ing forward in a furious canyon.

The edge and interior of the ravine was lined with immense bowlders and rocks, while large and stunted trees seemed to grow everywhere.

"Yar's what I call Wolf Ravine," said Baldy when they had spent some time in looking about them.

"And be the same towken, where is the goold?" inquired Mickey.

"Yes, that there is what I call the important question," added Ethan.

"That it is, of the greatest account, as me grandmither observed, whin she fell off the staaple, and axed whether her pipe was broke."

"It's in thar," was the reply of the hunter, as he pointed to the wildest-looking portion of the ravine.

"Let's git it then."

"Thar be some other things that have got to be looked after first," was the reply, "and we've got to find a place to stow ourselves away."

This was a matter of considerable difficulty; but they succeeded at last in discovering a retreat in the rocks, where they were secure from any attack, no matter by how formidable a number made.

After this, they hunted up a grazing place for their animals, which were turned loose.

They soon found that the trapper had not de-ceived them. There was an unusually rich de-posit of gold in one portion of the ravine, and the men fell to work with a will, conscious that they would reap a rich reward for their labor.

The name, Wolf Ravine, had been given to it by the trapper, because on his first discovery of it he had shot a large mountain wolf, that was clambering up the side; but none others were seen afterward.

But there was one serious drawback to this brilliant prospect of wealth. Indians of the most treacherous and implacable kind were all around them, and were by no means disposed to let them alone.

On the second day after their labor, a horde of them came screeching down upon them; and had it not been for the safe retreat, which the trapper's foresight had secured, all three would have been massacred.

As it was, they had a severe fight, and were penned up for the better part of two days, by which time they had slain so many of their enemies that the remaining ones were glad to withdraw.

But when the trapper stole out on a visit to his horses he found that every one had been completely riddled by balls. The treacherous dogs had taken every means of revenge at hand.

"Skin me fur a skunk, but we've stood this long as we ought to!" exclaimed Baldy Bicknell, when he returned. "You take care of yourselves till I come back again!"

With which speech he slung his rifle over his shoulder and started for St. Louis.

CHAPTER VII.
THE STEAM MAN ON HIS TRAVELS.

YOUNG Brainerd had a mortal fear that the existence of the steam man would be discovered by some outsider, when a large crowd would probably collect around his house, and his friends would insist on a display of the powers of the extraordinary mechanism.

But there was no one in the secret except his mother, and there was no danger of her revealing it. So the boy experimented with his invention until there was nothing more left for him to do, except to sit and watch its workings.

Finally, when he began to wonder at the prolonged delay of the trapper, who had visited him some weeks before, he made his appearance as suddenly as if he had risen from the ground, with the inquiry:

"Have you got that thundering old thing ready?"

"Yes; he has been ready for a week, and waiting."

"Wal, start her out then, fur I'm in a hurry."

"You will have to wait awhile, for we can't get ready under half a day."

It was the hunter's supposition that the boy was going to start the man right off up street, and then toward the West; but he speedily revealed a far different plan.

It was to box up the man and take it to Independence by steamboat. At that place they would take it out upon the prairie, set it up and start it off, without any fear of disturbance from the crowds which usually collect at such places, as they could speedily run away from them.

When the plan was explained to Baldy, he fully indorsed it, and the labor was begun at once. The legs of the steam man being doubled up, they were able to get it in a box, which gave it the appearance of an immense piano under transportation. This, with considerable difficulty, was transported to the wharf, where, with much grumbling upon the part of the men, it was placed on board the steamboat, quickly followed by the wagon and the few necessary tools.

The boy then bade his mother good-by, and she, suspecting he would be gone but a short time, said farewell to him, with little of the regret she would otherwise have felt, and a few hours later the party were steaming rapidly up the "Mad Missouri."

Nothing worthy of notice occurred on the passage, and they reached Independence in safety. They secured a landing somewhat above the town, on the western side, where they had little fear of disturbance.

Here the extraordinary foresight and skill of the boy was manifest, for, despite the immense size of the steam man, it was so put together that they were able to load it upon the wagon, and the two, without any other assistance, were able to drag it out upon the prairie.

"You see, it may break down entirely," remarked young Brainerd, "and then we can load it on the wagon and drag it along."

"That must be a powerful strong wagon to carry such a big baby in it as that."

"So it is; it will hold five times the weight without being hurt in the least."

It was early in the forenoon when they drew it out upon the prairie in this manner, and began putting it together. It certainly had a grotesque and fearful look when it was stripped of all its bandages, and stood before them in all its naked majesty.

It had been so securely and carefully put away, that it was found uninjured in the least. The trapper could not avoid laughing when the boy clambered as nimbly up its shoulder as another Gulliver, and made a minute examination of every portion of the machinery.

While thus employed, Baldy took the shafts of the wagon, and trotted to a farm-house, which he descried in the distance, where he loaded it down with wood and filled the tank with water. By the time he returned, Johnny had everything in readiness, and they immediately began "firing up."

In this they bore quite a resemblance to the modern steam fire engines, acquiring a head of steam with remarkable quickness. As the boy had never yet given the man such an opportunity to stretch his legs as he was now about to do, he watched its motions with considerable anxiety.

Everything was secured in the most careful manner, a goodly quantity of fuel piled on, the boiler filled with water, and they patiently waited the generation of a sufficient head of steam.

"Is it all good prairie land in that direction?" inquired the boy, pointing to the West.

"Thar's all yer kin want."

"Then we'll start. Look out!"

Despite the warning thus kindly given, the steam man started with a sudden jerk, that both of them came near being thrown out of the wagon.

The prairie was quite level and hard, so that everything was favorable, and the wagon went bounding over the ground at a rate so fast that both the occupants were considerably frightened, and the boy quickly brought it down to a more moderate trot.

This speed soon became monotonous, and as it ran so evenly, Baldy said:

"Let her go, younker, and show us what she can do."

The rod controlling the valve was given a slight pull, and away they went, coursing like a locomotive over the prairies, the wheels spinning round at a tremendous rate, while the extraordinary speed caused the wind thus created almost to lift the caps from their heads, and a slight swell in the prairie sent the wagon up with a bound that threatened to unseat them both.

It worked splendidly. The black smoke puffed rapidly from the top of the hat, and the machinery worked so smoothly that there was scarcely a click heard. The huge spiked feet came lightly to the ground, and were lifted but a short distance from it, and their long sweep and rapid movement showed unmistakably that the steam man was going at a rate which might well defy anything that had yet swept the prairies.

As there was no little risk in running at this speed, and as young Brainerd had not yet become accustomed to controlling it, he slackened the rate again, so that it sank to an easy gliding motion, equal to the rapid trot of an ordinary horse.

Fully ten minutes were passed in this manner, when steam was entirely shut off, whereupon the giant came to such a sudden halt that both were thrown violently forward and bruised somewhat.

"Skulp me! but don't stop quite so sudden like," said the hunter. "It's a little onhandy fur me to hold up so quick!"

"I'll soon learn to manage it," replied Johnny. "I see it won't do to shut off all at once."

Descending from his perch, he examined every portion of the engine. Several parts were found heated, and the fuel was getting low. The water in the boiler, however, was just right, the engineer having been able to control that from his seat in the wagon.

Throwing in a lot of wood, they remounted to their perch and started forward again. There was an abundance of steam, and the boy readily acquired such a familiarity with the working of his man, that he controlled it with all the skill of an experienced engineer.

The speed was slackened, then increased. It stopped and then started forward again with all the ease and celerity that it could have done if really human, while it showed a reserve of power and velocity capable of performing wonders, if necessary.

As yet they had seen nothing of any travelers. They were quite anxious to come across some, that they might show them what they were capable of doing.

"There must be some passing over the plains," remarked Johnny, when they had passed some thirty or forty miles.

"Plenty of 'em; but we've got out of the track of 'em. If you'll turn off summat to the left, we'll run foul of 'em afore dark."

The boy did as directed, and the rattling pace was kept up for several hours. When it was noon they helped themselves to a portion of the food which they brought with them, without checking their progress in the least. True, while the boy was eating, he kept one eye on the giant who was going at such rapid strides; but that gentleman continued his progress in an unexceptionable manner, and needed no attention.

When the afternoon was mostly gone, Baldy declared that they had gone the better part of a hundred miles.

The boy could hardly credit it at first; but, when he recalled that they had scarcely paused for seven hours, and had gone a portion of the distance at a very high rate, he saw that his friend was not far out of the way.

It lacked yet several hours of dusk, when the trapper exclaimed:

"Yonder is an emigrant train—now make for 'em!"

CHAPTER VIII.
INDIANS.

THE steam man was headed straight toward the emigrant train, and advanced at a speed which rapidly came up with it.

They could see, while yet a considerable distance away, that they had attracted notice, and the emigrants had paused and were surveying them with a wonder which it would be difficult to express.

It is said that when Robert Fulton's first steamboat ascended the Hudson, it created a consternation and terror such as had never before been known—many believing that it was the harbinger of the final destruction of the world.

Of course, at this late day, no such excitement can be created by any human invention—but the sight of a creature speeding over the country, impelled by steam, and bearing such a grotesque resemblance to a gigantic man, could not but startle all who should see it for the first time.

The steam man advanced at a rate which was quite moderate, until within a quarter of a mile of the astonished train, when the boy let on a full head of steam and instantly bounded forward like a meteor. As it came opposite the amazed company, the whistle was pulled, and it gave forth a shriek hideous enough to set a man crazy.

The horses and animals of the emigrant train could be seen rearing and plunging, while the men stood too appalled to do anything except gaze in stupid and speechless amazement.

There were one or two, however, who had sense enough to perceive that there was nothing at all very supernatural about it, and they shouted to them to halt; but our two friends concluded it was not desirable to have any company, and they only slackened their speed, without halting.

But there was one of the emigrants who determined to know something more about it, and, mounting his horse, he started after it on a full run. The trapper did not perceive him until he had approached quite close, when they again put on a full head of steam, and they went bounding forward at a rate which threatened to tear them to pieces.

But the keen perception of the boy had detected what they were able to do without real risk; and, without putting his invention to its very best, he kept up a speed which steadily drew them away from their pursuer, who finally became discouraged, checked his animal, and turned round and rode back to his friends, a not much wiser man.

This performance gave our friends great delight. It showed them that they were really the owners of a prize whose value was incalculable.

"Ef the old thing will only last," said Baldy, when they had sunk down to a moderate trot again.

"What's to hinder?"

"Dunno; yer oughter be able to tell. But these new-fangled things generally go well at first, and then, afore yer know it, they bu'st all to blazes."

"No fear of this. I made this fellow so big that there is plenty of room to have everything strong and give it a chance to work."

"Wal, you're the smartest feller I ever seen, big or little. Whoever heard of a man going by steam?"

"I have, often; but I never saw it. I expect when I go back to make steam horses—"

"And birds, I s'pose?"

"Perhaps so; it will take some time to get such things in shape, but I hope to do it after awhile."

"Skulp me! but thar must be some things that you can't do, and I think you've mentioned 'em."

"Perhaps so," was the quiet reply.

"When you git through with this Western trip, what are you goin' to do with this old feller?"

"I don't know. I may sell him, if anybody wants him."

"No fear of that; I'll take him off your hands, and give you a good price for him."

"What good will he do you?"

"Why, you can make more money with him than Barnum ever did with his Woolly Horse."

"How so?" inquired the boy, with great simplicity.

"Take him through the country and show him to the people. I tell yer they'd run after such things. Git out yer pictures of him, and the folks would break thar necks to see him. I tell yer, thar's a fortune thar!"

The trapper spoke emphatically like one who knows.

As it was growing dusk, they deemed it best to look for some camping-place. There was considerable danger in running at night, as there was no moon, and they might run into some gully or ravine and dislocate or wrench some portion of their machinery, which might result in an irreparable catastrophe.

Before it was fairly dark they headed toward a small clump of trees, where everything looked favorable.

"You see we must find a place where there is plenty water and fuel, for we need both," remarked the boy.

"Thar's plenty of wood, as yer see with yer eyes," replied Baldy, "and when trees look as green as that, thar's purty sure sign thar's water not fur off."

"That's all we want," was the observation of the engineer as he headed toward the point indicated.

Things were growing quite indistinct, when the steam man gave its last puff, and came to rest in the margin of the grove.

The fires were instantly drawn, and everything was put in as good shape as possible, by the boy, while the trapper made a tour of examination through the grove. He came back with the report that everything was as they wished.

"Thar's a big stream of water runnin' right through the middle, and yer can see the wood fur yourself."

"Any signs of Indians?" asked the boy, in a low voice, as if fearful of being overheard.

"Dunno; it's too dark to tell."

"If it's dangerous here, we had better go on."

"Yer ain't much used to this part the world. You may keep powerful easy till mornin'."

As they could not feel certain whether in danger or not, it was the part of prudence to believe that some peril threatened them. Accordingly they ate their evening meal in silence, and curled up in the bottom of their wagon, first taking the precaution to fill their tank with water, and placing a portion of wood and kindlings in the bowels of the steam man, so that in case of danger, they would be able to leave at a short notice.

Johnny Brainerd was soon sound asleep, and the trapper followed, but it was with that light, restless slumber which is disturbed by the slightest noise.

So it came about that, but a few hours had passed, when he was aroused by some slight disturbance in the grove. Raising his head he endeavored to peer into the darkness, but he could detect nothing.

But he was certain that something was there, and he gently aroused the boy beside him.

"What is it?" queried the latter in a whisper, but fully wide-awake.

"I think thar ar Ingins among the trees."

"Good heavens! what shall we do?"

"Keep still and don't git skeart—'sh!"

At this juncture he heard a slight noise, and cautiously raising his head, he caught the outlines of an Indian, in a crouching position, stealing along in front of the wagon, as though examining the curious contrivance. He undoubtedly was greatly puzzled, but he remained only a few minutes, when he withdrew as silently as he had come.

"Stay yer, while I take a look around!" whispered Baldy, as he slid softly out the wagon, while the boy did the same, waiting until sure that the trapper would not see him.

Baldy spent a half-hour in making his reconnoissance. The result of it was that he found there were fully twenty Indians, thoroughly wide-awake, who were moving stealthily through the grove.

When he came back, it was with the conviction that their only safety lay in getting away without delay.

"We've got to learn," said he, "how long it will take yer to git up steam, youngster?"

"There is a full head on now. I fired up the minute you left the wagon."

"Good!" exclaimed Baldy, who in his excitement did not observe that the steam man was seething, and apparently ready to explode with the tremendous power pent up in its vitals.

CHAPTER IX.

THE STEAM MAN AS A HUNTER.

At this juncture the trapper whispered that the Indians were again stealing around them. Johnny's first proceeding was to pull the whistle wide open, awaking the stillness of the night by a hideous, prolonged screech.

Then, letting on the steam, the man made a bound forward, and the next moment was careering over the prairie like a demon of darkness, its horrid whistle giving forth almost one continual yell, such as no American Indian has ever been able to imitate.

When they had gone a few hundred yards, Johnny again slackened the speed, for there was great risk in going at this tremendous rate, where all was entire blank darkness, and there was no telling into what danger they might run. At the speed at which they were going they would have bounded into a river before they could have checked themselves.

"Yer furgot one thing," said Baldy, when they had considerably moderated their gait, and were using great caution.

"What is that?"

"Yer oughter had a lamp in front, so we could travel at night, jist as well as day."

"You are right; I don't see how I came to forget that. We could have frightened the Indians more completely, and there would have been some consolation in traveling at such a time."

"Is it too late yet?"

"Couldn't do it without going back to St. Louis."

"Thunderation! I didn't mean that. Go ahead."

"Such a lamp or head-light as the locomotives use would cost several hundred dollars, although I could have made one nearly as good for much less. Such a thing in the center of a man's forehead, and the whistle at the end of his nose, would give him quite an impressive appearance."

"Yer must do it, too, some day— My God!"

The boy instantly checked their progress, as the trapper uttered his exclamation; but quickly as it was done, it was none too soon, for another long step and the steam man would have gone down an embankment, twenty feet high, into a roaring river at the base. As it was, both made rather a hurried leap to the ground, and ran to the front to see whether there was not danger of his going down.

But fortunately he stood firm.

"I declare that was a narrow escape!" exclaimed the boy as he gazed down the cavernous darkness, looking doubly frightful in the gloom of the night.

"Skulp me if that wouldn't have been almost as bad as staying among the red-skins," replied the trapper. "How are we goin' to get him out of this?"

"We've got to shove him back ourselves."

"Can't we reverse him?"

"No; he isn't gotten up on that principle."

By great labor they managed to make him retrograde a few steps, so that he could be made to shy enough to leave the dangerous vicinity, and once more started upon the broad firm prairie.

"Do you suppose these Indians are following us?" inquired the boy.

"No fear of it."

"Then we may as well stay here."

The fires were drawn again, everything made right, and the two disposed themselves again for spending the night in slumber.

No disturbance occurred, and both slept soundly until broad daylight. The trapper's first proceeding upon awakening was to scan the prairie in every direction in quest of danger.

He was not a little amused to see a dozen or so mounted Indians about a third of a mile to the west. They had reined up on the plain, and were evidently scanning the strange object, with a great deal of wonder, mixed with some fear.

"Do you think they will attack us?" inquired the boy, who could not suppress his trepidation at the sight of the warlike savages, on their gayly-caparisoned horses, drawn up in such startling array.

"Ef thar war any danger of that, we could stop 'em by 'tacking 'em.

"Jest fire up and start toward 'em, and see how quick they will scatter."

The advice was acted upon on the instant, although it was with no little misgiving on the part of the engineer.

All the time that the "firing up" process was under way the savages sat as motionless as statues upon their horses. Had they understood the real nature of the "animal," it cannot be supposed that they would have hesitated for a moment to charge down upon it and demolish it entirely.

But it was a *terra incognita*, clothed with a terror such as no array of enemies could wear, and they preferred to keep at a goodly distance from it.

"Now, suppose they do not run?" remarked Johnny, rather doubtingly, as he hesitated whether to start ahead or not.

"What if they don't? Can't we run another way? But yer needn't fear. Jist try it on."

Steam was let on as rapidly as possible, and the momentum gathering quickly, it was soon speeding over the prairie at a tremendous rate, straight toward the savages.

The latter remained motionless a few moments, before they realized that it was coming after them, and then, wheeling about, they ran as though all the legions of darkness were after them.

"Shall I keep it up?" shouted Johnny in the ear of the hunter.

"Yas; give 'em such a skear that they won't be able to git over it ag'in in all thar lives."

There is some fun in chasing a foe, when you know that he is really afraid of you, and will keep running without any thought of turning at bay, and the dwarf put the steam man to the very highest notch of speed that was safe, even at the slight risk of throwing both the occupants out.

The prairie was harder and nearer level than any over which they had passed since starting, so that nothing was in the way of preventing the richest kind of sport.

"Are we gaining?" inquired Johnny, his eyes glowing with excitement.

"Gaining? Thar never was a red-skin that had such a chase in all the world. Ef they don't git out the way mighty soon, we'll run over 'em all."

They were, in truth, rapidly overhauling the red-skins, who were about as much terrified as it was possible for a mortal to be, and still live.

To increase their fears, the boy kept up a constant shrieking of his whistle. If there had been any other contrivance or means at his command, it is possible the red-skins would have tumbled off their horses and died; for they were bearing almost all the fright, terror and horror that can possibly be concentrated into a single person.

Finding there was no escape by means of the speed of their horses, the Indians sensibly did what the trapper had prophesied they would do at first.

They "scattered," all diverging over the prairie. As it was impossible for the steam man to overtake all of these, of course, this expedient secured the safety of the majority.

Neither Baldy nor the boy were disposed to give up the sport in this manner; so, they singled out a single "noble red-man," who was pursuing nearly the same direction as they were, and they headed straight for him.

The poor wretch, when he saw that he was the object of the monster's pursuit, seemed to become frantic with terror. Rising on his horse's back, he leaned forward until it looked as though there was danger of going over his head altogether. Then, whooping and shrieking to his terrified horse, that was already straining every nerve, he pounded his heels in its sides, vainly urging it to still greater speed.

In the mean time, the steam man was gaining steadily upon him, while to add variety to the scene, Johnny kept up the unearthly shrieking of the nose-whistle of the giant. It was difficult to tell which sounded the most hideously in this strange chase.

The remaining Indians had improved their advantage to the utmost. Fearful that their dreadful enemy might change its mind and single them out, they kept up their tearing flight, all regardless of the great extremity to which their companion was reduced, until finally they disappeared in the distance.

A short distance only separated pursuer and pursued, when the latter, realizing that there was no escape in flight, headed toward the river, which was a short distance on the right.

This saved him. When with a howl, horse and rider thundered over the bank and disappeared, the steam man could not follow him. He was compelled to give up the chase and draw off.

A few days later, and without further noteworthy incident, the steam man reached Wolf Ravine, being received in the manner narrated at the beginning of this story.

CHAPTER X.

WOLF RAVINE.

DURING the absence of Baldy Bicknell in search of the steam man, neither Mickey nor Ethan had been disturbed by Indians.

They had worked unceasingly in digging the gold mine to which they had gained access through the instrumentality of the trapper. When they had gathered together quite a quantity of the gravel and dirt, with the yellow sand glittering through it, it was carried a short distance to the margin of the river, where it underwent the "washing" process.

While thus engaged, one of them was constantly running up the bank, to make sure that their old enemies did not steal upon them unawares. Once or twice they caught sight of several moving in the distance, but they did not come near enough to molest them, doing nothing more than to keep them on the *qui vive*.

There was one Indian, however, who bestrode a black horse, who haunted them like a phantom. When they glanced over the river, at almost any time, they could see this individual cautiously circling about on his horse, and apparently waiting for a chance to get a shot at his enemies.

"Begarrah, but he loves us, that he does, as the lamb observed when speaking of the wolf," said Mickey, just after he had sent a bullet whistling about their ears.

"Jehosiphat! he loves us too much!" added the Yankee, who had no relish for these stolen shots. "If we ain't keerful, there'll be nuthin' of us left when Baldy comes back—that is, if he comes back at all."

This redskin on his black horse was so dangerous that he required constant watching, and the men could perform only half their usual work. It was while Mickey was on the lookout for him that he caught sight of the steam man coming toward him, as we have related in another place.

So long as that personage was kept puffing and tearing round the vicinity, they knew there was no fear of disturbance from the treacherous red-skins, who were so constantly on the alert to avenge themselves for the loss they had suffered in the attack; but it would hardly pay to keep an iron man as sentinel, as the wear and tear in all probability would be too much for him.

After consulting together upon the return of Baldy, and after they had ridden behind the steam man to their heart's content, they decided upon their future course. As the boy, Johnny, had no intention of devoting himself to manual labor, even had he been able, it was agreed that he should take upon himself the part of sentinel, while the others were at work.

In this way it was believed that they could finish within a couple of weeks, bidding good-by to the Indians, and quickly reach the States and give up their dangerous pursuits altogether, whereas, if compelled to do duty themselves as sentinels, their stay would be doubly prolonged.

This arrangement suited the boy very well, who was thereby given opportunity to exercise his steam man by occasional airings over the prairies. To the east and south the plains stretched away till the horizon shut down upon them, as the sky does on the sea. To the west, some twenty odd miles distant, a range of mountains was visible, the peaks being tinged with a faint blue in the distance, while some of the more elevated looked like white conical clouds resting against the clear sky beyond.

From the first, young Brainerd expressed a desire to visit these mountains. There was something in their rugged grandeur which invited a close inspection, and he proposed to the trapper that they should make a hunting excursion in that direction.

"No need of goin' so fur for game," he replied, "takes too much time, and thar's sure to be red-skins."

"But if we go with the steam man we shall frighten them all away," was the reply.

"Yas," laughed Baldy, "and we'll skear the game away too."

"But we can overtake that as we did the poor Indian the other day."

"Not if he takes to the mountains. Leastways yer isn't him that would like to undertake to ride up the mountain behind that old gintleman."

"Nor I either, but we can leave the wagon when we get to the base of the mountain."

"And give the reds time to come down and run off with yer whole team."

"Do you think there is danger of that?"

"Dunno as thar be, but ef they catched sight of yourself, they'd raise yer ha'r quicker'n lightning."

Seeing that the little fellow was considerably discouraged, Baldy hastened to add:

"Ef you're keerful, younker, and I b'lieve yer generally be, take a ride thar yerself, behind yer jumping-jack, but remember my advice and stick to yer wagon."

Having thus obtained permission of the hunter, Johnny Brainerd, as may well be supposed, did not wait long before availing himself of his privilege.

The weather, which had been threatening toward the latter part of the day, entirely cleared away, and the next morning dawned remarkably clear and beautiful. So the boy announced his intention of making the expected visit, after which, he promised to devote himself entirely to performing the duty of sentinel.

"Abeout what time may we look for you, neow?" asked Ethan, as he was on the point of starting.

"Sometime this afternoon."

"Come in before dark, as me mither used to observe to meself, when I wint out shparkin'," added Mickey.

The boy promised to heed their warnings, and began firing up again. The tank was completely filled with water, and the wagon filled nearly full of wood, so that the two were capable of running the contrivance for the entire day, provided there was no cessation, and that he was on the "go" continually.

Before starting, it was thoroughly oiled through and through, and put in the best possible condition, and then waving them all a pleasant farewell, he steamed gayly toward the mountains.

The ground was admirable, and the steam man traveled better than ever. Like a locomotive, he seemed to have acquired a certain smoothness and steadiness of motion, from the exercise he had already had, and the sharp eye of the boy detected it at once. He saw that he had been very fortunate indeed in constructing his wonderful invention, as it was impossible for any human skill to give it any better movement than it now possessed.

The first three or four miles were passed at a rattling gait, and the boy was sitting on the front of his wagon, dreamily watching the play of the huge engine, when it suddenly paused, and with such abruptness that he was thrown forward from his seat, with violence, falling directly between the legs of the monster, which seemed to stand perfectly motionless, like the intelligent elephant that is fearful of stirring a limb, lest he might crush his master lying beneath him.

The boy knew at once that some accident had happened, and unmindful of the severe scratch he had received, he instantly clambered to his feet, and began examining the machinery, first taking the precaution to give vent to the surplus steam, which was rapidly gathering.

It was some time before he could discover the cause of difficulty, but he finally ascertained that a small bolt had slipped loose, and had caught in such a manner as to check the motion of the engine on the instant.

Fortunately no permanent injury was done, and while he was making matters right, he recollected that in chatting with the trapper as he was on the point of starting, he had begun to screw on the bolt, when his attention had been momentarily diverted, when it escaped his mind altogether, so that he alone was to blame for the accident, which had so narrowly escaped proving a serious one.

Making sure that everything was right, he remounted the wagon, and cautiously resumed his journey, going very slowly at first, so as to watch the play of the engine.

Everything moved with its usual smoothness, and lifting his gaze he descried three buffaloes, standing with erect heads, staring wonderingly at him.

"If you want a chase you may have it!" exclaimed the boy as he headed toward them.

CHAPTER XI.

THE STEAM MAN ON A BUFFALO HUNT.

WITH a wild snort of alarm, the three buffaloes turned tail and dashed over the prairie, with the shrieking steam man in pursuit.

The boy had taken the precaution to bring a rifle with him. When he saw them flee in this terrified manner, the thought came to him at once that he would shoot one of them, and take a portion back to his friends for their supper.

It would be a grand exploit for him, and he would be prouder of its performance than he was of the construction of the wonderful steam man.

The lumbering, rolling gait of the buffaloes was not a very rapid one, and the boy found himself speedily overhauling them without difficulty. They did not know enough to separate, but kept close together, sometimes crowding and striking against each other in their furious efforts to escape.

But, after the chase had continued some time, one of the animals began to fall in the rear, and Johnny directed his attention toward him, as he would be the most easy to secure.

This fellow was a huge bull that was slightly lame, which accounted for his tardiness of gait. Frightened as he was, it was not that blind terror which had seized the Indians when they discovered the steam man so close at their heels. The bull was one of those creatures that if closely pressed would turn and charge the monster. He was not one to continue a fruitless flight, no matter who or what was his pursuer.

The boy was not aware of this sturdy trait in the animal, nor did he dream of anything like resistance.

So he steadily drew toward him, until within twenty yards, when he let go of his controlling rod, and picked up the rifle beside him. A bullet from this, he supposed, would kill any animal, however large, no matter at what portion of his body he aimed.

So raising partly to his feet, and steadying himself as well as he could, he aimed for the lumping haunch of the animal. The ball buried itself in his flank, and so retarded his speed, that the next moment the boy found himself beside him.

The instant this took place, the bull lowered his head, and without further warning, charged full at the steam man.

The boy saw the danger, but too late to stave it off. His immense head struck the rear of the monster with such momentum that he was lifted fully a foot from the ground—the concussion sounding like the crack of a pistol.

Fortunately the shock did not materially injure the machine, although the frightened boy expected to be capsized and killed by the infuriated buffalo.

The latter, when he had made his plunge, instantly drew back for another, which was sure to be fatal if made as fairly as the first. The boy retained his presence of mind enough to let on full steam, and the concern shot away at an extraordinary rate, bounding over the ground so furiously that the billets of wood were thrown and scattered in every direction, so that now, from being the pursuer, he had speedily become the pursued. The tables were turned with a vengeance!

It was only by providential good fortune that young Brainerd escaped instant destruction. The wonder was that the steam man was not so injured as to be unable to travel, in which case the maddened bull would have left little of him.

As it was, the experience of the boy was such as he could never forget. When he turned his affrighted glance behind he saw the enraged animal plunging furiously after him, his head lowered, his tongue out, his eyes glaring, and his whole appearance that of the most brutal ferocity.

Had the bull come in collision with the horse or man while in that mood he would have made short work of him.

But great as was his speed, it could not equal that of the wonderful steam man, who took such tremendous strides that a few minutes sufficed to carry him beyond all danger.

Johnny quietly slacked off steam, but he kept up a good swinging gait, not caring to renew his close acquaintance with his wounded enemy. The latter speedily discovered he was losing ground, and finally gave up the pursuit and trotted off at a leisurely rate to join his companions, apparently none the worse for the slight wound he had received.

As soon as the boy found himself beyond the reach of the animal's fury he halted the man and made a minute examination of the machinery.

The head and horns of the buffalo had dented the iron skin of the steam man, but the blow being distributed over a large area, inflicted no other damage—if indeed this could be called damage of itself.

The boy was greatly pleased, not only at his escape but at the admirable manner in which his invention had borne the shock of collision. It gave him a confidence in it which hitherto he had not felt.

Turning his face more toward the mountains, he again let on a good head of steam and rattled over the prairie at a stirring rate. An hour was sufficient to bring him to the base, where he halted.

He had not forgotten the warning of the trapper, but, like almost any inexperienced person, he could not see any cause for alarm. He scanned every part of the prairie and mountain that was in his field of vision, but could detect nothing alarming.

He supposed the parting admonition of Baldy was merely a general warning, such as a cautious person gives to one whom he has reason to fear is somewhat careless in his conduct.

It therefore required little self-argument upon his part after putting his man in proper "condition," to start off on a ramble up the mountain side. It was not his intention to remain more than an hour or so, unless he came across some game. He had a goodly quantity of ammunition, and was careful that his rifle was loaded, so as not to be taken unawares by any emergency.

Although Johnny Brainerd was afflicted with a misshapen form, yet he was very quick and active upon his feet, and bounded along over the rocks, and across the chasms like a deer, with such a buoyancy of spirits that he forgot all danger.

However, he had gone but a short distance, when he was startled by a low fierce growl, and turning his head, saw to his horror, that he had nearly run against a colossal animal, which he at once recognized as the dreaded grizzly bear.

Such a meeting would have startled an experienced hunter, and it was therefore with no steady nerve that he hastily brought his piece to his shoulder and fired.

The shot struck the bear in the body, doing just what his shot at the buffalo had done some time before. It thoroughly angered him, without inflicting anything like a serious wound. With a growl of fury the brute made straight for him.

What would the boy have given, as he sped down the mountain side, were he now in his wagon, whirled over the prairie at a rate which would enable him to laugh to scorn any such speed as that of the brute.

At first he had hopes of reaching his refuge, but he was not long in seeing that it was impossible, and found that if he escaped he must find some refuge very speedily.

When he suddenly found himself beneath a goodly-sized tree it looked like a providential indication to him, and throwing his gun to the ground, he ascended the tree in the shortest time that he had ever made.

He was none too soon as it was, for the bear was so close beneath him that he felt the brush of its claws along his feet, as he nervously jerked them beyond its reach.

Hastily scrambling to the very top of the tree, he secured himself among the limbs, and then glanced down to see what his enemy was doing. Great was his relief to find him sitting on his haunches, contenting himself with merely casting wistful glances upward.

The sensation of even temporary safety was a relief—but when a full hour had dragged by, with scarcely a single change of position upon the part of the brute, Johnny began to ask himself what was to be the end of all this.

It looked as though the grizzly had resolved on making his dinner upon the youngster who had dared to fire a shot at him. The patience of an animal is proverbially greater than that of a human being, and that of the bear certainly exceeded to a great degree that of his expected prey who crouched in the limbs above.

CHAPTER XII.
THE GRIZZLY BEAR.

FROM where young Brainerd was perched on the tree it was impossible to catch a glimpse of the steam man, so patiently awaiting his return. The distance was also too great for him to make himself heard by the miners, who were hard at work twenty miles away.

Fruitful in expedients, it was not long before the boy found a resource in his trouble. Tearing a large strip from his coat, he tore this into smaller strips, until he had secured a rope half a dozen yards in length. Upon the end of this he placed a loop, and then, descending to the lowest limb, he devoted himself to the task of looping it over the end of his gun. It fortunately had fallen in such a manner that the muzzle was somewhat elevated, so that here was a good opportunity for the exercise of his skill and patience.

When the first attempt was made the bear suddenly clawed at it and tore it from the boy's hand before he could jerk it beyond his reach. So he was compelled to make another one.

Nothing discouraged, the boy soon had this completed, and it was dropped down more cautiously than before. When the grizzly made a lunge at it, it was deftly twitched out of his way.

This was repeated several times, until the brute became disgusted with the sport, and dropping down behind the tree, let the boy do all the fishing he chose.

Now was his time, but the boy did not allow his eagerness to overcome the steadiness of his nerves. It required no little skill, but he finally succeeded in dropping the noose over the muzzle of the gun and jerked it up taut.

With a heart beating high with hope, Johnny saw it lifted clear of the ground, and he began carefully drawing it up. The grizzly looked curiously at his maneuvers, and once made as if to move toward the dangling rifle; but, ere his mind was settled, it was drawn beyond his reach, and the cold muzzle was grasped in the hand of the eagerly waiting boy.

While drawing it up, he had been debating with himself as to the best means of killing the brute. Remembering that his first shot had done no harm, he sensibly concluded that he had not yet learned the vulnerable part of the monster.

His gun was loaded very carefully, and when everything was ready he made a noise, to attract the attention of the brute. The bear looked up instantly, when the gun was aimed straight at his right eye.

Ere the grizzly could withdraw his gaze, the piece was discharged, and the bullet sped true, crashing into the skull of the colossal brute. With a howling grunt, he rose upon his hind feet, clawed the air a few moments, and then dropped dead.

Young Brainerd waited until he was certain that the last spark of life had fled, when he cautiously descended the tree, scarcely able to realize the truth that he had slain a grizzly bear—the monarch of the western wilderness. But such was the fact, and he felt more pride at the thought than if he had slain a dozen buffaloes.

"If I only had him in the wagon," he reflected, "I'd take him into camp, for they will never believe I killed a grizzly bear."

However, it occurred to him that he might secure some memento, and accordingly he cut several claws and placed them in his pocket. This done, he concluded that, as the afternoon was well advanced, it was time he started homeward.

His hurried flight from the ferocious brute had bewildered him somewhat, and, when he took the direction he judged to be the right one, he found nothing familiar or remembered, from which fact he concluded he was going astray.

But a little computation on his part, and he soon righted himself, and was walking along quite hopefully, when he received another severe shock of terror, at hearing the unmistakable whoop of an Indian, instantly followed by several others.

Immediately he recalled the warning given by the trapper, and looked furtively about, to make sure that he was not already in their hands. His great anxiety now was to reach the steam man and leave the neighborhood, which was rapidly becoming untenable.

So he began stealing forward as rapidly as possible, at the same time keeping a sharp lookout for danger. It required a half-hour, proceeding at this rate, before reaching the base of the mountain. The moment he did so, he looked all around in quest of the steam man, whom he had been compelled to desert for so long a time.

He discovered it standing several hundred yards away; but, to his dismay, there were fully a dozen Indians standing and walking about it, examining every portion with the greatest curiosity.

Here was a dilemma indeed, and the boy began to believe that he had gotten himself into an inextricable difficulty, for how to reach the steam man and renew the fire—under the circumstances—was a question which might well puzzle an older head to answer.

It was unfortunate that the machine should have been taken at this great disadvantage, for it was stripping it of its terror to those Indians, who were such inveterate enemies to the whites.

They had probably viewed it with wonder and fear at first; but finding it undemonstrative, had gradually gathered courage, until they had congregated around it, and made as critical a scrutiny as they knew how.

Whatever fear or terror they had felt at first sight was now gone; for they seemed on the most familiar terms with it.

Several climbed into the wagon—others passed in and around the helpless giant—and one valiant fellow hit him a thwack on the stomach with his tomahawk.

This blow hurt the boy far more than it did the iron man, and he could hardly repress a cry of pain, as he looked upon the destruction of his wonderful friend as almost inevitable.

The savage, however, contented himself with this demonstration, and immediately after walked away toward the mountain. The observant boy knew what this meant, and he withdrew from his temporary hiding-place, and started to watch him.

The fact that the Indian followed precisely the path taken by him, did not remove the uneasiness, and he made up his mind that nothing but danger was to come to him from this proceeding.

When the Indian had reached the spot where the dead grizzly bear lay, he paused in the greatest wonderment. Here was something which he did not understand.

The dead carcass showed that somebody had slain him, and the shot in the eye looked as though it had been done by an experienced hunter. A few minutes' examination of the ground showed further that he who had fired the shot was in the tree at the time, after which he had descended and fled.

All this took but a few minutes for the savage to discover, when he gave a whoop of triumph at his success in probing the matter, and started off on the trail.

Unluckily, this led straight toward the bowlder behind which the boy had concealed himself; and ere he could find a new hiding-place the Indian was upon him.

At sight of the boy, the savage gave a whoop, and raised his tomahawk; but the youngster was expecting this, and instantly raising his gun, he discharged it full into his heart.

As he heard the shriek of the Indian, and saw him throw up his arms, he did not wait to hear or see anything else, but instantly fled with might and main, scarcely looking or knowing whither he was going.

A short time after he found himself at the base of the mountain, very near the spot where he had first come, and glancing again toward the steam man, he saw him standing motionless, as before, and with not a single Indian in sight!

CHAPTER XIII.
AN APPALLING DANGER.

NOT a second was to be lost. The next moment the boy had run across the intervening space and pulled open the furnace door of the steam man. He saw a few embers yet smoldering in the bottom—enough to rekindle the wood. Dashing in a lot from the wagon, he saw it begin blazing up. He pulled the valve wide open, so that there might not be a moment's delay in starting, and held the water in the boiler at a proper level. The smoke immediately began issuing from the pipe or hat, and the hopes of the boy rose correspondingly.

The great danger was that the Indians would return before he could start. He kept glancing behind him, and it was with a heart beating with despair that he heard several whoops, and saw at the same instant a number of red-skins coming toward him.

The boy gave a jolt to the wagon, which communicated to the steam man, and it instantly started, at quite a moderate gait, but rapidly increased to its old-fashioned run.

It was just in the nick of time, for two minutes later the savages would have been upon him. As it was, when they saw the giant moving off they paused for a moment in amazement.

But their previous acquaintance with the apparatus had robbed it of all its supernatural attributes, and their halt lasted but a few seconds. The next moment they understood that there was some human agency about it, and uttering their blood-curdling yells, they started in full pursuit. But by this time the steam gentleman was getting down to his regular pace, and was striding over the prairie like a dromedary. For a time the Indians gained, then the intervening distance became stationary, and then he began pulling steadily away from them.

Still the savages maintained the chase until satisfied of its hopelessness, when they gave it up and sullenly withdrew in the direction of the mountains.

The young fellow, in his triumph, could not

avoid rising in the wagon, shouting and waving his hat defiantly at his baffled pursuers. The daring act came near costing his life, for it was instantly followed by the discharge of several guns, and the singing of the bullets about his ears caused him to duck back into his seat as suddenly as he had risen from it.

The afternoon was now quite well advanced, and besides feeling hungry, Johnny Brainerd was anxious to get back to camp.

The intervening distance was rapidly passed, and the sun was just setting as he slacked up within a short distance of Wolf Ravine.

For some unaccountable reason, the nearer he approached "camp," as it was called, a feeling akin to fear came over him. It was a presentiment of coming evil, which he found it impossible either to shake off or to define, and that was why he halted some distance away.

From where he stood it was impossible to see his two friends at work, but at that time of day he knew they were accustomed to stop work and come out upon the prairie for the purpose of enjoying the cool breeze of evening. At the same time, when such constant danger threatened, they were accustomed to have one of their number, either all or a part of the time, on the ground above, where the approach of enemies could be detected.

The absence of anything like a sentinel increased the boy's apprehensions, and when he had waited some fifteen minutes without seeing anything of his friends he became painfully uneasy.

What if they had been killed? What if they were prisoners? What if a hundred Indians were at that moment in the possession of Wolf Ravine?

Such and similar were the questions which the affrighted boy asked himself, and which, with all his shrewdness, he was unable to answer.

In the hope of attracting attention he set up a shrieking with the whistle, which sounded so loud on the still evening air that it must have gone miles away over the level prairie.

There being no response to this he kept it up for some time, but it still failed, and all this confirmed him in the belief that "something was up."

What that particular something was it was impossible to say, so long as he sat in the wagon, and for five minutes he endeavored to decide whether it was best to get out and make a reconnoissance on his own hook or remain where, in case of danger, he could seek safety in flight.

As the day wore rapidly away, and he still failed to see or hear anything of his friends, he finally concluded to get out and make an examination of the ravine.

Accordingly he sprung lightly to the ground, but had scarcely alighted when a peculiar signal—something resembling a tremulous whistle—reached his ear, and he instantly clambered back again, fully satisfied that the whistle was intended as a signal, and that it concerned him, although whether from friend or foe he could only conjecture.

However, his alarm was such that he moved a hundred yards or so further away from the ravine, where there was less likelihood of being surprised by any sudden rush upon the part of the thieving red-skins.

From this standpoint he carefully scanned what could be seen of the ravine. It descended quite gradually from the edge of the bank, so that he gained a partial view of the rocks and bowlders upon the opposite side. Some of the trees growing in the narrow valley rose to such a hight that one-half or two-thirds of them were exposed to view.

It was while the boy was gazing at these that he detected a peculiar movement in one of the limbs, which instantly arrested his attention.

A moment showed him that the peculiar waving motion was made by human agency, and he strained his eyes in the hope of detecting the cause of the curious movement.

The gathering darkness made his vision quite uncertain; but he either saw, or fancied he saw, a dark object among the limbs which resembled the form of Baldy Bicknell, the trapper.

Johnny Brainerd would have given almost anything in the world could he have understood what it all meant.

But the very fact of these singular demonstrations was *prima facie* evidence of the most unquestionable kind; and, after a moment's consultation with himself, he began moving away, just as the sharp crack of several rifles notified him of the fearful peril which he had escaped.

CHAPTER XIV.
THE HUGE HUNTER.

Simultaneous with the report of the rifles came the pinging of the bullets about the ears of young Brainerd, who, having started the steam man, kept on going until he was a considerable distance from the ravine.

All the time he kept looking back, but could see nothing of his enemies, nor could he detect the point from which the rifle-shots were fired.

Now, as night descended over the prairie, and the retreat of his friends became shrouded in impenetrable darkness, he fully appreciated the fact that not only were they in great danger, but so was he himself.

The heathenish terror with which the steam man had at first inspired the savages had rapidly worn away, the circumstances unfortunately having been such that they had very speedily learned that it was nothing more than a human invention, which of itself could accomplish little or no harm.

He could but reflect, as the man glided slowly along, that if he had the three friends beside him, how easily they could glide away in the darkness and leave all danger behind.

But they were in the extremity of peril already, and, reflect and cogitate as much as he chose, he could see no earthly way of assisting them out of their difficulty.

Besides the concern which he naturally felt regarding his friends, there was a matter that more clearly related to himself that demanded his attention.

The water in the tank was at its lowest ebb, and it would be dangerous for him to attempt to run more than one hour or so longer before replenishing it. Consequently he was unable to stand anything like another chase from the Indians.

As the part of prudence, therefore, he turned toward the river, following slowly along the bank, in quest of some place where it would be easy and safe for him to secure the much-needed water.

It was a long and discouraging hunt. The banks were so high that he could find no point where it was safe for him to descend to the water's edge. There was too great a risk of "upsetting his cart," a calamity which, in all probability, would be irreparable.

At length, however, when he had wandered about a mile distant from the Wolf Ravine, he discovered a place, where the bank had about six feet elevation, and sloped down gradually to the river.

Here he paused, and with a small vessel, descended to the stream, muttering to himself as he did so:

"Why didn't I think and put a pumping arrangement to the machine? I could have done it as well as not, and it would have saved me a good deal of trouble."

But regrets were now unavailing, and he lost no time in useless lamentations, setting to work at once. It was tedious labor, carrying up the water in a small vessel, and emptying it in the tank, but he persevered, and at the end of a couple of hours the task was completed.

"I can make the wood stand me another day," he added, as he stood looking at the greatly diminished pile—"although, if I knew where to get it, I would load up now, and then I should be prepared—"

He suddenly paused, for scarcely a dozen yards away, coming up the margin of the river, straight toward him, he descried the figure of a man fully six feet and a half high.

Young Brainerd's first impulse was to spring into the wagon and start away at full speed; but a second glance showed him that it was not an Indian, but a white man, in the garb of a hunter.

"Hullo, boss, thar, what yer doin'?"

He was at a loss what reply to make, and therefore made none. The next moment the giant hunter was beside him.

"B'ars and bufflers! younker, what ye got thar?" he demanded, eying the steam man with an expression of the most amazed wonder. "I say, what do yer call that thing?"

"That," laughed Johnny, who could not avoid a feeling of strong apprehension at the singular appearance of the strange hunter, "is a sort of peregrinating locomotive."

"Paggyratin' locomotive—what's that?" he asked, in a gruff voice, and with an expression of great disgust at the unfamiliar words employed.

"You have seen a locomotive, haven't you?"

"Reckon I hev, down in St. Louey."

"Well, this is something on the same principle, except that it uses legs instead of wheels."

"Can that ere thing walk?"

"Yes, sir, and run, too; it traveled all the way from the Missouri river to this place."

The huge hunter turned upon him with a fierce expression.

"Yer can't fool this yar hoss in that style."

"Don't you believe me?" asked the boy, who was fearful of offending the stranger.

"No, sar; not a word."

"How do you suppose we got it here?"

"Fotched in a wagon."

"Let me show you what he can do."

He was about to step into the wagon, when the hunter stopped him.

"See hyar, younker, who mought yer be?"

The boy gave his name and residence.

"What yer doin' hyar?"

"I'm traveling with this machine of mine."

"How do you git it along?"

"I was just going to show you when you stopped me."

"Hold on; no need of bein' in a sweat about it. Do yer come alone?"

"No. I came with a hunter."

"What war his name?"

"Baldy Bicknell."

"B'ars and bufflers! did yer come with him?"

"Yes; he was my companion all the way."

"Whar mought he be?"

Johnny Brainerd hesitated a moment. While the huge hunter might possibly be of great service to the beleaguered miners, yet he recollected that it was the desire of Baldy that the fact of gold existing in Wolf Ravine should be kept a secret from all except their own party.

Should it become known to any of the numerous hunters and emigrants who were constantly passing in the neighborhood, there would be such a flocking to the place that they would be driven away and probably killed for the treasure that they had already obtained.

The boy, therefore, chose to make a non-committal reply:

"Baldy is some distance away, in camp."

"And what are yer doin' hyar?"

"I stopped here to get water for this steam man, as we call him. You know anything that travels by steam must have the water to generate it."

"I say, younker, I don't want none of yer big words to me. Ef I h'ar any more, b'ars and bufflers, ef I don't crack yer over the head with Sweetlove, my shootin'-iron, so mind what yer say, fur I won't stand no nonsense."

"I didn't wish to offend you," returned the boy, in the meekest of tones.

"How far away might be Baldy?"

"I couldn't tell you exactly, but I think it is less than ten miles."

"Be you goin' back to camp to-night?"

"It was my intention—that is, I meant to do so."

"Guess I'll go with yer; but see hyar, younker, let's see yer try that old humbug of yourn."

The boy sprung into the wagon, glad of the opportunity of getting rid of what looked like a dangerous man. Before he could start he was again peremptorily stopped.

"Yer see, I b'leeve yar a humbug, but if that ole thing does run, and, mind, I tell yer, I don't b'leeve it will, do yer know what I'm goin' to do?"

"I do not."

"I'm goin' to take it myself to chase red-skins in. It won't bother yer much fur them long legs of yourn to carry that humpback home again. So, younker, start now, and let us see what yer can do."

The boy let on steam, and the man started off on a moderate gait, which rapidly increased to a swift one. The huge, wonder-stricken hunter watched it until it gradually faded out of sight in the gloom, and still watched the place where it had disappeared, and though he watched much longer, with a savage and vindictive heart, yet it never came back to him again.

CHAPTER XV.
THE ATTACK IN THE RAVINE.

IN the mean time, the situation of our friends in Wolf Ravine was becoming perilous to the last degree.

Before going to work, on the morning of the steam man's excursion to the mountains, Baldy Bicknell made a reconnoissance of the ravine, to assure himself that there was no danger of being suddenly overwhelmed, while delving for the precious yellow sand.

He saw abundant signs of Indians having recently visited the place, but he concluded there were none in the immediate vicinity, and that comparatively little risk was run in the boy making his wished-for visit to the mountains in the west.

Through the center of the ravine ran a small stream of water, hardly of enough volume to be used for washing gold without a dam being created. It looked as if this had once been the head of a large stream, and that the golden sand had been drifted to this spot, by the force of the powerful current.

The auriferous particles were scattered over the entire breadth of the ravine, for the distance of several hundred feet, being found in the richest deposits between the ledges and rocks, in the bottom of the channel, where, as may well be supposed, it was no easy matter to obtain.

A short distance back of the "diggings," where the vast masses of rocks assumed curiously grotesque forms, the miners discovered a rude cave, where they at once established their head quarters. A tiny stream ran through the bottom of it, and with a little placing of the loose bowlders, they speedily put it in the best condition of defense.

It was almost entirely surrounded 'by trees, and there was one spot where a thin man, like Hopkins or Baldy, could draw his body through and climb a luxuriant cottonwood, whose top gave a wide view of the surrounding plain.

The day passed away without any signs of Indians, Baldy occasionally ascending the side of the ravine, and scanning the plains in every direction, on the constant lookout for the insidious approach of their enemies.

Just before nightfall, while all three were at work, a rifle was discharged, and the bullet was imbedded in the tough oaken handle of the spade with which the trapper was digging.

"Whar in thunder did that come from?" he demanded, dropping the implement, catching up the rifle, and glaring savagely about him.

But neither of the others could answer him, and climbing up the bank, he looked fiercely around for some evidence of the whereabouts of his treacherous foe.

The latter remained invisible, but several hundred yards down the ravine, he caught a glimpse of enough Indians dodging hither and thither to satisfy him that there was quite a formidable force in the valley.

Giving the alarm to his companions, all three withdrew within the cave, not the less willingly, as it was very near their usual quitting time.

"Begorrah! and what'll becoom of the shtame man and the boy?" inquired Mickey, as he hastily obeyed orders.

"Jerusalem!" exclaimed the Yankee, in great trepidation, "if he isn't warned, they'll catch him sure, and then what'll become of us? We'll have to walk all the way hum."

As the best means of communicating with him, the trapper climbed through the narrow opening, and to the top of the tree, where he ensconced himself, just as the steam man uttered its interrogative whistle.

The trapper, as we have shown in another place, replied by pantomime, not wishing to discover his whereabouts to the enemy, as he had a dim idea that this means of egress might possibly prove of some use to him, in the danger that was closing around them.

When Johnny Brainerd recognized his signal, and beat a retreat, Baldy began a cautious descent to his cave again. At this time it was already growing dark, and he had to feel his way down again.

And so it came about, that not until he had reached the lowest limb, did his trained ear detect a slight rustling on the ground beneath. Supposing it to be either Mickey or Ethan, he continued his descent, merely glancing below. But at that moment something suspicious caught his eye, and peering down more carefully, he discovered a crouching Indian, waiting with drawn knife until he should come within his reach.

The trapper was no coward, and had been in many a hand-to-hand tussle before; but there was something in the character of the danger which would have made it more pleasant for him to hesitate awhile until he could learn its precise dimensions; but time was too precious, and the next moment, he had dropped directly by the side of the red-skin.

The latter intended to make the attack, but without waiting for him, Baldy sprung like a panther upon him and bore him to the earth. There was a silent but terrific struggle for a few moments, but the prodigious activity and power of the trapper prevailed, and when he withdrew from the grasp of the Indian, the latter was as dead as a door nail.

The struggle had been so short that neither Mickey nor Ethan knew anything of it, until Baldy dropped down among them, and announced what had taken place.

"Jerusalem! have they come as close as that?" asked the Yankee in considerable terror.

"Skulp me, if they ain't all around us!" was the reply of the hunter. "How we ar' to git out o' hyar, ar' a hard thing to tell jist now."

"It's meself that thinks the rid gentlemin have a love fur us, as me mither obsarved, when she cracked the head of me father," remarked Mickey, who had seated himself upon the ground with all the indifference of an unconcerned spectator.

It was so dark in their cave-like home that they could not see each other's faces, and could only catch a sort of twilight glimpse of their forms when they passed close to each other.

It would have made their quarters more pleasant had they struck a light, but it was too dangerous a proceeding, and no one thought of it. They could only keep on the alert, and watch for the movement of their enemies.

The latter, beyond all doubt, were in the immediate vicinity, and inspired as they were by hate of the most vindictive kind, would not allow an opportunity to pass of doing all the harm in their power.

The remains of their food was silently eaten in the darkness, when Baldy said:

"Do yer stay hyar whar ye be till I come back."

"Where might ye be going naow?" inquired Hopkins.

"I'm goin' outside to see what the reds are doin', and to see whether thar's a chance fur 'em to gobble us up hull."

"Do yees mind and take care of y'urself, as me mither cautioned me when I went a shparkin'," said Mickey, who naturally felt some apprehension, when he saw the trapper on the point of leaving them at such a dangerous time.

"Yes. Baldy, remember that my fate is wrapped up in yours," added the Yankee, whose sympathies were probably excited to a still greater extent.

"Never mind about Baldy; he has been in such business too often not to know how to take care of himself."

"How long do you expect to be gone?" inquired Ethan.

"Mebbe all night, if thar ain't much danger. Ef I find the varments ar' too thick I'll stay by yer, and if they ain't I'll leave fur several hours. Leastways, whatever I do, you'll be sure to look out fer the skunks."

With this parting admonition, the trapper withdrew.

In going out, he made his exit by the same entrance by which all had come in. He proceeded with great caution, for none knew better than he the danger of a single misstep. He succeeded, after considerable time, in reaching a portion of the valley so shrouded in gloom that he was able to advance without fear of discovery.

He thoroughly reconnoitered every part of the ravine in the immediate vicinity of the cave, but could discover nothing of the Indians, and he concluded that they were some distance away.

Having assured himself of this, the trapper cautiously ascended the side of the ravine, until he reached the open prairie, when he lost no time in leaving the dangerous place behind him.

He had no intention, however, of deserting his friends, but had simply gone in quest of the steam man. He comprehended the difficulty under which they all labored, so long as they were annoyed in this manner by the constant attacks of the savages, and he had an idea that the invention of the dwarfed Johnny Brainerd could be turned to a good account in driving the miscreants away so thoroughly that they would remain away for a long enough time for them to accomplish something in the way of gathering the wealth lying all about them.

He recalled the direction which he had seen the puffing giant take, and he bent his steps accordingly, with only a faint hope of meeting him without searching the entire night for him.

Baldy was shrewd enough to reason that as the boy would wish some water for his engine, he would remain in the immediate vicinity of the river until at least that want could be supplied.

Acting on this supposition, he made his way to the river bank, and followed so closely to the water that its moonlit surface was constantly visible to him.

The night was still, and, as he moved silently along, he often paused and listened, hoping to hear the familiar rattle of the wheels, as the youngster sped over the prairie.

Without either party knowing it, he passed within a few yards of Duff McIntosh, the huge trapper, whom he had known so intimately years before.

But had he been aware of the fact, he would only have turned further aside, to avoid him; for, when the two trappers, several years previous, separated, they had been engaged in a deadly quarrel, which came near resulting fatally to both.

At length the faint rattle of the wheels caught his ear, and he bent his steps toward the point where he judged the steam man to be.

CHAPTER XVI.

THE REPULSE.

A FEW minutes more satisfied the trapper that he was right. Gradually out from the darkness the approaching figure resolved itself into the steam man.

Johnny Brainerd, after leaving the huge trapper so neatly, continued wandering aimlessly over the prairie at a moderate speed, so as to guard against the insidious approach of the Indians, or the hunter who had threatened to confiscate his property in so unjustifiable a manner.

Fortunately he did not see Baldy until the latter cautiously hailed him, otherwise he would have fled before ascertaining his identity; but the moment he recognized his voice he hastened toward him, no less surprised than pleased at meeting him so unexpectedly.

"Where are Mickey and Ethan?" he inquired, as he leaped alongside of him.

"In the cave."

"How is it you are here?"

The trapper briefly explained that he had crept out to hunt him up; but as there seemed no imminent danger, he deemed it best to leave his companions there, as if the Indians once gained possession of the golden ravine, it would be difficult, if not impossible, to displace them.

Besides, in order to carry out the scheme which he had formed, it was necessary that two at least should remain in the cave, while the others were on the outside.

Under the direction of the trapper, the steam man slowly approached the ravine, keeping at a respectful distance, but so near that if any sudden emergency should arise, they would be able to render assistance to their friends.

The boy gave several whistles so as to inform the Irishman and Yankee of their wher abouts. A few seconds after, and while the noise of the instrument was echoing over the prairie, a fainter whistle reached their ears.

"That's the long-legged Yankee!" instantly remarked the trapper; "he knows how to make any kind of noise."

"What does it mean?"

"It means that all's right."

"Where are the Indians?"

"They ain't fur off. I wish they war further, fur ef it warn't fur them, we'd had half the yaller metal out of thar by this time."

Young Brainerd had the reputation of possessing a remarkably keen vision; but, peer as much as he might, he could detect nothing unusual. The trapper, however, affirmed that numerous forms could be seen creeping along the edge of the prairie, and that these same forms were more nor less than so many redskins.

"What are they trying to do?"

"Dunno."

"Hadn't we better withdraw?" inquired Johnny, showing a little nervousness.

"Not till we know they're arter us," was the quiet reply.

By and by the boy himself was able to get an occasional glimpse of the shadowy figures moving to and fro.

"I think they are going to surround us," he added, "and I feel as though we ought to get out while we can do so."

The only reply to this, was by the trapper suddenly bringing his gun to his shoulder and firing. An agonizing screech, as the savage threw himself in the air, showed that the shot had not been in vain.

Rather curiously at the same moment the report of a gun in the ravine reached their ears, followed by the same death-shriek.

"They ain't sleepin' very powerful down thar," was the pleased remark of the trapper, as he leisurely reloaded his piece, while the boy remained in that nervous state, awaiting the permission of Baldy to go spinning away over the prairie at a rate that would very quickly carry him beyond all danger.

But the trapper was in no hurry to give the ardently desired permission. He seemed to have a lingering affection for the place, which prevented his "tearing himself away."

The boy's timidity was not in the least diminished, when several return shots were fired, the bullets pinging all around them.

"My gracious, Baldy, let's get out of this!" he instantly pleaded, starting the man himself.

"Go about fifty feet," was the reply, "but not any further."

It may be said that the steam man fairly leaped over this space, and somewhat further, like a frightened kangaroo, and even then it would not have halted had not the trapper given peremptory orders for it to do so.

The sky was now clear and the moon, riding high and nearly full, illumined the prairie for a considerable distance, and there was no fear but that they could detect the approach of the most treacherous savage, let him come in whatever disguise he chose.

The night wore gradually away, without any particular demonstration upon the part of either the Indians or white men, although dropping shots were occasionally exchanged, without any particular result on either side.

Now and then a red-skin, creeping cautiously along, made his appearance on the edge of the ravine; but there was too much light for him to expose himself to the deadly rifle of the trapper, who took a kind of savage pleasure in sending his leaden messengers after the aborigines.

This species of sport was not without its attendant excitement and danger; for the last creature to take a shot quietly is an American Indian; and they kept popping away at the steam man and its train whenever a good opportunity offered.

Owing to the size and peculiar appearance of the steamer, he was a fair target for his enemies; and, indeed, so uncomfortably close did some of the bullets come, that the boy almost continually kept his head lowered, so as to be protected by the sides of the wagon.

Finally morning came, greatly to the relief of all our friends. As soon as it was fairly light the Irishman and Yankee were notified that a move was about to be made, by means of the steam-whistle. An answering signal coming back to them, the steam man at once advanced to the very edge of the ravine.

The trapper peering cautiously down the gulch, caught sight of several red-skins crouching near the cave, and, directing young Brainerd to discharge his piece at a certain one, the two fired nearly together. Scarce five seconds had elapsed, when both Ethan and Mickey did the same. All four, or rather three—as the boy gave his principal attention to the engine, began loading and firing as rapidly as possible.

The red-skins returned a few scattering shots; but they were taken at such disadvantage, that they immediately began a precipitate retreat down the ravine.

Ere they had withdrawn a hundred yards, Ethan and Mickey emerged from the cave, shouting and excited, firing at every red-skin they could see, the Irishman occasionally swinging his gun over his head, and daring the savages to a hand-to-hand encounter.

While the two were thus engaged, the trapper was not idle. The steam man maintained his place but a short distance behind the enemies, and his deadly rifle scarcely ever failed of its mark.

The moment an Indian was killed or helplessly wounded, his companions caught and dragged him away, there being a great fear upon the part of all that some of their number might fall into the hands of their enemies, and suffer the ineffaceable disgrace of being scalped.

The savages were followed a long distance, until their number had diminished down to a fraction of what it was originally, and the survivors had all they could do in taking care of their disabled comrades.

Never was victory more complete. The Indians were thoroughly discomfited, and only too glad to get away after being so severely punished. During this singular running fight the steam man kept up a constant shrieking, which doubtless contributed in no slight degree to the rout of the red-skins. They fired continually at the fearful-looking monster, and, finding their shots produced no effect, invested the thing with a portion of the supernatural power which they had given it at first sight.

When the last glimpse of the retreating Indians was seen, the trapper turned triumphantly toward the boy.

"Warn't that purty well done, younker?"

"It was indeed."

"They'll now stay away awhile."

"We would have failed if we had waited any longer."

"Why so, boy?"

"Because the last stick is burned, and the steam man couldn't be made to run a mile further without more fuel."

CHAPTER XVII.
HOMEWARD BOUND.

THE punishment administered to the Indians who had so greatly annoyed the miners proved a very beneficial one.

Nothing more was seen of them, except one or two glimpses of the red-skin upon his black horse. He, however, maintained a respectful distance, and at the end of a day or two disappeared altogether.

These were golden moments indeed to the miners, and they improved them to the utmost. From earliest light until the darkness of night they toiled almost unceasingly. Half the time they went hungry rather than stop their work to procure that which was so much needed. When, however, the wants of nature could no longer be trifled with, Baldy took his rifle and started off on a hunt, which was sure to be brief and successful.

Sometimes he caught sight of some game in the gulch, and sometimes something in the air drew the fire of his unerring rifle, and the miners feasted and worked as only such violently laboring men can do.

Although the boy was unable to assist at the severe labor, yet he soon demonstrated his genius and usefulness. He not only constructed a dam, but made a "rocker," or machine, of an original style, that did the work far more expeditiously and thoroughly than it had yet been done.

While the men were getting the auriferous sand, he separated it from the particles of dirt and gravel, without any assistance from them, and without any severe labor for himself.

There was some apprehension upon the part of all that the huge trapper, whom young Brainerd had met at night, would make his appearance. Should he do so, it would be certain to precipitate a difficulty of the worst kind, as he was morose, sullen, treacherous, envious and reckless of danger.

Baldy Bicknell really feared him more than he did the Indians, and the constant watchfulness he exercised for several days showed how great was his apprehension.

Fortunately, indeed, for all concerned, the giant hunter continued his travels in a different direction, and the miners were undisturbed by him.

Two weeks passed, by the end of which time the ravine was about exhausted of its precious stuff, and the miners made their preparations for going home.

It was impossible to do anything more than conjecture the amount of wealth they had obtained, but Baldy was sure that there was enough, when sold, to buy each of them a handsome farm.

"Jerusalem! but naow ain't that good?" exclaimed the delighted Ethan Hopkins, as he mopped off his perspiring forehead. "That 'ere encourages me to take a step that I've often contemplated."

"What might the same be?"

"Git married; me and Seraphenia Pike hev been engaged for the last ten years, and now I'll be hanged ef I don't go home and get spliced."

"And it's myself that'll do the same," added Mickey, as he executed an Irish jig on the hard earth in front of their cavern home, after they had concluded to leave the place.

"Where does she reside?" inquired Ethan.

"Ballyduff, Kings county, in the Gim of the Sea; it's there that lives the lass that's to have the honor of becoming Mrs. McSquizzle, and becomin' the mither of her own children. Arrah, but isn't the same a beauty?"

"The same as my own, Michael," ventured the Yankee, who deemed it his duty to correct this general remark of his friend.

"Arrah, now, get out wid ye! she can't begin wid Miss Bridget Moghlaghighogh that resides wid her mit er and two pigs on the outskirts of Ballyduff, in the wee cabin that has the one room and the one windy. Warrah, warrah, now isn't she a jewel?"

"And so is Seraphenia."

"But has she the rid hair, that makes it onnecessary for them to have the candle lit at night? and has she the same beautiful freckles, the size of a ha'penny, on the face and the nose, that has such an iligant turn up at the end, that she used to hang her bonnet on it? Arrah, now, and didn't she have the swate teeth—six of the same that were so broad that they filled her mouth—and it was none of yer gimblet holes that was her mouth, but a beautiful one, that when she smiled went round to her ears, did the same. And her shoes! but you orter seen them."

"Why so?"

"What was the matter with her shoes?"

"Nothing was the same. They was the shoes that the little pigs went to slaap in, afore they got so big that they couldn't git in them, and then it was her brother that used one of them same for a trunk when he imigrated to Ameriky. Arrah, now, but wasn't me own Bridget a jewel?"

"Jehosephat! I should think she was!" exclaimed Hopkins, who had listened in amazement to this enumeration of the beauties of the gentle Irish lass, who had won the affections of Mickey McSquizzle. "No doubt she had a sweet disposition."

"Indeed she had, had she; it was that of an angel, was the same. It was niver that I staid there a night coorting the same that she didn't smash her shillaleh to smithereens over me head. Do yees observe that?" asked Mickey, removing his hat, and displaying a scar that extended half way across his head.

"I don't see how any one can help seeing that."

"Well, that was the parting salute of Bridget, as I started for Ameriky. Arrah, now, but she did the same in style."

"That was her parting memento, was it?"

"Yes; I gave her the black eye, and she did the same fur me, and I niver takes off me hat to scratch me head that I don't think of the swate gal that I left at home."

And thereupon the Irishman began whistling "The Girl I Left Behind Me," accompanying it with a sort of waltzing dance, kept with remarkably good time.

"And so you intend to marry her?" inquired Hopkins, with no little amazement.

"It's that I do, ef I finds her heart fraa when I return to Ballyduff. You know, that the loikes of her is sought by all the lads in Kings county, and to save braaking their hearts, she may share the shanty of some of 'em."

"Jerusalem! but she is the all-firedest critter I ever heard tell on."

"What does ye maan by that?" demanded the Irishman, instantly flaring up; "does ye maan to insinooate that she isn't the most charming craater in the whole counthry?"

"You'll allow me to except my own Seraphenia?"

"Niver a once."

"Then I'll do it whether you like it or not. Your gal can't begin with mine, and never could."

"That I don't allow any man to say."

And the Irishman immediately began divesting himself of his coat, preparatory to settling the difference in the characteristic Irish manner. Nothing loth, the Yankee put himself in attitude, determined to stand up for the rights of his fair one, no matter by whom assailed.

Matters having progressed so far, there undoubtedly would have been a set-to between them, had not the trapper interfered. He and the boy were engaged in preparing the steam man and wagon for starting, when the excited words drew their attention, and seeing that a fight was imminent, Baldy advanced to where they stood and said:

"Not another word, or skulp me! ef I don't hammer both of you till thar's nothin' left o' you."

This was unequivocal language, and neither of the combatants misunderstood it. All belligerent manifestations ceased at once, and they turned to in assisting in the preparations for moving.

When all four were seated in the wagon, with their necessary baggage about them, it was found that there was comparatively little room for the wood. When they had stored all that they could well carry, it was found that there was hardly enough to last them twelve hours, so that there was considerable risk run from this single fact.

The steam man, however, stepped off with as much ease as when drawing the wagon with a single occupant. The boy let on enough of steam to keep up a rattling pace, and to give the assurance that they were progressing homeward in the fastest manner possible.

Toward the middle of the afternoon a storm suddenly came up and the rain poured in torrents. As the best they could do, they took refuge in a grove, where, by stretching the canvas over themselves and the steam man, they managed to keep free from the wet.

The steam man was not intended to travel during stormy weather, and so they allowed him to rest.

CHAPTER XVIII.

THE ENCAMPMENT.

The storm proved the severest which the steam man had encountered since leaving St. Louis, and it put an effectual veto on his travels during its continuance, and for a short time afterward.

The prairie was found so soft and slippery that they were compelled to lie by until the sun had hardened it somewhat, when they once more resumed their journey.

As they now had thousands of dollars in their possession, and as all sorts of characters were found on the western plains, it may be said that none of the company ever felt easy.

Baldy Bicknell, the trapper, from his extensive experience and knowledge of the West, was the guide and authority on all matters regarding their travels. He generally kept watch during the night, obtaining what sleep he could through the day. The latter, however, was generally very precarious, as at sight of every horseman or cloud of smoke, they generally awakened him, so as to be sure and commit no serious error.

As the steam man would in all probability attract an attention that might prove exceedingly perilous to the gold in their possession, the trapper concluded it prudent to avoid the regular emigrant routes. Accordingly they turned well to the northward, it being their purpose to strike the Missouri, where they would be pretty sure of intercepting some steamer. Reaching such a place they would unjoint and take apart the steam man, packing it up in such a manner that no one could suspect its identity, and embark for St. Louis.

While this relieved them of the danger from their own race, it increased the probability of an attack upon the Indians, who scarcely ever seemed out of sight.

Their watchfulness, however, was constant, and it was due to this fact, more than any other, that they escaped attack at night for the greater part of their return journey.

Their position in the wagon was so cramped, that the party frequently became excessively wearied, and springing out, trotted and walked for miles alongside the tireless steam giant. Water was abundant, but several times they were put to great inconvenience to obtain wood. On three occasions they were compelled to halt for half a day in order to obtain the necessary supply.

Once the steam man came to a dead standstill in the open prairie, and narrowly escaped blowing up. A hasty examination upon the part of the inventor, revealed the fact that a leak had occurred in the tank, and every drop had run out.

This necessitated the greatest work of all, as water was carried the better part of a mile, and nearly an entire day consumed before enough steam could be raised to induce him to travel to the river, to procure it himself, while the miners acted as convoys.

Late one afternoon, they reached a singular formation in the prairie. It was so rough and uneven that they proceeded with great difficulty and at a slow rate of speed. While advancing in this manner, they found they had unconsciously entered a small narrow valley, the bottom of which was as level as a ground floor. The sides contracted until less than a hundred feet separated them, while they rose to the hight of some eight or ten feet, and the bottom remained compact and firm, making it such easy traveling for the steam man, that the company followed down the valley, at a slow pace, each, however, feeling some misgiving as to the propriety of the course.

"It runs in the right direction," said young Brainerd, "and if it only keeps on as it began, it will prove a very handy thing for us."

"Hyar's as afeared it ain't goin' to keep on in that style," remarked Baldy; "howsumever, you can go ahead awhile longer."

"Naow, that's what I call real queer," remarked Ethan Hopkins, who was stretching his legs by walking alongside the steamer.

"And it's meself that thinks the same," added Mickey, puffing away at his short black pipe. "I don't understand it, as me father obsarved when they found fault with him for breaking another man's head."

"Ef we git into trouble, all we've got to do is to back out," remarked Baldy, as a sort of apology for continuing his advance.

"This fellow doesn't know how to go backward," said Johnny, "but if it prove necessary, we can manage to turn him round."

"All right—go ahead."

At the same moment, the limber Yankee sprung into the wagon, and the steam man started ahead at a speed which was as fast as was prudent.

However, this delightful means of progress was brought to an unexpected standstill, by the sudden and abrupt termination of the valley. It ended completely as though it were an uncompleted canal, the valley rising so quickly to the level of the prairie, that there was no advancing any further, nor turning, nor in fact was there any possible way of extricating themselves from the difficulty, except by working the steam man around, and withdrawing by the same path that they had entered by.

"Well, here we are," remarked the boy, as they came to a standstill, "and what is to be done?"

"Get out of it," was the reply of Hopkins, who advanced several yards further, until he came up on the prairie again, so as to make sure of the exact contour of the ground.

"Did yer ever try to make the thing go up hill?" asked the trapper.

Young Brainerd shook his head.

"Impossible! he would fall over on us, the minute it was attempted. When I was at work at first making him, what do you think was the hardest thing for me to do?"

"Make him go, I s'pose."

"That was difficult, but it was harder work to balance him—that is, so when he lifted up one foot he wouldn't immediately fall over on the same side. I got it fixed after a while, so that he ran as evenly and firmly as an engine, but I didn't fix upon any plan by which he could ascend or descend a hill."

"Can't you make him do it?"

"Not until he is made over again. I would be afraid to attempt to walk him up a moderate inclination, and know it would be sure destruction to start him up such a steep bank as that."

"Then we must work him round, I s'pose."

"There is nothing else that can be done."

"Let's at it, then."

This proved as difficult a job as they imagined. The steam man was so heavy that it was impossible to lift him, but he was shied around as much as possible; and, by the time he had walked across the valley he had half turned round.

He was then coaxed and worked back a short distance, when, with the "leverage" thus gained, the feat was completed, and the steam man stood with his face turned, ready to speed backward the moment that the word might be given.

By this time, however, the day was gone, and darkness was settling over the prairie. Quite a brisk breeze was blowing, and, as the position of the party was sheltered against this annoyance, Hopkins proposed that they should remain where they were until morning.

"We couldn't get a better place," said Johnny Brainerd, who was quite taken with the idea.

"It's a good place and it's a bad one," replied the trapper, who had not yet made up his mind upon the point.

They inquired what he meant by calling it a bad place.

"Ef a lot of the varmints should find we're hyar, don't you see what a purty fix they'd have us in?"

"It would be something like the same box in which we caught them in Wolf Ravine," said young Brainerd.

"Jist the same, perzactly."

"Not the same, either," said Hopkins; "we've got a better chance of getting out than they had. We can jump into the wagon and travel, while they can't; there's the difference."

"S'pose they git down thar ahead of us—how ar' we goin' to git away from them then?"

"Run over them."

"Don't know whether the younker has fixed the engine so it'll run over the skunks, ef it doesn't run up hill."

"It can be made to do that, I think," laughed young Brainerd.

"Afore we stay hyar, I'll take a look round to make sure that thar's some show for us."

The trapper ascended the bank, and, while his companions were occupied in their preparations for encamping, he examined the whole horizon and intervening space, so far as the human eye was capable of doing it. Finding nothing suspicious, he announced to his companions that they would remain where they were until morning.

CHAPTER XIX.

THE DOINGS OF A NIGHT.

It was soon found that the camping ground possessed another advantage which, during the discussion, had been altogether overlooked.

During the afternoon they had shot a fine-looking antelope, cooking a portion at the time upon the prairie. A goodly portion was left, and they now had an opportunity of kindling their fire without the liability of its being seen, as would have been the case had they encamped in any other place.

This being agreed to, the fire was speedily kindled, and the trapper himself began the culinary performance. It was executed with the characteristic excellence of the hunter, and a luscious meal was thus provided for all. At its conclusion, all stretched themselves upon the ground for the purpose of smoking and chatting, as was their usual custom at such times.

The evening whiled pleasantly away, and when it had considerably advanced, the question of who should act as sentinel was discussed. Up to this, young Brainerd had never once performed that duty at night, although he had frequently solicited the privilege. He now asked permission to try his hand. After considerable talk it was agreed that he might do. The trapper had lost so much sleep, that he was anxious to secure a good night's rest, and the careful scrutiny which he had taken of the surrounding prairie convinced him that no danger threatened. So he felt little apprehension in acceding to the wish of the boy.

At a late hour the three men stretched themselves upon the ground, with their blankets gathered about them, and they were soon wrapped in profound slumber, while Johnny, filled with the importance and responsibility of his duty, felt as though he should never need another hour's sleep. He was sure of being able to keep up an unintermitting watch several days and nights, should it become necessary.

Following the usual custom of sentinels, he shouldered his gun and paced back and forth before the smoldering camp-fire, glancing in every direction, so as to make sure that no enemy stole upon him unawares.

It formed a curious picture—the small fire burning in the valley—motionless forms stretched out before it, the huge steam man silent and grim standing near, the dwarfed boy, pacing slowly back and forth, and, above all, the moon shining down upon the silent prairie.

The moon was quite faint, so that only an indistinct view of objects could be seen. Occasionally Johnny clambered up the bank and took a survey of the surrounding plains; but seeing nothing at all suspicious, he soon grew weary of this, and confined his walks to the immediate vicinity of the camp-fire, passing back and forth between the narrow breadth of the valley.

As the hours dragged slowly by, the boy gradually fell into a reverie, which made him almost unconscious of external things. And it was while walking thus that he did not observe a large wolf advance to the edge of the gully, look down, and then whisk back out of sight before the sentinel wheeled in his walk and faced him.

Three separate times was this repeated, the wolf looking down in such an earnest, searching way that it certainly would have excited the remark and curiosity of any one observing it.

The third glance apparently satisfied the wolf; for it lasted for a few seconds, when he withdrew, and lumbered away at an awkward rate, until a rod or two had been passed, when the supposed wolf suddenly rose on its hind legs, the skin and head were shifted to the arms of the Indian, and he continued on at a leisurely gait until he joined fully fifty comrades, who were huddled together in a grove, several hundred yards away.

In the mean time young Brainerd, with his rifle slung over his shoulder, was pacing back and forth in the same deliberate manner, his mind busily engaged on an "improvement" upon the steam man, by which he was to walk backward as well as forward, although he couldn't satisfactorily determine how he was to go up and down hill with safety.

Still occupied in the study of the subject, he took a seat by the half-extinguished camp-fire and gazed dreamily into the embers. It had been a habit with him, when at home, to sit thus for hours, on the long winter evenings, while his mind was so busily at work that he was totally oblivious to whatever was passing around him.

It must have been that the boy seated himself without any thought of the inevitable result of doing so; for none knew better than he that such a thing was fatal to the faithful performance of a sentinel's duty; and the thought that his three companions, in one sense, had put their safety in his hands, would have prevented anything like a forgetfulness of duty.

Be that as it may, the boy had sat thus less than half an hour when a drowsiness began stealing over him. Once he raised his head and fancied he saw a large wolf glaring down upon him from the bank above, but the head was withdrawn so quickly that he was sure it was only a phantom of his brain.

So he did not rise from his seat, but sitting still he gradually sunk lower, until in a short time he was sleeping as soundly as either of the three around him.

Another hour wore away, and the fire smoldered lower and all was still.

Then numerous heads peered over the edge of the ravine for a few seconds, and as suddenly withdrew.

A few minutes later a curious sight might have been seen—a sight somewhat resembling that of a parcel of school-boys making their gigantic snow-balls. The fifty Indians, the greater portion of whom had patiently waited in the adjoining grove, while their horses were securely fastened near, issued like a swarm of locusts and began rolling huge bowlders toward the valley. Some of them were so large that half a dozen only succeeded in moving them with the greatest difficulty.

But they persevered, working with a strange persistency and silence, that gave them the appearance of so many phantoms engaged at their ghostly labor. Not a word was exchanged, even in the most guarded of tones, for each understood his part.

In time half a dozen of these immense stones reached the edge of the ravine. They were ranged side by side, a few feet apart, so as not to be in each other's way, and the Indians stood near, waiting until their work should be completed.

Some signal was then made, and then one of these bowlders rolled down in the ravine. Even this scarcely made any perceptible noise, the yielding ground receiving it like a cushion, as it came to a halt near the center of the valley.

When this was done a second followed suit, being so guided that it did not grate against its companion, but came to rest very near it.

Then another followed, and then another and another, in the same stealthy manner, until over a dozen were in the valley below.

This completed, the phantom-like figures descended like so many shadows, and began tugging again at the bowlders.

Not a word was exchanged, for each knew what was required of him. Fully an hour more was occupied, by which time the labor was finished.

The bowlders were arranged in the form of an impassable wall across the narrow valley, and the steam man was so thoroughly imprisoned that no human aid could ever extricate him.

CHAPTER XX.

THE CONCLUDING CATASTROPHE.

Baldy Bicknell, the trapper, was the first to discover the peril of himself and party.

When the Indians had completed their work it lacked only an hour of daylight. Having done all that was necessary, the savages took their stations behind the wall, lying flat upon the ground, where they were invisible to the whites, but where every motion of theirs could be watched and checkmated.

When the trapper opened his eyes he did not stir a limb—a way into which he had got during his long experience on the frontiers. He merely moved his head from side to side, so as to see anything that was to be seen.

The first object that met his eye was the boy Brainerd, sound asleep. Apprehensive then that something had occurred, he turned his startled gaze in different directions, scanning everything as well as it could be done in the pale moonlight.

When he caught sight of the wall stretched across the valley, he rubbed his eyes, and looked at it again and again, scarcely able to credit his senses. He was sure it was not there a few hours before, and he could not comprehend what it could mean; but it was a verity, and his experience told him that it could be the work of no one except the Indians, who had outwitted him at last.

His first feeling was that of indignation toward the boy who had permitted this to take place while he was asleep, but his mind quickly turned upon the more important matter of meeting the peril, which, beyond all doubt, was of the most serious character.

As yet he had not stirred his body, and looking toward the prison wall, he caught a glimpse of the phantom-like figures, as they occasionally flitted about, securing the best possible position, before the whites should awake.

This glimpse made everything plain to the practical mind of Baldy Bicknell. He comprehended that the red-skins had laid a plan to entrap the steam man, more than to entrap themselves, and that, so far as he could judge, they had succeeded completely.

It was the tightest fix in which he had ever been caught, and his mind, fertile as it was in expedients at such crises, could see no way of meeting the danger.

He knew the Indians had horses somewhere at command, while neither he nor his comrades had a single one. The steam man would be unable to pass that formidable wall, as it was not to be supposed that he had been taught the art of leaping.

Whatever plan of escape was determined upon it was evident that the steamer would have to be abandoned; and this necessitated, as an inevitable consequence, that the whites would have to depend upon their legs. The Missouri river was at no great distance, and if left undisturbed they could make it without difficulty, but there was a prospect of anything sooner than that they would be allowed to depart in peace, after leaving the steam man behind.

The trapper, as had been his invariable custom, had carefully noted the contour of the surrounding prairie, before they had committed the important act of encamping in the gorge or hollow. He remembered the grove at some distance, and was satisfied that the barbarians had left their horses there, while they had gathered behind the wall to wait the critical moment.

By the time these thoughts had fairly taken shape in his brain it was beginning to grow light, and with a premonitary yawn and kick he rose to his feet and began stirring the fire. He was well aware that although he and his companions were a fair target for the rifles of their enemies, yet they would not fire. Their plan of action did not comprehend that, though it would have settled everything in their favor without delay.

"I declare I have been asleep!" exclaimed Brainerd, as he began rubbing his eyes.

"Yes. You're a purty feller to make a sentinel of, ain't you?" replied the trapper, in disgust.

"I hope nothing has happened," answered Johnny, feeling that he deserved all the blame that could be laid upon him.

"Not much, exceptin' while yer war snoozin' the reds have come down and got us all in a nice box."

The boy was certain he was jesting until he saw the expression of his face.

"Surely, Baldy, it is not as bad as that?"

"Do you see that ar?" demanded the trapper, pointing toward the wall, which the youngster could not help observing.

"How comes that to be there?"

"The red-skins put it thar. Can yer steam man walk over that?"

"Certainly not; but we can remove them."

"Do yer want to try it, younker?"

"I'm willing to help."

"Do yer know that ar' somethin' less nor a hundred red-skins ahind them, jist waitin' fur yer to try that thing?"

"Good heavens! can it be possible?"

"Ef you don't b'l'eve it, go out and look for yerself, that's all."

The boy, for the first time, comprehended the peril in which he had brought his friends by his own remissness, and his self-accusation was so great, that, for a few moments, he forgot the fact that he was exposed to the greatest danger of his life.

By this time Ethan and Mickey awoke, and were soon made to understand their predicament. As a matter of course, they were all disposed to blame the author of this; but when they saw how deeply he felt his own shortcoming, all three felt a natural sympathy for him.

"There's no use of talkin' how we came to get hyar," was the philosophical remark of the trapper; "it's 'nough to know that we are hyar, with a mighty slim chance of ever gettin' out ag'in."

"It's enough to make a chap feel down in the mouth, as me friend Jonah observed when he went down the throat of the whale," said Mickey.

"How is it they don't shoot us?" asked Hopkins; "we can't git out of their way, and they've got us in fair range."

"What's the use of doin' that? Ef they kill us, that'll be the end on't; but ef they put thar claws on us, they've got us sure, and can have a good time toastin' us while they yelp and dance around."

All shuddered at the fearful picture drawn by the hunter.

"Jerusalem! don't I wish I was to hum in Connect'cut!"

"And it's myself that would be plaised to be sitting in the parlor at Ballyduff wid me own Bridget Maghlaghaghighagh, listenin' while she breathed swate vows, afther making her supper upon praties and inions."

"I think I'd ruther be hyar," was the commentary of the trapper upon the expressed wish of the Irishman.

"Why can't yees touch up the staam man, and make him hop owver them shtones?" asked Mickey, turning toward the boy, whom, it was noted, appeared to be in deep reverie again.

Not until he was addressed several times did he look up. Then he merely shook his head, to signify that the thing was impossible.

"Any fool might know better than that," remarked the Yankee, "for if he could jump over, where would be the wagon?"

"That 'ud foller, av coorse."

"No; there's no way of getting the steam man out of here. He is a gone case, sure, and it looks as though we were ditto. Jerusalem! I wish all the gold was back in Wolf Ravine, and we war a thousand miles from this place."

"Wishing 'll do no good; there's only one chance I see, and that ain't no chance at all."

All, including the boy, eagerly looked up to hear the explanation.

"Some distance from hyar is some timbers, and in thar the reds have left their animals. Ef we start on a run for the timbers, git thar ahead of the Ingins, mount thar hosses and put, thar'll be some chance. Yer can see what chance thar is fur that."

It looked as hopeless as the charge of the Light Brigade.

Young Brainerd now spoke.

"It was I who got you into trouble, and it is I, that, with the blessing of Heaven, am going to get you out of it."

The three now looked eagerly at him.

"Is there no danger of the Indians firing upon us?" he asked of the hunter.

"Not unless we try to run away."

"All right; it is time to begin."

The boy's first proceeding was to kindle a fire in the boiler of the steam man. When it was fairly blazing, he conti ued to heap in wood, until a fervent heat was produced such as it had never experienced before. Still he threw in wood, and kept the water low in the boiler, until there was a most prodigious pressure of steam, making its escape at half a dozen orifices.

When all the wood was thrown in that it could contain, and portions of the iron sheeting could be seen becoming red-hot, he ceased this, and began trying the steam.

"How much can he hold?" inquired Hopkins.

"One hundred and fifty pounds."

"How much is on now?"

"One hundred and forty-eight, and rising."

"Good heavens! it will blow up!" was the exclamation, as the three shrunk back, appalled at the danger.

"Not for a few minutes; have you the gold secured, and the guns, so as to be ready to run?"

They were ready to run at any moment; the gold was always secured about their persons and it required but a moment to snatch up the weapons.

"When it blows up, run!" was the admonition of the boy.

The steam man was turned directly toward the wall, and a full head of steam let on. It started away with a bound, instantly reaching a speed of forty miles an hour.

The next moment it struck the bowlders with a terrific crash, shot on over its face, leaving the splintered wagon behind, and at the instant of touching ground upon the opposite side directly among the thunderstruck Indians, it exploded its boiler!

The shock of the explosion was terrible. It was like the bursting of an immense bomb-shell, the steam man being blown into thousands of fragments, that scattered death and destruction in every direction. Falling in the very center of the crouching Indians, it could but make a terrible destruction of life, while those who escaped unharmed, were beside themselves with consternation.

This was the very thing upon which young Brainerd had counted, and for which he made his calculations. When he saw it leap toward the wall in such a furious manner, he knew the inevitable consequence, and gave the word to his friends to take to their legs.

All three dashed up the bank, and reaching the surface of the prairie, Baldy Bicknell took the lead, exclaiming:

"Now for the wood yonder!"

As they reached the grove, one or two of the number glanced back, but saw nothing of the pursuing Indians. They had not yet recovered from their terror.

Not a moment was to be lost. The experienced eye of the trapper lost no time in selecting the very best Indian horses, and a moment later all four rode out from the grove at a full gallop, and headed toward the Missouri.

The precise result of the steam man's explosion was never learned. How many were killed and wounded could only be conjectured; but the number certainly was so great that our friends saw nothing more of them.

They evidently had among their number those who had become pretty well acquainted with the steam man, else they would not have laid the plan which they did for capturing him.

Being well mounted, the party made the entire journey to Independence on horseback. From this point they took passage to St. Louis, where the gold was divided, and the party separated, and since then have seen nothing of each other.

Mickey McSquizzle returned to Ballyduff Kings county, Ireland, where, we heard, he and his gentle Bridget, are in the full enjoyment of the three thousand pounds he carried with him.

Ethan Hopkins settled down with the girl of his choice in Connecticut, where, at last accounts, he was doing as well as could be expected.

Baldy Bicknell, although quite a wealthy man, still clings to his wandering habits, and spends the greater portion of his time on the prairies.

With the large amount of money realized from his western trip, Johnny Brainerd is educating himself at one of the best schools in the country. When he shall have completed his course, it is his intention to construct another steam man, capable of more wonderful performances than the first.

So let our readers and the public generally be on the lookout.

THE END.

Waverley Library.

1 The Masked Bride. By Mrs. Mary R. Crowell.
2 Was It Love? By Wm. Mason Turner.
3 The Girl Wife. By Bartley T. Campbell.
4 A Brave Heart. By Arabella Southworth.
5 Bessie Raynor. By Wm. Mason Turner, M. D.
6 The Secret Marriage. By Sara Claxton.
7 A Daughter of Eve. By Mrs. Crowell.
8 Heart to Heart. By Arabella Southworth.
9 Alone in the World. By author of "Clifton."
10 A Pair of Gray Eyes. By Rose Kennedy.
11 Entangled. By Henrietta Thackeray.
12 His Lawful Wife. By Mrs. Stephens.
13 Madcap. By Corinne Cushman.
14 Why I Married Him. By Sara Claxton.
15 A Fair Face. By Bartley T. Campbell.
16 Trust Her Not. By Margaret Leicester.
17 A Loyal Lover. By Arabella Southworth.
18 His Idol. By Mrs. Mary Reed Crowell.
19 The Broken Betrothal. By Mary G. Halpine.
20 Orphan Nell. By Agile Penne.
21 Now and Forever. By H. Thackeray.
22 The Bride of an Actor. By the author of "Alone in the World," etc., etc.
23 Leap Year. By Sara Claxton.
24 Her Face Was Her Fortune. By E. Blaine.
25 Only a Schoolmistress. By A. Southworth.
26 Without a Heart. By Col. P. Ingraham.
27 Was She a Coquette? By H. Thackeray.
28 Sybil Chase. By Mrs. Ann S. Stephens.
29 For Her Dear Sake. By Sara Claxton.
30 The Bouquet Girl. By Agile Penne.
31 A Mad Marriage. By Mary A. Denison.
32 Mariana, the Prima Donna. By A. Southworth.
33 The Three Sisters. By Alice Fleming.
34 A Marriage of Convenience. By Sara Claxton.
35 All Against Her. By Clara Augusta.
36 Sir Archer's Bride. By Arabella Southworth.
37 The Country Cousin. By Rose Kennedy.
38 His Own Again. By Arabella Southworth.
39 Flirtation. By Ralph Royal.
40 Pledged to Marry. By Sara Claxton.
41 Blind Devotion. By Alice Fleming.
42 Beatrice, the Beautiful. By A. Southworth.
43 The Baronet's Secret. By Sara Claxton.
44 The Only Daughter. By Alice Fleming.
45 Her Hidden Foe. By Arabella Southworth.
46 The Little Heiress. By M. A. Denison.
47 Because She Loved Him. By Alice Fleming.
48 In Spite of Herself. By S. R. Sherwood.
49 His Heart's Mistress. By Arabella Southworth.
50 The Cuban Heiress. By Mrs. Mary A. Denison.
51 Two Young Girls. By Alice Fleming.
52 The Winged Messenger. By Mary Reed Crowel.
53 Agnes Hope. By W. M. Turner, M. D.
54 One Woman's Heart. By George S. Kaime.
55 She Did Not Love Him. By Arabella Southworth.
56 Love-Mad. By Wm. M. Turner, M. D.
57 A Brave Girl. By Alice Fleming.
58 The Ebon Mask. By Mary Reed Crowell.
59 A Widow's Wiles. By Rachel Bernhardt.
60 Cecil's Deceit. By Jennie Davis Burton.
61 A Wicked Heart. By Sara Claxton.
62 The Maniac Bride. By Margaret Blount.
63 The Creole Sisters. By Anna E. Porter.
64 What Jealousy Did. By Alice Fleming.
65 The Wife's Secret. By Col. Juan Lewis.
66 A Brother's Sin. By Rachel Bernhardt.
67 Forbidden Bans. By Arabella Southworth.
68 Weavers and Weft. By Mrs. M. E. Braddon.
69 Camille. By Alexander Dumas.
70 The Two Orphans. By D'Ennery.
71 My Young Wife. By My Young Wife's Husband.
72 The Two Widows. By Annie Thomas.
73 Rose Michel. By Maude Hilton.
74 Cecil Castlemaine's Gage. By Ouida.
75 The Black Lady of Duna. By J. S. Le Fanu.
76 Charlotte Temple. By Mrs. Rowson.
77 Christian Oakley's Mistake. By Miss Mulock.
78 My Young Husband. By Myself.
79 A Queen Amongst Women. By the author of "Dora Thorn."
80 Her Lord and Master. By Florence Marryat.
81 Lucy Temple.
82 A Long Time Ago. By Meta Orred.
83 Playing for High Stakes. By Annie Thomas
84 The Laurel Bush. By Miss Mulock.
85 Led Astray. By Octave Feuillet.
86 Janet's Repentance. By George Eliot.
87 Romance of a Poor Young Man. By O. Feuillet.
88 A Terrible Deed. By Emma G. Jones.
89 A Gilded Sin.
90 The Author's Daughter. By Mary Howitt.
91 The Jilt. By Charles Reade.
92 Eileen Alanna. By Dennis O'Sullivan.
93 Love's Victory. By B. L. Farjeon.
94 The Quiet Heart. By Mrs. Oliphant.
95 Lettice Arnold. By Mrs. Marsh.
96 Haunted Hearts. By Rachel Bernhardt.
97 Hugh Melton. By Catharine King.
98 Alice Learmont. By Miss Mulock.
99 Marjorie Bruce's Lover. By Mary Patrick.
100 Through Fire and Water. By Fred. Talbot.
101 Hannah. By Miss Mulock.
102 Peg Woffington. By Charles Reade.
103 A Desperate Deed. By Erskine Boyd.
104 Shadows on the Snow. By B. L. Farjeon.
105 The Great Hoggarty Diamond. By W. M. Thackeray.
106 From Dreams to Waking. By E. Lynn Linton.
107 Poor Zeph. By F. W. Robinson.
108 The Sad Fortunes of the Rev. Amos Barton. By George Eliot.
109 Bread-and-Cheese and Kisses. By B. L. Farjeon
110 The Wandering Heir. By C. Reade.
111 The Brother's Bet. By E. F. Carlen.
112 A Hero. By Miss Mulock.
113 Paul and Virginia. From the French of Bernardin de St. Pierre.
114 'Twas in Trafalgar's Bay. By Walter Besant and James Rice.
115 The Maid of Killeena. By William Black.
116 Hetty. By Henry Kingsley.
117 The Wayside Cross. By Capt. E. A. Milman.
118 The Vicar of Wakefield. By Oliver Goldsmith
119 Maud Mohan. By Annie Thomas.
120 Thaddeus of Warsaw. By Miss Jane Porter.
121 The King of No-Land. By B. L. Farjeon.
122 Lovel the Widower. By W. M. Thackeray.
123 An Island Pearl. By B. L. Farjeon.
124 Cousin Phillis.
125 Leila; or, The Siege of Grenada. By Edward Bulwer, (Lord Lytton.)
126 When the Ship Comes Home. By Walter Besant and James Rice.
127 One of the Family. By James Payn.
128 The Birthright. By Mrs. Gore.
129 Motherless; or, The Farmer's Sweetheart. By Colonel Prentiss Ingraham.
130 Homeless; or, The Two Orphan Girls in New York. By Albert W. Aiken.
131 Sister against Sister; or, The Rivalry of Hearts. By Mrs. Mary Reed Crowell.
132 Sold for Gold; or, Almost Lost. By Mrs. M. V. Victor.
133 Lord Roth's Sin; or, Betrothed at the Cradle. By Mrs. Georgiana Dickens.
134 Did He Love Her? By Bartley T. Campbell.
135 Sinned Against; or, Almost in His Power. By Lillian Lovejoy.
136 Was She His Wife? By Mary Reed Crowell.
137 The Village on the Cliff. By Miss Thackeray.
138 Poor Valeria; or, The Broken Troth. By Margaret Blount.
139 Margaret Graham. By G. P. R. James.
140 Without Mercy. By Bartley T. Campbell.
141 Honor Bound. By Lillian Lovejoy.
142 Fleeing from Love. Mrs. Harriet Irving.
143 Abducted. By Rett Winwood.
144 A Strange Marriage. By Lillian Lovejoy.
145 Two Girls' Lives. By Mrs. Mary Reed Crowell.
146 A Desperate Venture. By Arabella Southworth
147 The War of Hearts. By Corinne Cushman.
148 Which Was the Woman? By Sara Claxton.
149 An Ambitious Girl. By Frances H. Davenport.
150 Love Lord of All. By Alice May Fleming.
151 A Wild Girl. By Corinne Cushman.
152 A Man's Sacrifice. By Harriet Irving.
153 Did She Sin? By Mrs. Mary Reed Crowell.

A new issue every week.

For sale by all Newsdealers, price five cents each, or sent, postage paid, on receipt of six cents.

BEADLE AND ADAMS, Publishers,
98 William street, Y. N.

BEADLE AND ADAMS'

STANDARD DIME PUBLICATIONS.

Speakers.

Beadle and Adams have now on their lists the following highly desirable and attractive text-books, prepared expressly for schools, families, etc. Each volume contains 100 large pages, printed from clear, open type, comprising the best collection of Dialogues, Dramas and Recitations, (burlesque, comic and otherwise.) The Dime Speakers for the season of 1882—as far as now issued—embrace twenty-four volumes, viz.:

1. American Speaker.	13. School Speaker.
2. National Speaker.	14. Ludicrous Speaker.
3. Patriotic Speaker.	15. Komikal Speaker.
4. Comic Speaker.	16. Youth's Speaker.
5. Elocutionist.	17. Eloquent Speaker.
6. Humorous Speaker.	18. Hail Columbia Speaker.
7. Standard Speaker.	
8. Stump Speaker.	19. Serio-Comic Speaker.
9. Juvenile Speaker.	20. Select Speaker.
10. Spread-Eagle Speaker	21. Funny Speaker.
11. Dime Debater.	22. Jolly Speaker.
12. Exhibition Speaker.	23. Dialect Speaker.

24. Dime Book of Recitations and Readings.

These books are replete with choice pieces for the School-room, the Exhibition, for Homes, etc. They are drawn from fresh sources, and contain some of the choicest oratory of the times. 75 to 100 Declamations and Recitations in each book.

Dialogues.

The Dime Dialogues, each volume 100 pages, embrace twenty-nine books, viz.:

Dialogues No. One.	Dialogues No. Fifteen.
Dialogues No. Two.	Dialogues No. Sixteen.
Dialogues No. Three.	Dialogues No. Seventeen.
Dialogues No. Four.	Dialogues No. Eighteen
Dialogues No. Five.	Dialogues No. Nineteen.
Dialogues No. Six.	Dialogues No. Twenty.
Dialogues No. Seven.	Dialogues No. Twenty-one.
Dialogues No. Eight.	Dialogues No. Twenty-two.
Dialogues No. Nine.	Dialogues No. Twenty-three.
Dialogues No. Ten.	Dialogues No. Twenty-four.
Dialogues No. Eleven.	Dialogues No. Twenty-five.
Dialogues No. Twelve.	Dialogues No. Twenty-six.
Dialogues No. Thirteen.	Dialogues No. Twenty-seven.
Dialogues No. Fourteen	Dialogues No. Twenty-eight.

Dialogues No. Twenty-nine.

15 to 25 Dialogues and Dramas in each book.

These volumes have been prepared with especial reference to their *availability* in *all* school-rooms, They are adapted to schools with or without the furniture of a stage, and introduce a range of characters suited to scholars of every grade, both male and female. It is fair to assume that no volumes yet offered to schools, *at any price*, contain so many *available* and useful dialogues and dramas, serious and comic.

Dramas and Readings.

164 12mo Pages. 20 Cents.

For Schools, Parlors, Entertainments and the Amateur Stage, comprising Original Minor Dramas, Comedy, Farce, Dress Pieces, Humorous Dialogue and Burlesque, by noted writers; and Recitations and Readings, new and standard, of the greatest celebrity and interest. Edited by Prof. A. M. Russell.

DIME HAND-BOOKS.

Young People's Series.

Beadle's Dime Hand-Books for Young People cover a wide range of subjects, and are especially adapted to their end. They constitute at once the cheapest and most useful works yet put into the market for popular circulation.

Ladies' Letter-Writer.	Book of Games.
Gents' Letter-Writer.	Fortune-Teller.
Book of Etiquette.	Lovers' Casket.
Book of Verses.	Ball-room Companion.
Book of Dreams.	Book of Beauty.

Hand-Books of Games.

Beadle's Dime Hand-Books of Games and Popular Hand-Books cover a variety of subjects, and are especially adapted to their end.

Handbook of Summer Sports.

Book of Croquet.	Yachting and Rowing
Chess Instructor.	Riding and Driving.
Cricket and Football.	Book of Pedestrianism.
Guide to Swimming.	

Handbook of Winter Sports—Skating, etc.

Manuals for Housewives.

Beadle's Dime Family Series aims to supply a class of text-books and manuals fitted for every person's use—the old and the young, the learned and the unlearned. They are of conceded value.

1. Cook Book.	4. Family Physician.
2. Recipe Book.	5. Dressmaking and Millinery
3. Housekeeper's Guide.	

Lives of Great Americans

Are presented complete and authentic biographies of many of the men who have added luster to the Republic by their lives and deeds. The series embraces:

I.—George Washington.	VII.—David Crockett.
II.—John Paul Jones.	VIII.—Israel Putnam.
III.—Mad Anthony Wayne	X.—Tecumseh.
IV.—Ethan Allen.	XI.—Abraham Lincoln.
V.—Marquis de Lafayette.	XII.—Pontiac.
VI.—Daniel Boone.	XIII.—Ulysses S. Grant.

The above publications for sale by all newsdealers or will be sent, post-paid, on receipt of price, by BEADLE & ADAMS, 98 William St., N. Y.

ON THE DECK OF THE STEAMER THAT STRANGE DUEL BEGAN.

TIP TOP WEEKLY

AN IDEAL PUBLICATION FOR THE AMERICAN YOUTH

Issued Weekly—By Subscription $2.50 per year. Entered as Second Class Matter at the N. Y. Post Office, by STREET & SMITH, 238 William St., N. Y. Entered According to Act of Congress, in the year 1899 in the Office of the Librarian of Congress, Washington, D. C.

No. 158.   NEW YORK, April 22, 1899.   Price Five Cents.

Contents of This Number. Page.
FRANK MERRIWELL'S NOBILITY; or, The Tragedy of the Ocean Tramp. - - - 1.

Frank Merriwell's Nobility

OR, THE

TRAGEDY OF THE OCEAN TRAMP

By BURT L. STANDISH.

CHAPTER I.

OFF FOR EUROPE.

"Off——"

"At last!"

"Hurrah!"

The tramp steamer "Eagle" swung out from the pier and was fairly started on her journey from New York to Liverpool.

On the deck of the steamer stood a group of five persons, three of whom had given utterance to the exclamations recorded above.

On the pier swarmed a group of Yale students, waving hands, hats, handkerchiefs, bidding farewell to their five friends and acquaintances on the steamer. Over the water came the familiar Yale cheer. From the steamer it was answered.

In the midst of the group on deck was Frank Merriwell. Those around him were Bruce Browning, Jack Diamond, Harry Rattleton and Tutor Wellington Maybe.

It was Frank's scheme to spend the summer months abroad, while studying in the attempt to catch up with his class and pass examinations on re-entering college in the fall. And he had brought along his three friends, Browning, Diamond and Rattleton. They were on their way to England.

Frank was happy. Fortune had dealt him a heavy blow when he was compelled by poverty to leave dear old Yale, but he had faced the world bravely, and he had struggled like a man. Hard work, long hours and poor pay had not daunted him.

At the very start he had shown that he possessed something more than ordinary ability, and while working on the railroad he had forced his way upward step by step till it seemed that he was in a fair way to reach the top of the ladder.

Then came disaster again. He had lost his position on the railroad, and once more he was forced to face the world and begin over.

Some lads would have been discouraged. Frank Merriwell was not. He set his teeth firmly and struck out once more. He kept his mouth shut and his eyes open. The first honorable thing that came to his hand to do he did. Thus it happened that he found himself on the stage.

Frank's success as an actor had been phenomenal. Of course, to begin with, he had natural ability, but that was not the only thing that won success for him. He had courage, push, determination, stick-to-it-iveness. When he started to do a thing he kept at it till he did it.

Frank united observation and study. He learned everything he could about the stage and about acting by talking with the members of the company and by watching to see how things were done.

He had a good head and plenty of sense. He knew better than to copy after the ordinary actors in the road company to which he belonged. He had seen good acting enough to be able to distinguish between the good and bad. Thus it came about that the bad models about him did not exert a pernicious influence upon him.

Frank believed there were books that would aid him. He found them. He found one on "Acting and Actors," and from it he learned that no actor ever becomes really and truly great that does not have a clear and distinct enunciation and a correct pronunciation. That is the beginning. Then comes the study of the meaning of the words to be spoken and the effect produced by the manner in which they are spoken.

He studied all this, and he went further. He read up on "Traditions of the Stage," and he came to know all about its limitations and its opportunities.

From this it was a natural step to the study of the construction of plays. He found books of criticism on plays and playwriting, and he mastered them. He found books that told how to construct plays, and he mastered them.

Frank Merriwell was a person with a vivid imagination and great mechanical and constructive ability. Had this not been so, he might have studied forever and still never been able to write a successful play. In him there was something study could not give, but study and effort brought it out. He wrote a play.

"John Smith of Montana" was a success. Frank played the leading part, and he made a hit.

Then fate rose up and again dealt him a body blow. A scene in the play was almost exactly like a scene in another play, written previously. The author and owner of the other play called on the law to "protect" him. An injunction was served on Merry to restrain him from playing "John Smith." He stood face to face with a lawsuit.

Frank investigated, and his investigation convinced him that it was almost certain he would be defeated if the case was carried into the courts.

He withdrew "John Smith."

Frank had confidence in himself. He had written a play that was successful, and he believed he could write another. Already he had one skeletonized. The frame work was constructed, the plot was elaborated, the characters were ready for his use.

He wrote a play of something with which he was thoroughly familiar—college life. The author or play-maker of ability who writes of that with which he is familiar stands a good chance of making a success. Young and inexperienced writers love to write of those things with which they are unfamiliar, and they wonder why it is that they fail.

They go too far away from home for their subject.

At first Frank's play was not a success. The moment he discovered this he set himself down to find out why it was not a success. He did not look at it as the author, but as a critical manager to whom it had been offered might have done.

He found the weak spots. One was its name. People in general did not understand the title, "For Old Eli." There was nothing "catchy" or drawing about it.

He gave it another name. He called it, "True Blue: A Drama of College Life."

The name proved effective.

He rewrote much of the play. He strengthened the climax of the third act, and introduced a mechanical effect that was very ingenious. And when the piece next went on the road it met with wonderful success everywhere.

Thus Frank snatched success from defeat.

It is a strange thing that when a person fights against fate and conquers, when fortune begins to smile, when the tide fairly turns his way, then everything seems to come to him. The things which seemed so far away and so impossible of attainment suddenly appear within easy reach or come tumbling into his lap of their own accord.

It was much this way with Frank. He had dreamed of going back to college some time, but that time had seemed far, far away. Success brought it nearer.

But then it came tumbling into his lap. No one had been found to claim the fortune he discovered in the Utah Desert. Investigation had shown that there were no living relatives of the man who had guarded the treasure till his death. That treasure had been turned over to Frank.

Frank had brought his play to New Haven, and his old college friends had given him a rousing welcome. And now he had made plans to return to college in the fall, while his play was to be carried on the road by a well-known and experienced theatrical manager.

The friends who had been with Frank when he discovered the treasure, with the exception of Toots, the colored boy, had refused to accept shares of the fortune. Then Merry had insisted on taking them abroad with him, and here they were on the stamer "Eagle," bound for Liverpool.

Toots, dressed like a "swell," was on the pier. He shouted with the others, waving his silk hat.

The crowd was cheering now:

"Beka Co ax Co ax Co ax!
Breka Co ax Co ax Co ax!
O——up! O——up!
Parabolou!
Yale! Yale! Yale!
'Rah! 'rah! 'rah!
Yale!"

CHAPTER II.

SURPRISING THE FRENCHMAN.

"Bah! Ze American boy, he make me —what you call eet?—vera tired!"

Frank turned quickly and saw the speaker standing near the rail not far away. He was a man between thirty-five and forty years of age, dressed in a traveling suit, and having a pointed black beard. He was smoking.

An instant feeling of aversion swept over Merry. He saw the person was a supercilious Frenchman, critical, sneering, insolent, a man intolerant with everything not of France and the French.

This man was speaking to another person, who seemed to be a servant or valet, and who was very polite and fawning in all his retorts.

"Ah! look at ze collectshung on ze pier," continued the sneering speaker. "Someone say zey belong to ze great American college. Zey act like zey belong to ze—ze—what you call eet?—ze menageray. Zey yell, shout, jump—act like ze lunatic."

"It is possible, monsieur," said Frank, with a grim smile, "that they are copying their manners after Frenchmen at a Dreyfus demonstration."

The foreigner turned haughtily and stared at Frank. Then he shrugged his shoulders, turned away and observed to his companion:

"Jes' like all ze Americans—ah!—what eez ze word?—fresh."

The other man bowed and rubbed his hands together.

"Haw!" grunted Browning, lazily. "How do you like that, Frank?"

"Oh, I don't mind it," murmured Merry. "I consider the source from which it came, and regard it as of no consequence."

Diamond was glaring at the Frenchman, for it made his hot Southern blood boil to hear a foreigner criticize anything American. Like all youthful Americans, his great admiration and love for his own country made him intolerant of criticism.

Frank had a cooler head, and he was not so easily ruffled.

Rattleton was unable to express his feelings.

Tutor Maybe looked somewhat perturbed, for he was an exceedingly mild and peaceable man, and the slightest suggestion of trouble was enough to agitate him.

But the Frenchman did not deign to look toward Frank again, and it seemed that all danger of trouble was past.

The "Eagle" sailed slowly down the harbor, signaling now and then to other boats.

Frank, Jack, Bruce and Harry formed a fine quartette, and they sang:

"Soon we'll be in London town;
  Sing, my lads, yo! heave, my lads, ho!
And see the queen, with her golden crown;
  Heave, my lads, yo-ho!"

The Frenchman made an impatient gesture, and showed annoyance, which caused Frank to laugh.

Behind them Brooklyn Bridge spanned the river, looking slender and graceful, like a thing hung in the air by delicate threads.

Close at hand were Governor's Island and the Statue of Liberty. The Frenchman was pointing it out.

"Ze greatest work of art in all America,'" he declared, enthusiastically; "an' France give zat to America. Ze Americans nevare think to put eet zere themselves. France do more for America zan any ozare nation, but ze Americans forget. Zey forget Lafayette. Zey forget France make it possibul for zem to conquaire Engalande an' get ze freedom zey ware aftaire. An' now zey—zey—what you call eet?—toady to Engalande. Zey pretende to love ze Engaleesh. Bah! Uncale Sam an' John Bull both need to have some of ze conaceit taken out away from zem."

"It would take more than France, Spain, Italy and all the rest of the dago nations to do the job!" spluttered Harry Rattleton, who could not keep still longer.

"Maurel," said the Frenchman, speaking to his companion, "t'row ze insolent dog ovareboard!"

"Oui, monsieur!"

Quick as thought the man sprang toward Harry, as if determined to execute the command of his master.

He did not put his hands on Rattleton, for Frank was equally swift in his movements, and blocked the fellows' way, coolly saying:

"I wouldn't try it if I were you."

"Out of ze way!" snarled the man, who was an athlete in build. "If you don't, I put you ovare, too!"

"I don't think you will."

"Put him ovare, Maurel, ordered the Frenchman, with deadly coolness.

The athletic servant clutched Frank, but, with a twist and a turn, Merry broke the hold instantly, kicked the fellow's feet from beneath him, and dropped him heavily to the deck.

Bruce Browning stooped and picked the man up as if he were an infant. Every year seemed to add something to the big collegian's wonderful strength, and now the astounded Frenchman found himself unable to wiggle.

Browning held the man over the rail, turning to Frank to ask:

"Shall I give him a bath, Merriwell?"

"I think you hadn't better," laughed Frank. "Perhaps he can't swim, and ——"

"He can swim or sink," drawled Bruce. "It won't make any difference if he sinks. Only another insolent Frenchman out of the way."

The master was astounded. Up to that moment he had regarded the young Americans as scarcely more than boys, and he had fancied his athletic servant could easily frighten them. Instead of that, something quite unexpected by him had happened.

The astounded servant showed signs of terror, but in vain he struggled. He was helpless in the clutch of the giant collegian.

The master seemed about to interfere, but Frank Merriwell confronted him in a manner that spoke as plainly as words.

"Out of ze way!" snarled the man.

"Speaking to me?" inquired Merry, lifting his eyebrows.

"Oui! oui!"

"I am sorry, but I can't accommodate you till my friend gets through with your servant, who was extremely fresh, like most Frenchmen."

"Zis to me!"

"Yes."

"Sare, I am M. Rouen Montfort, an' I ——"

"It makes no difference to me if you are the high mogul of France. You are on the deck of an English vessel, and you are dealing with Americans."

The Frenchman flung his cigar aside and seemed to feel for a weapon.

Frank stood there quietly, his eyes watching every movement.

"If you have what you are seeking about your person," he said, with perfect calmness, "I advise you not to draw it. If you do, as sure as you are sailing down New York harbor, I'll fling you over the rail, weapon and all!"

That was business, and it was not boasting. Frank actually meant to throw the man into the water if he drew a weapon.

M. Rouen Montfort paused and stared at Frank Merriwell, beginning to understand that he was not dealing with an ordinary youth.

"Fool!" he panted. "You geeve me ze eensult I will haf your life!"

"You have already insulted me, my friends and everything American. It's your turn to take a little of the medicine."

"Eef we were een France——"

"Which we are not. We are still in America, the land of the free. But I don't care to have a quarrel with you.

Bruce put the fellow down. If he minds his business in the future, don't throw him overboard."

"All right," grunted the big fellow; "but I was just going to drop him in the wet."

He put the man down, and the fellow seemed undecided what to do.

Harry Rattleton laughed.

"Now wake a talk—no, I mean take a walk," he cried. "It will be a good thing for your health."

"Come, Maurel," said the master, with an attempt at dignity; "come away from ze fellows!"

Maurel was glad enough to do so. He had thought to frighten the youths without the least trouble, but had been handled with such ease that even after it was all over he wondered how it could have happened.

M. Montfort walked away with great dignity, and Maurel followed, talking savagely and swiftly in French.

"Well, it wasn't very hard to settle them," grinned Browning.

"But we have not settled them," declared Frank. "There will be further trouble with M. Rouen Montfort and his man Maurel."

CHAPTER III.

A FRESH YOUNG MAN.

Frank and his three friends had a stateroom together. The tutor was given a room with other parties.

The weather for the first two days was fine, and the young collegians enjoyed every minute, not one of them having a touch of sea-sickness till the third day.

Then Rattleton was seized, and he lay in his bunk, groaning and dismal, even though he tried to be cheerful at times.

Browning enjoyed everything, even Rattleton's misery, for he could be lazy to his heart's content.

They had enlivened the times by singing songs, those of a nautical flavor, such as "Larboard Watch" and "A Life on the Ocean Wave," having the preference.

Now it happened that the Frenchman occupied a room adjoining, and he was very much annoyed by their singing. He pounded on the partition, and expressed his feelings in very lurid language, but that amused them, and they sang the louder.

"M. Montfort seems to get very agitated,'" said Frank, laughing.

"But I hardly think there is any danger that he will do more than hammer on the partition," grunted Bruce. "He's kept away from us since he found he could not frighten anybody."

"He's a bluffer," was Diamond's opinion.

"He's a great fellow to play cards," said Merry. "But he seems to ply for something more than amusement."

"How's that?" asked Jack, interested

"I've noticed that he never cares for whist or any game where there are no stakes. He gets into a game only when there's something to be won."

"Well, it seems to me that he's struck a poor crowd on this boat if he's looking for suckers. He should have shipped on an ocean liner. What does he play?"

"He seems to have taken a great fancy to draw poker. 'Pocaire' is what he calls it. He pretended at first that he didn't know much of anything about the game, but, if I am not mistaken, he's an old stager at it. I watched the party playing in the smoking-room last night."

"Who played?" asked Bruce.

"The Frenchman, a rather sporty young fellow named Bloodgood, a small, bespectacled man, well fitted with the name of Slush, and an Englishman by the name of Hazleton."

"That's the crowd that played in the Frenchman's stateroom to-day," groaned Rattleton from his berth.

"Played in the stateroom?" exclaimed Frank. "I wonder why they didn't play in the smoking-room?"

"Don't know," said Harry; "but I fancy there was a rather big game on, and you know the Frenchman has the biggest stateroom on the boat, so there was plenty of room for them. They could play there without interruption."

"There seems to be something mysterious about that Frenchman," said Frank.

"I think there's something mysterious about several passengers on this boat," grunted Browning. "I haven't seen much of this young fellow Bloodgood, but he strikes me as a mystery."

"Why?"

"Well he seems to have money to burn, and I don't understand why such a fellow did not take passage on a regular liner."

"As far as that goes," smiled Merry, "I presume some people might think it rather singular that we did not cross the pond in a regular liner; but then they might suppose it was a case of economy with us."

While they were talking there came a rap on their door which Frank threw open.

Just outside stood a young man with a flushed face and distressed appearance. He was dressed in a plaid suit, and wore a red four-in-hand necktie, in which blazed a huge diamond. There were two large solitaire rings on his left hand, and he wore a heavy gold chain strung across his vest.

"Beg your pardon, dear boys," he drawled. "Hope I'm not intruding."

Then he walked in and closed the door.

"My name's Bloodgood," he said—"Raymond Bloodgood. I've seen you fellows together, and you seem like a jolly lot. Heard you singing, you know. Great voices—good singing."

Then he stopped speaking, and they stared at him, wondering what he was driving at. For a moment there was an awkward pause, and then Bloodgood went on:

"I was up pretty late last night, you know. Had a little game in the smoking-room. Plenty of booze, and all that, and I'm awfully rocky to-day. Got a splitting headache. Didn't know but some of you had a bromo seltzer, or something of the sort. You look like a crowd that finds such things handy occasionally."

At this Frank laughed quietly, but Diamond looked angry and indignant.

"What do you take us for?" exclaimed the Virginian, warmly. "Do you think we are a lot of boozers?"

Bloodgood turned on Jack, lifting his eyebrows.

"My dear fellow——" he began.

But Frank put in:

"We have no use for bromo seltzer, as none of us are drinkers."

"Oh, of course not," said the intruder, with something like a sneer. "None of us are drinkers, but then we're all liable to get a little too much sometimes, especially when we sit up late and play poker."

Frank saw that Diamond had taken an instant dislike to the youth with the diamonds and the red necktie, and he felt like averting a storm, even though he did not fancy the manner of the intruder.

"We do not sit up late and play poker," he said.

"Eh? Oh, come off! You're a jolly lot of fellows, and you must have a fling sometimes."

"We can be jolly without drinking or gambling."

"Why, I'm hanged if you don't talk as if you considered it a crime to take a drink or have a little social game!"

Frank felt his blood warm up a bit, but he held himself in hand, as he quietly retorted:

"Intemperance is a crime. I presume there are men who take a drink, as you call it, without being intemperate; but I prefer to let the stuff alone entirely, and then there is no danger of going over the limit."

"And I took you for a sport! That shows how a fellow can be fooled. But you do play poker occasionally. I know that."

"How do you know it, Mr. Bloodgood?"

"By your language. You just spoke of going over the limit. That is a poker term."

"And one used by many people who never played a game of cards in their lives."

"But you have played cards? You have played poker? Can you deny it?"

"If I could, I wouldn't take the trouble, Mr. Bloodgood. I think you have made a mistake in sizing up this crowd."

"Guess I have," sneered the fellow. "You must be members of the Y. M. C. A."

"Say, Frank!" panted Jack; "open the door and let me——"

But Frank checked the hot-headed youth again.

"Steady, Jack! It is not necessary. He will go directly. Mr. Bloodgood, you speak as if it were a disgrace to belong to the Y. M. C. A. That shows your ignorance and narrowness. The Y. M. C. A. is a splendid organization, and it has proved the anchor that has kept many a young man from dashing onto the rocks of destruction. Those who sneer at it should be ashamed of themselves, but, as a rule, they are too bigoted, prejudiced, or narrow-minded to recognize the fact that some of the most manly young men to be found belong to the Y. M. C. A."

Bloodgood laughed.

"And I took you for a sport!" he cried. "By Jove! Never made such a blunder before in all my life! Studying for the ministry, I'll wager! Ha! ha! ha!"

Frank saw that Diamond could not be held in check much longer.

"One last word to you, Mr. Bloodgood," he spoke. "I am not studying for the ministry, and I do not even belong to the Y. M. C. A. If I were doing the one or belonged to the other, I should not be ashamed of it. I don't like you. I can stand a little freshness; in fact, it rather pleases me; but you are altogether too fresh. You are offensive."

Merry flung open the door.

"Good-day, sir."

Bloodgood stepped out, turned round, laughed, and then walked away.

"Hang it, Merriwell!" grated Diamond, as Frank closed the door; "why didn't you let me kick him out onto his neck!"

CHAPTER IV.

WHO IS BLOODGOOD?

Diamond was thoroughly angry. So was Rattleton. In his excitement, Harry said something that caused Frank to turn quickly, and observe:

"Don't use that kind of language, old man, no matter what the provocation. Vulgarity is even lower than profanity."

Harry's face flushed, and he looked intensely ashamed of himself.

"I peg your bardon—I mean I beg your pardon!" he spluttered. "It slipped out. You know I don't say anything like that often."

"I know it," nodded Frank, "and that's why it sounded all the worse. I don't know that I ever heard you use such a word before."

Harry did not resent Frank's reproof, for he knew Frank was right, and he was ashamed.

Every young man who stoops to vulgarity should be ashamed. Profanity is coarse and degrading; vulgarity is positively low and filthy. The youth who is careful to keep his clothes and his body clean should be careful to keep his mouth clean. Let nothing go into it or come out of it that is in any way lowering.

Did you ever hear a loafer on a corner using profane and obscene language? I'll warrant most of you have, and I'll warrant that you were thoroughly disgusted. You looked on the fellow as low, coarse, cheap, unfit to associate with respectable persons. The next time you use a word that you should be ashamed to have your mother or sister hear just think that you are following the example of that loafer. You are lowering yourself in the eyes of somebody, even though you may not think so at the time. Perhaps one of your companions may be a person who uses such language freely, and yet he has never before heard it from you. He laughs, he calls you a jolly good fellow to your face; but he thinks to himself that you are no better than anybody else, and behind your back he tells somebody what he thinks. He is glad of the opportunity to show that you are no better than he is. Never tell a vulgar story. Better never listen to one, unless your position is such that you cannot escape without making yourself appear a positive cad. If you have to listen to such a story, forget it as soon as possible. Above all things, do not try to remember it.

Some young men boast of the stories they know. And all their stories are of the "shady" sort. It is better to know no stories than to know that kind. It is better not to be called a good fellow than to win a reputation by always having a new story of the low sort ready on your tongue.

There are other and better ways of winning a reputation as a good fellow. There are stories which are genuinely humorous and funny which are also clean. No matter how much of a laugh he may raise, any self-respecting person feels that he has lowered himself by telling a vulgar story. It is not so if he has told a clean story. He is satisfied with the laughter he has caused and with himself.

Frank Merriwell was called a good fellow. It was not often that he told a story, but when he did, it was a good one, and it was clean. He had an inimitable way of telling anything, and his stories were all the more effective because they came at rare intervals. He did not cheapen them by making them common.

And never had anybody heard him tell a story that could prove offensive to the ears of a lady.

Not that he had not been tempted to do so. Not that he had not heard such stories. He had been placed in positions where he could not help hearing them without making himself appear like a thorough cad.

Frank's first attempt to tell a vulgar story had been the lesson that he needed. He was with a rather gay crowd of boys at the time, and several had told "shady" yarns, and then they had called for one from Frank. He started to tell one, working up to the point with all the skill of which he was capable. He had them breathless, ready to shout with laughter when the point was reached. He drew them on and on with all the skill of which he was capable. And then, just as the climax was reached, he suddenly realized just what he was about to say. A thought came to him that made his heart give a great jump.

"What if my mother were listening?"

That was the thought. His mother was dead, but her influence was over him. A second thought followed. Many times he had seemed to feel her hovering near. Perhaps she was listening! Perhaps she was hearing all that he was saying!

Frank Merriwell stopped and stood quite still. At first he was very pale, and then came a rush of blood to his face. He turned crimson with shame and hung his head.

His companions looked at him in astonishment. They could not understand what had happened. Some of them cried, "Go on! go on!"

After some seconds he tried to speak. At first he choked and could say nothing articulate. After a little, he muttered:

"I can't go on—I can't finish the story! You'll have to excuse me, fellows! I'm not feeling well!"

And he withdrew from the jolly party as soon as possible.

From that day Frank Merriwell never attempted to tell a story that was in the slightest degree vulgar. He had learned his lesson, and he never forgot it.

Some boys swagger, chew tobacco, talk vulgar, and swear because they do not wish to be called "sissies." They fancy such actions and language make them manly, but nothing could be a greater mistake.

Frank did nothing of the sort, and all who knew him regarded him as thoroughly manly. Better to be called a "sissy" than to win reputed manliness at the cost of self-respect.

Frank had forced those who would have regarded him with scorn to respect him. He could play baseball or football with the best of them; he could run, jump, swim, ride, and he excelled by sheer determination in almost everything he undertook. He would not be beaten. If defeated once, he did not rest, but prepared himself for another trial and went in to win or die. In this way he showed himself manly, and he commanded the respect of enemies as well as friends.

Rattleton was ashamed of the language he had used after the departure of Bloodgood, and he did not attempt to excuse himself further. He lay back in his berth, looking sicker than ever.

"I'd give ten dollars for the privilege of helping Mr. Bloodgood out with my foot!" hissed Jack Diamond. "Never saw anybody so fresh!"

"Oh, I've seen lots of people just like him," grunted Browning, getting out a pipe and lighting it.

"Don't smoke, Bruce!" groaned Rattleton, as the steamer gave an unusually heavy roll. "I'm sick enough now. That will make me worse."

"Oh, we'll open the port."

"Open the port!" laughed Frank. "And we just told Bloodgood we did not drink."

"Port-hole, not port wine," said the big fellow, with a yawn. "We'll let in some fresh air."

"We can't let in anything fresher than just went out," declared the Virginian, as he flung open the round window that served to admit light and air.

"There's something mighty queer about that fellow," said Frank. "Did you notice the diamonds he was wearing, fellows?"

"Yes," said Bruce, beginning to puff away at his new briarwood. "Regular eye-hitters they were."

"Who knows they were genuine?" asked Jack.

"Nobody here," admitted Frank. "It is impossible to distinguish some fake stones from real diamonds, unless you examine them closely. But, somehow, I have a fancy that those were genuine diamonds."

"What makes you think so?"

"I don't know just why I think so, but I do. Something tells me that for all of his swagger Bloodgood is a fellow who would scorn to wear paste diamonds."

"What do you make out of the fellow, anyway?" asked Bruce.

"I'm not able to size him up yet," admitted Frank. "I'm not certain whether he came of a good family or a bad one, but I'm inclined to fancy it was the former."

"I'd like to know why you think so?" from Jack. "He did not show very good breeding."

"But there is a certain something about

his face that makes me believe he comes from a high-grade family. I think he has become lowered by associating with bad companions."

"Well, I don't care who or what he is," declared Jack; "if he gets fresh around me again, I'll crack him one for luck. I can't stand him for a cent!"

"Better turn him over to me," murmured Bruce, dozily. "I'll sit on him."

"And he'll think he's under an elephant," laughed Merry. "Bruce cooked M. Montfort, and I reckon he'd have less trouble to cook Mr. Bloodgood."

At this moment there was a hesitating, uncertain knock on the door.

"Another visitor, I wonder?" muttered Frank.

CHAPTER V.

THE SUPERSTITIOUS MAN.

A little man hesitated outside the door when it was opened. He had a sad, uncertain, mournful drab face, puckered into a peculiar expression about the mouth. He was dressed in black, but his clothes were not a very good fit or in the latest style. He fingered his hat nervously. His voice was faltering when he spoke.

"I—I beg your pardon, gentlemen. I—I hope I am not—intruding?"

He had not crossed the threshold. He seemed in doubt about the advisability of venturing in.

There was something amusing in the appearance of the little man. Frank recognized a "character" in him, and Merry was interested immediately. He invited the little man in, and closed the door when that person had entered.

"I—I know it's rather—rather—er—bold of me," said the stranger, apologetically. "But you know people on shipboard—er—take many—liberties."

"Oh, yes, we know it!" muttered Diamond.

Browning grunted and looked the little man over. He was a curiosity to Bruce.

"What can we do for you, sir?" asked Frank.

The little man hesitated and looked around. He sidled over and put his hand on the partition.

"The—ah—next room is occupied by the—er—the French gentleman, is it not?" he asked.

"Yes, sir."

"I—I presume—presume, you know—that you are able to hear any—ah—conversation that may take place in that room, unless—er—the conversation is—guarded."

"Not unless we take particular pains to listen," said Merry. "Even then, it is doubtful if we can hear anything plainly."

"And we are not eavesdroppers," cut in Diamond. "We do not take pains to listen."

"Oh, no—er—no, of course not!" exclaimed the singular stranger. "I—I didn't insinuate such a thing! Ha! ha! ha! The idea! But you know—sometimes—occasionally—persons hear things when they—er—do not try to hear."

"Well, what in the world are you driving at?" asked Frank, not a little puzzled by the man's singular manner.

"Well, you see, it's—this way: I—I don't care to be—overheard. I don't want anybody to—to think I'm prying into their—private business. You understand?"

"I can't say that I do."

"Perhaps I can make myself—er—clearer."

"Perhaps you can."

"My name is—er—Slush—Peddington Slush."

"Holy cats! what a name!" muttered Browning, while Rattleton grinned despite his sickness.

"I—I'm taking a sea voyage—for—for my health," explained Mr. Slush. "That's why I didn't go over on a—a regular liner. This way I shall be longer at—at sea. See?"

"And you are keeping us at sea by your lingering way in coming to a point," smiled Merry.

"Eh?" said the little man. Then he seemed to comprehend, and he broke into a sudden cackle of laughter, which he shut off with startling suddenness, looking frightened.

"Beg your pardon!" he exclaimed. "Quite—ah—rude of me. I don't do it—often."

"You look as if it wouldn't hurt you to do it oftener," said Merry, frankly. "Laughter never hurt anyone."

"I—I can't quite agree with—you, sir. I beg your pardon! No offense! I—I don't wish to be offensive—you understand. I once knew a man who died from —er—laughing. It is a fact, sir. He laughed so long—and so hard—that he— he lost his breath—entirely. Never got it back again. Since then I've been very —cautious. It's a bad sign to laugh—too hard."

Merry felt like shouting, but Jack was looking puzzled and dazed. Diamond could not comprehend the little man, and he failed to catch the humor of the character.

"Now," said Mr. Slush, "I will come directly to the—point."

"Do," nodded Frank.

"I just saw a—er—person leave this room. I wish to know if—— Good gracious, sir! Do you know that is a bad sign!"

He pointed a wavering finger at Frank.

"What is a bad sign?" asked Merry, surprised.

"To wear a—a dagger pin thrust through a—a tie in which there is the least bit of—red. It is a sign of—of bloodshed. I—I beg you to remove that —that pin from that scarf!"

The little man seemed greatly agitated.

After a moment of hesitation, Frank laughed lightly and took the pin from the scarf.

Immediately the visitor seemed to breathe more freely.

"Ah—er—thank you!" he said. "I— I've seen omens enough. Everything seems to point to—to a—tragedy. I regret exceedingly that I ever sailed—on this steamer. I—I shall be thankful when I put my feet on dry land—if I ever do again."

"You must be rather superstitious," suggested Frank.

"Not at all—that is, not to any extent," Mr. Slush hastened to aver. "There are a few signs—and omens— which I know—will come true."

"Indeed!"

"Yes, sir!" asserted the little man, with surprising positiveness. "I know something will happen—to this boat. I —I am positive of it."

"Why are you so positive?"

"Everything foretells it. At the very start it was—foretold. I was foolish then that I did not demand—demand, sir—to be set ashore, even after the steamer had left—her pier."

"How was that?"

"There was a cat, sir—a poor, stray cat—that came aboard this steamer. They did not let her stay—understand me? They—they drove her off!"

"And that was a bad omen?"

"Bad! It was—ah—er—frightful! Old sailors will tell you that. Always—er— let a cat remain on board a vessel—if— she—comes on board. If you—if you do not—you will regret it."

"And you think something must happen to this steamer?"

"I'm afraid so—I feel it. There is— something mysterious about the vessel, gentlemen. I don't know—just what it is —but it's something. The—the captain looks worried. I—I've noticed it. I've talked with him. Couldn't get any satisfaction—out of him. But I—I know!"

"I'm afraid you are a croaker," said Diamond, unable to keep still longer.

"You may think so—now; but wait and see—wait. Keep your eyes—open. I—I think you will see something. I think you will find there are—mysterious things going on."

"Well, you have not told us what you want of us, Mr. Slush," said Frank.

"That's so—forgot it." Then, of a sudden, to Bruce: "Don't twirl your thumbs—that way. Do it backward—backward! It—it's a sure sign of—disaster to twirl your thumbs—forward."

"All right," grunted the big fellow; "backward it is." And he reversed the motion.

"Thank you," breathed Mr. Slush, with a show of relief. "Now, I'll tell you—why I called. I—er—saw a young man—leaving this room—a few minutes ago."

"Yes."

"Mr. Bloodgood."

"Yes."

"I—I have taken an interest in—Mr. Bloodgood. I—I think he is—a rather nice young man."

"I don't admire your taste," came from Jack.

"Eh? I don't know him—very well. You understand. Met him—in the smoking-room. Sometimes I—er—play cards—for amusement. Met him that way."

"Does he play for amusement?" asked Frank.

"Oh, yes—ah—of course. That is—he—he likes—a little stake."

"I thought so."

"I—I don't mind that."

"Great Scott!" thought Merry. "I don't see how he ever gets round to play cards for money. I shouldn't think he'd know what to do. It would take him so long to make up his mind."

"But I—I don't care to make a—a companion of anybody about whom I know—nothing. That's why I—came to you. I—I thought it might be you could give me—some information—about Mr. Bloodgood."

"You've come to the wrong place."

"Really? Don't you know—anything about him? You are—er—well acquainted with him?"

"On the contrary, to-day is the first time we have ever spoken to him."

"Is that so?" said Mr. Slush, in evident disappointment. "You are—er—young men about—about his age, and—and——"

"Not in his class," put in Diamond.

"No?" said Mr. Slush, looking at Jack queerly. "I didn't know—I thought——"

There the queer little man stopped, seeming quite unable to proceed. Then, in his hesitating, uncertain way, he tried to make it clear that he did not care to play cards for money with anybody about whom he knew nothing. He was not very effective in his explanation, and seemed himself rather uncertain concerning his real reason for wishing to make inquiries concerning Bloodgood.

Frank studied Mr. Slush closely, but could not take the measure of the man. Somehow, Merry seemed to feel that there was more to the queer little fellow than appeared on the surface.

"Well, you have come to the wrong parties to get information about Mr. Bloodgood," said Frank. "But, if you are so particular about your company, it might be well to learn something concering the other members of your party."

"Oh—er—I know all about them," asserted Mr. Slush.

"Indeed?"

"Yes. Hugh Hazleton is the younger son of an English nobleman, and he is—is all—right."

"Who told you this?"

"He did."

"Then it must be true," grunted Browning, with a grin on his broad face.

"Yes," nodded the little man, innocently, "that is—ah—settled. M. Rouen Montfort is a—a great French journalist and—er—writer of books."

"Is that so?" smiled Merry. "Queer, I never heard of him. I suppose he told you this?"

"Oh, yes. He is a very fine—gentleman. Ah—did Mr. Bloodgood invite—er—any of you to come into the—ah—game?"

Frank fancied he saw a sudden light. Was it possible Mr. Slush was looking for "suckers?"

Was it possible he had been sent there to inveigle them into the party, so that some sharp might "skin" them? It did not seem improbable.

Harry seemed to catch onto the same idea, for he popped up in his bunk suddenly, but a sudden roll of the steamer caused him to sink down again with a groan.

Diamond's eyes began to glitter. He, too, fancied he saw the little game.

"No," said Merry, slowly, "he did not invite any of us to come in."

The litlte man seemed relieved.

"I—I didn't know," he faltered. "If he had—I—I was going to say something. Perhaps it is not—necessary."

"Perhaps not," said Frank; "but it may not do any hurt to say it."

"And it may do some hurt—to you," muttered Diamond under his breath. "I will kick this fellow!"

But, to the surprise of all, the superstitious man cackled out a short, broken laugh, and said:

"Oh, I was going to—to warn you—that's all. It—it's liable to be a pretty—stiff game. I thought it would be a—good thing for you to—keep out of it. It started—light, but it's working—upright along. Almost any time somebody is liable to—to propose throwing off the—the limit, and then somebody is going to get—hurt. If you are—not in it, why you won't be in any—danger."

There was a silence. The four youths looked at the visitor and then at each other.

What did it mean?

If he was playing them for "suckers," surely he was doing it in a queer manner.

"Thank you," said Frank, stiffly. "You are kind!"

"More than kind!" muttered Diamond.

"Don't mention it," said the little man, trying to look pleasant, but making a dismal failure. "I—I dont' like to see respectable young men caught in a—trap. That's all. Thought I'd tell you. Didn't know that you would—thank me. Took my chances on that. Well, I think I'll—be going."

He turned, falteringly, seemed about to say something more, opened the door part way, hesitated, then said "good-day," and went out.

CHAPTER VI.

THE CARGO OF THE "EAGLE."

'Well?"

"Well!"

"Well!"

The same word, but from three different persons, and spoken in three different inflections.

"Will somebody please hit me with something hard!" murmured Jack.

"What does it mean, Merry?" asked Rattleton.

"You may search me!" exclaimed Frank, in rather expressive slang, something in which he seldom indulged, unless under great provocation.

Browning had said nothing. He was pulling steadily at his pipe, quite unaware that it had gone out.

"What do you make of Mr. Peddington Slush?" asked Jack.

"I don't know what to make of him," confessed Frank. "About the only thing of which I am sure is that he has a corker for a name. That name is enough to make any man look sad and dejected."

"What did he come here for, anyhow?" asked Rattleton.

"To find out about Raymond Bloodgood—he said."

"I know he said so, but I don't stake any talk—I mean take any stock in that. What difference does it make to him who Bloodgood is?"

"That was something he did not make clear."

"He didn't seem to make anything clear," declared Jack. "I thought for sure that he was going to throw out some hooks to drag us into that game of poker. If he had, I should have known he was sent here, and I'd kicked him out, whether you had been willing or not, Merry!"

"I'd opened the door and held it wide for you," smiled Frank.

"What do you think of him, Browning?" asked Harry.

"His way of talking made me very tired," yawned the big fellow. "He seemed to work so hard to get anything out."

"I'll allow that we have had two rather queer visitors," said the Virginian.

"And I shall take an interest in them both after this," declared Frank.

"Talk about superstitious persons, I believe he heads the list," from Jack.

"He said he was not superstitious," laughed Merry.

"But the cat worried him."

"And my twiddling my thumbs," put in Bruce.

"And this dagger pin in my scarf," said Frank.

"It's a wonder he didn't prophecy shipwreck, or something of that sort," groaned Rattleton, who had settled at full length in his berth. "If this rolling motion keeps up, I shall get so I won't care if we are wrecked."

"He must be a dandy in a good swift game of poker!" laughed Frank. "I shouldn't think he'd be able to make up his mind how to discard. He'd be a drawback to the game, or I'm much mistaken."

"It strikes me that he'd be easy fruit," said Rattleton.

"He looks like a 'sucker' himself, but sometimes it is impossible to tell about a man till after you see him play. Anyhow, these two visits were something to break the monotony of the voyage. It promised to be pretty lively at the start, but it has settled down to be rather quiet."

Bloodgood and Slush proved good food for conversation, but the boys tired of that after a while.

Diamond went out by himself, and Frank went to Tutor Maybe's room, where he spent the time till the gong sounded for supper.

"Come, Harry," said Frank, appearing in the stateroom, "aren't you ready for supper?"

Rattleton gave a groan.

"Don't talk to me about eating!" he exclaimed. "It makes me sick to think about it. Leave me—let me die in peace!"

Jack was not there, so Frank and Bruce washed up and went out together. They were nearly through eating when the Virginian came in and took his place near them at the table.

Usually the captain sat at the head of that table, but he was not there now.

"Where have you been?" asked Frank.

"Getting onto a few things," said Jack, in a peculiar way.

"Why, what's the matter with you?" asked Bruce, pausing to stare at the Southerner. "You are pale as a ghost!"

"Am I?" said Diamond, his voice sounding rather strained and unnatural.

"Sure thing. I wouldn't advise you to eat any more, and perhaps you hadn't better look at the chandaliers while they are swinging. You'll be keeping Rattleton company."

"Oh, I'm not sick—at least, not seasick," averred Jack.

"Then what ails you? I was going to prescribe ginger ale if it was the first stage of seasickness. Sometimes that will brace a person up and straighten out his stomach."

"Oh, don't talk remedies to me. I took medicine three days before I started on this voyage, and everybody I saw told me something to do to keep from being sick. I'm wearing a sheet of writing paper across my chest now."

When supper was over Jack motioned for his friends to follow him. The three went on deck and walked aft till they were quite alone.

The "Eagle" was plowing along over a deserted sea. The waves were running heavily, and night was shutting down grimly over the ocean.

"What's the matter with you, Diamond?" asked Browning. "Why have you dragged us out here? It's cold, and I'd rather go into our stateroom and take a loaf after eating so heartily. By Jove! if this keeps up, they won't have provisions enough on this boat to feed me before we get across."

"I wanted to have a little talk without," said Jack; "and I didn't care about talking in the stateroom, where I might be overheard."

"What's up, anyway?" demanded Frank, warned by the manner of the Virginian that Jack fancied he had something of importance to tell them.

"I've been investigating," said Jack.

"What?"

"Well, I found out that there is something the matter on this boat."

"Did you learn what it was?"

"I don't know that I have, but I've discovered one thing. I've learned the kind of cargo we carry."

"What is it?"

"Petroleum and powder!"

CHAPTER VII.

PREMONITIONS OF PERIL.

"Well, that's hot stuff when it's burning," said Merriwell, grimly.

"Rather!" grunted Browning.

'If I'd known what the old boat carried, I think I'd hesitated some about shipping on her," declared Jack. "What if she did get on fire?"

"We'd all go up in smoke," said Merriwell, with absolute coolness. "That is about the size of it."

"Well," said Jack, "I heard two of the sailors talking in a very mysterious manner. They say the 'Eagle' is hoodooed and the captain knows it. They say he has not slept any to speak of since we left New York."

"Sailors are always superstitious. They are ignorant, as a rule, and ignorance breeds superstition."

"Do you consider Mr. Slush ignorant?" asked Bruce.

"Didn't have time to size him up, but he's queer."

"I shall feel that I am over a volcano during the rest of the voyage," said Jack. "What if there was somebody on board who wished to destroy the ship?"

"It wouldn't be much of a job," grunted Browning. "A match touched to a powder keg would do the trick in a hurry."

"But he'd go up with the rest of us," said Frank.

"Unless he used a slow match," put in Jack. "These captains always have their enemies, who are desperate fellows and ready to do almost anything to injure them. The steamer might be set afire by means of a slow match, which would give the villain time enough to get away."

"I hardly think there's anybody desperate enough to do that kind of a trick, for it would be a case of suicide."

"Perhaps not. The chap who did the trick might have some plan of escaping. Then I have known men desperate enough to commit suicide if they could destroy an enemy at the same time."

"Well, it's likely all this worry about this vessel and cargo is entirely needless and foolish."

"I don't believe it," said the Virginian. "I know now that the captain has been worried. I have noticed it in his manner. He is pale and restless."

"Well, it's likely he may be rather anxious, for it's certain he cannot carry any insurance on such a cargo."

"He was not at the table to-night."

"No."

"I'd give something to be on solid ground and away from this powder mill. You know that sometimes there is such a thing as an unaccountable explosion. A heavy sea must cause motion or friction in the cargo, and friction often starts a fire on shipboard. Fire on this vessel means a quick road to glory."

"Huah!" grunted Bruce. "I'm not in the habit of worrying about things that may happen. It's cold out here. Let's go back to the stateroom."

"It will be well enough to keep still about the nature of the cargo, Diamond," said Frank.

"Oh, I shall keep still about that all right!" assured Jack.

As they moved back along the deck they discovered somebody who was leaning over the rail and making all sorts of dismal sounds and groans.

"The next time I go to Europe I'll stay at home!" moaned this individual. "Oh, my! oh, my! How bad I feel! Next that comes will be the shaps of my twos—I mean the taps of my shoes!"

"It's Rattles!" laughed Frank, softly; "and he is sicker than ever. He's tried to crawl out to get some air."

At this moment a man opened the door near Rattleton, and asked:

"Is the—ah—er—moon up yet?"

"I don't know," moaned Harry. "But it is if I swallowed it. Everything else is up, anyhow."

"If the—ah—moon comes up red to-night, it will mean— —"

"I don't give a rap what it means!" snorted Rattleton. "Don't talk to me! Let me die without torturing me! I'm sick enough without having you make me worse!"

Mr. Slush, for he was the anxious inquirer about the moon, dodged back into the cabin, closing the door hesitatingly.

Then Rattleton, unaware of the proximity of his amused friends, hung over the rail and groaned again.

Frank walked up and spoke:

"I see, my dear boy, that you are heeding the Bible admonition."

"Hey?" groaned Harry. "'What is it?"

"'Cast thy bread upon the waters!' You are doing it all right, all right."

"Now, don't carry this thing too far!" Rattleton tried to say in a fierce manner, but his fierceness was laughable. "The worm will turn when trodden upon."

"But the banana peel knows a trick worth two of that. Did you ever hear that touching little poem about the man who stepped on a banana peel? Never did? Why, that is too bad! You don't know what you've missed. Listen, and you shall hear it."

Then Frank solemnly declaimed:

"He walked along one summer day,
  As stately as a prince;
He stepped upon a banana peel,
  And he hasn't 'banana' where since."

Rattleton gave a still more dismal groan.

"You are conspiring with the elements to hasten my death!" he said. "I can't stand many more like that."

"You should wear a sheet of writing paper across your breast, same as I do," said Diamond. "Then you won't be sick."

"I've got two sheets of writing paper across mine," declared Harry.

"You should drink a bottle of ginger ale to settle your stomach," put in Frank.

"Just drank three bottles of ginger ale, and they've turned my stomach wrong side out," gurgled the sick youth.

"You should allow yourself perfect relaxation, and not try to fight against it," from Browning.

"Oh, I haven't allowed myself anything else but perfect relaxation," came from Harry. "You all make me tired!"

Then he staggered into the cabin and disappeared on his way back to the stateroom.

Diamond and Browning followed, but Frank lingered behind.

Although he had kept the fact concealed, Merry was troubled with a strange foreboding of coming disaster. In every way he tried to overcome anything like superstition, but he remembered that, on many other occasions, he had been warned of coming trouble by just such feelings.

"I'd like to know just what is going on upon this steamer," he muttered, as he walked forward. "I feel as if something was wrong, and I shall not be satisfied till I investigate."

CHAPTER VIII.

IN THE STOKE-HOLE.

Frank found the chief engineer taking some air. Merry fell into conversation with the man, who was smoking and seemed quite willing to talk.

Having a pleasant and agreeable way, Frank easily led the engineer on, and it was not long before the man was quite taken with the chatty passenger.

Frank was careful not to seem inquisitive or prying, for he knew it would be easy to arouse the engineer's suspicions if there should be anything wrong on the steamer.

However, Merry was working for a privilege, and he obtained it. When he expressed a desire to go below and have a look at the engines and furnaces, the engineer invited him to come along.

They passed through a door, and then began a descent by means of iron ladders. The clanking roar of the machinery came up to them. Frank could hear and feel the throbbing heart beats of the great boat.

The engine room was quickly reached, and there the engineer showed him the massive machinery that moved with the regularity of clockwork and the grace and ease that came from great power and perfect adjustment.

All this was interesting, but Frank was anxious to go still deeper.

"Go ahead," said the engineer, showing him the way. "Down that ladder there. You'll be able to see the furnaces and the stokers at work. I don't believe you'll care to go into the stoke-hole."

Frank descended. Great heat came up to him, accompanied by a glow that shifted and changed, dying down suddenly at one moment and glaring out at the next. He could hear the ring of shovels and the clank of iron doors.

He reached an iron grating, where a fierce heat rolled up and seemed to scorch him. From that position he could look down into the stoke-hole and see the black, grimy, sweating, half-clad men at work there.

Above him, at the head of the ladder he had just descended, a pair of shining eyes glared down, but he saw them not. He had not observed a cleaner who was at work on the machinery in the engine-room, and who kept his hat pulled over his eyes till Frank departed.

The blackened stokers looked like grim demons of the fiery pit as they labored at the coal, which they were shoveling into the mouths of the greedy furnaces.

The shifting glow was caused by the opening and closing of the furnace doors, which clanged and rang.

For a moment the pit below would seem shrouded in almost Stygian darkness, save for some bar of light that gleamed out from a crack or draft, and then there would be a rattle of iron and a flare of blood-red light that came with the flinging open of a furnace door.

In the glare of light the bare-armed, dirt-grimed stokers would shovel, shovel, shovel, till it seemed a wonder that the fire was not completely deadened by so much coal.

Sometimes the doors of all the furnaces would seem open at once, and the glare and heat that came up from the place was something awful.

Merry wondered how human beings could live down there in that terrible place.

Some of the men were raking out ashes and hoisting it by means of a mechanism provided for the purpose.

Frank pitied the poor creatures who were forced to work down in that place. Yet he remembered it was not so many months since he had applied for the position of wiper in an engine round-house, obtained the job, and worked there with the grimiest and lowest employees of the railroad.

There was something fascinating in the black pit and the grimy men who labored down there in the glare and heat. Frank was so absorbed that he heard no sound, received no warning of danger.

Merry leaned out over the edge of the iron grating. Something struck on his back, he was clutched, thrust out, hurled from the grating!

It was done in a twinkling. He could not defend himself, but he made a clutch to save himself, caught something, swung in, struck against the iron ladder, and went tumbling and sliding downward.

At the moment when Frank was attacked, a glare of light had filled the pit. One of the stokers had turned his back to the gleaming mouths of the furnaces and looked upward, as if to relieve his aching eyes.

He saw everything that occurred on the grating. He saw a man slip down the ladder behind Frank and spring on his back. He saw that man hurl Frank from the grating.

The stoker uttered a shout and ran toward the foot of the ladder, expecting to find Frank laying there, severely injured or killed. He was astounded when he saw the ready-witted youth grasp the grating, swing in, strike the ladder, cling and slide.

Down Frank came with a rush, but he did not fall. He landed in the stoke-hole without being severely injured. He was on his feet in a twinkling, and up that ladder he went like a cat.

His assailant had darted up the ladder above and disppeared. Merry reached the grating from which he had been hurled, and then he ran up the other ladder.

He was soon in the engine-room.

In that room there was no excitement. The machinery was sliding and swinging in a regular manner, while the engineer sat watching its movements, talking to an assistant. Oilers and cleaners were at work.

"Where is he?" cried Frank, his voice sounding clear and distinct.

They looked at him in amazement.

"What's the matter?" asked the engineer, coming forward.

"I was attacked from behind and thrown into the stoke-hole," Merry explained. "The fellow who did it came in here."

"Thrown into the stoke-hole?"

"Yes."

"From where?"

"The grating at the foot of the first ladder."

The engineer looked doubtful.

"My dear fellow," he said, "you would have been maimed or killed. You do not seem to be harmed."

Frank realized that the engineer actually doubted his word.

"He might have fallen," said the assistant; "but it would have broken his neck."

"I tell you I was attacked from behind and thrown down!" exclaimed Frank. "I managed to get hold of the ladder and slide, so I was not killed."

The engineer looked annoyed.

"This is what comes of letting a passenger in here," he said. "It's the last time I'll do it on my own responsibility. Now if you go out and tell you were thrown into the stoke-hole, there'll be any amount of fuss over it."

"I am telling it right here," said Frank, grimly, "and I want to know who did the trick. Somebody who came from this room must have done it."

"Impossible!"

"Then where did he come from?"

The engineer and his assistant looked at each other, and the former began to swear.

"What do you think of it, Joe?" he asked.

"Think you made a mistake, Bill; but his story won't go. Nobody'll take any stock in it."

Frank was angry. It was something unusual for his word to be doubted, and he felt like expressing his feelings decidedly.

He was saved the trouble. The grimy stoker who had witnessed the struggle and the fall appeared in the door of the engine-room. He saw Frank and cried:

"Hello, you! So you're all right? Wonder you wasn't killed. You came down with a rush, young feller, but you went back just as quick."

Frank understood instantly.

"Here is a man who saw it!" he cried. "He will tell you that I am not lying."

The engineer turned to the stoker.

"How did he happen to fall?" he asked.

"He didn't fall," declared the begrimed coal heaver.

"No? What then——"

"'Nother chap jumped on his back and flung him down. It's wonderful he wasn't killed."

Frank was triumphant. He regarded the engineer and his assistant with a grim smile on his face.

"This is incredible!" exclaimed the engineer. "Who could have done such a thing?"

"Somebody who came from this room!" rang out Merry's clear voice.

"This shall be investigated!" declared the engineer. "Look around! See if you can find the man who attacked you. The only ones here are myself, Mr. Gregory, and the wipers."

"I want a look at those wipers," said Frank.

"You shall have it. Mr. Gregory and I were talking together over here all the time you were gone."

"Oh, I do not suspect you," said Merry; "but I want a good look at those wipers."

"Did you see the man who threw you into the stoke-hole?"

"No, but——"

"Then how will you know who it was if you see him?"

"Whoever did so had a reason for the act—a motive. He must have known me before. I may know him."

"Come," invited the engineer.

He called one of the wipers down from amid the sliding shafts and moving machinery. The man came unhesitatingly.

Frank took a square look at this man, who did not seek to avoid inspection.

"Never saw him before," confessed Merry.

The wiper was dismissed.

"Hackett," called the engineer.

The other wiper did not seem to hear. He pretended to be very busy, and kept at work.

"Hackett!"

He could not fail to hear that. He kept his face turned away, but answered:

"Yes, sir."

"Come here. I want you."

The wiper hesitated. Then he turned and slowly approached. His face was besmeared till scarcely a bit of natural color showed, and his hat was pulled low over his eyes. He shambled forward awkwardly, and stood in an awkward position, with his eyes cast down.

Frank looked at him closely and started. Then, in a perfectly calm manner, but with a trace of triumph in his voice, he declared:

"This is the fellow who did the job!"

CHAPTER IX.

IN IRONS.

"What?" cried the engineer, in astonishment.

"How do you know?" asked the engineer's assistant, incredulously.

"That's it—how do you know?" demanded the engineer. "You said you did not see the person who attacked you."

"I did not."

"Yet you say this is the man."

"Yes."

"How do you know?"

"I know him."

"You do?"

"Yes."

"You have seen him before?"

"I should say so, on several occasions. He is one of my bitterest enemies. This is not the first time he has tried to kill or injure me. He has made the attempt many times before. He is the only person here who would do such a thing."

"If this is true," said the engineer, grimly, "he shall pay dearly for his work!"

The assistant nodded.

"What have you to say, Hackett?" demanded the engineer.

"I say it's a lie!" growled the fellow. "I never saw this chap before he came into the engine-room. He doesn't know me, and I don't know him."

"You hear what Hackett has to say," said the engineer, turning to Frank.

"I hear what this fellow has to say, but his name is not Hackett."

"Is not?"

"No, no more than mine is Hackett."

"Then what is his name?"

"His name is Harris!" asserted Merry, "and he is a gambler and a crook. I'll guarantee that he has not been long on the 'Eagle.'"

"No; we took him on in New York scarcely two hours before we sailed. We needed a man, and he applied for any kind of a job. Found he had worked round machinery, and we took him as wiper and general assistant."

"It was not so many weeks ago that he attacked me at New Haven," said Frank. "He failed to do me harm. When he found I was going abroad he declared he would go along on the same steamer. At the time he must have thought I was going by one of the regular liners; but it is plain he followed me up pretty close and found I was going over this way. As there is no second-class passage on this boat, he decided he could not travel in the same class with me without being discovered, and he resolved to go as one of the crew, if he could get on that way. That's how he happens to be here."

"If what you say is true, it will go pretty hard with Mr. Harris. We'll have him ironed and——"

A cry of rage broke from the lips of the accused.

"There is no proof!" he snarled. "No one can swear I attacked this fellow and threw him into the stoke-hole!"

"Oh, yes!" said the stoker who had come up from below. "I saw the whole business. By the light from the furnaces, I plainly saw the man who did it, and you are the man!"

"That settles it!" declared the engineer. "You'll make the rest of the voyage in irons, Mr. Harris!"

"Then I'll give you something to iron me for!" shouted the furious young villain.

He leaped on Frank Merriwell with the fierceness of a wounded tiger.

Frank was not expecting the assault, and, for the moment, he was taken off his guard.

They were close to the moving machinery. Within four feet of them a huge plunging rod was playing up and down, moved by a steel bar that weighed many tons. Harris attempted to fling Frank beneath this bar, where he would be struck and crushed.

The villain nearly succeeded, so swift and savage was his attack.

Frank realized that the purpose of the wretch was to fling him into the machinery, and he braced himself to resist as quickly as possible.

Shouts of consternation broke from the engineer and his assistant. They sprang forward to seize Harris and help Frank.

But, before they could interfere, Frank broke the hold of his enemy, forced him back and struck him a terrible blow between the eyes felling him instantly.

Merriwell stood over Harris, his hands clenched his eyes gleaming.

"Get up!" he cried. "Get up you dog! I can't strike you when you are down, and I'd give a hundred dollars to hit you just once more!"

But Harris did not get up. He realized that his second attempt had failed, and he stood in awe of Frank's terrible fists. He looked up at those gleaming eyes, and turned away quickly, feeling a sudden great fear.

Did Frank Merriwell bear a charmed life?

Surely it seemed that way to Harris just then. For the first time, perhaps, the young rascal began to believe that it was not possible to harm the lad he hated with all the intensity of his nature.

The engineer and his assistants grabbed Harris and held him, the former swearing savagely. They dragged the fellow to his feet, but warned him to stand still.

Harris did so. For the moment, at least, he was completely cowed.

A man was sent for the captain, with instructions to tell him just what occurred. Of course the captain of the steamer was the only person who could order one of the men placed in irons.

The captain came in in a little while, and he listened in great amazement to the story of what had taken place. His face was hard and grim. He asked Frank a few questions, and then he ordered that Harris be ironed and confined in the hold.

"Mr. Merriwell," said the captain, "I am very sorry that this happened on my ship."

"It's all right, captain," said Frank. "You are in no way to blame. The fellow shipped with the intention of doing just what he did, if he found an opportunity."

"It will go hard with him," declared the master. "He'll not get out of this without suffering the penalty."

Harris was sullen and silent. Frank spoke to him before he was led away.

"Harris," he said, "you have brought destruction on yourself. I can't say that I am sorry for you, for, by your persistent attacks on me, you have destroyed any sympathy I might have felt. You have ruined your own life."

"No!" snarled Sport. "You are the one! You ruined me! If I go to prison for this, I'll get free again sometime, and I'll not forget you, Frank Merriwell! All the years I am behind the bars will but add to the debt I owe you. When I come forth to freedom, I'll find you if you are alive, and I'll have your life!"

Then he was marched away between two stout men, his irons clanking and rattling.

CHAPTER X.

THE GAME IN THE NEXT ROOM.

When Merry appeared in his stateroom he was greeted with a storm of questions.

"Well, what does this mean?"

"Trying to dodge us?"

"Running away?"

"Muts the whatter with you—I mean what's the matter?"

"Where have you been?"

"Stand and give an account of yourself!"

Then he told them a little story that astounded them beyond measure. He explained how he had taken a fancy to look the steamer over and had fallen in with the engineer. Then he related how he had visited the engine room and been thrown into the stoke-hole.

But when he told the name of his assailant the climax was capped.

"Harris?" gasped Rattleton, incredulously.

"Harris?" palpitated Diamond, astounded.

"Harris?" roared Browning, aroused from his lazy languidness.

"On this steamer?" they shouted in unison.

"On this steamer," nodded Frank, really enjoying the sensation he had created.

"He—he attacked you?" gurgled Rattleton, seeming to forget his recent sickness.

"He did."

"And you escaped after being thrown into the stoke-hole?" fluttered Diamond.

"I am here."

"And you didn't kill the cur on sight?" roared Browning.

"He is in the hold in irons."

"Serves him right!" was the verdict of Frank's three friends.

"Well, this is what I call a real sensation!" said the Virginian. "You certainly found something, Frank!"

"Well, that fellow has reached the end of his rope at last," said Harry, with intense satisfaction, once more stretching himself in his bunk.

"That's pretty sure,'" nodded Jack. "Attempted murder on the high seas is a pretty serious thing."

"He'll get pushed for it all right this time," grunted Browning, beginning to recover from his astonishment.

Then they talked the affair over, and Frank gave them his theory of Sport's presence on the steamer, which seemed plausible.

"This is something rather more interesting than the superstitious man or the Frenchman," said Diamond.

"The superstitious man was interesting at first," observed Merry; "but I've a fancy that he might prove a bore."

Then Bruce grunted:

"Say, does Fact and Reason err,
And, if they both err, which the more?
The man of the smallest calibre
Is sure to be the greatest bore."

While they were talking, the sound of voices came from the stateroom occupied by the Frenchman. Soon it became evident that quite a little party had gathered in that room.

The boys paid no attention to the party till it came time to turn in for the night. Then they became aware that something was taking place in the adjoining room, and it was not long before they made out that it was a game of poker.

As they became quiet, they could hear the murmur of voices, and, occasionally, some person would speak distinctly, "seeing," "raising" or "calling."

Diamond began to get nervous.

"Say," he observed, "that makes me think of old times. Many a night I've spent at that."

"What's the matter with you?" said Frank. "Do you want to go in there and take a hand?"

"Well," Jack confessed, "I do feel an itching."

"I feel like getting some sleep," grunted Bruce, "and they are keeping me awake."

"Why are they playing in a stateroom, anyhow?" exclaimed Frank. "It's no place for a game of cards at night."

"That's so," agreed Rattleton, dreamily. "But you are keeping me awake by your chatter a good deal more than they are. Shut up, the whole lot of you!"

There was silence for a time, and then, with a savage exclamation, Diamond sprang out of his berth and thumped on the partition, crying:

"Come, gentlemen, it's time to go to bed! You are keeping us awake."

There was no response.

Jack went back to bed, but the murmuring continued in the next stateroom, and the rattle of chips could be heard occasionally.

"What are we going to do about it, Merriwell?" asked Jack, savagely.

"We can complain."

But making a complaint was repellant to a college youth, who was inclined to regard as a cheap fellow anybody who would do such a thing, and Diamond did not agree to that.

"Well," said Frank, "I suppose I can go in there and clean them all out."

"How?"

"At their own game," laughed Merry, muffledly.

"If anybody in this crowd tackles them that way I'll be the one," asserted the Virginian.

"Then nobody here will tackle them that way," said Frank, remembering how he had once saved Diamond from sharpers in New Haven.

Frank was a person who believed that knowledge of almost any sort was likely to prove of value to a man at some stage of his career, and he had made a practice of learning everything possible. He had studied up on the tricks of gamblers, so that he knew all about their methods of robbing their victims. Being a first-class amateur magician, his knowledge of card tricks had become of value to him in more than one instance. He felt that he would be able to hold his own against pretty clever card-sharps, but he did not care or propose to have any dealings with such men, unless forced to do so.

The boys kept still for a while. Their light was extinguished, but, up near the ceiling, a shaft of light came through the partition from the other room.

Diamond saw it. He jumped up and dragged a trunk into position by that partition. Mounted on the trunk, he applied his eye to the orifice and discoverd that he could see into the Frenchman's room very nicely.

"What can you see?" grunted Browning.

"I can see everyone in there," answered Jack.

"Name them."

"The Frenchman, the Englishman, the superstitious man, and our fresh friend, Bloodgood."

"Same old crowd," murmured Frank.

"Yes, and a hot old game!" came from the youth on the trunk. "My! my! but they are whooping her up! They've got plenty to drink, and they are playing for big dust."

"Tell them to saw up till to-morrow," mumbled Bruce.

Jack did not do so, however. He remained on the trunk, watching the game, seeming greatly interested.

A big game of poker interested him any time. It was through the influence of Frank that he had been led to renounce the game, but the thirst for its excitements and delights remained with him, for he had come from a family of card-players and sportsmen.

"Come, come!" laughed Frank, after a while; "I can hear your teeth chattering, old man. Get off that trunk and turn in."

"Wait!" fluttered Jack—"wait till I see this hand played out."

In less than half a minute he cried:

"It's a skin game! I knew it was!"

"What's the lay?" asked Merry.

"That infernal Frenchman is a card-sharp!"

"I suspected as much."

"His pal is the Englishman. They are standing in together."

"Yes?"

"Sure thing. They are bleeding Bloodgood and Slush. Bloodgood thinks he's pretty sharp, and I have not much sympathy for him; but I am sorry for poor little Slush. He should have paid attention to some of his signs and omens. He knew something disastrous would happen during this voyage, and I rather think it will happen to him."

Then Diamond thumped the wall again, crying:

"Stop that business in there! Mr. Slush, you are playing cards with crooks —you are being robbed! Get out of that game as soon as you can!"

There was a sudden silence in the adjoining room, and then M. Rouen Montfort was heard to utter an exclamation in French, following which he cried:

"I see you to-morrow, saire! I make you swallow ze lie!"

"You may see me any time you like!" Diamond flung back.

CHAPTER XI.

THE HORRORS OF THE HOLD.

To the surprise of the four youths, M. Montfort utterly ignored them on the following day, instead of seeking "trouble," as had been anticipated.

"Well," said Jack, in disgust, "he has less courage than I thought. He is just a common boasting Frenchman."

"He is not a common Frenchman," declared Frank. "I believe he is a rascal of more than common calibre."

"But he lacks nerve, and I have nothing but contempt for him," said the Virginian. "I didn't know but he would challenge me to a duel."

"What if he had?"

"What if he had?" hissed the hot-blooded Southern youth. "I'd fought him at the drop of the hat!"

"That's all right, but you know most Frenchmen fight well in a duel."

"I don't know anything of the kind. They are expert fencers, but I notice it is mighty seldom one of them is killed in a duel. They sometimes draw a drop of blood, and then they consider that 'honor is satisfied,' and that ends it."

It was midway in the forenoon that

Frank met Mr. Slush on deck. The little man was looking more doleful and dejected than ever, if possible.

"The—ah—the moon showed rather yellow last night," he said. "That is a —a sure sign of disaster."

"Well," said Merry, with a smile, "I think the disaster will befall you, sir, if you do not steer clear of the crowd you were in last night."

Mr. Slush looked surprised.

"Might I—ah—inquire your meaning?" he faltered.

"I mean that you are playing poker with card-sharps, and they mean to rob you," answered Frank, plainly.

"I—I wonder how you—er—know so much," said the little man, with something like faint sarcasm, as Frank fancied.

"It makes little difference how I know it, but I am telling you the truth. I am warning you for your good, sir."

"Er—ahem! Thank you—very much."

Mr. Slush walked away.

"Well, I'm hanged if he doesn't take it coolly enough!" muttered Frank, perplexed.

Frank felt an interest to know how Sport Harris was getting along. He walked forward and found the captain near the steps that led to the bridge.

In reply to Merry's inquiry, the captain said:

"Oh, don't worry about him. There are rats down there in the hold, but I guess he'll be able to fight them off. He'll have bread and water the rest of the voyage."

After that Merry could not help thinking of Harris all alone in the darkness of the hold, with swarms of rats around him, eating dry bread, washed down with water.

Frank felt that the youthful villain did not deserve any sympathy, but, despite himself, he could not help feeling a pang of pity for him.

When he expressed himself thus to his friends, however, they scoffed at him.

"Serves the dog right!" flashed Diamond. "He is getting just what he deserves, and I'm glad of it!"

"He will get what he deserves when we reach the other side," grunted Browning.

"No," said Merry; "he is an American, and he'll have to be taken back to the United States for punishment."

"Well, he'll get it all right."

"Well, I don't care to think that he may be driven mad shut up in the dark hold with the rats."

This feeling grew on Frank. At last he went to the captain and asked liberty to see Harris.

The request was granted, and, accompanied by two men, Frank descended into the hold.

Down there, amid barrels and casks, they came upon Harris. Frank heard the irons rattle, and then a gaunt-looking, wild-eyed creature rose up before them, shown by the yellow light of the lanterns.

Frank Merriwell had steady nerves, but, despite himself, he started.

The appearance of the fellow had changed in a most remarkable manner. Harris looked as if he was overcome with terror.

"There he is," said one of the men, holding up his lantern so the light fell more plainly on the wretched prisoner.

"Have you come to take me out of here?" cried Harris, in a tone of voice that gave Frank a chill. "For God's sake, take me out of this place! I'll go mad if I stay here much longer! It is full of rats! I could not sleep last night—I dare not close my eyes for a minute! Please—please take me out of here!"

Then he saw and recognized Frank.

"You?" he screamed. "Have you come here to gloat over me, Frank Merriwell?"

"No," said Frank; "I have come to see if I can do anything for you."

"Ha! ha! ha!" laughed Harris, in a manner that made Frank believe madness could not be far away. "You wouldn't do that! I know why you are here! You have triumphed over me! You wish to see me in all my misery! Well, look at me! Here I have been thrown into this hellish hole, amid rats and vermin, ironed like a nigger! Look till you are satisfied! It will fill your heart with satisfaction! Mock me! Sneer at me! Deride me!"

"I have no desire to do anything of the sort," declared Frank. "I am sorry for you, Harris."

"Sorry! Bah! You lie! Why do you tell me that?"

"It is the truth. You brought this on yourself, and so——"

"Don't tell me that again! You have told it enough! If I'd never seen you, I'd not be here now. You brought it on me, Frank Merriwell. If I die here in this cursed hole, you'll have something pleasant to think about! You can laugh over it!"

"You shall not die here, Harris, if I can help it. I'll speak to the captain about you."

The wretch stared at Merry, his eyes looking sunken and glittering. Then, all at once, he crouched down there, his chains clanking, covered his face with his hands and began to cry.

No matter what Harris had done, Frank was deeply pitiful then.

"I shall go directly to the captain," he promised, "and I'll ask him to have you taken out of this place. I will urge him to have it done."

Harris said nothing.

Frank had seen enough, and he turned away. As they were moving off, Harris began to scream and call to them, begging them not to leave him there in the darkness.

Those cries cut through and through Frank Merriwell. He knew he was in no way responsible for the fate that had befallen the fellow, and yet he felt that he must do something for Harris.

He kept his word, going directly to the captain.

CHAPTER XII.

THE FINISH OF A THRILLING GAME.

The captain listened to what Frank had to say, but his sternness did not seem to relax in the least, as Merry described the sufferings the prisoner was enduring. But Frank would not be satisfied till the captain had made a promise to visit Harris himself and see that the fellow was taken out and cared for if he needed it.

Needless to say that the captain forgot to make the visit right away.

Frank did not tell his friends where he had been and what he had seen. He did not feel like talking about it, and they noticed that he looked strangely grim and thoughtful.

Tutor Maybe tried to talk to him about studies, but Merry was in no mood for that, as his instructor soon discovered.

Despite the fact that the sea was running high, Rattleton seemed to have recovered in a great measure from his sickness, so he was able to get on deck with the others. At noon, he even went to the table and ate lightly, drinking ginger ale with his food.

An hour after dinner Frank found a game of poker going on in the smoking-room. Mr. Slush was in the game. So were the Frenchman, the Englishman, and Bloodgood.

No money was in sight, but it was plain enough from the manner in which the game was played that the chips each man held had been purchased for genuine money, and the game was one for "blood."

M. Montfort looked up for a moment as Frank stopped to watch the game. Their eyes met. The Frenchman permitted a sneer to steal across his face, while Frank looked at him steadily till his eyes dropped.

At a glance, Merry saw that Bloodgood was "shakey." The fellow had been growing worse and worse as the voyage progressed, and now he seemed on the verge of a break-down.

A few minutes after entering the room Frank heard one of the spectators whisper to another that Bloodgood was "bulling the game," and had lost heavily.

Bloodgood was drinking deeply. Mr. Slush seemed to be indulging rather freely. The Frenchman sipped a little wine now and then, and the Englishman drank at regular intervals.

The Frenchman was perfectly cool. The Englishman was phlegmatic. Slush hesitated sometimes, but, to the surprise of the boys, seemed rather collected. Bloodgood was hot and excited.

Frank took a position where he could look on. He watched every move. After a time he discerned that the Englishman and the Frenchman were playing to each other, although the trick was done so skillfully that it did not seem apparent.

Bloodgood lost all his chips. The game was held up for a few moments. He stepped into the next room and returned with a fresh supply.

"This is the bottom," he declared. "You people may have them as soon as you like. To blazes with them! Let's lift the limit."

"Ah—er—let's throw it off—entirely," suggested Mr. Slush.

Bloodgood glared at the little man in astonishment.

"What?" he cried. "You propose that? Why, you didn't want to play a bigger game than a quarter limit at the start!"

"Perhaps you are—er—right," admitted Mr. Slush. "I—er—don't deny it. But I have grown more—more interested, you understand. I—I don't mind playing a good game—now."

"Well, then, if the other gentlemen say so, by the gods, we'll make it no limit!" Bloodgood almost shouted.

The Frenchman bowed suavely, a slight smile curling the ends of his pointed mustache upward.

"I haf not ze least—what you call eet?—ze least objectshong," he purred.

"I don't mind," said the Englishman.

Now there was great interest. Somehow, Frank felt that a climax was coming. He watched everything with deep interest.

Luck continued to run against Bloodgood. To Frank's surpirse, it was plain Mr. Slush was winning. This seemed to surprise and puzzle both the Englishman and the Frenchman.

It was hard work to draw the little man in when Hazleton or Montfort dealt. On his own deal or that of Bloodgood, he seemed ready for anything.

"By Jove!" whispered Frank, in Diamond's ear. "That man is not such a fool as I thought! I haven't been able to understand him at all, and I don't understand him now."

At length there came a big jack-pot. It was passed round several times. Then Hazleton opened it on three nines.

Bloodgood sat next. He had two pairs, aces up, and he raised instantly.

Montfort was the next man. He held a pair of deuces, but he saw all that had been bet, and doubled the amount!

Mr. Slush hesitated a little. He seemed ready to lay down, but finally braced up and came in, calling.

Hazleton did not accept the call. He raised again.

Bloodgood looked at his hand and cursed under his breath. It was just good enough to make him feel that he ought to make another raise, but he began to think there were other good hands out, and it was not possible to tell where continued raising would land him, so he "made good."

With nothing but a pair of deuces in his hand, Montfort "cracked her up" again for a good round sum.

The hair on the head of Mr. Slush seemed to stand. He swallowed and looked pale. Then he "made good."

Hazleton had his turn again, and he improved it. For the next few minutes, Montfort and Hazleton had a merry time raising, but neither Slush nor Bloodgood threw up.

"This is where they are sinking the knife in the suckers!" muttered Jack Diamond.

Frank Merriwell said not a word. His eyes were watching every move.

At last the betting stopped, and Slush picked up the pack to give out the cards.

Hazleton called for two. He received them, and remained imperturbable.

He had caught nothing with his three nines.

Bloodgood had tumbled to the fact that he was "up against" threes, and he had discarded his pair of low cards, holding only the two aces. To these he drew a seven and two more aces!

Bloodgood turned pale and then flushed. He held onto himself with all his strength. Here was his chance to get back his losings. Everything was in his favor. He was confident there were some good hands out, and it was very likely some of them might be improved on the draw, but he felt the pot was the same as his.

The Frenchman drew two cards.

Slush took one.

Then hot work began. Within three minutes Hazleton, with his three nines, had been driven out. Bloodgood, Montfort and Slush remained, raising steadily.

There was intense excitement in that room. The captain of the steamer had come in, and he was looking on. Some of the spectators were literally shaking with excitement.

Bloodgood's chips were used up. He flung money on the table.

All that he had went into the pot, and still he would not call. He offered his

I. O. U.'s, but Mr. Slush declined to agree.

"Money or its equivalent," said the little man, with such decisiveness that all were astonished.

"I haven't any money," protested Bloodgood.

"Then you are out," said Slush.

"It's robbery!" cried Bloodgood.

"Why, you can't kick; you haven't even called once."

"Not even once, saire," purred the Frenchman.

"By blazes! I have the equivalent!" shouted Bloodgood.

Into an inner pocket he plunged. He brought out a velvet jewel box. When this was opened, there was a cry of wonder, for a magnificent diamond necklace was revealed.

"That is worth ten thousand dollars!" declared Bloodgood, "and I'll bet as long as it lasts!"

Mr. Slush held out his hand.

"Please let me examine it," he said.

He took a good look at it.

"Ees it all right, sair?" asked the Frenchman, eagerly.

"It is," said Mr. Slush, "and I will take charge of it!"

He thrust the case into his pocket, rose quickly, stepped past Montfort and clapped a hand on Bloodgood's shoulder.

"I arrest you, Benton Hammersley, for the Clayton diamond robbery!" he said. "It is useless for you to resist, for you are on shipboard, and you cannot escape."

Bloodgood uttered a fierce curse.

"Who in the fiend's name are you?" he snarled, turning pale.

And "Mr. Slush" answered:

"Dan Badger, of the New York detective force! Permit me to present you with a pair of handsome bracelets, Mr. Hammersley."

Click—the trapped diamond thief was ironed!

CHAPTER XIII.

FIRE IN THE HOLD.

Everyone except the detective himself seemed astounded. The clever officer, who had played his part so well, was as cool as ice.

The Frenchman cried:

"But zis pot—eet ees not settailed to whom eet belong yet!"

The detective stepped back to his chair.

"The easiest way to settle that is by a show-down," he ssaid. "Under the circumstances, further bettering is out of the question."

"And I rather think I am in the show-down," choked out the prisoner. "I'll need this money to defend myself when I come to trial."

"You shall have it," assured Dan Badger—"if you win it."

"Well, I think I'll win it," said the ironed man, spreading out his hand. "I have four aces, and you can't beat that."

"Oh, my dear saire!" cried the Frenchman. "Zat ees pretty gude, but I belief zis ees battaire. How you like zat for a straight flush?"

He lay his cards on the table, and he had the two, three, four, five and six of hearts.

There was a shout of astonishment.

"Ze pot ees mine!" exultantly cried the Frenchman.

"Stop!" rang out Frank Merriwell's clear voice. "That pot is not yours!"

Everyone looked at Merry.

"He is using a table 'hold-out!'" accused Frank, pointing straight at Montfort. "I saw him make the shift. The five cards that really belong in his hands will be found in the hold-out under the table!"

There was dead silence. The Frenchman turned sallow.

"It makes no difference," said the quiet voice of the detective, breaking the silence. "I have a higher straight flush of clubs here. Mine runs up to the eight spot, and so I win the pot."

He showed his cards and raked in the pot.

With a savage cry, M. Montfort flung his hand aside, leaped to his feet, sprang at Frank, and struck for Merry's face.

The blow was parried, and he was knocked down instantly.

A sailor, pale and shaking, came dashing into the room and whispered a word in the captain's ear.

An oath broke from the capain's lips, and he whirled about and rushed from the room.

Slowly Montfort picked himself up.

There was a livid mark on his cheek. He glared at Frank with deadly hatred.

"Cursed meddlaire!" he grated. "You shall pay for this."

There was consternation outside. On the deck was heard the sound of running feet.

"Something has happened!" said Diamond, hurrying to the door. "I wonder what it is."

The "Eagle" was plunging along through a heavy sea. On the deck some men were running to and fro. Everyone seemed in the greatest consternation.

Jack sprang out and stopped a man.

"What is the matter?" he demanded.

"The ship is on fire!" was the shaking answer. "There is a fire in the hold!"

Diamond staggered. He whirled about and sprang into the smoking-room. In a moment he was at Frank's side.

"Merry," he said, "what I feared has come! The steamer is on fire!"

"Where?"

"In the hold."

Frank remembered the barrels and casks he had seen there.

"Then we are liable to go scooting skyward in a hurry!" he said. "It can't take the fire long to reach the petroleum and powder!"

CHAPTER XIV.

SAVING AN ENEMY.

In truth, there was a fire in the "Eagle's" hold. The captain and the crew seemed perfectly panic-stricken. The thought of the explosion that might come any moment seemed to rob them of all reason.

Frank Merriwell and his friends rushed out of the smoking-room.

The hold had been opened in an attempt to get water onto the flames. Smoke was rolling up from the opening.

"Close down the hatch!" shouted somebody. "It is producing a draft, and that helps the fire along!"

Then faint cries came from the hold —cries of a human being in danger and distress!

"It's Harris!" exclaimed Diamond. "He is down there, and his time has come at last!"

"A rope!" shouted Frank Merriwell, flinging off his coat.

"What are you going to do?" demanded Bruce Browning.

"By heavens! I am going down there and try to bring Harris out!"

"You're a fool!" chattered Harry Rattleton. "Think of the oil and powder down there! The stuff is liable to explode any moment! You shall not go!"

Frank saw a coil of rope at a distance. He rushed for it, brought it to the hold, let an end drop and dangle into the darkness from whence the smoke rolled up.

"You are crazy!" roared Bruce Browning, attempting to get hold of Frank. "I refuse to let you go down there!"

"Don't put your hands on me, Browning!" cried Frank. "If you do, I shall knock you down!"

They saw that he meant just what he said. He would not be stopped then. Bruce Browning, giant that he was, felt that he would be no match for Frank then.

The rope was made fast, and down into the smoke and darkness slid Frank, disappearing from view.

Barely had he done so when some sailors came rushing forward and attempted to close the hatch.

"Hold on!" thundered Browning. "You can't do that now!"

"Get out of the way!" comamnded one of them, who seemed to be an officer. "We must close this hatch to hold the fire in check long enough for the boats to be lowered."

"A friend of mine has gone down there. You can't close it till he comes out!"

"To blazes with your friend!" snarled the man. "What business had he to go down there? If he's gone, he will have to stay there. His life does not count against all the others."

Then, under his directions the men started to close the hatch.

Browning sailed into them. He was aroused to his full extent by the thought of what would happen if the hatch was closed and Frank was shut down there with the fire and smoke. He knocked them aside, he hurled them away as if they were children. They could not stand before him for an instant.

There was a cry from below.

"Pull away, up there!"

It was Frank's voice.

Willing hands seized the rope. There was a heavy weight at the end of it. They dragged the weight up, with the smoke rolling into their faces in a cloud that grew denser and denser.

And up through the smoke came Sport Harris, irons and all, with the ends of the rope tied about his waist!

Frank had found Harris, and here the fellow was.

They untied the rope from Sport's waist in a hurry. Then they lowered it again.

"Pull away!"

Frank Merriwell was dragged up through the smoke.

"Now," said Browning, "down goes the hatch!"

And it was slammed into place in a hurry, holding the smoke back.

CHAPTER XV.

THE SEA GIVES UP.

The pumps were going, in an attempt to flood the hold, but the men did not attempt to fight the fire in anything like a reasonable manner.

The knowledge of the cargo down there in the hold turned them to cowards and unreasoning beings. They were expecting to be blown skyward at any moment.

Of a sudden the engines stopped and the "Eagle" began to lose headway. Men were making preparations to lower the boats.

"Well, I'll be hanged if they are not going to abandon the ship!" exclaimed Frank. "The case must be pretty bad. I wonder how the fire started."

"I set it!"

At his feet was Harris, whom he had just rescued from the hell below, and the fellow had declared that he set the fire!

"You?"

"Yes," said the wretch. "I was crazy. I found a match in my pocket, and I thought I was willing to roast if I could destroy you, so I set the fire. Pretty soon I realized what I had done, but then I found it too late when I tried to beat it out. The old steamer will go into the air in a few minutes, and we'll all go with it, unless we can get off in the boats right away."

"It would have served you right had I left you to your fate!" grated Frank, as he turned away.

He ran down to his stateroom to gather up some of the few little valuables he hoped to save. He was not gone long, but when he returned, he found two boats had been launched and were pulling away, the persons in them being in great haste to get as far from the steamer as they could before the explosion.

Three or four women were in the first boat.

It was rather difficult to lower the boats in the heavy sea that was running, but the men were working swiftly, pushed by the terror of the coming disaster.

A little smoke curled up from the battened-down hatches.

As Frank reached the deck, he nearly ran against M. Rouen Montfort, who was carrying a pair of swords in scabbards, which seemed to be treasures he wished to save.

The Frenchman stopped and glared at Merry.

"Cursed Yankee!" he grated. "I would like to put one of zese gude blades t'rough your heart!"

"Haven't a doubt of it," said Merriwell, coolly. "That's about the kind of a man I took you to be."

Another boat got away, and the last boat was swung from the davits.

A sailor counted the men who remained and spoke to the captain. The latter said:

"At best, the boat will not hold them all. There is one too many, at least. Let the fellow in irons stay behind."

Harris heard this, and fancied his doom was sealed. He began to beg to be taken along, but one of the men gave him a kick.

The Frenchman turned on Frank.

"Do you hear?" he cried. "One cannot go. Do you make eet ze poor deval in ze iron? or do you dare fight me to see wheech one of us eet ees? Eef you make eet ze poor devval, eet show you are ze cowarde. Ha! I theenk you do not dare to fight!"

He spat toward Merry to express his contempt.

"Let me fight him!" panted Diamond at Frank's elbow.

"See that Harris is put into the boat!" ordered Merriwell. "I fancy I can take care of this Frenchman. If you do not get Harris into the boat I swear I will not enter it if I conquer Montfort!"

Then he whirled on the Frenchman.

"I accept your challenge!" he cried in clear tones.

Montfort uttered an exclamation of satisfaction. He flung off his coat, saying:

"Choose ze weapon, saire."

Frank did not pause to look them over in making a selection. He caught up one of them and drew it from the scabbord.

Montfort took the other.

"Ready?" cried the American youth.

"Ready!" answered the Frenchman.

Clash!—the swords came together and there on the deck of the burning steamer the strange duel began.

Frank fought with all the coolness and skill he could command. He fought as if he had been standing on solid ground instead of the deck of a ship that might be blown into a thousand fragments at any moment.

The Frenchman had fancied that the Yankee would prove easy to conquer, but he soon discovered Frank possessed no little skill, and he saw that he must do his best.

More than once Montfort thrust to run Frank through the body, and once his sword passed between the youth's left arm and his side.

Merry saw that the Frenchman really meant to kill him if possible.

Then men were getting into the boat. There were but few seconds left in which to finish the duel. Rattleton called to him from the boat, shouting above the roar of the wind:

"Finish him, Frank! Come on, now! Lively!"

The tip of Montfort's sword slit Frank's sleeve and touched his arm.

"Next time I get you!" hissed the vindictive Frenchman.

But right then Frank saw his opportunity. He made a lunge and drove his sword into the Frenchman's side.

Montfort uttered a cry, dropped his sword, flung up his hands, and sunk bleeding to the deck.

Merry flung his blood-stained weapon aside and bent over the man, saying sincerely:

"I hope your wound is not fatal, M. Montfort."

"It makes no difference!" gasped the man. "You are ze victor, so I must stay here an' die jus' ze same."

But Frank Merriwell was seized by a feeling of horror at the thought of leaving this man whom he had wounded. In a moment he realized he would be haunted all his life by the memory if he did so.

Quickly he caught M. Montfort up in his arms. He sprang to the side of the steamer. The boat was holding in for him. His friends shouted to him. The captain ordered him to jump at once.

"Catch this man!"

He lifted M. Montfort, swung him over the rail, and dropped him fairly into the boat!

"He has chosen," said the captain. "The boat will hold no more. Pull away!"

It was useless for Frank's friends to beg and plead. Away went the boat, leaving the noble youth to his doom.

Forty minutes later there was a terrible flare of fire and smoke, a thunderous explosion, and the ill-fated steamer had blown up.

Harry Rattleton was crying like a baby.

"Poor Frank!" he sobbed. "Noblest fellow in all the world—good-by! I'll never see you again!"

Tears rolled down Bruce Browning's face, and Jack Diamond, grim and speechless, looked as if the light of the world had gone out forever.

. . . . . .

Some days later the passengers and crew from the lost "Eagle" were landed at Liverpool by the steamer "Seneca," which had picked them up at sea. The "Seneca" was a slow old craft, but she got there all right.

A little grimy tender carried Bruce, Jack, Harry and the tutor from the "Seneca" to the floating dock. It was a sad and wretched-looking party.

On the dock stood a young man who shouted to them and waved his hand.

Jack Diamond started, gasped, clutched Browning and whispered:

"Look—look there, Bruce! Tell me if

I am going crazy, or do you see somebody who looks like——"

Harry Rattleton clutched the big fellow by the other side, spluttering:

"Am I doing gaffy—I mean going daffy? Look there! Who is that waving his hand to us?"

"It's the ghost of Frank Merriwell, as true as there are such things as ghosts!" muttured Browning.

But it was no ghost. It was Frank Merriwell in the flesh, alive and well! He greeted them as they came off the tender. He caught them in his arms, laughing, shouting, overjoyed. And they, realizing it really was him, hugged him and wept like a lot of big-hearted, manly young men.

Frank explained in a few words. He told how, after they had left him, he had belted himself well with life-preservers and left the "Eagle" in time to get away before the explosion. Then he was picked up by an Atlantic liner, which brought him to Liverpool in advance of his friends.

Thus he was there to receive them, and it seemed that the sea had given up its dead.

[THE END.]

The next number (159) of the TIP TOP WEEKLY will contain "Frank Merriwell's Backer; or, Among London Sports," by Burt L. Standish.

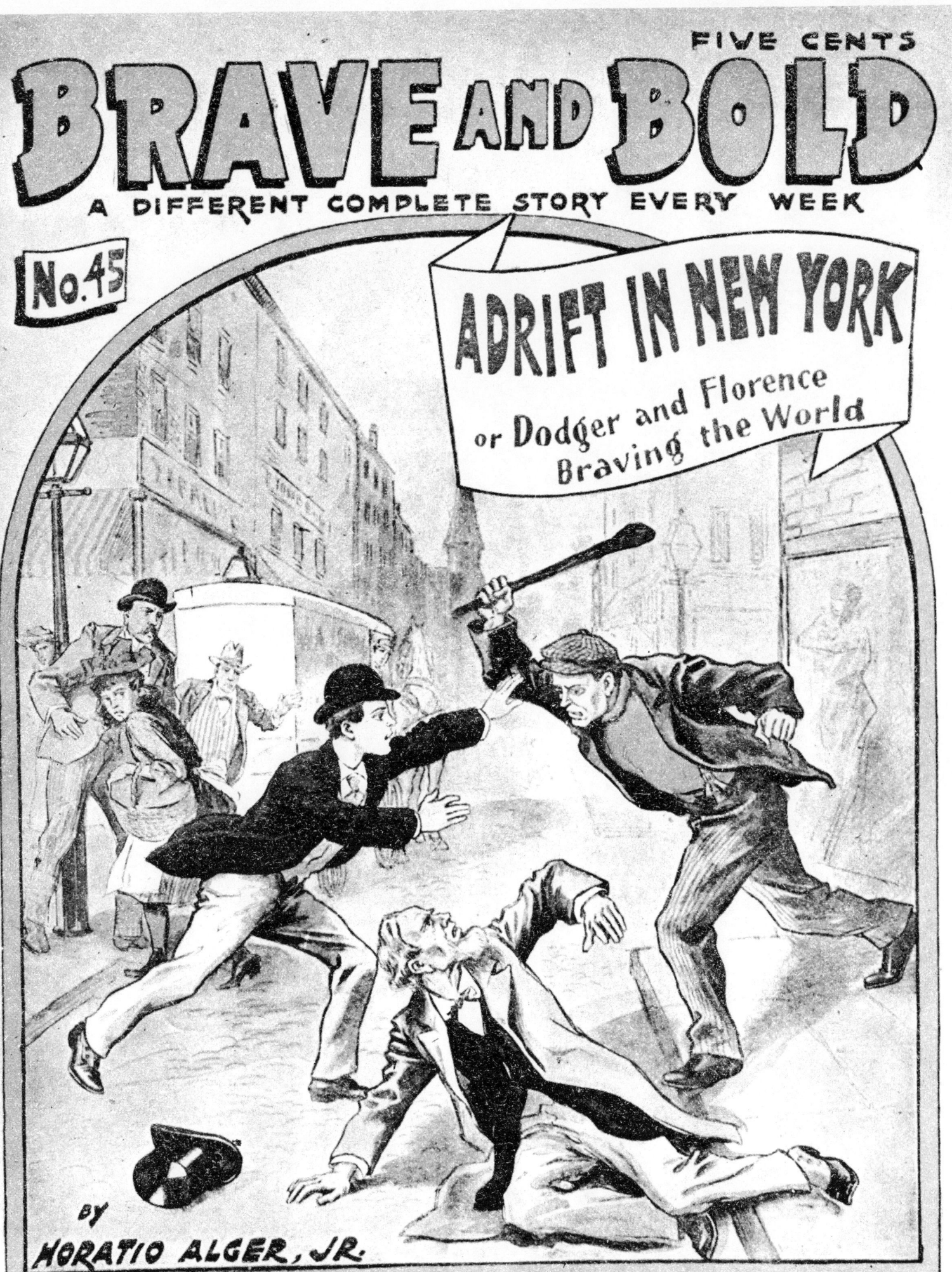

On the sidewalk lay the prostrate figure of a man. Over him, bludgeon in hand, bent a ruffian, whose purpose was only too clearly evident.

BRAVE & BOLD

A Different Complete Story Every Week

Issued Weekly. By Subscription $2.50 per year. Entered according to Act of Congress in the year 1903, in the Office of the Librarian of Congress, Washington, D. C. STREET & SMITH, 238 William St., N. Y.

No. 45.   NEW YORK, October 31, 1903.   Price Five Cents.

ADRIFT IN NEW YORK;

OR,

Dodger and Florence Braving the World.

By HORATIO ALGER, JR.

CHAPTER I.

THE MISSING HEIR.

"Uncle, you are not looking well to-night."

"I am not well, Florence. I sometimes doubt if I shall ever be any better."

"Surely, uncle, you cannot mean——"

"Yes, my child, I have reason to believe that I am nearing the end."

"I cannot bear to hear you speak so, uncle," said Florence Linden, in irrepressible agitation. "You are not an old man. You are but fifty-four."

"True, Florence, but it is not years only that make a man old. Two great sorrows have embittered my life. First, the death of my dearly-loved wife, and next, the loss of my boy, Harvey."

"It is long since I have heard you refer to my cousin's loss. I thought you had become reconciled—no, I do not mean that—I thought your regret might be less poignant."

"I have not permitted myself to speak of it, but I have never ceased to think of it day and night."

John Linden paused sadly, then resumed:

"If he had died, I might, as you say, have become reconciled; but he was abducted at the age of four by a revengeful servant whom I had discharged from my employment. Heaven knows whether he is living or dead, but it is impressed upon my mind that he still lives, it may be in misery, it may be as a criminal, while I, his unhappy father, live on in luxury which I cannot enjoy, with no one to care for me——"

Florence Linden sank impulsively on her knees beside her uncle's chair.

"Don't say that, uncle," she pleaded. "You know that I love you, Uncle John."

"And I, too, uncle."

There was a shade of jealousy in the voice of Curtis Waring as he entered the library through the open door, and, approaching his uncle, pressed his hand.

He was a tall, dark-complexioned man, of perhaps thirty-five, with shifty, black eyes and thin lips, shaded by a dark mustache. It was not a face to trust.

Even when he smiled, the expression of his face did not soften. Yet he could moderate his voice so as to express tenderness and sympathy.

He was the son of an elder sister of Mr. Linden, while Florence was the daughter of a younger brother.

Both were orphans, and both formed a part of Mr. Linden's household, and owed everything to his bounty.

Curtis was supposed to be in some business downtown; but he received a liberal allowance from his uncle, and often drew upon him for outside assistance.

As he stood with his uncle's hand in his, he was necessarily brought near Florence, who instinctively drew a little away, with a slight shudder, indicating repugnance.

Slight as it was, Curtis detected it, and his face darkened.

John Linden looked from one to the other.

"Yes," he said, "I must not forget that I have a nephew and a niece. You are both dear to me, but no one can take the place of the boy I have lost."

"But it is so long ago, uncle," said Curtis. "It must be fourteen years."

"It is fourteen years."

"And the boy is long since dead!"

"No, no!" said John Linden, vehemently. "I do not, I will not, believe it. He still lives, and I live only in the hope of one day clasping him in my arms."

"That is very improbable, uncle," said Curtis, in a tone of annoyance. "There isn't one chance in a hundred that my cousin still lives. The grave has closed over him long since. The sooner you make up your mind to accept the inevitable, the better."

The drawn features of the old man showed that the words had a depressing effect upon his mind, but Florence interrupted her cousin with an indignant protest.

"How can you speak so, Curtis?" she exclaimed. "Leave Uncle John the hope that he has so long cherished. I have a presentiment that Harvey still lives."

John Linden's face brightened up.

"You, too, believe it possible, Florence?" he said, eagerly.

"Yes, uncle, I not only believe it possible, but probable. How old would Harvey be if he still lived?"

"Eighteen—nearly a year older than yourself."

"How strange! I always think of him as a little boy."

"And I, too, Florence. He rises before me in his little velvet suit, as he was when I last saw him, with his sweet, boyish face, in which his mother's looks were reflected."

"Yet, if still living," interrupted Curtis, harshly, "he is a rough street boy, perchance serving his time at Blackwell's Island, and a hardened young ruffian whom it would be bitter mortification to recognize as your son."

"That's the sorrowful part of it," said his uncle, in a voice of anguish. "That is what I most dread."

"Then, since, even if he were living, you would not care to recognize him, why not cease to think of him, or else regard him as dead?"

"Curtis Waring, have you no heart?" demanded Florence, indignantly.

"Indeed, Florence, you ought to know," said Curtis, sinking his voice into softly modulated accents.

"I know nothing of it," said Florence, coldly, rising from her recumbent position, and drawing aloof from Curtis.

"You know that the dearest wish of my heart is to find favor in your eyes. Uncle, you know my wish, and approve of it, do you not?"

"Yes, Curtis; you and Florence are equally dear to me, and it is my hope that you may be united. In that case, there will be no division of my fortune. It will be left to you jointly."

"Believe me, sir," said Curtis, with faltering voice, feigning an emotion which he did not feel, "believe me, that I fully appreciate your goodness. I am sure Florence joins with me——"

"Florence can speak for herself," said his cousin, coldly. "My uncle needs no assurances from me. He is always kind, and I am always grateful."

John Linden seemed absorbed in thought.

"I do not doubt your affection," he said; "and I have shown it by making you my joint heirs in the event of your marriage; but it is only fair to say that my property goes to my boy, if he still lives."

"But, sir," protested Curtis, "is not that likely to create unnecessary trouble? It can never be known, and meanwhile——".

"You and Florence will hold the property in trust."

"Have you so specified in your will?" asked Curtis.

"I have made two wills. Both are in yonder secretary. By the first the property is bequeathed to you and Florence. By the second, and later, it goes to my lost boy, in the event of his recovery. Of course, you and Florence are not forgotten, but the bulk of the property goes to Harvey."

"I sincerely wish the boy might be restored to you," said Curtis; but his tone belied his words. "Believe me, the loss of the property would affect me little, if you could be made happy by realizing your warmest desire; but, uncle, I think it only the part of a friend to point out to you, as I have already done, the baselessness of any such expectation."

"It may be as you say, Curtis," said his uncle, with a sigh. "If I were thoroughly convinced of it, I would destroy the later will, and leave my property absolutely to you and Florence."

"No, uncle," said Florence, impulsively, "make no change; let the will stand."

Curtis, screened from his uncle's view, darted a glance of bitter indignation at Florence.

"Is the girl mad?" he muttered to himself. "Must she forever balk me?"

"Let it be so for the present, then," said Mr. Linden, wearily. "Curtis, will you ring the bell? I am tired, and shall retire to my couch early."

"Let me help you, Uncle John," said Florence, eagerly.

"It is too much for your strength, my child. I am growing more and more helpless."

"I, too, can help," said Curtis.

John Linden, supported on either side by his nephew and niece, left the room, and was assisted to his chamber.

Curtis and Florence returned to the library.

"Florence," said her cousin, "my uncle's intentions, as expressed to-night, make it desirable that there should be an understanding between us. Take a seat beside me"—leading her to a sofa—"and let us talk this matter over."

With a gesture of repulsion, Florence declined the proffered seat, and remained standing.

"As you please." she answered, coldly.

"Will you be seated?"

"No; our interview will be brief."

"Then I will come to the point. Uncle John wishes to see us united."

"It can never be!" said Florence, decidedly.

Curtis bit his lip in mortification, for her tone was cold and scornful.

Mingled with his mortification was genuine regret, for as he was capable of loving any one, he loved his fair, young cousin.

"You profess to love Uncle John, and yet you would disappoint his cherished hope!" he returned.

"Is it his cherished hope?"

"There is no doubt of it. He has spoken to me more than once on the subject. Feeling that his end is near, he wishes to leave you in charge of a protector."

"I can protect myself," said Florence, proudly.

"You think so. You do not consider the hapless lot of a penniless girl in a cold and selfish world."

"Penniless?" repeated Florence, in an accent of surprise.

"Yes, penniless. Our uncle's bequest to you is conditional upon your acceptance of my hand."

"Has he said this?" asked Florence, sinking into an armchair, with a helpless look.

"He has told me so more than once," returned Curtis, smoothly. "You don't know how near to his heart this marriage is. I know what you would say: If the property comes to me, I could come to your assistance, but I am expressly prohibited from doing so. I have pleaded with my uncle in your behalf, but in vain."

Florence was too clear-sighted not to penetrate his falsehood.

"If my uncle's heart is hardened against me," she said, "I shall be too wise to turn to you. I am to understand, then, that my choice lies between poverty and a union with you?"

"You have stated it correctly, Florence."

"Then," said Florence, arising, "I will not hesitate. I shrink from poverty, for I have been reared in luxury, but I will sooner live in a hovel——"

"Or a tenement house," interjected Curtis, with a sneer.

"Yes, or a tenement house, than become the wife of one I loathe."

"Girl, you shall bitterly repent that word!" said Curtis, stung to fury.

She did not reply, but, pale and sorrowful, glided from the room, to weep bitter tears in the seclusion of her chamber.

CHAPTER II.

A STRANGE VISITOR.

Curtis Waring followed the retreating form of his cousin with a sardonic smile.

"She is in the toils! She cannot escape me!" he muttered. "But"—and here his brow darkened—"it vexes me to see how she repels my advances, as if I were some loathsome thing. If only she would return my love—for I do love her, cold as she is—I should be happy. Can there be a rival? But no! we live so quietly that she has met no one who could win her affections. Why can she not turn to me? Surely, I am not so ill-favored, and, though twice her age, I am still a young man. Nay, it is only a young girl's caprice. She shall yet come to my arms, a willing captive."

His thoughts took a turn, as he arose from his seat, and walked over to the secretary.

"So it is here that the two wills are deposited!" he said to himself; "one making me a rich man, the other a beggar! While the last is in existence I am not safe. The boy may be alive, and liable to turn up at any moment. If only he were dead—or the will destroyed——" Here he made a suggestive pause.

He took a bunch of keys from his pocket, and tried one after another, but without success. He was so absorbed in his work that he did not notice the entrance of a dark-browed, broad-shouldered man, dressed in a shabby corduroy suit, till the intruder indulged in a short cough, intended to draw attention.

Starting with guilty consciousness, Curtis turned sharply around, and his glance fell on the intruder.

"Who are you?" he demanded, angrily. "And how dare you enter a gentleman's house unbidden?"

"Are you the gentleman?" asked the intruder, with intentional insolence.

"Yes."

"You own this house?"

"Not at present. It is my uncle's."

"And that secretary—pardon my curiosity—is his?"

"Yes; but what business is it of yours?"

"Not much. Only it makes me laugh to see a gentleman picking a lock. You should leave such business to men like me."

"Look here, fellow," said Curtis, thoroughly provoked, "I don't know who you are, nor what you mean, but let me inform you that your presence here is an intrusion, and the sooner you leave this house the better!"

"I will leave it when I get ready."

Curtis started to his feet, and advanced toward his visitor with an air of menace.

"Go at once," he exclaimed, angrily, "or I will kick you out of the door!"

"Oh, no, you won't!"

"And why not?" asked Curtis, with a feeling of uneasiness for which he could not account.

"Why not? Because, in that case, I should seek an interview with your uncle, and tell him——"

"What?"

"That his son still lives—and that I can restore him to his——"

The face of Curtis Waring blanched; he staggered as if he had been struck, and he cried out, hoarsely:

"It is a lie!"

"It is the truth, begging your pardon. Do you mind my smoking?" and he coolly produced a common clay pipe, filled it, and lighted it.

"Who are you?" asked Curtis, scanning the man's features with painful anxiety.

"Have you forgotten Tim Bolton?"

"Are you Tim Bolton?" faltered Curtis.

"Yes; but you don't seem glad to see me?"

"I thought you were——"

"In Australia. So I was, three years since. Then I got homesick, and came back to New York."

"You have been here three years?"

"Yes," chuckled Bolton. "You didn't suspect it, did you?"

"Where?" asked Curtis, in a hollow voice.

"I keep a saloon on the Bowery. There's my card. Call around when convenient."

Curtis was about to throw the card into the grate, but on second thought dropped it into his pocket.

"And the boy?" he asked, slowly.

"Is alive and well. He hasn't been starved. Though I dare say you wouldn't have grieved if he had."

"And he is actually in this city?"

"Just so."

"Does he know anything of—you know what I mean?"

"He doesn't know that he is the son of a rich man, and heir to the property which you look upon as yours. That's what you mean, isn't it?"

"Yes. What is he doing? Is he at work?"

"He helps me some in the saloon, sells papers in the evenings, and makes himself generally useful."

"Has he any education?"

"Well, I haven't sent him to boarding school or college," answered Tim. "He don't know no Greek, or Latin, or mathematics—phew! that's a hard word! You didn't tell me you wanted him made a scholar of."

"I didn't. I wanted never to see or hear from him again. What made you bring him back to New York?"

"Couldn't keep away, governor. I got homesick, I did. There ain't but one Bowery in the world, and I hankered after that——"

"Didn't I pay you money to keep away, Tim Bolton?"

"I don't deny it; but what's three thousand dollars? Why, the kid's cost me more than that. I've had the care of him for fourteen years, and it's only about two hundred a year."

"You have broken your promise to me!" said Curtis, sternly.

"There's worse things than breaking your promise," retorted Bolton.

"Look here, Tim Bolton," said Curtis, drawing up a chair, and lowering his voice to a confidential pitch, "you say you want money?"

"Of course I do."

"Well, I don't give money for nothing."

"I know that. What's wanted now?"

"You say the boy is alive?"

"He's very much alive."

"Is there any necessity for his living?" asked Curtis, in a sharp, hissing tone, fixing his eyes searchingly on Bolton, to see how his hint would be taken.

"You mean that you want me to murder him?" said Bolton, quickly.

"Why not? You don't look overscrupulous."

"I am a bad man, I admit it," said Bolton, with a gesture of repugnance, "a thief, a low blackguard, perhaps, but, thank Heaven! I am no murderer! And if I was, I wouldn't spill a drop of that boy's blood for the fortune that is his by right."

"I didn't give you credit for so much sentiment, Bolton," said Curtis, with a sneer. "You don't look like it, but appearances are deceitful. We'll drop the subject. You can serve me in another way. Can you open this secretary?"

"Yes; that's in my line."

"There is a paper in it that I want. It is my uncle's will. I have a curiosity to read it."

"I understand. Well, I'm agreeable."

"If you find any money or valuables, you are welcome to them. I only want the paper. When will you make the attempt?"

"To-morrow night. When will it be safe?"

"At eleven o'clock. We all retire early in this house. Can you force an entrance?"

"Yes; but it will be better for you to leave the outer door unlocked."

"I have a better plan. Here is my latchkey."

"Good! I may not do the job myself, but I will see that it is done. How shall I know the will?"

"It is a big envelope, tied with a narrow tape. Probably it is inscribed, 'My will.'"

"Suppose I succeed, when shall I see you?"

"I will come around to your place on the Bowery. Good-night."

Curtis Waring saw Bolton to the door, and let him out. Returning, he flung himself on a sofa.

"I can make that man useful!" he reflected. "There is an element of danger in the boy's presence in New York, but it will go hard if I can't get rid of him! Tim Bolton is unexpectedly squeamish, but there are others to whom I can apply. With gold, everything is possible. It's time matters came to a finish. My uncle's health is rapidly failing—the doctor hints that he has heart disease—and the fortune for which I have been waiting so long will soon be mine, if I work my cards right. I can't afford to make any mistakes now."

CHAPTER III.

FLORENCE AND DODGER.

Florence Linden sat in the library the following evening in an attitude of depression. Her eyelids were swollen, and it was evident she had been weeping. During the day she had had an interview with her uncle, in which he harshly insisted upon her yielding to his wishes, and marrying her Cousin Curtis.

Florence had absolutely refused.

"I see you are incorrigible," finally said John Linden, stormily. "Do you know what will be the consequences?"

"I am prepared for all."

"Then listen! If you persist in balking me, I shall leave the entire estate to Curtis."

"Do with your money as you will, uncle. I have no claim to more than I have received."

"You are right there; but that is not all."

Florence fixed upon him a mute look of inquiry.

"I will give you twenty-four hours more to come to your senses. Then, if you persist in your ingratitude and disobedience, you must find another home."

"Oh, uncle, you do not mean that?" exclaimed Florence, deeply moved.

"I do mean it, and I shall not allow your tears to move me. Not another word, for I will not hear it. Take twenty-four hours to think over what I have said."

Florence bowed her head on her hands, and gave herself up to sorrowful thoughts.

After a brief pause, Florence seated herself at the table, and drew toward her writing materials.

"My heart is broken!" she murmured; "I, who am driven from the only home I have ever known. What can have turned against me my uncle, usually so kind and considerate? It must be that Curtis has exerted a baleful influence upon him. I cannot leave him without one word of farewell."

She took up a sheet of paper, and wrote, rapidly:

"DEAR UNCLE: You have told me to leave your house, and I obey. I cannot tell you how sad I feel, when I reflect that I have lost your love, and must go forth among strangers—I know not where. I was but a little girl when you gave me a home. I have grown up in an atmosphere of love, and I have felt very grateful to you for all you have done for me. I have tried to conform to your wishes, and I would obey you in all else—but I cannot marry Curtis; I think I would rather die. Let me still live with you as I have done. I do not care for any part of your money—leave it all to him, if you think best—but give me back my place in your heart. You are angry now, but you will some time pity and forgive your poor Florence, who will never cease to bless and pray for you. Good-by!
FLORENCE."

After completing the note, Florence let her head fall upon the table, and sobbed herself to sleep.

An hour and a half passed, the servant looked in, but noticing that her mistress was sleeping, contented herself with lowering the gas, but refrained from waking her.

And so she slept on till the French clock upon the mantel struck eleven.

Five minutes later, and the door of the room slowly opened, and a boy entered on tiptoe. He was roughly dressed. His figure was manly and vigorous, and despite his stealthy step and suspicious movements, his face was prepossessing.

He started when he saw Florence.

"What, a sleeping gal!" he said to himself. "Tim told me I'd find the coast clear; but I guess she's sound asleep, and won't hear nothing. I don't half like this job, but I've got to do as Tim told me. He says he's my father, so I s'pose it's all right. All the same, I shall be nabbed some day, and then the family'll be disgraced. It's a queer life I've led ever since I can remember. Sometimes I feel like leaving Tim and settin' up for myself. I wonder how 'twould seem to be respectable?"

The boy approached the secretary, and with some tools he had brought essayed to open it. After a brief delay, he succeeded, and lifted the cover. He was about to explore it, according to Tim's directions, when he heard a cry of fear, and turning swiftly, saw Florence, her eyes dilated with terror, gazing at him.

"Who are you?" she asked, in alarm, "and what are you doing there?"

The boy sprang to the side of Florence, and seized her wrists in his strong, young grasp.

"Don't you alarm the house," he said, "or I'll——"

"What will you do?" gasped Florence, in alarm.

The boy was evidently softened by her beauty, and answered, in a tone of hesitation:

"I don't know. I won't harm you if you keep quiet."

"What are you here for?" asked Florence, fixing her eyes on the boy's face; "are you a thief?"

"I don't know—yes, I suppose I am."

"How sad, when you are so young."

"What! miss, do you pity me?"

"Yes, my poor boy; you must be very poor, or you wouldn't bring yourself to steal."

"No. I ain't poor; leastways, I have enough to eat, and I have a place to sleep."

"Then why don't you earn your living by honest means?"

"I can't; I must obey orders."

"Whose orders?"

"Why, the guv'nor's, to be sure."

"Did he tell you to open that secretary?"

"Yes."

"Who is the gov'nor, as you call him?"

"I can't tell; it wouldn't be square."

"He must be a very wicked man."

"Well, he ain't exactly what you call an angel, but I've seen wuss men than the guv'nor."

"Do you mind telling me your own name?"

"No; for I know you won't peach on me. Tom Dodger."

"Dodger?"

"Yes."

"That isn't a surname."

"It's all I've got. That's what I'm always called."

"It is very singular," said Florence, fixing a glance of mingled curiosity and perplexity upon the young visitor.

While the two were earnestly conversing in that subdued light, afforded by the lowered gaslight, Tim Bolton crept in through the door unobserved by either, tiptoed across the room to the secretary, snatched the will and a roll of bills, and escaped, without attracting attention.

"Oh, I wish I could persuade you to give up this bad life," resumed Florence, earnestly, "and become honest."

"Do you really care what becomes of me, miss?" asked Dodger, slowly.

"I do, indeed."

"That's very kind of you, miss; but I don't understand it. You are a rich young lady, and I'm only a poor boy, livin' in a Bowery dive."

"What's that?"

"Never mind, miss; such as you wouldn't understand. Why, all my life I've lived with thieves, and drunkards, and bunco men, and——"

"But I'm sure you don't like it. You are fit for something better."

"Do you really think so?" asked Dodger, doubtfully.

"Yes; you have a good face. You were meant to be good and honest, I am sure."

"Would you trust me?" asked the boy, earnestly, fixing his large, dark eyes eloquently on the face of Florence.

"Yes, I would, if you would only leave your evil companions, and become true to your better nature."

"No one ever spoke to me like that before, miss," said Dodger, his expressive features showing that he was strongly moved. "You think I could be good if I tried hard, and grow up respectable?"

"I am sure you could," said Florence, confidently.

There was something in this boy, young outlaw though he was, that moved her powerfully, and even fascinated her, though she hardly realized it. It was something more than a feeling of compassion for a wayward and misguided youth.

"I could if I was rich like you, and lived in a nice house, and 'sociated with swells. If you had a father like mine——"

"Is he a bad man?"

"Well, he don't belong to the church. He keeps a gin-mill, and has ever since I was a kid."

"Have you always lived with him?"

"Yes; but not in New York."

"Where, then?"

"In Melbourne."

"That's in Australia."

"Yes, miss."

"How long since you came to New York?"

"I guess it's about three years."

"And you have always had this man as a guardian? Poor boy!"

"You've got a different father from me, miss?"

Tears forced themselves to the eyes of Florence, as this remark brought forcibly to her mind the position in which she was placed.

"Alas!" she answered, impulsively, "I am alone in the world."

"What! ain't the old gentleman that lives here your father?"

"He is my uncle; but is very, very angry with me, and has this day ordered me to leave the house."

"Why, what a cantankerous old ruffian he is, to be sure!" exclaimed the boy, indignantly.

"Hush! you must not talk against my uncle. He always been kind to me till now."

"Why, what's up? What's he mad about?"

"He wants me to marry my Cousin Curtis—Curtis Waring—a man I do not even like."

"That's a shame! I've seen him. He's got dark hair and a dark complexion, and a wicked look in his eyes."

"You, too, have noticed that?"

"I've seen such as him before. He's a bad man."

"Do you know anything about him?" asked Florence, eagerly.

"Only his looks."

"I am not deceived," murmured Florence. "It's not wholly prejudice. The boy distrusts him, too. So you see, Dodger," she added, aloud, "I am not a rich young lady, as you suppose. I must leave this house, and work for my living. I have no home any more."

"If you have no home," said Dodger, impulsively, "come home with me."

"To the home you have described, my poor boy? How could I do that?"

"No; I will hire a room for you in a quiet street, and you shall be my sister. I will work for you, and give you my money."

"You are kind, and I am glad to think I have found a friend when I need one most. But I could not accept stolen money. It would be as bad as if I, too, were a thief."

"But I am not a thief! That is, I won't be any more."

"And you will give up your plan of robbing my uncle?"

"Yes, I will; though I don't know what my guv'nor will say. He'll half murder me, I expect. He'll be sure to cut up rough."

"Do right, Dodger, whatever happens. Promise me that you will never steal again?"

"There's my hand, miss—I promise. Nobody ever talked to me like you. I never thought much about bein' respectable, and growin' up to be somebody, but if you take an interest in me, I'll try hard to do right."

At this moment Mr. Linden, clad in a long morning gown, and holding a candle in his hand, entered the room, and started in astonishment when he saw Florence clasping the hand of one whose appearance led him to stamp as a young rough.

"Shameless girl!" he exclaimed, in stern reproof. "So this is the company you keep when you think I am out of the way!"

CHAPTER IV.
A TEMPEST.

The charge was so strange and unexpected that Florence was overwhelmed. She could only murmur:

"Oh, uncle!"

Her young companion was indignant. Already he felt that Florence had consented to accept him as a friend, and he was resolved to stand by her.

"I say, old man," he bristled up, "don't you go to insult her! She's an angel!"

"No doubt you think so," rejoined Mr. Linden, in a tone of sarcasm. "Upon my word, miss, I congratulate you on your elevated taste. So this is your reason for not being willing to marry your Cousin Curtis?"

"Indeed, uncle, you are mistaken. I never met this boy till to-night."

"Don't try to deceive me. Young man, did you open my secretary?"

"Yes, sir."

"And robbed it, into the bargain," continued Linden, going to the secretary and examining it. He did not, however, miss the will, but only the roll of bills. "Give me back the money you have stolen from it, you young rascal!"

"I took nothing, sir."

"It's a lie! The money is gone, and no one else could have taken it."

"I don't allow no one to call me a liar. Just take that back, old man, or I——"

"Indeed, uncle, he took nothing, for he had only just opened the secretary when I woke up and spoke to him."

"You stand by him, of course, shameless girl! I blush to think that you are my niece. I am glad to think that my eyes are opened before it is too late."

The old merchant rang the bell violently, and aroused the house. Dodger made no attempt to escape, but stood beside Florence, in the attitude of a protector. But a short time elapsed before Curtis Waring and the servants entered the room, and gazed with wonder at the *tableau* presented by the excited old man and the two young people.

"My friends," said John Linden, in a tone of excitement, "I call you to witness that this girl, whom I blush to acknowledge as my niece, has proved herself unworthy of my kindness. In your presence, I cut her off, and bid her never again darken my door."

"But what has she done, uncle?" asked Curtis. He was prepared for the presence of Dodger, whom he rightly concluded to be an agent of Tim Bolton, but he could not understand why Florence should be in the library at this late hour. Nor was he able to understand the evidently friendly relations between her and the young visitor.

"What has she done?" repeated John Linden. "She has introduced that young ruffian into the house to rob me. Look at that secretary! He has forced it open, and stolen a large sum of money."

"It is not true, sir," said Dodger, calmly; "about taking the money, I mean. I haven't taken a cent."

"Then why did you open the secretary?"

"I did mean to take money, but she stopped me."

"Oh, she stopped you?" repeated Linden, with withering sarcasm. "Then, perhaps, you will tell me where the money is gone?"

"He hasn't discovered about the will," thought Curtis, congratulating himself; "if the boy has it, I must manage to give him a chance to escape."

"You can search me if you want to," continued Dodger, proudly. "You won't find any money on me."

"Do you think I am a fool, you young burglar?" exclaimed John Linden, angrily.

"Uncle, let me speak to the boy," said Curtis, soothingly. "I think he will tell me."

"As you like, Curtis; but I am convinced that he is a thief."

Curtis Waring beckoned Dodger into an adjoining room.

"Now, my boy," he said, smoothly, "give me what you took from the secretary, and I will see that you are not arrested."

"But, sir, I didn't take nothing—it's just as I told the old duffer. The girl waked up just as I'd got the secretary open, and I didn't have a chance."

"But the money is gone," said Curtis, in an incredulous tone.

"I don't know nothing about that."

"Come, you'd better examine your pockets. In the hurry of the moment you may have taken it without knowing it."

"No, I couldn't."

"Didn't you take a paper of any kind?" asked Curtis, eagerly. "Sometimes papers are of more value than money."

"No, I didn't take no paper, though Tim told me to."

Curtis quietly ignored the allusion to Tim, for it did not suit his purpose to get Tim into trouble. His unscrupulous agent knew too much that would compromise his principal.

"Are you willing that I should examine you?"

"Yes, I am. Go ahead."

Curtis thrust his hand into the pockets of the boy, who, boy as he was, was as tall as himself, but was not repaid by the discovery of anything. He was very much perplexed.

"Didn't you throw the articles on the floor?" he demanded, suspiciously.

"No, I didn't."

"You didn't give them to the young lady?"

"No; if I had, she'd have said so."

"Humph! this is strange. What is your name?"

"Dodger."

"That's a queer name. Have you no other?"

"Not as I know of."

"With whom do you live?"

"With my father. Leastways, he says he's my father."

There was a growing suspicion in the mind of Curtis Waring. He scanned the boy's features with attention.

Could this ill-dressed boy—a street boy in appearance—be his long-lost and deeply-wronged cousin?

"Who is it that says he is your father?" he demanded, abruptly.

"Do you want to get him into trouble?"

"No, I don't want to get him into trouble, or you, either. Better tell me all, and I will be your friend."

"You're a better sort than I thought at first," said Dodger. "The man I live with is called Tim Bolton."

"I thought so," quickly ejaculated Curtis. He had scarcely got out the words before he was sensible that he had made a mistake.

"What! do you know Tim?" inquired Dodger, in surprise.

"I mean," replied Curtis, lamely, "that I had heard of this man, Bolton. He keeps a saloon on the Bowery, doesn't he?"

"Yes."

"I thought you would be living with some such man. Did he come to the house with you to-night?"

"Yes."

"Where is he?"

"He stayed outside."

"Perhaps he is there now."

"Don't you go to having him arrested," said Dodger, suspiciously.

"I will keep my promise. Are you sure you didn't pass out the paper and the money to him? Think, now."

"No, I didn't. I didn't have a chance. When I came into the room yonder, I saw the gal asleep, and I thought she wouldn't hear me, but when I got the desk open, she spoke to me, and asked me what I was doin'."

"And you took nothing?"

"No."

"It seems very strange. I cannot understand it. Yet my uncle says the money is gone. Did any one else enter the room while you were talking with Miss Linden?"

"I didn't see any one."

"What were you talking about?"

"She said the old man wanted her to marry you, and she didn't want to."

"Upon my word, she was very confidential. You are a queer person for her to select as a confidant."

"Maybe so, sir; but she knows I'm her friend."

"You like the young lady, then? Perhaps you would like to marry her yourself?"

"As if she'd taken any notice of a poor boy like me. I told her if her uncle sent her away, I'd take care of her, and be a brother to her."

"How would Mr. Tim Bolton—that's his name, isn't it?—like that?"

"I wouldn't take her to where he lives."

"I think, myself, it would hardly be a suitable home for

a young lady brought up on Madison Avenue. There is certainly no accounting for tastes. Miss Florence——"

"That's her name, is it?"

"Yes; didn't she tell you?"

"No; but it's a nice name."

"She declines my hand, and accepts your protection. It will certainly be a proud distinction to become Mrs. Dodger."

"Don't you laugh at her!" said Dodger, suspiciously.

"I don't propose to. But I think we may as well return to the library."

"Well?" said Mr. Linden, as his nephew returned with Dodger.

"I have examined the boy, and found nothing on his person," said Curtis; "I confess I am puzzled. He appears to have a high admiration for Florence——"

"As I supposed."

"She has even confided to him her dislike for me, and he has offered her his protection."

"Is this so, miss?" demanded Mr. Linden, sternly.

"Yes, uncle," faltered Florence.

"Then you can join the young person you have selected whenever you please. For your sake, I will not have him arrested for attempted burglary. He is welcome to what he has taken, since he is likely to marry into the family. You may stay here to-night, and he can call for you in the morning."

John Linden closed the secretary, and left the room, leaving Florence sobbing. The servants, too, retired, and Curtis was left alone with her.

"Florence," he said, "accept my hand, and I will reconcile my uncle to you. Say but the word, and——"

"I can never speak it, Curtis! I will take my uncle at his word. Dodger, call for me to-morrow at eight, and I will accept your friendly services in finding me a new home."

"I'll be on hand, miss. Good-night!"

"Be it so, obstinate girl!" said Curtis, angrily. "The time will come when you will bitterly repent your mad decision."

CHAPTER V.

FLORENCE LEAVES HOME.

Florence passed a sleepless night. It had come upon her so suddenly, this expulsion from the home of her childhood, that she could not fully realize it. She could not feel that she was taking her last look at the familiar room, and well-remembered dining-room where she had sat down for the last time to breakfast. She was alone at the breakfast table, for the usual breakfast hour was half-past eight, and she had appointed Dodger to call for her at eight.

The bell rang. She went out into the hall, and when the door was opened, the visitor proved to be Dodger. He had improved his appearance so far as his limited means would allow. His hands and face were thoroughly clean; he had bought a new collar and necktie; his shoes were polished, and despite his shabby suit, he looked quite respectable. Getting a full view of him, Florence saw that his face was frank and handsome, his eyes bright, and his teeth like pearls.

"Come, Miss Florence," said Dodger; "if you don't mind walking over to Fourth Avenue, we'll take the horse cars."

So, under strange guidance, Florence Linden left her luxurious home, knowing not what awaited her. What haven of refuge she might find she knew not. She, like Dodger, was adrift in New York.

Florence, as she stepped on the sidewalk, turned, and fixed a last sad look on the house that had been her home for so many years. She had never anticipated such a sundering of home ties, and even now she found it difficult to realize that the moment had come when her life was to be rent in twain, and the sunlight of prosperity was to be darkened and obscured by a gloomy and uncertain future.

She had hastily packed a few indispensable articles in a valise, which she carried in her hand.

"Let me take your bag, Miss Florence," said Dodger, reaching out his hand.

"I don't want to trouble you, Dodger."

"It ain't no trouble, Miss Florence. I'm stronger than you, and it looks better for me to carry it."

"You are very kind, Dodger. What should I do without you?"

"There's plenty that would be glad of the chance of helping you," said Dodger, with a glance of admiration at the fair face of his companion.

"I don't know where to find them," said Florence, sadly. "Even my uncle has turned against me."

"He's an old chump!" ejaculated Dodger, in a tone of disgust.

"Hush! I cannot hear a word against him. He has always been kind and considerate till now. It is the evil influence of my Cousin Curtis that has turned him against me. When he comes to himself, I am sure he will regret his cruelty."

"He would take you back if you would marry your cousin?"

"Yes; but that I will never do!" exclaimed Florence, with energy.

"Bully for you!" said Dodger. "Excuse me," he said, apologetically. "I ain't used to talkin' to young ladies, and perhaps that ain't proper for me to say."

"I don't mind, Dodger; your heart is in the right place."

"Thank you, Miss Florence. I'm glad you've got confidence in me. I'll try to deserve it."

"Where are we going?" asked the young lady, whose only thought up to this moment had been to get away from the presence of Curtis and his persecutions.

They had now reached Fourth Avenue, and a surface car was close at hand.

"We're going to get aboard that car," said Dodger, signaling with his free hand. "I'll tell you more when we're inside."

Florence entered the car, and Dodger, following, took a seat at her side.

They presented a noticeable contrast, for Florence was dressed as beseemed her station, while Dodger, in spite of his manly, attractive face, was roughly attired, and looked like a working boy.

"Now, I'll tell you where we are goin'," said Dodger. "A friend of mine, Mrs. O'Keefe, has a lodgin' house, just off the Bowery. I saw her last night, and she says she's got a good room that she can give you for two dollars a week—I don't know how much you'd be willing to pay, but——"

"I can pay that for a time, at least. I have a little money, and I must find some work to do soon. Is this Mrs. O'Keefe a nice lady?"

"She ain't a lady at all," answered Dodger, bluntly. "She keeps a apple-stand near the corner of Bowery and Grand Street; but she's a good, respectable woman, and she's good-hearted. She'll be kind to you, and try to make things pleasant; but if you ain't satisfied——"

"It will do—for the present. Kindness is what I need, driven as I am from the home of my childhood. But you, Dodger, where do you live?"

"I'm goin' to take a small room in the same house, Miss Florence."

"I shall be glad to have you near me."

"I am proud to hear you say that. I'm a poor boy, and you're a rich lady, but——"

"Not rich, Dodger. I am as poor as yourself."

"You're a reg'lar lady, anyway. You ain't one of my kind, but I'm going to improve and raise myself. I was readin' the other day of a rich man that was once a poor boy, and sold papers like me. But there's one thing in the way—I ain't got no eddication."

"You can read and write, can't you, Dodger?"

"Yes, I can read pretty well, but I can't write much."

"I will teach you in the evenings, when we are both at leisure."

"Will you?" asked the boy, with a glad smile. "You're very kind—I'd like a teacher like you."

"Then it's a bargain, Dodger," and Florence's face, for the first time, lost its sad look, and she saw an opportunity of helping one who had befriended her. "But you must promise to study faithfully."

"That I will. I've made up my mind I won't live with Tim no longer. I can earn my own livin' sellin' papers, or smashin' baggage, and keep away from Tim. I'd have done it before if I'd had a friend like you to care for me."

"We will stand by each other, Dodger. Heaven knows I need a friend, and if I can be a friend to you, and help you, I will."

"We'll get out here, Miss Florence. I told Mrs. O'Keefe I'd call at her stand, and she'll go over and show you your room."

They left the car at the corner of Grand Street, and Dodger led the way to an apple-stand, presided over by a lady of ample proportions, whose broad, Celtic face seemed to indicate alike shrewd good sense and a kindly spirit.

"Mrs. O'Keefe," said Dodger, "this is the young lady I spoke to you about—Miss Florence Linden."

"It's welcome you are, my dear, and I'm very glad to make your acquaintance. You look like a rale leddy, and I don't know how you'll like the room I've got for you."

"I cannot afford to be particular, Mrs. O'Keefe. I have had a—a reverse of circumstances, and I must be content with an humble home."

"Then I'll go over and show it to you. Here, Kitty, come and mind the stand," she called to a girl about thirteen, across the street, "and don't let anybody steal the apples. Look out for Jimmy Mahone; he stole a couple of apples right under my nose this mornin', the young spalpeen!"

They went to a four-story tenement of shabby brick, which was evidently well filled up by a miscellaneous crowd of tenants—shop girls, mechanics, laborers and widows, living by their daily toil.

Florence had never visited this part of the city, and her heart sank within her as she followed Mrs. O'Keefe through a dirty hallway, up a rickety staircase, to the second floor.

"One more flight of stairs, my dear," said Mrs. O'Keefe, encouragingly. "I've got four rooms upstairs; one of them is for you, and one for Dodger."

Florence did not reply. She began to understand at what cost she had secured her freedom from a distasteful marriage.

In her Madison Avenue home all the rooms were light, clean and luxuriously furnished. Here—— But words were inadequate to describe the contrast.

Mrs. O'Keefe threw open the door of a back room, about twelve feet square, furnished in the plainest manner, uncarpeted, except for a strip that was laid, like a rug, beside the bedstead.

There was a washstand, with a mirror, twelve by fifteen inches, placed above it, a pine bureau, a couple of wooden chairs, and a cane-seated rocking-chair.

"There, my dear, what do you say to that?" asked Mrs. O'Keefe, complacently. "All nice and comfortable as you would wish to see."

"It is—very nice," said Florence, faintly, sacrificing truth to politeness.

But Mrs. O'Keefe was kind, and Florence appreciated it.

"I must be goin'," said Dodger. "I've got to work, or I can't pay room rent when the week comes around."

"What are you going to do, Dodger?" asked Florence.

"It isn't time for the evenin' papers yet, so I shall go 'round to the piers, and see if I can't get a job at smashin' baggage. Good-by, Miss Florence; I'll be back some time this afternoon."

"And I must be goin', too," said Mrs. O'Keefe. "I can't depend on that Kitty; she's a wild slip of a girl, and just as like as not I'll find a dozen apples stole when I get back. I hope you won't feel lonely, my dear."

"I think I will lie down a while," said Florence. "I have a headache."

She threw herself on the bed, and a feeling of loneliness and desolation came over her.

Her new friends were kind, but they could not make up to her for her uncle's love, so strangely lost, and the home she had left behind.

CHAPTER VI.
FLORENCE OBTAINS EMPLOYMENT.

In the house on Madison Avenue, Curtis Waring was left in possession of the field. Through his machinations, Florence had been driven from home and disinherited.

He was left sole heir to his uncle's large property, with the prospect of soon succeeding, for, though only fifty-four, John Linden looked at least ten years older, and was as feeble as many men past seventy.

Yet, as Curtis seated himself at the breakfast table, an hour after Florence had left the house, he looked far from happy or triumphant.

One thing he had not succeeded in—the conquest of his cousin's heart. Though he loved himself best, he was really in love with Florence, so far as he was capable of being in love with any one.

She was only half his age—scarcely that—but he persuaded himself that the match was in every way suitable.

He liked to fancy her at the head of his table, after the death of his uncle, which he anticipated in a few months, at latest.

The more she appeared to dislike him, the more he determined to marry her, even against her will.

She was the only other one likely to inherit John Linden's wealth, and by marrying her, he would make sure of it.

Besides that, now that Florence was really gone, her uncle regretted, and would gladly have had her back again.

"I shall have to humor and deceive him," thought Curtis, after a talk with Mr. Linden. "I shall have a difficult part to play, but I am sure to succeed at last."

* * * * * * *

For a few days, after being installed in her new home, Florence was like one dazed.

She could not settle her mind to any plan of self-support.

She was too unhappy in her enforced exile from her home, and it saddened her to think that the uncle who had always been so kind was perhaps permanently estranged from her.

Though Mrs. O'Keefe was kind, and Dodger was her faithful friend, she could not accustom herself to her poor surroundings.

She had not supposed luxury so essential to her happiness.

It was worse for her because she had nothing to do but give way to her morbid fancies.

This Mrs. O'Keefe was clear-sighted enough to see.

"I am sorry to see you so downcast like, my dear young lady," she said.

"How can I help it, Mrs. O'Keefe?" returned Florence.

"Try not to think of your wicked cousin, my dear."

"It isn't of him that I think—it is of my uncle. How could he be so cruel, and turn against me after years of kindness?"

"It's that wicked Curtis that is settin' him against you, take my word for it, Miss Florence. Shure, he must be wake-minded, to let such a spalpeen set him against a swate young lady like you."

"He is weak in body, not in mind, Mrs. O'Keefe. You are right in thinking that it is Curtis that is the cause of my misfortunes."

"Your uncle will come to his right mind some day, never fear! And now, my dear, shall I give you a bit of advice?"

"Go on, my kind friend. I will promise to consider whatever you say."

"Then you'd better get some kind of work to take up your mind—a bit of sewin', or writin', or anything that comes to hand. I suppose you wouldn't want to mind my apple-stand a couple of hours every day?"

"No," answered Florence, "I don't feel equal to that."

"It would do you no end of good to be out in the open air. It would bring back the roses to your pale cheeks. If you coop yourself up in this dark room, you'll fade away and get thin."

"You are right. I will make an effort and go out. Besides, I must see about work."

Here Dodger entered the room in his usual breezy way. In his hand he brandished a morning paper.

"How are you feelin', Florence?" he asked; he had given up saying Miss Florence, at her request. "Here's an advertisement that'll maybe suit you."

"Show it to me, Dodger," said Florence, beginning to show some interest.

The boy directed her attention to the following advertisement:

"WANTED—A governess for a girl of twelve. Must be a good performer on the piano, and able to instruct in French and the usual English branches. Terms must be moderate. Apply to Mrs. Leighton, at 127 W—— Street."

"There, Florence, what do you say to that? That's better than sewin'."

"I don't know, Dodger, whether I am competent."

"You play on the pianner, don't you?"

"Yes."

"Well enough to teach?"

"I think so; but I may not have the gift of teaching."

"Yes, you have. Haven't you been teachin' me every evening? You make everything just as clear as mud—no, I don't mean that. You just explain so that I can't help understandin'."

"Then," said Florence, "I suppose I am at liberty to refer to you?"

"Yes; you can tell the lady to call at the office of Dodger, Esq., any mornin' after sunrise, and he'll give her full particulars."

Florence did not immediately decide to apply for the situation, but the more she thought of it, the more she felt inclined to do so. The little experience she had had with Dodger satisfied her that she should enjoy teaching better than sewing or writing.

Accordingly, an hour later, she put on her street dress and went uptown, to the address given in the advertisement.

No. 127 was a handsome brownstone house, not unlike the one in which Florence had been accustomed to live. It was a refreshing contrast to the poor tenement in which she lived at present.

"Is Mrs. Leighton at home?" inquired Florence.

"Yes, miss," answered the servant, respectfully. "Whom shall I say?"

"I have come to apply for the situation of governess," answered Florence, feeling rather awkward as she made the statement.

"Ah," said the servant, with a perceptible decline in respect. "Won't you step in?"

"Thank you."

"Well, she do dress fine for a governess," said Nancy to herself. "It's likely she'll put on airs."

The fact was that Florence was dressed according to her past social position—in a costly street attire—but it had never occurred to her that she was too well dressed for a governess.

She took her seat in the drawing-room, and five minutes later there was a rustling heard, and Mrs. Leighton walked into the room.

"Are you the applicant for the position of governess?" she asked, surveying the elegantly attired young lady seated on the sofa.

"Yes, Mrs. Leighton," answered Florence, easily, for she felt more at home in a house like this than in the tenement.

"Have you taught before?"

"Very little," answered Florence, smiling to herself, as she wondered what Mrs. Leighton would say if she could see Dodger, the only pupil she ever had. "However, I like teaching, and I like children."

"Pardon me, but you don't look like a governess, Miss——"

"Linden," suggested Florence, filling out the sentence. "Do governesses have a peculiar look?"

"I mean as to dress. You are more expensively dressed than the average governess can afford."

"It is only lately that my circumstances required me to support myself. I should not be able to buy such a dress out of my present earnings."

"I am glad to hear you say that, for I do not propose to give a large salary."

"I do not expect one," said Florence, quietly.

"You consider yourself competent to instruct in music, French and the English branches?"

"Oh, yes."

"Do you speak French?"

"Yes, madam."

"Would you favor me with a specimen of your piano playing?"

There was a piano in the back parlor. Florence removed her gloves, and taking a seat before it, dashed into a spirited selection from Strauss.

Mrs. Leighton listened with surprised approval.

"Certainly you are a fine performer," she said. "What—if I should engage you—would you expect in the way of compensation?"

"How much time would you expect me to give?"

"Three hours daily—from nine to twelve."

"I hardly know what to say. What did you expect to pay?"

"About fifty cents an hour."

Florence knew very well, from the sums that had been

paid for her own education, that this was miserably small pay, but it was much more than she could earn by sewing.

"I will teach a month on those terms," she said, after a pause.

Mrs. Leighton looked well pleased. She knew that she was making a great bargain.

"Oh, by the way," she said, "can you give references?"

"I can refer to Madam Morrison," naming the head of a celebrated female seminary. "She educated me."

"That will be quite satisfactory," said Mrs. Leighton, graciously. "Can you begin to-morrow?"

"Yes, madam."

"You will then see your pupil. At present she is out."

Florence bowed and withdrew.

She had been afraid Mrs. Leighton would inquire where she lived, and she would hardly dare to name the humble street which she called home.

CHAPTER VII.

TIM BOLTON'S SALOON.

Not far from Houston Street, on the west side of the Bowery, is an underground saloon, with whose proprietor we are already acquainted.

It was kept by Tim Bolton, whose peculiar tastes and shady characteristics well fitted him for such a business.

It was early evening, and the gas jets lighted up a characteristic scene.

On the sanded floor were set several tables, around which were seated a motley company, all of them with glasses of beer or whiskey before them.

Tim, with a white apron on, was moving about behind the bar, ministering to the wants of his patrons. There was a scowl upon his face, for he was not fond of work, and he missed Dodger's assistance.

The boy understood the business of mixing drinks as well as he, and often officiated for hours at a time, thus giving his guardian and reputed father a chance to leave the place and meet outside engagements.

On this particular evening, there was an unexpected arrival at the saloon.

A well-dressed gentleman descended the stairs gingerly, looked about him with fastidious disdain, and walked up to the bar.

Tim Bolton was filling an order, and did not immediately observe him.

When at length he turned around, he exclaimed, in some surprise:

"Mr. Waring!"

"Yes, Bolton, I have found my way here."

"I have been expecting you."

"I came to you for some information."

"Well, ask your questions. I don't know whether I can answer them."

"First, where is my Cousin Florence?"

"How should I know? She wasn't likely to place herself under my protection."

"She's with that boy of yours—Dodger, I believe you call him. Where is he?"

"Run away," answered Bolton, briefly.

"Do you mean that you don't know where he is?"

"Yes, I do mean that. I haven't set my eyes on him since that night."

"What do you mean by such negligence? Do you remember who he is?"

"Certainly I do."

"Then why do you let him get out of your reach?"

"How could I help it? Here I am tied down to this bar day and night! I'm nearly dead for want of sleep."

"It would be better to close up your place for a week, and look for him."

"Couldn't do it. I should lose all my trade. People would say I was closed up."

"And have you done nothing toward his recovery?"

"Yes, I have sent out two men in search of him."

"Have you any idea where he is, or what he is doing?"

"Yes, he has been seen in front of the Astor House, selling papers. I have authorized my agent, if he sees him again, to follow him home, and find out where he lives."

"That is good! Astor House? I may see him myself."

"But why do you want to see him? Do you want to restore him to his rights?"

"Hush!" said Curtis, glancing around him apprehensively. "What we say may be overheard, and excite suspicion. One thing may be secured by finding him—the knowledge of Florence's whereabouts."

"What makes you think she and the boy are together?"

"He came for her trunk. I was away from home, or I would not have let it go——"

"It is strange that they two are together, considering their relationship."

"That is what I am afraid they will find out. She may tell him of the mysterious disappearance of her cousin, and he——"

"That reminds me," interrupted Bolton. "He told Hooker—Hooker was the man that saw him in front of the Astor House—that he didn't believe I was his father. He said he thought I must have stolen him when he was a young kid."

"Did he say that?" asked Curtis, in evident alarm.

"Yes, so Hooker says."

"If he has that idea in his head, he may put two and two together, and guess that he is the long-lost cousin of Florence. Tim, that boy must be got rid of."

"If you mean what I think you do, Mr. Waring, I'm not with you. I won't consent to harm the boy."

"You said that before. I don't mean anything that will shock your tender heart, Bolton," said Curtis, with a sneer. "I mean carried a distance—Europe or Australia, for instance. All I want is to keep him out of New York till my uncle is dead. After that, I don't care what becomes of him."

"That's better. I've no objection to that. How is the old gentleman?"

"He grieved so much at first over the girl's loss that I feared he would insist on her being recalled at once. I soothed him by telling him that he had only to remain firm, and she would come around, and yield to his wishes."

"Do you think she will?" asked Tim, doubtfully.

"I intend she shall!" said Curtis, significantly. "Bolton, I love that girl all the more for her obstinate refusal to wed me. I have made up my mind to marry her, with her consent or without it."

"I thought it was only the estate you were after?"

"I want the estate, and her with it. Mark my words, Bolton, I will have both!"

"You will have the estate, no doubt; Mr. Linden has made his will in your favor, has he not?" and Bolton looked intently in the face of his visitor.

"Hark you, Bolton. There is a mystery I cannot fathom. My uncle made two wills. In the earlier, he left the estate to Florence and myself, if we married; otherwise, to me alone."

"That is satisfactory."

"Yes, but there was another, in which the estate goes to his son, if living. That will has disappeared."

"Is it possible?" asked Bolton, in astonishment. "When was it missed?"

"On the night of the burglary."

"Then you think——"

"That the boy, Dodger, has it. Good Heaven! if he only knew that by this will the estate goes to him!" and Waring wiped the perspiration from his brow.

"You are sure that he did not give you the will?" he demanded, eying Bolton, sharply.

"I have not seen him since the night of the robbery."

"If he has read the will, it may lead to dangerous suspicions."

"He would give it to your Cousin Florence, would he not?"

"Perhaps so. Bolton, you must get the boy back, and take the will from him, if you can."

"I will do my best; but you must remember that Dodger is no longer a small kid. He is a boy of eighteen, strong and well grown. He wouldn't be easy to manage. Besides, as long as he doesn't know that he has any interest in the will, his holding it won't do any harm. Is the old gentleman likely to live long?"

"I don't know. I sometimes hope—— Pshaw! why should I play the hypocrite when speaking to you? Surely, it is no sin to wish him better off, since he can't enjoy life!"

"He might if Florence and his son were restored to him."

"What do you mean, Bolton?" asked Curtis, suspiciously.

"What could I mean? It merely occurred to me," said Bolton, innocently. "You say he is quiet, thinkin' the girl will come around?"

"Yes."

"Suppose time passes, and she doesn't? Won't he try to find her? As she is in the city, that won't be hard."

"I shall represent that she has left the city. That estate I must have."

"Suppose you get it, what is there for me?" asked Bolton.

"I will see that you are recompensed if you help me to it."

"Will you put that in writing?"

"Do you take me for a fool? To put it in writing would be to place you in your power! You can trust me."

"Well, perhaps so," said Tim Bolton, slowly.

"At any rate, you will have to. Well, good-night. I will see you again soon. In the meantime, try to find the boy."

Tim Bolton followed him with his eyes, as he left the saloon.

"What would he say," said Bolton to himself, "if he knew that the will he so much wishes to find is in my hands, and that I hold him in my power already?"

CHAPTER VIII.

DODGER BECOMES AMBITIOUS.

"Wish me luck, Dodger!"

"So I do, Florence. Are you goin' to begin teachin' this mornin'?"

"Yes; and I hope to produce a favorable impression. It is very important to me to please Mrs. Leighton and my future pupil."

"I'm sure you'll suit. How nice you look!"

Florence smiled, and looked pleased. She had taken pains with her dress and personal appearance, and, being luckily well provided with handsome dresses, had no difficulty in making herself presentable. As she stepped out of the shabby doorway upon the sidewalk, no one supposed her to be a tenant, but she was generally thought to be a visitor, perhaps the agent of some charitable association.

"Perhaps all will not judge me as favorably as you do, Dodger," said Florence, with a laugh.

"If you have the headache any day, Florence, I'll take your place."

"You would look rather young for a tutor, Dodger, and I am afraid you would not be dignified. Good-morning! I shall be back to dinner."

"I am glad to find you punctual, Miss Linden," said Mrs. Leighton, graciously, as Florence was ushered into her presence. "This is your future pupil, my daughter, Carrie."

Florence smiled, and extended her hand.

"I hope we shall like each other," she said.

The little girl eyed her with approval. This beautiful young lady was a pleasant surprise to her, for, never having had a governess, she expected to meet a stiff, elderly lady, of stern aspect. She readily gave her hand to Florence, and looked relieved.

Florence found her a nice child, and the new duties of governess were by no means disagreeable.

Florence was not only an excellent scholar, but she had the art of imparting knowledge, and, what is very important, she was able in a few luminous words to explain difficulties and make clear what seemed to Carrie obscure.

In the evening, Dodger spent an hour, and sometimes more, pursuing his studies, under the direction of Florence. At first his attention was given chiefly to improving his reading and spelling, for Dodger was far from fluent in the first, while his style of spelling many words was strikingly original.

"Ain't I stupid, Florence?" he asked one day, after spelling a word of three syllables with such ingenious incorrectness as to convulse his young teacher with merriment.

"Not at all, Dodger. You are making excellent progress; but sometimes you are so droll that I can't help laughing."

"I don't mind that, if you think I am really gettin' on."

"Undoubtedly you are!"

"I make a great many mistakes," said Dodger, dubiously.

"Yes, you do; but you must remember that you have taken lessons only a short time. Don't you think you can read a good deal more easily than you did?"

"Yes; I don't trip up half so often as I did. I'm afraid you'll get tired of teachin' me."

"No fear of that, Dodger. As long as I see that you are improving, I shall feel encouraged to go on."

"I wish I knew as much as your other scholar."

"You will in time if you go on. You mustn't get discouraged."

"I won't!" said Dodger, stoutly. "If a little gal like her can learn, I'd ought to be ashamed if I don't—a big boy of eighteen."

"It isn't the size of the boy that counts, Dodger."

"I know that, but I ain't goin' to give in, and let a little gal get ahead of me!"

"Keep to that determination, Dodger, and you will succeed in time, never fear."

On the whole, Florence enjoyed both her pupils. She had the faculty of teaching, and she became very much interested in both.

As for Dodger, she thought, rough diamond as he was, that she saw in him the making of a manly man, and she felt that it was a privilege to assist in the development of his intellectual nature.

Again, he had picked up a good deal of slang from the nature of his associates, and she set to work to improve his language, and teach him refinement.

It was necessarily a slow process, but she began to find after a time that a gradual change was coming over him.

"I want you to grow up a gentleman, Dodger," she said to him one day.

"I'm too rough for that, Florence. I'm only an ignorant street boy."

"You are not going to be an ignorant street boy all your life. I don't see why you should not grow up a polished gentleman."

"I will keep on, Florence," said Dodger, earnestly. "If I ever find my relations I don't want them to be ashamed of me."

It was not the first time he had referred to his uncertain origin.

"Won't Tim Bolton tell you anything about your family?"

"No; I've asked him more'n once. He always says he's my father, and that makes me mad."

"It is strange," said Florence, thoughtfully. "I had a young cousin stolen many years ago."

"Was it the son of the old gentleman you lived with on Madison Avenue?"

"Yes; it was the son of Uncle John. It quite broke him down. After my cousin's loss he felt that he had nothing to live for."

"I wish I was your cousin, Florence," said Dodger, thoughtfully.

"Well, then, I will adopt you as my cousin, or brother, whichever you prefer!"

"I would rather be your cousin."

"Then cousin let it be! Now we are bound to each other by strong and near ties."

"But when your uncle takes you back you'll forget all about poor Dodger."

"No, I won't, Dodger. There's my hand on it. Whatever comes, we are friends forever."

"Then I'll try not to disgrace you, Florence. I'll learn as fast as I can, and see if I don't grow up to be a gentleman."

CHAPTER IX.

IN A TRAP.

Several weeks passed without changing in any way the position or employment of Dodger or Florence.

They had settled down to their respective forms of labor, and were able not only to pay their modest expenses, but to save up something for a rainy day.

Florence had but one source of regret.

She enjoyed her work, and did not now lament the luxurious home which she had lost.

But she did feel sore at heart that her uncle made no sign of regret for their separation.

From him she received no message of forgiveness or reconciliation.

"He has forgotten me!" she said to herself, bitterly. "He has cast me utterly out of his heart. I do not care for his money, but I do not like to think that my kind uncle—for he was always kind till the last trouble—has steeled his heart against me forever."

It was about this time that the quiet tenor of Dodger's life was interrupted by a startling event.

One afternoon about six o'clock, he stood on the pier awaiting the arrival of the day boat from Albany, with a small supply of evening papers under his arm.

He had sold all but half a dozen when the boat touched the pier. He stood watching the various passengers as they left the boat and turned their steps in different directions, when some one touched him on the shoulder.

Looking up, he saw standing at his side a man of slender figure, with gray hair and whiskers.

"Boy," he said, "I am a stranger in the city. Can I ask your assistance?"

"Yes, sir; certainly," answered Dodger, briskly.

"Do you know where the nearest station of the elevated road is?

"I want to go uptown, but I know very little about the city. Will you accompany me as guide? I will pay you well."

"All right, sir," answered Dodger.

It was just the job he was seeking.

"We shall have to walk a few blocks, unless you want to take a carriage."

"It isn't necessary. I am strong, in spite of my gray hair."

And indeed he appeared to be.

Dodger noticed that he walked with the elastic step of a young man, while his face certainly showed no trace of wrinkles.

"I live in the West," said the stranger, as they walked along. "I have not been here for ten years."

"Then you have never ridden on the elevated road?" said Dodger.

"N-no," answered the stranger, with curious hesitation.

Yet when they reached the station he went up the staircase and purchased his ticket with the air of a man who was thoroughly accustomed to doing it.

"I suppose you won't want me any longer," said Dodger, preparing to resign the valise he was carrying, and which, by the way, was remarkably light considering the size.

"Yes, I shall need you," said the other, hurriedly. "There may be some distance to walk after we get uptown."

"All right, sir."

Dodger was glad that further service was required, for this would of course increase the compensation which he would feel entitled to ask.

They entered one of the cars, and sat down side by side.

They got out at One Hundred and Twenty-fifth Street, and struck down toward the river, Dodger carrying the valise.

"I wonder where we're going?" he asked himself.

At length they reached a wooden house of three stories, standing by itself, and here the stranger stopped.

He rang the bell, and the door was opened by a humpbacked negro, who looked curiously at Dodger.

"Is the room ready, Julius?" asked the old man.

"Yes, sir."

"Boy, take the valise upstairs, and I will follow you."

Up two flights of stairs walked Dodger, followed by the old man and the negro.

The latter opened the door of a back room, and Dodger, obedient to directions, took the valise inside and deposited it on a chair.

He had hardly done so when the door closed behind him, and he heard the slipping of a bolt.

"What does all this mean?" Dodger asked himself, in amazement.

"Hold on, there! Open that door!" he exclaimed aloud.

There was no answer.

"I say, let me out!" continued our hero, beginning to kick at the panels.

This time there was an answer.

"Stop that kicking, boy! I will come back in fifteen minutes and explain all."

"Well," thought Dodger, "this is about the strangest thing that ever happened to me. However, I can wait fifteen minutes."

He sat down on a cane chair—there were two in the room—and looked about him.

He was in an ordinary bedroom, furnished in the usual manner. There was nothing at all singular in its appearance.

Dodger waited impatiently for the time to pass.

Seventeen minutes had passed when he heard the bolt

drawn. Fixing his eyes eagerly on the door he saw it open, and two persons entered.

One was the hump-backed negro, carrying on a waiter a plate of buttered bread, and a cup of tea; the other person was—not the old man, but, to Dodger's great amazement, a person well remembered, though he had only seen him once—Curtis Waring.

"Set down the waiter on the table, Julius," said Waring.

Dodger looked on in stupefaction. He was getting more and more bewildered.

"Now you can go!" said Curtis, in a tone of authority.

The negro bowed, and after he had disposed of the waiter withdrew.

"Do you know me, boy?" asked Curtis, turning now and addressing Dodger.

"Yes; you are Mr. Waring."

"You remember where you last saw me?"

"Yes, sir. At your uncle's house on Madison Avenue."

"Quite right."

"How did you come here? Where is the old man whose valise I brought from the Albany boat?"

Curtis smiled, and drew from his pocket a gray wig and whiskers.

"You understand now, don't you?"

"Yes, sir; I understand that I have been got here by a trick."

"Yes," answered Curtis, coolly. "I have deemed it wise to use a little stratagem. But you must be hungry. Sit down and eat your supper while I am talking to you."

Dodger was hungry, for it was past his usual supper time, and he saw no reason why he should not accept the invitation.

Accordingly, he drew his chair up to the table and began to eat. Curtis seated himself on the other chair.

"I have a few questions to ask you, and that is why I arranged this interview. We are quite by ourselves," he added, significantly.

"Very well, sir; go ahead."

"Where is my Cousin Florence? I am right, I take it, in assuming that you know where she is?"

"Yes, sir; I know," answered Dodger, slowly.

"Very well, tell me."

"I don't think she wants you to know."

Curtis frowned.

"It is necessary I should know!" he said, emphatically.

"I will ask her if I may tell you."

"I can't wait for that. You must tell me at once."

"I can't do that."

"You are mistaken; you can do it."

"Then I won't!" said Dodger, looking his companion full in the face.

Curtis Waring darted a wicked look at him, and seemed ready to attack the boy who was audacious enough to thwart him, but he restrained himself and said:

"Let that pass for the present. I have another question to ask. Where is the document you took from my uncle's desk on the night of the burglary?"

And he emphasized the last word.

Dodger looked surprised.

"I took no paper," he said.

"Do you deny that you opened the desk?"

"No."

"When I came to examine the contents in the presence of my uncle, it was found that a document—his will—had disappeared, and with it a considerable sum of money."

And he looked sharply at Dodger.

"I don't know anything about it, sir. I took nothing."

"You can hardly make me believe that. Why did you open the desk if you did not propose to take anything?"

"I did intend to take something. I was under orders to do so, for I wouldn't have done it of my own free will; but the moment I got the desk open I heard a cry, and looking around, I saw Miss Florence looking at me."

"And then?"

"I was startled, and ran to her side."

"And then you went back and completed the robbery?"

"No, I didn't. She talked to me so that I felt ashamed of it. I never stole before, and I wouldn't have tried to do it then, if—if some one hadn't told me to."

"I know whom you mean—Tim Bolton."

"Yes, Tim Bolton, since you know."

"What did he tell you to take?"

"The will and the money."

"Exactly. Now we are coming to it. You took them, and gave them to him?"

"No, I didn't. I haven't seen him since that night."

Curtis Waring regarded the boy thoughtfully. His story was straightforward, and it agreed with the story told by Tim himself. But, on the other hand, he denied taking the missing articles, and yet they had disappeared.

Curtis decided that both he and Tim had lied, and that this story had been concocted between them.

Probably Bolton had the will and the money—the latter he did not care for—and this thought made him uneasy, for he knew that Tim Bolton was an unscrupulous man, and quite capable of injuring him, if he saw the way clear to do so.

Curtis regarded the boy in some perplexity.

He had every appearance of telling the truth.

Dodger had one of those honest, truthful countenances which lend confirmation to any words spoken. If the boy told the truth, what could have become of the will—and the money? As to the former, it might be possible that his uncle had destroyed it, but the disappearance of the money presented an independent difficulty.

"The will is all I care for," he said, at length. "The thief is welcome to the money, though there was a considerable sum."

"I would find the will for you if I could," said Dodger, earnestly.

"You are positive you didn't give it to Tim Bolton?"

"Positive, sir. I haven't seen Tim since that night."

"You may be speaking the truth, or you may not. I will talk with you again to-morrow," and Curtis arose from his chair.

"You don't mean to keep me here?" said Dodger, in alarm.

"I shall be obliged to do so."

"I won't stay!" exclaimed Dodger, in excitement, and he ran to the door, meaning to get out; but Curtis drew a pistol from his pocket and aimed it at the boy.

"Understand me, boy," he said, "I am in earnest, and I am not to be trifled with."

Dodger drew back, and Curtis opened the door and went out, bolting it after him.

Dodger threw himself on the bed at an early hour, but he did not undress, thinking there might possibly be a chance to escape during the night.

But the morning came and found him still a prisoner, but not in the solitary dwelling.

CHAPTER X.

A MIDNIGHT RIDE.

Curtis Waring had entrapped Dodger for a double purpose.

It was not merely that he thought it possible the boy had the will, or knew where it was.

He had begun to think of the boy's presence in New York as dangerous to his plans.

John Linden might at any time learn that the son, for whose disappearance he had grieved so bitterly, was still living in the person of this street boy. Then there would be an end of his hopes of inheriting the estate.

Only a few months more and the danger would be over, for he felt convinced that his uncle's tenure of life would be brief. The one essential thing, then, seemed to be to get Dodger out of the city.

The first step had already been taken; what the next was will soon appear.

At eleven o'clock a hack stopped in front of the house, and Curtis Waring descended from it.

"Stay here," said he to the driver. "There will be another passenger. If you are detained I will make it right when I come to pay you."

"All right, sir," said the hackman. "I don't care how long it is if I am paid for my time."

Curtis opened the door with a pass-key, and found Julius dozing in a chair in the hall.

"Wake up, you sleepy-head," he said. "Has anything happened since I left here?"

"No, sir. De boy is still upstairs."

"He ought to be in a deep sleep by this time. I will go up and see. Go up with me, Julius, for I may have to ask you to help me bring him down."

They went up together.

Curtis drew the bolt, and, entering the chamber, his glance fell upon Dodger, fast asleep on the bed.

"I am glad the boy did not undress," he said. "It will save me a great deal of trouble. Now, Julius, you can take his feet and I will lift his head, and we will take him downstairs."

"S'pos'n he wakes up, Massa Curtis?"

"He won't wake up. I took care the sleeping potion should be strong enough to produce profound slumber for eighteen hours."

"Seems as if he was dead," said Julius, nervously.

"Tush, you fool! He's no more dead than you or I."

The hackman looked curious when the two men appeared with their sleeping burden, and Curtis felt that some explanation was required.

"The boy has a very painful disease," he said, "and the doctor gave him a sleeping draught. He is going abroad for his health, and, under the circumstances, I think it best not to wake him up. Drive slowly and carefully to Pier No. —, as I don't want the boy aroused if it can be helped."

"All right, sir."

"Julius, you may lock the door and come with me. I shall need your help to get him on board the ship."

"All right, Massa Curtis."

The journey was successfully accomplished, but it took an hour, for, according to directions, the hackman did not force his pace, but drove slowly, till he reached the North River pier indicated.

At the pier was a large, stanch vessel—the *Columbia*—bound for San Francisco, around Cape Horn.

All was dark, but the second officer was pacing the deck. Curtis Waring hailed him.

"What time do you get off?"

"Early to-morrow morning."

"So the captain told me. I have brought you a passenger."

"The captain told me about him."

"Is his stateroom ready?"

"Yes, sir. You are rather late."

"True; and the boy is asleep, as you will see. He is going to make the voyage for his health, and, as he has been suffering some pain, I thought I would not wake him up. Who will direct me to his stateroom?"

The mate summoned the steward, and Dodger, still unconscious, was brought on board and quietly transferred to the bunk that had been prepared for him.

It was a critical moment for poor Dodger, but he was quite unconscious of it.

"What is the boy's name?" asked the mate.

"Arthur Grant. The captain has it on his list. Is he on board?"

"Yes; but he is asleep."

"I do not need to see him. I have transacted all necessary business with him—and paid the passage money. Julius, bring the valise."

Julius did so.

"This contains the boy's clothing. Take it to the stateroom, Julius."

"All right, Massa Curtis."

"What is your usual time between New York and San Francisco?" asked Curtis, addressing the mate.

"From four to six months. Four months is very short,

six months very long. We ought to get there in five months, or perhaps a little sooner, with average weather."

"Very well. I believe there is no more to be said. Good-night!"

"Good-night, sir."

"So he is well out of the way for five months!" soliloquized Curtis. "In five months much may happen. Before that time I hope to be in possession of my uncle's property. Then I can snap my fingers at fate."

CHAPTER XI.

OUT AT SEA.

The good ship *Columbia* had got fifty miles under way before Dodger opened his eyes.

He looked about him languidly at first, but this feeling was succeeded by the wildest amazement, as his eyes took in his unusual surroundings.

He had gone to sleep on a bed—he found himself on awakening in a ship's bunk.

He half arose in his berth, but the motion of the vessel and a slight feeling of dizziness compelled him to resume a recumbent position.

"I must be dreaming," thought Dodger. "It's very queer. I am dreaming. I am at sea. I suppose that explains it."

He listened and heard the swish of the waters as they beat against the sides of the vessel.

He noted the pitching of the ship, and there was an unsteady feeling in his head, such as those which have gone to sea will readily recall.

Dodger became more and more bewildered.

"If it's a dream, it's the most real dream I ever had," he said to himself.

At this moment the steward opened the cabin.

"Hello, young man! Have you got up?" he asked.

"Where am I?" asked Dodger, looking at him with a dazed expression.

"Where are you? You're on the good ship *Columbia*, to be sure."

"Are we out to sea?"

"Of course you are."

"How far from land?"

"Well, about fifty miles, more or less, I should judge."

"How long have I been here?"

"It seems to me you have a poor memory. You came on board last evening."

"I suppose Curtis Waring brought me," said Dodger, beginning to get his bearings.

"There was a gentleman came with you—so the mate told me. I don't know his name."

"Where is the ship bound?"

"To San Francisco, around Cape Horn. I supposed you knew that."

"I never heard of the ship *Columbia* before, and I never had any idea of making a sea voyage."

The steward looked surprised.

"I suppose your guardian arranged about that? Didn't he tell you?"

"I have no guardian."

"Well, you'll have to ask Capt. Barnes about that. I know nothing, except that you are a passenger, and that your fare has been paid."

"My fare paid to San Francisco?" asked Dodger, more and more at sea, both mentally and physically.

"Yes; we don't take any deadheads on the *Columbia*."

"Can you tell me what time it is?"

"About twelve o'clock. Do you feel hungry?"

"N—not very," returned Dodger, as a ghastly expression came over his face, and he tumbled back into his berth, looking very pale.

The next day Dodger felt considerably better, and ventured to go upon deck.

Though his head did not feel exactly right, the strong wind entered Dodger's lungs, and he felt exhilarated. His eyes brightened, and he began to share in the excitement of the scene.

Pacing the deck was a stout, bronzed seaman, whose dress made it clear even to the inexperienced eyes of Dodger that he was the captain.

"Good-morning, Master Grant," he said, pleasantly. "Are you getting your sea legs on?"

The name was unfamiliar to Dodger, but he could see that the remark was addressed to him.

"Yes, sir," he answered.

"Ever been to sea before?"

"No, sir."

"You'll get used to it. Bless me, you'll stand it like an old sailor before we get to 'Frisco."

"Is it a long voyage, captain?" asked Dodger.

"Five months, probably. We may get there a little sooner. It depends on the winds and weather."

"Five months!" said Dodger to himself, in a tone of dismay.

The captain laughed.

"It'll be a grand experience for a lad like you, Arthur!" said the captain, encouragingly.

Arthur! So his name was Arthur! He had just been called Master Grant, so Arthur Grant was his name on board ship.

Dodger was rather glad to have a name provided, for he had only been known as Dodger heretofore, and this name would excite surprise. He had recently felt the need of a name, and didn't see why this wouldn't answer his purpose as well as any other.

"I must write it down so as not to forget it," he resolved. "It would seem queer if I forgot my own name."

"I shouldn't enjoy it much if I were going to be seasick all the time," he answered.

"Oh, a strong, healthy boy like you will soon be all right. You don't look like an invalid."

"I never was sick in my life."

"But your guardian told me he was sending you on a sea voyage for your health."

"Did Mr. Waring say that?"

"Yes; didn't you know the object of your sea trip?" asked Capt. Barnes, in surprise.

"No."

"There may be some tendency to disease in your system—some hereditary tendency," said the captain, after a pause. "Were your parents healthy?"

"They—died young," answered Dodger, hesitatingly.

"That accounts for your guardian's anxiety. However, you look strong enough, in all conscience; and if you're not healthy, you will be before the voyage ends."

"I don't know what I am to do for clothes," said

Dodger, as a new source of perplexity presented itself. "I can't get along with one shirt and collar for five months."

"You will find plenty of clothes in your valise. Hasn't it been given you?"

"No, sir."

"You may ask the steward for it. You didn't think your guardian would send you on a five months' voyage without a change of clothing, did you?"

And the captain laughed heartily.

"I don't know Mr. Waring very well," said Dodger, awkwardly.

As he went downstairs to inquire about the valise, this question haunted him:

"Why did Curtis Waring send him on a sea voyage?"

CHAPTER XII.
THE OTHER PASSENGER.

Dodger took the valise to his stateroom, and, finding a key tied to the handles, he opened it at once.

It proved to contain a very fair supply of underclothing, socks, handkerchiefs, etc., with a toothbrush, a hairbrush and comb, and a sponge. Never in his life had Dodger been so well supplied with clothing before. There were four white shirts, two tennis shirts, half a dozen handkerchiefs and the same number of socks, with three changes of underclothing.

"I begin to feel like a gentleman," said Dodger to himself, complacently.

That was not all. At the bottom of the valise was an envelope, sealed, on which was inscribed the name: "Dodger."

"That is for me, at any rate," thought our hero. "I suppose it is from Curtis Waring."

He opened the envelope, and found inclosed twenty-five dollars in bills, with a few lines written on a half sheet of paper. These Dodger read, with interest and curiosity. They were as follows:

"DODGER: The money inclosed is for you. When you reach California you will find it of use. I have sent you out there because you will find in a new country a better chance to rise than in the city of New York. I advise you to stay there and grow up with the country. In New York you were under the influence of a bad man, from whom it is best that you should be permanently separated. I know something of the early history of Tim Bolton. He was detected in a crime, and fled to escape the consequences. Your mother was his sister, but quite superior to himself. Your right name is Arthur Grant, and it will be well for you to assume it hereafter. I have entered you in the list of passengers under that name.

"I thought you had taken the will from my uncle's desk, but I am inclined to think you had nothing to do with it. If you know where it is, or whether Bolton has it, I expect you to notify me in return for the money I have expended in your behalf. In that case you can write to me, No. — Madison Avenue.
"CURTIS WARING."

Dodger read this letter over twice, and it puzzled him.

"He seems from the letter to take an interest in me," he soliloquized. "At any rate, he has given me money and clothes, and paid my passage to California. What for, I wonder? I don't believe it is to get me away from the bad influence of Tim. There must be some other reason."

He had just closed up his valise, when a young man of dark complexion, and of an attractive, intellectual expression, entered the cabin.

He nodded pleasantly to Dodger, and said:

"I suppose this is Arthur Grant?"

"Yes, sir," answered Dodger, for he had decided to adopt the name.

"We ought to become close friends, for we are, I believe, the only passengers."

"Then you are a passenger, too?" said Dodger, deciding, after a brief scrutiny, that he should like his new acquaintance.

"Yes. My name is Randolph Leslie. I have been, for the last five years, a reporter on leading New York daily papers, and worked so closely that my health has become somewhat affected. My doctor recommended a sea voyage, and I have arranged for a pretty long one. Do you intend to remain in California?"

"I don't know what I do intend," replied Dodger. "I didn't know I was going to California at all until I woke up in my stateroom."

The young man looked surprised.

"Didn't you know the destination of the vessel when you came on board?" he asked.

"I was brought aboard in my sleep."

"This is curious. It looks to me as if you had a story to tell.

"Of course, I don't want to be curious, but if there is any way in which I can help you, by advice, or in any other way, I am quite ready to do so."

Dodger paused, but only briefly. This young man looked friendly, and might help him to penetrate the mystery which at present baffled him.

At any rate, his experience qualified him to give friendly advice, and of this Dodger felt that he stood in need.

"I ought to tell you, to begin with," he said, "that I am a poor boy, and made my living as best I could, by carrying baggage, selling papers, etc."

"I don't think any the worse of you for that. Tell me your story, if you don't mind."

Thus invited, Dodger told his story to Randolph Leslie, keeping nothing back.

"Well, I suppose," said Leslie, after he had heard the strange tale, "there is no use in speculating about the matter now. The important point is, what are we to do with ourselves during the four or five months we must spend on shipboard?"

"I don't know what I can do," said Dodger. "I can't sell papers, and I can't smash baggage."

"Suppose I take you as a scholar?"

"I should like it very much, Mr. Leslie, but I'm afraid I haven't got money enough to pay you."

"That is true. You will need all the money you have when you land in California. Twenty-five dollars won't go far—still you have all the money that is necessary, for I do not intend to charge you anything."

"You are very kind to me, Mr. Leslie, considerin' you don't know me," said Dodger, gratefully.

"On the contrary, I think I know you very well. In four months a great deal can be accomplished. I don't know how quick you are to learn. After we have had one or two lessons I can judge better."

Two days later Mr. Leslie pronounced his opinion, and a favorable one.

"You have not exaggerated your ignorance," he said to Dodger. "You have a great deal to learn, but on the other hand you are quick, have a retentive memory, and are very anxious to learn. I shall make something of you."

"I learn faster with you than with Florence," said Dodger.

"Probably she would succeed better with girls, but I hold that a male teacher is better for boys. I think you have talent for arithmetic. I don't expect to make you fit for a bookkeeper, but I hope to make you equal to most office boys by the time we reach San Francisco."

"I wish you would, Mr. Leslie. What do you mean to do when you get to San Francisco?"

"I shall seek employment on one of the San Francisco daily papers. Six months or a year so spent will restore my health, and enable me to live without drawing upon my moderate savings."

"I expect I shall have to work, too, to get money to take me back to New York."

And now we must ask the reader to imagine four months and one week passed.

There had been favorable weather on the whole, and the voyage was unusually short.

Dodger and the reporter stood on deck, and with eager interest watched the passage through the Golden Gate. A little later and the queen city of the Pacific came in sight, crowning the hill on which a part of the city is built, with the vast Palace Hotel a conspicuous object in the foreground.

CHAPTER XIII.

FLORENCE IN SUSPENSE.

We must now return to New York to Dodger's old home.

When he did not return at the usual hour, neither Florence nor Mrs. O'Keefe was particularly disturbed.

It was thought that he had gone on some errand of unusual length, and would return an hour or two late.

Eight o'clock came, the hour at which the boy was accustomed to repair to Florence's room to study, and still he didn't make his appearance.

"Dodger's late this evening, Mrs. O'Keefe," said Florence, going up to the room of her landlady.

"Shure he is. It's likely he's gone to Brooklyn or up to Harlem, wid a bundle. He'll be comin' in soon."

"I hope he will be well paid for the errand, since it keeps him so long."

"I hope so, too, Florence, for he's a good boy, is Dodger."

Nine o'clock came, and Florence became alarmed. She had not been aware how much she depended upon the company of her faithful friend, humble as his station was.

Again she went into Mrs. O'Keefe's room. The apple-woman had been out to buy some groceries and had just returned.

"I am getting anxious about Dodger," said Florence. "It is nine o'clock."

"And what's nine o'clock to a boy like him? Shure he's used to bein' out at all hours of the night."

"I shall feel relieved when he comes home. What should I do without him?"

"Shure I'd miss him myself—but it isn't the first time he has been out late."

"Perhaps that terrible Tim Bolton has got hold of him," suggested Florence.

"Tim isn't so bad, Florence. He isn't fit company for the likes of you, but there's worse men nor Tim."

"Didn't he send out Dodger to commit a burglary?"

"And if he hadn't you'd never made Dodger's acquaintance."

"That's true; but it doesn't make burglary any more excusable. Don't you really think Tim Bolton has got hold of him?"

"If he has, he won't keep him long, I'll make oath of that. He might keep him overnight, but Dodger would come back in the morning."

Florence was somewhat cheered by Mrs. O'Keefe's refusal to believe that Dodger was in any serious trouble, but she could not wholly free herself from uneasiness. When eleven o'clock came she went to bed very unwillingly, and got very little rest during the night. Morning came, and still Dodger did not show up. As we know, he was fairly started on his long voyage, though he had not yet recovered consciousness.

Florence took a very light breakfast, and at the usual time went to Mrs. Leighton's to meet her pupil. When the study hours were over, she did not remain to lunch, but hurried back, stopping at Mrs. O'Keefe's apple-stand just as that lady was preparing to go home to prepare dinner.

"Have you seen anything of Dodger, Mrs. O'Keefe?" asked Florence, breathlessly.

"No, I haven't, Florence. I've had my eye out watchin' for him, but he hasn't showed up."

"Is there anything we can do?" asked Florence, anxiously.

"Well, we might go around and see Tim—and find out whether he's got hold of him."

"Let us go at once."

A short walk brought the two strangely assorted companions to the entrance of Tim Bolton's saloon.

"I'm afraid to go in, Mrs. O'Keefe," said Florence.

"Come along wid me, my dear; I won't let anything harm you. You ain't used to such a place, but I've been here more than once to fill the growler. Be careful as you go down the steps, Florence."

Tim Bolton was standing behind the bar, and as he heard steps he looked carelessly toward the entrance, but when he saw Florence, his indifference vanished. He came from behind the bar, and advanced to meet her.

"Miss Linden," he said.

Florence shrank back and clung to her companion's arm.

"Is there anything I can do for you? I am a rough man, but I'm not so bad as you may think."

"That's what I told her, Tim," said Mrs. O'Keefe. "I told Florence there was worse men than you."

"Thank you, Mrs. O'Keefe."

"Oh, Mr. Bolton," broke in Florence, unable to bear the suspense longer, "where is Dodger?"

Tim Bolton looked at Florence in undisguised astonishment.

"Dodger!" he repeated. "How should I know? I supposed that you had lured him away from me."

"He didn't like the business you were in. He preferred to make a living in some other way."

"Then why do you ask me where he is?"

"Because he did not come home last night. Shure he rooms at my house," put in Mrs. O'Keefe, "and he hasn't showed up since——"

"And you thought I might have got hold of him?" said Bolton, inquiringly.

"Then you are mistaken. I haven't seen the boy for weeks."

Tim Bolton spoke so straightforwardly that there was no chance to doubt his word.

"When he was living with you, Mr. Bolton," continued Florence, "did he ever stay away like this?"

"No," answered Bolton, "Dodger was always very regular about comin' home."

"Then something must have happened to him," said Florence, anxiously.

"What do you think, Mr. Bolton?" asked Florence.

Tim Bolton seemed busy thinking. Finally he brought down his hand forcibly on the bar, and said:

"I begin to see through it."

Florence did not speak, but she fixed an eager look of inquiry on the face of the saloon-keeper.

"I believe Curtis Waring is at the bottom of this," he said.

"My cousin!" exclaimed Florence, in astonishment.

"Yes, your cousin, Miss Linden."

"But what can he have against poor Dodger? Is it because the boy has taken my part and is a friend to me?"

"He wouldn't like him any better on account of that; but he has another and a more powerful reason."

"Would you mind telling me what it is? I cannot conceive what it can be."

"At present," answered Bolton, cautiously, "I prefer to say nothing on the subject. I will only say that the boy's disappearance interferes with my plans, and I will see if I can't find out what has become of him."

"If you only will, Mr. Bolton, I shall be so grateful. I am afraid I have misjudged you. I thought you were an enemy of Dodger's."

"Then you were mistaken. I have had the boy with me since he was a kid, and though I've been rough with him at times, maybe, I like him, and I may some time have a chance to show him that old Tim Bolton is one of his best friends."

"I will believe it now, Mr. Bolton," said Florence, impulsively, holding out her hand to the burly saloon-keeper.

He was surprised, but it was evident that he was pleased, also, and he took the little hand respectfully in his own ample palm, and pressed it in a friendly manner.

"There's one thing more I want you to believe, Miss Linden," he said, "and that is, that I am your friend, also."

"Thank you, Mr. Bolton. And now let us all work together to find Dodger."

"You can count on me, Miss Linden. If you'll tell me where you live I'll send or bring you any news I may hear."

"I live with Mrs. O'Keefe, my good friend, here."

"I haven't my kyard with me, Tim," said the apple-woman, "but I'll give you my strate and number. You know my place of business?"

"Yes."

"If you come to me there I'll let Florence know whatever you tell me. She is not always at home."

The two went away, relieved in mind, for, helpless and bewildered as they were, they felt that Tim Bolton would make a valuable ally.

CHAPTER XIV.

BOLTON MAKES A DISCOVERY.

"I see it all," Bolton said to himself, thoughtfully. "Curtis Waring is afraid of the boy—and of me. He's circumvented me neatly, and the game is his—so far my little plan is dished. I must find out for certain whether he's had anything to do with gettin' Dodger out of the way, and then, Tim Bolton, you must set your wits to work to spoil his little game."

Bolton succeeded in securing the services of a young man who had experience at tending bar, and about eight o'clock, after donning his best attire, he hailed a Fourth Avenue surface car and got aboard.

Getting out at the proper street, he made his way to Madison Avenue, and ascended the steps of John Linden's residence.

He asked for Mr. Waring.

He paused on the threshold, and frowned when he saw who it was that awaited him.

He was ushered into the library, and at the end of a short time, Curtis Waring appeared.

"Jane told me that a gentleman was waiting to see me," he said.

"Well, she was right."

"And you, I suppose, are the gentleman?" said Curtis, in a sneering tone.

"Yes; I am the gentleman," remarked Bolton, coolly.

"I am not in the habit of receiving visits from gentlemen of your class. However, I suppose you have an object in calling."

"It shall go hard with me if I don't pay you for your sneers some day," thought Bolton; but he remained outwardly unruffled.

"Well," he answered, "I can't say that I have any particular business to see you about. I saw your cousin recently."

"Florence?" asked Curtis, eagerly.

"Yes."

"What did she say? Did you speak with her?"

"Yes. She doesn't seem any more willin' to marry you."

Curtis Waring frowned.

"She is a foolish girl," he said. "She doesn't know her own mind."

"She looks to me like a gal that knows her own mind particularly well."

"Pshaw! what can you know about it?"

"Then you really expect to marry her some time, Mr. Waring?"

"Certainly I do."

"And to inherit your uncle's fortune?"

"Of course. Why not?"

"I was thinkin' of the boy."

"The boy is dead——"

"What?" exclaimed Bolton, jumping to his feet in irresistible excitement.

"Don't be a fool. Wait till I finish my sentence. He is dead so far as his prospects are concerned. Who is there than can identify him with the lost child of John Linden?"

"I can."

"Yes; if any one would believe you. However, it is for your interest to keep silent."

"That is just what I want to know. I suppose you can make it for my interest."

"Yes, and will—after I get the property. I don't believe in counting my chickens before they are hatched."

"Of course you know that the boy has left me?"

"Yes," answered Curtis, indifferently. "He is with my cousin, I believe."

"Yes; and through her I can learn where he is, and get hold of him if I desire."

A cynical smile played over the face of Curtis Waring.

"Do you propose to get him back?" he asked, shrugging his shoulders."

"I am right," thought Bolton, shrewdly. "From his manner it is easy to see that Curtis is quite at ease as regards Dodger. He knows where he is!"

"You asked me what business I came about, Mr. Waring," he said, after a pause.

"Yes."

"Of course, I am devoted to your interests, but is it quite fair to make me wait till you come into your fortune before allowing me anything?"

"I think so."

"You don't seem to consider that I can bring the boy here and make him known to your uncle as the son he lost so long ago?"

"You are quite sure you can bring the boy here?" asked Curtis.

"Why not? I have only to go to Florence and ask her to send the boy to me."

"You are quite at liberty to do so, if you like, Tim Bolton," said Curtis, with a mocking smile. "I am glad, at any rate, that you have shown me what is in your mind. You are very sharp, but you are not quite so sharp as I am."

"I don't understand you."

"Then I will be more explicit. It's out of your power to make use of the boy against me, because——"

"Well?"

"Because he is not in the city."

"Where is he, then?"

"Where you are not likely to find him."

"If you have killed him——" Bolton began, but Curtis interrupted him.

"The boy is safe—I will tell you that much," he said; "but for reasons which you can guess, I think it better that he should be out of New York. When the proper time comes, and all is safe, he may come back, but not in time to help you in your cunning plans, Mr. Tim Bolton."

"Then, I suppose," said Bolton, assuming an air of mortification and discomfiture, "it is no use for me to remain here any longer."

"You are quite right. I wish you a pleasant journey home. Give my love to Florence when you see her."

"That man is a fiend!" soliloquized Bolton, as he walked back, leisurely, to his place of business. "Let me get hold of Dodger and I will foil him yet!"

CHAPTER XV.

FLORENCE RECEIVES A LETTER.

The discovery, through Tim Bolton, that Curtis Waring had a hand in the disappearance of Dodger, partially relieved the anxiety of Florence—but only partially.

He might be detained in captivity, but even that was far better than an accident to life or limb.

She knew that he would try to get word to her at the earliest opportunity, in order to relieve her fears.

But week after week passed, and no tidings came.

At length, at the end of ten weeks, a note came to her, written on a rough sheet of paper, the envelope marked by a foreign stamp.

It ran thus:

"DEAR FLORENCE: I am sure you have worried over my disappearance. Perhaps you thought I was dead, but I was never better in my life. I am on the ship *Columbia*, bound for San Francisco, around Cape Horn; and just now, as one of the officers tells me, we are off the coast of Brazil.

"There is a ship coming north, and we are going to hail her and give her letters to carry home, so I hope these few lines will reach you all right. I suppose I am in for it, and must keep on to San Francisco. But I haven't told you yet how I came here.

"It was through a trick of your cousin, Curtis Waring. I haven't time to tell you about it; but I was drugged and brought aboard in my sleep; when I woke up I was fifty miles at sea.

"Don't worry about me, for I have a good friend on board, Mr. Randolph Leslie, who has been a reporter on one of the New York daily papers. He advises me to get something to do in San Francisco, and work till I have earned money enough to get home. He says I can do better there, where I am not known, and can get higher pay. He is giving me lessons every day, and he says I am learning fast.

"The ship is almost here, and I must stop. Take good care of yourself, and remember me to Mrs. O'Keefe, and I will write you again as soon as I get to San Francisco.
"DODGER.

"P. S.—Don't let on to Curtis that you have heard from me, or he might try to play me some trick in San Francisco."

Florence's face was radiant when she had read this letter.

Dodger was alive, well, and in good spirits. The letter

arrived during the afternoon, and she put on her street dress at once and went over to the apple-stand and read the letter to Mrs. O'Keefe.

"Well, well!" ejaculated the apple-woman. "So it's that ould thafe of the world, Curtis Waring, that has got hold of poor Dodger, just as Tim told us. It seems mighty quare to me that he should want to stale poor Dodger. If it was you, now, I could understand it."

"It seems strange to me, Mrs. O'Keefe," said Florence, thoughtfully. "I thought it might be because Dodger was my friend, but that doesn't seem to be sufficient explanation. Don't you think we ought to show this letter to Mr. Bolton?"

"I was goin' to suggest that same. If you'll give it to me, Florence, I'll get Mattie to tend my stand, and slip around wid it to Tim's right off."

"I will go with you, Mrs. O'Keefe."

Mattie, who was playing around the corner, was summoned.

Arrived at the front of the saloon, Mrs. O'Keefe penetrated the interior, and met Tim near the door.

"Have you come in for some whiskey, old lady?" asked Tim, in a jesting tone.

"I'll take that by and by. Florence is outside, and we've got some news for you."

"Won't she come in?"

"No; she don't like to be seen in a place like this. She's got a letter from Dodger."

"You don't mean it!" ejaculated Tim, with sudden interest. "Where is he?"

"Come out and see."

"Good-afternoon, Miss Linden," said Tim, gallantly. "So you've news from Dodger?"

"Yes; here is the letter."

Bolton read it through attentively.

"Curtis is smart," he said, as he handed it back. "He couldn't have thought of a better plan for getting rid of the boy. It will take several months for him to reach 'Frisco, and after that he can't get back, for he won't have any money."

"Dodger says he will try to save money enough to pay his way back."

"It will take him a good while."

"It doesn't take long to come back by cars, does it?"

"No; but it costs a great deal of money. Why, it may take Dodger a year to earn enough to pay his way back on the railroad."

"A year!" exclaimed Florence, in genuine dismay—"a year, in addition to the time it takes to go out there! Where will we all be at the end of that time?"

"Not in jail, I hope," answered Bolton, jocularly. "I am afraid your uncle will no longer be in the land of the living."

A shadow came over Florence's face.

"Poor Uncle John!" she said, sadly. "It is terrible to think he may die thinking hardly of me."

"Well, I am glad to hear from the lad. If Curtis had done him any harm, I'd have got even with him if it sent me to jail."

A quiet, determined look replaced Tim Bolton's usual expression of easy good humor. He could not have said anything that would have ingratiated him more with Florence.

"Thank you, Mr. Bolton," she said, earnestly. "I shall always count upon your help. Now, Mr. Bolton, tell me what can I do to help Dodger?"

"I don't see that you can do anything now, as it will be most three months before he reaches 'Frisco. You might write to him toward the time he gets there."

"I will."

"Direct to the post office. I think he'll have sense enough to ask for letters."

"I wish I could send him some money. I am afraid he will land penniless."

"If he lands in good health you can trust him for makin' a livin'. A New York boy, brought up as he was, isn't goin' to starve where there are papers to sell and errands to run. Why, he'll light on his feet in 'Frisco, take my word for it."

Florence felt a good deal encouraged by Tim's words of assurance, and she went home with her heart perceptibly lightened.

But she was soon to have trials of her own, which for the time being would make her forgetful of Dodger.

CHAPTER XVI.

FLORENCE DISCHARGED.

"Miss Linden," said Mrs. Leighton, one day in the fourth month of Dodger's absence, "Carrie has perhaps told you that I give a party next Thursday evening."

"She told me," answered the governess.

"I expected Prof. Bouvier to furnish dancing music—in fact, I had engaged him—but I have just received a note stating that he is unwell, and I am left unprovided. It is very inconsiderate on his part," added the lady, in a tone of annoyance.

Florence did not reply. She took rather a different view of the professor's letter, and did not care to offend Mrs. Leighton.

"Under the circumstances," continued the lady, "it has occurred to me that, as you are really quite a nice performer, you might fill his place. I shall be willing to allow you a dollar for the evening. What do you say?"

Florence felt embarrassed. She shrank from appearing in society in her present separation from her family, yet could think of no good excuse. Noticing her hesitation, Mrs. Leighton added, patronizingly:

"On second thought, I will pay you a dollar and a half"—Prof. Bouvier was to have charged ten dollars—"and you will be kind enough to come in your best attire. You seem to be well provided with dresses."

"Yes, madam, there will be no difficulty on that score."

"Nor on any other, I hope. As governess in my family, I think I have a right to command your services."

"I will come," said Florence, meekly. She felt that it would not do to refuse after this.

But it would have been much better for her, if she had, as it turned out. Florence was very pretty and she attracted the attention of a certain rich young man, a Mr. De Brabazon, who insisted upon dancing with her several times. This aroused the jealousy of Mrs. Leighton's niece, who proceeded to find out what she could about the governess and reported her discoveries to Mrs. Leighton.

Mrs. Leighton sat in her boudoir with a stern face and tightly compressed lips. Miss Carter, her niece, had called the previous afternoon and informed her of the astounding discoveries she had made respecting the governess.

So when Florence entered the house she was told that Mrs. Leighton wished to see her at once.

"I wonder what's the matter now?" she asked herself.

When she entered the room she saw at once that something was wrong.

"You wished to see me, Mrs. Leighton?" she said.

"Yes," answered Mrs. Leighton, grimly. "Will you be seated?"

Florence sat down a few feet from her employer and waited for an explanation.

She certainly was not prepared for Mrs. Leighton's first words:

"Miss Linden, where do you live?"

Florence started, and her face flushed.

"I live in the lower part of the city," she answered, with hesitation.

"That is not sufficiently definite."

"I live at No. 27 —— Street."

"I think that is east of the Bowery."

"You are right, madam."

"You lodge with an apple-woman, do you not?"

"I do," answered Florence, calmly.

"In a tenement house?"

"Yes, madam."

"And you actually come from such a squalid home to instruct my daughter!" exclaimed Mrs. Leighton, indignantly. "It is a wonder you have not brought some terrible disease into the house."

"There has been no case of disease in the humble dwelling in which I make my home. I should be as sorry to expose your daughter to any danger of that kind as you would be to have me."

"It is a merciful dispensation of Providence, for which I ought to be truly thankful. But the idea of receiving in my house an inmate of a tenement house! I am truly shocked. Is this apple-woman your mother?"

"I assure you that she is not," answered Florence, with a smile which she could not repress.

"Or your aunt?"

"She is in no way related to me. She is an humble friend."

"Miss Linden, your tastes must be low to select such a home and such a friend."

"The state of my purse had something to do with the selection, and the kindness shown me by Mrs. O'Keefe, when I needed a friend, will explain my location further. I am at present suffering reversed circumstances. It is but a short time since I was very differently situated."

"I won't inquire into your change of circumstances. I feel compelled to perform an unpleasant duty."

Florence did not feel called upon to make any reply, but waited for Mrs. Leighton to finish speaking.

"I shall be obliged to dispense with your services as my daughter's governess. It is quite out of the question for me to employ a person who lives in a tenement house."

Florence bowed acquiescence, but she felt very sad. She had become attached to her young charge, and it cost her a pang to part from her.

Besides, how was she to supply the income of which this would deprive her?

"I bow to your decision, madam," she said, with proud humility.

"You will find here the sum that I owe you, with payment for an extra week in lieu of notice."

"Thank you. May I bid Carrie good-by?"

"It is better not to do so, I think. The more quietly we dissolve our unfortunate connection the better!"

Florence's heart swelled, and the tears came to her eyes, but she could not press her request.

When she reached her humble home she had a severe headache and lay down. Mrs. O'Keefe came in later to see her.

"And what's the matter with you, Florence?" she asked.

"I have a bad headache, Mrs. O'Keefe."

"You work too hard, Florence, wid your teachin'. That is what gives you the headache."

"Then I shan't have it again, for I have got through with my teaching."

"What's that you say?"

"I am discharged."

"And what's it all about?"

Florence explained matters. Mrs. O'Keefe became indignant.

"She's a mean trollop, that Mrs. Leighton!" she exclaimed, "and I'd like to tell her so to her face. Where does she live?"

"It will do no good to interfere, my good friend. She is not willing to receive a governess from a tenement house."

"Shure you used to live in as grand a house as herself."

"But I don't now."

"Don't mind it too much, mavourneen. You'll soon be gettin' another scholar. Go to sleep now, and you'll sleep the headache away."

Florence finally succeeded in following the advice of her humble friend.

She resolved to leave till the morrow the cares of the morrow.

She had twelve dollars, and before that was spent she hoped to be in a position to earn some more.

CHAPTER XVII.

AN EXCITING ADVENTURE.

Dodger soon became accustomed to his duties in his new San Francisco home. He found Mr. Tucker an exacting, but not an unreasonable, man. He watched his new assistant closely for the first few days, and was quietly taking his measure.

At the end of the first week he paid the salary agreed upon—fifteen dollars.

"You have been with me a week, Arthur," he said.

"Yes, sir."

"And I have been making up my mind about you."

"Yes, sir," said Dodger, looking up inquiringly. "I hope you are satisfied with me?"

"Yes, I think I may say that I am. You don't seem to be afraid of work."

"I have always been accustomed to work."

On their arrival in San Francisco, both Dodger and his new friend, Randolph Leslie, were very fortunate. Randolph had no trouble in finding work as a reporter. And

Dodger, to his great joy, obtained a position in the express office of a Mr. Tucker.

Dodger felt proud of his success, and put away the fifteen dollars with a feeling of satisfaction. He had never saved half that sum in the same time before.

"Curtis Waring did me a favor when he sent me out here," he reflected; "but as he didn't mean it, I have no occasion to feel grateful."

Dodger found that he could live for eight dollars a week, and he began to lay by seven dollars a week with the view of securing funds sufficient to take him back to New York.

He was in no hurry to leave San Francisco, but he felt that Florence might need a friend. But he found that he was making progress slowly.

About this time he met with an adventure which deserves to be noted.

It was about seven o'clock one evening that he found himself in Mission Street.

At a street corner his attention was drawn to a woman poorly dressed, who held by the hand a child of three.

Her clothing was shabby, and her attitude was one of despondency. It was clear that she was ill and in trouble.

Dodger possessed quick sympathies, and his own experience made him quick to understand and feel for the troubles of others.

Though the woman made no appeal, he felt instinctively that she needed help.

"I beg your pardon," he said, with as much deference as if he were addressing one favored by fortune, "but you seem to be in need of help?"

"God knows, I am!" said the woman, sadly.

"Perhaps I can be of service to you. Will you tell me how?"

"Neither I nor my child has tasted food since yesterday."

"Well, that can be easily remedied," said Dodger, cheerfully. "There is a restaurant close by. I was about to eat supper. Will you come in with me?"

"I am ashamed to impose upon the kindness of a stranger," murmured the woman.

"Don't mention it. I shall be very glad of company," said Dodger, heartily.

"Then I will accept your kind invitation."

It was a small restaurant, but neat in its appointments, and, as in most San Francisco restaurants, the prices were remarkably moderate.

At an expense of twenty-five cents each, the three obtained a satisfactory meal.

The woman and child both seemed to enjoy it, and Dodger was glad to see that the former became more cheerful as time went on.

There was something in the child's face that looked familiar to Dodger. It was a resemblance to some one that he had seen, but he could not for the life of him decide who it was.

"How can I ever thank you for your kindness?" said the lady, as she arose from the table. "You don't know what it is to be famished——"

"Don't I?" asked Dodger. "I have been hungry more than once, without money enough."

"You don't look it," she said.

"No, for now I have a good place and am earning a good salary."

"Are you a native of San Francisco?"

"No, madam. I can't tell you where I was born, for I know little or nothing of my family. I have only been here a short time. I came from New York."

"So did I," said the woman, with a sigh. "I wish I were back there again."

"How came you to be here? Don't answer if you prefer not to," Dodger added, hastily.

"I have no objection. My husband deserted me, and left me to shift for myself and support my child."

"How have you done it?"

"By taking in sewing. But that is a hard way of earning money. There are too many poor women who are ready to work for starvation wages, and so we all suffer."

"Mamma, I am tired. Take me up in your arms," said the child.

"Poor child! He has been on his feet all day," sighed the mother.

She tried to lift the child, but her own strength had been undermined by privation, and she was clearly unable to do so.

"Let me take him!" said Dodger. "Here, little one, jump up!"

He raised the child easily, and despite the mother's protest carried him in his arms.

"I will see you home, madam," he said.

"I fear the child will be too heavy for you."

"I hope not. Why, I could carry a child twice as heavy."

They reached the room at last—a poor one, but a welcome repose from the streets.

"Don't you ever expect to see your husband again?" asked Dodger. "Can't you compel him to support you?"

"I don't know where he is," answered the woman, despondently.

"If you will tell me his name, I may come across him some day."

"His name," said the woman, "is Curtis Waring."

Dodger stared at her, overwhelmed with surprise.

CHAPTER XVIII.

AN IMPORTANT DISCOVERY.

"Curtis Waring!" ejaculated Dodger, his face showing intense surprise. "Is that the name of your husband?"

"Yes. Is it possible that you know him?" asked the woman, struck with Dodger's tone.

"I know a man by that name. I will describe him, and you can tell me whether it is he. He is rather tall, dark hair, sallow complexion, black eyes, and a long, thin nose."

"It is like him in every particular. Oh, tell me where he is to be found?"

"He lives in New York. He is the nephew of a rich man, and is expecting to inherit his wealth."

"There was a time when he treated me well, when he appeared to love me," murmured the woman. "I cannot forget that he is the father of my child."

"Do you mind telling me how you came to marry him?" Dodger asked.

"It was over four years ago that I met him in this city," was the reply. "I am a San Francisco girl. I had never been out of California. I was considered pretty then," she added, with a remnant of pride, "faded as I am to-day."

Looking closely in her face, Dodger was ready to believe this.

"We married, securing apartments on Kearney Street. We lived together till my child was born, and for three months afterward. Then Mr. Waring claimed to be called away from San Francisco on business. He said he might be absent six weeks. He left me a hundred dollars, and urged me to be careful of it, as he was short of money, and needed considerable for the expenses of the journey. He left me, and I have never seen or heard from him since."

Dodger then told the woman something of his connection with Waring and of the latter's desire to marry his Cousin Florence.

"She ought to know, and her uncle ought to know," said Dodger. "Mrs. Waring, I can't see my way clear yet. If I were in New York I would know just what to do. Will you agree to stand by me, and help me?"

"Yes, I will," answered the woman, earnestly.

"I will see you again to-morrow evening. Here is some money to help you along for the present. Good-night."

Dodger, as he walked away, pondered over the remarkable discovery he had made.

It was likely to prove of the utmost importance to Florence.

Her uncle's displeasure was wholly based upon her refusal to marry Curtis Waring, but if it should be proved to him that Curtis was already a married man, there would seem no bar to reconciliation.

It was easy to decide what plan was best, but how to carry it out presented a difficulty which seemed insurmountable.

The expenses of a journey to New York for Dodger, Mrs. Waring and her child would not be very far from five hundred dollars, and where to obtain this money was a problem.

The time might come when Dodger, by his own efforts, could accumulate the needed sum, but it would require a year at least, and in that time Mr. Linden would probably be dead.

Absorbed and disturbed by these reflections, Dodger walked slowly through the darkened streets till he heard a stifled cry, and looking up, beheld a sight that startled him.

On the sidewalk lay the prostrate figure of a man. Over him, bludgeon in hand, bent a ruffian, whose purpose was only too clearly evident.

CHAPTER XIX.

JUST IN TIME.

Dodger, who was a strong, stout boy, gathered himself up and dashed against the ruffian with such impetuosity that he fell over his intended victim, and his bludgeon fell from his hand.

It was the work of an instant to lift it, and raise it in a menacing position.

The discomfited villain broke into a volley of oaths, and proceeded to pick himself up.

He was a brutal-looking fellow, but was no larger than Dodger, who was as tall as the majority of men.

"Give me that stick," he exclaimed, furiously.

"Come and take it," returned Dodger, undaunted.

The fellow took him at his word, and made a rush at our hero, but a vigorous blow from the bludgeon made him cautious about repeating the attack.

"Curse you!" he cried, between his teeth. "I'd like to chaw you up."

"I have no doubt you would," answered Dodger; "but I don't think you will. Were you going to rob this man?"

"None of your business!"

"I shall make it my business. You'd better go, or you may be locked up."

"Give me that stick, then."

"You'll have to do without it."

He made another rush, and Dodger struck him such a blow on his arm that he winced with pain.

"Now I shall summon the police, and you can do as you please about going."

Dodger struck the stick sharply on the sidewalk three times, and the ruffian, apprehensive of arrest, ran around the corner just in time to rush into the arms of a policeman.

"What has this man been doing?" asked the city guardian, turning to Dodger.

"He was about to rob this man."

"Is the man hurt?"

"Where am I?" asked the prostrate man, in a bewildered tone.

"I will take care of him, if you will take charge of that fellow."

"Can you get up, sir?" asked Dodger, bending over the fallen man.

The latter answered by struggling to his feet and looking about him in a confused way.

"Where am I?" he asked. "What has happened?"

"You were attacked by a ruffian. I found you on the sidewalk, with him bending over you with this club in his hand."

"He must have followed me. I was imprudent enough to show a well-filled pocketbook in a saloon where I stopped to take a drink. No doubt he planned to relieve me of it."

"You have had a narrow escape, sir."

"I have no doubt of it. I presume the fellow was ready to take my life, if he found it necessary."

"I will leave you now, sir, if you think you can manage."

"No, stay with me. I feel rather upset."

"Where are you staying, sir?"

"At the Palace Hotel. Of course you know where that is?"

"Certainly. Will you take my arm?"

"Thank you."

Little was said till they found themselves in the sumptuous hotel, which hardly has an equal in America.

"Come to my room, young man; I want to speak to you."

It was still early in the evening, and Dodger's time was his own.

He had no hesitation, therefore, in accepting the stranger's invitation.

On the third floor the stranger produced a key and opened the door of a large, handsomely-furnished room.

"If you have a match, please light the gas."

Dodger proceeded to do so, and now, for the first time, obtained a good view of the man he had rescued. He was a man of about the average height, probably not far from fifty, dressed in a neat business suit, and looked like a substantial merchant.

"Please be seated."

Dodger sat down in an easy-chair conveniently near him.

"Young man," said the stranger, impressively, "you have done me a great favor."

Dodger felt that this was true, and did not disclaim it.

"I am very glad I came up just as I did," he said.

"How large a sum of money do you think I had about me?" asked his companion.

"Five hundred dollars?"

"Five hundred dollars! Why, that would be a mere trifle."

"It wouldn't be a trifle to me, sir," said Dodger.

"Are you poor?" asked the man, earnestly.

"I have a good situation that pays me fifteen dollars a week, so I ought not to consider myself poor."

"Suppose you had a considerable sum of money given you, what would you do with it?"

"If I had five hundred dollars, I should be able to defeat the schemes of a villain, and restore a young lady to her rights."

"That seems interesting. Tell me the circumstances."

Dodger told the story as briefly as he could. He was encouraged to find that the stranger listened to him with attention.

"I asked you how much money you supposed I had," said the stranger, when Dodger had finished. "I will tell you. In a wallet I have eleven thousand dollars in bank notes and securities."

"That is a fortune," said Dodger, dazzled at the mention of such a sum.

"If I had lost it, I have plenty more, but the most serious peril was to my life. Through your opportune assistance I have escaped without loss. I fully appreciate the magnitude of the service you have done me. As an evidence of it, please accept these bills."

He drew from the roll two bills and handed them to Dodger.

The boy, glancing at them mechanically, started in amazement. Each bill was for five hundred dollars.

"You have given me a thousand dollars!" he gasped.

"I am aware of it. I consider my life worth that, at least. James Swinton never fails to pay his debts."

"But, sir, a thousand dollars——"

"It's no more than you deserve. When I tell my wife, on my return to Chicago, about this affair, she will blame me for not giving you more. There is my card, and if you ever come to Chicago, call upon me."

"I will, sir."

When Dodger left the Palace Hotel he felt that he was a favorite of fortune.

It is not always that the money we need is so quickly supplied.

He resolved to return to New York as soon as he could manage it, and take with him the wife and child of Curtis Waring.

This would cost him about five hundred dollars, and he would have the same amount left.

Mrs. Waring was overjoyed when Dodger called upon her and offered to take her back to New York.

"I shall see Curtis again," she said. "How can I ever thank you?"

But Dodger, though unwilling to disturb her dreams of happiness, thought it exceedingly doubtful if her husband would be equally glad to see her.

CHAPTER XX.

THE DARKEST DAY.

When Florence left the employ of Mrs. Leighton she had a few dollars as a reserve fund. As this would not last long, she at once made an effort to obtain employment.

She desired another position as governess, and made application in answer to an advertisement.

But she was unsuccessful.

"Well, Florence, did you get a place?" asked Mrs. O'Keefe, as she passed that lady's stand.

"No, Mrs. O'Keefe," answered Florence, wearily.

"And what will you be doin' now?"

"Do you think I can get some sewing to do, Mrs. O'Keefe?"

"Yes, Miss Florence—I'll get you some vests to make; but it's hard work and poor pay."

"I must take what I can get," sighed Florence. "I cannot choose."

The result was that Mrs. O'Keefe brought Florence in the course of the day half a dozen vests, for which she was to be paid the munificent sum of twenty-five cents each.

Florence had very little idea of what she was undertaking.

She was an expert needlewoman, and proved adequate to the work, but with her utmost industry she could only make one vest in a day, and that would barely pay her rent.

True, she had some money laid aside on which she could draw, but that would soon be expended, and then what was to become of her?

"Shure, I won't let you starve, Florence," said the warm-hearted apple-woman.

"But, Mrs. O'Keefe, I can't consent to live on you."

"And why not? I'm well and strong, and I'm makin' more money than I nade."

"I couldn't think of it, though I thank you for your kindness."

"Shure, you might write a letter to your uncle."

"He would expect me, in that case, to consent to a marriage with Curtis. You wouldn't advise me to do that?"

"No; he's a mane blackguard, and I'd say it to his face."

Weeks rolled by, and Florence began to show the effects of hard work and confinement.

She grew pale and thin, and her face was habitually sad.

She had husbanded her savings as a governess as closely as she could, but in spite of all of her economy it dwindled till she had none left.

Henceforth, she must depend on twenty-five cents a day, and this seemed well-nigh impossible.

In this emergency the pawnbroker occurred to her.

She had a variety of nice dresses, and she had also a handsome ring given her by her uncle on her last birthday.

This she felt sure must have cost fifty dollars. It was a trial to part with it, but there seemed to be no alternative.

This she took to a pawnbroker's, but the most the man would give her was five dollars.

She left the place, half timid, half ashamed, and wholly discouraged.

But the darkest hour is sometimes nearest the dawn. A great and overwhelming surprise awaited her. She had scarcely left the shop when a glad voice cried:

"I have found you at last, Florence!"

She looked up and saw—Dodger.

But not the old Dodger. She saw a nicely dressed young gentleman, larger than the friend she had parted with six months before, with a brighter, more intelligent, and manly look.

"Dodger!" she faltered.

"Yes, it is Dodger."

"Where did you come from?"

"From San Francisco. But what have you been doing in there?"

And Dodger pointed in the direction of the pawnbroker's shop.

"I pawned my ring."

"Then I shall get it back at once. How much did you get on it?"

"Five dollars."

"Give me the ticket, and go in with me."

The pawnbroker was very reluctant to part with the ring, which he made sure would not be reclaimed; but there was no help for it.

As they emerged into the street, Dodger said:

"I've come back to restore you to your rights, and give Curtis Waring the most disagreeable surprise he ever had. Come home, and I'll tell you all about it. I've struck luck, Florence, and you're going to share it."

CHAPTER XXI.

MRS. O'KEEFE IN A NEW ROLE.

No time was lost in seeing Bolton and arranging a plan of campaign.

Curtis Waring, nearing the accomplishment of his plans, was far from anticipating impending disaster.

His uncle's health had become so poor, and his strength had been so far undermined, that it was thought desirable to employ a sick nurse. An advertisement was inserted in a morning paper, which luckily attracted the attention of Bolton.

"You must go, Mrs. O'Keefe," he said to the applewoman. "It is important that we have some one in the house—some friend of Florence and the boy—to watch what is going on."

"Bridget O'Keefe is no fool. Leave her to manage."

The result was that among a large number of applicants Mrs. O'Keefe was selected by Curtis as Mr. Linden's nurse, as she expressed herself willing to work for four dollars a week, while the lowest outside demand was seven.

We will now enter the house, in which the last scenes of our story are to take place.

Mr. Linden, weak and emaciated, was sitting in an easy-chair in his library.

Mrs. O'Keefe, who had taken the name of Mrs. Barnes, was with him.

"Is there anything I can do for you, Mr. Linden?" asked the new nurse, in a tone of sympathy.

"Can you minister to a mind diseased?"

"I'll take the best care of you, Mr. Linden, but it isn't as if you had a wife or daughter."

"Ah, that is a sore thought! I have no wife or daughter; but I have a niece."

"And where is she, sir?"

"I don't know. I drove her from me by my unkindness. I repent bitterly, but it's now too late."

"And why don't you send for her to come home?"

"I would gladly do so, but I don't know where she is. Curtis has tried to find her, but in vain. He says she is in Chicago."

"And what should take her to Chicago?"

"He says she is there as a governess in a family."

"By the brow of St. Patrick!" thought Mrs. O'Keefe, "if that Curtis isn't a natural-born liar. I'm sure she'd come back if you'd send for her, sir."

"Do you think so?" asked Linden, eagerly.

"I'm sure of it."

"But I don't know where to send."

"I know of a party that would be sure to find her."

"Who is it?"

"It's a young man. They call him Dodger. If any one can find Miss Florence, he can."

"You know my niece's name?"

"I have heard it somewhere. From Mr. Waring, I think."

"And you think this young man would agree to go to Chicago and find her?"

"Yes, sir, I make bold to say he will."

"Tell him to go at once. He will need money. In yonder desk you will find a picture of my niece and a roll of bills. Give them to him and send him at once."

"Yes, sir, I will. But if you'll take my advice, you won't say anything to Mr. Curtis. He might think it foolish."

"True! If your friend succeeds, we'll give Curtis a surprise."

"And a mighty disagreeable one, I'll be bound," soliloquized Mrs. O'Keefe.

"I think, Mrs. Barnes, I will retire to my chamber, if you will assist me."

She assisted Mr. Linden to his room, and then returned to the library.

"Mrs. Barnes, there's a young man inquiring for you," said a maid servant, entering.

"Send him in, Jane."

The visitor was Dodger, neatly dressed.

"How are things going, Mrs. O'Keefe?" he asked.

"Splendid, Dodger. Here's some money for you."

"What for?"

"You're to go to Chicago and bring back Florence."

"But she isn't there."

"Nivir mind. You're to pretend to go."

"But that won't take money."

"Give it to Florence, then. It's hers by rights. Won't we give Curtis a surprise? Where's his wife?"

"I have found a comfortable boarding house for her. When had we better carry out this programme? She's very anxious to see her husband."

"The more fool she. Kape her at home and out of his sight, or there's no knowin' what he'll do. And, Dodger, dear, kape an eye on the apple-stand. I mistrust Mrs. Burke that's runnin' it."

"I will. Does the old gentleman seem to be very sick?"

"He's wake as a rat. Curtis would kill him soon if we didn't interfere. But we'll soon circumvent him, the snake in the grass! Miss Florence will soon come to her own, and Curtis Waring will be out in the cold."

"The most I have against him is that he tried to marry Florence when he had a wife already."

"He's as bad as they make em, Dodger. It won't be my fault if Mr. Linden's eyes are not opened to his wickedness."

Mrs. O'Keefe was a warm-hearted woman, and the sad, drawn face of Mr. Linden appealed to her pity.

"Why should I let the poor man suffer when I can relieve him?" she asked herself.

So the next morning, after Curtis had, according to his custom, gone downtown, being in the invalid's sick chamber, she began to act in a mysterious manner. She tiptoed to the door, closed it, and approached Mr. Linden's bedside with the air of one about to unfold a strange story.

"Whist, now," she said, with her finger on her lips.

"What is the matter?" asked the invalid, rather alarmed.

"Can you bear a surprise, sir?"

"Have you any bad news for me?"

"No; it's good news, but you must promise not to tell Curtis."

"Is it about Florence? Your messenger can hardly have reached Chicago."

"He isn't going there, sir."

"But you promised that he should," said Mr. Linden, disturbed.

"I'll tell you why, sir. Florence is not in Chicago."

"I—don't understand. You said she was there."

"Begging your pardon, sir, it was Curtis that said so, though he knew she was in New York."

"But what motive could he have had for thus misrepresenting matters?"

"He doesn't want you to take her back."

"I can't believe you, Mrs. Barnes. He loves her, and wants to marry her."

"He couldn't marry her if she consented to take him."

"Why not? Mrs. Barnes, you confuse me."

"I won't deceive you as he has done. There's rason in plinty. He's married already."

"Is this true?" demanded Mr. Linden in excitement.

"It's true enough; more by token, to-morrow, whin he's out, his wife will come here and tell you so herself."

"But who are you who seem to know so much about my family?"

"I'm a friend of the pore girl you've driven from the house, because she would not marry a rascally spalpeen that's been schemin' to get your property into his hands."

"You are a friend of Florence? Where is she?"

"She's in my house, and has been there ever since she left her home."

"Is she—well?"

"As well as she can be whin she's been workin' her fingers to the bone wid sewin' to keep from starvin'."

"My God! what have I done?"

"You've let Curtis Waring wind you around his little finger—that's what you've done, Mr. Linden."

"How can I see Florence?"

"How soon can you bear it?"

"The sooner the better."

"Then it'll be to-morrow, I'm thinkin', that is if you won't tell Curtis."

"No, no; I promise."

"I'll manage everything, sir. Don't worry now."

Mr. Linden's face lost its anxious look—so that when, later in the day, Curtis looked into the room, he was surprised.

"My uncle looks better," he said.

"Yes, sir," answered the nurse. "I've soothed him like."

"Indeed! You seem to be a very accomplished nurse."

"Faith, that I am, sir, though it isn't I that should say it."

"May I ask how you soothed him?" inquired Curtis, anxiously.

"I told him that Miss Florence would soon be home."

"I do not think it right to hold out hopes that may prove ill founded."

"I know what I am about, Mr. Curtis."

"I dare say you understand your business, Mrs. Barnes, but if my uncle should be disappointed, I am afraid the consequences will be lamentable."

Curtis went into his uncle's chamber.

"How are you feeling, uncle?" he asked.

"I think I am better," answered Mr. Linden, coldly, for he had not forgotten Mrs. Barnes' revelations.

"That is right. Only make an effort, and you will soon be strong again."

"I think I may. I may live ten years to annoy you."

"I fervently hope so," said Curtis, but there was a false ring in his voice that his uncle detected. "How do you like the new nurse?"

"She is helping me wonderfully. You made a good selection."

"I will see that she is soon discharged," Curtis inwardly resolved. "If her being here is to prolong my uncle's life, and keep me still waiting for the estate, I must clear the house of her."

"You must not allow her to buoy you up with unfounded hopes. She has been telling you that Florence will soon return."

"Yes; she seems convinced of it."

"Of course, she knows nothing of it. She may return, but I doubt whether she is in Chicago now. I think the family she was with has gone to Europe."

"Where did you hear that, Curtis?" asked Mr. Linden, with unwonted sharpness.

"I have sources of information which at present I do not care to impart. Rest assured that I am doing all I can to get her back."

"You still want to marry her, Curtis?"

"I do, most certainly."

"I shall not insist upon it. I should not have done so before."

"Have you changed your mind, uncle?"

"Yes; I have made a mistake, and I have decided to correct it."

"What has come over him?" Curtis asked himself. "Some innuence hostile to me has been brought to bear. It must be that nurse. I will quietly dismiss her to-morrow, paying her a week's wages, in lieu of warning. She's evidently a meddler."

CHAPTER XXII.

THE CLOSING SCENE.

The next day Tim Bolton, dressed in a jaunty style, walked up the steps of the Linden mansion.

"Is Mr. Waring at home?" he asked.

"No, sir; he has gone downtown."

"I'll step in and wait for him. Please show me to the library."

Jane, the maid, who had been taken into confidence by the nurse, showed him at once into the room mentioned.

Half an hour later Curtis entered.

"How long have you been here, Bolton?"

"But a short time. You sent for me?"

"I did."

"On business?"

"Well, yes."

"Is there anything new?"

"Yes, my uncle is failing fast."

"Is he likely to die soon?"

"I shouldn't be surprised if he died within a week."

"I suspect Curtis means to help him! Well, what has that to do with me?" he asked. "You will step into the property, of course?"

"There's a little difficulty in the way which I can overcome with your help."

"What is it?"

"I can't get him to give up the foolish notion that the boy he lost is still alive."

"It happens to be true."

"Yes; but he must not know it. Before he dies I want him to make a new will, revoking all others, leaving all the property to me."

"Will he do it?"

"I don't know. As long as he thinks the boy is living, I don't believe he will. You see what a drawback that is."

"I see. What can I do to improve the situation?"

"I want you to sign a paper confessing that you abducted the boy——"

"At your instigation!"

"That must not be mentioned. You will go on to say that a year or two later—the time is not material—he died of typhoid fever. You can say that you did not dare to reveal this before, but do so now, impelled by remorse."

"Have you got it written out? I can't remember all them words."

"Yes; here it is."

"All right,". said Bolton, taking the paper and tucking it into an inside pocket. "I'll copy it out in my own handwriting. How much are you going to give me for doing this?"

"A thousand dollars."

"Cash?"

"I can't do that. I have met with losses at the gaming table, and I don't dare ask money from my uncle at this time. He thinks I am thoroughly steady."

"At how much do you value the estate?"

"At four hundred thousand dollars. I wormed it out of my uncle's lawyer the other day."

"And you expect me to help you to that amount for only a thousand dollars?"

"A thousand dollars is a good deal of money."

"And so is four hundred thousand. After all, your uncle may not die."

"He is sure to."

"You seem very confident."

"And with good reason. Leave that to me. I promise you, on my honor, to pay you two thousand dollars when I get the estate."

"But what is going to happen to poor Dodger, the rightful heir?"

"Well, let it be three hundred dollars a year."

"Where is he now?"

"I don't mind telling you, as it can do no harm. He is in California."

"Whew! That was smart. How did you get him there?"

"I drugged him, and had him sent on board a ship bound for San Francisco, around Cape Horn. The fact is, I was getting a little suspicious of you, and I wanted to put you beyond the reach of temptation."

"You are a clever rascal, Curtis. After all, suppose the prize should slip through your fingers?"

"It won't. I have taken every precaution."

"When do you want this document?"

"Bring it back to me this afternoon, copied and signed. That is all you have to do; I will attend to the rest."

While this conversation was going on there were unseen listeners.

Behind a portière Mrs. Barnes, the nurse, and John Linden heard every word that was said.

"And what do you think now, sir?" whispered Mrs. O'Keefe (to give her real name).

"It is terrible. I would not have believed Curtis capable of such a crime. But is it really true, Mrs. Barnes? Is my lost boy alive?"

"To be sure he is."

"Have you seen him?"

"I know him as well as I know you, sir, and better, too."

"Is he—tell me, is he a good boy? Curtis told me that he might be a criminal."

"He might be, but he isn't. He's as dacent and honest a boy as iver trod shoe leather. You'll be proud of him, sir."

"But he's in California."

"He was; but he's got back. You shall see him to-day, and Florence, too. Hark! I hear the door bell. They're here now. I think you had better go in and confront Curtis."

"I feel weak, Mrs. Barnes. Let me lean on you."

"You can do that, and welcome, sir."

The nurse pushed aside the portière, and the two entered the library—Mrs. Barnes rotund and smiling, Mr. Linden gaunt and spectral, looking like one risen from the grave.

Curtis eyed the pair with a startled look.

"Mrs. Barnes," he said, angrily, "what do you mean by taking my uncle from his bed and bringing him down here? It is as much as his life is worth. You seem unfit for your duties as nurse. You will leave the house to-morrow, and I will engage a substitute."

"I shall lave whin I git ready, Mr. Curtis Waring," said the nurse, her arms akimbo. "Maybe somebody else will lave the house. Me and Mr. Linden have been behind the curtain for twenty minutes, and he has heard every word you said."

Curtis turned livid, and his heart sank.

"It's true, Curtis," said John Linden's hollow voice. "I have heard all. It was you who abducted my boy, and have made my life a lonely one all these years. Oh, man! man! how could you have the heart to do it?"

Curtis stared at him with parched lips, unable to speak.

"Not content with this, you drove from the house my dear niece, Florence. You made me act cruelly toward her. I fear she will not forgive me."

But just then the door opened, and Florence, rushing into the room, sank at her uncle's feet.

"Oh, uncle," she said, "will you take me back?"

"Yes, Florence, never again to leave me. And who is this?" he asked, fixing his eyes on Dodger, who stood shyly in the doorway.

"I'll tell you, sir," said Tim Bolton. "That is your own son, whom I stole away from you when he was a kid, being hired to do it by Curtis Waring."

"It's a lie," said Curtis, hoarsely.

"Come to me, my boy," said Linden, with a glad light in his eyes.

"At last Heaven has heard my prayers," he ejaculated. "We will never be separated. I was ready to die, but now I hope to live for many years. I feel that I have a new lease of life."

With a baffled growl Curtis Waring darted a furious look at the three.

"That boy is an impostor," he said. "They are deceiving you."

"He is my son. I see his mother's look in his face. As for you, Curtis Waring. my eyes are open at last to your villainy. You deserve nothing at my hands; but I will make some provision for you."

There was another surprise.

Curtis Waring's deserted wife, brought from California by Dodger, entered the room, leading by the hand a young child.

"Oh, Curtis," she said, reproachfully. "How could you leave me? I have come to you, my husband, with our little child."

"Begone! woman!" said Curtis, furiously. "I will never receive nor recognize you!"

"Oh, sir!" she said, turning to Linden, "what shall I do?"

"Curtis Waring," said Linden, sternly, "unless you receive this woman and treat her properly, you shall receive nothing from me."

"And if I do?"

"You will receive an income of two thousand dollars a year, payable quarterly. Mrs. Waring, you will remain here with your child till your husband provides another home for you."

Curtis slunk out of the room, but he was too wise to refuse his uncle's offer.

He and his wife are living in Chicago, and he treats her fairly well, fearing that, otherwise, he will lose his income.

Mr. Linden looks ten years younger than he did at the opening of the story.

Florence and Dodger—now known as Harvey Linden—live with him.

Dodger, under a competent private tutor, is making up the deficiencies in his education.

It is early days yet to speak of marriage, but it is possible that Florence may marry a cousin, after all.

Tim Bolton has turned over a new leaf, given up his saloon, and is carrying on a country hotel within fifty miles of New York.

He has five thousand dollars in the bank, presented by Dodger, with his father's sanction, and is considered quite a reputable citizen.

As for Mrs. O'Keefe, she still keeps the apple-stand, being unwilling to give it up; but she, too, has a handsome sum in the bank, and calls often upon her two children, as she calls them.

In the midst of their prosperity Florence and Dodger will never forget the time when they were adrift in New York.

THE END.

The next issue, No. 46, will contain "A Lad of Steel; or, Running Down the Tiger," by Matt Royal. This is a most marvelous story of a brave, clever boy, whom nothing can down. Almost unassisted, he performs remarkable deeds of valor. Surprise follows surprise, and the reader is led on in breathless suspense from one scene of excitement to another. It is a tale you cannot afford to miss.

B&T 2807